JENNIE GERHARDT

The University of Pennsylvania
Dreiser Edition

THOMAS P. RIGGIO
General Editor

James L. W. West III
Lee Ann Draud
Textual Editors

JENNIE GERHARDT

THEODORE DREISER

Edited by
JAMES L. W. WEST III

University of Pennsylvania Press

Philadelphia

Copyright © 1992 by the University [of Pennsylvania Pre]ss

Library of Congress Cataloging-in-Pu[blication Data]

Dreiser, Theodore, 1871–1945.
    Jennie Gerhardt / Theodore Dreiser ; edited by James L. W. West III.
        p.   cm. — (University of Pennsylvania Dreiser edition)
    Originally published: New York : Harper, 1911.
    Includes bibliographical references and index.
    ISBN 0-8122-8164-0
    I. West, James L. W.   II. Title.   III. Series: Dreiser, Theodore, 1871–1945.
University of Pennsylvania Dreiser edition.
PS3507.R55J4   1992
813'.52—dc20   92-20462
                                                                                      CIP

Printed in the United States of America

CONTENTS

ILLUSTRATIONS

PREFACE

On 6 January 1901 Theodore Dreiser began work on his second novel, *Jennie Gerhardt*. Like *Sister Carrie*, the book took its inspiration from events in the unruly life of one of his sisters. Nearly eleven years separated this start from the publication of the novel in October 1911 by the firm of Harper and Brothers. The reasons for the long hiatus have by now become a familiar part of Dreiser biography. So too is the tangled history of composition that led Dreiser through two sets of major revisions: the first in the time between the spring of 1901 and the winter of 1902, after which a debilitating depression forced him to put aside the novel; and then in the crucial months between January 1911, when he had completed an initial version of the novel, and the spring of that year, when he submitted the manuscript to Harpers. In the latter period, the novel continued to undergo a number of significant changes. Relying on readers as diverse as the critic James G. Huneker, the editor Fremont Rider, and Lillian Rosenthal (a sensitive reader in her early twenties), Dreiser reshaped his story, altering the original "happy ending" that has Jennie marry Lester Kane to a darker version that leaves her alone and bereft. Dreiser then submitted the manuscript to further readings by H. L. Mencken and others before delivering it to Harpers.

Harpers editor Ripley Hitchcock had convinced the firm to consider the novel, despite Dreiser's reputation as a personally difficult author of morally dubious fiction. But acceptance had its price. What happened to Dreiser's text at Harpers is a story that has not been told before in its entirety. This edition places that story in sharper focus, and it offers for the first time a text that Dreiser and his trusted advisers agreed upon before it underwent considerable editorial emendation at Harpers. In fact, the version of the story that Dreiser had brought to closure by April 1911 was altered and cut by more than 16,000 words for the first edition. With an eye to the demands of the literary marketplace, Hitchcock's editorial staff bowdlerized the text and removed a good deal of Dreiser's social and philosophical commentary. Perhaps the most important change had to do with the character of Jennie, who in Dreiser's original version is a much fuller, more clearly defined figure than she is in the published book. All later editions of *Jennie Gerhardt* are based upon the Harpers text.

The present edition is meant to complement the first edition of 1911. That book can now be read as a work of art that is a product of its time and of publishing conditions that did not allow Dreiser to issue his novel in the state in which he had completed it in the spring of 1911. The novelist's habit of preserving his personal and professional papers makes the present edition possible. Based on the manuscripts and typescripts at the University of Pennsylvania and the Barrett Collection at the University of Virginia, this edition offers the novel in a form that has never been available to readers. It is the version that so excited Mencken and that prompted him to write his historic *Smart Set* review—even while he complained in private of the "ruthless slashing" to which Harpers had subjected Dreiser's original text.

This edition will undoubtedly lead readers to reexamine historical problems such as Dreiser's relation to the naturalistic and sentimental forms of his day. In addition, it provides an occasion to consider the novel in terms that are critically relevant to our times. *Jennie Gerhardt* is challenging—perhaps more so than any other Dreiser novel—as a text that encourages inquiries relevant to recent debates about the literary canon. In particular, the novel opens up the question of how a canonical author like Dreiser may be viewed in relation to issues of gender and emerging literary minorities.

Dreiser thought of Jennie as "my pet heroine," and in listing for Mencken his books and the various types of readers they attracted, he named *Jennie Gerhardt* as appealing to "emotionalists—especially women" (13 May 1916). Mencken, who read the book as a grim, naturalistic novel, did not argue with Dreiser's assessment of the published work, but he clearly read it with more emphasis on Lester Kane's philosophical skepticism than on Jennie's spirituality. In the present text Jennie is still the embodiment of spiritual idealism. She is also, however, more of a force to be reckoned with; her power as a woman is clearer, and we are less likely to see her as a weak sentimental heroine. This edition gives the reader a fuller idea of Dreiser's characterization of Jennie. It allows us to examine the nature of the cuts made by Harpers and to ask questions about the rationale behind them. Why, for instance, did the character of Jennie undergo a more thorough revision than that of Lester? What assumptions about gender dominated the literary marketplace and led the Harpers editors to turn Jennie into the more passive, nebulously drawn figure upon which much modern criticism has focused?

This edition also offers us a chance to test the limits of traditional concepts of naturalism that have been used to describe Dreiser's departure from the normative fiction of his day. Although *Jennie Gerhardt* rarely falls within the purview of contemporary studies of multicultural literature, this aspect of the novel was apparent to many of its first readers. The early reviewers—particularly those who were hostile to Dreiser—often remarked that Jennie is a "Teutonic type of woman" or "a middle class German American," that she represents the "perverted ideal of feminine character which naturalism has fathered in the earnest German mind," and that "the milieu in which the author has set his people is untouched with Americanism." These reviewers, however biased, were sensitive to what we have forgotten: Dreiser's brand of naturalism is yoked to class and ethnic perspectives that represented something new and challenging in American literature.

Although Dreiser himself later claimed the novel to be his major contribution to the "treatment of German-American subjects" (Dreiser to A. E. Zucker, 14 September 1942), he did not emphasize this aspect of *Jennie Gerhardt* in 1911. Among other reasons, Dreiser's ambivalent feelings about the culture of his immigrant German father led him away from the standard treatments of German-Americans by writers in the first decade of this century. By temperament and background, he could not write a version of the newly emerging Horatio Alger form of the German-American success story—like George Grimm's *Pluck* (1904; 1911), which celebrated both the author's immigrant German heritage and his community's assimilation into American life. Neither could Dreiser follow the benign but condescending nativist view of German-American life typified by Brand Whitlock's *The Turn of the Balance* (1907), a novel that Dreiser later said had depicted "the career of an unfortunate German family which might almost have been ours." The response to *Jennie Gerhardt* by Dreiser's sister Claire—"I can readily recognize . . . many well known characters and feel an old acquaintance with Jennie"— underlines the cluster of family memories that went into the making of the novel. The present edition allows us to consider, in a more comprehensive way, the narrative strategies Dreiser used to translate his own minority heritage into the mainstream of American fiction.

This volume continues the Pennsylvania Dreiser Edition's tradition of publishing authoritative texts of writings that either survive in manuscript or are not easily accessible to the specialist and general reader alike. Such an undertaking would be unimaginable without the goodwill of the administration and the special training of the staff at the Van Pelt-Dietrich Library Center of the University of Pennsylvania. Paul H. Mosher, Director of Libraries at the University of Pennsylvania, has provided continuing support to the Dreiser Edition as well as considerable professional encouragement. Equally important has been the commitment of the University of Pennsylvania Press. Director Thomas Rotell has in both the best and worst of times devoted the resources of his staff to making this project something other than a scholarly fantasy.

Together with the Pennsylvania Edition of *Sister Carrie* (1981), this edition of *Jennie Gerhardt* is one of a projected series of volumes that will provide scholarly texts of Dreiser's novels. Volume editor James L. W. West III wrote the historical and textual commentaries, assembled the historical notes, devised the editorial principles, emended the text, and supervised the collations and the compilation of the apparatus. Textual editor Lee Ann Draud reviewed all work on the volume, supplemented the emendations and textual notes, copyedited the book, and served as liaison with the production staff at the University of Pennsylvania Press. The general editor, the textual editor, and James M. Hutchisson proofread the text and verified the contents at each stage of preparation.

THOMAS P. RIGGIO
General Editor
The University of Pennsylvania
Dreiser Edition

ACKNOWLEDGMENTS

For permission to reproduce previously unpublished sections from the various manuscripts and typescripts of *Jennie Gerhardt,* I am grateful to the Trustees of the University of Pennsylvania. I wish also to thank Daniel H. Traister, Nancy M. Shawcross, Christine Ruggere, Georgianna Ziegler, and the staff of the Special Collections Department at the Van Pelt-Dietrich Library Center, University of Pennsylvania, for assistance throughout this project. I owe a special debt of gratitude to Neda M. Westlake, retired Curator of Rare Books at the Van Pelt, for her advice and help during the early stages of this project.

For permission to examine and use the surviving typescript of *Jennie Gerhardt* in the Theodore Dreiser Collection (#6220), Clifton Waller Barrett Library, I am grateful to the Manuscripts Division, Special Collections Department, Alderman Library, University of Virginia. Permission to publish letters by Frederick A. Duneka and Hamilton Wright Mabie (Harper Collection, accession number 2347) has been granted by The Pierpont Morgan Library. Dreiser's inscription in the Rider copy of *Jennie Gerhardt* is published here with the permission of the George Arents Research Library for Special Collections at Syracuse University. Permission to publish Sara W. Dreiser's letter to Grant Richards has been given by the Rare Book and Special Collections Library, University of Illinois at Urbana-Champaign. Jay Hoster, president of the Columbus Historical Society, was most helpful with matters of local history in Columbus, Ohio, around 1880.

Among my fellow Dreiserians I am especially grateful to Richard Lingeman, whose detailed account of the composition of *Jennie Gerhardt* in his recent two-volume biography of Dreiser served as a guide for much of my work here. I thank Thomas P. Riggio for liaison work and for some useful suggestions about the historical commentary. Lee Ann Draud has been immensely helpful throughout with matters textual. Other Dreiser scholars who have offered advice, information, and friendship are Nancy Warner Barrineau, Frederic Rusch, James M. Hutchisson, Arthur D. Casciato, and Philip Gerber. Colleagues at my own and other universities to whom I am grateful for various kinds of assistance include Joseph J. Kockelmans, Catherine Barlet, Noel Polk, Peter L. Shillingsburg, Robert H. Hirst, Joseph R. McElrath, Jr., and Lucia Kinsaul. My friends Sheldon and Lucy Hackney, Alan Filreis and Susan Albertine, and Frank and Gretta Casciato were most hospitable to me during various visits to Philadelphia.

At The Pennsylvania State University, University Park, I wish to thank the director and staff of the Institute for the Arts and Humanistic Studies, where much of this work was performed. I am also grateful to the Department of English and to the College of the Liberal Arts at Penn State for significant research support. For diligent and accurate labor on the collations and textual apparatus, I thank La Verne Kennevan Maginnis. I am grateful to Robert M. Myers for his invaluable work on the maps, chronology, and historical notes. Tracy Simmons Bitonti and Flora Buckalew also labored faithfully on the project, assisting with library legwork and performing important textual chores.

J.L.W.W. III
State College, Pennsylvania

JENNIE
GERHARDT

CHAPTER I

One morning, in the fall of 1880, a middle-aged woman, accompanied by a young girl of eighteen, presented herself at the clerk's desk of the principal hotel in Columbus, Ohio, and made inquiry as to whether there was anything about the place that she could do. She was of a helpless, fleshy build, with a frank open countenance and an innocent, diffident manner. Her eyes were large and patient, and in them dwelt such a shadow of distress as only those who have looked sympathetically into the countenances of the distraught and helpless poor know anything about. Any one could see where the daughter behind her got the timidity and shamefacedness which now caused her to stand back and look indifferently away.

The fancy, the feeling, the innate affection of an untutored, but poetic mind, were all blended in the mother, but poverty was driving her. Excepting a kind of gravity and poise, which were characteristic of her father, the daughter inherited her disposition from her mother. Together they presented so appealing a picture of honest necessity, that even the clerk was affected.

"What is it you would like to do?" he said.

"Maybe you have some cleaning or scrubbing," she replied, timidly. "I could wash the floors."

The daughter, hearing the statement, turned uneasily, not because it irritated her to work, but because she hated people to know. The clerk interrupted because he did not like to see the mother strain so nervously at explaining. Manlike, he was affected by the evidence of beauty in distress. The innocent helplessness of the daughter made their lot seem hard.

"Wait a moment," he said, and, stepping into a back office, called the head housekeeper.

There was work to be done. The main staircase and parlor hall were unswept because of the absence of the regular scrubwoman.

"Is that her daughter with her?" asked the housekeeper, who could see them from where she was standing.

"Yes, I suppose so," returned the clerk.

"She might come this afternoon, if she wants to. The girl helps her I suppose."

"You go see the housekeeper," said the clerk pleasantly, as he came back to the desk. "Right through there"—pointing to a nearby door. "She'll arrange with you about it."

The succession of events of which this little scene might have been called the tragic culmination, had taken place in the life and family of William Gerhardt, a glass-blower by trade. Having suffered the reverses so common in the lower fields of endeavor, this man was forced, for the present, to see his wife, his six children, and himself depending for the necessaries of life upon whatever windfall of fortune the morning of each successive day might bring. He was sick in bed. His oldest boy, Sebastian, worked as an apprentice to a local freight-car builder, but received only four dollars a week. Genevieve, the oldest of the girls, was past eighteen, but had not as yet been taught any special work. The other children, George, aged fourteen; Martha, twelve; William, ten; and Veronica, eight, were too young to do anything, and only made the problem of existence the more complicated. It was the ambition of both the father and mother to keep them in school, but the method of supplying clothes, books and monthly dues for this purpose, was practically beyond solution. The father, being an ardent Lutheran, insisted that the parochial schools were essential, and there, outside of the prayers and precepts of the Evangelical faith, they learned little. One child, Veronica, was already forced to remain at home for the want of shoes. George, old enough to understand and suffer from distinction made between himself and those better dressed, often ran away and played "hookey." Martha complained that she had nothing to wear, and Genevieve was glad that she was out of it all. Their one mainstay was the home, which, barring a six-hundred-dollar mortgage, the father owned. He had borrowed this money at a time when he had saved enough to buy the house and lot, in order that he might add three rooms and a porch, and make it large enough for them to live in. A few years were still to run on the mortgage, but times had been so bad he had been forced to use up not only the little he had saved to pay off the principal, but that meant for the annual interest also. Helpless as he was, the doctor's bill, children's school, interest on the mortgage about to fall due, and sums owed butcher and baker, who, though knowing him to be absolutely honest, had trusted him until they could trust no longer—all these perplexities weighed upon his mind and racked him so nervously as to delay his recovery.

Mrs. Gerhardt was no weakling. For a time she took in washing, what little she could get, devoting the intermediate hours to dressing the children, cooking, seeing that they got off to school, mending their clothes, waiting on her husband, and occasionally weeping. Not infrequently she went personally to some new grocer, each time farther and farther away, and starting an account with a little cash, would receive credit, until other grocers warned the philanthropist of his folly. Corn was cheap. Sometimes she would make a kettle of lye hominy, and this would last, with scarcely anything else, for an entire week. Corn-meal also, when made into mush, was better than nothing, and with a little milk, sometimes seemed rich. Potatoes fried was the nearest they ever came to luxurious food, and coffee was a treat. Coal was got by picking it up in buckets and baskets along the maze of tracks in the nearby railroad yard. Wood, by similar journeys to surrounding lumber yards. Thus they lived from day to day, each hour hoping their father would get well and that the glass works would start up. The whole commercial element seemed more or less paralyzed in this district. Gerhardt was facing the approaching winter and felt desperate.

"George," he would say, when the oldest of those attending school would come home at four o'clock, "we must have some more coal," and seeing Martha, William and Veronica unwillingly gather up the baskets, would hide his face and wring his hands. When Sebastian, or "Bass," as his associates had transformed it, would arrive streaked and energetic from the shop at half-past six, he would assume a cheerful air of welcome.

"How are things down there?" he would inquire. "Are they going to put on any more men?"

Bass did not know, and had no faith in its possibility, but he went over the ground with his father and hoped for the best.

"I must get out of this now pretty soon," was the sturdy Lutheran's regular comment, and his anxiety found but weak expression in the modest quality of his voice.

To add to all this trouble little Veronica took the measles, and, for a few days, it was thought that she would die. The mother neglected everything else to hover over her and pray for the best. Dr. Ellwanger came every day, out of humane sympathy, and gravely examined the child. The Lutheran minister, Pastor Wundt, called to offer the consolation of the Church. Both of these men brought an atmosphere of grim ecclesiasticism into the house. They were the black-garbed, sanctimonious emissaries of superior forces. Mrs. Gerhardt felt as if she were going to lose her child, and watched sorrowfully by the cot-side. After three days the worst was over, but there was no bread in the house. Sebastian's wages had been spent for medicine. Only coal was free for the picking, and several times the children had been scared from the railroad yards. Mrs. Gerhardt thought of all the places to which she might apply, and despairingly hit upon the hotel. Her son had often spoken of its beauty, and she was a resourceful woman. Genevieve helped her at home, why not here?

"How much do you charge?" the housekeeper asked her.

Mrs. Gerhardt had not thought this would be left to her, but need emboldened her.

"Would a dollar a day be too much?"

"No," said the housekeeper. "There is only about three days' work to do every week. If you would come every afternoon you could do it."

"Very well," said the applicant. "Shall we start today?"

"Yes. If you'll come with me now, I'll show you where the cleaning things are."

The hotel into which they were thus summarily introduced, was a rather remarkable specimen for the time and place. Columbus, being the state capital, and having a population of fifty thousand, and a fair passenger traffic, was a good field for the hotel business, and the opportunity had been improved; so at least the Columbus people proudly thought. The structure, five stories in height, and of imposing proportions, stood at one corner of the central public square, where were the capitol building and principal stores, and, naturally, the crowd and hurry of life, which, to those who had never seen anything better, seemed wondrously gay and inspiriting. Large plate-glass windows looked out upon both the main and side streets, through which could be seen many comfortable chairs scattered about for those who cared to occupy them. The lobby was large, and had been recently redecorated. Both floor and wainscot were of white marble, kept shiny by frequent polishing. There was an imposing staircase with hand-rails of walnut and toe strips of brass. An inviting corner was devoted to a news and cigar stand. Where the staircase curved upward the clerk's desk and offices had been located, all done in hardwood and ornamented by novel gas fixtures. One could see through a door at one end of the lobby to the barber-shop, with its chairs and array of shaving mugs. Outside were usually to be seen two or three buses, arriving or departing in accordance with the movement of the trains.

To this caravansary came the best of the political and social patronage of the state. Several governors had made it their permanent abiding place during their terms of office. The two United States Senators, whenever business called them to Columbus, invariably maintained parlor chambers at the hotel. One of them, Senator Brander, was looked upon by the proprietor as more or less of a permanent resident, because he was not only a natural inhabitant of the city, but an otherwise homeless bachelor. Other and more transient guests were congressmen, state legislators and lobbyists, merchants, professional men, and, after them, the whole raft of indescribables, who, coming and going, make up the glow and stir of this kaleidoscopic world.

Mother and daughter, brought into this realm of brightness, saw only that which was far off and immensely superior. They went about too timid to touch anything, for fear of giving offense. The great red-carpeted hallway, which they were set to sweep, overawed them so that they constantly kept their eyes down and spoke in their lowest tones. When it came to scrubbing the steps, and polishing the brass work of the splendid stairs, both needed to steel themselves, the mother against her timidity, the daughter against her shame at so public an exposure. Wide beneath lay the imposing lobby, and men, lounging, smoking, passing constantly in and out, could see them both.

"Isn't it fine?" said Genevieve nervously, more to be dulling the sound of her own conscience than anything else.

"Yes," returned her mother, who, upon her knees, was wringing out her cloth with earnest but clumsy hands.

"It must cost a good deal to live here, don't you think?"

"Yes," said her mother. "Don't forget to rub into these little corners. Look here what you've left."

Jennie, actually reassured by this correction, fell earnestly to her task, and polished vigorously without lifting her eyes.

In this manner they worked carefully downward until about five o'clock, when it was dark outside, and all the lobby was brightly lighted. Now they were very near the bottom of the stairway.

Through the big swinging doors there entered from the chilly world without a tall, distinguished, middle-aged gentleman, whose silk hat and loose military cape-coat marked him at once, among the crowd of general idlers, as some one of importance. His face was of a dark and solemn cast, but broad and sympathetic in its lines, and his bright eyes were heavily shaded with thick, bushy, black eye-brows. He carried a polished walking-stick, evidently more for the pleasure of the thing than anything else. Passing to the desk, he picked up the key that had already been laid out for him, and coming to the staircase, started up.

The middle-aged woman, scrubbing at his feet, he acknowledged by not only walking around her, but by graciously waving his hand, as much as to say, "Don't move for me."

The daughter, however, caught his eye by standing up, her troubled glance showing that she feared that she was in his way.

He bowed, smiled pleasantly, and addressing her said:

"You shouldn't have troubled yourself."

Jennie only smiled.

When he had reached the upper landing, a sidewise glance told him, more keenly than even his first view, of her uncommon features. He saw the high, white forehead, with its smoothly parted and plaited hair. The eyes he knew were blue, the complexion fair. He had even time to admire the mouth and full cheeks, but most of all, the well-rounded, graceful form, full of youth, health, and all that futurity of hope, which to the middle-aged and waning, is so suggestive of all that is worth begging of Providence. Without another look, he went dignifiedly upon his way, carrying her impression with him. This was the Honorable George Sylvester Brander, junior senator from Ohio.

A few moments after he had gone, and Jennie had become engrossed with her labor as before, the fact that she also had observed him disclosed itself.

"Wasn't that a fine-looking man who went up just now?"

"Yes, he was," said her mother.

"He had a gold-headed cane."

"You mustn't stare at people when they pass," cautioned her mother wisely. "It isn't nice."

"I didn't stare at him," returned Jennie innocently. "He bowed to me."

"Well, don't you pay any attention to anybody," said her mother. "They may not like it."

Jennie fell to her task in silence, but the finery of the world was having its say. She could not help giving ear to the sounds, the brightness, and the buzz of conversation and laughter which went about. In one section of the parlor floor was the dining-room, and from the clink of dishes one could tell that supper was being prepared. In another was the parlor proper, and there someone came to play on the piano. All that feeling of rest and relaxation which comes before the evening meal pervaded the place. It touched the heart of the innocent working-girl with hope, for hers were the years, and poverty could not as yet fill her young mind with cares. She rubbed diligently always, and sometimes forgot the troubled mother at her side, whose kindly eyes were becoming invested with crow's-feet, and whose lips half-repeated the hundred cares of the day. She could only think that all of this was very fascinating, and wish that a portion of it might come to her.

At half-past five, the housekeeper, remembering them, came and told them that they might go. The fully finished stairway was relinquished by both with a sigh of relief, and passing out into the side street, by the rear entrance, after putting their implements away, the couple hastened homeward, the mother, at least, pleased to think that at last she had something to do.

As they passed several fine houses, Jennie was again touched by something of that which the unwonted novelty of the hotel life had driven swiftly home.

"Isn't it fine to be rich?" she said.

"Yes," answered her mother, who was thinking of the suffering Veronica.

"Did you see what a big dining-room they had there?"

"Yes."

They went on past the low cottages and among the dead leaves of the year.

"I wish we were rich," murmured Jennie with a sigh.

"I don't know just what to do," confided her mother after a time, when her own deep thoughts would no longer bear silence. "I don't believe there's a thing to eat in the house."

"Let's stop and see Mr. Bauman again," exclaimed Jennie, her natural sympathies restored by the hopeless quality in her mother's voice.

"Do you think he would trust us any more?"

"Let's tell him where we're working. I will."

"Well," said her mother wearily.

Into the small, dimly lighted grocery store, which was two blocks from their house, both of the wayfarers ventured nervously. Mrs. Gerhardt was about to begin, but Jennie spoke first.

"Will you let us have some bread tonight, and a little bacon? We're working now at the Columbus House, and we'll be sure to pay you Saturday."

"Yes," added Mrs. Gerhardt, "I have something to do."

Bauman, who had long supplied them before illness and trouble began, knew that they told the truth.

"How long have you been working there?" he asked.

"Just this afternoon."

"You know, Mrs. Gerhardt," he said, "how it is with me. I don't want to refuse you. Mr. Gerhardt is good for it, but I am poor, too. Times are hard," he explained further. "I have my family to keep."

"Yes, I know," said Mrs. Gerhardt weakly.

Her old red cotton shawl hid her rough hands, red from the day's work, but they were working nervously. Jennie stood by strained and silent.

"Well," concluded Mr. Bauman eventually, "I guess it's all right this time. Do what you can for me Saturday."

He laid out the bread and bacon, and when about to hand it to them added, with a touch of cynicism:

"When you get money again, I guess you'll go and trade somewhere else."

"No," returned Mrs. Gerhardt, "you know better than that." But she was too nervous to parley long.

They went out into the shadowy street again, and on past the low cottages to their own home.

"I wonder," said the mother wearily, when they neared the door, "if they've got any coal?"

"Don't worry," said Jennie. "If they haven't, I'll go."

"A man run us away," was almost the first greeting that the perturbed George offered, when the children had gathered in the kitchen to discuss developments with their mother. "I got some though," he added. "I threw it off a car."

Mrs. Gerhardt only smiled, but Jennie laughed.

"How is Veronica?" she inquired.

"She seems to be sleeping," said the father. "I gave her medicine again at five."

While the scant meal was being thus tardily prepared, the mother went to the cot-side, taking up another night's vigil that was almost without sleep.

During the preparation of the meal, such as it was, Sebastian made a suggestion. His larger experience in social and commercial matters made this valuable. Though only a car-builder's apprentice, without any education, except such as pertained to Lutheran doctrine, to which he objected very much, he was imbued with American color and energy. His transformed name of Bass suited him exactly. Tall, athletic and well-featured for his age, he had already received those favors and glances from the young girls that tend to make the bright boy a dandy. With the earliest evidence of such interest, he had begun to see that appearances were worth something, and from that to the illusion that they were more important than anything else, was but an easy step. At the car-works he got in with a half-dozen other young boys, who knew Columbus and its possibilities thoroughly, and with them he fraternized until he was a typical stripling of the town. He knew all about ball-games and athletics, had heard that the state capital contained the high and mighty of the land, loved the theatre, with its suggestion of travel and advertisement, and was not unaware that to succeed one must do something—associate, or at least, seem to, with those who were foremost in the world of appearances.

For this reason, the young boy loved to hang about the Columbus House. It seemed to him that this hotel with its glow and shine was the centre and circumference of all that was worth while in the social sense. He would go downtown evenings, when he first secured money enough to buy a decent suit of clothes, and stand around the hotel entrance with his friends, kicking his heels, smoking a two-for-five-cent cigar, preening himself on his stylish appearance and looking after the girls. Others were there with him, town dandies and nobodies, those who gambled, or sought other pleasures, and young men who came there to get shaved or to drink a glass of whiskey. And all of these he both admired and sought to emulate. Clothes were the main persuasion. If they wore nice clothes and had rings and pins, whatever they did seemed appropriate. He wanted to be like them, and act like them, and so his experience of the more pointless forms of life rapidly broadened.

It was he who had spoken to his mother more than once of the Columbus House, and now that she was working there, much to his mortification, he thought that it would be better if they only took laundry from it. Work they had to, in some such difficult way, but if they could get some of these fine gentlemen's laundry to do, how much better it would be. Others did it.

"Why don't you get some of those hotel fellows to give you their laundry?" he asked of Jennie after she had related the afternoon's experiences to him. "It would be better than scrubbing the stairs."

"How do you get it?" she replied.

"Why, ask the clerk, of course."

This struck her as very much worth while.

"Don't you ever speak to me if you meet me around there," he cautioned her a little later, privately. "Don't you let on that you know me."

"Why?" she asked, innocently.

"Well, you know why," he answered, having indicated before that when they looked so poor he did not want to be disgraced by having to own them as relatives. "Just you go on by. Do you hear?"

"All right," she returned, meekly, for although this youth was not much over a year her senior, his superior will dominated.

The next day on their way to the hotel, Jennie spoke to her mother.

"Bass said we might get some of the laundry of the men at the hotel to do."

Mrs. Gerhardt, whose mind had been straining all night at the problem of adding something to the three dollars which her six afternoons would bring her, approved of the idea.

"So we might," she said. "I'll ask that clerk."

When they reached the hotel, however, no immediate opportunity presented itself. They worked on until late in the afternoon. Then, as fortune would have it, the housekeeper sent them in to scrub up the floor behind the clerk's desk. That individual felt very kindly toward both mother and daughter. He liked the former's sweetly troubled countenance, and the latter's pretty face. When they were working about him on their knees, he did not feel irritated at all. Finally they got through, and Mrs. Gerhardt ventured very meekly to put the question which she had been anxiously revolving in her mind all the afternoon.

"Is there any gentleman here," she said, "who would give me his washing to do? I'd be so very much obliged for it."

The clerk looked at her, and again saw what was written all over her face, absolute want.

"Let's see," he answered, thinking of Senator Brander and Marshall Hopkins. Both were men of large, charitable mould who would be more than glad to aid a poor woman. "You go up and see Senator Brander. He's in twenty-two. Here," he added, writing out the number, "you go up and tell him I sent you."

Mrs. Gerhardt took the card with a tremor of gratefulness. Her eyes looked the words she could not say.

"That's all right," said the clerk, observing her emotion. "You go right up. You'll find him in his room now."

With the greatest diffidence Mrs. Gerhardt knocked at number twenty-two. Jennie stood silently at her side.

After a moment the door was opened, and in the full radiance of the bright room stood the senator. He was as faultlessly attired as before, only this time, because of a fancy smoking coat, he looked younger.

"Well, madam," he said, recognizing the couple, and particularly the daughter, he had seen upon the stairs, "what can I do for you?"

Very much abashed, the mother hesitated in her reply.

"We would like to know if you have any washing you could let us have to do?"

"Washing," he repeated after her, in a voice which had a peculiarly resonant quality. "Washing? Come right in. Let me see."

He stepped aside with much grace, waved them in, and closed the door. While the two stood half-confused amid the evidences of comfort and finery, he repeated, "Let me see."

Mrs. Gerhardt looked principally at his handsome head, but Jennie studied the room. Such an array of knick-knacks and things that seemed of great value on mantel and dressing-case she had never seen. The senator's easy chair, with a green-shaded lamp beside it, the rich heavy carpet and rugs upon the floor, and all the scattered evidence of mannish comfort were to her distinctly ideal.

While they were standing he moved over to a corner of the room, but turned about to say, "Sit down; take those two chairs there."

Still overawed, mother and daughter thought it more polite to disobey.

He disappeared into a large closet, but came out again, and after advising them to sit down, said, with a glance at Mrs. Gerhardt and a smile at Jennie:

"Is this your daughter?"

"Yes, sir," said the mother. "She's my oldest girl."

"Oh, she is," he returned, turning his back now and opening a bureau drawer. While he was rummaging and extracting several articles of apparel, he asked:

"Is your husband alive?"

"What is his name?"

"Where does he live?"

To all of these questions Mrs. Gerhardt very humbly answered.

"How many children have you?" he inquired very earnestly.

"Six," said Mrs. Gerhardt.

"Well," he returned, "that's quite a family. You've certainly done your duty to the nation."

"Yes, sir," returned Mrs. Gerhardt, who was touched by his genial and interested manner.

"And you say this is your oldest daughter?"

"Yes, sir."

"What does your husband do?"

"He's a glass-blower. But he's sick now."

During the colloquy Jennie's large blue eyes were wide with interest. Whenever he looked at her, she turned upon him such a frank, unsophisticated gaze, and smiled in such a vague, sweet way, that he could not help repeating his attentions.

"Well," he said, "that is too bad. I have some washing

here—not very much, but what there is, you are welcome to. Next week there may be more."

He went about now, stuffing things into a blue cotton bag with a pretty design on the side, and all the while asking questions. In some indefinable way, these two figures appealed to him. He wanted to know just how their home condition stood and why this innocent looking mother, with the pathetic eyes, came to be scrubbing hotel stairways.

In trying to question closely, without giving offense, he bordered upon the ridiculous:

"Where is it you live?" he said, recalling that the mother had only vaguely indicated.

"On 13th Street," she returned.

"North or South?"

"South."

He paused again, and bringing over the bag said:

"Well, here they are. How much do you charge for your work?"

Mrs. Gerhardt started to explain, but he saw how aimless his question was. He really did not care about the price. Whatever such humble souls as these might charge, he would willingly pay.

"Never mind," he said, sorry that he had mentioned the subject.

"Do you want these any certain day?" questioned the mother.

"No," he said, scratching his head reflectively, "any day next week will do."

She thanked him with a simple phrase, and started to go.

"Let me see," he said, stepping ahead of them and opening the door. "You may bring them back Monday."

"Yes, sir," said Mrs. Gerhardt. "Thank you."

They went out and the senator returned to his reading, but it was with a peculiarly disturbed mind.

"Too bad," he said, closing his volume. "There's something very pathetic about those people."

He brooded awhile, the ruck of his own trivial questions coming back, and then arose. Somehow their visit seemed for the time being to set clearly before him his own fortunate condition. Jennie's spirit of wonder and appreciation was abroad in the chamber.

As for Mrs. Gerhardt, she forgot the other washing in the

glee of getting this one. She and Jennie made their way anew through the shadowy streets.

"Didn't he have a fine room?" whispered Jennie.

"Yes," answered her mother. "He's a great man."

"He's a senator, isn't he?" continued the daughter.

"Yes."

"It must be nice to be famous," said the girl, softly.

CHAPTER II

The spirit of Jennie—who shall express it? This daughter of poverty, who was now to fetch and carry the laundry of this distinguished citizen of Columbus, was a creature of a mellowness which words can but vaguely suggest. There are natures born to the inheritance of flesh that come without understanding, and that go again without seeming to have wondered why. Life, as long as they endure it, is a true wonderland, a thing of infinite beauty, which could they but wander into it, wonderingly, would be heaven enough. Opening their eyes, they see a conformable and perfect world. Trees, flowers, the world of sound and the world of color. These are the valued inheritance of their state. If no one said to them "Mine," they would wander radiantly forth, singing the song which all the earth may some day hope to hear. It is the song of goodness.

Caged in the world of the material, however, such a nature is almost invariably an anomaly. That other world of flesh, into which has been woven pride and greed, looks with but blinded eyes, and sees but little. If one says it is sweet to look at the clouds, the answer is a word against idleness. If one seeks to give ear to the winds, it shall be well with his soul, but they will seize upon his possessions. If all the world of the so-called inanimate delay one, calling with tenderness in sounds that seem to be too perfect to be less than understanding, it shall be ill with the body. The hands of the actual are forever reaching toward such as these—forever seizing greedily upon them. It is of such that the bondservants are made.

In the world of the actual, Jennie was such a spirit. From her earliest youth, goodness and mercy had moulded her impulses. Did Sebastian fall and injure himself, it was she who struggled with straining anxiety to carry him safely to his mother. Did George complain that he was hungry, she gave him all of her bread. Many were the hours in which she had rocked her younger brothers and sisters to sleep, singing whole-heartedly betimes and dreaming far dreams. Since her earliest walking period, almost, she had been as the right hand of her mother. What scrubbing, baking, errand-running and nursing there had been to do, she did. No one had ever heard her rudely complain, though she often thought of the hardness of it. Others did not have to do it, that she knew. There were girls whose lives were more beautifully environed, and her fancy reached out to them, but sympathy left her singing where she was. When the days were fair, she looked out of her kitchen window and longed to go where the meadows were. Nature's fine curves and shadows touched her as a song itself. There were times when she had gone with George and the others, leading them away to where a patch of hickory trees flourished, because there were open fields, with shade for comfort and a brook of living water. No artist in the formulating of conceptions, her soul still responded to these things, and every sound and every sigh were welcome to her because of their beauty.

When the soft, low call of the wood-doves, those spirits of the summer, came out of the distance, she would incline her head and listen, the whole spiritual quality of it dropping like silver bubbles into her own great heart.

Where the sunlight was warm, and the shadows flecked with its splendid radiance, she delighted to wonder at the pattern of it, to walk where it was most golden, and follow with instinctive appreciation the holy corridors of the trees.

Color was not lost upon her. That wonderful radiance which fills the western sky at evening, touched and unburdened her heart.

"I wonder," she said once with girlish simplicity, "how it would feel to float away off there among those clouds."

She had discovered a natural swing of a wild grape-vine, and was sitting in it with Martha and George.

"Oh, wouldn't it be nice if you had a boat up there," said George.

She was looking with uplifted face at a far-off cloud, a red island in a sea of silver.

"Just supposing," she said, "people could live on an island like that."

Her soul was already up there, and its elysian paths knew the lightness of her feet.

"There goes a bee," said George, noting a bumbler winging by.

"Yes," she said dreamily, "it's going home."

"Does everything have a home?" asked Martha.

"Nearly everything," she answered.

"Do the birds go home?" questioned George.

"Yes," she said, deeply feeling the poetry of it herself, "the birds go home."

"Do the bees go home?" urged Martha.

"Yes, the bees go home."

"Do the dogs go home?" said George, who saw one travelling lonesomely along the nearby road.

"Why, of course," she said, "you know that dogs go home."

"Do the gnats?" he persisted, seeing one of those curious spirals of minute insects turning energetically in the waning light.

"Yes," she said, half believing her remark. "Listen."

"Oho!" exclaimed George incredulously. "I wonder what kind of houses they live in."

"Listen," she gently persisted, putting out her hand to still him.

It was that halcyon hour when the Angelus falls like a benediction upon the waning day. Far off the notes were sounding gently, and nature, now that she listened, seemed to have paused also. A scarlet-breasted robin was hopping in short spaces upon the green of the grass before her. A humming bee hummed, a cowbell tinkled, while some suspicious cracklings about told of a secretly reconnoitering squirrel. Keeping her pretty hand weighed in the air, she listened until the long soft notes spread and faded, and her heart could hold no more. Then she arose.

"Oh," she said, clenching her fingers in an agony of poetic feeling. There were crystal tears of mellowness in her eyes. The wondrous sea of feeling in her had stormed its banks. Of such was the spirit of Jennie.

CHAPTER III

The junior senator from Ohio, George Sylvester Brander, was a man of peculiar mould. In him there were joined, to a remarkable degree, the wisdom of the opportunist and the sympathies of the true representative of the people. Born a native of southern Ohio, he had been raised and educated there, if one might except the two years in which he had studied law at Columbia University, and the other years in which he had received polish and breadth at Washington. Not over-wise in the sense of absolute understanding, he could still be called a learned man. He knew common and criminal law, perhaps, as well as any citizen of his state, but he had never practised with that assiduity which brought to so many others distinguished notoriety. He was well informed in the matter of corporation law, but had too much humanity and general feeling for the people to convince himself that he could follow it. He had made money, and had had splendid opportunities to make a great deal more if he had been willing to stultify his conscience, but that he had never been able to do. *Right* seemed a great thing to talk about. He loved the sounding phrases with which he could pour off, to the satisfaction of his hearers, the strong conceptions and feelings he had on this divine topic, but he could never reason clearly enough to discover for himself whether he was following it or not. Friendship called him to many things which courteous reason could have honorably prevented. Only in the last presidential election he had thrown his support to a man for governor who, as he well knew, had no claim which a strictly honorable conscience could have honored. Friends did it. He felt, in the last resort, that he could not go back of the protestations of his friends. They would vouch for the individual this time. Why not believe them?

In the same way, he had been guilty of some very questionable, and one or two actually unsavory, appointments. Personal interest dictated a part of this—friendship for friends of the applicants, the rest. Whenever his conscience pricked him too keenly, he would endeavor to cheer himself with his pet spoken phrase: "All in a lifetime." Thinking over things quite alone in his easy chair, he would sometimes rise up with these words on his lips, and smile sheepishly as he did so. Conscience was not, by any means, dead in him. His sympathies, if anything, were keener than ever.

This man, three times congressman from the district of which Columbus was a part, and twice senator, had never married. In his youth, he had had a serious love affair, but there was nothing discreditable to him in the fact that it came to nothing. The lady found it inconvenient to wait for him. He was too long in earning a competence upon which they might subsist.

Tall, straight-shouldered, neither lean nor stout, he was today an imposing figure. Having received his hard knocks and endured his losses, there was that about him which touched and awakened the sympathies of the imaginative. People thought him naturally agreeable, and his senatorial peers looked upon him as not any too heavy mentally, but personally a fine man.

His presence in Columbus at this particular time was due to the fact that his political fences needed careful repairing. The general election had weakened his party in the state legislature. There were enough votes to re-elect him, but it would require the most careful political manipulation to hold them together. Other men were ambitious. There were a half-dozen available candidates, any one of whom would have rejoiced to step into his shoes. He realized the exigencies of the occasion. They could not well beat him, he thought; but if so, the president could be induced to give him a ministry abroad. The clinching of this, even, required party consultation and pledges.

It might be supposed that, under such circumstances, a man would be satisfied, bringing to bear the logic of life, and letting the world wag as it would. Such men exist in theory only. Brander, like all the rest of his fellow-men, felt the drag of the unsatisfied. He had wanted to do so many things. Here he was—fifty-two years of age, clean, honorable, highly distinguished, as the world takes it, but single. He could not help looking about him now and then and speculating upon the fact that he had no one to care for him. His chamber seemed strangely hollow at times—his own personality exceedingly disagreeable.

In the world of his associates, he knew many men who had lovely wives. He could see plainly that these women were all in all to their husbands. Homes, the finest and most comfortable he had ever known, were founded solidly on such. Sons, daughters, nephews and nieces, in merry and comforting array, all seemed to be gathered round some people, but he—he was alone.

"Fifty!" he often thought to himself. "Alone—absolutely alone."

Sitting in his chamber that Saturday afternoon, he was aroused by a rap at his door. He had been speculating upon the futility of all of his political energy, in the light of the impermanence of life and fame.

"What a great fight we make to sustain ourselves," he thought. "How little difference it will make to me a few years hence."

He arose, and opening wide his door, perceived Jennie. She had come, as she had suggested to her mother, at this time, instead of on Monday, in order to give a more favorable impression of promptness.

"Come right in," said the senator, and, as on the first occasion, graciously made way for her.

Jennie passed in, momentarily expecting some comment upon the brevity of time in which the washing had been done. The senator never noticed it at all.

"Well, my young lady," he said when she had put the bundle down, "how do you find yourself this evening?"

"Very well," replied Jennie. "We thought we'd better bring your clothes today instead of Monday."

"Oh, that would not have made any difference," replied Brander, who thus lightly waved aside what to her seemed so important. "Just leave them on the chair."

Jennie stood up a moment, and considering that not even the fact of having received no recompense was an excuse for lingering, would have gone out, had not the senator detained her.

"How is your mother?" he asked pleasantly, the whole condition of the family distinctly coming back to him.

"She's very well," said Jennie simply.

"And your little sister? Is she any better?"

"The doctor thinks so," replied Jennie, who was greatly concerned over the youngest.

"Sit down," he went on entertainingly. "I want to talk to you."

Stepping to a nearby chair, the young girl seated herself.

"Hem!" he went on, clearing his throat lightly. "What seems to be the matter with her?"

"She has the measles," returned Jennie. "We thought once that she was going to die."

Brander studied her face as she said this, and he thought he saw something exceedingly pathetic there. The girl's poor clothes and her wondering admiration for his state affected him. He felt again that thing which she had made him feel before—the far way he had come along the path of comfort. How high up he was in the world, indeed!

Not recognizing the innate potentiality of any creature, however commonplace, who could make him feel this, he went glibly on, lured, and in a way, controlled by an unconscious power in her. She was a lodestone of a kind, and he was its metal; but neither she nor he knew it.

"Well," he said after a moment or two of reflection, "that's too bad, isn't it."

The spirit in which he said this was entirely conventional. He did not, by a hundredth part, feel the quality which it conveyed to her. Somehow, it brought to Jennie a general picture of her mother and father, and of all the stress and worry they were undergoing at present. She hardened herself intensely against the emotion, lurking so closely behind the surface in her, and silently let the comment pass. It was not lost on him, however. He put his hand to his chin, and in a cheery, legal way said:

"She is better now, though, of course. How old is your father?"

"Fifty-seven," she replied.

"And is he any better?"

"Oh, yes sir. He's around now, although he can't go out just yet."

"I believe your mother said he was a glass-blower by trade?"

"Yes sir."

Brander well knew the depressed local conditions in this branch of manufacture. It had been part of the political issue in the last campaign. They must be in a bad way truly.

"Do all of the children go to school?" he inquired.

"Why, yes sir," returned Jennie, stammering. She was too shamefaced to own that one was left out for the lack of shoes. The utterance of the falsehood troubled her.

He studied awhile and finding that he had no good excuse for further detaining her, arose and came over to her. Out of his pocket he took a thin layer of bills, and removing one, handed it to her.

"You take that," he said, "and tell your mother that I said she should use it for whatever she wants."

Jennie took it with mingled feelings, but did not see how much it was. The great man was so near her, the wonderful chamber in which he dwelt so impressive, she scarcely realized what she was doing.

"Thank you," she said. And then, "Is there any day you want your washing called for?"

"Oh, yes," he answered, "Monday—Monday evenings."

She went away, and half in a reverie he closed the door behind her. The interest that he felt in these people was unusual. Poverty and beauty certainly made up an affecting combination. He sat down in his chair and gave himself over to the pleasant speculations which her coming had aroused. Why should he not help them? Why not study this fine girl who had such a striking head?

He mused and as he did so, the quarters and half hours passed. There were pictures in his mind of a low cottage, a cheerless chamber, a lovely girl carrying a bundle to him through the shadows of a dreary November evening.

"I'll find out where they live," he thought to himself at last, waking up and standing.

In the days that followed, Jennie regularly came for the clothes. On Monday and again on Saturday evening she appeared with her air of cleanly beauty and innocence, which pleased the able senator greatly. He found himself more and more interested to talk to, or rather, at her, as it was in the beginning; but in time he managed to remove from her mind that timidity and fear which had made her feel uncomfortable in his presence. Much of her charm was her utter unaffectedness.

One thing he did which helped toward this was to call her by her first name. This began with her third visit, and thereafter he used it with almost unconscious frequency.

It could scarcely be said that he did this in a fatherly spirit, for he had little of that attitude toward any one. The man felt young, and could never see why time should insist on making alterations in his body while his tastes and spirits remained unchanged. He felt exceedingly young sometimes as he talked to this girl, and wondered whether she could not perceive and appreciate him on his youthful side.

As for Jennie, she admired the conditions surrounding this man, and subconsciously the man himself, the most attractive she had ever known. Everything he had was fine, everything he did was gentle, distinguished, and considerate. From some far source, perhaps old German ancestors, she inherited an understanding and appreciation of this. Life ought to be lived as he lived it. One should have things of ornament and beauty about. The privilege of being generous as he was, that she would have liked most.

Part of her attitude was due to that of her mother, whom sympathy rather than reason guided. For instance, when she brought to her the ten dollars, Mrs. Gerhardt was transported with joy.

"Oh," said Jennie, "I didn't know until I got outside that it was so much. He said I should give it to you."

Mrs. Gerhardt took it, and holding it loosely in her folded hands, saw distinctly before her the tall senator with his fine manners, remembering her.

"What a fine man he is," she said. "He has a good heart."

Frequently throughout the evening and the next day, she commented upon this, repeating how good he must be, or how large was his heart. When it came to washing his clothes, she was like to have rubbed them to pieces, feeling that whatever she did, she could scarcely do enough. Gerhardt was not to know. He had such stern views about accepting money without earning it that even in their distress, she would have experienced difficulty in getting him to take it. Consequently, she said nothing, but used it to buy bread and meat, and going as it did such a little way, the sudden windfall was never noticed.

Jennie, from now on, reflected this attitude toward the senator, and feeling so generously, talked more freely. They came to be on such good terms that he gave her a little leather picture-case from his dresser which he thought he saw her admiring. Every time she came he found excuse to detain her, and soon discovered that, for all her soft girlishness, there lay deep-seated in her a conscious deprecation of poverty and a shame of having to own to any need. He began to honestly admire her for this, but seeing that her clothes were poor and her shoes worn, to wonder how he could help her without offending.

Not infrequently, he thought to follow her some evening, and see for himself what the condition of the family might be. He was a United States Senator, however. The neighborhood they lived in must be very poor. He stopped to consider how his prowling thereabouts might be taken. Little considerations like these are very large in the case of a public citizen. His enemies might readily observe, and then manufacture anything. Consequently, this was put off.

Early in December he returned to Washington for three weeks, and both Mrs. Gerhardt and Jennie were surprised to learn one day that he had gone. Never had he given them less than two dollars a week for his washing, and several times it had been five. He had not realized, perhaps, what a breach his absence would make in their finances. Left thus, they pinched along. Gerhardt, now better, searched for work at the various mills, and finding nothing, procured a saw-buck and saw, and going from door to door, sought for the privilege of sawing wood. There was not a great deal of this to do, but he managed by the most earnest labor to earn two, and sometimes three dollars a week. This, added to what his wife earned and Sebastian gave, was enough to keep bread in their mouths, but scarcely more.

It was at the opening of the joyous Christmas-time, that the bitterness of their poverty affected them most. The Germans love to make a great display at Christmas. It is the one season of the year when the fulness of their large family affection manifests itself. Warm in the appreciation of the joys of childhood, they love to see the little ones have toys and games. Father Gerhardt, at his saw-buck during the weeks before Christmas, thought of this often. What would little Veronica not deserve after her long illness? How he would have liked to give each of the children a stout pair of shoes, the boys a warm cap, the girls a pretty hood. Toys and games and candy they had always had before. He hated to think of the snow-covered Christmas morning, and no table richly piled with what their young hearts would most desire.

As for Mrs. Gerhardt, one could better imagine than describe her feelings. She felt so keenly about it that she could hardly bring herself to speak of the dreaded hour to her husband. Three dollars she had laid aside in the hope of getting enough to buy a ton of coal and so put an end to poor George's daily pilgrimage to the coal yard, but now as the Christmas week drew near, she decided to abandon the coal idea, and use it for gifts. Gerhardt senior was also secreting two dollars even from her, in the hope that Christmas evening he could produce it at a critical moment and relieve her anxiety.

When the actual time arrived, however, there was very little to be said for the comfort they got out of the occasion. The whole city was rife with the Christmas atmosphere. Grocery stores and meat markets were strung with holly. The toy-shops and candy-stores were radiant with fine displays of everything that a self-respecting Santa Claus should have about him. Both parents and children observed it all. The former with serious thoughts of need and anxiety; the latter with wild fancy and only partially suppressed longings.

Frequently had Gerhardt said in their presence:

"Kriss Kringle is very poor this year. He hasn't so very much to give."

But no child, however poverty-stricken, could be made to believe this. Every time after so saying he looked into their eyes, but in spite of the warning, expectation flamed in them undiminished.

Christmas coming on Tuesday, the Monday before there was no school. Before going to the hotel, Mrs. Gerhardt had cautioned George that they must bring enough coal from the yards to last over Christmas day. The latter went once with his two younger sisters, but there being a dearth of picking for some reason, it took them a long time to fill their baskets, and by night they had scarcely gathered enough.

"Did you go for the coal?" asked Mrs. Gerhardt, the first thing when she returned from the hotel that evening.

"Yes," said George.

"Did you get enough for tomorrow?"

"Yes," he replied, "I guess so."

"Well, now, I'll go and look," she replied, and taking the lamp, they went out into the woodshed where the coal was deposited.

"Oh, my!" she exclaimed when she saw it. "Why, that isn't enough. You must go right off and get some more."

"Oh," said George, pouting his lips, "I don't want to go. Let Bass go."

Bass, who had returned promptly at a quarter past six, was already busy in the back bedroom washing and dressing preparatory to going downtown.

"No," said Mrs. Gerhardt, "Bass has worked hard all day. You must go."

"Oh, I don't want to," pouted George. "Let him go along anyhow."

"Now," she said, realizing at the same time how hard it all was, "what makes you so stubborn?"

"Well, I don't want to go," returned the boy. "I've been over there three times today."

"All right," said Mrs. Gerhardt, "maybe tomorrow you'll be without a fire, and then what?"

They went back to the house, but George's conscience was too troubled to allow him to consider the case as closed.

"Bass, you come go," he called to his elder brother when he was inside.

"Go where?" said Bass.

"To get some coal."

"No," said the former, "I guess not. What do you take me for?"

"Well, then, I'll not," said George, with an obstinate jerk of his head.

"Why didn't you get it up this afternoon?" questioned his brother sharply. "You've had all day to do it."

"Aw, I did get it up," said George. "We couldn't get any. I can't get any when there ain't any, can I?"

"I guess you didn't try very hard," said the dandy.

"What's the matter now?" asked Jennie, who, coming in after having stopped at the grocer's for her mother, saw George with a solemn pout on his face.

"Oh, Bass won't go with me to get any coal."

"Didn't you get any this afternoon?"

"Yes," said George, "but Ma says I didn't get enough."

"I'll go with you," said his sister. "Bass, will you come along?"

"No," said the young man, indifferently, "I won't." He was adjusting his necktie and felt irritated.

"There ain't any," said George, "unless we get it off the cars. There wasn't any cars where I was."

"There are, too!" exclaimed Bass.

"There ain't," said George.

"Didn't I see 'em just as I came across the tracks, now?"

"Well, they just run 'em in then," said George.

"Well they're there, if you want to look."

"Oh, don't quarrel," said Jennie. "Get the baskets, and let's go right now before it gets too late."

The other children, who had a fondness for their big sister, got out the implements of supply—Veronica a basket, Martha and William buckets, and George a big clothes-basket, which he and Jennie were to fill and carry between them. Bass, moved by his sister's willingness and the little respect he maintained for her, now made a suggestion.

"Now, I'll tell you what you do, Jen. You go over there with the kids to 8th Street and wait around those cars. I'll be along in a minute. When I come by, don't any of you pretend to know me. Just you say, 'Mister, won't you please throw us some coal down?' and then I'll get up on the cars and throw you off enough. D'ye hear?"

"All right," said Jennie, very much pleased.

"Don't you let on that you know me, now, any of you, do you hear?"

"Yes," said George, indifferently. "Come on, Mart."

Out into the snowy night they went, visible because of the snow and the moonlight seeping through fleecy clouds, and made their way to the railroad tracks. At the intersection of the street and the broad railroad yard were many heavily laden cars of bituminous coal newly backed in. All of the children gathered within the shadow of one. While they were standing there, waiting the arrival of their brother, the Washington Special arrived, a long, fine train with several of the new-style drawing-room cars, the big plate-glass windows shining, and the passengers looking out from the depths of their comfortable chairs. The children instinctively drew back as it thundered past.

"Oh, wasn't it long?" said George.

"Wouldn't I like to be a brakeman, though," said William.

Jennie, alone, kept silent, but the suggestion of travel and comfort was the most appealing to her of all.

Sebastian now appeared in the distance, a mannish spring in his stride, and with every evidence that he took himself seriously.

He was of that peculiar stubbornness and determination that, had the children now failed to carry out his suggestion, he would have gone deliberately by, and refused to help them at all.

Martha, however, took the situation as it needed to be taken, and piped childishly, "Mister, won't you please throw us down some coal?"

Sebastian stopped abruptly, and looking sharply at them as a stranger well might, exclaimed, "Why, certainly!" and proceeded to climb up on the car from whence he cast down with remarkable celerity more than enough chunks to fill their baskets, after which, not caring to linger any longer amid such plebeian company, he hastened across the net work of tracks, and was lost to view.

Upon this trail, however, when they had their baskets well filled and carried to the side-walk, came another gentleman, this time a real one, with high hat and distinguished cape-coat, whom Jennie immediately recognized. This was the honorable senator himself, newly returned from Washington, and anticipating a very unprofitable Christmas. He had arrived upon the express which had enlisted the attention of the children, and was carrying his light grip, for the pleasure of it, to the hotel. When he drew near, he thought he recognized Jennie, and paused to be more certain.

"Is that you, Jennie?" he said.

The latter, who had discovered him even more quickly than he had her, exclaimed, "Oh, there is Mr. Brander!" and, dropping her end of the basket, with a caution to the children to take it right home, hurried away in the opposite direction.

The senator followed, calling three or four times "Jennie! Jennie!" but losing hope of overtaking her, and, suddenly recognizing, and thereupon respecting, her simple, girlish shame, stopped, and turning back, decided to follow the children. Being gentle and tenderly human, the significance of the present situation was not lost upon him. Anew he felt that same sensation which he seemed always to get from this girl—the far cry between her estate and his. It was something to be a senator tonight, here where these children were picking coal. What could the joyous holiday of the morrow hold for them? He tramped along sympathetically, an honest lightness coming into his step, and soon saw them enter the gateway of the low cottage. Crossing the street, he stood in the weak shade of the snow-laden trees. The light was burning with a yellow glow in a rear window. All about was the white snow. In the woodshed he could hear the voices of the children, and once he thought he detected the form of Mrs. Gerhardt. After a time another form came shadow-like through the side gate. He knew who it was. It touched him to the quick, and he bit his lip sharply to avoid any further show of emotion. Then he turned vigorously on his heel and walked away.

The chief grocery of the city was conducted by one Manning, a staunch adherent of Brander, and one who felt honored by his senator's acquaintance. To him, at his busy desk, came the senator this night.

"Manning," he said, "could I get you to undertake a little work for me this evening?"

"Why certainly, Senator, certainly," said the groceryman. "When did you get back? Glad to see you. Certainly."

"I want you to get everything together that would make a nice Christmas for a family of eight—father and mother and six children—Christmas tree, groceries, toys—you know what I mean."

"Certainly, certainly, Senator," said Mr. Manning.

"Never mind the cost now. Send plenty of everything. I'll give you the address," and he picked up a note book to write it.

"Why, I'll be delighted, Senator," went on Mr. Manning, rather affected himself. "I'll be delighted. You always were generous."

"Here you are, Manning," said the senator, grimly, from the mere necessity of it. "Send everything now, and the bill to me."

"I'll be delighted," was all the astonished and approving groceryman could say.

The senator passed out, but remembering the old people, visited a clothier and shoe man, and finding that he could only guess at what sizes might be required, ordered the several articles with the privilege of exchange. When his labors were over, he returned to his room.

"Carrying coal," he thought, over and over. "Really, it was very thoughtless in me. I mustn't forget them any more."

CHAPTER IV

The desire to flee, which Jennie experienced upon seeing the senator again, was attributable to what she considered the disgrace of her position. She was ashamed to think that he, who thought so well of her, should discover her doing so common a thing. Girl-like, she was inclined to imagine that his interest in her depended upon things which were better than this.

When Jennie reached home, Mrs. Gerhardt had heard of her flight from the other children.

"What was the matter with you, anyhow?" asked George, when she came in.

"Oh, nothing," she answered, but immediately turned to her mother, who was near, and said, "Mr. Brander came by and saw us."

"Oh, did he?" softly exclaimed her mother. "He's back then. What made you run, though, you foolish girl?"

"Well, I didn't want him to see me."

Mrs. Gerhardt could not help laughing at her daughter's predicament and the children's description of her flight, but she secretly appreciated and sympathized with her feelings. It was too bad, she thought, that the distinguished senator should know.

"Well, maybe he didn't know you, anyhow," she said.

"Oh, yes he did, too," whispered Jennie. "He called after me three or four times."

Mrs. Gerhardt shook her head.

"What is it?" said Gerhardt, who had been hearing the conversation from the adjoining room, and now came out.

"Oh, nothing," said the mother, who hated to explain the significance which the senator's personality had come to have in their lives. "A man frightened them when they were bringing the coal."

Gerhardt looked the distress he felt, but could say nothing. It was all too bad that his children must be subjected to this, but what could he do? Seeing the rest of them laughing over it and looking upon it in the light of a joke, he smiled also.

"We'll buy some coal pretty soon, maybe," he added.

The arrival of the Christmas presents, later in the evening, threw the household into an uproar of excitement. Neither Gerhardt nor the mother could believe their eyes when a grocery wagon halted in front of their cottage, and a lusty clerk began to carry in the gifts. After failing to persuade the clerk to hesitate, or to convince him that he had made a mistake, the large assortment of things was looked into with exceedingly human glee.

"Just you never mind," were the clerk's authoritative words. "I know what I'm about. Gerhardt, isn't it? Well, you're the people."

Mrs. Gerhardt moved about, rubbing her hands in her excitement, and giving vent to an occasional "Well, isn't that nice now!"

Gerhardt himself was melted at the thought of the generosity of the unknown benefactor, and was inclined to lay it all to the goodness of a great local mill owner, who knew him and wished him well. Mrs. Gerhardt tearfully suspected the source, but said nothing. Jennie knew by instinct the author of it all.

The afternoon of the day after Christmas, Brander encountered the mother in the hotel, Jennie having been left at home to look after the house.

"How do you do, Mrs. Gerhardt!" he exclaimed genially, extending his hand. "How did you enjoy your Christmas?"

Poor Mrs. Gerhardt took it nervously, and tried to look at him in an appreciative way, but it was impossible. Her eyes filled rapidly with tears.

"There, there," he said, patting her on the shoulder. "Don't cry. You mustn't forget to get my laundry today."

"Oh, no sir," she returned, and would have said more, had he not walked away.

From this on, Gerhardt heard continually of the fine senator at the hotel, how pleasant he was, and how much he paid for his washing. He was inclined, with the simplicity of a German working-man, to believe that only superior qualities could exist in one so distinguished.

Jennie, whose attitude needed no encouragement in this direction, was more than ever prejudiced in his favor.

There was developing in her that perfection of womanhood, the mould of form, which could not help but attract any man. She gave evidence of much that would develop into a fine matronly bearing later in life. Already, she was nearly perfect, well-built, and tall for a girl. Had she been dressed in the trailing skirts of a woman of fashion, she would have made a fitting companion for a man the height of the senator. Her eyes were wondrously clear and bright, her skin fair, and her teeth white and even. She was clever, too, in a sensible way, and by no means deficient in observation. All that she lacked was training and that assurance of which the knowledge of utter dependency despoils one. Carrying washing, though, and being compelled to acknowledge almost anything as a favor, put her at a disadvantage.

Nowadays when she came to the hotel upon her semi-weekly errand, Senator Brander took her presence with easy grace, and to this she responded. He urged her to examine the knick-knacks of his chamber freely, gave her little presents for herself, or her brothers and sisters, and talked to her so unaffectedly, that finally the over-awing sense of the great difference between them was brushed away, and she looked upon him more as a generous friend than as a distinguished senator. He asked her once how she would like to go to a seminary, thinking all the while how attractive she would be when she came out. Finally, one evening, he called her to his side.

"Come over here, Jennie," he said, "and stand by me."

She came, and having her so near, he took her hand.

"Well, Jennie," he said, studying her face in a quizzical, interrogative way, "what do you think of me anyhow?"

"Oh," she answered, looking consciously away, "I don't know. What makes you ask me that?"

"Oh, yes, you do," he returned. "You have some opinion of me. Tell me now, what is it?"

"No, I haven't," she said innocently.

"Oh, yes, you have," he went on pleasantly, interested because thus eluded. "You must think something of me. Now, what is it?"

"Do you mean do I like you?" she asked frankly, looking down at the big mop of black hair well streaked with gray which hung about his forehead, and gave an almost leonine cast to his fine face.

"Well, yes," he said with a sense of disappointment. She was barren of the art of the coquette.

"Why, of course I like you," she replied prettily.

"Haven't you ever thought anything else about me?" he went on.

She paused a moment while he shook her hand up and down, little conscious of the peculiar advantage he was thus lightly taking.

"I think you're very kind," she went on, even more bashfully; she realized now that he was still holding her hand.

"Is that all?" he asked.

"Well," she said with a blink of her big eyes, "isn't that enough?"

He looked at her, and the playful, companionable way in which she seemed to take him, thrilled him. It was the essence of human comfort in another that he was feeling. How long had it been since the touch of a human hand had the thrill and warmth in it for him that hers did. How cold was the general material of life beside this warm, human factor, a woman dealing sympathetically with him. He studied her face in silence, while she turned and twisted, feeling, but scarcely understanding, the deep import of his scrutiny.

"Well," he said at last, "I think you're a fine girl. Don't you think I'm a pretty nice man?"

"Yes," said Jennie, promptly.

He leaned back in his chair and laughed at the unconscious drollery of her reply. She looked at him curiously, and smiled.

"What made you laugh?" she inquired.

"Oh, your answer," he returned. "I really ought not to laugh, though. You don't appreciate me in the least. I don't believe you like me at all."

"But I do, though," she replied earnestly. "I think you're so good." Her eyes showed very plainly that she felt what she was saying.

"Well," he said, drawing her gently down to him, and the same instant, he pressed his lips to her cheek.

"Oh!" she cried, straightening up, both startled and frightened.

It was a new note in their relationship. The senatorial quality vanished in an instant. She recognized in him what she had not felt before. He seemed younger, too. She was a woman to him, and he was playing the part of a lover. She hesitated, but not knowing just what to do, did nothing at all.

"Well," he said, "did I frighten you?"

She looked at him, but moved by her underlying respect for this great man, she said with a smile, "Yes, you did."

"I did it because I like you so much."

She meditated upon this a moment, and then said, "I think I'd better be going."

"My, now," he pleaded, "are you going to run away because of that?"

"No," she said, moved by a curious feeling of ingratitude, "but I ought to be going. They'll be wondering where I am."

"You're sure you're not angry about it?"

"No," she replied with more of a womanish air than she had ever shown before. It was a novel experience to be in so authoritative a position. It was so remarkable that it was almost confusing to both.

"You're my girl anyhow," the senator said, rising. "I'm going to take care of you in the future."

Jennie heard this, and it pleased her. He was so able, she thought, to do something wondrous—so much in the nature of a magician. She looked about her, and the thought of coming into such a life and such an atmosphere was heavenly. Not that she fully understood his meaning, however. He meant to be good and generous, and give her fine things. Naturally she was happy. She took up the package that she had come for, not seeing or feeling the incongruity of her position, while he felt it as a direct reproof.

"She ought not to carry that," he thought. A great wave of sympathy swept over him. He took her cheeks between his hands, this time in a superior and more generous way. "Never mind, little girl," he said. "You won't have to do this always. I'll see what I can do."

The outcome of this was simply a more sympathetic relationship between them. He did not hesitate to ask her to sit beside him on the arm of his chair the next time she came, and to question her intimately about the family's condition, and her own desires. Several times he noticed that she was evading things, particularly in regard to what her father was doing. She was ashamed to own that he was sawing wood. Fearing lest something more serious was impending, he decided to go out some day and see for himself.

This he did, when a comfortable morning presented itself,

and his other duties did not press upon him. It was three days before the great fight in the legislature began, which ended in his defeat. Nothing could be done in these few remaining days. He knew he had everything as secure as such things could be made—which was never very secure. He took his cane and strolled forth, coming to the cottage in the course of a half-hour, and knocked boldly at the door.

Mrs. Gerhardt opened it.

"Good morning," he said, cheerily; then, seeing her hesitate, he added, "May I come in?"

The good mother, who was all but overcome by his astonishing presence, wiped her hands furtively upon her much-mended apron, and seeing that he waited for a reply, said:

"Oh, yes. Come right in. Have this chair."

She hurried forward, forgetting to close the door, and, offering one of the common chairs, asked him to be seated.

Genially, Brander looked at her, and feeling sorry that he was the occasion of so much confusion, said, "Don't trouble yourself, Mrs. Gerhardt. I was passing and thought I'd come in. How is your husband?"

"He's well, thank you," returned the mother. "He's out working today."

"Then he has found employment?"

"Yes sir," said Mrs. Gerhardt, who hesitated, like Jennie, to say what it was.

"The children are all well now, and in school, I hope?"

"Yes," replied the mother, who had by now unfastened her apron, and was nervously turning it in her lap.

"That's good, and where is Jennie?"

The latter, who had been ironing, had abandoned the board and concealed herself in the bedroom, where she was busy tidying herself in the fear that her mother would not have fore-thought enough to say that she was out, and so let her escape.

"She's here," returned her mother, who had hopes of her daughter rescuing her. "She'll be right in soon. I'll call her."

Using this as an excuse, she passed out of the room and, finding Jennie, said:

"Oh, my, you go in for a moment. I must put off these old slippers, anyway."

"What did you tell him I was here for?" said Jennie weakly.

"What could I do?" asked the mother.

Together they hesitated while the senator surveyed the room. It was nothing uncommon to him, this evidence of poverty, but they thought it was. He felt sorry to think that such deserving people must suffer so, but intended, also, in a vague way, to ameliorate their condition, if possible.

"Good morning," the senator said to Jennie, when she came into his presence. "How do you do today?"

Jennie came forward, extending her hand and blushing. She found herself so much disturbed by this visit that she could hardly find tongue to answer his questions.

"I thought," he said, "I'd come out and find where you live. This is a quite comfortable house. How many rooms have you?"

"Five," said Jennie. "You'll have to excuse their looks this morning. We've been ironing and it's all upset."

"I know," said Brander, gently. "Don't you think I understand, Jennie? You mustn't feel nervous about me."

She noticed the comforting, personal tone he always used with her when she was at his room, and it tended in a way to subdue her flustered senses.

"You mustn't think it anything if I come here occasionally. I intend to come. I want to meet your father."

"Oh," said Jennie, "he's out today."

While they were talking, however, the honest wood-cutter was coming in at the gate with his buck and saw. Brander saw him, and at once recognized him by a slight resemblance to his daughter.

"There he is now, I believe," he said.

"Oh, is he?" said Jennie, looking out.

Gerhardt, who was given to speculation these days, passed by the window without looking up. He put his wooden buck down, and hanging his saw on a nail on the side of the house, came in.

"Mother," he called in German, and then not seeing her, came to the door of the front room and looked in.

Brander arose and extended his hand. The knotted and weatherbeaten German came forward, and took it with a very questioning expression of countenance.

"This is my father, Mr. Brander," said Jennie, all her diffidence dissolved by sympathy. "This is the gentleman from the hotel, Papa—Mr. Brander."

"What's the name?" said the German, turning his head.

"Brander," said the senator.

"Oh, yes," he said with a considerable German accent. "Since I had the fever, I don't hear good. My wife, she spoke to me of you."

"Yes," said the senator, "I thought I'd come out and make your acquaintance. You have quite a family."

"Yes," said the father, who was conscious of his very poor garments and anxious to get away. "I have six children—all young. She's the oldest girl."

Mrs. Gerhardt now came back and Gerhardt, seeing his chance, said:

"Well, if you'll excuse me, I'll go. I broke my saw, and so I had to stop work."

"Certainly," said Brander, graciously, realizing now why Jennie never wanted to explain. He half wished that she were courageous enough not to conceal anything.

"Well, Mrs. Gerhardt," he said, when the mother was stiffly seated, "I want to tell you that you mustn't look on me as a stranger. Hereafter I want you to keep me informed of how things are going with you. Jennie won't always do it."

Jennie smiled quietly. Mrs. Gerhardt only rubbed her hands.

They talked for a few minutes and then the senator said:

"Tell your husband to come and see me next Monday at my office in the hotel. I want to do something for him."

"Thank you," she said.

"I'll not stay any longer now," he added. "Don't forget to have him come."

"Oh, he'll come," she returned.

He arose and adjusting a glove on one hand, extended the other to Jennie.

"Here is your finest treasure, Mrs. Gerhardt," he said. "I think I'll take her."

"Well, I don't know," said her mother, "whether I could spare her or not."

"Well," said the senator, going toward the door, and giving Mrs. Gerhardt his hand, "good morning."

He nodded and walked out, while a half-dozen neighbors, who had observed his entrance, peeked from behind curtains and drawn blinds at the astonishing sight.

"Who can that be, anyhow?" was the general query.

"See what he gave me," said the innocent mother to her daughter the moment he had closed the door.

It was a ten-dollar bill. He had placed it in her hand as he said goodbye.

CHAPTER V

Having been conducted by circumstances into so obligated an attitude toward the senator, it was not unnatural for Jennie to conceive most generously of everything he had done, or, from now on, did. New benefactions contributed to this feeling. The senator gave her father a letter to a local mill-owner, who saw that he received something to do. It was not much, to be sure, a mere job as night-watchman, but it had significant results. One of these was the extreme gratefulness of the latter, who could anticipate, from now on, only good flowing from such a quarter.

Another agreeable influence was due to gifts made to the mother, through the daughter. Once, he sent her a dress, and another time, a shawl. All these things were given in a spirit of mingled charity and self-gratification, but to Mrs. Gerhardt, they glowed with but one motive. Senator Brander was good-hearted.

As for Jennie, he drew nearer to her in every possible way, so that at last, she came to see him in a light which would require considerable analysis to make clear. This fresh, young soul, however, had too much innocence and buoyancy to consider for a moment the world's view. Since that one notable and halcyon visit upon which he had robbed her of her original shyness, and implanted a tender kiss upon her cheek, they had lived in a different atmosphere. Jennie was his companion now, and as he more and more unbended, and even joyously flung aside the habiliments of dignity, her perception of him grew clearer. They laughed and chatted in a natural way, and he was comforted by the world of youth into which he had thus found entrance.

One thing that disturbed him, however, was the occasional

thought, which he could not repress, that he was not doing right. Other people must soon discover that he was not confining himself strictly to conventional relations with this washer-woman's daughter. He suspected that the housekeeper was not without knowledge that Jennie almost invariably lingered from a quarter to three quarters of an hour, whenever she came for or returned his laundry. He knew that it might come to the ears of the hotel clerks and so, in a general way, get about town and work serious injury, but the reflection did not cause him to modify his conduct. Sometimes he consoled himself with the thought that he was not doing her any actual harm, and at other times argued that he could not put this one delightful tenderness out of his life. Did he not wish honestly to do her much good?

He thought of these things occasionally, and decided that he could not stop. The private self-glorification which this achievement might bring him was hardly worth while. He had not so very many more years to live. Why die unsatisfied?

One evening he put his arm around her and strained her to his breast. Another time he drew her to his knee, and told her of the life at Washington. Always he had a caress and a kiss for her now, but it was still in a tentative, uncertain way. He did not want to reach for her soul too deeply.

Jennie enjoyed it all innocently. Elements of fancy and novelty entered into her life. She was an unsophisticated creature, emotional, totally inexperienced in the matter of the affections and yet large enough mentally to enjoy the attentions of this great man who had thus bowed, from his high position, to make friends with her.

One evening, she pushed his hair back from his forehead as she stood by his chair, and, finding nothing else to do, took out his watch. The great man thrilled as he looked at her pretty innocence, and said:

"Would you like to have a watch, too?"

"Yes, indeed, I would," said Jennie, with a deep breath.

The next day he stopped as he was passing a jewelry store, and bought one. It was gold, and had pretty ornamented hands.

"Come here now," he said, when she came the next time; "I want to show you something. See what time it is by my watch."

Jennie drew out the watch from his waistcoat pocket and started in surprise.

"This isn't your watch!" she exclaimed, her face full of innocent wonder.

"No," he said, pleased with his thought of putting it there, "it's yours."

"Mine!" exclaimed Jennie. "Mine! Oh, isn't it lovely!"

"Do you think so?" he said.

Her ecstasy in its customary vein was one of the most grateful things he knew. Her face shone with light, and her eyes fairly danced.

"That's yours," he said. "See that you wear it now, and don't lose it."

Jennie took it, and seeing him looking at her so kindly, paused as she was fastening it on.

"You're so good!" she exclaimed.

"No," he said, but he held her at arm's length by the waist, to study out what his reward might be. Slowly he drew her toward him until, when very close, she put her arms about his neck, and laid her cheek in gratitude against his own. This was the quintessence of pleasure for him. He felt as he had been longing to feel for years.

This affectional progress suffered a change when the great senatorial fight came on in the legislature. Attacked by a combination of rivals, Brander was given the fight of his life. To his amazement he discovered that a great railroad corporation, which had always been friendly, was secretly throwing its strength in behalf of an already too powerful candidate. Shocked by this defection, he was thrown into the deepest gloom, and next, into a paroxysm of wrath. These slings of fortune, however well he pretended to know them, never failed to lacerate him. It had been too long since he had endured one.

During this period, Jennie received her earliest lesson in the vagaries of men. For two weeks she did not even get to see him, and one evening, after an extremely comfortless conference with his leader, he met her with the most chilling formality. When she knocked at his door he only troubled to open it a foot and exclaimed almost harshly, "I can't bother about the clothes tonight! Come tomorrow."

Jennie turned, shocked and surprised by this reception. She did not know what to think of it. He was restored on the instant to his far-off, mighty throne, and left to rule in peace. Why should he not cut her off shortly if he pleased? But why—

A day or two later he repented mildly, but had no time to readjust things. His washing was taken and delivered with considerable formality, and he went on toiling forgetfully until at last he was miserably defeated by two votes. Astounded by this result, he lapsed into gloom, and brooded mightily, wondering what move he could now make that would be of value to him.

Into this atmosphere came Jennie, bringing with her the lightness and fascination of her own hopeful disposition. Nagged to desperation by his thoughts, Brander first talked to her to amuse himself, but soon got caught by the relief which she supplied. Looking at her, his distress vanished, and he found himself observing that youth was best. Was not this human exhilaration which he found in her presence the greatest thing in the world?

"Ah, Jennie," he said, talking to her as he might have to a child, "youth is on your side. You have the most valuable thing in life."

"Do I?"

"Yes, but you don't realize it. You never will, until it is too late."

Finding himself wonderfully relieved, he now leaned toward her slightly, and, in these bitter days, waited for her coming. If he should go away now, as minister, to a foreign country, he wondered what he should do.

"I love that girl," he thought. "I wish I could have her with me."

Fortune had another fling for him to endure. It got about the hotel that Jennie was, to use the mildest expression, conducting herself strangely. A girl who carries washing must expect criticism if anything not befitting her station is observed in her apparel. Jennie was seen wearing the gold watch. Her mother was informed by the housekeeper of the state of things.

"I thought I'd speak to you about it," she said. "People are talking. You'd better not let your daughter go to his room for the laundry."

Mrs. Gerhardt was too astonished and hurt for utterance. Jennie had told her nothing, but even now she did not believe there was anything to tell. The watch had been both approved of and admired by her. She had not thought that it was endangering her daughter's reputation.

Going home she worried almost incessantly, and talked with Jennie about it. The latter did not admit the implication that things had gone too far. In fact, she did not look at it in that light. She did not own, it is true, what really had happened while she was visiting the senator.

"It's so terrible that people should begin to talk!" said her mother. "Did you really stay so long in the room?"

"I don't know," returned Jennie, compelled by her conscience and the dire import people attach to such things to admit at least part of the truth. "Perhaps I did."

"He has never said anything out of the way to you, has he?"

"No," answered her daughter, who did not attach any suspicion of evil to what had passed between them.

If the mother had only gone a little bit further, she might have learned more, but she was only too glad, for her own peace of mind, to hush the matter up. People were slandering a good man, that she knew. Jennie had been the least bit indiscreet. People were always so ready to talk. How could the poor girl, amid such unfortunate circumstances, do otherwise than she did. It made her cry to think of it.

The result of it all was that she decided to get the washing herself.

She came to his door the next Monday after this decision. Brander, who was expecting Jennie, was both surprised and disappointed.

"Why," he said to her, "what has become of Jennie?"

Having hoped that he would not notice, or, at least, not comment upon the change, Mrs. Gerhardt did not know what to say. She looked up at him weakly in her innocent, motherly way, and said, "She couldn't come tonight, very well."

"Not ill, is she?" he inquired.

"No," she said.

"I'm glad to hear that," he said resignedly. "How have you been?"

Mrs. Gerhardt explained to him, in answer to his pleasant question, the condition of the family, and then went away. After she had gone, he got to thinking the matter over, and wondered at the change. Something had happened, he felt, but he was in no position to say what. It seemed rather odd that he should be wondering over it.

On Saturday, however, when she returned the clothes, he felt that there must be something wrong.

"What's the matter, Mrs. Gerhardt?" he inquired. "Has anything happened to your daughter?"

"No, sir," she returned, too troubled to wish to deceive him.

"Isn't she coming for the laundry any more?"

"I,—I,—" ventured the mother, stammering in her perturbation—"she—they have been talking about her," she at last forced herself to say.

The senator looked down upon her with considerable gravity, and said:

"Who has been talking?"

"The people here in the hotel."

"Who, what people?" he interrupted, a touch of the choler that was in him showing itself.

"The housekeeper."

"The housekeeper, eh!" he exclaimed. "What has she got to say?"

The mother related to him her experience.

"And she told you that, did she?" he remarked in wrath. "She ventures to trouble herself about my affairs. I wonder people can't mind their own business without interfering with mine. Your daughter, Mrs. Gerhardt, is perfectly safe with me. I have no intention of doing her an injury. It's a shame," he added, though in almost a classic manner, "that a girl can't come to my room in this hotel without having her motive questioned. I'll look into this matter."

"I hope you don't think that I have anything to do with it," said the mother apologetically. "I know you like Jennie and wouldn't injure her. You've done so much for her and all of us, Mr. Brander, I feel ashamed to keep her away."

"That's all right, Mrs. Gerhardt," he said, quietly. "You did perfectly right. I don't blame you in the least. It is the lying accusation passed about in this hotel that I object to. We'll see about that."

Mrs. Gerhardt stood there, pale with excitement. She was afraid she had deeply offended this man who had done so much for them. If she could only say something, she thought, that would clear this matter up, and make him feel that she was no tattler. Scandal was awful to her.

"I thought I was doing everything for the best," she said at last.

"So you were," he replied. "I like Jennie very much. I have always enjoyed her coming here. It is my intention to do well by her, but perhaps it will be better to keep her away, at least for the present."

After he had expressed himself somewhat further to this effect, he opened the door and saw her out, but it was only the beginning of his real mental labor in the matter.

Again that evening the senator sat in his easy chair and brooded over this new development. Jennie was really much more precious to him than he had thought. Now that he had no hope of seeing her there any more, he began to realize how much these little visits of hers had meant. He thought the matter over very carefully, realized instantly that there was nothing to be done so far as the hotel gossip was concerned, and concluded that he had really placed the girl in a very unsatisfactory position.

"Perhaps I had better end this little affair," he thought. "It isn't a wise thing to pursue."

On the strength of this conclusion he went to Washington and finished his term. Then he returned to Columbus to await the friendly recognition from the president which was to send him upon some ministry abroad. Jennie had not been forgotten in the least. The longer he stayed away, the more interested he was to get back. When he was again peaceably settled in his old quarters, he took up his cane one morning and strolled out in the direction of the cottage. Arriving there, he made up his mind to go in, and, knocking at the door, he was greeted by Mrs. Gerhardt and her daughter with astonished and diffident smiles. He explained vaguely that he had been away, and mentioned his laundry as if that were the object of his visit. Then, when chance gave him a few moments with Jennie alone, he said:

"How would you like to take a drive with me tomorrow evening?"

"I'd like it," said Jennie, to whom the proposition was a decided novelty.

He smiled and patted her cheek, because he was happy to see her again. Every day seemed to be adding to her beauty. Graced with her cleanly white apron this morning, and rounded in the face by the simple plaiting of her hair, she was a pleasing sight.

He waited genially until Mrs. Gerhardt returned and then, having accomplished the purpose of his visit, arose.

"I'm going to take your daughter out riding tomorrow evening," he explained. "I want to talk to her about her future."

"Won't that be nice?" said the mother. She saw nothing incongruous in the proposal. They parted with smiles and much handshaking.

"That man has the best heart," said Mrs. Gerhardt. "Doesn't he always speak so nicely of you? He may help you to an education. You ought to be proud."

"I am," said Jennie frankly.

"I don't know whether we had better tell your father, or not," concluded Mrs. Gerhardt. "He doesn't like for you to be out evenings."

It was for this reason that the deeply religious Gerhardt did not know of the ride.

Jennie was ready when the ex-senator called. When she opened the door for him, that helpless sort of loveliness which rested in her eyes touched him as sharply as ever. He could see by the weak-flamed, unpretentious parlor-lamp that she was dressed for him, and that the occasion had called out the best she had. A pale lavender gingham, starched and ironed until it was a model of laundering, set off her pretty figure and gave that atmosphere of superior cleanliness which her spirit deserved. There were little lace-edged cuffs and a rather high collar attached to it. She had no gloves, nor any jewelry, nor yet a jacket good enough to wear, but her hair was done up in such a dainty way that it set off her well-shaped head better than any hat, and the few ringlets that could escape crowned her as with a halo. When Brander suggested that she wear a jacket, she hesitated a moment, but went in and borrowed her mother's cape—a plain gray woolen one. Brander realized now that she had no jacket, and suffered keenly to think that she had contemplated going without one.

"She would have endured the raw night air," he thought, "and said nothing of it."

He looked at her and shook his head reflectively.

Her cheeks flushed, warmly, as she looked at him. He soon made her feel as if he were delighted to have her go with him, and her many shortcomings of dress would, perhaps, never be thought of.

On the way, he talked to her of her family, and wanted to know how her father was getting on.

"He's doing real well," she said; "they like him where he's working."

Brander kept silent awhile, for he was content to have this girl beside him again. The absence he had endured had made his heart grow fonder. She seemed even more delightful than when he had last seen her. Everything she did was so gentle.

For an hour the senator thrilled with such pleasure as he had not known in years. Jennie was not silent, and every word she said showed the natural feeling and interest she took in everything in life.

"Well, Jennie," he said, when she asked him to notice how soft the trees looked, where outlined dimly against the new rising moon they were touched with its yellow light, "you're a great one. I believe you would write poetry if you were schooled a little."

"Do you suppose I could?" she asked innocently.

"Do I suppose, little girl?" he said, taking her hand. "Do I suppose? Why, I know. You're the dearest little day-dreamer in the world. Of course you could write poetry. You live it. You are poetry, my dear. Don't you worry about writing any."

This eulogy touched her as nothing else possibly could have. He was always saying such nice things. No one ever seemed to like or appreciate her half as much as he did. And how great he was! Everybody said that. Her own father.

They rode still further, until suddenly remembering, he said, "I wonder what time it is. Perhaps we had better be turning back. Have you your watch?"

Jennie started, for this watch had been the one thing of which she had hoped he would not speak. Ever since he had returned, it had been on her mind.

In his absence, the family finances had become so strained, she had been compelled to pawn it. Martha had got to that place in the matter of apparel where she could no longer go to school unless something new were provided for her. Mrs. Gerhardt had spoken of this in her hopeless, helpless way, and Jennie had felt heart-tugs many a morning when little Martha had gone forth, her old clothes demeaning her every feature.

"I don't know what to do," said her mother.

"You might pawn my watch," said Jennie. "I guess Bass could take it."

Mrs. Gerhardt objected, but need is a stern commander. She thought more calmly over it after a day or two, and finally Jennie persuaded her to let her give Bass the watch.

"Get as much as you can," she said. "I don't know whether we'll be able to get it out again."

Secretly Mrs. Gerhardt wept.

Bass took it, and having argued with the local pawnbroker, was able to bring home ten dollars. Mrs. Gerhardt took the money, and, after expending it all upon her children, heaved a sigh of relief. Martha looked very much better. Naturally, Jennie was glad.

Now, however, when the senator spoke of it, her hour of retribution seemed at hand. She actually trembled, and he noticed the quaver.

"Why, Jennie," he said gently, "what made you start like that?"

"Nothing," she answered.

"Haven't you your watch?"

She paused, for it seemed impossible to tell a deliberate falsehood. There was a strained silence, in which he suspected something of the truth, and then she said, with a voice that had too much of a sob in it for him not to hear, "No, sir."

Seriously he weighed the matter, and then suspecting some further generosity toward her family, finally made her confess.

"Well," he said, "dearest, don't feel badly about it. There never was such another girl. I'll get your watch for you. Hereafter when you need anything, I want you to come to me. Do you hear? I want you to promise me that. If I'm not here, I want you to write me. I'll always be in touch with you from now on. You will have my address. Just let me know, and I'll help you. Do you understand?"

"Yes," said Jennie.

"You'll promise to do that now, will you?"

"Yes," she replied.

For a time neither of them spoke.

"Jennie," he said at last, the spring-like quality of the night moving him to a burst of feeling, "I've about decided that I can't do without you. Do you think you could make up your mind to live with me from now on?"

Jennie looked away, not clearly understanding his words as he meant them. It was a strong statement for him. The man had got to the place where that wondrous something about her made it constantly more difficult for him to keep his hands off of her. She was so much of a grace and a naiad, he longed to fold her in his arms. Oh, that youth could only come back to him, so that he might be worthy of this girl.

"I don't know," she said, vaguely feeling that it all meant something finer and better.

"Well now, you think about it," he said pleasantly. "I'm serious. Would you be willing to marry me and let me put you away in a seminary for a few years?"

"Go away to school?"

"Yes, after you marry me."

"I guess so," she replied. Her mother came into her mind. Maybe she could help the family.

He looked around at her, and tried to make out her face clearly in the shadow. It was not dark. The moon was now above the trees in the east, and already the vast host of stars were paling before it.

"Don't you care for me at all, Jennie?" he asked.

"Yes!"

"You never come for my laundry any more though," he returned pathetically. It touched her to hear him say this.

"I didn't do that," she answered. "I couldn't help it. Mother thought it was best."

"So it was," he said, feeling her sorrow over the matter. "I was only joking with you. You'd be glad to come if you could, wouldn't you?"

"Yes, I would," she answered frankly.

He took her hand and pressed it so feelingly that all his kindly words seemed doubly re-enforced to her. Reaching impulsively up, she put her arms about him. "You're so good to me," she said with the loving tone of a daughter.

"There, there," he exclaimed, the weakest and loveliest portion of his disposition manifesting itself. "It isn't that. You're my girl, Jennie. I'd do anything in the world for you."

CHAPTER VI

The father of this unfortunate family, William Gerhardt, was a man of considerable interest on his personal side. Born in the Dukedom of Saxony, he had had character enough to oppose the army-conscription iniquity, and flee, in his eighteenth year, to Paris. From there he had set forth for America, the land of promise.

Arrived in this country, he had made his way by slow stages from New York to Philadelphia and thence westward, working for a time in the various glass factories of Pennsylvania, and found, in one romantic village of this new world, his heart's ideal. With her, a simple American girl, of immediate German extraction, he had removed to Youngstown, and thence to Columbus, each time following a glass manufacturer by the name of Hammond, whose business prospered and waned by turns.

It is to some purpose that the natural romance of such a progress is indicated, for this man had now become extremely religious; and this feeling was directly due to the pensive, speculative chord re-echoing in a nature incapable of a broad mental perspective, but producing such actions and wanderings as his life, up to this time, had been full of. Gerhardt felt, rather than reasoned. He had always done so. A slap on the back, accompanied by enthusiastic protestations of affection or regard, was always worth more to him than mere cold propositions concerning his own individual advancement. He loved companionship, and was easily persuaded by it, but never beyond the limit of honesty.

"William," his employer used to say to him, "I want you because I can trust you," and this, to him, was more than silver and gold.

He might sometimes get so overwrought by praise of this sort that he would talk about it, but ordinarily it was a deep-seated happiness which he found in realizing that he was honest.

This honesty, like his religious propensity, was wholly due to inheritance. He had never reasoned about it. Father and grandfather before him were sturdy German artisans who had never cheated anybody out of a dollar, and this honesty of intention came into his veins undiminished.

His Lutheran proclivities had been strengthened by years of

church-going and home religious service. In his father's cottage, the influence of the Lutheran minister had been all-powerful, and from that situation he inherited the feeling that the Lutheran Church was a perfect institution, and its teachings of all-importance when it came to the matter of future life. Having neglected it during the ruddiest period of his youth, he took it up again when it came to the matter of selecting a wife, and was insistent enough to have his sweetheart change her faith at his behest. She would naturally have aligned herself with the Mennonite or perhaps the Dunkard religion, had theology been of equal weight with love. As it was, she came heartily over to the Lutheran denomination, was resoundingly instructed by a preacher of that faith in Beaver Falls, and thereafter came modestly to believe in it—the positive thunderings of the local pulpit seeming scarcely explicable to her on any other grounds than that of absolute truth. Why should these men rage and roar if what they said was not dangerously true? Why wear black, and forever struggle in so solemn a cause? Regularly she attended the small local church with her husband; and the several ministers, who had come and gone in their time, had been regular visitors, and, in a sense, inspectors of this household.

Pastor Wundt, the latest minister, saw to it personally that they gave a good account of themselves. He was a sincere and ardent churchman, but his bigotry and domineering orthodoxy were all outside the pale of rational religious conception. He considered that the members of his flock were jeopardizing their eternal salvation if they danced, played cards or went to theatres, and he did not hesitate to declare vociferously that hell was yawning for those who disobeyed his injunctions. Drinking, even temperately, was a sin. Smoking—well, he smoked himself. Right conduct in marriage, however, and innocence in the matter of youthful virtue until marriage was reached, were the last essence of Christian necessity. Let no one talk of salvation, he had said, for a daughter who had failed to keep her chastity unstained, or for the parents who, by negligence, had permitted her to fall. Hell was yawning for all such. You must walk the straight and narrow way if you would escape eternal punishment through his theology, and there was scarcely a Sunday in which he did not refer to the iniquitous license which was observable among American young men and women.

"Such shamelessness!" he used to say. "Such indifference to all youthful reserve and innocence!—Here they go, these young boys, loafing about the street corners, when they should be at home helping their fathers and mothers, or studying and improving their minds." And the girls—what bitter scenes had he of late not been compelled to contemplate. There was laxness somewhere. These fathers and mothers, whose daughters walked the streets after seven at night, and were seen strolling in the shadowy path of the trees and hanging over gates and fences talking to young men, would rue it some day. There was no possible good to come out of anything like that. The boys could only evolve into loafers and scoundrels, the daughters into something too shameless to name. Let there be heed taken of this.

Gerhardt and his wife and Jennie heard this, and, so indeed, did all the others except Sebastian, but the little ones were, of course, not able to understand very well. Sebastian could not be made to go to church. He was vigorous and self-willed, and his father, from whipping him, unavailingly, and occasionally threatening to turn him out of doors, had come, out of sympathy for the lad's mother, merely to complain tempestuously about him every Sunday morning. Jennie herself was convinced that it was terrible the way he acted. She knew that he was honest, and worked steadily, but she thought that he should not neglect the church, and particularly should not offend and grieve his parents. Religion had, as yet, no striking hold upon her. In fact, she felt its claims most lightly. It was a pleasant thing to know that there was a heaven, a fearsome one to realize that there was a hell. Young girls and boys ought to be good, and be genial toward their parents, when they had to work so hard. Otherwise, the whole religious problem was badly jumbled in her mind, and she did not know what to make of it.

Gerhardt was convinced that everything spoken from the pulpit of his church was literally true. He believed now that he had been rather wild and irreligious in his youth, and that the problem of the future life was the all-important question for man. Death was an awesome thing to him. He had lived in dread of the icy marvel of it ever since his youth, and now that the years were slipping away and the problem of the world was becoming more and more inexplicable, he clung with pathetic anxiety to the doctrines which contained a solution. Oh, if he could only be so honest and upright, he thought, that the Lord would have no excuse for ruling him out. He trembled not only for himself, but for his wife and children. Would he not some day be held responsible for them? Would not his own laxity and lack of system in inculcating the laws of eternal life to them end in his and their damnation? He pictured to himself the torments of hell, and wondered how it would be with him and his in the final hour.

Naturally, such a deep religious feeling made him stern with his children. He was prone to hold them close to the line of religious duty, and scan with a narrow eye the pleasures and foibles of youthful desire. Jennie was never to have any lover, it seemed. Any flirtation she might have had with the youths she met upon the streets of Columbus could have had no continuation in her home. Her father forgot that he was once young himself, and looked only to the welfare of her spirit. So the senator was a novel factor in her life, and had an open field.

When he first began to take an interest in their family affairs, the conventional religious standards of Father Gerhardt were set at naught, because he had no means of judging such a character. He was no common corner-boy, coquetting with his pretty daughter. The manner in which he was inducted was so radically original, and so subtle, that he was in and active before any one, so to speak, thought anything about it. Gerhardt himself was deceived, and, expecting nothing but honor and profit to flow to his family from such a source, accepted the interest and the service which this man did him, and plodded peacefully on. His wife did not tell him of the numerous benefactions which had come from the same source before and since the wonderful Christmas.

The result of this was serious from several points of view. It was not long before the neighbors began to talk, for, of course, the presence of a man like Brander in the life of a girl like Jennie was of too conspicuous a nature to go unobserved. A watchful old friend of Gerhardt's informed that worthy of the current drift of events. It was from the front of his small front yard that Mr. Otto Weaver addressed Mr. Gerhardt as the latter was setting off to work one evening.

"Gerhardt, I want to speak a word with you. As a friend of yours, I want to tell you what I hear. The neighbors, you know, they talk about the man who comes to see your daughter."

"My daughter?" said Gerhardt, more puzzled and pained by

this confidential interruption than mere words could indicate. "Whom do you mean? I don't know of anyone who comes to see my daughter."

"No?" inquired Weaver, as astonished nearly as the recipient of his confidences. "The middle-aged man, with gray hair. He carries a cane sometimes. You don't know him?"

Gerhardt racked his memory with a puzzled face.

"They say he was a senator once," went on Weaver, doubtful of what he had got into. "I don't know."

"Ah," returned Gerhardt, measurably relieved. "Senator Brander. Yes. He has come sometimes so. Well, what of it?"

"It is nothing," returned the neighbor, "only they talk. He is no longer a young man, you know. Your daughter, she goes out with him now a few times. These people, they see that, and now they talk about her. I thought you might want to know."

Gerhardt was of so deep a religious feeling that the matter of right conduct was the most active thing in his nature. Unfortunately, he was not wise enough to disassociate it from public opinion. When a thing like this happened, the very first of its kind in his married life, he was shocked to a terrible degree. People must have a reason for saying such things. Jennie and her mother were seriously at fault. Still he did not hesitate to defend his daughter.

"He is a friend of the family," he said confusedly. "People should not talk until they know. My daughter has done nothing."

"That is so. It is nothing," continued Weaver. "People talk before they have any grounds. You and I are old friends. I thought you might want to know. It is like it is with my own family."

Gerhardt stood there another minute or so, his jaw fallen and a strange helplessness upon him. The world was such a grim thing to have antagonistic to you. Its opinions and good favor were so essential. How hard he tried to live up to its rules! Why would it not be satisfied, and let him alone?

"I am glad you told me," he murmured as he started to extricate himself. "I will see about it. Good-night."

For those who are not familiar with the German idea of association, this transcript from life may seem in a measure strained. Everywhere, however, the German from the old country combines a genial clannishness with a desire to regulate the conduct of his fellows. Particularly is this true of fathers of families who are moderately successful. They combine charity toward their poorer neighbors with a grade of positive advice, which they are only too anxious to see enforced. Thus, Father Wundt would come time and again, solely to see whether his directions for maintaining respectability were being positively fulfilled. Others only advised in a milder sense. With Gerhardt, however, who was in a way a reflection of the attitude of others, it went far. Being one who would accept such things, it was natural that he should also be one whom they should lacerate. In that respect, he dreaded that his condition, or that of his family, should offend or cause comment. It seemed to him as if he would rather die than have his private affairs become a matter of public scorn.

When he came home the next morning, his first deed was to question his wife.

"What is this about Senator Brander coming out to call on Jennie?" he asked in German. "The neighbors are talking about it."

"Why, nothing," answered Mrs. Gerhardt, in the same language. She was decidedly taken aback at his question. "He did call two or three times."

"You didn't tell me that," he returned, a sense of her frailty in tolerating and shielding such weakness in one of their children irritating him.

"No," she replied, absolutely nonplussed. "He has only been here two or three times."

"Two or three times!" exclaimed Gerhardt, the German tendency to talk loud coming upon him. "Two or three times! The whole neighborhood talks about it. What is this, then?"

Mrs. Gerhardt paused a moment, her fears rising. It seemed as if something dreadful was pending.

"He only called two or three times," she repeated weakly.

"Weaver comes to me on the street," continued Gerhardt, "and tells me that my neighbors are talking of the man my daughter is going with. I didn't know anything about it. There I stood. I didn't know what to say. What kind of a way is that? What must the man think of me?"

While he was going on in this strain, Mrs. Gerhardt was collecting her troubled thoughts. How was it that this strange predicament had come upon her? What had she done? Suddenly, it shone as a light that she was not at fault. Had not this man been an emissary of kindness to them? Did not she know that Jennie was improving innocent opportunities and conducting herself without blame? Why should these neighbors talk? Why send their insinuations home to her through her husband?

"There is nothing the matter," she declared suddenly, using an effective German idiom. "Jennie has done nothing. The man has only called at the house once or twice. There is—"

"What is this then?" interrupted Gerhardt, who was anxious to discover what had been going on.

"Jennie has gone walking with him once or twice. He has called here at the house. What is there now in that for the people to talk about? Can't the girl have any pleasure at all?"

"But he is an old man," returned Gerhardt, voicing the words of Weaver. "He is a public citizen. What should he want to call on a girl like Jennie for?"

"I don't know," said Mrs. Gerhardt, defensively. "He comes here to the house. I don't know anything but good about the man. Can I tell him not to come?"

Gerhardt paused at this. All that he knew of the senator was excellent. What was there now that was so terrible about it?

"The neighbors are so ready to talk. They haven't got anything else to talk about now, so they talk about Jennie. You know whether she is a good girl or not. Why should they say such things?" and tears came into the soft little mother's eyes.

"That is all right," said Gerhardt, who could scarcely be mellow enough in his zeal for his family honor to sympathize with her. "He ought not to want to come around and take a girl of her age out walking. It looks bad, even if he don't mean any harm."

At this moment Jennie came in.

She had heard the talking from the little front bedroom, where she slept with one of the other children, but had not suspected its import. Now her mother turned her back and bent over the table where she was making biscuit, in order that her daughter might not see her eyes.

"What's the matter?" she inquired when she saw how peculiarly they both stood there.

"Nothing," said Gerhardt firmly.

Mrs. Gerhardt made no sign, but her very stillness told something. Jennie went over, and, peeping about, saw the tears.

"What's the matter?" she repeated wonderingly, gazing at her father.

Gerhardt only stood there, his daughter's innocence dominating his terror of evil.

"What's the matter?" she urged softly of her mother.

"Oh, it's the neighbors," returned the mother brokenly. "They're always ready to talk about something they don't know anything about."

"Is it me again?" inquired Jennie, her face flushing faintly.

"You see," observed Gerhardt, apparently addressing the world in general, "she knows. Now, why didn't you tell me that he was coming here? The neighbors talk, and I hear nothing about it until today. What kind of a way is that, anyhow?"

"Oh," exclaimed Jennie, out of the purest sympathy for her mother. "What difference does it make?"

"What difference?" cried Gerhardt, still talking in German, although Jennie answered in English. "Is it no difference that men stop me on the street and speak of it? You should be ashamed of yourself to say that. I always thought well of this man, but now, since you don't tell me about him, and the neighbors talk, I don't know what to think. Must I get my knowledge of what is going on in my own home from my neighbors?"

Mother and daughter paused. Jennie had already begun to think that their error was serious. Mrs. Gerhardt's only thought was that Jennie was being maligned.

"I didn't keep anything from you because it was evil," she said. "Why, he only took me out riding once."

"Yes, but you didn't tell me that," answered her father.

"You know you don't like for me to go out after dark," replied Jennie. "That's why I didn't. There wasn't anything else to hide about it."

"He shouldn't want you to go out after dark with him," observed Gerhardt, always mindful of the world outside. "What can he want with you, taking you after dark? Why does he come here? He is too old, anyhow. I don't think you ought to have anything to do with him—such a young girl as you are."

"He doesn't want to do anything except help me," murmured Jennie. "He wants to marry me."

"Marry you? Ha! Why doesn't he tell me that!" exclaimed Gerhardt. "I shall look into this. I won't have him running around with my daughter and the neighbors talking. Besides he is too old. I shall tell him that. He ought to know better than to put a girl where she gets talked about. It is better he should stay away altogether."

This threat of Gerhardt's, that he would tell Brander to stay away, seemed simply terrible to Jennie and to her mother. What good could come of any such attitude? Why must they be degraded before him? Of course Brander did call again, while Gerhardt was away at work, and they trembled lest he should hear of it. A few days later the senator came and took Jennie for a long walk. Neither she nor her mother said anything to Gerhardt. But he was not to be put off the scent for long.

"Has Jennie been out again with that man?" he inquired of Mrs. Gerhardt the next evening.

"He was here last night," returned the mother, evasively.

"Did she tell him he shouldn't come any more?"

"I don't know. I don't think so."

"Well, now, I will see for myself once whether this thing will be stopped or not," said the determined father. "I shall talk with him. Wait till he comes again."

In accordance with this, he took occasion to come up from his factory on three different evenings, each time carefully surveying the house, in order to discover whether any visitor was being entertained. On the fourth evening Brander came, and, inquiring for Jennie, who was exceedingly nervous, he took her out for a walk. She was afraid of her father, lest some unseemly thing should happen, but did not know exactly what to do.

Gerhardt, who was on his way to the house at the time, observed her departure. That was enough for him. Walking deliberately in upon his wife, he said:

"Where is Jennie?"

"She is out somewhere," said her mother.

"Yes, I know where," said Gerhardt. "I saw her. Now wait till she comes home. I will tell him."

He sat down calmly, reading a German paper and keeping an eye upon his wife until, at last, the gate clicked, and the front door opened. Then he got up.

"Where have you been?" he exclaimed in German.

Brander, who had not suspected that any trouble of this

character was pending, felt irritated and uncomfortable. Jennie was covered with confusion. Her mother was suffering an agony of torment in the kitchen.

"Why, I have been out for a walk," she answered confusedly.

"Didn't I tell you not to go out any more after dark?" said Gerhardt, utterly ignoring Brander.

Jennie colored furiously, unable to speak a word.

"What is the trouble?" inquired Brander gravely. "Why should you talk to her like that?"

"She should not go out after dark," returned the father rudely. "I have told her two or three times now. I don't think you ought to come here any more, either."

"And why?" asked the senator, pausing to consider and choose his words. "Isn't this rather peculiar? What has your daughter done?"

"What has she done!" exclaimed Gerhardt, his excitement growing under the strain he was enduring, and speaking almost unaccented English in consequence. "She is running around the streets at night when she oughtn't to be. I don't want my daughter taken out after dark by a man of your age. What do you want with her anyway? She is only a child yet."

"Want!" said the senator, straining to retain his ruffled dignity. "I want to talk with her, of course. She is old enough to be interesting to me. I want to marry her, if she will have me."

"I want you to go out of here and stay out of here," returned the father, losing all sense of logic, and descending to the ordinary level of parental compulsion. "I don't want you to come around my house any more. I have enough trouble without my daughter being taken out and given a bad name."

"I tell you frankly," said the senator, drawing himself up to his full height, "that you will have to make clear your meaning. I have done nothing that I am ashamed of. Your daughter has not come to any harm through me. Now, I want to know what you mean by conducting yourself in this manner."

"I mean," said Gerhardt, excitedly repeating himself, "I mean, I mean that the whole neighborhood talks about how you come around here, and have buggy-rides and walks with my daughter when I am not here—that's what I mean. I mean that you are no man of honorable intentions, or you would not come taking up with a little girl who is only old enough to be your daughter. People tell me well enough what you are. Just you go and leave my daughter alone."

"People!" said the senator. "Well, I care nothing for your people. I love your daughter, and I am here to see her because I do love her. It is my intention to marry her, and if your neighbors have anything to say to that, let them say it. There is no reason why you should conduct yourself in this manner before you know what my intentions are."

Unnerved by this unexpected and terrible altercation, Jennie had backed away to the door leading out into the dining-room, and her mother, seeing her, came forward.

"Oh," said the latter, breathing excitedly, "he came home when you were away. What shall we do?"

Jennie only gazed with a nervous intensity and terror of abasement, which was soon to dissolve in tears.

"Marry, eh!" exclaimed the father. "Is that it?"

"Yes," said the senator, "marry, that is exactly it. Your daughter is eighteen years of age and can decide for herself. You have talked and acted in a manner tonight which I would have deemed impossible in you. I can only lay it to some unfounded prejudice which has no ground in fact. You have insulted me and outraged your daughter's feelings. Now, I wish you to know that it cannot stop here. If you have any cause to say anything against me outside of mere hearsay, I wish you to say it."

The senator stood before him, a very citadel of righteousness. He was neither loud-voiced nor angry-mannered, but there was a tightness about his lips and a coolness and laxity about his hands which bespoke the man of force and determination.

"I don't want to talk to you any more," returned Gerhardt, who was checked but not over-awed. "My daughter is my daughter. I am the one who will say whether she shall go out at night, or whether she shall marry you either. I know what you politicians are. When I first met you I thought you were a fine man, but now, since I see the way you conduct yourself with my daughter, I don't want anything more to do with you. Just you go and stay away from here. That's all I ask of you."

"I am sorry, Mrs. Gerhardt," said Brander, turning deliberately away from the angry father, "to have had such an argument in your home. I had no idea that your husband was opposed to my visits. However, I will leave the matter as it stands for the present. You must not take all this as badly as it seems."

Gerhardt looked on in astonishment at his coolness.

"I will go now," he said, addressing Gerhardt; "but you mustn't think that I am leaving this matter for good. You have made a serious mistake this evening. I hope you will realize that. I bid you good-night." He bowed slightly and went out.

Gerhardt closed the door firmly. "Now," he said, turning to his daughter and wife, "we will see whether we are rid of him or not. I will show you how to go after night upon the streets when everybody is talking already."

In so far as words were concerned, the argument ceased, but looks and feelings ran strong and deep, and for days thereafter scarcely a word was spoken in the little cottage. Gerhardt began to brood over the fact that he had accepted his place from the senator and decided to give it up. He made it known that no more of the senator's washing was to be done in their house, and if he had not been sure that Mrs. Gerhardt's hotel work was due to her own efforts in finding it, he would have stopped that. No good would come out of it, anyway. The outer door of the hostelry was a place for loafers. Sebastian proved that. If she had never gone there, all this talk would never have come upon them.

As for the senator, he went away decidedly ruffled by this crude occurrence. Strong as was his interest in Jennie, and fine as were his words, there remained an unavoidable sense of stooping, and of being involved among unfortunate and tainted circumstances. Neighborhood slanders are bad enough on their own plane, but for a man of his standing to descend and become involved in one, struck him now as being a little bit common. He did not understand the religious disposition of the father. Only the ripening and alluring beauty of his protégée remained, a subtle fragrance hanging over all, which saved him from absolute disgust with himself. He thought that he would do something about it in the future, but did not know the variation and vacillation of his own disposition. Time went by, and he lingered speculating. A week or so later, he was called to Washington. The life of the girl he left behind him was now exceedingly bare.

In the meantime the Gerhardt family struggled along as before. Gerhardt, not having known how much money had been steadily contributed by his benefactor, felt that the family ought to get along about as before. They were poor, indeed, but he was willing to face such poverty when it could be endured with honor. The grocery bills were of the same size, however. The children's clothing was steadily wearing out. Economy had to be practised, and payments stopped on old bills that Gerhardt was trying to adjust.

There came a day when the annual interest on the mortgage was due, and yet another when two different grocerymen met Gerhardt on the street and asked about their little bills. He did not hesitate to explain just what the situation was, and tell them, with convincing honesty, that he would try hard and do the best he could, but his spirit was unstrung by it. Many a time he prayed for the favor of heaven while at his labor, and did not hesitate to use the daylight hours that he should have had for sleeping to go about—either looking for a more remunerative position or to obtain such little jobs as he could now and then pick up. One of them was that of cutting grass.

Mrs. Gerhardt protested against these things, but he only explained his procedure by pointing to their necessity.

"When people stop me on the street and ask me for money, I have no time to sleep."

Mrs. Gerhardt could not help noting the perverse, unreasoning zealotry that had brought them to this, but neither could she help seeing and sympathizing with the anxiety that brought such marked lines of care to his face.

It was a distressing situation for all of them.

To cap it all, Sebastian got in jail. Fate brought it about in such a way that there was no actual blame attached, but communities usually do not look further than the material evidences. It was the old coal-stealing ruse of his, practiced once too often. He got up on a car one evening while Jennie and the children waited for him, and a railroad detective arrested him. There had been a good deal of coal-stealing during the past two years, but as long as it was confined to moderate quantities, the railroad took no notice. When, however, customers of shippers complained that cars from the Pennsylvania fields lost thousands of pounds in transit to Cleveland, Cincinnati, Chicago and other points, detectives were set to work. Gerhardt's children were not the only ones who preyed upon the railroad in this way. Other families in Columbus—many of them—were constantly doing the same thing, but Sebastian happened to be seized upon as the Columbus example. He was taken up, and the whole community could have noticed the item in the daily papers if they had wanted to.

"You come off that car now," said the detective, suddenly appearing out of the shadow. Jennie and the other children dropped their baskets and buckets and fled for their lives. Sebastian's first impulse was to jump and run, but when he tried it the detective grabbed him by the coat.

"Hold on here!" he exclaimed. "I want you."

"Aw, let go," said Sebastian savagely, for he was no weakling. There was nerve and determination in him, as well as a keen sense of his awkward predicament.

"Let go, I tell you," he reiterated, and, giving a jerk, he almost upset his captor.

"Come here now," said the detective, pulling him viciously in an effort to establish his authority.

Sebastian came, but it was with a blow which staggered his adversary.

There was more struggling, and then a passing railroad hand came to the detective's assistance. Together they hurried Sebastian toward the depot, and, there discovering the local officer, turned him over. It was with a torn coat, scarred hands and face, and a black eye that he was locked up for the night.

The consequence of this was something dreadful in the little world in which it happened.

When the children came home, they could not say what had happened to their brother, but as nine o'clock came, and then ten, and eleven, and Sebastian did not return, Mrs. Gerhardt was beside herself. He had stayed out many a night as late as twelve and one, but his mother had a foreboding of something terrible tonight. When half-past one arrived, and no Sebastian, she began to cry.

"Some one ought to go up and tell your father," she said. "He may be in jail."

Jennie volunteered, but George, who was soundly sleeping, was awakened to go along with her.

"What!" said Gerhardt, astonished to see his two children.

"Bass hasn't come yet," said Jennie, and then told the story of the evening's adventure in explanation.

Gerhardt left right away with his two children, walking

excitedly back with them to a point where he could turn off to go to the jail. He was so worked up by the possibility of the thing that he was almost numb.

"Is that so, now!" he repeated nervously, rubbing his clumsy hands across his wet forehead.

At the station house, the sergeant in charge, who did not know anything about Gerhardt or his condition, told him curtly that Bass was under arrest.

"Sebastian Gerhardt?" he said, looking over his blotter. "Yes, here he is. Stealing coal and resisting an officer. Is he your boy?"

"Oh, my!" said Gerhardt, "*Ach Gott!*" He actually wrung his hands in distress.

"Want to see him?" asked the sergeant.

"Yes, yes," said the father.

"Take him back, Fred," said the other to the old watchman in charge, "and let him see the boy."

When Gerhardt stood in the back room, and Sebastian was brought out all marked and tousled, he broke down and began to cry. No word could cross his lips, because of his emotion.

"Don't cry, Pop," said Sebastian bravely. "I couldn't help it. It's all right. I'll be out in the morning."

Gerhardt only shook with his grief.

"Don't cry," continued Sebastian, doing his very best to restrain his own tears. "I'll be all right. What's the use crying?"

"I know, I know," said the gray-headed parent brokenly, "but I can't help it. It is my fault that I should let you do that."

"No, no, it isn't," said Sebastian. "You couldn't help it. Does Mother know anything about it?"

"Yes, she knows," he returned. "Jennie and George just came up where I was and told me. I didn't know anything about it until just now," and he began to cry again, recovering himself after a moment with difficulty.

"Well, don't you feel badly, now," went on Bass, the finest part of his nature coming to the surface. "I'll be all right. Just you go back to work now, and don't worry. I'll be all right."

"How did you hurt your eye?" asked the father, looking at him with red eyes.

"Oh, I had a little wrestling match with the man who nabbed me," said the boy, smiling bravely. "I thought I could get away."

"You shouldn't do that, Sebastian," said his father. "It may go harder with you on that account. When does your case come up?"

"In the morning, they told me," said Bass. "Nine o'clock."

"This is awful, awful," repeated Gerhardt, getting back to the horror of the thing. His voice vibrated with emotion.

"You go on back to your work now, and take it easy. I won't come out so bad," consoled his boy.

Gerhardt, however, stood there for some time and spoke of bail, fine, and the whole medley of court details, without seeing exactly what he could do. Finally, he was persuaded by Bass to go away, but the starting was another occasion for a burst of feeling, and he was led away shaking, but trying to conceal it.

"It's pretty tough," said Bass to himself as he was led back to his cell. He was thinking solely of his father. "I wonder what Ma will think."

The thought of this touched him tenderly. "I wish I'd knocked the dub over the first crack," he said. "What a fool I was not to get away."

CHAPTER VII

The outcome of this was in true keeping with the dictates of poverty. Gerhardt had no time to act. He did not know any one to whom he could appeal between the hours of two and nine o'clock in the morning. He went back to talk with his wife, and then to his post of duty. But it almost strained his heart cords to the point of snapping. With her, he had discussed ways and means, but who does not know the modest resources of the poor? Only one man could they think of who was able, or possibly willing, to do anything. This was the glass manufacturer, Hammond; but he was not in the city. Gerhardt did not know this, however.

When nine o'clock came, he went alone to the court, for it was thought advisable for the others to stay away. Mrs. Gerhardt was to hear immediately what happened. He would come right back.

The judge of the city court was a lean, wiry little individual who loved to take life with a cackling jocosity, which was a humorous thing in itself. He considered that such whims as these, in which he frequently interpreted the law, were good and natural, and that nothing, after all, really depended upon his mood.

When Sebastian was lined up inside the dock, he had a number of inmates to wait for. There were seven ahead of him. Gerhardt had been forced to take a rear seat, as he could say nothing in his boy's defense. When the officer, who had relieved the detective of this prisoner, heard the justice inquire, "What's the next case?" he pushed Sebastian before the inner railing, and said:

"Stealing coal, Your Honor, and resisting arrest."

The magistrate looked at Sebastian closely, his left eye squinted, and his mind unfavorably impressed by the lad's scratched and wounded face.

"Well, young man," he said, "what have you to say for yourself?"

At the sight of the shuffling and pushing which attended his son's presentation, Gerhardt arose. He could not stay away. Making his way forward, he came near to the railing, but was seized by a court officer, who exclaimed, pushing him back—"Here, where are you going?"

"That is my boy," said Gerhardt. "I want to see the judge."

"Who's the witness in this case?" the court was asking. When he heard the shuffling, he stopped to look about the room. "What's the noise about?" he asked.

"This man says he's the young man's father, and wants to testify," said the nearest officer.

"Tell him to stand outside the dock and wait till he's called," returned the magistrate irritably. "Now then, how did you get your black eye?"

Sebastian looked at him, but did not answer at once. The detective who had arrested him leaned forward and began to explain.

"I arrested him," he said. "He was on one of the company's cars. He tried to break away from me, and when I held him he assaulted me. This man here was a witness," he added, turning to the railroad hand who had helped him.

"Stealing coal and fighting when you're caught, eh," observed the magistrate, looking over his bench at the prisoner.

"Well, Gerhardt, you look as though you might like to fight. That's how you got your black eye, I suppose."

Sebastian, in his youthful pride and shame, looked down, but said nothing. He did not see just what he could say without lying.

"Is that where he struck you?" asked the court, observing the detective's swollen jaw.

"Yes, sir," he returned, glad of an opportunity to be further revenged.

"If you please," put in Gerhardt, leaning forward, "he is my boy. He was sent to get the coal. He—"

"We don't mind when they pick up around the yard," put in the detective, "but he was throwing it off the cars to half-a-dozen others."

"Can't you earn enough to keep from taking coal off the coal cars?" asked the court, but before either father or son had time to answer, he added, "What is your business?"

"Car builder," said Sebastian.

"And what do you do?" he questioned, addressing the father.

"I am watchman at Miller's furniture factory."

"Um," said the court, still feeling that Sebastian was sullen and contentious. "Well, this young man might be let off on this coal-stealing charge, but he seems to be altogether too free with his fists. Columbus is altogether too rich in that sort of thing. Ten dollars."

"If you please," began Gerhardt, but the court officer was already pushing him away.

"I don't want to hear any more about it," said the court. "He's stubborn, anyhow. What's the next case?"

Gerhardt made his way over to his boy, abashed and yet very glad it was no worse. Somehow, he thought, he could raise the money. Sebastian looked at him solicitously when he came forward.

"It's all right," said Bass soothingly. "He didn't give me half a chance to say anything."

"I'm only glad it wasn't more," said Gerhardt nervously. "We will try and get the money."

He explained about going to see Hammond, and tried to offer consolation, but Bass gave more of that than he received.

"I will go now," Gerhardt said at last, and started off with a promise to be right back.

Going first home to his wife, he informed the troubled household of the result. Mrs. Gerhardt stood white and yet relieved, for ten dollars seemed something that might be had. Jennie heard the whole story with open mouth and wide eyes. It was a terrible blow to her. Poor Bass. He was always so lively and good-natured. It seemed terrible that he should be in jail.

Gerhardt went hurriedly to Hammond's fine residence, but he was not in the city. He thought then of a lawyer by the name of Jenkins, whom he knew in a casual way, but Jenkins was not in at his office. There were several grocers and coal merchants whom he knew well enough, but he owed them money. Pastor Wundt might let him have it, but the agony such a disclosure to that worthy would entail held him back. He did call on one or two acquaintances, but these, surprised at the unusual and peculiar request, excused themselves. At four o'clock he returned home temporarily, weary and exhausted.

"I don't know what to do," he observed after detailing his efforts. "If I could only think."

Jennie thought of Brander, but the situation had not accentuated her desperation to the degree where she could brave her father's opposition, and his terrible insult to the senator, to go and ask. Her watch had been pawned a second time, and she had no other means of obtaining money.

"If we don't get the money there by five o'clock," said Gerhardt, "he will have to stay all night again." He was thinking of the wages that were tied up until the end of the week, the use of which for this purpose would leave them without anything.

It was eight in the evening when he returned for good, tired and footsore, but so overwrought in spirit that neither of these weaknesses appeared as definite pains. It was a fact, most forcefully apparent to him now, that his poverty was a grinding thing. He really did not know which way further to look. The situation had been canvassed fully by himself and his wife, but neither had any additional suggestion to make. Ten dollars is ten dollars, and when one who is a day laborer is wanting it there are not so many resources. The family sat together in the kitchen in council but nothing came of it. Only Jennie kept thinking over and over of Brander and what he would do if he knew.

But he had gone, or she thought he had. She had read in the paper shortly after her father's quarrel with him that he had departed. There had been no notice of his return. She wondered what she could do, thinking of Bass the while in his narrow cell. To think of Bass, so smart and clean as a rule, his eye cut, as her father had said, lying in prison. And for trying to get them coal!

The family council lasted until ten-thirty, but there was still nothing decided. Mrs. Gerhardt persistently and monotonously turned one hand over in the other and stared at the floor. Gerhardt ran his hand through his reddish brown hair and now and then pulled at the chin of his distraught face. "It's no use," he said finally. "I can't think of anything."

"Go to bed, Jennie," said her mother solicitously. "Get the others to go. There's no use their sitting up. I may think of something. You go on to bed."

They stood about awhile longer—Jennie and the children, but finally after repeated urgings from her mother she persuaded them to accompany her and retired into the little rooms where they slept two and two.

This daughter of poverty, although she outwardly acquiesced in the suggestion that she retire, could not so easily agree that there was nothing more to be done. Brander had pleaded with her so often to come to him if she were in trouble. Bass was in jail. Her father and mother distraught in the kitchen. Her father was opposed to the ex-senator—but if he did not know? Over and over in her sympathetic, girlish mind she turned this thought. If he did not know.

But supposing the ex-senator were not in the city?—She could do nothing then. But could she sleep and not know? She stood before a narrow, half-tall mirror that surmounted a shabby bureau, thinking. Her sister Veronica, with whom she slept, was already composing herself to dreams. The others had retired—all except Gerhardt and his wife—and she fumbled at her collar, but her face was white. If they would only go to bed—her father and mother. Finally a grim resolution fixed itself in her consciousness. She would go and see Senator Brander. If *he* were in town he would help Bass. Why shouldn't she—he loved her. He had asked over and over to marry her, said he would. In the deep of her soul she had always expected him to return. And he would. Why should she not go and ask him for help?

She hesitated a little while, then hearing Veronica breathing regularly, she took her hat and jacket from off a hook behind the door and noiselessly opened the door into the sitting room to see if anyone were stirring.

There was no sound save that of Gerhardt rocking nervously to and fro in the kitchen. There was no light save that of her own small room-lamp and a gleam from under the kitchen door. She turned and blew the former out,—then slipped quietly to the front door, opened it and stepped out into the night.

The problem which this daughter of the poor had undertaken to solve was a difficult one, though she did not see it wholly in that light. She was compounded at this moment of a sense of pity and a sense of hope. A waning moon was shining, almost full, and a hushed sense of growing life filled the air, for it was nearing spring again. As she hurried along the shadowy streets—the arc light had not yet been invented—she had a sinking sense of fear, a numbness to danger, and quavering thoughts as to what her noble benefactor would think. What would he think? Sometimes she almost turned at the thought and then the recollection of Bass in his night cell would come to her and she would hurry on.

The character of the Columbus House was such that it was not difficult for a maiden of Jennie's age (or any other woman for that matter) to find ingress, through the ladies' entrance, to the various floors of the hotel at that hour of the night. The hotel, not unlike many others of the time, was in no sense loosely conducted, but its method of supervision was lax. For instance there was no individual supervision of the hotel laundry service, but certain authorized washer-women could come and go as they pleased. There was no hired servitor to guard the ladies' entrance, its use not being of such a multiplied character as to seem to require that service. Any person could enter and, by applying at a rear entrance to the lobby, gain the attention of the clerk. Otherwise not much notice was taken of those who came and went. The character of the patronage, principally men, and they of a certain commercial standing and ability, guaranteed a standard of conservatism which had hitherto not been infringed upon.

When she came to the door it was dark save for a low light burning in the entry-way. The distance to the senator's room was only a short way along the hall of the second floor. She hurried up the steps, nervous and pale, but giving no other outward sign of the storm that was surging within her. When she came to his familiar door she paused from fear that he was, fear that he was not, present. A glow overhead assured her of the former fact and she knocked timidly. A man coughed and bestirred himself.

The very comfortable statesman had been thinking of her at the time. His room, whenever he came back to Columbus, was redolent of joy that had been—memories of her own simple ways, her, to him, perfect beauty. He wanted to go out some day and have a talk with her again. He was determined that her foolish German father should not ultimately interfere with his plans in regard to her. She was his. She belonged to him—so he argued. Why should her father interfere?

In the midst of these thoughts came the knock and he coughed and rose.

His surprise as he opened the door knew no bounds. Fate had realized his dream for him. "Why, Jennie!" he exclaimed. "How delightful! I was thinking of you. Come in—Come in."

He welcomed her with an eager embrace.

"I was coming out to see you, believe me, I was. I was thinking all along how I could straighten this matter out. And now you come. But what's the trouble?"

He held her at arm's length and studied her troubled face. The beauty of her moved him as did cut lilies, wet with dew.

He felt a great surge of tenderness.

"I have something to ask you," she at last brought herself to say. "My brother is in jail. We need ten dollars to get him out, and I didn't know where else to go."

"My poor child," he said, chafing her hands. "Where else should you go? Where else would you want to go? Haven't I told you always to come to me? Don't you know, Jennie, I would do anything in the world for you?"

"Yes," she gasped.

"Well, then, don't worry about that any more. But won't fate ever cease striking at you, poor child? How did your brother come to get in jail?"

"They caught him throwing coal down from the cars," she replied.

"Ah!" he sighed, his sympathies touched and awakened. Here was this boy arrested and fined for what fate was practically driving him to do. Here was this girl pleading with him at night, in his room, for what to her was a great necessity—ten dollars— to him, a mere nothing. "I will arrange about your brother," he said quickly. "Don't worry. I can get him out in half an hour. You sit here now and be comfortable until I return."

He waved her to his easy chair beside a large lamp and hurried out of the room.

The entire arrangement of the administration of criminal law in Columbus was quite familiar to him. He knew the sheriff who had personal supervision of the county jail. He knew the judge who had administered the fine. It was but a five minutes' task to write a note to the judge asking him to revoke the fine, for the sake of the boy's character, and send it by a messenger to his home. Another ten minutes' task to go personally to the jail and ask his friend, the sheriff, to release the boy then and there.

"Here is the money," he said. "If the fine is revoked you can return it to me. Let him go now."

The sheriff was only too glad to comply. He hastened below to personally supervise the task, and Bass, an astonished boy, was set forth in the night with no one to explain to him immediately how it had happened.

"That's all right now," said the turnkey. "You're free now. Run along home and don't let them catch you at anything like that again."

Bass went his way, wondering, and the ex-senator returned to his hotel brooding as to just how this situation should be handled. Obviously Jennie had not told her father of her mission. She had come as a last resource. She was waiting for him in his room now.

There are crises in all men's lives when they waver between the strict fulfillment of justice and duty and the great possibilities for personal happiness which another line of conduct seems to ensure. And the issues are not always marked and clear. At this moment he knew that Jennie was in his hands. He knew that the issue of taking her, even as his wife, was complicated by the senseless opposition of her father. The opinion of the world offered another complication. Supposing he should take her openly, what would the world say? She was a big woman, basically, that he knew. There was something there which was far and away beyond the keenest suspicion of the common herd. He did not know what it was—some bigness of emotion not altogether squared with intellect—or perhaps, better yet, experience—which was worthy of any man's desire. It gripped him like a magnet. It pulled him firmly. "This wonderful girl," he thought, "this wonderful girl."

Meditating as to what he should do he returned to his hotel and the room. As he entered he was struck anew with her beauty and, what was more significant yet, the appeal of her personality. In the glow of the shaded lamp she seemed a figure of marvelous potentiality.

"Well," he said, endeavoring to appear calm, "I have looked after your brother. He is out."

She rose.

"Oh!" she exclaimed, clasping her hands and stretching her arms out toward him. There were tears of gratefulness in her eyes.

He saw them and stepped close to her quickly. "Jennie, for heaven's sake don't cry. You angel! You sister of mercy! To think you should have to add tears to your other sacrifices."

He drew her to him and then all the caution of years deserted him. There was a sense of need and of fulfillment in his mood. At last, in spite of other losses, fate had brought him what he most desired—love, a woman whom he could love. He pulled her to him close and kissed her again and again.

The Englishman Jefferies has told us that it requires a hundred and fifty years to make a perfect maiden. "From all enchanted things of earth and air, this preciousness has been drawn. From the south wind that breathed a century and a half ago over the green wheat; from the perfume of the growing grasses waving over honey-laden clover and laughing veronica, hiding the green-finches, baffling the bee; from rose-loved hedges, woodbine and corn-flower azure-blue, where yellowing wheat-stalks crowd up under the shadow of green firs. All the devious brooklet's sweetness, where the iris stays the sunlight; all the wild wood's hold of beauty; all the broad hill's thyme and freedom—thrice a hundred years repeated.

"A hundred years of cowslips, bluebells, violets; purple spring and golden autumn; sunshine, shower and dewy mornings; the night immortal; all the rhythm of time unrolling. A chronicle unwritten and past all power of writing; who shall preserve a record of the petals that fell from the roses a century ago? The swallows to the housetop three hundred times—think of that!

Thence she sprang, and the world yearns towards her beauty as to flowers that are past. The loveliness of seventeen is centuries old. That is why passion is almost sad."

If you have understood and appreciated the beauty of harebells three hundred times repeated; if the quality of the roses, of the music, of the ruddy mornings and evenings of the world has ever touched your heart; if all beauty were passing, and you were given these things to hold in your arms before the world slipped away, would you give them up?

CHAPTER VIII

It cannot be said that at this time a clear sense of what had happened—of what social and physical significance this new relationship to the senator entailed, was present in Jennie's mind. She was not conscious as yet of that shock which the possibility of maternity, even under the most favorable conditions, brings to the average woman. The astonishing awakening which comes to one who has not thought of the possibilities of the situation, has not dreamed that the time is ripe or the hour has come, was for a later period. Her present attitude was one of surprise, wonder, uncertainty—and at the same time a sense of beauty and pleasure in this new thing. Brander, for all he had done, was a good man, closer to her than ever. He loved her. His protest was definite and convincing. Because of this new relationship, a change in her social condition was to come about. Life was to be radically different from now on—was different at this moment. The able ex-senator had assured her over and over of his enduring affection.

"I tell you, Jennie," he said as it came time for her to leave, "I don't want you to worry. This emotion of mine has gotten the best of me, but I'll marry you. I've been carried off my feet by what you are. It's best for you to go home tonight. Say nothing at all. Caution your brother, if it isn't too late. Keep your peace and I will marry you and take you away from here shortly. I can't do it right now. I don't want to do it here. But I'm going to Washington and I'll send for you. And here,"—he reached for his purse and took from it a hundred dollars, practically all he had with him, "take that. I'll send you more tomorrow. You're my girl now—remember that. You belong to me."

He embraced her tenderly.

She went out into the night, thinking. No doubt he would do as he said. There were the possibilities of a charming and comfortable life. Suppose he did marry her. Oh, dear. She would go to Washington—that far-off place. And her father and mother, they would not need to work so hard any more. She could help them. And Bass, and Martha—she fairly glowed as she recounted to herself the possibilities of helpfulness.

The pity of this world's affairs is that they are not as easily adjusted as the fancy of man would dictate. The hour of the night, it was past one, the ignorance or perhaps knowledge by now of her parents, the storm that would ensue once Gerhardt knew that she had gone to the senator and remained so late, the big, dark, important new fact which she could not tell—all troubled her soul to the point of wretchedness as she neared her home. Brander kept her company to her own gate, suggested that he enter and make an explanation, but the house being dark, the thought occurred to both that possibly the Gerhardts had not heard Bass come in—she had left the door open and Bass had his own key anyhow. Had he unconsciously locked her out?

She slipped up the steps and tried the door. It was open. She paused a moment to indicate to her lover that it was and entered. All was silent within. She slipped to her own room and heard Veronica breathing. She went next to where Bass slept with George. He was there, stretched out as if asleep. When she entered he asked, "Is that you, Jennie?"

"Yes."

"Where have you been?"

"Listen," she murmured. "Have you seen Papa and Mama?"

"Yes."

"Did they know I had gone out?"

"Ma did. She told me not to ask after you. Where have you been?"

"I went to see Senator Brander for you."

"Oh, that was it. They didn't tell me why they let me out."

"Don't tell any one," she pleaded. "I don't want any one to know. You know how Papa feels about him."

"All right," he replied. But he was curious as to what the ex-senator thought, what he had done, how she had appealed to him.

"He didn't say much," she said. "He went to get you out. How did Mama know I was gone?"

"I don't know," he replied.

She was so glad to see him back that she stroked his hair, all the time, however, thinking of her mother. So she knew. She must tell her—what?

As she was thinking, her mother came to the door.

"Jennie," she whispered.

Jennie went out.

"Oh, why did you go?" she asked.

"I couldn't help it, Ma," she replied. "I thought I must do something."

"Why did you stay so long?"

"He wanted to talk to me," she answered evasively.

Her mother looked at her nervously, wanly.

"I have been so afraid, oh, so afraid. Your father went to your door, but I said you were asleep. He locked the front door, but I opened it again. When Bass came in he wanted to call you, but I persuaded him not."

She looked again wistfully at her daughter.

"I'm all right, Mama," said Jennie encouragingly. "I'll tell you all about it tomorrow. Go to bed. How does he think Bass got out?"

"He doesn't know. He thought maybe they just let him go because he couldn't pay the fine."

Jennie laid her hand lovingly on her mother's shoulder.

"Go to bed," she said.

She was already years older in thought and act. She felt as though she must help her mother now, somehow, as well as herself.

The days which followed were of dreamy uncertainty to Jennie. She went over in her mind these dramatic events time and time and time and again. It was not such a difficult matter to tell her mother that the senator had talked of marriage again, that he proposed to come and get her after a trip to Washington, that he had given her a hundred dollars and intended to give her more, but of the other—she could not bring herself to speak of that. It was too sacred. The balance of the money he had promised her arrived by messenger the following day, four hundred dollars in bills, with the admonition in letter form that she put it in a local bank. The ex-senator explained also that he was already on his way to Washington, but that he would come back or send for her and that meanwhile he would write. "Keep a stout heart," he wrote. "There are better days in store for you."

Mrs. Gerhardt was dubious of all this generosity—of what it all might mean, but in view of what had gone before, his declaration of love, his announcement of his desire to marry her, it seemed, at worst, plausible. Jennie had always been a truthful and open girl. She seemed frank enough to her now. There was a certain wistfulness which worried her, at times. She had not noted this in her daughter's moods before.

Then came days for Jennie which, because of the possibility of tidings, the Arabian-like character of which were scarcely explainable, were most attractive to her. Brander was gone, her fate was really in the balance, but because her mind still retained all of the heart-innocence and unsophistication of her youth, she was truthful, and even without sorrow at times. He would send for her. There was the mirage of a distant country and wondrous scenes looming up in her mind. She had a little fortune in the bank, more than she had ever dreamed of, with which to help her mother. There were natural, girlish anticipations of good still holding over, which made her less apprehensive than she could otherwise possibly have been. All nature, life, possibility was in the balance. It might turn good, or ill, but with so inexperienced a soul it would not be entirely evil until it was so.

How a mind under such uncertain circumstances could retain so comparatively placid a vein is one of those marvels which finds its explanation in the inherent trustfulness of the spirit of youth. It is not often that the minds of men retain the perceptions of their younger days. The marvel is not that one should thus retain, but that any should ever lose them. Go the world over, and, after you have put away the wonder and tenderness of youth, what is there left? The few sprigs of green that sometimes invade the barrenness of your materialism, the few glimpses of summer which flash past the eye of the wintry soul, the half-hours off during the long tedium of burrowing, these reveal to the hardened earth-seeker the universe which the youthful mind has with it always. No fear and no favor; the open fields and the light upon the hills; morning, noon, night; stars, the bird-calls, the water's purl—these are the natural inheritance of the mind of the child. Men call it poetic, those who are hardened, fanciful. In the days of their youth, it was natural, but the receptiveness of youth has departed and they cannot see.

How this worked out in her personal actions was to be seen only in a slightly accentuated wistfulness, a touch of which was in every task. Did she wash, sew, walk with her brothers and sisters, it was always the same, a wood-dove kind of wistfulness prevailing. Sometimes she would wonder that no letter came, but at the same time she would recall the fact that he had specified a few weeks, and hence the six that actually elapsed did not seem so long.

In the meanwhile the distinguished ex-senator had gone cheerily to his conference with the president, had joined in a pleasant round of social calls, and was about to pay a short country visit to some friends in Maryland, when he was seized with a slight attack of fever, which confined him to his room for a few days. He felt a little irritated that he should be laid up just at this time, but never suspected that there was anything serious in his indisposition. Then the doctor discovered that he was suffering from a virulent form of typhoid, the ravages of which took away his senses for a time and left him very weak. He was thought to be convalescing, however, when, just six weeks after he had last parted with Jennie, he was seized with a sudden attack of heart failure and never regained consciousness. Jennie remained blissfully ignorant of his illness and did not even see the heavy-typed headlines of the announcement of his death until Bass came home that evening.

"Look here, Jennie," he said, when he came in, "Brander's dead."

He held up the newspaper, on the first column of which was printed in heavy block type:

DEATH OF EX-SENATOR BRANDER.

Sudden Passing of Ohio's Distinguished Son.
Succumbs to Heart-failure at the Arlington, in
Washington. Recent attack of typhoid from which he was thought
to be recovering proves fatal. Notable phases
of a remarkable career.

Jennie looked at it in blank amazement.

"Dead?" she exclaimed.

"There it is in the paper," returned Bass, his tone being that of one who is imparting a very interesting piece of news. "He died at ten o'clock this morning."

Jennie took the paper with but ill-concealed trembling and went into the adjoining room. There she stood by the front window and looked at it again, a sickening sensation of dread holding her as in a trance.

"He is dead," was all her mind could formulate for the time, and as she stood there, the voice of Bass recounting the fact to Gerhardt in the adjoining room sounded in her ears. "Yes, he is dead," she heard him say, and once again she tried to get some conception of what it meant to her.

The vigor of the blow which Fate thus dealt to Jennie was too much for her to ever get a full conception of it. The human mind is limited in its capacity to receive impressions. She was literally stunned, and in this condition her mind was not capable of feeling either sorrow or pain to any great extent.

It was while she was standing there that Mrs. Gerhardt came in. She had heard Bass's announcement and had seen Jennie leave the room, but her trouble with Gerhardt over the senator had caused her to be careful of any display of interest, and now she came in to see what effect it would have upon Jennie. No conception of the real state of affairs ever having crossed her mind, she was largely interested in the loss Jennie would feel in this sudden annihilation of her hopes. She could never be a foreign minister's wife now, and the influence of the man who had been so kind to them all was completely obliterated.

"Isn't it too bad?" she said, with real sorrow. "To think that he should have to die just when he was going to do so much."

She paused, expecting some word of agreement, but finding the latter unwontedly dumb, she continued with:

"I wouldn't feel badly, if I were you. It can't be helped. He meant to do a good deal, but you mustn't think of that now. It's all over, and it can't be helped, you know."

She paused again and still Jennie remained dumb, whereupon, seeing how useless her words were, she concluded that Jennie wished to be alone, and she went away.

Still Jennie stood there, and now, as the real significance of the news began to formulate itself into consecutive thoughts, she began to see the wretchedness of her position, the helplessness. She went into her bedroom after her mother had gone and sat down upon the side of the bed, from which position, by the dim evening light here prevailing, she saw a very pale, distraught face staring at her from out of the small mirror. She looked at it uncertainly, then put her hands up to her forehead and leaned over toward her knee.

"I'll have to go away," she thought, and began, with the courage of despair, to wonder where.

In the meantime the evening meal was announced, and, to maintain appearances, she went out and joined the family. The naturalness of her part was very difficult to sustain. Mrs. Gerhardt noted her effort to conceal her feelings. Gerhardt observed her subdued condition without guessing the depth of feeling which it covered. Bass was too much interested in his own affairs to pay much attention to anybody.

During the days that followed, Jennie pondered over the difficulties of her position and wondered what she should do. Money she had, it was true, but no friends, no experience, no place to go. She had always lived with her family. While she was lingering in this state, she began to feel unaccountable sinkings of spirit, nameless and formless dreads which seemed to lurk about and haunt her. Once when she arose in the morning she felt an uncontrollable desire to cry, and frequently thereafter this feeling would seize upon her at varying times, the inability to conceal which aroused Mrs. Gerhardt's interest. The latter began to note her moods, and upon coming into the room one afternoon found her eyes wet, a thing which moved her to the closest and most sympathetic inquiry.

"Now you must tell me what's the matter with you," she said, greatly distressed.

Jennie, to whom confession at first seemed impossible, under the sympathetic persistence of her mother broke down at last and made the fatal confession, whereupon Mrs. Gerhardt only stood there, too dumb with misery for a time to give vent to a word.

"Oh!" she said at last, a great wave of self-accusation sweeping over her. "It is all my fault. I might have known."

The crowding details of this miserable discovery were too numerous and too pathetic to record. Concealment was one thing the mother troubled over. Her husband's actions, another. Brander, the world, her beautiful, good Jennie—all returned to her mind in rapid succession. That Brander should have betrayed her daughter seemed horrible.

She went back after a time to the washing she had to do, and stood over her tub, rubbing and crying. The tears ran down her cheeks and dropped into the suds. Once in awhile she would stop and lift the corner of her apron in an effort to dry her eyes, but emotion soon filled them again.

When the first shock had passed, there came a vivid consciousness of approaching danger with always the need of thinking about it. Mrs. Gerhardt was no fine reasoner for such a situation. She thought and thought, but always the necessity of telling her husband haunted her. He had often said that if ever one of his daughters should act like some of those he knew, he would turn her out of doors. "She should not stay under my roof!" he had exclaimed.

Now that this evil was truly upon him, he would be as good as his word. Had he not driven Brander away? Would he have any use for her, or Jennie, once he knew that they had countenanced the senator after his warning, and with such terrible results? Jennie herself had no idea of trying to escape.

"I'm so afraid of your father," Mrs. Gerhardt often said to Jennie in this intermediate period. "I don't know what he'll say."

"Perhaps I'd better go away," suggested her daughter.

"No," she said, "he needn't know just yet. Wait awhile."

The difficulty of this is neither easily understood by, nor indicated to, those who do not know. In all Columbus Mrs. Gerhardt knew no one to whom she could send Jennie, if her father refused to endure her. It was not a village, but, even so, wherever she went, a wave of gossip was likely to spread and reach all about. Brander's money would keep her, but where? Thinking it over, she decided to tell her husband, and hope for the best.

One day then, when her own suspense had reached the place where it could no longer be endured, she sent Jennie away with the children, hoping to be able to tell her husband before they returned. All the morning she fidgeted about, dreading the opportune moment and letting him retire to his slumber without speaking. When afternoon came she did not go out to work, because she could not leave and see her duty unfulfilled. Gerhardt arose at four and still she hesitated, knowing full well that Jennie would soon return, and the specially prepared occasion be lost. It is almost certain that she would not have had the heart to say anything if he himself had not brought up the subject of Jennie's appearance.

"She doesn't look well," he said. "There seems to be something the matter with her."

"Oh," began Mrs. Gerhardt, visibly struggling under her fears, and moved to make an end of it at any cost, "Jennie is in trouble. I don't know what to do. She—"

Gerhardt, who had unscrewed a door-lock and was trying to mend it, brought the hand which held the screwdriver lightly to the table and stopped.

"What do you mean?" he asked.

Mrs. Gerhardt had her apron up in her hands at the time, her nervous tendency to roll it coming upon her. She tried to summon sufficient courage to explain, but fear and misery dominating, she lifted the apron to her eyes and began to cry.

Gerhardt looked at her and got up. He was a man with the Calvin type of face, rather spare, and sallow as to skin, a result of age and work in the wind and rain. When he was surprised or angry, a spark of light would come in his eye. He frequently pushed his hair back when he was troubled, and almost invariably walked the floor. Just now he looked alert and dangerous.

"What is that you say?" he inquired in German, his voice straining to a hard note. "In trouble—has someone—" he paused and flung his hand upward. "Why don't you speak?" he demanded.

"I never thought," went on Mrs. Gerhardt, frightened, and yet following her own train of thought, "that anything like that would happen to her. She was such a good girl. Oh!" she concluded, "to think he should ruin Jennie."

"By thunder!" shouted Gerhardt, giving way to a fury of feeling, "I thought so! Brander! Ha! Your fine man! That comes of letting her go running around at nights, buggy-riding, walking the streets. I thought so. God in heaven—!"

He broke from his dramatic attitude and struck out in a fierce stride across the narrow chamber, turning like a caged animal.

"Ruined!" he exclaimed. "Ruined! Ha! So he has ruined her, has he!"

Suddenly he stopped like an image jerked by a string. He was directly in front of Mrs. Gerhardt, who had retired to the table at the side of the wall and was standing there pale with fear.

"He is dead now!" he shouted, as if this fact had now first occurred to him. "He is dead!"

He put both hands to his temples as if he feared his brain would give way, and stood looking at her, the mocking irony of the situation seeming to burn in his brain like fire.

"Dead!" he repeated, and Mrs. Gerhardt, fearing for the reason of the man, shrank still farther away, her wits taken up more with the tragedy of the figure he presented than with the actual substance of his woe.

"He intended to marry her," she pleaded nervously. "He would have married her, if he had not died."

"Would have!" shouted Gerhardt, coming out of his trance at the sound of her voice. "Would have! That's a fine thing to talk about now. Would have! The hound! May his soul burn in hell—the dog! Ah, God! I hope—I hope—If I was not a Christian—" He clenched his hands, the awfulness of the thought of what he could wish for Brander's soul shaking him like a leaf.

Too strained by the fury of this mental tempest, Mrs. Gerhardt now burst into tears, and the old German turned away from her, his own feelings far too intense for him to have any sympathy with her. He walked to and fro, his heavy step shaking the kitchen floor. After a time he came back, a new phase of the dread calamity having offered itself to his mind.

"When did this happen?" he demanded.

"I don't know," returned Mrs. Gerhardt, too terror-stricken to tell the truth. "I only found it out the other day."

"You lie!" he exclaimed in his excitement, the painful accusation escaping him almost without consciousness on his part. "You were always shielding her. It is your fault that she is where she is. If you had let me have my way there would have been no cause for our trouble tonight."

He turned away from her, a vague sense of the dreadful assault he had made breaking into his mind, but his feeling was still too high to allow him to reason.

"A fine ending," he went on to himself. "A fine ending. My boy gets into jail; my daughter walks the streets and gets herself talked about; the neighbors come to me with open remarks about my children; and now she comes and lets this scoundrel ruin her. By the God in heaven, I don't know what has got into my children!"

He paused, rather saddened by the last reflection, and turned in a more pathetic strain, the substance of which was self-commiseration.

"I don't know how it is," he said. "I try, I try! Every night I pray that the Lord will let me do right, but it is no use. I might work and work. My hands," he said, putting them out, "are rough with work. All my life I have tried to be an honest man. Now—now—" his voice broke, and it looked for a moment as if he would give way to tears. Suddenly he turned on his wife, the major passion of anger possessing him.

"You are the cause of this," he exclaimed. "You are the sole cause. If you had done as I told you to do, this would not have happened. No, you wouldn't do that. She must go out! out!! out!!! She must have something to do. Well, she has had something to do now. She has become a street-walker, that's what she has become. She has set herself right to go to hell. Let her, now. Let her go. I wash my hands of the whole thing. This is enough for me."

He made as if to go off to his little bedroom, but he had no sooner reached the door than he came back.

"I throw back his job to him, the scoundrel!" he said, thinking of his own part in the miserable procession of events. "I would rather starve on the streets than take anything from such a hound as that. My family seems accursed."

He went on a little while longer, all the weakness and passion of his nature manifesting itself, when suddenly he thought of Jennie in connection with the future. Mrs. Gerhardt had been expecting this, a keen, nervous tension holding her to the point. It was none the less painful as a shock, however, when it came.

"She shall get out!" he said electrically. "She shall not stay under my roof! Tonight! At once! I will not let her enter my door again! I will show her whether she will disgrace me or not!"

"You mustn't turn her out on the streets tonight," pleaded Mrs. Gerhardt. "She has no place to go."

"Tonight!" he repeated. "This very minute! Let her find a home! She did not want this one. Let her get out now. We will see how the world treats her."

There seemed to be an element of satisfaction in this for him, for he quieted down to a dull, silent pace, giving vent only to a few short ejaculations. The minutes passed, and he asked other questions, upbraiding Mrs. Gerhardt, pouring invective upon Brander, reaffirming his opinion and intention concerning Jennie.

At half-past five, when Mrs. Gerhardt was tearfully going about the duty of getting supper, Jennie returned. Her mother started when she heard the door open, for now she knew the storm would burst afresh. Jennie was prepared though, if pallor and depression make suitable preparation for the expected.

"Get out of my sight!" he said, when he saw her coming into the room. "You shall not stay another hour in my house. I don't want to see you any more. Get out!"

Jennie stood before him pale, trembling a little, and silent. The children she had brought home with her ranged about in frightened amazement. Veronica and Martha, who loved her dearly, began to cry.

"What's the matter?" George asked, his mouth open in wonder.

"She shall get out," reiterated Gerhardt. "I don't want her under my roof. If she wants to be a street-walker, let her be one, but she shall not stay here. Pack your things," he added, staring at her.

Jennie moved, but the children cried loudly.

"Be still," said Gerhardt. "Go into the kitchen."

He drove them all out and followed stubbornly himself.

Knowing what had been coming, Jennie was partially prepared. She gathered up her few little belongings and began, with tears, to put them into a valise her mother brought her. The little girlish trinkets that she had accumulated, all were left in their places. She saw them but thought of her younger sisters and let them stay. Martha and Veronica thought of her deeply, and wanted to go in the room where she was working, but when they started, their father exclaimed, "Stay here!" It was a trying hour, and in it she seemed to move absolutely forsaken.

At six o'clock Bass came in, and seeing the queer nervous assembly in the kitchen, inquired what the trouble was.

Gerhardt looked at him oppressively, for he was in a grim, determined mood, but did not answer.

"What's the trouble?" insisted Bass. "What are you all sitting around for?"

Gerhardt was getting ready to make a speech, but Mrs. Gerhardt whispered, with tears but ill-concealed:

"He is driving Jennie away."

"What for?" asked Bass, opening his eyes in astonishment.

"I shall tell you what for," said Gerhardt, still speaking in German. "Because she's a street-walker, that's what for. She goes and gets herself ruined by a man thirty years older than she is, a man old enough to be her father. Let her get out of this. She shall not stay here another minute."

Bass looked about him, and the children opened their eyes. All felt clearly that something terrible had happened, even the little ones. None but Bass understood.

"What do you want to send her out tonight for?" he inquired. "This is no time to send a girl out on the streets. Can't she stay here until morning?"

"No," said Gerhardt.

"He oughtn't to do that," put in the mother.

"She goes now," said Gerhardt. "Let that be an end of it."

Bass stood still, feeling that it was too bad to have her go out in the night, but no thought of his own responsibility for her condition afflicting him. What the father had said about age proved that her seducer was Brander, but that anything had happened to her the night of his jailing did not cross his mind. In a vague way, he thought it was a pretty bad scrape that Jennie had got herself into, but did not want to see her harshly abused. Still, no fine magnanimity called him to any striking action.

"Where is she going to go?" he asked.

"I don't know," Mrs. Gerhardt interpolated weakly.

Bass looked around, but did nothing until Mrs. Gerhardt motioned him toward the front door when her husband was not looking.

"Go in! Go in!" was the import of her gesture.

Bass went in, and then Mrs. Gerhardt dared to leave her work and follow. The children stayed awhile, but, one by one, even they slipped away, leaving Gerhardt alone. When he thought that time enough had elapsed, he arose.

In the interval, Jennie had been hastily coached by her mother. She should go to a private boarding-house somewhere and send her address. Bass would not go directly with her, but she should wait a little way up the street, and he would follow. When her father was away, the mother might get to see her, or Jennie could come home. All was to be postponed until they could meet again.

While the instructions were still going on, Gerhardt came in. "Is she going?" he asked harshly.

"Yes," answered Mrs. Gerhardt, with her first and only note of defiance.

Bass said, "What's the hurry?" But Gerhardt frowned too mightily to permit him to venture more. Jennie, attired in the one good dress she had, and carrying her valise, came in, a pale gentle flower, toned to the melancholy of the occasion. Rich pathos was in her soulful eyes, and a tenderness that was not for herself at all. Fear was there now, for she was passing through a fiery ordeal, but she had already grown more womanly. The strength of love, too, was there; the dominance of patience and the ruling sweetness of sacrifice. Out she passed into the shadow, after kissing her mother goodbye, and the tears fell fast. Then she recovered herself, and on the instant began the new life.

CHAPTER IX

The world into which Jennie was thus unduly sent forth was that in which virtue has always struggled since time imme-morial, for virtue is the wishing well and the doing well unto others. Since time immemorial, those who have been gentle enough to carry the burdens have been allowed to carry them, and the tendency to be lamblike has usually made for the shambles. Virtue is that quality of generosity which offers itself willingly for service to others, and, being this, it is held by society to be nearly worthless. Sell yourself cheaply and you shall be used lightly and trampled under foot. Hold yourself dearly, however unworthily, and it will come about that you will be respected—how quickly depends upon your power to seize and retain. Society, in the mass, lacks woefully in the matter of discrimination. Its one criterion is the opinion of others. Its one test, that of self-preservation. Has he preserved his fortune? Has she preserved her maidenhood?

Only in rare instances, and with rare individuals, does there seem to be any guiding light from within.

Jennie had not sought to hold herself dear. Innate feeling in her made for self-sacrifice. She could not be readily corrupted by the world's selfish lessons on how to preserve oneself from the evil to come.

Going to the corner, Jennie waited in the falling shadows until at last Bass came up. She did not know where to go or what to do. Her wide eyes were filled with vague wonder and pain. She was outside now. There was no one to tell her how.

It is in such supreme moments that growth is greatest. It comes as with a vast surge, this feeling of strength and sufficiency. We may still tremble, the fear of doing wretchedly may linger, but we grow. Flashes of inspiration come to guide the soul. In nature there is no outside. When cast from a group or a condition, we have still the companionship of all that is. Nature is not ungenerous. Its winds and stars are fellows with you. Let the soul be but gentle and receptive, this vast truth will come home; not in set phrases, perhaps, but as a feeling, a comfort, which, after all, is the last essence of knowledge. In the universe, peace is wisdom.

"Give me your grip," said Bass, coming up; and, seeing that she was brimming with unutterable feeling, added, "I think I know where I can get you a room."

He led the way to the southern part of the city, where they were not known, and up to the door of an old lady whose parlor clock had been recently purchased from an installment firm he had started to work for. She was not well off, he knew, and had a room to rent.

"Is that room of yours still vacant?" he asked.

"Yes," she said, looking at Jennie.

"I wish you'd let my sister have it. We're moving away and she can't go yet."

The old lady expressed her willingness, and Jennie was soon temporarily installed.

"Don't worry now," said Bass, who felt rather sorry for her. "Pop won't keep this up always."

He was feeling quite worldly in his attitude.

"Don't call him 'Pop,'" said Jennie.

"Well, 'Pa,' then," he returned. "This'll blow over. Ma said I should tell you not to worry. Come up tomorrow when he's gone."

Jennie said she would, maybe, and, after giving her further verbal encouragement, he spoke to the old lady about board for Jennie, and left.

"It's all right now," he said encouragingly as he went out. "You'll come out all right. Don't worry. I've got to go back, but I'll come around in the morning."

He went away, and the bitter stress of it blew rather lightly above his head, for he was thinking that Jennie had made a mistake. This was shown by the manner in which he had asked her questions as they had walked together, and that in the face of her sad and doubtful mood.

"What'd you want to do that for?" and "Didn't you ever think what you were doing?" he inquired.

"Please don't ask me tonight," Jennie had said to him, which put an end to the sharpest form of his queries. She had no excuse to offer and no complaint to make. If any blame attached, very likely it was hers. His own misfortune and the family's and her sacrifice were alike forgotten.

Being left alone in her strange abode, Jennie gave way to her saddened feelings. The shock and shame of being turned out finally subdued her, and she wept. Although of a naturally long-suffering and uncomplaining disposition, the catastrophic wind-up of all her hopes was too much for her. She found herself turning in memory to the dead senator and the dire consequence of her relationship with him, as well as to the harsh and yet deserved wrath of her father. What was this element in life that could seize and overwhelm one as does a great wind? Why this sudden intrusion of death to shatter all that had seemed most promising?

As she thought over these things, a very clear recollection of the details of her long relationship with Brander came back to her, and for all her suffering she could only feel a loving affection for him. After all, he had not deliberately willed her any harm. The graciousness of his demeanor, the generosity of his disposition, the uniformly affectionate manner toward her, all came back to clear his memory. He had been essentially a good man, and she could but feel sorry, more for his sake than for her own, that his end had been so untimely.

These cogitations, while not at all reassuring, were, nevertheless, a source of beguilement, the use of which was to cause the night to pass, and the next morning Bass stopped on his way to work to say that Mrs. Gerhardt wished her to come home that same evening. Gerhardt would not be present, and they could talk it over.

The reception of this intelligence was most grateful to Jennie. Of all things, the most painful seemed that of not being able to go home again, and this word now opened that door to her. She spent the day lonesomely enough, but when night fell her spirits brightened, and at a quarter of eight she set out.

The details of this reunion and of several subsequent visits which she made were of a kind somewhat to sustain her drooping spirits, even though they did not bring her much comforting intelligence. Gerhardt, she learned, was still in a direfully angry and outraged mood. He had already decided to throw up his place on the following Saturday and go over to Youngstown, the possibility of getting work there luring him as a refuge from evil. Any place was better than Columbus after this, Mrs. Gerhardt confessed he had said. He could never expect to hold up his head here again. Its memories were odious. He would go away now, and, if he succeeded in finding work, the family should follow, a decision which meant the abandoning of the little home. He was not going to try to meet the mortgage on the house—he could not hope to.

Poor as this intelligence was, Mrs. Gerhardt's kindly disposition succeeded in making some capital out of it. If he went, as he said, Jennie could of course return. Jennie had the money Brander had given her, as she well knew. They could get along. She should only wait until Saturday and then return, after which they would have ample time to decide what was best.

The sudden turn of affairs transformed one portion of Jennie's troubles,—that of being compelled to go away, into grief for her father's pain-racked and conscience-driven body, but, as she could not fail to see that whatever befell now could neither receive let nor hindrance from her, she decided to avail herself of her mother's offer.

At the end of the week, Gerhardt took his leave and Jennie returned, after which, for a time at least, there was a restoration of the old order, a condition which of course could not endure.

Bass saw it. The trouble that had so recently manifested itself was decidedly odious to him. The thought of the possible developments, the certainty of talk and the intention of Gerhardt to move the family, with the exception of Jennie, to Youngstown, all weighed upon him disagreeably. Columbus was no place to stay. Youngstown was no place to go. If they could all move away to some larger city, it would be much better.

He pondered over this and hearing, through first one and then another, that a manufacturing boom was on in Cleveland, thought it might be wise if they, or at least he, went there. He might go, and if he succeeded, the others might come. If Gerhardt still worked on in Youngstown, as he was now doing, and the family came to Cleveland, it would save Jennie from being turned out in the streets.

Bass waited a little while before making up his mind but finally announced his purpose.

"I believe I'll go up to Cleveland," he said to his mother one evening as she was getting supper.

"Why?" she asked, looking up in an uncertain manner. She was rather afraid that Bass would desert her.

"I think I can get work there," he returned. "We oughtn't to stay in this darned old town."

"Don't swear," she returned.

"Oh, I know," he said, "but it's enough to make any one swear. We've never had anything but rotten luck here. I'm going to go, and maybe if I get anything, we can all move. We'd be better off if we'd get some place where people don't know us. We can't do anything here."

Mrs. Gerhardt listened with a strong hope for a betterment of their miserable life creeping into her heart. If Bass would only do this. If he would go and get work, and come to her rescue as a strong, bright young son might, what a thing it would be. They were in the rapids of a life which was moving toward a dreadful calamity. If only something would happen.

"Do you think you could get something to do?" she asked interestedly.

"I ought to," he said. "I've never looked for a place yet that I didn't get it. Other fellows have gone up there and done all right. Look at the Millers."

He shoved his hands into his pockets and looked out the window, then said:

"Do you think you could get along until I try my hand up there?"

"I guess we could," she replied. "Papa's at work now and we have some money that, that—" she hesitated to name the source, so ashamed was she of their predicament.

"Yes, I know," said Bass grimly.

"We won't have to pay any rent here before fall and then we'll have to give it up anyhow," she added.

She was referring to the mortgage on the house, which fell due the next September and which unquestionably could not be met. "If we could move away from here before then, I guess we could get along."

"I'll do it," said Bass determinedly. "I'll go."

Accordingly, he threw up his place at the end of the month, and the day after he left for Cleveland.

CHAPTER X

The incidents of the days that followed, relating as they did peculiarly to Jennie, were of an order which the morality of our day has agreed to taboo. Certain processes of the All-mother, the great artificing wisdom of the power that in silence and darkness works and weaves—when viewed in the light of the established opinion of some of the little individuals created by it, are considered very vile. "How is it," we ask ourselves, "that any good can come of contemplating so disagreeable a process?" And we turn our faces away from the creation of life, as if that were the last thing that man should dare to interest himself in, openly.

It is curious that a feeling of this sort should spring up in a world whose very essence is generative, the vast process dual, and where wind, water, soil and light alike minister to the fruition of that which is all that we are. Although the whole earth, not we alone, is moved by passions hymeneal, and everything terrestrial has come into being by the one common road, yet there is that ridiculous tendency to close the eyes and turn away the head as if there were something unclean in the method of nature. "Conceived in iniquity and born in sin," is the unnatural interpretation put upon the process by the extreme religionist, and the world, by its silence, gives assent to a judgement so marvelously warped.

Surely there is something radically wrong in this attitude. The teachings of philosophy and the deductions of biology should find more practical application in the daily reasoning of man. No process is vile, no condition unnatural. The accidental variation from a given social practice does not make a sin. It is the indifference to duty entailed, the ignorance of the highest wisdom which would care and make provision for the happiness of every creature conceived, that is either contemptible or pitiable. No poor little earthling, caught in the enormous grip of chance, and so swerved from the established customs of men, could possibly be guilty of that depth of vileness which the attitude of the world would seem to predicate so inevitably.

And yet Jennie, no conscious wisher of evil, was now to witness the unjust interpretation of that wonder of nature, which, but for the intervention of death, or the possible changing of an opinion of a man, might have been consecrated and hallowed as one of the ideal functions of life. Although herself unable to distinguish the separateness of this from every other normal process of life, yet was she made to feel, by the actions of all about her, that degradation was her portion, and sin the foundation as well as the condition of her state. Almost, not quite, was the affection, the consideration, the care—which afterward the world would demand of her for her child—now sought to be extinguished in her. Almost, not quite, was the budding and essential love looked upon as evil. She must contemn herself, contemn that which in the more approved limits of society is of all things the most sacred and holy.

As yet, we are dwelling in a most brutal order of society, against the pompous and loud-mouthed blusterings of which the temperate and tender voice of sympathy seems both futile and vain. Although able to look about him, and in the vast ordaining of nature read a wondrous plea for closer fellowship, yet, in the teeth of all the winds of circumstance, and between the giant legs of chance, struts little man—the indifference, the non-understanding, the selfishness of whom make his playground too often a field of despair. Winds to whisper that it is with the sum and not the minute individual of life that nature is concerned; waters to teach that of her bounty no man may be honestly deprived. All the beauty, the sweetness, the light poured forth with so lavish a hand that all may see the lesson of eternal generosity, and yet, unseeing man, narrowly drawing himself up in judgement, still seizes his brother by the throat, exacts the last tittle of form or custom and, finding him unable or unwilling to comply, drags him helpless and complaining to the gibbets and the jails.

Jennie, no unwilling but only a helpless victim, was now within the purview of this same unreasoning element of society, the judgers of those who do not judge, the blamers of those who do not blame. Although it was neither the gibbet nor the jail of a few hundred years before, there was that, in the ignorance and immobility of the human beings about her, which made it impossible for them to see anything but a vile and premeditated infraction of the social code, the punishment of which was ostracism. All she could do now was to withdraw and hide away, to shun the piercing and scornful gaze of men, to bear all in silence and, at the proper time, go hence a marked example of the result of evil-doing.

Heaven be praised for this truth, however—that in the natural innocence of the good heart is neither understanding of the petty prejudices of society, nor room for cavilling against fate. Although a mark for the wit and a butt for the scorn of men, such a heart is so allied with the larger perception of things that it cannot see. Not with weeping or self-berating, therefore, was her heart now filled. Not with selfish regrets as a vain remorse. Sorrow there was, it is true, but only a mellow phase of it, a vague uncertainty and wonder, which would sometimes cause her eyes to fill with tears.

You have heard the wood-dove calling in the lone stillness of the summertime, you have found the unheeded brooklet singing and babbling where no ear comes to hear. Under dead leaves and snowbanks the delicate arbutus unfolds its simple blossom, answering some heavenly call for color. So, too, this other flower of womanhood.

Jennie was left alone, but like the wood-dove she was a voice of sweetness in the summertime. Going about her household duties, she was content to await without murmur the fulfillment of that process for which, after all, she was but the sacrificial implement. When her duties were lightest, she was content to sit in quiet meditation, the marvel of life holding her as in a trance. When she was heaviest pressed to aid her mother, she would sometimes find herself quietly singing, the pleasure of work lifting her out of herself. Always she was content to face the future with an earnest desire to struggle and make amends.

To those who cannot understand this attitude in one not sheltered by the conventions, not housed in comfort and protected by the love and care of a husband, it must be explained again that we are not dealing with the ordinary temperament. The latter—the customary small nature, even when buoyed by communal advice and assistance—is apt to see in a situation of this kind only terror and danger. Nature is unkind to permit the minor type of woman to bear a child at all. The larger natures in their maturity welcome motherhood, see in it the immense possibilities of racial fulfillment, find joy and satisfaction in being the handmaiden of so immense a purpose or direction.

Jennie, a child in years, was potentially a woman physically and mentally, but not yet come into rounded conclusions as to life and her place in it. She had not come into a realization of her own ability and self-reliance for the simple reason that thus far compulsion to think and act for herself had not been literally present. Instances there were, minor in the main, which required her personal judgement, but, when so required, judgement was not all wanting. The great situation which had drawn her into this anomalous position was from one point of view a tribute to her individual capacity. It proved her courage, the largeness of her sympathy, her willingness to sacrifice for what she considered a worthy cause. That it resulted in an unexpected consequence which placed a larger and more complicated burden upon her was due to the fact that her sense of self-protection had not been squared with her emotions. At times the prospective coming of the child resulted only in a sense of fear and confusion, because she did not know but that the child might eventually reproach her; but at the same time there was always that saving sense of possible justice in life which would not permit her to be utterly crushed. To her way of thinking, people were not all intentionally cruel. Vague thoughts of sympathy and divine goodness permeated her soul. Life at worst or best was beautiful—had always been so. How could a thing, so lovely in its outward seeming, produce only brutality and terror?

These thoughts did not come to her all at once, but through the months during which she watched and waited. It was a wonderful thing to be a mother—even when the family was shunned by all save the component members and the family physician. She felt that she would love this child, would be a good mother to it if life permitted. That was the problem—what would life permit?

There were many things to be done—clothes to be made, secrecy to be observed, care in her personal conduct of hygiene and diet observed. One of her fears was that Gerhardt might unexpectedly return, but he did not. The old family doctor who had nursed the various members of the Gerhardt family through their multitudinous ailments—Dr. Ellwanger—was taken into consultation and gave sound and practical advice. Despite his Lutheran upbringing, the practise of medicine in a large and kindly way had led him to the conclusion that there are more things in heaven and earth than are dreamed of in our philosophies and our small neighborhood relationships. "So it is," he observed to Mrs. Gerhardt when she confided to him nervously what the trouble was. "Well, you mustn't worry. These things happen in more places than you think. If you knew as much about life as I do, and about your neighbors, you would not cry. There are few places I go that there is not something. Your girl will be all right. She is very healthy. She can go away somewhere else afterwards and live, and people will never know. Why should you worry about what your neighbors think? It is not so uncommon as you imagine."

Mrs. Gerhardt marveled. He was such a wise man. It gave her a little courage. As for Jennie, she listened to his advice with interest and without fear. She wanted things not so much for herself as for her child, and she was anxious to do whatever she was told. The doctor was curious to know who the father was and when informed lifted his eyes. "Indeed!" he commented. "That ought to be a bright baby. I think it will be a girl." He was judging by a peculiar conformation of the muscles of the back which at this period was to him an invariable sign. "You need not worry," he said. "You will have an easy time. You are a strong girl." He tried to cheer the helpless family in other ways for he was a kindly man.

So it proved. There came the final hour when, the structural work having been accomplished, the child was ushered into the world. It was Dr. Ellwanger who presided, assisted by the worried mother who, having borne six herself, knew exactly what to do. There was no difficulty, and at the first cry of the new-born infant, which came with its appearance, there awakened in Jennie a tremendous yearning toward it which covered all phases of her responsibility. This was *her* child! It was weak and feeble—a little girl, as Dr. Ellwanger had predicted, and it needed her care. She took it to her breast, when it had been bathed and swaddled, with a tremendous sense of satisfaction and joy. This was her child, her little girl. She wanted to live and be able to work for it, and she rejoiced, even in her weakness, that she was so strong. Dr. Ellwanger predicted a quick recovery, which was the case. He thought two weeks would be the outside limit of her need to stay in bed. As a matter of fact in ten days she was up and about, as vigorous and healthy as ever. She had been born with strength and with that nurturing quality which makes the ideal mother.

There were months thereafter in which the child was as carefully looked after as any baby possibly could be. With the money which Brander had left, there was no worry as to the means of supplying such necessities of clothing as the child needed, and being of supreme motherly instincts herself there was no worry as to its care. The children, outside of Bass, who had gone long before, were too young to understand fully, and had been deceived by the story that Jennie was married to Senator Brander, who had died. They did not know that a child was coming until it was there. Jennie's chief distress was for her mother and these younger members who, at so early an age, had been compelled to move in the atmosphere of a tragedy. The neighbors were feared by Mrs. Gerhardt, for they were ever watchful and really knew all. Jennie would never have braved this local atmosphere except for the advice of Bass, who, being in Cleveland and having secured a place there some time before Jennie's confinement, had written that he thought when she got through her trouble and was well enough, it would be advisable for the whole family to seek a new start in life in the latter place. Things were flourishing there. What difference if things were temporarily bad? They would soon be out of it. Once away they would never hear of these neighbors any more and Jennie could find something to do. So she stayed at home.

CHAPTER XI

It is marvelous with what rapidity facts take hold upon the young mind and how new phases of life will sometimes create the illusion of a new and different order of society.

Bass was no sooner in Cleveland than the marvel of that growing city was sufficient to completely restore his equanimity of soul, and stir up new illusions as to the possibility of joy and rehabilitation for himself and the family. "If only they could come here," he thought. "If only they could all get work and do right." Here was no evidence of any of their recent troubles, no acquaintances who could come before them and suggest by their mere presence the troubles of the past. All was business, all activity. The very turning of the corner seemed to rid one of old times and crimes. It was as if a new world existed in every block.

When he had first come he had briskly looked about him and had soon found a place in a cigar store, and it was after working a few weeks that he began to write home the cheering ideas he had in mind. Jennie ought to come as soon as she was able, and then, if she found something to do, the others might follow. There was plenty of work for girls of her age to do. She could live in the same house with him temporarily; or maybe they could take one of the fifteen-dollar-a-month cottages he saw. There were great general furnishing houses where one could buy everything needful for a small house on very easy monthly terms. His mother could come and keep house for them. They would all be in a clean, new atmosphere, unknown, untalked about. They could start life all over, as it were. They could be decent, honorable, prosperous.

Filled with this hope, the glamour which new scenes and new environment invariably throw over the unsophisticated mind, he wrote a final letter in which he suggested that Jennie should come at once. This was when the baby was six months old. There were theatres here, he said, and beautiful streets. Vessels from the lakes came into the heart of the city. It was a wonderful city and growing very fast. It was thus that the new life appealed to him.

The effect which all this had upon Mrs. Gerhardt, Jennie, and the rest of the family was phenomenal. Mrs. Gerhardt, long weighed upon by the misery which Jennie's error had entailed, was for taking measures for carrying out this plan at once. So buoyant was her natural temperament that she was completely carried away by the glory of Cleveland, and already saw fulfilled therein not only her own desires for a nice home, but for the prosperous advancement of her children. "Of course they could get work," she said. Bass was right. She had always wanted Gerhardt to go to some large city, but he would not. Now it was necessary, and they would go and become better off than they ever had been. The crowds, the tinkling street-car bells, the measure of joy suggested by Bass in his mention of the theatres and beautiful streets, nicely furnished houses and the like, all these reached out to her, and their accomplishment was as if it were a mere matter of moving into the city. Let them but once get started and all these things would be added unto them.

Jennie was not less sanguine. Mrs. Gerhardt said she would talk to their father and, if it were agreeable to him, they would go and one of these days he could come after them. She knew that he would not now object to any arrangement by which the children could be placed in some position where they could earn a living. Undoubtedly he would refuse to leave his present position, where he was earning ten dollars a week, to go on any wild-goose chase for work in Cleveland. If they were successful and he should happen to get out of work, he might come. That she knew.

These ideas of hers were exactly in accordance with the fact. Gerhardt had no sooner read the letter of George's writing, after his mother's dictation, than he answered that it was not advisable for him to leave his place, but if Bass saw a way for them, it might be a good thing to go. He the more readily acquiesced in this plan for the single reason that he was half distracted with the worry of supporting the family and of paying the debts already outstanding. Every week he laid by five dollars out of his salary, which he sent in the form of a postal order to his wife. Three dollars he paid over for board, without room, and fifty cents he kept for spending money, church dues, a little tobacco and occasionally a glass of beer. A dollar and fifty cents he put in a little iron bank he had, saving thus meagrely against a rainy day. His room was a corner in the topmost loft of the mill where he worked, he having been permitted to stay there after becoming acquainted with the proprietor, who respected his honesty as well as his value as a watchman. To this he would ascend, after sitting alone on the doorstep of the mill in this lonely, forsaken neighborhood until nine o'clock of an evening; and here, amid the odor of machinery wafted up from the floor below, by the light of a single tallow candle, he would conclude his solitary day, reading his German paper, folding his hands and thinking, kneeling by an open window in the shadow of the night to say his prayers, and silently stretching himself to rest. Long were the days, dreary the prospect. Still he lifted his hands most reverentially in utmost faith to God, praying that he might be forgiven his sins, permitted a few years of comfort, made whole once again and happy in his family life.

From this eyrie he answered by a letter, composed with difficulty, that they might go. It would be a good thing if George could get work.

The effect of this was merely to increase the excitement of the family. There was the greatest longing and impatience among the children, the minds of whom were enticed by what to them were the heavenly wonders of the world without. Mrs. Gerhardt shared their emotions in a suppressed way, and when a last letter in the correspondence, by which all preliminaries had been arranged, came from Bass saying when he would expect Jennie, Mrs. Gerhardt could scarcely contain herself.

"Now, you go," she said, "and then when you've gone, I'll begin to get things ready."

She knew that nothing was definitely settled, and she depended upon Jennie's obtaining employment, but she could not help feeling that the drag of events was sweeping them into the great city almost above their reasoning. The putting off of old difficulties and old troubles, as this seemed to be, was perfect delight to her. This leaving the old shell and setting forth into the world of larger possibilities gripped her as it grips every heart. She was as happy as if all of her troubles had passed—had never been, in fact. Anticipation, expectation, these cleared away the fogs of doubt and sorrow, and created for her once again a happy world.

When the hour came for Jennie's departure there was great excitement in the household.

"How long you going to be 'fore you send for us?" was Martha's inquiry, several times repeated.

"Tell Bass to hurry up," said the eager George.

"I want to go to Cleveland, I want to go to Cleveland," Veronica was caught singing to herself.

"Listen to her!" exclaimed George sarcastically.

"Aw, you hush up," was her displeased rejoinder.

When the final hour came, however, in which Jennie must depart, it required all of her strength to go through with the farewells. Though everything was being done in order to bring them all together again under better conditions, she could not help feeling depressed. Her little one, now six months old, was being left behind. The great world was to her one undiscovered bourne. It frightened her.

"You mustn't worry, Ma," she found courage enough to say. "I'll be all right. I'll write you just as soon as I get there. It won't be so very long."

When it came to bending over her baby for the last time, her courage went out like a blown lamp, and Mrs. Gerhardt's urgent words of strength were unheeded. Stooping over the cradle in which the little one was resting, she looked into its face with passionate, motherly yearning.

"Is it going to be a good little girl?" she cooed.

Then she caught the child up into her arms, and hugging it closely to her neck and bosom, buried her face against its little body. Mrs. Gerhardt observed her shake and tremble.

"Come now," she said, coaxingly, "you mustn't act that way. She will be all right with me. I'll take care of her. If you're going to act that way, you'd better not try to go at all."

She turned her own head away after she had said this, her voice being near to a tremulous vibration.

Jennie lifted her head, her blue eyes wet with tears, and handed the little one to her mother.

"I can't help it," she said, half crying, half smiling.

Quickly she kissed her mother another time, and the children, then hurried out.

As she went down the street with George, she looked back and bravely waved her hand. Mrs. Gerhardt responded, noticing how much more like a woman she looked. It had been necessary to invest some of her money in new clothes to wear on the train. She had selected a neat, ready-made suit of brown, which fitted her nicely. She wore the skirt of this with a white shirtwaist, and a sailor hat with a white veil wound around it in such a fashion that it could be easily drawn over her face. As she went farther and farther away, Mrs. Gerhardt followed her lovingly with her glance, and when she disappeared from view she said tenderly, through her own tears:

"I'm glad she looked so nice, anyhow."

CHAPTER XII

The details of this family transfer were not long in working themselves out. At the depot, where Bass met Jennie, he at once began that explanation of things which led to the final arrangement of matters as originally planned. She was to get work.

"That's the first thing," he said, while the jingle of sound and color, which the body of the great city presented to her, was confusing and almost numbing her senses. "Get something to do. It doesn't matter what, so long as you get something. If you don't get more than three or four dollars a week, it will pay the rent. Then, with what George can earn, when he comes, and what Pop sends, we can get along all right. It'll be better than being down in that hole," he concluded.

"Yes," said Jennie, vaguely, her mind so hypnotized by the new display of life about her that she could not bring it forcibly to bear upon the topic under discussion. "I know what you mean. I'll get something."

She was much older now, in understanding if not in years. The remarkable ordeal through which she had so recently passed had aroused in her a clearer conception of the responsibilities of life. Her mother was always in her mind, her mother and the children. The latter, instead of objects to lead forth and amuse, had now become objects of study to her. Would Martha and Veronica have a better opportunity to do for themselves than she had had? They should be dressed better. During all that difficult period which she had given up to rumination and the consideration of her fate, she had come to understand that they ought to have more companionship, more opportunity to broaden their lives and make something of themselves. More than once she had said to her mother:

"It will be too bad if they can't be kept in school until they're old enough to know what to do for themselves."

Now that she was here on the threshold of this larger world

in which they were to find something better, she hoped—she felt rather weak. Confronted by the necessity of effort which this ponderous world revealed, she was somewhat uncertain. To work, to look for work, tomorrow. How would her earnest effort end?

The city of Cleveland, like every other growing city at this time, was crowded with those who were seeking employment. New enterprises were constantly springing up, but those who were seeking to fulfill the duties they provided were invariably in excess of the demand. A stranger coming to the city might walk into a small position of almost any kind on the very day he arrived, and he might as readily wander in search of employment for weeks and even months, if he were not exceedingly diligent, and not find it. The necessity, in the more common forms of work, which alone Jennie could do, of inquiring here, there and everywhere, involved considerable walking and the danger of fatigue, with the consequent sinking of spirits which such fatigue is certain to produce. Bass suggested the shops and department stores as a first field in which to inquire. The factories and other modes of employment were to be second choice.

"Don't pass a place, though," he had cautioned her, "if you think there's any chance of getting anything to do. Go right in."

"What must I say?" asked Jennie, nervously.

"Tell them you want work. You don't care what you do to begin with."

Reassured by this hearty grasp of the situation, now that he was satisfactorily installed himself, she set out the very first day and was rewarded by some very chilly experiences. Wherever she went, no one seemed to want any help. She applied at the stores, the factories, the little single businesses that lined the outlying thoroughfares, but was always met by a rebuff. As a last resource she turned to housework, although she had hoped to avoid that, and, studying the want columns, selected four which because of location seemed more promising than the others. To these she decided to apply. One had already been filled when she arrived, but the lady who came to the door was so taken by her appearance that she invited her in and questioned her as to her ability.

"I wish you had come a little earlier," she said. "I like you better than I do the girl I have taken. Leave me your address, anyhow."

Jennie went away, smiling at her reception. She was not

quite so youthful looking as she had been before her recent trouble, but the thinner cheeks and slightly deeper eyes added to the pensiveness and delicacy of her countenance. She was a model of neatness. Her clothes, all newly cleaned and ironed before leaving home, gave her a fresh and inviting appearance. There was growth coming to her in the matter of height, but already in appearance and intelligence she looked to be a young woman of twenty. Best of all, she was of that naturally sunny disposition, which, in spite of duties and deprivations, made her appear cheerful. Any one in need of a servant girl or house companion would have been delighted to have had her.

The second place she applied was a large residence in Euclid Avenue, which, once she saw it, seemed far too imposing for anything she might have to offer in the way of services, but having come so far she decided to apply. The servant who met her at the door directed her to wait a few moments and finally ushered her into the boudoir of the mistress of the house on the second floor. The latter, a Mrs. Bracebridge, a rather chill but prepossessing brunette of the conventionally fashionable type, had a keen eye for feminine values and was not at all unfavorably impressed by this latest applicant. In fact she was rather taken by her, in a cold way, and reached the conclusion that she might like to have her about in the general capacity of maid, if she knew anything. She talked with her a little while and finally decided to try her.

"I will give you four dollars a week, and you can sleep here if you wish."

Jennie protested that she was living with her brother and would soon have her family with her.

"Oh, very well," replied her mistress. "Do as you like about that. Only I expect you to be here promptly."

She wished her to remain for the day and begin her duties at once, and Jennie agreed. Mrs. Bracebridge provided her a dainty cap and apron, and then spent some little time in instructing her in her duties. She was, principally, to wait on her mistress, to brush her hair, help her dress, answer the bell if need be, wait on the table if need be (although there was a servant for that), and do any other errand which her mistress indicated. Mrs. Bracebridge seemed a little hard and formal to her prospective servant, but for all that Jennie admired the dash and go, and the obvious executive capacity of her employer.

At eight o'clock that evening Jennie was dismissed for the day and slipped out wondering at the beauty and the order of the things she had seen. The force and capacity of her employer's husband (a cool, shrewd, handsome man of fifty, who had arrived at seven) almost startled her. She wondered if she could be of any use in such a household and marveled that she had got along as well as she had. Her mistress had set her to cleaning her jewelry and boudoir ornaments, as an opening task, and though she had worked steadily and diligently, she had not finished by the time she left. She hurried away to her brother's apartment, delighted to be able to report that she had something. Now her mother could come to Cleveland. Now she could have her baby with her. Now they could really begin that new life which was to be so much better and finer and sweeter than anything they had ever had before.

The elation which followed this good fortune, slight as it was, was of some duration. Jennie wrote her mother, at Bass's suggestion, that she might come soon now, and a week or so later they found a house. Mrs. Gerhardt looked after the packing and shipping of the furniture and in due time announced the day of her departure from Columbus. No one was present to see her off. George and the other children had been employed to the fullest capacity of their strength in packing or helping mind the baby, and now, when the single load of furniture had been sent to the depot and the expressman had come and taken away the one trunk, Mrs. Gerhardt stood in the little old vacant house and cried. Grief over what she had suffered here, and what was now being apparently left behind, could not have been the logical source of her tears; but feeling is more subtle than intellect. Something about it—the few joys, perhaps, the mellowed aspect of certain sorrows, time, age, the fact that life and its relationships were thus slipping away one by one—had something to do with it.

"Don't cry, Ma," said George, pulling at her sleeve.

"I can't help it," she said.

Then gradually she recovered herself, smiled a little, looked after the thin ribbons that fastened on her small bonnet, took the little one from Martha and, urging her four children to keep in order, set out to meet the train.

It is always fascinating to think how the feelings of our lives change and interchange. At the depot, a new zest for living seized upon her, a new hope grew. In a few minutes the train would be here. In a few hours she would be in Cleveland with Jennie and Bass. Jennie had secured work, and Bass had a good place. George could possibly get something, or maybe he would not need to leave school so early. She would see. The other children could probably be provided with suitable clothing and sent to school. What a heaven this earth would be if only from now on they could get along nicely.

Mrs. Gerhardt had always had a keen desire for a nice home. Solid furniture, upholstered and trimmed, a thick, soft carpet of some warm, pleasing color, plenty of chairs, settees, pictures, a lounge and a piano had often come definitely into her mind, and as often they had been put sharply away by the rigor of her surroundings. Still she did not despair. Some day, maybe, before she died, these things would be added to her, and she would be happy. Her feelings at this time were colored by the possibility that this old hope would now be fulfilled.

When she arrived at Cleveland, much of her feeling was encouraged by the sight of Jennie's cheerful face. Bass assured her that they would get along all right. He took them out to the house, and George was shown the way to go back to the depot and have the freight looked after. Mrs. Gerhardt had still fifty dollars left out of the money which Senator Brander had sent to Jennie, and with this a way of getting a little extra furniture on the installment plan was provided. Bass had already paid the first month's rent, and Jennie had spent her evenings for the last few days washing the windows and floors of this new house and getting it in a state of perfect cleanliness. Now, when the first night fell, they had two new mattresses and comfortables spread upon a clean floor; a new lamp purchased from one of the nearby stores; a single box, borrowed by Jennie from a grocery store for cleaning purposes, upon which Mrs. Gerhardt could sit; and some sausages and bread to stay them until morning. They talked and planned their way for the future until nine o'clock came, when all but Jennie and her mother retired. These two talked on, the burden of responsibilities resting on the daughter. Mrs. Gerhardt had come to feel in a way dependent upon her.

How the furniture was all finally arranged is a detail needless to go into here. In the course of a week the entire cottage was in order, with a half-dozen pieces of new furniture, a new carpet, and some necessary utensils to improve the woeful lack the kitchen would have felt without them. The most disturbing thing was the need of a new cooking stove, the cost of which added greatly to the bill. Once settled, Bass and Jennie were got off regularly to their work by Mrs. Gerhardt. George was sent out by Bass to look for something to do. Both Jennie and her mother felt the injustice of this keenly, but knew no way of remedying it.

"We will let him go to school next year, if we can," said Jennie.

Her heart was really torn by what was now looked upon by her as the crying essential of these children's lives, an education. George was her favorite. The other children were sent off to the public school.

Auspiciously as all things seemed to have begun, the closeness with which their expenses were matching their income was a suspended menace to the welfare and peace of this family arrangement. Bass, originally very generous in his propositions, soon declared the fact that he felt four dollars a week for his room and board to be a sufficient contribution from himself. Jennie gave everything she earned and protested that she did not stand in need of anything, so long as the baby was properly taken care of. George secured a place as an overgrown cash-boy, and brought in two dollars and fifty cents a week, all of which he at first gladly contributed. Later on he was allowed fifty cents for himself as being meet and just. Gerhardt, from his lonely laboring post, contributed five dollars by mail, always arguing that a little money ought to be saved in order that his honest debts back in Columbus might be shortly paid. Out of this total income of fifteen dollars a week, all of these eight individuals had to be fed and clothed, the rent paid, coal purchased, and the regular monthly installment of three dollars paid on the outstanding furniture bill of fifty dollars.

How it was done, those comfortable individuals, who frequently discuss the social aspects of poverty, might well trouble to inform themselves. Rent, coal and light alone consumed the goodly sum of twenty dollars a month. Food, another unfortunately necessary item, used up twenty-five more. Clothes, installments, dues, occasional items of medicine and the like were met out of the remaining twelve dollars,—how, the ardent imagination of the comfortable reader can guess. It was done, however, and for a time the hopeful members considered that they were doing fairly well.

During this time the little family presented a picture of honorable and patient toil, which was interesting to contemplate. Every day Mrs. Gerhardt, who worked like a servant and received absolutely no compensation either in clothes, amusements or anything else, arose in the morning while the others slept, and built the fire. Next she went noiselessly about getting the breakfast. Fear of waking either Jennie, Bass or George before the necessary moment caused her considerable anxiety. Often as she moved about in her thin, worn slippers, cushioned with pieces of newspaper to make them fit, she looked in on their sleeping faces and with that divine sympathy which is born in heaven wished that they did not need to rise so early or yet work so hard. Sometimes she would pause before touching her beloved Jennie, look at her white face so calm in sleep, and wish that circumstances had been more kindly to her and that life would serve her well. Then she would lay her hand gently upon her and whisper, "Jennie, Jennie," until the weary sleeper would wake.

When they arose, breakfast was always ready. When they returned at night, supper was waiting. Evenings she would sit and entertain them, glad that she could work for them at home instead of going out by the day. Each of the children received a share of her attention. The little baby was closely looked after by her. She protested that she needed neither clothes nor shoes so long as one of the children would run errands for her.

What this beneficent presence meant to Jennie, only those possessed of a heart as great as hers may hope to understand. She of all the children fully understood her mother. She alone of all of them grieved for her, and strove with the fullness of a perfect affection to ease her burden. She of all women had the perfect mother instinct inborn.

"Ma, you let me do this."

"Now, Ma, I'll 'tend to that."

"You go sit down, Ma."

These were the every-day expressions of the enduring affection that existed between them. Always there was perfect understanding between Jennie and her mother, and, as the days passed, this naturally widened and deepened. Jennie could not bear to think of her mother as being always confined to the house. Daily she thought, as she worked, of that other spot in Cleveland where her mother was watching and waiting. How she longed to give her those comforts which she had always craved!

The days spent in the employ of the Bracebridge household were of a broadening character. Mrs. Bracebridge, worldly wise and of good insight, inquired into Jennie's family affairs and, while learning nothing of the true history of her servant or of her recent difficulties, learned enough to know that they were in exceedingly straitened circumstances. She was not among those who aid people with material substance, but she did have an occasional worth while suggestion to offer—more by way of example than by direct address. For this house was a school to Jennie, not only in the matter of dress and manners, but in a theory of existence. Mrs. Bracebridge, for a woman, and her husband, for a man, were the last word in the matter of self-sufficiency, definiteness of point of view, taste in the matter of appointments, care in the matter of dress, good form in the matter of reception, entertainment and what not. There were lessons here in the matter of modes, materials, seasonableness of things to wear, shops, the care of the hands, the preparation of a complexion, the wearing of the hair and so on. Now and then, apropos of nothing save her own mood, Mrs. Bracebridge would indicate her philosophy of life in a sentence.

"Life is a battle, my dear; if you gain anything you will have to fight for it."

"In my judgement it is silly not to take advantage of any aid which will help you to be what you want to be." (This while applying a faint suggestion of rouge.)

"Most people are born silly; they are exactly what they are capable of being."

"I despise lack of taste: it is the worst crime."

Most of these things were not said to Jennie. She overheard them, but to her quiet and reflective mind they had their import. Like seeds fallen upon good ground they took root and grew. She began to see in a vague way how the world wagged. She began to get a faint perception of hierarchies and powers. They were not for her perhaps, she thought, but they were in the world, and if fortune were kind one might better one's state. She worked on—wondering, however, for she did not see how anything was to be made really better for her. Who would have her, knowing her history? How would she ever explain the presence of her child?

Her child, her child, the one transcendent gripping theme of joy and fear. If she could only do something for it eventually.

CHAPTER XIII

For the first winter things went smoothly enough. By the closest economy the children were clothed and kept in school, the rent paid and the installments met. Once it looked as though there might be some difficulty about the continuance of the home life, and that was when Gerhardt wrote that he would be home for Christmas. The mill was to close down for a short period at that time. He was naturally anxious to see what the new life of his family at Cleveland was like.

Mrs. Gerhardt and all the rest would have welcomed his return with unalloyed pleasure had it not been for the fear they entertained of his creating a scene. Jennie talked it over with her mother, and Mrs. Gerhardt in turn spoke of it to Bass, whose advice was to brave it out.

"Don't worry," he said, "he won't do anything about it. I'll talk to him if he says anything."

The scene anticipated did not turn out as badly as expected, however. Gerhardt came home during the afternoon while Bass, Jennie and George were at work. Two of the younger children went to the train to meet him. When he entered, Mrs. Gerhardt greeted him affectionately, but she trembled for the discovery which was sure to come. Her suspense was not for long. Gerhardt opened the front bedroom door only a few minutes after he arrived. On the white counterpane of the bed was a pretty child, sleeping. He could not but know on the instant whose it was, but he pretended not to, and came out.

"Whose child is that?" he questioned.

"It's Jennie's," said Mrs. Gerhardt, weakly.

"When did that come here?"

"Not so very long ago," answered the mother, nervously.

"I guess she is here, too," he declared, a fact which he had already anticipated.

"She's working in a family," returned his wife in a pleading tone. "She's doing so well now. She had no place to go. Let her alone."

Gerhardt had received a light since he had been away. Certain inexplicable thoughts and feelings had come to him in his religious meditations. In his prayer he had admitted to the All-seeing that he might have done differently by his daughter. Yet he could not make up his mind how to treat her for the future. She had committed a great sin; it was impossible to get away from that.

When Jennie came home that night, a meeting was unavoidable. Gerhardt saw her coming and pretended to be deeply engaged in a newspaper. Mrs. Gerhardt, who had ventured to beg him not to ignore Jennie entirely when she came in, trembled for fear he would say or do something which would hurt her feelings.

"She is coming now," she said, crossing to the door of the front room where he was sitting, but he didn't look up. "Speak to her, anyhow," was her last appeal before the door opened, but he made no reply.

When Jennie came in her mother whispered, "He is in the front room."

Jennie paled, put her thumb to her lip and stood there, not knowing how to meet the situation.

"He knows you are here," said Mrs. Gerhardt tenderly, anxious to soften, as much as possible, the ordeal through which her daughter must pass. "I told him you were here."

"Has he seen—?"

Jennie paused as she recognized from her mother's face and nod that Gerhardt knew of the child's existence.

"Well, I guess I'd better go in," she ventured, weakly, but stood there, unable for the moment to summon up courage to move.

"Go ahead," said Mrs. Gerhardt; "it's all right. He won't say anything."

Jennie finally went to the door, and, seeing her father, his brow wrinkled as if in serious, unkindly thought, she hesitated, but made her way forward.

"Papa," she said, unable to formulate a thought.

Gerhardt looked up, his grayish brown eyes a study under their heavy sandy lashes. At the sight of his daughter, he weak-

ened internally, but with the self-adjusted armor of resolve about
him, he showed no sign of pleasure at seeing her. All the forces of
his conventional understanding of morality and his naturally
sympathetic and fatherly disposition were battling within him,
but, as in so many cases where the average mind is concerned,
convention was temporarily the victor.

"Yes," he said.

Jennie wanted to approach him and beg his forgiveness, and
then be allowed to put her arms around his neck and kiss him, as
she had been accustomed to do on his return after absences in the
past. But his demeanor made it only too plain that it was not to
be. Realizing that anything she could say would avail little, she
came forward and ventured:

"Won't you forgive me, Papa?"

"I do," he returned grimly.

She hesitated a moment and then stepped forward, for what
purpose he well understood.

"There," he said, pushing her gently away, as her lips barely
touched his grizzled cheek.

It was a frigid meeting.

When Jennie went out into the kitchen, after this very
trying ordeal, she lifted her eyes to her waiting mother and tried
to make it seem as if all had been well, but her tender emotional
disposition got the better of her.

"Did he make up to you?" her mother was about to ask, but
the words were only half out of her mouth before her daughter
sank down into one of the chairs close to the kitchen table and,
laying her head on her arms, burst forth into a series of convul-
sive, inaudible sobs.

"Now, now," said Mrs. Gerhardt. "There now, don't cry.
What did he say?"

It was some time before Jennie recovered herself sufficiently
to answer, but the situation was not one of such seeming difficulty
to her mother.

"I wouldn't feel bad," she said. "He'll get over it. It's his
way."

The return of Gerhardt brought forward the child question
in all its bearings. Although opposed to the presence of it and
irritated by the thought of having it in the house, he felt as if he
ought not to say anything. Jennie was working. Still he could not

help considering it from a grand-parental standpoint, particularly since the child was a human being possessed of a soul, and subject to baptism and union with the church. He thought it over and wondered if the baby had been baptized. Then he inquired.

"No, not yet," said his wife, who had not forgotten this duty, but had been uncertain, as had Jennie, whether the little one would be welcome in the faith. Things had been so bad in Columbus that they could not bring themselves to a public function of the sort there, and here only a few months had elapsed.

"No, of course not," said Gerhardt, whose faith in his wife's religious devotion was not any too great. "Such carelessness! Such irreligion! That is a fine thing."

He thought it over a few moments and then, as the irreligion and the danger of eternal damnation involved came home to him, he felt that this evil should be forcibly corrected at once.

"It should be baptized," he said. "Why don't she take it and have it baptized?"

Mrs. Gerhardt then reminded him that someone would have to stand godfather to the child, and there was no way to have the ceremony performed without expressing the fact that it was without a legitimate father.

Gerhardt listened to this, and it quieted him for a few moments, but his religion was something which he could not see put in the background by any difficulty. How would the Lord look upon any such quibbling as this! Up to this time, he had never looked upon the child directly and interestedly. Mrs. Gerhardt had attended to it inconspicuously, and, when this was impossible, he made it convenient for himself to be or look elsewhere. When the baby cried, a thing that seldom happened, he was apt to break out into some form of irritating comment or complaint, usually involving the fact that his wife was unnecessarily made to suffer, and yet that she deserved just what she was getting. When the child was silent or gurgling, he pretended to ignore her.

Now, when it came to the question of this religious ceremony, he had to take an interest, however stern, in the necessary details. The child had to have a name. There had to be an explanation offered for the absence of its parents. The child must be taken forthwith to the church—with Jennie, himself and his wife accompanying it as sponsors, or, if he did not want to condescend to his daughter in that manner, he must see that the baby was baptized when she was not present. He brooded over this difficulty and finally decided that the child must be taken on one of these weekdays between Christmas and New Year's, when Jennie would be at her work. This he broached to his wife and, receiving her approval, made his next announcement. "It has no name," he said.

Jennie and her mother had talked over this very matter, and Jennie had expressed a preference for Vesta. Now her mother made bold to suggest it as her own choice.

"How would Vesta do?"

Gerhardt heard this with indifference. He really had not asked so much because he wanted advice, but rather to bring up the question and furnish him his opportunity. He had a name in store, left over from the halcyon period of his youth, and never opportunely available in the case of his own children,—Wilhelmina. He had thought of it a number of times secretly, never associating it with unbending or with weakening in the direction of affection—never! He merely liked the name, and the child ought to be grateful to get it. With a far-off, gingery air he brought forward this first offering upon the altar of natural affection, for an offering it was, after all.

"That is nice," he said, forgetting his indifference. "But how would Wilhelmina do?"

Mrs. Gerhardt did not dare cross him when he was thus unconsciously weakening. Her woman's tact came to the rescue.

"We might give her both names," she suggested.

"It makes no difference to me," he replied, drawing back into the shell of opposition from which he had been inadvertently drawn. "Just so she is baptized."

Jennie heard of this with pleasure, for she was anxious that the child should have every advantage, religious or otherwise, that it was possible to obtain. She took great pains to starch and iron the clothes it was to wear on the appointed day.

Gerhardt sought out the minister of the nearest Lutheran church, a round-headed, thick-set theologian of the most formal type, to whom he stated his errand.

"Your grandchild?" inquired the minister.

"Yes," said Gerhardt, "her father is not here."

"So," replied the minister, looking at him curiously.

Gerhardt was not to be disturbed in his purpose. He explained that he and his wife would bring her. The minister, realizing the probable difficulty, did not question him further.

"The church cannot refuse to baptize her so long as you, as grandparent, are willing to stand sponsor for her," he said.

Gerhardt came away, hurt by the disgrace which he felt his position to involve, but satisfied in the fact that he had done his duty. Now he would take the child and have it baptized, and when that was over his present responsibility was done with.

When it came to the hour of the baptism, however, he found that another influence was working to guide him into greater interest and responsibility. The stern religion with which he was enraptured, its insistence upon a higher law, was there, and he heard again the precepts which had helped to bind him to his own children.

"Is it your intention to educate this child in the knowledge and love of the gospel?" asked the black-gowned minister, as he stood before them in the silent little church, whither they had brought the infant, reading from the form provided for such occasions.

Gerhardt answered "Yes," and Mrs. Gerhardt added her affirmative.

"Do you engage to use all necessary care and diligence, by prayerful instruction, admonition, example and discipline, that this child may renounce and avoid everything that is evil and that she may keep God's will and commandments as declared in His sacred word?"

A thought flashed through Gerhardt's mind, as the words were uttered, of how he had fared with his own children. They, too, had been thus sponsored. They, too, had heard his solemn pledge to care for their spiritual welfare. He was silent.

"We do," prompted the minister.

"We do," repeated Gerhardt and his wife weakly.

"Do you now dedicate this child by the rite of baptism unto the Lord, who brought it?"

"We do."

"And, finally, if you can conscientiously declare before God that the faith to which you have assented is your faith, and that the solemn promises you have made are the serious resolutions of your heart, please to announce the same in the presence of God, by saying, 'Yes.'"

"Yes," they replied.

"I baptize thee, Wilhelmina Vesta," concluded the minister, stretching out his hand over her, "in the name of the Father and of the Son and of the Holy Ghost. Let us pray."

Gerhardt bent his gray head and followed with humble diligence the beautiful invocation which followed:

"Almighty and everlasting God! We adore Thee as the great Parent of the children of men, as the Father of our spirits and the Former of our bodies. We praise Thee for giving existence to this infant and for preserving her until this day. We bless Thee that she is called to virtue and glory, that she has now been dedicated to Thee, and brought within the pale of the Christian church. We thank Thee, that by the Gospel of the Son, she is furnished with everything necessary to her spiritual happiness; that it supplies light for her mind, and comfort for her heart, encouragement and power to discharge her duty, and the precious hope of mercy and immortality to sustain and make her faithful. And we beseech Thee, O most merciful God, that this child may be enlightened and sanctified from her early years, by the Holy Spirit, and be everlastingly saved by Thy mercy. Direct and bless Thy servants, who are entrusted with the care of her, in the momentous work of her education. Inspire them with just conception of the absolute necessity of religious instruction and principles. Forbid that they should ever forget that this offspring belongs to Thee; and that if through their criminal neglect or bad example Thy reasonable creature be lost, Thou wilt require it at their hands. Give them a deep sense of the dignity of her nature, of the worth of her soul, of the dangers to which she will be exposed; of the honor and felicity to which she is capable of ascending with Thy blessing, and of the ruin in this world and the misery in the world to come which spring from wicked passion and conduct. Give them grace to check the first risings of forbidden inclinations in her breast, to be her defence against the temptations incident to childhood and youth, and, as she grows up, to enlarge her understanding, and to lead her to an acquaintance with Thee and with Jesus Christ, whom Thou hast sent. Give them grace to cultivate in her heart a supreme reverence and love for Thee, a grateful attachment to the gospel of Thy Son, his Saviour, a due regard for all its ordinances and institutions, a temper of kindness and goodwill to all mankind, and an invincible love of sincerity and truth. Help them to watch continually over her with tender solicitude, to be studious that by their conversation and deportment her heart may not be corrupted, and at all times to set before her such an example that she may safely tread in their footsteps. If it please Thee to prolong her days on earth, grant that she may prove an honor and a comfort to her parents and friends, be useful in the world, and find in Thy Providence an unfailing defence and support. Whether she live, let her live to Thee; or whether she die, let her die to Thee. And, at the great day of account, may she and her parents meet each other with rapture and rejoice together in Thy redeeming love, through Jesus Christ, forever and ever, Amen."

As this solemn admonition was read, not with the haste of a mere form, but the slowness and solemnity of manner which characterize those who are sincere in any belief, a feeling of obligation descended upon the grandfather of this little outcast; a feeling that he was bound to give the tiny creature lying on his wife's arm the care and attention which God in His sacrament had commanded. He bowed his head in utmost reverence, and when the service was concluded and they left the silent church, he was without words to express his feelings. Religion was a consuming thing with him. God was a person, a dominant reality. In life, as he looked about him, all the forms and laws by which his fellow creatures had their existence and their activity seemed to him the direct expression of Him. Religion was not a thing of words or interesting ideas to be listened to on Sunday, but a strong, vital expression of the Divine Will, handed down from a time when men were in personal contact with God. Its fulfillment was a matter of salvation and joy with him, the one consolation of a creature sent to wander in a vale whose explanation was not here but in heaven. Slowly Gerhardt walked on, and, as he brooded on the words and the duties which the sacrament involved, the shade of lingering disgust that had possessed him when he had taken the child to church disappeared and a feeling of natural affection took its place. However much the daughter had sinned, the infant was not to blame. It was a helpless, puling, tender thing, demanding his sympathy and his love. Gerhardt felt his heart go out to the little child, and yet he could not yield his position all in a moment.

"That is a nice man," he said of the minister to his wife as they walked along, rapidly softening in his conception of his duty.

"Yes, he was," said Mrs. Gerhardt, who was under the impression that he was held in silence by some grim rumination.

"It's a good-sized little church," he continued.

"Yes."

Gerhardt looked around him, at the street, the houses, the show of brisk life on this sunshiny, winter's day, and then finally at the child that his wife was carrying.

"She must be heavy," he said, in his characteristic German. "Let me take her."

Mrs. Gerhardt, who was rather weary, did not refuse.

"There!" he said as he looked at her and then fixed her comfortably upon his shoulder. "Let us hope she proves worthy of all that has been done today."

Mrs. Gerhardt listened, and the meaning in his voice interpreted itself plainly enough. The presence of the child in the house might be the cause of recurring spells of depression and unkind words, but there would be another and greater influence restraining him. There would always be her soul to consider. He would never again be utterly unconscious of her soul.

CHAPTER XIV

The difficulty after this was not so much concerning Gerhardt's attitude toward Jennie, for time seemed inclined to mend this gradually, but with the financial problem. It is true he did not recognize her presence, but this was a part of the unsubdued element of a storm that was on the wane. All during his stay he was shy in her presence and endeavored to make it appear as if he were unconscious of her being. When the time came for parting he even went away without bidding her goodbye, telling his wife she might do that for him, but, after going, he was not unconscious of having done wrong. "I might have bade her goodbye," he thought to himself, then became lost in the multitude of reasons for and against his not having done so.

For the time being the affairs of the Gerhardt family drifted. Jennie continued her work with Mrs. Bracebridge. Sebastian fixed himself firmly in his clerkship in the cigar store. George was promoted to the noble sum of three dollars a week and then three-fifty. It was a narrow, humdrum life the family led, however, for they had nothing to "do with." Coal, groceries, the wherewithal to buy shoes and clothing were the uppermost topics—if not in words then in thought. It gave a peculiar atmosphere of stress with no obvious signs of relief.

The thing which worried Jennie most, and there were many things which weighed heavy on a sensitive soul such as hers, was the outcome of her own life—not so much for herself but for her baby and the family. Working as she was, getting daily wiser as to the world's arrangement, she could not see really where she fitted in. "Who would have me?" she asked herself over and over. How was she to dispose of Vesta in any possible love affair? She did not immediately anticipate anything of the kind, but she was young, good-looking, and men were inclined to flirt with her, or rather attempt it. There had been occasions in the Bracebridge home when guests had secretly approached her with a view to luring her into some unlicensed relationship. Of course she rebuffed them firmly, but as gently as possible. This did not end the difficulty for her, however. Men were naturally attracted to her.

"My dear, you're a very pretty girl," said one old rake of fifty when she knocked at his door one morning to give him a message from his hostess.

"I beg your pardon," she said confusedly, and colored.

"Indeed you're quite sweet. And you needn't beg my pardon. I'd like to talk to you some time."

He attempted to chuck her under the chin, but Jennie hurried away. She would have reported the matter to her mistress, but a nervous shame deterred her. "Why will men always be doing this?" she thought.

There was another man, a very much younger one, who annoyed her greatly but whom she did not like or even consider sufficiently to fear. He was the son of a neighbor, a scion of wealth who bustled in and out much as he pleased, bringing this and that neighborly proposition. Mrs. Bracebridge seemed to like him very well. He was constantly looking for opportunities to speak to Jennie, to waylay her in the halls or on the stairs. His opportunities were not numerous, but, such as they were, he made the most of them.

"Why won't you be nice to me?" he one day asked her pleadingly.

"I don't like you," she said firmly. "Please don't. You mustn't speak to me this way. I'll tell Mrs. Bracebridge."

He straightened up nervously. "Oh, you wouldn't do that."

"You mustn't annoy me," she said and went her way, nervous and quite like a doe at bay.

He did not trouble her any more. Men seemed to think she would do these things. Was she innately bad and wrong herself?

It is a curious characteristic of the non-defensive disposition that it is like a honey-pot to flies. Nothing is brought to it, and much is taken away. Around a soft, yielding disposition, where beauty is and sweetness, men swarm. They sense this generosity, this non-protective attitude from afar. A girl like Jennie is like a comfortable fire to the average masculine mind; it is like warmth after the freezing attitude of harder dispositions. They gravitate to it, seek its sympathy. Yearn to possess it. Hence she was annoyed.

She got along well enough for some time, however, until there arrived from Cincinnati one day a certain Lester Kane, the son of a wholesale carriage builder of great trade distinction in that city and elsewhere throughout the country, who was wont to visit this house frequently in a social way. He was a friend of Mrs. Bracebridge more than of her husband, for the former had been raised in Cincinnati and as a girl had visited at his father's house. She knew his mother, his brother and his sisters and to all intents and purposes socially had always been considered one of the family.

"Lester's coming tomorrow, Henry," Jennie heard Mrs. Bracebridge tell her husband. "I had a wire from him this noon. He's such a scamp. I'm going to give him the big east front room upstairs. Do be sociable and give him some attention. His father was so good to me."

"I know it," said her husband calmly. "I like Lester. He's the biggest one in that family. But he's too indifferent. He doesn't care enough."

"I know; but he's so nice. I do think he's one of the nicest men I ever knew."

"I'll be decent to him. Don't I always do pretty well by your people?"

"Yes, pretty well."

"Oh, I don't know about that," he replied dryly.

When this notable person arrived Jennie was prepared to see someone of real ability and force, and she was not disappointed.

There came into the reception hall to greet her mistress a man of perhaps thirty-six years of age, above the medium in height, clear-eyed, firm-jawed, athletic, direct and vigorous. He had a deep, resonant voice that carried clearly everywhere and bespoke a presence, whether you saw him or not. He was simple and abrupt in his speech.

"Oh, there you are," he began. "I'm glad to see you again. How's Mr. Bracebridge? How's Fannie?"

He asked his questions forcefully, whole-heartedly, and his hostess answered as quickly and warmly as she could. "I'm glad to see you, Lester," she said. "George will take your things upstairs. Come up into my room. It's more comfy. How are Grandpa and Louise?"

He followed her up the stairs, and somehow Jennie, who had been standing at the head of the stairs listening, warmed to his presence. It seemed, why she could hardly say, that a personage of real worth had arrived. The house was cheerier. The attitude of her mistress was much more complaisant. Everybody seemed to feel that something must be done for this man.

Jennie herself bustled about her affairs—why, she could not have said. And his name ran in her mind. Lester Kane. And he was from Cincinnati. She looked at him now and then on the sly, and felt, for the first time in her life, an interest in a man on his own account. He was so big, so handsome, so forceful. She wondered what his business was, what he did. At the same time she felt a little dread of him. Once she caught him looking at her with a steady, incisive stare. She quailed inwardly and took the first opportunity to get out of his presence. Another time he tried to address a few remarks to her, but she pretended duty some-where else. He watched her at other times, however, particularly when she was not looking, and she could feel his gaze. She knew that his eyes were on her when her back was turned, and it made her nervous. She tried to think there was nothing to it, but every now and then in going about her work she came upon him, that steady gaze of his fascinating her. She felt as though she wanted to run away, although there was no very definite reason.

As a matter of fact, this man, who was so superior to her in his social position, so far removed from what might have been called her social opportunities, was greatly smitten with her. Like the others he was drawn by the peculiar softness of her disposition and her mood. There was that about her which spoke to him of the luxury of love. He felt as if somehow there were some way in which she could be quickly reached—why, he could not have said. She did not bear any outward marks of her previous experience. There were no evidences of coquetry about her, but still he "felt that he might." He was inclined to act on his first visit, but, business calling, he left after four days and was gone for three weeks. Jennie thought possibly he was gone for good and felt a sense of relief as well as regret. Then, suddenly, he was back again. He came apparently unexpectedly and explained to Mrs. Bracebridge that he had a number of things to do which he had not previously attended to. He looked at Jennie sharply, and she felt as if somehow his presence might concern her a little too.

On this second visit she had various opportunities of seeing him—at breakfast where she sometimes served, at dinner when she could see the guests at the table from the parlor or sitting-room, when he came to Mrs. Bracebridge's boudoir to talk things over. They were very friendly.

"Why don't you settle down, Lester, and get married?" Jennie heard her say to him the second day he was there. "You know it's time."

"I know," he replied, "but I'm in no mood for that. I want to browse around a little while yet."

"Yes, I know about your browsing. You ought to be ashamed of yourself. Your father is really worried."

He chuckled amusedly. "Father doesn't worry much about me. He has got all he can tend to to look after the business."

Jennie looked at him curiously. There was a note of real appeal in him for her. She scarcely understood what she was thinking, but this man drew her. If she had realized in what way, she would have fled his presence then and there.

Now he was more insistent in his observation of her—addressed an occasional remark to her, engaged her in brief, magnetic conversations. She could not help answering him—he was pleasing to her. Once he came across her in the hall on the second floor, searching in a locker for some linen. They were all alone, Mrs. Bracebridge having gone to do some morning shopping and the other servants being below stairs. On this occasion he made short work of the business that concerned him most. He approached her in a commanding, unhesitating and thoroughly determined way and said:

"I want to talk to you. Where do you live?"

"I— I—" she started to stammer, and blanched perceptibly. "I live out on Lorrie Street."

"What number?" he questioned, as though she were compelled to tell him.

She quailed and shook inwardly. "Thirteen fourteen," she replied mechanically.

He looked into her big, soft eyes with his dark, vigorous brown ones. There was a flash that was hypnotic, significant, insistent.

"You belong to me," he said. "I've been looking for you. When can I see you?"

"Oh, you mustn't," she said, her fingers going nervously to her lips. "I can't see you— I—"

"Oh, I mustn't, mustn't I? Look here"—he took her arm and drew her slightly closer—"you and I might as well understand each other right now. I like you. Do you like me? Say?"

She looked at him, her eyes wide, filled with wonder, with fear, with a growing terror.

"I don't know," she gasped, her lips dry.

"Do you?" He fixed her grimly, firmly with his eyes.

"I don't know."

"Look at me," he said.

"Yes," she replied.

He pulled her to him quickly. "I'll talk to you later," he said, and put his lips forcefully to hers.

She was horrified, stunned, like a bird in the grasp of a cat, but somehow through it all something terrific, inviting, urging, was speaking to her. He released her from his grasp. "We won't do any more of this here, but you belong to me."

He squeezed her arm, realizing the panic he was leaving her in, and turned and walked nonchalantly down the hall.

CHAPTER XV

The shock of this sudden encounter was so great to Jennie that she was hours in recovering herself. She did not understand clearly at first just what had happened. This man had appeared attractive to her truly, but she did not know that it warranted any more than a passing glance from her, certainly nothing from him. And yet, suddenly, out of clear sky, as it were, this astonishing thing had happened. She had yielded herself to another man. Why? Why? she asked herself, and yet within her own consciousness there was an answer. Though she could not explain, she belonged to him temperamentally and he belonged to her.

There is a fate in love and a fate in fight. This strong, intellectual bear of a man, son of a wealthy manufacturer, stationed as far as material conditions were concerned in a world immensely superior to that in which Jennie moved, was nevertheless instinctively, magnetically and chemically drawn to her. She was his natural affinity, though he did not know it,—the one woman who answered somehow the biggest need of his nature—a quiet, sympathetic, non-resisting attitude of mind. If Lester Kane had ever examined his own mental attitude toward women up to this time, he would have known that this was so. He had known all sorts of women, rich and poor, the highly bred maidens of his own class, the daughters of the proletariat, but he had never yet found one who to him seemed to combine the traits of an ideal woman—sympathy, kindliness of judgement, youth and beauty. He found many who had beauty—a number who had youth and beauty, a few who had sense and some beauty, but never one who combined all that he thought he needed. Somehow this ideal was located fixedly in the back of his brain, and when he thought he was in the presence of the right one he instinctively drew near. He had the notion that, for purposes of marriage, he ought perhaps to find this woman on his own plane. For purposes of temporary or permanent happiness he might take her from anywhere, leaving marriage, of course, out of the question. He had no idea of making anything like a serious proposal to a servant girl. He wanted to find one who would like him—love him perhaps—without anything really serious in the matter of a matrimonial relationship being considered. Hence he was not opposed to trying even in a field such as this, and particularly where he was so instinctively drawn. Jennie appeared exceptionally beautiful to him. He had never seen a servant quite like her. And she was lady-like and lovely without appearing to know it. Why, this girl was a rare flower. Why shouldn't he try to seize her?

For the purpose of avoiding a hasty and ill-conceived opinion on the part of those who are inclined to judge quickly, and from a single action, it will be necessary to present a competent analysis of this man here and now. Although on the face of things he appeared to be a hunter and destroyer of undefended virtue, he was yet a man of such a complicated and interesting turn of mind that those who are inclined to be radically intolerant of his personality had best suspend judgement until some further light can be thrown upon it. Not every mind is to be calculated by the weight of a single folly, not every personality judged by the drag of a single passion. There are some minds, fairly endowed with the power to see into things, that are nevertheless overwhelmed by the evidences of life and are confused. We live in an age in which the impact of materialized forces is well-nigh irresistible; the spiritual nature is overwhelmed by the shock. The tremendous and complicated development of our material civilization, the multiplicity and variety of our social forms, the depth, subtlety and sophistry of our mental cogitations, gathered, remultiplied and phantasmagorically disseminated as they are by these other agencies—the railroad, the express and post-office, the telegraph, telephone, the newspaper and, in short, the whole art of printing and distributing—have so combined as to produce what may be termed a kaleidoscopic glitter, a dazzling and confusing showpiece which is much more apt to weary and undo than to enlighten and strengthen the observing mind. It produces a sort of intellectual fatigue by which we see the ranks of the victims of insomnia, melancholia and insanity recruited. Our modern brain-pan does not seem capable of receiving, sorting and storing the vast army of facts and impressions which present themselves daily. The white light of publicity, which is as much the flaring-out of new church dogmas and architectural forms as it is the little news-item from which the expression has been borrowed, is too white. We are weighed upon by many things. Our hearts and souls no more than our brains can stand it. It is as if the wisdom of the infinite were struggling to beat itself into finite and cup-big minds.

It would not be too much to say that Lester Kane was, in a way, an example of the influence of this condition which we have described. His was a naturally observing mind, Rabelaisian in its strength and tendencies, but confused by the multiplicity of evidences of things, the vastness of the panorama of life, the glitter of its details, the unsubstantial nature of its forms, the uncertainty

of their justification. Raised a Catholic, he was no longer a believer in the Divine inspiration of Catholicism; raised a member
of the social elect, he was not altogether a believer in that innate
superiority which is too often supposed to exist in those socially
elect; brought up as the heir to a comfortable fortune and with the
opportunity of taking unto himself a money-endowed maiden of
his own plane, he was not a believer in the necessity or wisdom of
such a choice. Marriage itself was not an institution which he by
any means was ready to justify. It was established. Yes, certainly.
But what of it? The whole nation believed in it. True, but other
nations believed in polygamy. There were other questions that
bothered him—such questions as the belief in a single deity or
ruler of the universe, and whether a republican, monarchial or
aristocratic form of government was best. In short, the whole
gamut of things material, social, spiritual had come under the
knife of his mental surgery and been left but half dissected. Life
was not proved to him. Not a single idea of his, unless it were the
need of being honest, was finally settled. In all other things he
wavered, questioned, procrastinated, leaving to time and the
powers back of the universe that which he could not solve.

The genesis, growth and effect of such a mental condition is
not to be easily traced or explained, and yet Lester Kane was of so
much interest socially and morally in his day that it would be
interesting if some light could be thrown upon him. He was a
product of a combination of elements—religious, commercial,
social—modified by the overruling, circumambient atmosphere
of liberty in our national life which is productive of almost un-
counted freedoms of thought and action. Although thirty-six
years of age and apparently a man of vigorous, aggressive and
sound personality, he was, nevertheless, an essentially animal
man, pleasantly veneered by the social opportunities which the
family's position afforded him. Like the hundreds of thousands of
Irishmen who, in his father's day, had worked on the railroad
tracks, dug in the mines, picked and shoveled in the ditches,
carried up bricks and mortar on the endless structures of a new
land, he was strong, hairy, axiomatic and witty.

"Do you want me to come back here next year?" he had
asked of Brother Ambrose in a very defiant tone when, in his
seventeenth year, that intellectual grind was about to chastise
him for some schoolboy misdemeanor.

The other stared at him in astonishment. "Your father will have to look after that," he replied.

"Well, my father won't look after it," Lester returned. "If you touch me with that whip, I'll take things into my own hands. I'm not committing any punishable offences, and I'm not going to be knocked around any more."

Words, unfortunately, did not avail in this case, but a good, vigorous Irish-American wrestle did, in which the whip was broken and the discipline of the school so fractured that he was compelled to take his clothes and leave. After that, he looked his father in the eye and told him that he was not going to school any more.

"I'm perfectly willing to go to work," he explained. "There's nothing in a classical education for me. Let me go into the office, and I guess I'll pick up enough to carry me through."

Old Archibald Kane, keen, single of mind and unsullied of commercial honor, admired his son's determination and did not attempt to send him back.

"Come down to the office," he said; "perhaps there is something you can do."

Entering upon a business life at the age of eighteen, Lester had worked faithfully, rising in his father's estimation until now he had come to be, in a way, his personal representative. Whenever there was a contract to be entered upon, an important move to be decided, or a representative of the manufactory to be sent anywhere with power to consummate a deal, Lester was the one to go. His father trusted him implicitly, and so diplomatic and earnest was he in the fulfillment of his duties that this trust had never been impaired.

"Business is business," a favorite axiom with him, was, in the way he pronounced it, a flashing light of his ability as a man of affairs.

The trouble with Lester was that the complicated and incisive nature of his mind, coupled with his very robust physique, as well as the social and somewhat unintellectual nature of his duties, tended to produce a rather unbalanced condition.

There were molten forces in him, flames which burst forth now and then in spite of the fact that he was sure that he had them under control. One of these was a taste for liquor, of which he was perfectly sure he had the upper hand. He drank but very little, he thought. He drank only in a social way among friends, in greeting to the good health and the success of those he admired.

Another was his leaning toward women, a weakness he also thought he had well in hand. He was a man of breadth, he fancied; of vigor. His powers as a man and a well-favored one were self-conscious with him. If he chose to have relations with different women, he was capable of deciding how many, and where the danger point lay. If men were only guided by a sense of the brevity that all such relationships must have, there would not be as many troubles for them as some endured. Furthermore, he flattered himself that he had a grasp upon a right method of living, a method which was nothing more than a quiet acceptance of the social conditions as they were, tempered by a little personal judgement as to the right and wrong of individual conduct. Not to fuss and fume, not to cry out about anything, not to be mawkishly sentimental; to be vigorous and sustain your personality intact. Such was his theory of life, and he was satisfied that it was a good one.

The weight which these facts would have in adjusting his relationship with a girl like Jennie was to be seen in the manner in which he looked upon her difficulties. Although his original object in approaching her was one of pleasure-seeking purely, and his feeling—when he first discovered her shy, retreating, fearsome acceptance of him—one of prideful exultation in his own powers, yet now that he had thus summarily seized upon her, he could not help noting something finer than the merely commonplace in her character. She was lovely, no doubt of that, far above the average. Scraps of impressions concerning her, which were very pleasing, came back to him. A sense of a very agreeable presence was one thing; remembrance of how simply she had answered him another; how soft and retreating she was a third; all of which were coupled with so much that was natural and womanly.

"Such eyes," he recalled. "Such a pretty face. And she is so poor," a fact which cost him some few thoughts on the inequalities of life; thoughts not nearly so interesting as the girl herself.

There is a time in some men's lives when, owing to the rudeness of their own experiences or the delving power of their critical faculties, they begin to view feminine youth and beauty not so much in relation to the ideal of the eternal bliss which is to spring therefrom, but rather with regard to the social laws and customs by which they are environed.

"Must it be," they ask themselves in speculating concerning the possibility of taking a maiden to wife, "that I shall be compelled to swallow the whole social code, make a covenant with society, sign a pledge of abstinence, and give another a life interest in all my affairs, when I know too well that I am but taking to myself a variable creature like myself, whose wishes are apt to become insistent and burdensome in proportion to the decrease of her beauty and interest?"

At the same time there is a social or, rather, unsocial code, by which a man such as this can arrange to modify the chiefest phase of his difficulties under such circumstances, and that is by taking youth and beauty, not so environed by these social difficulties, and thus securing to himself the joys without the penalties which his own plane would attach thereto. There are many men who look upon women outside their own circle as creatures suited for the purposes of a temporary companionship, as it were. These men, and they comprise a fraction of the American body politic, secretly believe that you may sin if you so wish, taking your choice of feminine beauty as you may find it, if you are not unconscious of the danger that lurks in following such a course too closely. True support and comfort must be reserved as a matter of necessity for the woman who shall come in the more conventional way—herself seeking position and establishment, you adding somewhat to your personal dignity by accepting her as your wife.

If such a woman be finally acquired as a wife, the errors of the past do not matter. Your life is now adjusted to the needs of society. Obeisance to that national idol, the home, once paid, you may live in peace and honor until you offend against it.

Lester, for all his geniality, was such a man. He was past the youthful love period and knew it. The innocence and unsophistication of younger ideals had gone. Today he saw the women from whom it was considered policy for him to choose a wife in a more rounded way. Some of them were blessed with beauty, it is true, but beauty, with all these social manacles attached, was no longer so inviting. Besides, he knew the attention a courtship on this upper plane would require—the loverlike gallantry in the wooing, the broad, unconsidered assertions and poetic flights of fancy which he was no longer prepared to give. He could see where the

beauty of the lovers under the window in the moonlight necessarily figured in their souls, that their dalliance was sweet because
it was new and never before gone through with. Alas, for him it
seemed a hollow proposition at best.

A short course, a more direct way, a geometrician's straight
line to a woman's heart was more to his liking, and now that he
had found an opportunity to proceed on this basis, he was not
willing to give it up. He waited a few hours, thinking. He strolled
out to the place where she told him she lived, getting a wonderful
impression of the poverty and commonplace that was back of her.
When he inclined to be generous and fair and honorable because
of this, the thought of her beauty swept over him and changed his
mood. No, he must have her if he could—today, quickly, as soon
as possible. It was in that mood that he returned to Mrs. Bracebridge's home.

CHAPTER XVI

Meanwhile Jennie was going through the agony of one who
has a varied and complicated problem to confront. Her
baby, her father, her brothers and sisters all rose up to confront
her. What was this thing she was doing? What other wretched
relationship was she allowing herself to slip into? How was she to
explain to this man, if at all, why she did not want to have
anything to do with him—could not. How to explain to her
family about him if she did. He would not marry her, that was
sure, if he knew. He would not marry her anyhow, a man of his
station and position. Yet here she was parleying with him, when
she had no right. What was the thing for her to do? She pondered
over this until evening, deciding first that it was best to run away,
but remembering painfully that she had told him where she lived.
Then she decided that she would summon up her courage and
refuse him—tell him she couldn't, wouldn't have anything to do
with him. This last seemed quite all right in his absence. She said
to herself over and over that she would do that. And she would
get herself some work where he could not follow her up so easily.
It all seemed simple enough as she put on her things to go home in
the evening.

Her aggressive lover was not without his own conclusion in this matter, however. Since leaving her, as has been shown, he had thought concisely and to the point. It was his conclusion that he must act at once. She might tell her family, she might tell Mrs. Bracebridge, she might leave the city. He wanted to know more of the conditions which surrounded her, and there was only one way to do that—talk to her. He must persuade her to come and live with him. She would, he thought. She admitted she liked him. That soft, yielding note which he had first commented on to himself rather foreboded that he could win her for himself without much formality, if he wished to try. He decided to do so anyhow for, truly, he desired her greatly.

At five-thirty he returned to the Bracebridge home to see if she was still there. At six he had an opportunity to say to her, unobserved, "I am going to walk home with you. Wait for me at the next corner, will you?"

"Yes," she said, a sense of compulsion to do his bidding seizing her. She explained to herself afterward that she ought to talk to him, to tell him finally of her decision not to see him again, and that this was as good a time and place as any. At six-thirty he left the house on a pretext—a forgotten engagement—and a little after seven he was waiting for her in a closed carriage near the appointed spot. He was calm, absolutely satisfied as to the result, and curiously elate beneath a sturdy, shock-proof exterior. It was as if he breathed some fragrant perfume, soft, grateful, entrancing.

A few minutes after eight he saw Jennie coming along. The flare of the gaslamp was not strong, but it gave sufficient light to make her out. A wave of sympathy passed over him, for there was a great appeal in her personality. He stepped out as she neared the corner and confronted her. "Come, get in this carriage with me. I'll take you home."

"No," she replied. "I don't think I'd better."

"Come with me. I'll take you home. It's a better way to talk."

Once more that sense of dominance on his part, that power of compulsion. She yielded, feeling that she should not, and in a moment they were driving. He said to the cabman, "Anywhere for a little while." When she was seated beside him he began at once.

"Listen to me, Jennie, I want you. Tell me something about yourself."

"I have to talk to you," she replied, trying to stick to her original line of defence.

"About what?" he inquired, trying to fathom her expression in the half light.

"I can't do this way," her lips formulated. "I can't act this way. You don't know how it all is. I shouldn't have done what I did this morning. I mustn't see you any more. Really I mustn't."

"You didn't do what you did this morning," he remarked paradoxically, going back to that particular thought. "I did that. And as for seeing me any more, I'm going to see you." He seized her hand. "You don't know me, but I like you. I'm crazy about you, that's all. You belong to me. Now listen. I'm going to have you. Are you going to come to me?"

"No, no, no!" she replied in an agonized voice. "I can't do anything like that, Mr. Kane. Please listen to me. It can't be. You don't know. Oh, you don't know. I can't do what you want. I don't want to. I couldn't, even if I wanted to. You don't know how things are. But I don't want to do anything wrong. I mustn't. I can't. I won't. Oh, no! no!! no!!! Please let me go home."

He listened to this troubled, feverish outburst with sympathy, with even a little pity.

"What do you mean by you can't?" he asked curiously, his interest aroused.

"Oh, I can't tell you," she replied. "Please don't ask me. You oughtn't to know. But I mustn't see you any more. It won't do any good."

"But you like me," he retorted.

"Oh, yes, yes, I do. I can't help that. But you mustn't come near me any more. Please don't."

He turned this proposition over in his mind with the solemnity of a judge. Strongly aroused affectionally he was almost irresistible, and he knew it. This girl liked him—loved him really, brief as their contact had been. He was drawn to her strongly, he knew, not irrevocably but with exceeding strength. What was this she was saying about not being able to do what he wanted, and was it really so, and did it make any difference? What prevented her from yielding, especially since she wanted to? He was curious.

"See here, Jennie," he replied. "I hear what you say. I don't know what you mean by 'can't' if you want to. You say you like me. Why can't you come to me? You're my sort. We will get along beautifully together. You're suited to me temperamentally. I'd like to have you with me. What makes you say you can't come?"

"I can't," she replied. "I can't. I don't want to. I oughtn't. Oh, please don't ask me any more. You don't know. I can't tell you why." She was thinking of her baby.

The man had a keen sense of justice and fair play. Above all things he wanted to be decent in his treatment of people. In this case he wanted to be tender and considerate and yet win her. He turned this over in his mind.

"Listen to me," he said finally, still holding her hand. "I may not want you to do anything immediately. I want you to think it over. But you belong to me. You say you care for me. You admitted that this morning. I know you do. Now why should you stand out against me? I like you. I can do a lot of things for you. I'd like to. Why not let us be good friends now? Then we can talk the rest of this over later."

"But I mustn't do anything wrong," she insisted. "I don't want to. Please don't come near me any more. I can't do what you want."

"Now, look here," he said. "You don't mean that. Why did you say you liked me? Have you changed your mind? Look at me." (She had lowered her eyes.) "Look at me! You haven't, have you?"

"Oh no, no, no," she half sobbed, swept by some force beyond her control.

"Well, then, why stand out against me? I love you, I tell you—I'm crazy about you. That's why I came back this time. It was to see you!"

"Was it?" asked Jennie, surprised.

"Yes, it was. And I would have come again and again if necessary. I tell you I'm crazy about you. I've got to have you. Now tell me you'll come with me."

"No, no, no," she pleaded. "I can't. I must work. I want to work. I don't want to do anything wrong. Please don't ask me. You mustn't. You must let me go. Really you must. I can't do what you want."

"Tell me, Jennie," he said, changing the subject, "what does your father do?"

"He's a glass-blower."

"Here in Cleveland?"

"No, he works in Youngstown."

"Is your mother alive?"

"Yes, sir."

"You live with her?"

"Yes, sir."

He smiled at the "sir." "Don't say 'sir' to me, sweet," he pleaded in his gruff way. "And don't insist on the *Mr.* Kane. I'm not 'mister' to you any more. You belong to me, little girl, me," and he pulled her to him.

"Please don't Mr. Kane," she pleaded. "Oh, please don't. I can't! I can't! You mustn't."

But he sealed her lips with his own.

"Listen to me, Jennie," he repeated, using his favorite expression. "I tell you you belong to me. I like you better every moment. I haven't had a chance to know you. I'm not going to give you up. You've got to come to me eventually. And I'm not going to have you working as a lady's maid. You can't stay in that place except for a little while. I'm going to take you somewhere else. And I'm going to leave you some money, do you hear? You have to take it."

At the word money she quailed and withdrew.

"No, no, no!" she repeated. "No, I won't take it."

"Yes, you will. Give it to your mother. I'm not trying to buy you. I know what you think. I'm not. I want to help you. I want to help your family. I know where you live. I saw the place today. How many are there of you?"

"Six," she replied, quieting.

"The families of the poor," he thought.

"You take this from me," he insisted, drawing a purse from his coat. "And I'll see you very soon again. There's no escape, sweet."

"No, no," she protested. "I won't. I don't need it. No, you mustn't ask me. I won't do that."

He insisted further, but she was firm and finally he put it away.

"One thing is sure, Jennie, you're not going to escape me," he said. "You'll have to come to me eventually. Don't you know you will? Your own attitude shows that. I'm not going to leave you alone."

"Oh, if you knew the trouble you're causing me."

"I'm not causing you any real trouble, am I?" he asked. "Surely not."

"Yes. I can never do what you want."

"You will! You will!" he exclaimed eagerly, the thought of this prize escaping him heightening his passion. "You'll come to me." And he drew her close in spite of all her protests.

"There," he said when, after the struggle, that mystic something between them spoke again, and she relaxed. Tears were in her eyes, but he did not see them. "Don't you see how it is? You like me too."

"I can't," she repeated with a sob.

The note caught him. "You're not crying, little girl, are you?"

She made no answer.

"I'm sorry," he went on. "I'll not do anything more tonight. We're almost at your home. I'm leaving tomorrow, but I'll see you again. Yes, I will, sweet. I can't give you up now. I'll do anything in reason to make it easy for you, but I can't, do you hear?"

She shook her head.

"Here's where you get out," he said as the carriage drew up near the corner. He could see the evening lamp gleaming behind the Gerhardt cottage curtains.

"Goodbye," he said as she stepped out.

"Goodbye," she murmured.

"Remember," he said, "this is just the beginning."

"Oh, no, no!" she pleaded.

He looked after her as she walked away.

"The beauty!" he exclaimed.

Her whole body hurt as she walked, to say nothing of her mind. She stepped into the house—weary, discouraged, ashamed. What had she done? There was no denying she had compromised herself irretrievably. He would come back.

He would come back. And he had offered her money. That was the worst of all.

CHAPTER XVII

The inconclusive nature of this interview, exciting as it was, did not leave any doubt in either Lester Kane's or Jennie's mind; certainly this was not the end of the affair. Kane knew that he was deeply fascinated. This girl was lovely. She was sweeter than he had had any idea of. Her hesitancy, her repeated protests, her gentle no, no, no's, moved him as music might. This girl was for him, depend on that. He would get her. He would get her by any method he could, but he proposed to get her. She was too sweet to let go. What did he care about what his family might think, or the world? This girl was for him. What was his next move to be?

It was curious, in this connection, that he had the rather well-founded idea that Jennie would yield to him physically, as she had already affectionately, if he followed her closely enough—why, he could not say. Something about her—a warm womanhood, a guileless expression of countenance, a sympathy toward the sex relationship which had nothing to do with hard, brutal immorality—permeated her being. She was the kind of woman who was made for a man—one man. All her attitude toward sex was bound up with love, tenderness, service. When the one man arrived—and she did not figure sharply on any of the requisites that go with the average marriage calculations: wealth, social standing, personal force and what not—she would love him. He would be something like her—would love her, and then the rest would be all his—everything that she was. That was Jennie, and Lester understood this. He felt it. He felt that he was the one. She would yield to him.

On her part there was a great sense of complication and possible disaster. If he followed her, of course, he would learn all. She had not told him about Brander because she was under the vague illusion, as she talked, that she might escape. When she left him she knew he would come back. She knew, in spite of herself, that she wanted him to. If he had gone away and never communicated with her any more she would have been sorry, and yet she was afraid. She felt that she must not yield—she must escape—go on leading a humdrum life. Such was her situation, such her punishment for having made a mistake. She had made her bed and must lie on it.

The Kane family mansion at Cincinnati to which Lester returned after leaving Jennie was an imposing establishment which contrasted strangely with the Gerhardt home. Here was a great, rambling two-story affair, done after the manner of the French chateaux, but in red brick and brownstone. It was set down among flowers and trees in an almost park-like inclosure, and its very stones spoke of a splendid dignity and a refined luxury. Old Archibald Kane, the father, was a man of most serene mood. He had built a tremendous fortune, not by grabbing and browbeating and threatening, but by seeing a big need and filling it. Early in life he had realized that America was a growing country. There was going to be a big demand for vehicles—wagons, carriages, drays—and he knew that someone would have to supply them. Having founded a small wagon industry, he had built it up into a great business; he made good wagons, and he sold them at a good profit. It was his theory that most men were honest, that at bottom they wanted honest things, and if you gave them these they would buy of you and come back and buy again and again until you were an influential and rich man. He believed in the measure "heaped full and running over." He often said so, and he had now in his old age and all through his life the respect and approval of everyone who knew him. "Archibald Kane," you would hear his competitors say—"Ah, there is a fine man. Shrewd but honest. He's a big man."

This man was the father of two sons and three daughters, all healthy, all good-looking, all blessed with exceptional minds, but not all as generous and forceful as their long-living and big-hearted sire. Robert, the eldest, a man of forty years of age, was his father's right-hand man from a financial point of view, having a certain hard incisiveness which somehow fitted him for the inside direction of what might be called the money relationship of the concern. He was medium tall, of a rather spare build, with a high forehead slightly inclined to baldness, bright, liquid-blue eyes, an eagle nose, and thin, firm, even lips. He was a man of few words, rather slow to action and of deep thought. He sat close to his father as vice-president of the big company, which occupied two whole blocks in an outlying section of the city. He was a strong man—a coming man, as his father well knew.

Lester, the second boy, was his father's favorite. He was not by any means the financier that Robert was, but he had a bigger mental grasp of the subtleties which compose life. He was not hard and grasping like his brother, who was married, safely settled with his wife and three children, and fixed in his attention to business, but rather softer, more human, more good-natured about everything. He could not see his brother's attitude, could only think that life was meant to be more than mere work, and conducted himself, as has been seen, in an easier and less conventional way. Yet old Archibald admired him more as a man because he knew he had the bigger vision. Robert was perhaps more to be trusted in the solution of any financial difficulty, but Lester was to be most loved as a son.

Then there was Amy, thirty-two years of age, married, handsome, the mother of one child, a boy; Imogene, twenty-eight, also married, but as yet without children; and Louise, twenty-five, single, the best-looking of the girls but also the coldest and most critical. She was the most eager of all for social distinction, the most vigorous of all in her love of family prestige, the most desirous that the Kane family should outshine every other. She was proud to think that the family was so well placed socially and carried herself with an air and a hauteur which was sometimes amusing, sometimes irritating to Lester. He liked her—in a way she was his favorite sister—but he thought she might take herself with a little less seriousness and not do the family standing any harm.

Mrs. Kane, the mother, was a quiet, refined woman of sixty years of age, who, having come up from comparative poverty with her husband, was not as much for social show as her children but who in a way rejoiced that they should be. It seemed but fitting that the children of her able husband should be distinguished— that she should be, as his wife. They had always conducted themselves well, had given evidence of mental and moral qualities which were admirable. Why should not the community look up to them? It should. And in consequence she carried herself everywhere proudly.

The interior atmosphere of this home was most charming. The furniture, the rugs, the hangings and the pictures were of course of the best. Kane senior had learned years before that the thing to do in any case where you were in doubt as to your own judgement was to put the task or the work in the hands of someone who was not in doubt and whose judgement was certified by public approval. Hence this house, both from the point of view of construction and decoration, had been put into the hands of competent architects and decorators. It was well-built and well-furnished, with a great old Nuremberg clock in the hall which chimed the hours mellifluously, with some charming landscapes by Corot and Troyon and Daubigny on the walls, with soft, charmingly colored rugs and silken hangings at the windows. There was a grand piano for the daughters to play on, a chamber large enough for social dancing (though, all being Catholics, they were conservative in their attitude toward worldly pleasures), and suites of bedrooms where friends and guests could be entertained in number. There was a splendid dining-room, furnished after the period of Louis Quinze, and a library full of interesting, albeit standard, books. It was a fine home, a really comfortable American mansion, and was so known to be by all who knew anything about social life in Cincinnati.

The position Lester Kane held in this atmosphere was plainly indicated by the nature of his reception on this particular return. When he drove up from the depot, where he arrived early in the evening, he was greeted by an old Irish servitor who kept guard over the door.

"Ah, Mister Kane. Sure I'm glad to see you back. I'll take your coat. Yes, yes, it's been fine weather we're having. Yes, yes, the family's all well. Sure your sister Amy is just after leavin' the house with the boy. Your mother's upstairs in her room. Yes, yes."

The old servitor was so glad to see this favorite son home again that he rubbed his hands much in the spirit that a dog might wag its tail. Lester smiled cheerily.

He went up to his mother's room. In the latter, which was done in white and gold and overlooked the garden to the south and east, sat his mother, a gray-haired woman, of considerable strength and youth yet however, who had been reading. She looked up when the door opened, laid the volume down as he entered, and rose to greet him.

"There you are, Mother," he said, putting his arms around her and kissing her. "How are you?"

"Oh, I'm just about the same, Lester. How have you been?"

"Fine. I was up with the Bracebridges for a few days again. I had to stop off in Cleveland to see Parsons. They all asked after you."

"How is Minnie?"

"Just the same. She doesn't change any that I can see. She's just as interested in entertaining as she ever was."

"She's a bright girl," remarked his mother, recalling Mrs. Bracebridge as a girl in Cincinnati. "I always liked her. She's so sensible."

"She hasn't lost any of that, I can tell you," replied Lester significantly. He liked Mrs. Bracebridge for what he considered her definite social capacity. She handled social life as a man handled business.

His mother talked to him a few minutes about the routine of home life. Imogene's husband was leaving for St. Louis on some errand. Robert's wife was sick with a cold. Old Zwingle, the yard watchman at the factory, who had been with Mr. Kane for over forty years, had died. Her husband was going to the funeral. It was a typical family talk.

As he left to go to his own room he encountered Louise in the hall. Smart was the word for her, for she was dressed in a beaded black-silk dress, fitting close to her form, with a burst of rubies at her throat which somehow contrasted effectively with her dark complexion and black hair. Her eyes were black and piercing.

"Oh, there you are, Lester," she exclaimed. "When did you get in? Be careful how you kiss me. I'm going out, and I'm all fixed, even to the powder on my nose. Oh, you bear!" Lester had gripped her firmly and kissed her soundly. She pushed him away with her strong hands.

"I didn't brush much of it off," he said. "You can always dust more on with that puff of yours. There's too much on anyhow."

"Oh, hush. Tell me, are you coming to the Knowles' to-night?"

"What's there?"

"Why, don't you know? There's a big party for Marie's coming-out. They're expecting you. I hope you haven't forgotten."

"I didn't promise to go to that," he said half-defiantly. "I don't think I will, either. I'm going to bed early tonight."

"Oh, come, go to this. Mrs. Knowles will be angry. She's been nice enough to you, in all conscience."

"Well, maybe I will, late. I'm in no mood to go anywhere tonight."

He passed into his own room to dress for dinner.

One of the customs that had been adopted by the Kane family in the last few years was this custom of dressing for dinner. Guests had become so common that in a way it was a necessity and Louise, in particular, made a point of it. If one were not inclined to dress, dinner could be served in the little private dining-room on the ground floor. Robert was coming tonight, though, and a Mr. and Mrs. Burnett, old friends of his father and mother, and so Lester decided to dress. He knew that his father was around somewhere, but he did not trouble to look him up now. He was thinking of his last two days in Cleveland and wondering when he would see Jennie again.

CHAPTER XVIII

This dinner, his conversation with his father, his visit to the Knowles' coming-out party still further emphasized the distinctive nature of his home life, so different from the quality of the liaison he had fallen on in Cleveland. As Lester came downstairs after making his toilet, he found his father in the library reading, as was the old gentleman's wont when waiting for his late dinner.

"Hello, Lester," he said, looking up from his paper over the top of his glasses and extending his hand. "Where do you come from?"

"Cleveland," replied his son, gripping his father's hand firmly and smiling.

"Robert tells me you've been to New York."

"Yes, I was there."

"How did you find my old friend Arnold?"

"Just about the same," returned Lester. "He doesn't look any older."

"I suppose not," said Archibald genially, as if the report were a compliment to his own hardy condition. "He's been a temperate man. A fine old gentleman."

He led the way back to the sitting-room where they browsed over interesting social and home news until the chime of the clock in the hall warned the guests upstairs that it was time to dine.

When they came in, Lester met Robert again, and Louise, and these old friends of the family. There was a late arrival in the shape of Amy, who came back to announce that she was going with Louise to the Knowles homestead. Her own house was only a little way down the street.

Lester sat down in great comfort amid this estimable company. He liked this home atmosphere—his mother and father and his sisters. It was grateful to his senses to be with them, to be here. So he smiled and was exceedingly genial.

Amy announced that the Leverings were going to give a dance on Tuesday and inquired whether he intended to go.

"You know I don't dance," he returned dryly. "Why should I go?"

"Don't dance? Won't dance, you mean. You're getting too lazy to move. If Robert is willing to dance occasionally, I think you might."

"Robert's got it on me in lightness," Lester replied airily.

"And politeness," put in Louise.

"Be that as it may," said Lester.

"Don't try to stir up a fight, Louise," observed Robert sagely.

After dinner they adjourned to the library, and Lester talked with his brother a little on business. There were some contracts coming up for revision. He wanted to see what suggestions his brother had to make. Louise and Amy were already leaving in a carriage. "Are you coming now?" asked Louise, putting her head in at the door.

"A little later on I think. You can tell 'em I'll be there."

"Letty Pace asked about you the other night," she called back from the door.

"Kind," replied Lester. "I'm greatly obliged."

"She's a nice girl, Lester," put in his father, who was standing near the open fire close by. "I only wish you would marry her and settle down. You'd have a good wife in her."

"She's charming," testified Mrs. Kane.

"What is this?" asked Lester jocularly—"a conspiracy? You know I'm not strong on the matrimonial business."

"And well I know it," replied his mother semi-seriously. "I wish you were."

Lester changed the subject.

At ten he left for the Knowles' for a few minutes' stay. This was one of those exclusive society homes which make up the inner circle of a city like Cincinnati. And of course the Kanes were closely identified with it. Lester was most heartily welcome, as could be seen by the attitude of the hostess, who exclaimed at sight of him: "Why, Lester Kane! How do you do? I'm so glad to see you. I was really afraid you wouldn't come, and George would have been so disappointed. He asked particularly after you. How have you been?"

"You know me," smiled Lester easily.

"Indeed I do, sir. It's high time you were bestirring yourself to find a wife. You're rapidly becoming an old bachelor."

"The most interesting men in the world," he returned. "But don't you begin this matrimonial badgering. I got enough of that at home tonight. I just left one group that wants me to get married. Won't you try to want me to stay single?"

"What a question, you imp! No, I won't. Now you go right over there and find a nice girl and propose to her. I'm just going to give you six more months, and then I'm going to pick one for you myself."

"Easy! Easy!" was his retort. "Make it ten years. I'd rather have a long sentence."

"Six months, and not a day longer," and she waved him along.

He went, smiling. This society world amused him a little. He met some interesting women but, better yet, he met interesting men. He liked men. He liked to play billiards and poker and shoot ducks and drive fast horses. In society he found a few men who liked the same thing, and then they told him funny stories. When he had time, which was not so often, he liked to get with these fellows.

Tonight, for some reason, he seemed doomed to be teased about his matrimonial possibilities. He had hardly left Mrs. Knowles when a Mrs. Windom, another of the clever matrons of the city, buttonholed him. "Now Lester," she said, "I have something nice to tell you. I want you to come over here and let me explain. It's something fine."

"What is it?" he asked suspiciously, as they reached a nearby window.

"I have a wife picked out for you."

"What, another!" he exclaimed. "Oh, Lord."

"Why do you act like that?" she asked. "I think it's very impolite, not so say unkind. Why, the very idea."

"I refuse to explain," he said wearily.

"Well then, now listen," she went on, when he appeared subdued. "She's just the kind of girl you would have picked for yourself. She's sweet and pretty and young and intelligent—in fact, all the virtues. She's just lovely."

"Glory be!" exclaimed Lester with an imitation of enthusiasm. "Who is she?"

"I'm not going to tell you her name—only that she's young, beautiful, has a fortune in her own right, and is altogether charming. Now don't you think I'm just the best friend you ever had?"

"Well, fairly so," he replied. "Anyhow, that's a combination that ought to produce a mild imitation of friendship. Where is the body?"

"Lester Kane!" she exclaimed. "Aren't you ashamed of yourself? Now you come right over here, and I'll introduce you."

"Don't I know her?" he inquired.

"No, you don't. You know her family only. She just made her début last fall."

"This isn't to be a matrimonial tête-à-tête between me and sweet sixteen, is it?" He dreaded callow youth.

"Nothing so lucky, kind sir. You'll sue for her hand. Now you pick her out of those five over there by the window."

"Never. I'd rather get out a writ of attachment," said Lester as he turned and gazed. "Five," he added. "That's a good hand to draw to. I hope I know an heiress when I see one."

"Attention, sir," she ordered.

He looked, turning suddenly with a mock light of inquiry in his eye to ask:

"An heiress, did you say?"

"I did."

"Trust me," he said, gaily. "I am what is known as the human lodestone for heiresses. I can close my eyes and pick them. Thus—the one with the aigrette in her hair."

"Right!" exclaimed his guide. Then, with a hysterical little rise in her voice, "I do believe I have made a match."

"Give it to me," he said, holding out his hand. "My pipe's gone out."

She looked at him with a puzzled twinkle in her eye.

"Now you wait right here until I return," she said. "I'll be back in a moment."

"On this spot?"

"This very spot."

"I'm afraid she'll spot me."

"Oh, Lester Kane! Don't be silly. Now, you wait."

She fluttered away, and he strolled off in another direction, coming back, after a conversation with another woman, to find her very eager to get hold of him.

"As I live," she exclaimed, "she expressed a partiality for you! Now, come with me and let me introduce you to her."

"With pleasure," he said.

"Then you talk with her."

"What are you?" he inquired. "A matrimonial agent?"

"Aren't you ashamed of yourself? When you want another wife, now you shan't have her."

"Heaven be—" he started to say, but as they came before the young lady in question he paused and bowed. "I was saying how much I owed to her for bringing me over to you and giving me the pleasure of this introduction."

The young lady, who was one of those ambitious flowers of the many newly grown rich of our country—ruddy with the ruddiness of roses, innocent with innocence that is instructed to guard and that still desires without knowing quite how to attain, fashionable with the well-groomed fashions not only of dresses but of ideas, looked at him with eyes that were not stars but mirrors only—and smiled.

"I do believe she is one woman who has my real interests at heart," he added, gayly.

"How so?" asked the young débutante, with a little pinch at her red lips with her white teeth.

He looked at her with one of those searching glances for intellect which he was inclined more frequently to give in these days, and found instead a sort of coquettish barrenness, which, at his experienced stage of life, was but slightly calculated to engage. He was soon anxious to get away.

"When you are a way-worn bachelor, like your humble servant, with more *embonpoint* than wit, you will feel the kindliness of such services as she has just rendered me," he went on jocularly. "Real bachelors always crave introductions to young ladies."

He wandered out into a path of more or less complimentary badinage, to which the young lady replied with ease, but he was at the point where he found that he was talking down rather than up to a certain standard, and realized the old feeling that youthful interests were beyond his ken. When he was getting a little worried as to how he should escape, he was relieved by a young bachelor friend. He immediately strolled out of the drawing room and upstairs to the billiard room, where he proposed to have a quiet smoke.

He really could not stand for this sort of thing any more, he told himself. It was a bore. Such youth. It was silly. While he thought, his mind wandered back to Jennie and her peculiar "Oh, no, no!" *There* was someone who appealed to him. That was a type of womanhood worth while. Not sophisticated, not self-seeking, not watched over and set like a man-trap in the path of men, but a sweet little girl—sweet as a flower, who was without anybody, apparently, to watch over her. That night in his room he composed a letter, which he dated a week later because he did not want to appear too urgent and because he could not again leave Cincinnati for two weeks anyhow.

My dear Jennie:
　　Although it has been a week and I have said nothing, I have not forgotten you—believe me. Was the impression I gave of myself very bad? I will make it better from now on, for I love you, little girl—I really do. There is a flower on my table which reminds me of you very much—white, delicate, beautiful. Your personality, lingering with me, is just that. You are the essence of many things beautiful to me. It is in your power to strew flowers in my path if you will.
　　But what I want to say here is that I shall be in Cleveland on the 18th, and I shall expect to see you. I arrive Thursday night, and I want you to meet me in the ladies' parlor of the Dornton at noon Friday. Will you? You can lunch with me.
　　You see, I respect your suggestion that I should not call. (I will not—on condition.) These separations are dangerous to good friendship. Write me that you will. You see, I throw myself on your generosity. But I can't take no for an answer, not now.
　　With a world of affection,
　　　　Lester Kane.

He sealed that and addressed it. "She's a remarkable girl in her way," he thought. "She really is."

CHAPTER XIX

The arrival of this letter, coming after a week of silence and after she had had a chance to think deeply, served to concentrate all Jennie's ideas and feelings, not only concerning Lester, but also concerning her home, her child and herself, and presented them in rapid order for immediate consideration and answer. What now did she truly feel about this gentleman? What did she intend to do and say? Did she sincerely wish to answer his letter? Could she? If so, what must she say, and how adjust her movements so that her father would not be offended, her family not injured, her child's future not jeopardized? Heretofore all her movements, even the one in which she had sought to sacrifice herself for the sake of Bass in Columbus, had not seemed to involve any one but herself. Now, strange to say, the whole welfare of the family seemed involved, and she felt as if this serious attention from one as eminent as Lester must result in a difficulty of some sort—just what she could not have said.

The manifestation of love which Lester's letter contained demanded a confession from her. She wondered whether it would not be better to write him and explain everything. She had told him that she did not wish to do wrong. Must she tell him she had a child and beg him not to come any more? Would he obey her if she did? She doubted it. Would he let her alone if she opposed him? He might. Did she really want him to?

The need of making this confession was a painful thing to her. It caused her to hesitate, to start a letter in which she tried to explain, and then tear it up.

She wavered and varied in her intention, her mind a perfect balance between conflicting emotions, an event being almost necessary as a weight to turn her either way. When she would be on the verge of penning the truth, some flood of shame would be incontinently loosed to sweep away her intention. When she decided not to write or to go to him, the startling feeling would come that he would surely pursue her here, in her own home perhaps. He was a determined man.

One event which in a way helped to solve the difficulty for her, though in a manner adverse to her best intentions, was the sudden homecoming of her father, seriously injured by an accident at the glass-works in Youngstown where he worked.

It was on a Wednesday afternoon, in the latter part of August, when a letter came from Gerhardt. It was time for the regular weekly remittance, but this time, instead of the regular fatherly communication, written in German and telling of his condition and enclosing five dollars, there was a communication from him in another's hand, explaining that only the day before he had received a severe burn on both hands, due to the accidental overturning of a dipper of molten glass, and that he would be home the next morning. No explanation of just how severely he was injured was made, but the letter intimated that it was very bad.

"What do you think of that?" exclaimed William, whose mouth was wide open.

"Poor Papa!" said Veronica, tears welling up in her eyes.

Mrs. Gerhardt sat down, clasped her hands in her lap and stared at the floor. The significance of it was more dreadful than tears could cope with, and she rose after a time, pale and still.

"Now, what to do?" she nervously exclaimed to herself. The possibility that Gerhardt was disabled for life opened long vistas of difficulties which she had not the courage to contemplate.

Bass came home at half-past six, Jennie at eight. The former heard the news with an astonished face. He was of the kind whose personal balance could not be upset unless he himself were stricken.

"Gee! That's tough, isn't it?" he exclaimed. "Did the letter say how bad he was hurt?"

"No," replied Mrs. Gerhardt.

"Well, I wouldn't worry about it," he said, when he saw the expression of care and anxiety upon her face. "It won't do any good. We'll get along somehow. I wouldn't worry like that if I were you."

The truth of it was that he wouldn't, because his nature was decidedly different. Life did not rest heavily upon his shoulders. Care was a non-understandable thing. His brain was not large enough to grasp the significance and weigh the results of things.

"I know," said Mrs. Gerhardt, endeavoring to recover herself. "I can't help it, though. To think that just when we were getting along fairly well this new calamity should be added. It seems sometimes as if we were under a curse. We have so much bad luck."

When Jennie came, her mother turned to her instinctively, for here was her one stay.

"What's the matter, Ma?" asked Jennie as she opened the door and observed her mother's face. "What have you been crying about?"

Mrs. Gerhardt looked at her and then turned half away.

"Pa's had his hands burned," put in Bass solemnly. "He'll be home tomorrow."

Jennie turned and stared at him. "His hands burned!" she exclaimed.

"Yes," said Bass.

"How did it happen?"

"A pot of glass was turned over," he said.

Jennie looked at him, then at her mother, and her eyes dimmed with tears. Instinctively she drew near to her mother and put her arm around her.

"Now don't you cry, Ma," she said, barely able to control herself. "Don't you worry. I know how you feel, but we'll get along. Don't cry now." Then her own lips lost control of their evenness and she struggled long before she could bring her courage to the assistance of the others.

The peculiar situation, coming at this time and consonant with Lester's letter, had a notable psychologic effect upon her. Without volition upon her part there leaped into her consciousness a connection—subtle, in a way unwarranted, she thought, and persistent. What about this man's offer of money now? What about his declaration of love? Somehow it came back to her—his affection, his personality, his desire to help her, his enthusiasm, much as Brander's had done when Bass was in jail. Was she doomed to a second sacrifice? Did it really make any difference? Wasn't her life a failure already? She thought all this while her mother sat there looking haggard, distraught, weary of life. What a pity, she thought, that her mother must always suffer! Wasn't it a shame that she could never have any real happiness?

"I wouldn't feel so badly," she said, after a time. "Maybe he isn't burned so badly as we think. Did the letter say he'd be home in the morning?"

"Yes," said Mrs. Gerhardt, recovering herself.

They talked more quietly from then on, and, gradually, as the details were exhausted, a kind of dumb peace settled down upon the household.

"One of us ought to go to the train to meet him in the morning," said Jennie to Bass. "I will. I guess Mrs. Bracebridge won't mind."

"No," said Bass gloomily, "you mustn't. I can go."

He was sour at this new fling of fate, and looked it.

They considered and advised. Jennie and her mother saw the others off to bed and then sat out in the kitchen talking.

"I don't see what's to become of us, now," said Mrs. Gerhardt at last, completely exhausted by this new financial complication, which this calamity had wrought. She looked so weak and help-less, so much as if age and fortune were playing upon her as a tool, and as if all her life's hopes were slowly fading into ashes, that Jennie could hardly contain herself. She knew for what her mother had always longed, how she had toiled and worn herself away for nothing.

"Don't worry, Mama dear," she said, a great resolve coming into her heart. The world was wide. There was comfort and ease in it, scattered by others with a lavish hand. Surely, surely misfor-tune could not press so sharply but that they could live!

She sat down with her mother, the difficulties of the future seeming to approach with audible and ghastly steps.

"What do you suppose will become of us now?" repeated her mother, who saw how her fanciful conception of this Cleveland home had crumbled before her eyes.

"Why," said Jennie, who saw clearly and knew what could be done, "it will be all right. I wouldn't worry about it. Something will happen. We'll get something."

She realized as she sat there that fate had shifted the burden of the situation to her.

The arrival of Gerhardt in person merely strengthened this conviction. He came home the next day, and Bass, who met him at the depot, was disturbed by the distress he evinced. He looked very pale and seemed to have suffered a great deal. His cheeks were slightly sunken and his bony profile looked rather gaunt. His hands were heavily bandaged, and altogether he presented such a picture of thoughtful distress that many stopped to look at him.

"By chops," he said to Bass, "that was a burn I got. I thought once I couldn't stand the pain any longer. Such pain I had! Such pain! By chops! I will never forget it."

Then he related just how the accident had occurred, and said that he did not know whether he would ever be able to use his hands again. His thumb on his right hand and the first two fingers on the left had been burned to the bone. The two fingers had been amputated at the first joint—the thumb he might save, but his hands would be in danger of being stiff.

"By chops!" he added, "just at the time when I needed the money most. Too bad! Too bad!"

Then he shook his head in a very mournful way.

Bass endeavored to reassure him, but he was very well aware of the calamity he was facing. It was a dreadful thing, and he didn't know what to do.

When they reached the house and Mrs. Gerhardt opened the door, the old mill-worker, now conscious of her extreme sympathy, began to cry. Mrs. Gerhardt sobbed also. Even Bass lost control of himself for a moment or two, but quickly recovered. The other children wept until Bass called a halt on all of them.

"Don't cry now," he said cheeringly. "What's the use of crying? It isn't so bad as all that. You'll be all right again. We can get along."

Bass's words had a soothing effect, temporarily; and now that her husband was home, Mrs. Gerhardt recovered her composure. Though his hands were bandaged, the mere fact that he could walk and was not otherwise injured was some consolation. He might recover the use of his hands. Outside of the question of a mere livelihood, she would not have worried so much; although, of course, any injury to him was a great grief to her.

When Jennie came home that night she wanted to come close to her father in this crisis and lay the treasury of her services and affection at his feet, but she trembled lest he might be as cold to her as formerly.

On his part, Gerhardt was also troubled. Never had he completely recovered from the shame which his daughter had brought upon him. The fact that she had been taken back, was here, and was leading an honest life were things which he was perfectly ready and willing to weigh in the balance, but, some-how, his own *pronunciamento* upon what she deserved had served to hold him from any personal contact with her the last time he was here. Now he tried to think of some way in which a peaceful dwelling under the same roof could be effected. Although he wanted to be kindly, his feelings were so tangled that he hardly knew what to do.

Jennie came in and, with that feeling of affection and sorrow, now so overwhelmingly strong in her, approached him.

"Papa," she said.

Gerhardt looked confused and tried to say something natural, but it was unavailing. As with a rush of air, the whole tangle of the situation came upon him—his helplessness, her sorrow for his state, his own responsiveness to her affection, his gratitude for her tears—and he broke down again and cried helplessly.

"Forgive me, Papa," she pleaded. "I'm so sorry. Oh, I'm so sorry."

He did not attempt to look at her, but in that swirl of feeling that their meeting created, he thought he could forgive, and did.

"I have prayed," he said brokenly. "It is all right."

When he recovered himself, he felt ashamed and was relieved to answer her single inquiry in a brief way. Jennie said no more, but went into the kitchen, and, from that time, although there was always a great reserve between them, Gerhardt tried not to ignore her completely, and she tried to be as simple and affectionate as a daughter should.

While this affectional relationship was gradually readjusting itself, the trouble of their physical maintenance became most sharp. Although in these tense days Bass should have contributed more of his weekly earnings, he did not feel called upon to do it, so the small sum of eleven dollars per week was left to meet, as best it could, the current expenses of rent, food, and coal, to say nothing of the need of incidentals, which now began to press very heavily. Gerhardt had to go to a doctor to have his hands dressed daily. George needed a new pair of shoes. The house had to be run on five dollars less per week, for that was the sum Gerhardt had contributed. There was but one result ahead. Either more money must come from some source, or the family must beg for credit and suffer the old tortures of want. It crystallized a peculiar thought in Jennie's mind.

She still had Lester's letter, unanswered. The day was drawing near. Should she write? He would help them. Had he not tried to force money on her? She decided after a long cogitation that she really ought to, and consequently wrote him the briefest note. She would meet him as requested. Please not to come to the house. This she mailed and then waited, with a sort of soul dread, the arrival of the day.

CHAPTER XX

The fatal Friday came, and with it the soul dread she had been suffering was heightened to the Nth power. She was overwrought with the necessity of this thing—the tragedy; really she was not herself, and she went through the details of her toilet in the morning with a sense of weariness such as had not been customary to her of late. She was turning over in her mind an excuse to Mrs. Bracebridge for going out, an explanation to her mother of her present conduct after she had done what she was going to do, an explanation to her father some time of something which would be a lie—all the many curious complications of her life which would follow. There was really no alternative, she thought. Her own life was a failure. Why go on fighting? If she could make her family happy, if she could give Vesta a good education, if she could conceal the true nature of this older story and keep Vesta in the background—perhaps, perhaps—well, rich men had married poor girls before, after a long time. Lester was very kind; he liked her. At seven o'clock she left to go to Mrs. Bracebridge's, and at eleven she excused herself on the pretext of some work for her mother and left the house for the hotel.

Lester, leaving Cincinnati a few days earlier than he expected, had failed to receive her reply, the contents of which would have cheered him considerably, and came to Cleveland, the unkindness of her conduct troubling him not a little. As he walked across the large and ornamental public square, he was hardly cheered by the knowledge that he was now on the ground of his previous exploit and that Jennie had awakened in him a real feeling of interest. He recalled the more salient features of her face and manner, but was not inclined to look upon them as charms which were to afford him immediate pleasure. She had not written. That was enough to make him feel as if his little experience was about over.

When he reached the hotel and found that there was no word, he dropped the matter temporarily, the feeling that he was really defeated in this desire causing him no little dissatisfaction. He was a man not easily wrought up by these affectional feelings, but tonight he felt depressed, and so went gloomily up to his room and changed his linen. After supper, he proceeded to drown his dissatisfaction in a very amiable game of billiards with some friends from whom he did not part until he was slightly more elated. The next morning he arose with a vague idea of abandoning the whole affair, but as the hours elapsed and the time of his appointment drew near he decided that it might not be unwise to take a look. She might come. Accordingly, when it still lacked a quarter of an hour of the time, he stepped down into the parlor to see. Great was his delight when he beheld her—pale, reclining in a chair and waiting, disconsolately, the outcome of her acquiescence. He walked briskly up, a satisfied, gratified smile on his face.

"So you did come after all," he said, gazing at her with the look of one who has lost and recovered a prize. "What do you mean by not writing me? I thought from the way you neglected me that you had made up your mind not to come at all."

"I did write," she replied.

"Where?"

"To the address you gave me. I wrote three days ago."

"That explains it. It came too late. You should have written me before. How have you been?"

"Oh, all right," she replied.

"You don't look it," he said. "You look worried. What's the trouble, Jennie? Nothing gone wrong out at your house, has there?"

It was a fortuitous question. He hardly knew why he had asked it. Yet it opened the door to what she wanted to say.

"My father's sick," she replied.

"What's happened to him?"

"He burned his hands at the glass-works. We've been terribly worried. It looks as though he won't be able to use them any more."

She paused, looking the distress she felt, and he saw plainly that she was facing a crisis.

"That's too bad," he said. "That certainly is. When did this happen?"

"Oh, almost three weeks ago now."

"It certainly is bad. Come in to lunch, though. I want to talk with you. I've been wanting to get a better understanding of your family affairs ever since I left." He led the way into the dining-room and selected a secluded table. He tried to divert her mind by suggesting dishes she might like, but finding her rather perplexed, made up their menu himself. Then he turned to her with a cheering air. "Now, Jennie," he said, "I want you to tell me all about your family. I got a little something of it last time, but I want to get it straight. Your father, you said, was a glass-blower by trade. Now he can't work any more at that, that's obvious."

"Yes," she said.

"How many children are there?"

"Six."

"Are you the oldest?"

"No, my brother Sebastian is. He's twenty-two."

"And what does he do?"

"He's a clerk in a cigar store."

"Do you know how much he makes?"

"I think it's twelve dollars," she replied thoughtfully.

"And the other children?"

"Martha, William and Veronica don't do anything yet. They're too young. My brother George works at Wilson's. He's a cash-boy. He gets three dollars and a half."

Lester made a mental calculation. "And how much do you make?"

"I make four."

He stopped, figuring it up to see what they had to live on. "How much rent do you pay?"

"Twelve dollars."

"How old is your mother?"

"She's nearly fifty now."

He turned a fork in his hands, back and forth, thinking.

"To tell you the honest truth, I fancied it was something like that, Jennie," he said. "I've been thinking about you a lot. Now I know. There's only one answer to your problem, and it isn't such a bad one, if you'll only believe me." He paused for an inquiry, but she made none. Her mind was running on her own difficulties.

"Don't you want to know?" he inquired.

"Yes," she said mechanically.

"It's me," he replied. "You have to let me help you. I wanted to last time. I thought there might be some situation of this kind. Now you have to, do you hear?"

"I thought I wouldn't," she said simply.

"I knew what you thought," he replied. "That's all over now. I'm going to 'tend to this family of yours. And I'll do it right now while I think of it."

He drew out his purse and extracted several ten- and twenty-dollar bills—two hundred and fifty dollars in all. "I want you to take this," he said. "It's just the beginning. I will see that your family is provided for from now on. Here, give me your hand."

"Oh, no," she said. "Not so much. Don't give me all that."

"Yes," he replied. "Don't argue. Here. Give me your hand."

She put it out in answer to the summons of his eyes, and he shut her fingers on it. "I want you to have it, sweet! Whatever else we do hasn't anything to do with this. I love you, little girl. I'm not going to see you suffer. Nor anyone belonging to you."

Her eyes looked a dumb thankfulness, and she bit her lips.

"I don't know how to thank you," she said.

"You don't need to," he replied. "The thanks are all the other way—believe me."

He paused and looked at her, the beauty of her face holding him. She looked at the table, wondering what would come next.

"Now tell me," he said, after a time, "what you have been thinking about me. Anything favorable? You see, I've been thinking about you a lot."

"I—" she opened her lips and then stopped.

"Yes," he said. " 'I'—what?"

"I don't know what to think," she said after a time. "My family wouldn't want me to do anything wrong. I couldn't and stay at home. You don't know what a terrible man my father is when he gets angry. He wouldn't let me stay there if he knew. I don't see what I could do and stay at home." She stared at the cloth hopelessly, and he gazed at her with sympathetic consideration of her difficulties.

"How would you like to leave what you're doing and stay at home?" he asked. "That would give you your freedom daytimes."

"I couldn't do that," she replied. "Papa wouldn't allow it. He knows I ought to work."

"That's true enough," he said. "But there's so little in what you're doing. Good heavens! Four dollars a week! I would be glad to give you fifty times that sum if I thought there was any way in which you could use it." He idly thrummed the cloth with his fingers.

"I couldn't," she said. "I hardly know how to use this. They'll suspect. I'll have to tell Mama."

From the way she said it, he judged there must be some bond of sympathy between her and her mother which would permit of a confidence such as this. He was by no means a hard man, and the thought touched him. But he would not relinquish his purpose.

"There's only one thing to be done about this, as far as I can see," he went on very gently after a time. "You're not suited for the kind of work you're doing. There's no chance of your ever accomplishing anything that way. Give it up and come with me down to New York; I'll take good care of you. I love you and want you. As far as your family is concerned, you won't have to worry about them any more. You can take a nice home for them and furnish it in any style you please. Wouldn't you like that?"

He paused, while Jennie, shocked and yet drawn by this siren song of aid, ran along in thought to the full significance as far as her mother was concerned. All her life long Mrs. Gerhardt had been talking of this very thing, a nice home. If they could just have a nice home, a larger house with good furniture and a yard filled with trees, how happy she would be. In it they would be free of the care of rent, the commonplaceness of poor furniture, the wretchedness of poverty. He would help them, and her mother would not be troubled any more.

She hesitated there while his keen eye followed her in spirit, and he saw what a power he had set in motion. This would do it. This would be the thing that would persuade her, if anything would. He waited a few moments longer and then said:

"Well, wouldn't you better let me do that?"

"It would be very nice," she said, "but it can't be done now. I couldn't leave home. Papa would want to know all about where I was going. I wouldn't know what to say."

"Why couldn't you pretend that you are going down to New York with Mrs. Bracebridge?" he suggested. "There couldn't be any objection to that, could there?"

"Not if they didn't find out," she said, her eyes opening in amazement. The possibility was not anything which she had contemplated. "But if they should!"

"They won't," he replied calmly. "They're not watching

Mrs. Bracebridge's affairs. Plenty of mistresses take their maids on long trips. Why not simply tell them you're invited to go—have to go, and then go?"

"Do you think I could?" she inquired.

"Certainly," he replied. "What is there peculiar about that?"

She thought, and, as she did so, it did not seem so strange. Mrs. Bracebridge might have done this before. But there was something else. She looked at this man and realized that any such relationship with him meant motherhood for her again. There was the tragedy of birth to go through, under similarly difficult conditions, unless things should be arranged very differently. She could not stay at home again. She could not bring herself to tell him about Vesta, but she must tell him this. There must be something done or she could not go. It was not possible.

"I—" she said, formulating the first word of her sentence and then stopping.

"Yes," he said. " 'I'—what?"

"I—" She paused again.

He loved her way. He loved her sweet, hesitating lips.

"What is it, Jennie?" he asked helpfully. "You're so delicious. Can't you tell me?"

Her hand was on the table. He reached over and laid his strong brown one on top of it.

"I couldn't—have a baby," she said finally and looked down.

He looked at her, and the charm of her frankness, her innate decency under conditions which were anomalous and compulsory, the simple unaffected recognition of the facts of life lifted her to a plane in his esteem which she had not occupied before for him.

"You're a great girl, Jennie," he said. "You're wonderful. But don't worry about that. You don't need to. I understand a number of things that you don't yet. It can be arranged. You don't need to have a child unless you want to. And I don't want you to."

He stopped and she opened her eyes in wonder and a kind of shame. She had never known that.

He saw the question written in her face.

"It's so," he said. "You believe me, don't you? You think I know, don't you?"

"Yes," she faltered.

"Well, I do. But if you did, I wouldn't let any trouble come to you. I'd take you away. There won't be any trouble about that. Only I don't want any children. There wouldn't be any satisfaction in that proposition for me at this time. I'd rather wait. But there won't be—don't worry. You believe me, don't you?"

"Yes," she said. She half-wondered what it was he knew and how he could be so sure, but he did not trouble to explain.

"Look here, Jennie," he said after a time. "You care for me, don't you? You don't think I'd sit here and plead with you if I didn't care for you. I'm crazy about you, and that's the literal truth. You're like wine to me. I want you to come with me. I want you to do it quickly. I know how difficult this family business is, but you can arrange it. Come with me down to New York. We'll work out something later. I'll meet your family. We'll pretend a courtship, anything you like—only come now."

"You don't mean right away, do you?" she asked, startled.

"Yes, tomorrow if possible. Monday sure. You can arrange it. Why, if Mrs. Bracebridge asked you, you'd go fast enough, and no one would think anything about it. Isn't that so?"

"Yes," she replied.

"Well, then, why not now?"

"It's always so much harder to work out a falsehood," she replied thoughtfully.

"I know it, but you can come. Won't you?"

"Won't you wait a little while?" she pleaded. "It's so very sudden. I'm afraid."

"Not a day, sweet, that I can help. Can't you see how I feel? Look at me. Look in my eyes. Will you?"

"Yes," she replied sorrowfully, and yet with a thrill of affection. "I will."

CHAPTER XXI

The business of arranging for this sudden departure was really not as difficult as it had appeared. Jennie proposed to tell her mother the whole truth, and there was nothing to say to her father except that she was going with Mrs. Bracebridge at the latter's request. He might question her, but he really could not doubt. There was no reason. Lester had convinced her of that.

Before going home, however, she accompanied Lester to a department store, where she was fitted out with a trunk, a travelling suit-case, a travelling suit and hat—the discriminating taste of her lover guiding her in the selection of the latter, although her own taste was sound. Lester was very proud of his prize and anxious to make her look beautiful, but he was sensible of the fact that much purchasing could not be done here. "When we get to New York I am going to get you some things," he said to her. "I am going to show you what you can be made to look like." He had all the purchased articles packed in the trunk and sent to his hotel. Then he arranged to have Jennie come there and dress Monday for the trip, which would begin in the afternoon.

Jennie was beside herself with the worry of telling her mother, excusing herself to Mrs. Bracebridge, preventing any of the family from accompanying her to the train, and telling her father, but it all came out all right, after all. She was worried about Vesta and the general outcome of her life, but after confiding in her mother, which was really the most difficult thing of all, she saw that it might be done.

When Jennie came home Mrs. Gerhardt, who was in the kitchen, received her with her usual affectionate greeting. "Have you been working very hard? You look tired."

"No," she said, "I'm not tired. It isn't that. I just don't feel good."

"What's the trouble?"

"Oh, I have to tell you something, Mama. It's so hard." She paused, looking inquiringly at her mother and then away.

"Why, what is it?" asked her mother nervously. So many things had happened in the past that she was always on the alert for additional troubles. "You haven't lost your place, have you?"

"No," replied Jennie, with an effort to maintain her mental poise, "but I'm going to leave it."

"No!" exclaimed her mother—"Why?"

"I'm going to New York."

Her mother's eyes opened. "Why, when did you decide to do that?"

"Today," said Jennie quietly.

Mrs. Gerhardt stared. "You don't mean it," she said.

"Yes, I do, Mama. Listen. I've got something I want to tell you. You know how poor we are. There isn't any way we can make things come out right. I have found someone who wants to help us. He says he loves me, and he wants me to go to New York with him Monday. I've decided to go."

"Oh, Jennie!" exclaimed her mother. "Surely not! You wouldn't do anything like that after all that's happened. Think of your father."

"Listen, Mama," went on Jennie. "Please let me tell you first. I've thought it all out. It's really for the best. He's a good man. I know he is. He has lots of money. I think he loves me. He wants me to go with him, and I'd better go. He will take a new house for us when we come back and help us to get along. He wants to help me."

"Why, Jennie, how you talk!" exclaimed her mother. "Don't you think your father will want to know? How are you going to explain your going?"

"Listen, Mama," continued Jennie almost tragically, "I've thought so long. I know how it will be. There really isn't any other way. No one will ever have me as a wife—you know that. It might as well be this way. He loves me. He will give me a good home some time—he says so. And I love him. Why shouldn't I go?"

"Does he know about Vesta?" asked her mother cautiously.

"No," said Jennie guiltily. "I thought I'd better not tell him about her. She oughtn't to be brought into it if I can help it."

"I'm afraid you're storing up trouble for yourself, Jennie," said her mother. "Don't you think he is sure to find it out some time?"

"I thought maybe that she could be kept here," suggested Jennie, "until she's old enough to go to school. Then maybe I could send her somewhere."

"She might," said her mother, "but don't you think it would be better to tell him now? He won't think any the worse of you."

"It isn't that. It's her," said Jennie passionately. "I don't want her brought into it."

Her mother shook her head. "Where did you meet him?" she inquired.

"At Mrs. Bracebridge's."

"How long ago?"

"Oh, it's been almost two months now."

"And you never said anything about him," reproached her mother.

"I didn't know that he cared for me this way," defended her daughter.

"Why didn't you wait and let him come out here first?" asked her mother. "It would make things so much easier. You can't go and not have your father find out."

"I thought I'd say I was going with Mrs. Bracebridge. She might take me. I wanted him to wait, but he won't. Papa can't object to my going with her."

"No," said her mother thoughtfully.

The two looked at each other in silence. Mrs. Gerhardt, with her imaginative nature, endeavored to formulate some picture of this wonderful personality that had intruded itself. He was wealthy; he wanted to take Jennie; he wanted to give them a good home. What a story! She drifted in her mood, contrasting their present state of poverty with that other of possible comfort.

"And he gave me this," put in Jennie, who somehow psychically had been following her mother's mood. She opened her dress at the neck and took out the two hundred and fifty dollars, which she gave to her mother.

The latter stared at it wide-eyed. Here was the solvent of all her woes, apparently—food, clothes, rent, coal, all the ills that poverty is heir to and all done up in one small package of green and yellow bills. If there were plenty of money in the house, Gerhardt need not worry about his burned hands; if there were means such as this, George and Martha and Veronica could be clothed in comfort and made happy. Jennie could dress better; there would be a future education for Vesta.

"Do you think he might ever want to marry you?" asked her mother finally.

"I don't know," replied Jennie. "He might. I know he loves me."

"Well," said her mother after a long pause, "if you're going to tell your father, you'd better do it right away. He'll think it's strange as it is."

Jennie realized that she had won. Her mother had acquiesced from sheer force of circumstances. She was sorry, but somehow it seemed to be better. "I think you'd better say something to him first," said Jennie, "and then I'll mention it afterward."

The difficulty of telling this lie was very great for Mrs. Gerhardt, but she went through the falsehood with a seeming nonchalance which allayed Gerhardt's suspicions. The children were also told, and when, after the general discussion, Jennie repeated the falsehood to her father, it seemed natural enough.

"How long do you think you'll be gone?" he inquired, a thing he had immediately asked her mother.

"About two or three weeks," she replied.

"That's a nice trip," he said. "I came through New York in 1844. It was a small place then compared to what it is now."

Secretly he was pleased that Jennie had this chance. Her employer must like her.

When Monday came, Jennie made the excuse that she would leave from the Bracebridge home with her employer and did not need any companionship. Mrs. Bracebridge would supply her with clothes. She bade her parents goodbye and left early, going straight to the Dornton, where Lester awaited her.

"So you came," he said gaily, greeting her as she entered the ladies' parlor.

"Yes," she said simply.

"You are my niece," he said. "I have engaged a room for you near mine. I'll call for the key, and you go dress. When you're ready, I'll have the trunk sent to the depot. That train leaves at one o'clock. We won't have so very long to wait after you're ready."

She went to her room and dressed, while he fidgeted about, read, smoked, and finally knocked at her door.

She replied by opening to him, fully clad.

"You look charming," he said.

She looked down, for she was nervous and distraught. The whole process of planning, lying, nerving herself to carry out her part had been hard on her. She looked tired and fearful.

"Not grieving, are you?" he asked, seeing how things were.

"No-o," she replied.

"Come now, sweet. You mustn't feel this way. It's all coming out all right." He took her arm, and they strolled down the hall. He was astonished to see how smart she looked in even these simple clothes—the best she had ever had.

When they reached the depot after a short carriage ride, he carried her grip, with quite a stride, through the waiting room to the train. All his accommodations had been arranged beforehand, and he had allowed just enough time to make the train.

When they settled themselves in a Pullman state-room it was with a keen sense of satisfaction on his part. Life looked rosy. Jennie was beside him. He had done successfully what he had started out to do. So might it always be.

The details of this long ride to New York, coming as a climax to her days of confusion, were enough to make her despondent for the time being. As the train rolled out of the depot and the long reaches of the fields succeeded, she studied them wistfully, the pathos of the landscape making her exceedingly sad. There were the forests, leafless and bare; the wide, brown fields, wet with the rains of winter; the low farm-houses sitting out amid the flat stretches of prairie, their low roofs making them look as if they were hugging the ground. Towns passed by, little hamlets with cottages of white and yellow and drab, their roofs blackened by frost and rain. Jennie looked out, and, seeing one such town, the outskirts of which bore some resemblance to the old neighborhood they had lived in at Columbus, and in which the lights of evening were already beginning to twinkle, put her handkerchief to her eyes and began silently to cry.

Lester, who was engrossed in a letter at the time, did not notice it, but happening to glance her way after a time and seeing the handkerchief, he said:

"I hope you're not crying, are you, Jennie?"

She did not answer. Something about the rain-washed fields, the low cottages and the poverty-stricken condition of her mother and father, whom she was leaving behind to struggle alone, filled her heart to breaking.

"Here! here!" he said, when he saw a faint tremor shaking her. "This won't do. You have to do better than this. You'll never get along if you act that way."

She still made no reply, and the depth of her silent grief filled him with strange sympathies.

"Don't cry," he continued soothingly. "Everything will be all right. I told you that. You needn't worry about anything."

Jennie, who could not help paying heed to one for whom she already had such a deep feeling, made a great effort to recover herself and began to dry her eyes.

"You don't want to give way like that," he continued. "It doesn't do you any good. I know how you feel about leaving home, but tears won't help it any. It isn't as if you were going away for good, you know. Besides, you'll be going back shortly. You care for me, don't you, sweet? I'm something?"

"Yes," she said.

He settled himself back reassuringly. Jennie, in whom the last remark had revivified the thought of their relationship, present and future, began to think of how she would dispose of Vesta in case her father discovered her liaison or refused to have anything to do with the new-house plan.

"I'll have to tell him some time," she thought with a sudden upwelling of feeling as regarded the seriousness of this duty. "If I don't do it soon, and I should go and live with him and he should find it out, he would never forgive me. He might turn me out, and then where would I go? I have no home now. What would I do with Vesta?"

She turned to contemplate him, a premonitory wave of terror sweeping over her, but she only saw that imposing and comfort-loving soul quietly reading his letters, his smoothly shaved red cheek and comfortable head and body looking anything but militant, or like an avenging nemesis. She was just withdrawing her gaze when he looked up.

"Well, have you washed all your sins away?" he inquired merrily.

She smiled faintly at the allusion. The touch of fact in it made it slightly piquant.

"I expect so," she replied.

"You'd make an excellent Mary Magdalene," he returned playfully. "You have the hair and the tears."

His countenance beamed with suppressed appreciation of his own humor, and Jennie smiled also, largely because he did.

"How can you talk that way?" she protested softly.

He only smiled and turned to some other topic while she looked out of the window, the realization dwelling in her mind that her impulse to tell him had proved unavailing. "I'll have to do it shortly," she thought, and consoled herself with the idea that she would surely find courage before long.

Their arrival in New York the next day raised the important question in Lester's mind as to where he would stop. New York was a very large place, and he was not in much danger of encountering people who would know him, but he thought it just as well not to take chances and had the cabman drive them to one of the more exclusive apartment hotels, where he engaged a suite of rooms. Here he was in no danger of meeting with any one who knew him and, accordingly, settled himself for a two or three weeks' stay, during which time he thought he would have inured Jennie to her new life and straightened things out for her at home.

"Better write your mother today," was one of the first suggestions he made after their arrival, and Jennie, who had been thinking of it more or less all the way, hastened to comply. She wanted to assure her mother that she was safe and happy as well as to relieve her mind of the burden of doubt as to how things were at home. If she could but establish relationship with her home now, so that her going would not have been in vain, she would be happy.

This atmosphere into which she was so quickly plunged was so wonderful, so illuminating, that she could scarcely believe this was the same world she had inhabited before. Kane was no lover of vulgar display. He had been raised in a conservative atmosphere and knew by instinct and training what true refinement and comfort consisted of. In the matter of dress his taste was exquisite. The appointments with which he surrounded himself were always simple and elegant. He selected the most exclusive hotels for his temporary resting places, patronized only the most reliable and judgement-worthy shops. He knew at a glance what Jennie needed, and he bought for her with discrimination and care. It was his pleasure on this occasion and afterward to explain forms and customs to her, to tell her quietly what she must and must not do. In a splendid suite of rooms, with shopkeepers delivering the purchases he made, with hats and dresses and shoes and lingerie to try on, she had little time to think, when she was with him, of the problems which had confronted her so recently. Could this be she, she asked herself, looking in the mirror of her boudoir at the figure of a girl clad in blue velvet, with yellow French lace at her throat and upon her arms? Could these be her feet, clad in soft, shapely shoes at ten dollars a pair, these her hands on which she was drawing gloves, which harmonized well with her dress? The hats he had purchased gave her face an archness of expression not dreamed of by her before. She, Jennie Gerhardt, the washer-woman's daughter. At the thought, tears sprang to her eyes. At least her mother should not want now any more.

It was Lester's pleasure in these days to see what he could do with her to make her look like someone truly worthy of him. He exercised his most careful judgement, and the result surprised even himself. People turned in the halls, in the dining-rooms, on the street, in their carriages when they were driving, to see her.

"That is a stunning woman that man has with him," was a frequent comment.

Despite her altered state, Jennie did not lose her judgement of life or her sense of perspective or proportion. She had known in a vague way that these things existed. Now she felt as though life were tentatively loaning her something which would be taken away after a time. There was no instilling vanity in her bosom. Lester realized this as he watched her. "You're a big woman in your way," he said. "You'll amount to something. Life hasn't given you much of a deal up to now."

He wondered how he would adjust this relationship with his family, if they heard about it, for he realized that this was no temporary thing. If he should ever decide to take a house in Chicago or St. Louis (there was such a thought running in his mind), could he maintain it secretly? Did he want to? He was half-persuaded that he really, truly loved her.

As the time drew near for their return be began to counsel her wisely. "You ought to get some method of introducing me as an acquaintance to your father," he said. "It will ease matters up. I think I'll call. I wish your people lived in a different sort of neighborhood. All your father wants to straighten this thing out is to see me once or twice. Then if you tell him you're going to marry me, he'll think nothing of it."

She blanched at the thought of deception in regard to Vesta, but decided afterward that perhaps her father could be persuaded to say nothing about the child for the time being. He might do that.

One of the sanest things Lester had suggested was for her to retain the clothes she had worn in Cleveland in order that she might wear them home when she reached there. "There won't be any trouble about this other stuff," he said. "I'll have it cared for until we make some other arrangement." It was all very simple and easy; he was a master strategist.

Jennie had written her mother almost daily since she had been East. She had enclosed little separate notes to be read by her mother only. In one she explained Lester's desire to call, and urged her mother to prepare the way by telling her father she had met someone who liked her. She spoke of the difficulty concerning Vesta, and her mother at once began to plan a campaign to have her husband keep silence. There must be no hitch now. Jennie must be given an opportunity to better herself.

When she returned there was great rejoicing. Of course she could not go back to her work, but Mrs. Gerhardt explained that Mrs. Bracebridge had given Jennie a few weeks' vacation in order that she might look for something better, something at which she could make more money.

CHAPTER XXII

The problem of the Gerhardt family and its relationship to himself comparatively settled, Kane betook himself to Cincinnati and those commercial duties that ordinarily held him in reasonable check. He was heartily interested in the immense plant, which occupied two whole blocks in the outskirts of the city, and the theory of its conduct and development was as much a problem and a pleasure to him as to either his father or brother. He liked to think of the immense office building in the heart of the business section of Cincinnati, of its far-reaching ramifications. Carriages were shipped to Australia and South America and China. He liked to feel that he was a part of it, necessary, vital. When he saw freight cars going by on the railroads labelled "The Kane Manufacturing Company—Cincinnati" or witnessed in the windows of minor carriage sales companies in the different cities displays of the company's products, he was conscious of a moderate glow of satisfaction. It was something to be a factor in an institution so stable, so distinguished, so honestly worth while. Everyone gladly recognized him as a personage because of this. He and his brother and his father were big men in consequence.

It is one thing to have a thought like this and another to live up to it, for every important business personage realizes that there is an obligation to energy, to decency, to right conduct and social appearance which comes with great commercial responsibility and may not easily be ignored. If one is not a stockholder merely but an active participant in the urgent conduct of a big business, it is necessary to observe the social conventions; for if one is in the commercial and social limelight, one's every deed and action is critically scanned. A man may not vary in honesty and prosper long—certainly not in *great* commercial matters—and in the arrangement of his private life he cannot afford to swing too far from the social understanding of what is right and proper. People begin to criticize even the scions of great carriage companies, and it is not possible to long lead a life of duplicity or subtlety in matters of sex relationship. The public is exceedingly critical— was perhaps more so at that time than later. He was conscious as he rode toward his home city that he was entering on a relation- ship which might involve disagreeable consequences. Still he was strong for the spirit and character of the girl he had found. He thought she was lovely. He proposed to make as hearty an effort to retain this relationship inconspicuously as he could. He was a little afraid of his father's attitude, and that of his mother and brother and sisters if they should find out. His father was such a good, religious, moral man. He hated to offend him.

Another personage whom he had to consider seriously in all that he did was his brother Robert. The latter being so straight- laced, so vital, so energetic, was in a way an uninvited standard of conduct thrust upon him, whether he would have it or no. Robert's strict attention to business; his constant observance of the conventions of trade progress; his insistence that men must conduct themselves righteously in matters, morals, and their private lives irritated Lester. He knew that his brother was not warm-hearted or generous—would in fact turn any trick which could be speciously, or at best necessitously, recommended to his conscience. How he reasoned Lester did not know—he could not follow the ramifications of a logic which could combine hard business tactics with social and moral rigidity, but his brother managed to do it. "He's got a Scotch Presbyterian conscience mixed with an Asiatic perception of the main chance," Lester once told somebody, and he had the situation accurately mea- sured. Nevertheless he could not rout his brother from his posi- tions or defy him, for somehow he had the public conscience with him. He was in line with convention—practically, advisably, perhaps sophisticatedly. There was no answer but to look out.

Actually Robert was not so anxious to see Lester prosper.

Although he liked him well enough personally, he did not trust his financial judgement, and, temperamentally, they did not agree as to how life and its affairs should be conducted. Lester had a secret contempt for his brother's chill, persistent chase of the almighty dollar. Robert was sure that Lester's easy-going ways were reprehensible, and bound to create trouble sooner or later. In the business they did not quarrel much,—there was not much chance with the old gentleman still in charge—but there were certain minor differences constantly cropping up which showed which way the wind blew.

For one thing, the treatment of old employés was a thing which had never been settled to their mutual satisfaction. Robert was for running the business on a hard and cold basis, dropping the aged, who had grown up with his father, and cleaning out the "dead wood" as he called it. Lester had stood in counsel for a more humane course.

"I'm not going to see these old fellows who have grown up with this business thrown out bag and baggage, without anything, if I can help it. It isn't right. This house has made money. It can afford to be decent. I know a business has got to be conducted on a hard and fast basis in the main, but this thing of cleaning them all out without anything don't appeal to me. We could afford to get up a pension scheme which would take care of the most deserving. This house has made money."

"There you go, Lester, saddling a new item on the cost of production," protested his brother. "But it isn't wise. This house is in the lead today, but there are other carriage companies. We can't afford to take any more chances or saddle ourselves with any more expense than if we were beginners. The business of this concern is to make money, just as much as it can. If you want to do something for these people privately afterward, that's your business. Besides, we won't own it all after father's death. It's got to be run in the interest of all concerned."

Nothing was done about this at the time—Kane senior was too kindly to let any radical action be taken—but he was rather inclined to agree with Robert commercially, though sympathetically and ethically he thought that Lester had the more decent end of the argument.

These two brothers clashed on other minor points, always in a rather good-natured way. Lester was for building up trade through friendly relationships, concessions, personal contacts and favors. Robert was for pulling everything tight, cutting down the cost of production, and offering such financial inducements as would throttle competition. "I believe there is something in your method," he would say. "Father worked that way pretty much. But *you* would have to do it. I think the other idea is better. It certainly is for me. If this business holds its own it's got to come to it, unless I'm greatly mistaken. But for heaven's sake don't listen to me—" (this to his father) "I don't own it. And I'm perfectly willing to get out eventually. There's money in other lines that interest me quite as much."

The old manufacturer always did his best to pour oil on these troubled waters, but he foresaw an eventual clash. One or the other would have to get out, or perhaps both. Perhaps it would be divided up and sold before he died. "If only you two boys could agree," he used to say.

"I like Lester," his brother would reply. "He's too easy for his own good, though. He won't get anywhere by taking the other fellow into consideration."

Kane senior agreed with this also, but he liked Lester's attitude. It was kindly. He wished it could be worked out in connection with the success of the company.

Another thing which disturbed Lester in his relationship to women was his father's attitude on the subject of marriage—*his* marriage, to be specific. Never, in all the years that Lester had been gaily flitting about, had his father ceased to insist on the fact that he ought to get married and that he was making a big mistake not to. All the other children, save Louise, were safely married. Why not his favorite son? It was doing him injury morally, socially, commercially—that he was sure of.

"The world expects it of a man in your position," his father had argued from time to time. "It makes for social solidity and prestige. You ought to pick a good woman and raise a family. Where will you be when you get to my time of life if you haven't any children, any home? God ordained one system of procedure. If you don't work it out that way, you'll be sorry."

"Don't argue, father," his son would retort. They were loving in their relationship to each other. "I know all about that. If the right woman came along, I suppose I'd marry her. But she hasn't come along. What do you want me to do?—take anybody?"

"No, not anybody, of course, but there are lots of good women. You can surely find someone if you try. There's that Pace girl. What about her? You used to like her. I wouldn't drift on this way, Lester; it can't come to any good."

His son would only smile. "There, father, let it go now. You see where we get. I'll come around some time, no doubt. I've got to be thirsty when I'm led to water."

The old gentleman gave over, time and again, but it was a sore point with him. He wanted his son to settle down and be a real man of affairs.

The fact that such a situation as this might militate against any permanent arrangement he might make with Jennie was obvious even to him at this time. In all his philanderings in times past, and there had been quite a respectable number of them, he had never allowed any woman to get a social grip on him. He had never taken an apartment or house for any one. He had contributed to one or two that had been established before his time, but in a round-about way. He was careful of what he wrote and what he said, but this affair with Jennie had somehow taken on a different turn, and he was not interested to see it work out any other way. Jennie was not dangerous. She was trying to run from him. She did not understand what he meant by lavishing things upon her. Hence it was a pleasure to do it. There was a real joy in it. It was like showing a child something of the joy of living.

As he worked at his desk in the office of the company, bringing his correspondence up to date, or sat about the house with his father and mother and sister, or joined in the social engagements which were always being planned or executed, he thought of this thing of living with Jennie,—of continuing this relationship. Where? Could he bring her to Cincinnati? What a scandal if it were ever found out! Could he install her in a nice home somewhere near the city? The family would probably, eventually, suspect something. Could he take her along on his numerous business journeys? This first one to New York had been successful. Would it always be so? He turned the question over in his mind. The very difficulty gave it zest. Perhaps St. Louis or Pittsburgh or Chicago would be best after all. He went to these places frequently, Chicago most of all. He decided finally that it should be Chicago, if he could arrange it. He could make excuses to run up there. It was only a night's ride. Besides, she could always come to him quickly if he wired. Yes, Chicago was best. The very largeness and hustle of it made concealment easy.

After two week's stay at Cincinnati he wrote her that he was coming to Cleveland soon and received word that she thought it would be all right for him to come out. Her father had been told of him. She had felt it unwise to stay about the house and had gotten a place in a store at four dollars a week, though her father and brothers and sisters thought it was more. He smiled as he thought of her working, and yet the decency and energy of it appealed to him. "She's all right," he said. "She's the best I've come across yet."

He ran up to Cleveland the following Saturday, and, calling at her place of business, made an appointment to see her that evening and to call the next day. He was anxious that his intro-duction, as her beau, should be gotten over with as quickly as possible. When he did call, the whole shabby condition of the house, its confined nature, disgusted him in a way; but somehow Jennie seemed as sweet to him as ever. Gerhardt came in the front room, after Lester had been there a few minutes, and shook hands with him, as did Mrs. Gerhardt, but Lester paid little attention to them. The old German appeared to him to be merely com-monplace. These were such people as his foremen hired. He suggested after a few minutes that they seek a livery stable and go for a drive. Jennie put on her things, and together they departed. As a matter of fact, they went to an apartment retained by him to store her clothes. When she returned at eight in the evening, the family considered it nothing amiss.

CHAPTER XXIII

I t was only a little time after this, a month in all, before Jennie was able to announce that Lester intended to marry her. Lester's visits had of course paved the way for this, and it seemed natural enough. She had come to be looked upon in the family as some-thing rather out of the ordinary, for somehow things seemed to happen to Jennie. She got in with astonishing people; she seemed to see more of the world; she was constantly doing something out of the ordinary. Gerhardt, the only one whom she was really anxious to placate, was of course doubtful. He did not know just how this might be. Perhaps it was all right. Lester seemed a fine enough man in all conscience—too fine, in fact—but after Brander, why not? If a United States Senator could fall in love with Jennie, even as terrible as he had been, why not a business man? He thought about this and finally concluded that it might be all right, but only after considerable talk between him and his wife. The latter had to explain the two drives which Jennie had taken on the two times when Lester had called. Her suggestion was that it was natural enough (and it was) that so fine a man should not want to stay in so poor a home, and Gerhardt to a certain extent acquiesced in that thought. Certainly there was no harm in their driving Sundays. When the announcement was made, through Mrs. Gerhardt, that he had asked her to marry him and was going to take her to Chicago for the time being, the children thought it was a great thing for her. Gerhardt frowned. "Has she told him about the child?" he asked.

"No," replied his wife, "not yet."

"Not yet, not yet. Always something underhanded. Do you think he wants her if he knows? That's what comes of such conduct in the first place. Now she has to slip around like a thief. The child cannot even have an honest name."

Gerhardt went back to his newspaper reading and brooding. His life seemed a complete failure to him.

However, there was nothing to do except wait. Time might not work things out so disastrously. As for him, he was only waiting to be well enough to hunt up another job as a watchman. He wanted to get out of this mess of poverty and earn something.

In another little while Jennie confided to her mother that Lester had written her to come to Chicago. He was not feeling well. He did not want to come to Cleveland. The two women explained to Gerhardt that Jennie was going away to be married to Mr. Kane. Gerhardt flared up at this, and his suspicions were again aroused. But he could do nothing but grumble over the situation; it would lead to no good end, of that he was sure.

When the time came, Jennie prepared to go without saying anything to her father. He was out looking for work until late in the afternoon, and before he had returned she had bid the others goodbye. "I will write a note to him when I get there," she said. She kissed her baby over and over. "Lester will take a better house for us soon," she said. "He wants us to move." She talked as though she might not be going to stay in Chicago herself. The night train bore her to Chicago; the old life had ended and the new one had begun.

A curious thing should be recorded here: although Lester's intimacy with her had relieved the stress of family finances since the night she gave her mother the money he had given her, the children and Gerhardt were actually none the wiser. It was easy for Mrs. Gerhardt to deceive her husband as to the purchase of necessities, and she had not yet indulged in any of the fancies which an enlarged purse permitted. Fear deterred her. But Jennie had given her mother nearly all she had received from Lester and had advised her, against the time when they could spend, that the children should have good clothes, that a comfortable sitting-room and dining-room should be arranged, and that her mother was to have her almost-faded dream, a parlor. After she had been in Chicago for a few days, this came to pass, for she wrote that Lester wanted them to take a new home. This letter was shown to Gerhardt, who had been merely biding her return to make a scene. He frowned, but somehow it seemed an evidence of regularity. If he had not married her, why should he want to help them? Mrs. Gerhardt spoke of the large sum of money Jennie had sent, all she had been saving, and this also seemed a pretty strong proof of something—affection certainly. Perhaps Jennie was well married after all. Had she really been lifted to a high station? The man was a strong man, no doubt of that. He was rather a nice fellow too. Really, Gerhardt almost forgave her—not quite; but she was generous, that was sure.

The end of it all, so far as the Gerhardt household was concerned, was that a new home was really taken. At the end of a month, because of an enforced absence on the part of Lester, and with his advice, Jennie returned to Cleveland to help her mother move. Together they searched the streets for a nice, quiet neighborhood and finally found one. A house of nine rooms, with a yard, which rented for thirty dollars, was secured; and suitable furniture was installed, for Lester had cautioned her that she might want to be there a part of the time—that he might want to come occasionally. He advised her how to buy intelligently. There was a complete and interesting set of fittings for the dining-room, a nice, quiet arrangement of furniture for the sitting-room, a parlor set to gratify her mother, and bedroom sets complete for each room. The kitchen was supplied with every convenience, and there was even a bath room, a luxury the Gerhardts had never enjoyed before. Altogether the house was attractive, though plain, and Jennie was happy to know that her family could be comfortable in it.

When the time came for the actual moving Mrs. Gerhardt was fairly beside herself with joy, for was not this now the realization of her dream? All through the long years of her life she had been waiting for this. Now it had come. A new house, new furniture, plenty of room—things finer than she had ever seen. Her eyes shone as she looked at the new beds and tables and bureaus and whatnots. "Dear, dear, isn't this nice!" she exclaimed. "Isn't it beautiful!" She rubbed her hands and looked at Jennie, and once she squeezed her arm. Jennie smiled and tried to pretend satisfaction without emotion, but there were tears in her eyes. She was so glad for her mother's sake. She could have kissed Lester's feet for this service he had rendered her family.

The day the furniture was being moved in, her mother, Martha, and Veronica were on hand to clean and arrange things. At the sight of the large rooms and pretty yard, bare enough in winter but giving promise of a delightful greenness in spring, as well as the array of new furniture standing about in excelsior, the whole family, with the exception of Gerhardt, caught a fever of delight. Such beauty, such expansiveness! George rubbed his feet over the new carpets when he came home. Bass examined the quality of the furniture critically. "Swell," was his comment. Mrs. Gerhardt roved to and fro like a person in a dream. She could not believe that this was the place she was to live from now on—these bright bedrooms, this beautiful parlor, this handsome dining-room. She finally settled herself in the kitchen, the best equipped of its kind she had ever had. "It's beautiful," she said.

Gerhardt came last of all. Somehow he desired to linger about the old place until all was moved out. When he was led through the new house, he was subtly affected by the comparative luxury which had descended upon him. Although he tried hard not to show it, he could scarcely refrain from enthusiastic comment. The sight of an opal-globed chandelier over the dining-room table shocked him into a realization of one luxury hitherto not enjoyed.

"Gas, yet!" he said.

He looked grimly around, under his shaggy eyebrows, at the new carpets under his feet, at the long oak extension table covered with a white cloth and set with new dishes, at the pictures on the walls, at the bright, clean kitchen. He shook his head. "By chops! it's fine," he said. "It's very nice. Yes, it's very nice. We want to be careful now not to break anything. It's so easy to scratch things up, and then it's all over."

Experience in raising a family had taught him that.

CHAPTER XXIV

The fact that Lester did not at this time permanently establish Jennie in a home of her own was due to certain chilling complications at the commercial and social ends of his life. It appeared that in spite of his personal precautions, someone had seen him in New York who knew him and had reported the fact that he was with a girl. The details had not been received straight but they were sufficiently circumstantial to give rise to the report that he was secretly married—this among a few intimate friends of the family. Kane senior was of course greatly shocked at this report, though he did not believe it. Mrs. Kane, a woman who had always retained the highest social ambitions for her children, was beside herself with chagrin and mortification. Both parents were good Catholics, and if there was nothing in the secret marriage report there was still the sin and disgrace of an immoral relationship. Kane senior had Robert write Lester for him about the report,—for Lester had already gone to Chicago— saying that he was sure there was nothing in it but would like to know from him direct. He proposed to talk to him when he returned.

Lester, living with Jennie at an inconspicuous but comfortable family hotel on the North Side, swore under his breath. "I would better do nothing about this at this time," he thought. "It's too warm a trail." It was for that reason that he urged Jennie to return to Cleveland and get her family located in a new home. Later he would adjust the relationship on a better basis. He used to kiss her and tell her that he thought he would be able eventually to marry her. "You don't know what's back of me, though," he said to her.

Jennie, loving consciously and deeply for the first time, felt the wonder and joy of this. "I would be so happy, Lester," she said.

At the same time there swept over her the cloud of misrepresentation, or non-representation, in regard to Vesta. "If he should find out now," she thought. Several times she thought of making a confession and then, not the fact that Vesta would be injured by this relationship (she did believe that now), but what Lester would think of her deterred her. He seemed decidedly antagonistic to children. He did not want to have any.

It was decided then that she should return to Cleveland and that later some other arrangement would be made.

It would be useless to chronicle the events of the three years that followed—events and experiences by which the family grew from an abject condition of want to a state of comparative self-reliance, based of course on the obvious prosperity of Jennie and the generosity (through her) of her *soi-disant* husband. Lester was seen now and then, a significant figure, coming to Cleveland, sometimes coming out to the house, where he occupied with Jennie the two best rooms of the second floor. There were hurried trips on her part, in answer to telegraph messages, to Chicago, to St. Louis, to New York. One of his favorite pastimes was to engage quarters at the great resorts—Hot Springs, Mt. Clemens, and Saratoga—and, for a period of a week or two at a stretch, enjoy the luxury of living with Jennie as his wife. There were other times when he would pass through Cleveland only for the privilege of seeing her for a day. All the time he was aware that he was throwing on her the real burden of a rather difficult situation, but he did not see how he could remedy it at this time. He was not sure as yet that he really wanted to. They were getting along fairly well.

The attitude of the Gerhardt family toward this condition of affairs was peculiar. At first, in spite of the irregularity of it, it seemed natural enough. Jennie said she was married. They had not seen her marriage certificate, but she said she was married, and she seemed to carry herself with the air of one who holds that relationship. Still she never went to Cincinnati, where his family lived, and none of his relatives ever came near her. Then, too, his attitude, in spite of the money which had first blinded them, was peculiar. He really did not carry himself like a married man. He was so indifferent. There were weeks in which she appeared to receive only perfunctory notes. There were times when she would only go away for a few days to meet him. Then there were the longer periods in which she absented herself—the only worth while testimony toward a real relationship, and that in a way unnatural.

Bass, who had grown to be a young man of twenty-five with some business judgement and a desire to get out in the world, was suspicious. He had come to have a pretty keen knowledge of life, and intuitively he felt that things were not right. George, nineteen, who had gained a slight foothold in a wall-paper factory and was looking forward to a career in that field, was also restless. He felt that something was wrong. Martha, seventeen, was still in school, as were William and Veronica—each offered an opportunity to study indefinitely—but there was unrest with life. They knew about Jennie's child. The neighbors were obviously drawing conclusions for themselves. They had few friends. Gerhardt himself finally concluded that there was something wrong, but he had let himself into this situation and was not in much of a position now to raise an argument. He wanted to ask her at times— proposed to make her do better if he could—but the worst had already been done. It depended on Lester now, he knew that.

Things were gradually nearing a state where a general upheaval would have taken place had not life stepped in with one of its fortuitous solutions. Mrs. Gerhardt's health failed. Although stout and formerly of a fairly active disposition, she had of late years become decidedly sedentary in her habits and this, coupled with a mind naturally given to worry, and weighed upon as it had been by a number of serious and disturbing ills, seemed now to culminate in a slow but very certain case of systemic poisoning. She became decidedly sluggish in her motions, wearied more quickly at the few tasks left for her to do, and finally complained to Jennie that it was very hard for her to climb stairs. "I'm not feeling well," she said. "I think I'm going to be sick."

Jennie now took alarm and proposed to take her to some nearby watering place, but Mrs. Gerhardt wouldn't go. "I don't think it would do any good," she said. She sat about or went buggy-riding with her daughter, but the fading autumn scenery depressed her. "I don't like to get sick in the fall," she said. "The leaves coming down make me think I am never going to get well."

"Oh, Ma, how you talk!" said Jennie, but she felt frightened nevertheless.

How much the average home depends upon the mother was seen when it was feared the end was near. Bass, who had thought of getting married and getting out of this atmosphere for good, abandoned this idea temporarily. Gerhardt, shocked and greatly depressed, hung about like one expectant of and greatly awed by the possibility of disaster. Jennie, too inexperienced in death to feel that she could possibly lose her mother, felt as if somehow her living depended on her. Hoping in spite of all opposing circumstances, she hung about, a white figure of patience, waiting and serving.

The end came one morning after a month of illness and several days of unconsciousness, during which silence reigned in the house and all the family went about on tiptoe. It was on a fine, bracing November morning, when the flaming light on the decaying leaves and clear water of the lake would have boded a delaying return of strength, that Mrs. Gerhardt breathed her last, looking at Jennie in a few minutes of consciousness that life vouchsafed her at the very end. Jennie stared into her eyes with a yearning horror. "Oh, Mama! Mama!" she cried. "Oh, no, no!"

Gerhardt came running in from the yard, and, throwing himself down by the bed, wrung his bony hands in anguish. "I should have gone first!" he cried. "I should have gone first!"

The end of Mrs. Gerhardt at once made certain the dissolution of the family. Although, hitherto, there had been some hesitancy on the part of the children to do anything which would actually disrupt this rather complete household, now it seemed almost the only thing to do. Jennie could not be there all the time. Bass was bent on getting married at once, having had a girl in tow for some time. Martha, whose views of life had broadened and hardened, was anxious to get out also. She felt that a sort of stigma attached to the home—to herself, in fact, so long as she remained there. The fact that Jennie was serviceable and kindly was neither here nor there. Her life had been a failure, made so by herself, Martha thought, and a bad life at that. So she looked to the public schools as a source of income and soon stated that she was going to be a teacher. Gerhardt, alone, scarcely knew which way to turn. He was now a night-watchman. Jennie found him crying one day alone in the kitchen and immediately cried herself. "Now, Papa!" she pleaded, "it isn't as bad as that. You will always have a home,—you know that—as long as I have anything. You can come with me."

"No, no," he protested. He really did not want to go with her. "It isn't that," he continued. "My whole life comes to nothing."

It was some little time before Bass, George and Martha finally left, but, one by one, they got out, leaving Jennie, her father, Veronica and William. Gerhardt thought of going when she should get a home of her own. He did not think Lester would want her to live in Cleveland. He came there so little. During all of this tragic readjustment, he had not been able to be there once, though Jennie had gone to see him.

The history of the little outcast Vesta during these three years of comparative prosperity had been one of growth and rehabilitation in so far as her original arch-opponent—Gerhardt—was concerned. From having been accepted as a human being with a soul worth saving at the time of his first visit to Cleveland and her baptism, on through the gloomy days of the Lorrie Street house where he had noted the progress of her growth (at those odd intervals when he could find it convenient to come home for a few days), on through the period when he had sat about the house with burned hands and watched her play, an irritating yet captivating bundle of activity, he had come by degrees to be immensely fond of her. It was not her fault that she was nameless. She had not willed to come into the world. It was Jennie who had committed the great crime against her, and it was Jennie who was still refusing to make things right for her. For her sake—Jennie's—during the time he thought she was going to be honestly married (had found an honest lover), he had consented, because of his wife's persuasion, to say nothing of Vesta or of Jennie's past history, to help keep her in the background and thoroughly concealed. He had continued to do this during these years in which they had lived in the new home because Lester, according to Jennie, was to be told some day when she was sure of herself. Mrs. Gerhardt had always pleaded for Jennie with him—that he should not make trouble. "She is getting along all right now. Why do you want to stir up a fuss? He might leave her. You don't know how hard it may be for her to fix this thing with him. She will when she can."

Gerhardt fumed. Such deception! Such crookedness! "The Lord God will surely punish her," he declared in German. "Mark my words. There will be punishment come to her for this."

"Oh, don't predict," demanded Mrs. Gerhardt. "She's had trouble enough. Why don't you let her alone?"

"Let her alone! Let her alone!" he emphasized. "As though I had not been letting her alone. It's just that. If I had not let her alone, she would be a better woman today." But he did not tell Lester.

And that worthy had never even seen the child. During the short periods in which he deigned to visit the house—two or three days at most, Mrs. Gerhardt took good care that Vesta was kept in the background. There was a playroom on the top floor and a bedroom there, and it was easy to do it. Lester rarely left his rooms. He preferred to be with Jennie, who served his meals to him in what might have been called the living room of the suite. He was not at all inquisitive or anxious to meet or see any of the other members of the family. He was perfectly willing to shake hands with them—to exchange a few perfunctory words, but perfunctory words only. It was generally understood that the child must not appear, and so she did not.

There was a lovelier side to her sordid story, however, for Gerhardt, who realized the pity of this, was both father and mother to her, though he did not outstrip Jennie in attentions and affection when opportunity permitted. She was sorry enough in all conscience, but unwitting as to how to bring about the desired result. Lester was boorish in his attitude at times—so gruff. She was afraid to tell him because of the terrific scene she imagined would follow.

There is an inexplicable affinity between old age and child-hood which is as lovely as it is pathetic. During that very first year in Lorrie Street, when no one was looking Gerhardt had carried Vesta on his shoulders and pinched her soft red cheeks. When she got old enough to walk, he it was who, with a towel pulled securely under her arms, led her cheerfully and patiently about, awaiting the time when she would be able to take a few steps of her own accord. When she actually reached the place where she could walk, he was the one who coaxed her to the effort, shyly, grimly, mostly when he was alone, but always lovingly. By some strange hocus-pocus of fate this stigma on his family's honor, this blotch on conventional morality, had twined its helpless baby fingers about the tendons of his heart. He loved this little outcast—vigorously, hopefully. She was the one bright ray in a gloomy, pathetic life, and he was always wondering what her fortune was to be—whether Jennie was going to eventually acknowledge her to Lester and give her a good home or whether the child, like so many others, was to be kicked from pillar to post in this world, made a by-word and a scoffing because of her history, and left without anything eventually to sanctify the fact that she had lived. It was a difficult line of thought.

It was during this most halcyon period, which now ensued after they moved into the new house, that Gerhardt showed his finest traits of fatherhood toward the little outcast. "He is trying to teach her to say her prayers," Mrs. Gerhardt had once informed Jennie after she had privately noted his progress in that direction with the lisping child for some little time.

"Say 'Our Father,'" he used to demand of the toddling infant when he had her alone with him.

"Ow Fowvah," was her vowel-like interpretation of his sounds.

"'Who art in heaven.'"

"Ooh ah in aven," repeated the child.

"Why do you teach her so early?" demanded Mrs. Gerhardt when she heard him—pity for the little one's struggles with consonants and vowels moving her.

"Because I want she should learn the Christian faith," returned Gerhardt determinedly. "She ought to know her prayers. If she don't begin now she never will know them."

Mrs. Gerhardt smiled. Many of her husband's religious idiosyncrasies were amusing to her. At the same time she liked to see this sympathetic interest he was taking in the child's upbringing. If he were only not so hard, so narrow at times. He made himself a torture to himself and everyone else.

Every night thereafter it was the same, and, now that he had disclosed his interest in her, his worry over her future got the better of him, and he was constantly talking about what ought to be done about her life.

On the earliest bright morning of returning spring, he was wont to take her for her first toddlings abroad. "Come, now," he would say, "we will go for a little walk."

"Walk," chirped Vesta.

"Yes, walk," echoed Gerhardt.

Mrs. Gerhardt would sometimes fasten on one of Vesta's little hoods, for in these days Jennie kept her wardrobe beautifully replete. Taking her by the hand, Gerhardt would issue forth, satisfied to drag first one foot and then the other in order that her toddling step should be accommodated.

Everywhere nature was budding and bustling—the birds twittering their arrival from the south, the insects making their lively, gay use of a brief life. Sparrows chirped in the road; robins strutted upon the grass; bluebirds built in the eaves of simple cottages. He was eager to explain the marvels of life as they appeared to her wondering eyes.

"Oooh!—ooh!" exclaimed Vesta, catching sight of a low flashing touch of red as a robin lighted upon a twig nearby. Her little hand was up, and her eyes wide.

"Yes," said Gerhardt, as happy as if he himself had but newly discovered this marvelous creature. "Robin. Bird. Robin. Say robin."

"Wobin," said Vesta.

"Yes, robin," he answered. "It is going to look for a worm now. It will build a nest. Do you know what a nest is?"

Vesta had no idea of what his learned exposition was all about, and was not paying the slightest attention. Her little head was twisted as far backwards as a short, yielding neck would allow, the receding wonders of the world behind receiving her strict attention.

"Yes, that is a robin," went on Gerhardt unheeded. "We will look once now, and see if we cannot find a nest. I think I saw a nest in one of these trees."

He plodded peacefully on, seeking to rediscover an old abandoned nest that he had observed, discoursing betimes. "Here it is," he said at last, coming to a small and still leafless tree in which a winter-beaten remnant of a home was still clinging. "Here, come now, see," and he lifted her high up.

Vesta rose into the empyrean, glad to be able to soar so, but not much understanding or caring for a reason.

"See," said Gerhardt, indicating the wisp of dead grasses with his free hand. "Nest. That is a bird's nest. See!"

"Ooh!" repeated Vesta, imitating his pointing finger with one of her own. "Ness—ooh."

"Yes," said Gerhardt, putting her down again. "That was a *wren's* nest. They have all gone now. They will not come any more."

Still further they plodded, he expounding the simple facts of life, she wondering with the wide wonder of a child. When they had gone a block or two he turned slowly about, as if the end of the world had been reached.

"We must be going back," he said.

So through her first, second, third, fourth and fifth years she had come up, growing in sweetness, intelligence, vivacity. He was fascinated by the questions she asked, the puzzles she propounded. "Such a girl!" he would exclaim to his wife. "What is it she doesn't want to know? 'Where is God? What does He do? Where does He keep His feet?' she asks me. I gotta laugh sometimes." From rising in the morning to dress her to laying her down at night after she had said her prayers, she came to be the chief source of comfort of his days. It was something of this thought that had wrought tears when Jennie found him. Without this child, this outcast, his life was surely coming to a lonely end.

CHAPTER XXV

In the home of the Kane family at Cincinnati there were also things transpiring which made it look as though readjustments would have to take place in that quarter. During the last three years in which Lester had been thus tentatively associated with Jennie at his convenience, his attitude had changed considerably, although he himself was not aware of it. Unconsciously and indifferently he had come to think more of her as a worth while companion—soul-mate or affinity, had those terms been invented at that time—had come to rely upon her services, which were legion, when he was with her, and to rather look forward to reunion with her from time to time, solely because her presence was grateful to him. On the other hand, the fascination of the world, toward which he should have drawn, was less. His interest in the social affairs of Cincinnati was practically *nil.* His interest in any matrimonial proposition which had himself as the object was the same. He looked on his father's business organization as offering a real chance for himself if he could get control of it, but he saw no way of doing it. Robert was in charge equally with him, and offering the same persistent opposition, the same criticism, the same arguments that the methods of the house ought to be changed. Lester thought once or twice of entering some other line of business or allying himself with some other carriage company, but he did not feel that he could conscientiously do this. On the other hand his brother was going ahead, making outside investments out of money made by investments he had made before. He was being spoken of as a coming man in Cincinnati, a budding financial genius. Certain rumors of profitable street-railway investments on his part were abroad. Lester heard of these, and it irritated him. What was Robert doing? At the same time he was not sure that he himself wanted to do anything much. He had his salary, fifteen thousand a year, as secretary and treasurer of the company—(his brother was vice-president)—and about five thousand from some outside investments. He had not been as lucky or as shrewd in the deals he had made as Robert had been; aside from the principal which yielded his five thousand, he had nothing. Robert, on the other hand, was unquestionably worth between three and four hundred thousand dollars aside from the interest in the business, which both brothers shrewdly suspected would be divided somewhat in their favor. Robert and himself would get a fourth each, they thought, their sisters a sixth. It seemed natural that Kane senior should do this, seeing that they were obviously in control and doing the work. Still there was no certainty. The old gentleman might do anything or nothing. The probabilities were that he would be very fair and liberal. At the same time, Robert was obviously beating Lester in the game of life. What did Lester intend to do about it?

There comes a time in every thinking man's life when he pauses and "takes stock" of his condition, when he asks himself how it fares with his individuality as a whole—mental, moral, physical, material. This time comes after the first heedless flights of youth have passed, when the initiative and powerful efforts have been made, and he begins to feel the uncertainty of result and final value which attaches to everything. There is a deadening thought of uselessness which creeps into many men's minds—a thought which has been best expressed in Ecclesiastes where the preacher finds nothing new under the sun.

Although Lester did not consider himself either a mental, moral or any other kind of failure at this time, nevertheless this great illusive glitter of the other man was in his eye. Although he knew as well as any one that the majority of public reputations were mere tinsel at best, that the sum and substance of every individual's life was unrest and dissatisfaction, nevertheless he was beset by hours of dissatisfaction with himself, with the smallness of his accomplishments and with the manner in which he was drifting along, having a good time.

"What difference does it make?" he used to say by way of self-consolation, "whether I live at the White House or here at home, or at the Grand Pacific?" But in the very question was the implication that there was some difference which he felt like consoling himself for. The White House represented the rise and achievement of a great public character. His home and the Grand Pacific were what had come to him without effort.

He decided for the time being—it was about the time of the death of Jennie's mother—that he would make some effort to rehabilitate himself. He would cut out idling—these numerous trips with Jennie had cost him considerable time. He would make some outside investments. If his brother could find avenues of financial profit, he could. He would endeavor to assert his authority more—to pull the control of things toward him rather than to let them drift toward Robert. Should he forsake Jennie?—that thought also came to him. She had no claim on him. She would make no protest. He thought of that, but somehow he did not see how it could be done. It seemed cruel, useless, but more than anything, though he disliked to admit it, uncomfortable for himself. He liked her—loved her, perhaps, in a selfish way. He didn't see how he could desert her very well.

A test case as to the probable control of the factory came up while he was in Cincinnati at about this time. His brother wanted to sever relations with an old and well-established paint company in New York which had manufactured paints especially for the house, and invest in a new concern in Chicago, which was growing and had methods and means which looked promising for the future. Lester, knowing the members of the eastern firm, their reliability, their long and friendly relationship to the house, was in opposition. His father at first seemed to agree with Lester. But Robert stood up before them in Kane senior's office and argued out the question in his cold, logical way, his blue eyes fixing his brother. "We can't go on forever standing by old friends, just because Father here has dealt with them or you like them. We must have a change. The business must be hard and strong."

"It's just as Father feels about that," said Lester. "I have no deep opposition. It won't hurt me one way or the other. You say the house is going to profit eventually. I've stated the arguments on the other side."

"I'm inclined to think Robert is right," said Archibald Kane calmly. "Most of the things he has suggested so far have worked out."

Lester colored. "Well, we won't have any more discussion about that, then," he said. He rose and strolled out of the office.

The shock of this defeat, coming at a time when he was considering pulling himself together, depressed Lester considerably. It wasn't much, but it was a straw, and his father's remark about his brother's business acumen was even more irritating. He was beginning to wonder whether his father would discriminate in any way in the ultimate distribution of the property. Had he heard anything about his entanglement with Jennie? Had he resented the long vacations he had taken from business? It did not appear to Lester that he had neglected any necessary details in the past. He had wisely handled every proposition which had come up to him. He was still the investigator of propositions put to the house, the student of contracts, the adviser in counsel of his father and mother—but he was being worsted. Where would it end? He thought about this but could reach no conclusion.

In the meantime his brother Robert had come to a very definite conclusion in regard to the business and was planning a coup, once his father should die, which would put it all definitely in his hand. As he understood it, his father was going to divide the stock of the company into halves first, giving himself and Lester one fourth each in order that they might remain the dominant factors, as at present. The other half was to be divided into three equal parts, one part for each of the three daughters, but the whole thing was to be held in trust until Mrs. Kane's death. Robert's idea was, after mature deliberation, to curry favor with his three sisters, putting them under financial obligation by reason of minor, successful investments he could make for them and so getting them to vote their stock through him. If he could pool it all, or sit as their close financial adviser, he would at once reorganize the company to suit himself. He saw himself naturally elected president. He saw visions of a union with several other carriage companies which would make him a magnate. The Kane Carriage Manufacturing Company was now, in its line, already the strongest concern in the country. If he could buy secretly into the stock of several others, he could exercise a powerful influence toward the general combination which he hoped to effect. Time was an essential and agreeable factor to him. He did not at all object to waiting. He was cold, cool, farseeing. Sitting in his office chair, as vice-president of the company, he could already see where his plans would end. He did not propose to force Lester out, but he proposed to use him to accomplish his ends, or possibly part with him agreeably, giving him a fair price for his holdings.

Lester was not unaware, on his part, that Robert might have some such scheme in view. It was perfectly plain to him—to any one, he thought—that his brother would like to be in charge of the business. He would himself. Personally he could not wage the vigorous financial campaign his brother was waging. It was not of sufficient interest to him. Why should he worry about a salary or an official connection or a financial supremacy? Would he really be any happier?

At this time Robert propounded a scheme which, while really very progressive on its face and single in its intention, was a plan to get Lester out of immediate contact with the business, as well as to push the interests of the company. He proposed, no less, that they build an immense exhibition and storage warehouse on Michigan Avenue in Chicago and transfer a portion of their completed stock there. Chicago was more central than Cincinnati. Buyers from the West and country merchants could be more easily reached and dealt with there. It would be a big advertisement for the house, a magnificent evidence of its standing and prosperity. Kane senior and Lester immediately approved of this. Both saw its advantages. Robert suggested that Lester undertake the construction of the new building and that possibly he might want to reside in Chicago a part of the time. They needed branch offices in Chicago.

Lester thought of this, and it appealed to him, though it took him away from Cincinnati, largely if not entirely. He could really do considerable that way commercially, he thought. It was dignified and not unrepresentative of his standing in the company. He could live in Chicago, and Jennie could be kept in the background. The scheme he had for taking an apartment could now be arranged without difficulty. He voted yes: Robert smiled. "I'm sure we'll get good results from this all around," he said.

The result of this was that the company decided to build, and Lester to transfer Jennie to Chicago. The plans of the architects were to be drawn at once and work begun immediately. Lester decided that he would spend most of his time in Chicago. He had many friends there. In consequence he wrote Jennie to meet him, and together they selected an apartment on the North Side—a very comfortable arrangement of rooms on a side street near the lake—and he had it fitted up to suit his taste. It did not worry him much that he might be seen. He was as cautious as he could reasonably be, but he had to do this work. He figured that, living in Chicago, he could pose as a bachelor. He would never need to invite his friends to his rooms. There were his offices, where he could always be found, his clubs and the hotels. To his way of thinking the arrangement was practically ideal. In consequence, the details of the furnishing were completed, and Jennie was advised to come on permanently.

The conclusion reached in regard to this brought, of course, the affairs of the Gerhardt family to a climax. Jennie reported that she would have to live in Chicago. Gerhardt was glad from one point of view—it seemed an augury of better things, although it meant the final dissolution of the home in Cleveland within a reasonable course of time. Bass, Martha and George's being away ensured this. Veronica, nearing fifteen, wondered whether she could keep house. She did not relish the idea very much. William was still happy in his school work and did not mind: everything was fair and pleasant to him as yet.

The one concern of Jennie and Gerhardt was Vesta. As has been narrated, Gerhardt had become exceedingly fond of her. Drawn by that peculiar fascination which youth has for age, he could not now contemplate her departure with anything short of suffering. It was his natural thought that Jennie must take her. What else should a mother do?

"Have you told him yet?" he asked her, the day she spoke of her contemplated departure.

"No, but I'm going to soon," she assured him.

"Always soon," he said.

He shook his head. His throat swelled.

"It's too bad," he went on. "It's a great sin. God will punish you, I'm afraid. The child needs someone. I'm getting old— otherwise I would keep her. There is no one here all day now to look after her right, as she should be." Again he shook his head.

"I know," said Jennie weakly. "I'm going to fix it now. I'm going to have her live with me soon. I won't neglect her,—you know that."

"But the child's name," he insisted. "She should have a name. Soon in another year she goes to school. People will want to know who she is. She can't go on forever like this."

Jennie understood well enough that she couldn't. She was crazy about her baby. The heaviest crosses she had borne were the constant separations, this logical charge of neglect, and this logical charge of injustice which could be brought against her. It did seem unfair on her part—and yet she did not see clearly how she might have done otherwise. Vesta had good clothes, everything she needed. She was at least comfortable. Jennie hoped to give her a good education. If only she had not concealed the fact of Vesta's presence from Lester in the first place! Now it was almost too late, and yet it had not seemed wise to tell then. She decided to find some good woman or family in Chicago with whom she could leave Vesta for a little while. Then, then— she looked at this prospect nervously and blanched. But she knew it must come some day. It must.

The problem of relocating Vesta—transferring her without detection, was not easy. Lester was now in Chicago, or likely to be, almost continuously. She hoped to find some home—some quiet family or truly good woman who would take her for a consideration. Before transferring Vesta, Jennie returned to Chicago and hunted, at such times as she could arrange, for the right person and the right neighborhood. Finally, in a Swedish colony to the west of La Salle Avenue, she found an old lady who seemed to embody all the virtues she required—cleanliness, simplicity, honesty. She was a widow, doing work by the day, but was perfectly willing, for the consideration Jennie was able to offer, to give her time to Vesta instead. The latter was to go to kinder-garten when one should be found. She was to have toys and kindly attention, and Mrs. Olsen was to inform Jennie of any change in the child's health. Jennie proposed to call every day. She thought that sometimes, when Lester was out of town, Vesta might be brought to the apartment. She had had Vesta with her at Cleveland, and he had never found out anything. There was in her mind the thought that Vesta was to be well-educated and given station under an assumed name, if not through Lester.

This understanding completed, she returned at the first op-portunity to Cleveland to take Vesta away. Gerhardt, who had been brooding over his approaching loss was even more solicitous about her future and her keeping than he had been before. "She should grow up to be a fine girl," he said. "You should give her a good education—she is so smart." He spoke of the need of send-ing Vesta to a Lutheran school and church, but Jennie was not so sure of that. Time and association with Lester had made her come to think that perhaps the public school was the best place of all. The Lutheran church she had no objection to, though religious forms did not exactly explain life to her now.

On the second day after her arrival, when she was about to leave again, she brought Vesta down, trim and neat, to say goodbye. Veronica and William were going with her to the train. Gerhardt had been wandering about, restless as a lost spirit, while the process of dressing was going on; now that the hour had actually struck he was doing his best to control his feelings. He could see that the five-year-old child had no conception of what it meant to him. She was eager and self-interested, chattering about the ride and the train.

Jennie felt it all. She ached for her father, but she did not see what else should be done. He had always insisted that she take her—did so now.

"Be a good little girl," he said, lifting her up and kissing her. "See that you study your catechism and say your prayers. And you won't forget the Grandpa—what—" He tried to go on, but his voice failed him.

Jennie, who had feared it would be this way, choked back her emotion. "There," she said, "if I thought you were going to act like that—" but she stopped.

"Go," said Gerhardt manfully. "Go. It is best this way," and he stood solemnly by as they went out the door. Then he turned back to his favorite haunt, the kitchen, and stood there staring at the floor. It all came over him again. One by one they were leaving him—Mrs. Gerhardt, Bass, Martha, Jennie, Vesta. He clasped his hands together, after his old-time fashion, and shook his head again and again. "So it is! So it is!" he repeated. "They all leave me. All my life goes to pieces."

CHAPTER XXVI

During the three years in which Jennie and Lester had been associated, there had grown up between them an understanding which, while it may have appeared rather weak and unsatisfactory to the outsider, had a number of elements of strength. It is true that, in the first place, Lester did not care for her in the wild way a young lover might, but he loved her, as Jennie well knew, in his way. It was a strong, self-satisfying, determined kind of way, based solidly in a big animal nature, but rearing itself through feelings and subtleties of understanding and appreciation which were far above the lowest animal desires. He liked her—he liked the shy, confused look which shimmered in her eyes at times; he liked the yielding, considerate disposition that could not and would not quarrel. He liked the subtlety of soul or face or whatever it was that was in a human being and that made this girl this way—retreating, sympathetic, tender. And when he would look at her form and face he was sometimes moved by passion, sometimes by sympathy, sometimes by the delicate aesthetic values of her beauty. She was charming, he knew that—not strong or able in any of the ways the world measures ability, but with something that was better than ability of any pushing, executive character. She was sweet, and wasn't there some great, deep controlling force in that? He thought so. There was enough to hold him, anyhow, that he knew, for the time being. How long it would last he could not say, but it was quite strong enough to have kept him coming back to her over and over for three years, and at this time he felt no diminution in his interest. She was charming.

On her part Jennie had sincerely, deeply, truly learned to

love this man. At first when he had swept her off her feet, overawed her soul, beat down the courage that was in her and used her necessity as a chain wherewith to bind her to him, she was a little doubtful, a little afraid of him, although she liked him—was really drawn to him. Now, however, by the process of little things—by living with him, knowing him better, watching his moods, she had come to love him. He was so big, so vocal, so handsome. His point of view and opinions of anything and everything were so positive. Here was a man who, if she crouched and ran mouselike, stood up forthright and direct before the world. He was apparently not afraid of anything—God, man or devil. His pet motto, "Hew to the line, let the chips fall where they will," had stuck in her brain as something immensely characteristic of him. He used to look at her, holding her chin between the thumb and fingers of his big brown hand, and say: "You're sweet, all right, but you need courage and defiance. You haven't enough of those things." And her eyes would meet his in dumb appeal. She knew that she did not have them—never would have them—that she needed a shield. But she wanted him to be big and strong as he was and let her be as she was. He felt this, and it made him want to be decent and kindly. "Never mind," he would add, "you have other things." And then he would kiss her.

Jennie was so impressed by his courage, his wisdom, his generosity, his obvious sense of big affairs that she came to love him earnestly, desperately. She had no way of showing it openly, for she could not express herself in words, had no subtlety of gesture, none of the arts of the coquette. Words and phrases were a mystery. She could only look and feel, but she could do that deeply. Her feeling could cut through the hide of this big animal, straight to his heart at times. He sensed what she felt—how, he could not say—but he knew it. And in her silent way she understood him, was big enough for him, was sweet enough for him. He liked to be with her in silence, for there was always the sense of her presence, as one might feel the presence of a flower. When they walked out together it was with the feeling, on his part, that he had someone with him who was good to look at and pleasant to be with. She understood. He had to explain, but she understood what he was talking about, what people were, how they acted, how life was organized, only she did not answer with argument. She seemed always to tolerate, to apologize for, to seem to think people were not as bad as some people thought. It appealed to him as a big, decent way to take life, even if it did eliminate aggressiveness and the ability to gather material things.

Once, he remembered, they were walking in 23rd Street, New York, and some played-out specimen of humanity whom he had scarcely noticed attracted her attention. She was quick to see ragged clothes, worn shoes, care-lined faces. "Oh, look," she said to him, pulling his sleeve, "let's give him something."

"You're a queer girl, Jennie," he said. "You're always seeing that sort of thing. It isn't always as bad as you think, though."

"Why?" she asked vaguely, thinking of the man who had now gone his way.

"They are not always poor. Some of these people are professional beggars. They make their living that way."

"Oh, no!" she replied incredulously.

"Oh—yes, I know it. They have been exposed time and again. You're just good-natured. There's a despondent note in your character, but you'll get over that."

She looked down, wondering if what he said could be true. When he saw her expression of doubt and sympathy, he went on with, "Fortune is a thing that adjusts itself automatically to a person's capabilities and desires. If you see anybody who wants anything very badly and is capable of enjoying it, he is apt to get it. Not always, but most people get what they are capable of enjoying. Anyhow, sympathizing and worrying won't help anybody. Action is better. A barrel of flour is worth a hundred barrels of tears."

He strolled ahead, quite sure he had expressed the whole logic of the case, and Jennie, who was overawed by his mighty sentences, only studied the crowd again.

One of the most appealing things to Lester in these three years was the simple way in which she tried to shield herself from exposure of her various shortcomings. She could not write very well, and once he found a list of words he had used written out on a piece of paper with the meanings opposite. He smiled. But he liked her better for it. Another time in the Southern Hotel in St. Louis, and before that at other places, he watched her pretending a loss or lack of appetite because she thought she was being studied by nearby diners and that her manners were poor. She could not always be sure of the right forks and knives and the right

ways of holding, cutting, sipping things; but he knew that she
studied him, followed his lead.

"Why don't you eat something?" he asked good-naturedly.
"You're hungry, aren't you?"

"Not very."

"You must be. Listen, Jennie. I know what it is. You mustn't
feel that way. Your manners are all right. I wouldn't bring you here
if they weren't. Your instincts are all right. Don't be uneasy. I'd
tell you quick enough when there was anything wrong." His
brown eyes held a friendly gleam.

She smiled gratefully. "I do feel a little nervous at times," she
admitted.

"Don't," he repeated. "You're all right. Don't worry. I'll show
you." And he did.

By degrees she grew into an understanding of the usages and
customs of comfort. All that the Gerhardt family had ever had
had been the bare necessities. Now she was surrounded with
whatever she wanted—trunks, clothes, toilet articles, the equip-
ment of comfort—and while she liked it all, it did not upset her
sense of proportion and the fitness of things. There was no element of vanity in her, only a sense of joy in privilege and opportunity. It pleased her so to think she could do things for people—
for her father, her sisters and brothers, her baby. She had lived
these years worrying about her family, her baby and her future, but
at the same time realizing that her life held opportunities and
privileges for which she might well be grateful. And love had
been added to her life—a real love. It seemed to her as if she could
never be thankful enough for having found Lester—for his having
been sent to her. It had all come about badly, perhaps, but if she
could keep him!—if she could only keep him!

The details of getting Vesta located near her once adjusted,
Jennie settled down into the routine of a home life such as she had
never really anticipated would come to her some day. Lester, busy
about his multitudinous affairs, was in and out. He had a suite of
rooms reserved for himself at the Grand Pacific, which was then
the exclusive hotel of Chicago, and this was his ostensible residence. His luncheon and evening appointments were kept at the
Union Club. An early patron of the telephone, he had one
installed in his rooms with Jennie so he could reach her quickly.
He was home two and three nights a week, sometimes oftener. If

there was nothing else on hand and he had not been home for a day or two, he would sometimes call Jennie up and come out to lunch. He insisted at first on her having a girl for general housework, but acquiesced in the more sensible arrangement which she suggested later of letting someone come in to do the cleaning. She liked to work around her own home. Her natural industry and love of order prompted this.

Lester liked his breakfast promptly at eight in the morning. He wanted dinner served nicely at seven. Silverware, cut glass, imported china—all the details had been gathered to suit him. He kept his trunks and wardrobe at the apartment.

During the first few months of this life, there was no hitch in the arrangement. Everything went smoothly. He was in the habit of taking Jennie to the theatre now and then, the danger of meeting any one being obviated by the fact that, when so met, he introduced her as Miss Gerhardt. He was utterly frank in making clear his relationship to her, or at least not concealing it. When he registered her as his wife, it was usually under an assumed name, where there was danger of detection. Where there was not, and he had tried to make arrangements which were inconspicuous and exclusive as often as possible, he did not mind using his own signature. No evil had resulted thus far.

In the mere living with her he found great satisfaction. He had long since become used to her ways and characteristics and she to his, though neither of them fully understood the other as yet. He did not quite grasp the depth of her emotional nature. She did not see how essentially kind he was underneath a gruff exterior. They were gradually winning their way to each other. Every morning that he was there he would rise shortly after she did and, when not shaving or making his toilet, would come idling about the kitchen or dining room, sometimes arrayed in a large, flowered dressing gown. Usually, on these occasions, he would be in a semi-crusty, semi-humorous mood, the proportion depending to a certain extent on the time he had reached home the night before; and he would sit about making remarks on how she was getting along.

"Now we'll see what your boasted art of cooking amounts to this morning," he would say. Or, "This home life may have its attractions, but it takes a tall lot of forbearance when you think of the amount of breakfast-waiting a man has to stand for."

Sometimes he would stand gazing idly out of the back windows, commenting on the probable life of their neighbors. Jennie, who understood his moods, would laugh or gossip with him about what she saw, the character of the butcher, the delinquencies or troubles of the milkman, the hard times her washer-woman was having and what not. He would occasionally pinch her cheeks in passing or squeeze her arm. Sometimes she would get his comb and military brushes when he had not parted his hair exactly. It was a loving, kindly atmosphere which only convention, the accident of chance, and social differences had kept from being regular from the very beginning.

The trouble with this situation was that it was criss-crossed with the danger and consequent worry which the deception in regard to Vesta had entailed, as well as with Jennie's natural worry in regard to her father and the disorganized home. Since her leaving she had had no word from him, never would have word for that matter, she knew, except under great stress; but Veronica was writing that he wanted to give up the large house now, considering it wasteful, and that he was getting more and more cranky and fussy and that there was no living with him. Jennie feared, as Veronica hinted, that she and William would go to live with Martha, who was installed in a boarding house in Cleveland, and that Gerhardt would be left alone. He was such a pathetic figure to her now, with his injured hands and his one ability—that of being a watchman—that she was hurt to think of his being left alone. Would he come to her? She knew he would not—feeling as he did at present. Would Lester have him?—she was not sure of that. If he came, Vesta would have to be accounted for. So she worried.

The situation in regard to Vesta was really complicated. Owing to the feeling she had that she was doing her daughter a grave injustice, Jennie was particularly sensitive in regard to her, anxious to do a thousand things to make up for the one she could not do. She daily paid a visit to the home of Mrs. Olsen, taking toys, candy or whatever came into her mind as being likely to interest and please her child. She liked to sit with Vesta and tell her stories of fairies and giants, which kept the little girl wideeyed. At last she went so far as to bring her to the apartment when Lester was away visiting his parents, and, finding that it worked without harm and being sure of his continued absence, brought her again. From then on, by easy steps, it was possible during his several absences to do this regularly. After that, as time went on and she began to know his habits and to fix them in her mind because of Vesta, she became more bold—although "bold" is scarcely the word to use in connection with Jennie. She became venturesome much as a mouse might. She would risk Vesta's presence on the assurance of even short absences—two or three days. The trouble with Jennie was that she had no guile. She could not be subtle. She did not know how to conceal.

During these several visits with her child she had a good opportunity to see just what a lovely thing her life would be if she could but adjust it—the charm that would exist in being an honored wife and a happy mother and having so comfortable a home. Vesta was a most observant little girl. She could by her innocent childish questions give a hundred turns to the dagger of self-reproach which was already planted deeply in Jennie's heart.

"Can I come to live with you?" was one of her simplest and most frequently repeated questions, to which Jennie would reply that Mama could not have her come just yet, but that very soon now, just as soon as she possibly could, she would be allowed to come.

"Don't you know just when?" Vesta would say.

"No dearest, not just when. Very soon now. You won't mind waiting a little while. Don't you like Mrs. Olsen?"

"Yes," replied Vesta, "but then she—now she—ain't got any nice things now. She's just got old things."

Jennie, who knew no way of answering her daughter's pleadings, endeavored to soothe her by saying that she could have anything that she wanted, and that she should come to see her often, answers which were not devoid of a residue of pain.

Lester was of course not in the least suspicious. His observations of things relating to this home were rather casual. He went about his work and his pleasures, believing Jennie to be the soul of sincerity and good-natured service, and it never occurred to him that there was anything underhanded in her actions. Once he did come home sick in the afternoon and found her absent—an absence which endured from two o'clock to five. He was a little irritated and grumbled on her return, but his irritation was as nothing to her astonishment and fright when she found him there. She blanched at the thought of his suspecting something and, finding that he did not suspect, explained as best she could. She had gone to see her washer-woman. She was slow about her marketing. She didn't dream he was there. She was sorry too that her absence had lost her an opportunity to serve him. It showed her what a mess she was likely to make of it all.

It so happened that about three weeks after the above occurrence, Lester had occasion to return to Cincinnati for a week, and during this time Jennie again brought Vesta to the flat, a thing she was tempted to do by the fact that, as in the first instance, Lester wrote her a letter saying that he had decided to extend his stay and giving her the exact day of his return. This letter, thoroughly to be depended upon in his case, was made even more certain by the added information that if he changed his mind he would let her know. Accordingly Vesta was brought, and for four days there were the happiest goings-on between the mother and child.

That this little reunion would have passed like the other one and nothing ever come of it was absolutely certain, had it not been for an oversight on Jennie's part, the far-reaching effects of which she could only afterward regret. This was the leaving of a little toy lamb under the large leather divan in the front room, where Lester was invariably wont to lie and smoke. It was a comic little creature, small and dusty, with a fixed stare and tiny feet. A little bell, held by a thread of blue ribbon, was fastened about its neck, and this tinkled feebly whenever it was shaken. Vesta had climbed up, and, with the unaccountable freakishness of children, had deliberately dropped it behind the divan, a move which Jennie did not notice at the time. Afterward when she gathered up the various playthings previous to Vesta's departure, she overlooked it entirely, and there it rested, its innocent eyes still staring upon the sunlit regions of toyland when Lester returned.

That same evening, when he was lying on the divan, quietly enjoying his cigar and his newspaper, he chanced to drop the former, fully lighted, and wishing to recover it before it should do any damage leaned over and looked under the divan. He was not able to see the cigar that way, however, so he rose and pulled the lounge out, a move which revealed to him the little lamb still standing where Vesta had dropped it. He stooped over and picked it up, turning it over and over and wondering how it had come there.

Lester was not by any means the objector to children which Jennie took him to be. For all his solemn assertions about his unfitness to be a father and his unwillingness to have the care of a child, there was something very mellow in his mood concerning them. Sometimes he thought that a child or two would be most pleasing to him if he were only inclined to pull himself together and assume a stable course, and this thought was now reawakened in him by the lamb he held in his hand.

"A lamb!" Some neighbor's child, perhaps, whom Jennie had introduced into the household, he thought. She was very fond of children. He would have to go and tease her about this.

Accordingly he held the toy jovially before him and, coming out into the dining-room where Jennie was working at the sideboard, exclaimed in a mock-solemn voice, "Where did this come from?"

Jennie, who was totally unconscious of the existence of this evidence of her duplicity, turned about and, seeing him holding it out toward her, was instantly possessed with the idea that he had suspected all and was now about to visit just wrath upon her. Instantly the blood flamed in her cheeks and as quickly left them. Fear blanched her countenance and took her courage away.

"Why, why—" she stuttered, "it's a little toy I bought."

"I see it is," he returned genially, her guilty tremor not escaping his observation, but having at the same time no explicable significance to him. "It's frisking around a mighty lonely sheepfold. It looks to me as if it would do for the star member of an animal wash."

He touched the little bell at its throat, while Jennie stood there, unable to speak. The bell tinkled feebly, and then he looked at her again. She was trying her best to recover herself before he should see. His manner was so humorous that she could tell he suspected nothing. It was almost impossible for her to recover, though, so limp was she.

"What's ailing you?" he said.

"Nothing," she replied.

"You look as though a lamb was a terrible shock to you."

"I forgot to take it out from there was all," she went on blindly.

"It looks as though it had been played with enough," he added more seriously, and then, seeing that the discussion was evidently painful to her, dropped it. The lamb had not furnished him the amusement that he had expected.

Lester went back into the front room and stretched himself out and thought it over. Why was she so nervous? What was there about a toy to make her grow pale? Surely there was no harm in her harboring some youngster of the neighborhood when she was alone—if she wanted to, having it come in and play. Why should she be so nervous?

CHAPTER XXVII

Nothing more was said about the incident of the toy lamb. Time might have wholly effaced the impression from Lester's memory had nothing else intervened to arouse his suspicions, but a mishap of any kind seems invariably to be linked with others which follow as a matter of course. One day it was a drawer which he thought she closed rather nervously upon his entering the room; another time it was a story-book concealed under a cloth, of which he made no remark although it seemed rather an odd thing to find. Lastly it was the discovery of a little dress, the examination of which by him was purely accidental. He was rummaging in the top drawer of the chiffonier for a handkerchief and, not finding one, pulled open the second and third drawers. In the third drawer he encountered a little pink bundle, the form of which was rather odd. Although not suspicious, he had seen so many odd things of late that he could not resist the temptation to unfold it, whereupon there was revealed to his gaze a little dress— very simple in the making, the meaning of which struck him as significant. There was either some little neighbor-child whom she was innocently befriending, and of whom, because of his expressions concerning children, she was afraid to tell him, or there was something in it all secret and concerning which she was trying to deceive him—a thought which was anything but pleasant when connected with Jennie.

This latter idea, while very disagreeable to him, was as yet scarcely well enough established by fact to warrant him in taking his stern and usually vigorous measures where deception was concerned. Although secrecy was an abomination to him and lying a crime, yet Jennie's relations with him had always been so frank, tender and apparently open that he could not bring himself to act at once. He would bide a little. Perhaps the matter would clear itself up of its own accord.

He put the dress back and went solemnly to his office, but the fates were not done with him yet. One evening when he happened to be lingering about the flat later than usual, the doorbell rang, and, Jennie being busy in the kitchen and not hearing, he went himself to open the door. He was greeted by a middle-aged woman who frowned very nervously upon him and inquired in broken Swedish accents for Jennie.

"Wait a moment," he said and, stepping to the rear door, called her.

Jennie came and, seeing who it was, stepped nervously out in the hall and closed the door after her, an action which instantly struck him as suspicious. He had not noticed her do anything like that before. He frowned and determined to inquire thoroughly into the matter. A moment later Jennie reappeared. Her face was white and very visibly affected, and her fingers seemed to be nervously seeking something to seize upon.

"What's the trouble?" he inquired, the irritation he had felt the moment before giving his voice a touch of gruffness.

Jennie paused a moment, not knowing how to begin, but visibly moved to say something.

"I've got to go out for a little while," she at last managed to say, and Lester, who was all the more puzzled and irritated by this secrecy and nervousness, put considerable emphasis in his tone as he replied:

"Very well. You can tell me what's the trouble with you, though, can't you? Where do you have to go?"

"I—I," began Jennie, stammering, "—I have—"

"Yes?" he said grimly.

"I have to go on an errand," she repeated, hopelessly struggling for a delay of this inquisition. "I—I can't wait. I'll tell you when I come back, Lester. Please don't ask me now."

She looked vainly at him, her troubled countenance still marked by preoccupation and anxiety to get away, and Lester, who had never seen this look of intense responsibility in her before, was moved and irritated by it.

"That's all right," he said, "but what's the use of all this secrecy? Why can't you come out and tell what's the matter with you? What's the use of this whispering behind doors?—Where do you have to go?"

He paused, checked by his own harshness, and Jennie, who

was intensely wrought-up by the information she had received as well as by the unwonted verbal castigation she was now enduring, rose to an emotional state never reached by her before.

"I will, Lester, I will!" she exclaimed. "Only not now. I haven't time. I'll tell you everything when I come back. Please don't stop me now."

She hurried to the adjoining chamber to get her wraps, and Lester, who had even yet no clear conception of what it all meant, followed her stubbornly to the door.

"See here!" he exclaimed in his vigorous, brutal way. "You're not acting right. What's the matter with you? I want to know."

He stood in the doorway, his whole frame exhibiting the pugnacity and settled determination of a man who is bound to be obeyed. Jennie, troubled and driven to bay, turned at last.

"It's my child, Lester!" she exclaimed. "It's dying. I haven't time to talk. Oh, please don't stop me. I'll tell you everything when I come back."

"Your child!" he exclaimed. "What the hell are you talking about?"

"I couldn't help it," she returned. "I was afraid—I should have told you long ago. I meant to only—only— Oh, let me go now, and I'll tell you all when I come back!"

He stared at her in amazement. Could this be the Jennie he had known? Was this the woman he had lived with for four years and never once suspected of duplicity? Surely there was some mistake here. He stepped aside, unwilling to force her any further now. "Well, go ahead. Don't you want someone to go along with you?"

"No," she replied. "Mrs. Olsen is right here. I'll go with her."

She hurried forth, white-faced, and he stood there, pondering. Could this be the woman he had thought that he knew? Why, she had been deceiving him for years. Jennie! The white-faced! The simple!

"Well I'll be damned!" he said. "Well I'll be God-damned!"

The reason why Jennie had been called was nothing more than one of those infantile seizures, the coming and result of which no man can predict two hours beforehand. Vesta had been seriously taken with membranous croup only a few hours before, and the development since had been so rapid that the poor old Swedish mother was half-frightened to death. Mrs. Kane was to come at once. This message, delivered as it was in a very nervous manner by one whose only object was to bring her, had induced the soul-racking fear of death in Jennie and caused her to brave the discovery by Lester in the manner described.

Jennie left the flat and hastened anxiously away, her one thought now being to reach her child before the arm of death could interfere and snatch it from her, her mind weighed upon by a legion of fears. What if it should already be too late when she reached there; what if Vesta should really be no more? Instinctively she quickened her pace and, as the street lamps came and receded into gloom, she forgot all the sting of Lester's words, forgot all fear that he might turn her out of doors and leave her alone in a great city with a little child to take care of; she remembered only the fact that her Vesta was very ill, possibly dying, and that she was the direct cause of the child's absence at present. But for her, perhaps but for the want of her care and attention, Vesta might be well and out of danger tonight.

"If I can only get there," she kept saying to herself. And then, with that frantic unreason which is the chief characteristic of the instinct-driven mother, "I might have known that God would punish me for my unnatural conduct. I might have known—I might have known."

She waited at the corner where the street-cars ran, every moment that passed between her reaching there and a street-car's quick arrival seeming like an age to her, and all the while she was busy heaping reproaches on herself, wondering whether the good God she believed in would vouchsafe her mercy enough to spare her child until she could reach her, saying over to herself that it was a visitation for all her past misconduct and promising that, no matter what happened, if God would spare Vesta now she would take her to herself as a mother should and never henceforward for one moment neglect her again.

When she reached the gate she fairly sped up the little walk and into the house, where her Vesta was lying pale, quiet, and weak but considerably better. Several Swedish neighbors and a middle-aged physician were in attendance, all of whom looked at her curiously as she dropped beside her child's bed and spoke to her. Vesta was awake and responded to her mother, at which Jennie, far too keyed up for any emotional display, only stroked her forehead and listened to the various explanations of the neighbors and the physician, practically all of whom agreed that no further danger was to be anticipated and that Vesta would unquestionably be much better in the morning.

This comforting intelligence, while serving to relax her nervous state, was not at all weakening in its effect upon her resolutions. She had sinned and sinned grievously against her daughter, but now she would make amends as far as possible. Lester was very dear to her, but she would no longer attempt to deceive him in anything. If he left her—(she could not help but ache at the thought)—she would be compelled to endure. Vesta must not be an outcast any longer. She must be given a home, with her, close by her side tomorrow, as soon as she was well. Where Jennie was, there must Vesta be.

Sitting by the bedside in this humble Swedish cottage, Jennie was now able to see the long and devious path on which her first groundless concealment had led her, the trouble and pain it had created in her own home, the months of suffering it had given her with Lester, the agony it had heaped upon her this night—and to what end? The truth had been discovered anyhow. Lester would be driven away from her by a deception which, in the beginning, might have as readily been avoided; Vesta had been neglected. She sat there and meditated, not knowing what next was to happen, while Vesta first quieted and then went soundly to sleep.

In the meanwhile Lester, after recovering from the first heavy impact of this discovery, spent some little time wondering at the significance of it. The need for some definite course of action was uppermost in his mind. Strange, now as he looked at it, a miserable shadow seemed suddenly to have descended upon him; a shadow, the evil of which seemed to rest almost entirely with Jennie. She had wantonly deceived him; had practised some miserable chicanery, the substance of which he was not even now clearly aware of. She had been living a lie, for how long he could not say, and now it had all come out—how tragically he had just been able to witness.

Almost the first questions he asked himself after she had gone were whose child it was—the father of it; in just what way he had been related to Jennie's life; how old it was; how and in what manner it came to be in Chicago, where Jennie had managed to look after it. All of which, by running up against a blank wall, so far as his own knowledge was concerned, only served to deepen the color of her duplicity.

Curiously now, as he thought, his first meeting with her at Mrs. Bracebridge's came back. What was it about her then that attracted him? Why did he think, after a few hours' observation, that he could seduce her to do his will? What was it—moral looseness or weakness or what? He thought and thought but he could not lay hold of any exact fact. Art was in this thing, the practised art of the cheat, and in deceiving such a confiding nature as his she had done even more than practise deception— she had been ungrateful.

Now the quality of ingratitude was a very objectionable thing to Lester—the last and most offensive trait of debased natures, and to be able to discover a trace of it in Jennie was very disturbing. She had not exhibited it in any other way before, it was true—quite the contrary—but nevertheless he saw strong evidence of it now, and it made him very sour in his feeling toward her. How could she be guilty of any such conduct toward him— he who had picked her up out of nothing, so to speak, and befriended her?

As he stood thus meditating, he went back in mind over the incidents of recent days and saw how convincingly they fitted together perfectly. Her coming home that day and exhibiting so much trepidation—yes, that was manifestly connected with this. Her turning pale when he brought out the little lamb—simple enough now. The sudden closing of the drawer, the finding of the story-book, the finding of the dress—one after another they all came back in order, and so she stood before him beautifully convicted. What did he intend to do about it?

He moved from his chair in this silent room and began to pace slowly to and fro, the weightiness of this subject exercising to the full his power of decision. She was guilty of a misdeed which he felt able to condemn. The original concealment was evil; the continued deception more. Lastly, there was the thought that her love after all had been divided, part for him, part for the child, a discovery which no man in his position could contemplate with serenity. He moved irritably as he thought of it, shoved his hands in his pockets and walked to and fro across the floor.

That a man of Lester's natural decency of temperament

should consider himself wronged by Jennie, merely because she concealed a child whose presence was due to no more evil intention than was involved later in the fact of her yielding herself to him, was evidence of one of those inexplicable perversions of judgement to which the human mind, in its capacity of keeper of the honor of others, seems almost permanently committed. "Judge not lest ye be judged" is the wisdom of tenderness, but the human mind will persist in doing this thing because it is preservative of things as they are so to do. Given a certain code of morals—true or false—if you wish to preserve them, the actions of all men must be judged accordingly. In so much as anyone has faith in any given doctrine or theory, in so far will he judge his fellow men by it, not more.

Now Lester, aside from his own personal conduct (for men seldom judge with that in the balance), had faith in the ideal that a woman should reveal herself to a man in love, perfectly, and the fact that she had not done so was a grief. He had asked her once tentatively about her past. She had begged him not to. That was the time she should have spoken of any child. Now—he shook his head.

His first impulse, after he had thought the thing out some, was to walk out and leave her. He was given to definite, determined action, and that quickly. At the same time he was curious to hear the rest of this business. He did put on his hat and coat, though, and strode out, stopping at the first convenient saloon. He took a car and went down to the club, strolling about the different rooms and chatting with several people whom he encountered. He was restless and irritated and, finally, after three hours of meditation, took a cab and returned. He wanted to hear the balance of the story.

The distraught Jennie, sitting by her sleeping child, was at last made to realize by its peaceful breathing that all danger was really over. There was no further call for anything she could do, and so gradually the claims of the flat she had deserted began to reassert themselves, the promise to Lester and the need of being loyal to her duties unto the very end. Lester might possibly be waiting for her. It was just probable that he wished to hear the remainder of her story before breaking with her entirely. Although anguished and frightened by the certainty, as she deemed it, of his forsaking her, she nevertheless felt that if it must be, it was no more than what she deserved—a just punishment for all her misdoings.

Pondering over the difficulty of facing him again, of finding something to do on the morrow when it would be all over, she finally arose and took her way back. When she arrived at the flat it was after eleven, and the hall light was already out. She ascended the stairs and, seeing a light over the transom, she first tried the door and then inserted her key. No one stirred, however, and opening the door she entered in the expectation of seeing Lester sternly confronting her. He was not there, however. The burning gas had been merely an oversight on his part. She glanced quickly about, but seeing only the empty room, she came instantly to the other conclusion that he had forsaken her—and so stood there, a meditative, helpless figure.

"Gone!" she thought.

It was while she was still lingering in this condition, haunting like a ghost the scene of vanished joys, that Lester's cab rolled up and that worthy ascended the stairs. He was in the same determined mood and came in with his derby hat pulled low over his broad forehead, close to his sandy eyebrows, and his overcoat buttoned up closely about his neck. He took off the coat without looking at her and hung it on the rack. Then he deliberately took off his hat and hung that up also. When he was through he turned to where she was watching him with wide eyes.

"I want to know about this thing now from beginning to end. Whose child is that?"

The directness and import of this question frightened Jennie even more. Although perfectly willing to confess—prepared as she thought she had been, this single remark served to show the whole revelation she was facing, all the darksome chapters of her life now to be revealed. She wavered a moment, as one who might be going to take a leap in the dark, then opened her lips mechanically and confessed.

"It's Senator Brander's."

"Senator Brander?" echoed Lester, the familiar name of the dead but still famous statesman ringing with shocking and unexpected force in his ears. "How did you come to know him?"

"We used to do his washing for him," she rejoined simply—"my mother and I."

Lester paused, the baldness of the statements issuing from

her sobering even his rancorous mood. Senator Brander's child, he thought to himself. So that great representative of the interests of the common people was the undoer of her—a self-confessed washer-woman's daughter. A fine tragedy of low life all this was.

"How long ago was this?" he demanded, his face the picture of a darkling mood.

"It's been nearly six years now," she returned.

He calculated the time that had elapsed since he had known her and then inquired, "How old is the child?"

"She's a little over five," returned Jennie.

Lester moved, the call for serious and consecutive thought made by these statements causing him to assume an even more peremptory though less bitter manner. Some of the flushness due to the spirits he had consumed had passed, and in its place came a cooler comprehension of what he was doing—of what she had been doing also.

"Where have you been keeping her all this time?"

"She was at home until you went to Cincinnati last spring. I went down and brought her then."

"Was she there the times I came to Cleveland?"

"Yes," said Jennie, "but I didn't let her come out anywhere where you could see her."

"I thought you said you told your people you were married!" he exclaimed, wondering how this relationship of the child to the family could have been adjusted.

"I did," she replied, "but I didn't want to tell you about her. They thought all the time I intended to."

"Well, why didn't you?"

"Because I was afraid."

"Afraid of what?"

"I didn't know what was going to become of me when I went with you, Lester. I didn't want to do her any harm if I could help it. I was ashamed. Afterward when you said you didn't like children, I was afraid."

"Afraid I'd leave you?"

"Yes."

He stopped, the simplicity of her answers removing a part of the suspicion of artful duplicity which had originally weighed upon him. After all, there was not so much of that in it as mere wretchedness of circumstance and cowardice of morals. What a family she must have! What queer non-moral values they must have to have brooked any such a combination of affairs.

"Didn't you know that you'd be found out in the long run?" he at last demanded. "Surely you might have seen that you couldn't raise her that way. Why didn't you tell me in the first place? I wouldn't have thought anything of it then."

"I know," she said. "I wanted to protect her."

"Where is she now?" he asked.

Jennie explained.

She stood there, the contradictory aspects of these questions and of his attitude puzzling even herself. She did try to explain them after a time, but all Lester could gain was that she had blundered along without any artifice at all—a condition so manifest that, had he been in any other position than that he was, he might have pitied her. As it was, the revelation concerning Brander was hanging over him, and he finally returned to that.

"You say your mother used to do washing for him. How did you come to get in with him?"

Jennie, who until now had borne his questions with unmoving pain, winced at this. He was now encroaching upon the period that was by far the most distressing memory of her life. What he had just asked seemed to be a demand upon her to make everything clear.

"I was so young, Lester," she pleaded. "I was only eighteen. I didn't know. I used to go to the hotel where he was stopping and get his laundry, and at the end of the week I'd take it to him again."

She paused, and as he took a chair, looking as if he expected to hear the whole story, she continued: "We were so poor. He used to give me money to give to my mother. I didn't know."

She paused again, totally unable to go on, and he, seeing that it would be impossible for her to explain without prompting, took up his questioning again—eliciting by degrees the whole pitiful story. Brander had intended to marry her, she confessed. He had written to her, but before he could come to her he died.

Throughout this recital, Lester, who could not help judging with his own family in the balance, was shocked and disagreeably weighed upon by the ignorance and misery it revealed. Such stooping on the part of a man like Brander—such almost criminal ineptitude on the part of her parents. They were common, there was no doubt of that. Certain people were simply unfit. His own family—what a feeling of disgust there would be in that quarter if they could see him mixed up with such an affair as this.

There was a period of five minutes in which he said nothing at all, put his arm on the mantel and stared at the wall, during which time Jennie waited, not knowing what would next follow—not wishing to make a single plea. During this time the clock ticked audibly, and Lester's face betrayed no sign of either thought or feeling. He was thinking of her story now—quite calm, quite sober, wondering what he should do. Jennie was before him as the criminal at the bar. He, the righteous, the moral, the pure of heart, was in the judgement seat. Now to sentence her—to make up his mind what course was most fit.

He sat there thinking, but, strange to relate, now that he had heard all, he could not quite make up his mind. It was a disagreeable tangle, to be sure—something that a man of his position and wealth ought really not to have anything to do with. This child, the actuality of it, put an almost unbearable face upon the whole matter—and yet—he was not quite prepared to speak. He turned after a time, the silvery tinkle of the French clock on the mantel striking three causing him to become aware of Jennie—pale, uncertain, still standing as she had stood all this while.

"Better go to bed," he said considerately and turned to his own thoughts.

Jennie stood there wide-eyed, expectant, ready to hear at any moment his decision as to her fate. She waited in vain, however. After a long time of musing, he rose and went to the coat rack near the door.

"Better go to bed," he said indifferently. "I'm going out."

She turned instinctively, feeling that even in this crisis there was some little service she might render, but he did not see her. He went out, vouching no further speech.

She looked after him and, as his footsteps sounded on the stair, she felt as if she were doomed and were hearing her own death knell. What had she done? What would he do now? She stood there, a dissonance of despair, and when the lower door clicked she moved her hand out of the agony of her suppressed despair.

"Gone!" she thought. "Gone!"

In the light of a late dawn she was still sitting there pondering, her speculations as to her future being far too urgent for tears.

CHAPTER XXVIII

The sullen, philosophic Lester was not as determined upon a course of action as he appeared to be. Solemn as was his mood and speculative, he did not see after all exactly what grounds he had for complaint. The child's existence complicated matters considerably. He did not like to see the evidence of Jennie's previous misdeeds walking about in the shape of a human being, but as a matter of fact he admitted to himself that he might have forced Jennie's story out of her before if he had gone about it in earnest. She would not have lied, he knew that. At the very outset he might have demanded the history of her past. He had not done so. Now—well, now it was too late. The one thing it did fix in his mind was that it would be useless to ever think of marrying her. It couldn't be done, not by a man in his station. The best thing to do was to make reasonable provision for her and then quit. He went to his hotel fully determined to do this, after a little time, but he did not actually say to himself that he would do it at once.

It is an easy thing for a man to theorize in a situation of this kind, quite another to act. Our comforts, appetites and passions grow on us with usage, and Jennie was not only a comfort but an appetite with him. Almost four years of constant association had taught him so much about her and himself that he was not prepared to let go easily or quickly. It was too much of a wrench. He could think of it, bustling about the work of a great organization during the daytime, but when night came it was a different matter. He could be lonely, too, he discovered much to his surprise, and it disturbed him.

One of the things that interested him in this situation was Jennie's early theory that the mixing of Vesta with him and her in this new relationship would have injured the child. Just how had she come by that feeling, he wanted to know? He was much better stationed than she was. Somehow it dawned on him after a time that there might have been something in her point of view. She did not know who he was or what he would do with her. He might have left her shortly. Being uncertain, she could have wished to protect her baby. That wasn't so bad. Then again, he was curious to know what the child was like. The daughter of a man like

Senator Brander might be something of an infant. He had been a brilliant man, and Jennie was a charming woman. He thought of this, and, while it irritated him, it also aroused his curiosity. He ought to go back and see the child—he was really entitled to a view of it, but he hesitated because of his own attitude in the beginning. It seemed to him that he really ought to quit, and here he was parleying with himself.

The truth was that he couldn't. Three years of living with Jennie had, by the very quality of the sympathetic, affectional service rendered, made him in an affectional way dependent. Now he had been close to someone who, at odd times and at his convenience, provided him exactly the service and the atmosphere which he needed to be comfortable and happy. Who had ever been so close to him before? His mother loved him, but she was always a socially ambitious woman whose attitude toward him had not so much to do with real love as with ambition. His father—well, his father was a man, like himself. All of his sisters were distinctly wrapped up in their own affairs; Robert and he were temperamentally uncongenial. With Jennie he had really been happy, he had truly lived. She was necessary to him; the more he stayed away from her the more he wanted her. He finally decided to have a straight-out talk with her, to arrive at some sort of understanding. She ought to get the child and take care of it. She must understand that he might eventually want to quit. She ought to be made to feel that a definite change had taken place, though no immediate break might occur. She was not, of course, in any immediate danger of want. He would always see that she was provided with money. He took his customary way to her there at the apartment the same evening that he thought these things out, determined to put matters to rights.

During his absence Jennie had been vastly disturbed about her fate. Although when he left she really did not know whether he would ever return, she did not feel able to make a move until he gave some indication of what he intended to do. The flat was still here with everything relating to his personal apparel, as well as his furniture, and until that was looked after by him she could not have gone if she had wanted to. Accordingly she went about as usual, prepared the breakfast and dinner that he did not come for, and between these, on the first day, ventured to pay a visit to Vesta, who was so nearly recovered that Jennie's apprehensions were almost entirely dispelled. She said nothing to the woman about taking her, but all the while her mind was busy with the thought of what she would do the moment Lester notified her that he was not coming back. This was that she would take Vesta and find something to do—possibly go back to Cleveland. She hardly knew what, but she would get something.

Her mind was at flood tide with these thoughts one evening when, from the dining room, where she was arranging some things preparatory to getting a dinner at a moment's notice, she heard the front door open and saw Lester enter. She put down her things and went in to meet him. He calmly took off his hat and coat before he turned to her.

"There's just one thing to be done about this as far as I can see," he began with characteristic directness and without further introduction. "Get the child and bring her here, where you can take care of her. There's no use leaving her in the hands of strangers."

"I will, Lester," said Jennie submissively. "I always wanted to."

"Very well, then, you'd better do it at once," and he took an evening newspaper out of his pocket and strolled toward one of the front windows; then he turned to her. "You and I might as well understand each other, Jennie. I can see how this thing came about. It was a piece of foolishness on my part not to have asked you before and made you tell me. It was silly for you to conceal it, even if you didn't want the child's life mixed with mine. You might have known that it couldn't be done. That's neither here nor there, though, now. The thing that I want to point out is that it is things like this which make the relationship between a man and a woman terribly unsatisfactory. You can't live and hold any relationship without confidence. You and I had that, I thought. I've told you about how things are with me. You haven't done that, you see. I don't see my way clear, all in all, to ever hold more than a tentative relationship with you on this basis. The thing is too tangled. There's too much cause for scandal."

"I know," said Jennie.

"Now, I don't propose to do anything hasty. For my part I don't see why things can't go on about as they are—certainly for the present, but I want you to see just how things stand with me. I want you to look the facts in the face."

Jennie sighed. "I know, Lester," she said, "I know."

He went to the window and stared out. There were some trees in the yard, where the darkness was settling. He wondered how this would really come out, for he liked a home atmosphere. Should he leave the apartment and go to his club?

"You'd better get the dinner," he suggested after a time, turning toward her irritably; but he did not feel as distant as he looked. It was a shame that life could not be more decently organized. He went back to his lounge, and Jennie went about her duties. She was thinking of Vesta, of her own ungrateful attitude toward Lester, of his final decision never to marry her. So that was how one dream had been wrecked by folly.

She spread the table, lit the pretty silver candles he liked to have burning, made his favorite biscuit, put a small leg of lamb in the oven to roast, and washed some lettuce leaves for a salad. She had been a diligent student of a cook-book for some time and had learned a good deal from her mother. All this time she was thinking how it would all work out. He would leave her, no doubt of that, eventually. He would go away and marry someone else. She was doomed to just this sort of thing, but had not her life been fated? Had she ever had exactly what she wanted for long? No. Well, then, this additional blow could be borne, although it would tear her heart. Her Lester.

"Oh, well," she thought finally, "he is not going to leave me right away—that is something. And I can bring Vesta here."

She sighed as she brought the things to the table. If life would only give her Lester and Vesta together—but that was all over. The best she could hope for now, eventually, was what he had implied. Vesta and herself alone.

CHAPTER XXIX

There was peace and quiet for some time after this storm. Jennie went the next day and brought Vesta away with her. She had no difficulty in explaining to the Swede mother, since Vesta's health offered a sufficient excuse. There was then the reunion of the mother and child in this still-uncertain home, the joy of which made up for many other worries. "Now I can do by her as I ought," she thought, and three or four times during the day she found herself humming a little song.

Lester came only occasionally at first. He was trying to make himself believe that he ought to do something toward reforming his life—toward bringing about that eventual separation he had suggested. He did not like the idea of a child being in this apartment—especially that particular child. He fought his way through a period of calculated neglect and then began to return to the apartment more regularly. In spite of all its drawbacks, it was a place of quiet, peace, and very notable personal comfort.

During the first days of Lester's return it was very difficult for Jennie to know how to adjust things—how to keep the lightsome, nervous, almost uncontrollable child from annoying the staid, emphatic, commercial-minded man. She knew that she would have to watch Vesta closely, for Vesta would be out and around him if she didn't. Jennie gave Vesta a severe talking-to the first night Lester telephoned that he was coming, telling her that he was a very bad-tempered man who didn't like children and that she mustn't go near him. "You mustn't talk," she said. "You mustn't ask questions. Let Mama ask you what you want. And don't reach, ever."

Vesta agreed solemnly, but the idea of necessarily complying was not very deeply impressed after all.

Lester came at seven. Jennie, who had taken great pains to array Vesta as attractively as possible, had gone into her bedroom to give her own toilet a last touch. Vesta was supposedly in the kitchen. As a matter of fact, she had followed her mother to the door of the sitting-room, where now she could be plainly seen. Lester hung up his hat and coat, then, turning, caught his first glimpse. She was very sweet—he admitted that at a glance, arrayed in a blue-dotted white flannel dress, enhanced by a blue-starred softly rolled collar and cuffs, and completed by white stockings and yellow shoes. Her corn-colored ringlets hung gaily about her face. Blue eyes, rosy lips, rosy cheeks completed the picture. Lester stared, almost inclined to say something, but restrained himself. Vesta shyly retreated.

When Jennie came out, he commented on the fact that Vesta had arrived. "Rather sweet-looking child," he said. "Do you have much trouble in making her mind?"

"Not much," she returned.

Jennie went on to the dining-room, and then he heard his first scrap of conversation between them.

"Who are he?" asked Vesta.

"Sh! That's your Uncle Lester. Didn't I tell you you mustn't talk?"

"Are he your uncle?"

"No, dear. Don't talk now. Run into the kitchen."

"Are he only my uncle?"

"Yes. Now run along."

"All right."

And in spite of himself Lester had to smile.

What might have followed if the child had been homely, misshapen, peevish, or all three, can scarcely be conjectured. Had Jennie been less tactful, even in the beginning, he might have obtained a disagreeable impression. As it was, the natural beauty of the child, combined with the mother's gentle tact in keeping her in the background, served to give him that fleeting glimpse of innocence and youth which is always pleasant. For three hours after he arrived, the only impression he had of the child was the one he had received from the front room when he came in, but the impression lingered with him sharply. So this was the daughter of the late lamented State Senator Brander, and he would have married Jennie if he had lived!

That so fortunate an introduction could not end without beneficial results was obvious. Jennie was most careful to arrange a little playroom out of a maid's bedroom and to keep Vesta there during Lester's visit. There did not appear to be very much evidence of suppression, so far as he could make out, and everything was peaceful. Jennie loved her little one and managed to control her through her affections. That fact was not beyond his observation.

The thought struck him one night as he sat at home, canvassing the situation in his mind, as he usually did, that Jennie had had Vesta all these years; she had never had her with her when she was with him, however, and had never given him the least impression that she had such a thing as a baby on her mind, and yet her affection for Vesta was obviously great, as was Vesta's love for Jennie. "It's queer," he said. "She's a peculiar woman."

One morning Lester was sitting in the parlor near the window, reading his paper, when he thought he heard something stir.

He turned and was surprised to see a large blue eye fixed upon him through the crack of a neighboring door—the effect of which was very disconcerting indeed. It was not like the ordinary eye, which, under any such embarrassing circumstances, would have been immediately withdrawn, but instead was one of a much bolder kind, keeping its position without a sign of an abasement and deliberately staring him out of countenance. At the same time it was a wild eye, innocent in its largeness, so that the combination of effrontery and simplicity rather robbed him of his ability to reason about the matter. He turned from his paper solemnly and looked again. There was the eye. He turned from it again. Still was the eye present. He crossed his legs and looked again. Lo, the eye was gone.

Now the appearance of this eye, while not a very important thing in itself, had in it the saving grace of drollery, a thing to which Lester was especially responsive. Although not in the least inclined to relax his attitude toward the situation, he found his mind in the minutest degree tickled by the mysterious appearance, and the corners of his mouth animated by a desire to turn up. He did not give way to the feeling and stuck by his paper, but the incident remained very clearly in his mind. The young wayfarer had made her first really important impression on him.

Not long after this Lester was sitting one morning at his breakfast, calmly eating his chop and conning his newspaper, when he was aroused by another visitation—this time not quite so simple. Jennie had given Vesta her breakfast earlier and set her to amuse herself alone until Lester should leave the house. Jennie was seated at the table, pouring out the coffee, when Vesta suddenly appeared, very businesslike in manner, and marched through the room. Lester looked up, and Jennie colored and arose.

"What is it, Vesta?" she inquired, following her.

By this time, however, Vesta had reached the kitchen, secured a little broom, and returned, a droll determination lighting her face.

"I want my little broom!" she exclaimed and marched sedately past, at which manifestation of spirit Lester again twitched internally, this time allowing the slightest suggestion of a smile to play across his mouth.

Other things happened after this, notably a window-cleaning episode in which Vesta figured, a bare-armed little Amazon scrubbing diligently at one of the front windows, and again as the principal in some little hallway disagreement in which she must have come off with some uncertainty, for he heard her exclaim to her mother, "She better not hit me, better she?" at which he could not repress a chuckle.

"That's pretty good!" he thought. " 'Better she,' " and smiled again.

The effect of these things was gradually to break down the feeling of distaste he had for the child and to establish in its place a sort of tolerant recognition of her possibilities as a human being, a thing which ended in his frankly suggesting that she be allowed to come to the table with them.

"If she's going to live here, she'll have to come some time," he suggested, and Jennie, whom by his speech he seemed to indicate as the one who had kept her away, duly brought her.

The developments of the next six months were of a kind to further relax the strain of opposition which still existed in Lester's mind. Although not at all resigned to the somewhat tainted atmosphere in which he was living, and secretly feeling that there was much of the low and common about all that had transpired, yet he still found himself so comfortable in the home so established that he could not persuade himself to give it up. It was too much like a bed of down. Jennie was too worshipful. The condition of unquestioned liberty, as far as all his old social relationships were concerned, coupled with the privilege of quiet, simplicity and affection in the home, was too inviting. He lingered on, and, lingering, came more and more into the feeling that perhaps it would be just as well to let matters rest as they were.

During this time his relations with the little Vesta were strengthened somewhat. Owing to her clever whimsicality and the manner in which Jennie still guarded against intrusion upon him, Vesta proved more of a diversion to him than he had dreamed a child—and such a child—could be. He was not used to children, had never had one close enough about him to really know what, in the case of a bright and pretty child, the attraction might be. He had been inclined to think a child must prove an annoyance, and in this he had already been agreeably disappointed. Now he discovered that there was a real flavor of humor about Vesta's doings, and so came to watch for its development.

Thus at the breakfast and dinner table, although at first he tried to show no sign of any interest in her doings one way or the other, her irrepressible individuality proved so much of a factor that he could not possibly hold his peace. She was forever doing something interesting, and although Jennie watched over her with a care that was in itself a revelation to him, nevertheless she managed to elude every effort to suppress her and came straight home with her remarks. Once, for example, she was sawing away at a small piece of meat upon her large plate with her large knife when Lester remarked to Jennie that it might be advisable to get her a little breakfast set.

"She can hardly handle these knives."

"Yes," said Vesta instantly, "I need a little knife. My hand is just so very little."

She held it up and Jennie, who never could tell what was to follow, reached over and put it down, while Lester with difficulty restrained a desire to laugh.

Another morning not long after, she was watching Jennie get the lumps of sugar in her own and Lester's cups when she broke in with: "I want two lumps in mine, Mama."

"No, dearest," replied Jennie, "you don't need any in yours. You have milk to drink."

"Uncle Lester has two," she protested.

"Yes," returned Jennie, "but you're only a little girl. Besides, you mustn't say anything like that at the table. It isn't nice."

"Uncle Lester eats too much sugar," was her immediate rejoinder, at which that fine gourmet smiled broadly.

"I don't know about that," he put in, for the first time deigning to answer her directly. "That sounds like the fox and grapes to me." Vesta smiled back at him, and now that the ice was broken she chattered on unrestrainedly.

There were other things that interested him. Once he came home and found Jennie sitting on the floor, building a house out of blocks for her baby, and Vesta vastly interested.

"Now where's the chimney, Mama?" she was saying as she scattered blocks about.

Jennie got up, smiling.

"Don't let me disturb you," said Lester. "Play on. I'll lie down and read."

"Don't go, Mama," cried Vesta. "Don't go, Mama."

"Mama'll build it some other time," said Jennie, and kissed her baby's cheek. He liked this. It appealed to him as something sweet and worth while.

Another time he heard Jennie telling Vesta a wonder story, "Old Mr. Pig and the Wolf," no less, the latter the one who "huffed and puffed" and tried his best to blow the pig's house in.

Vesta was all excitement over the progress of the yarn and was "huffing and puffing" with her mother at each critical stage. "And did the wolf catch him that time?" she asked eagerly, looking in her mother's face.

"No, dearest," he heard Jennie say. "He ran and he ran and the wolf ran right after him, but he got to the door first and slammed it in the old wolf's face—*bang!* like that!"

Lester smiled.

"Did he have far to run?" asked Vesta sympathetically.

"Yes, quite a way. Clear down a long hill," explained Jennie.

"Was he tired?" added the child quaintly.

"Haw! Haw!" chuckled Lester quietly. " 'Was he tired?' That's pretty good." He came out after a time and watched Jennie undress her baby and tuck her in bed. He was getting fond of the little waif because she was bright.

"That's a smart child," he once remarked to Jennie. "She won't need much showing to make her way."

He got so he tried to talk to Vesta himself and finally succeeded, telling her curious things about some clowns with big feet who were being postered about the city as a part of a coming circus, and about some performing seals he had once seen. "I would like a nice seal!" exclaimed Vesta when he was through describing.

"I believe that," he replied, "but you'd have a hard time keeping him. Seals like lots of water. We haven't much water here."

"Couldn't I keep him in the bath tub?" asked Vesta.

"A fine, merry life he'd lead in the bath tub," said Lester, laughing. "He'd have a joyous chance to swim."

Jennie came in and took her. She was amused herself, but she was afraid Vesta would wear on Lester. But Vesta was convinced that the seal proposition was feasible.

It got so at last that Lester felt as though the little girl belonged to him; he was willing to see that she shared in such opportunities as his position and wealth might make possible—provided, of course, that he stayed with Jennie and that they worked out some arrangement which would not conflict notably with the world which was back of him, and which he had to keep constantly in mind.

CHAPTER XXX

The following spring the new showrooms and warehouse were completed and Lester took up his work in the building proper. Heretofore, he had been transacting all his business affairs at the Grand Pacific and the club. From now on he felt himself to be firmly established in Chicago—as if that were to be his future home. A large number of details were thrown upon him—the control of a considerable office force and the handling of various important transactions. It took away from him the need of traveling, that duty going to Amy's husband, under the direction of Robert. The latter was doing his best to push his personal interests, not only through the influence he was bringing to bear upon his sisters but through his reorganization of the factory during his brother's absence. It was so easy for him now to gradually replace, one by one, the people who were objectionable to him—to surround himself by degrees with people in responsible positions who were under obligation to him for putting them there. Several men whom Lester was personally fond of were in danger of elimination. But Lester did not hear of this, and Kane senior was inclined to give Robert a free hand. Age was telling on him. He was glad to see someone with a strong policy come up and take charge. Lester did not seem to mind. He and Robert were apparently on better terms than ever before.

Things might have rested so without growing much worse except that Lester's private career with Jennie in Chicago was not a matter which could be easily concealed. At times he was seen out driving with her by people who knew him in a social and commercial way. He was for brazening it out on the ground that he was a single man and at liberty to associate with whom he pleased. Jennie might be any young woman of good family in whom he was interested. She was good-looking and well-mannered—he had

schooled her well. He did not propose to introduce her to anybody if he could help it, and he always made it a point to be a fast
traveler in driving, in order that others might not attempt to
detain and talk to him. At the theatre, as has been said, if he were
caught, she was simply "Miss Gerhardt."

The trouble was that many of his friends were as keen ob-
servers of life as he was. They had no quarrel to pick with his
conduct. Only he had been seen in other cities, in times past,
with this same woman. She must be someone he was keeping in
an illicit way. Well, what of it? Wealth and youthful spirits must
have their fling. Rumors came to Robert, who, however, kept his
own counsel. If Lester wanted to do this sort of thing, all well and
good. But he could see where it would eventually do him no good.
There must come a time when there would be a show-down.

The latter eventuated, in one form, about a year and a half
after Lester and Jennie had begun living in the North Side apartment. It so happened that during a stretch of inclement weather
in the fall, Lester was seized with a mild form of grippe. When he
felt the first symptoms, he thought that it would be a matter of
short duration and tried to overcome it at once by taking a hot
bath and a liberal dose of quinine. But the infection was stronger
than he had counted on, and by morning he was flat on his back
with a severe fever and a splitting headache.

His long period of association and residence with Jennie had
made him incautious. Policy would have dictated that he take
himself off to his hotel and endure his sickness alone. As a matter
of fact he was very glad to be in the house with her, had her call up
the office to say he was indisposed and would not be down for a
day or so, and then yielded himself comfortably to her patient
ministrations.

Jennie was, of course, delighted to have him with her, sick or
well. She persuaded him to see a doctor and have him prescribe.
She brought him potions of hot lemonade and bathed his face and
hands in cold water over and over. Later, when he was recovering, she gave him appetizing cups of beef tea or gruel.

It was during this illness that the first real contretemps
occurred. Lester's sister Louise, who had been visiting with friends
in St. Paul, and who had written him that she might stop off to see
him on his way home in a month, decided upon an earlier return
than she had originally planned. While Lester was sick at his

apartment, she arrived in Chicago and, calling up the office and finding that he was not there and would not be for several days, asked where he could be found.

"I think he is at his rooms in the Grand Pacific," said an incautious secretary. "He's not feeling well."

A number of people had inquired, or this last would not have been added. The latter remark incited Louise to look further and, calling up the Grand Pacific, she found that he had not been there for several days—did not, as a matter of fact, occupy his rooms more than one or two days a week. Piqued by this, she telephoned his club.

It so happened that at the club there was a telephone boy who had himself called up the apartment a number of times for Lester in the past. He had not been cautioned not to give its number—as a matter of fact, it had never been asked for by any one else. When Louise stated that she was Lester's sister and was anxious to find him at once, the boy replied, "I think he lives at 19 Schiller Street."

"Whose address is that you're giving?" inquired a passing clerk.

"Mr. Kane's."

"Well, don't be giving out addresses. Don't you know that yet?"

The boy apologized, but Louise had hung up the receiver and was gone.

About an hour later, curious as to her brother's third residence number, she arrived at Schiller Street and was surprised at finding it less pretentious than she thought it would be. Ascending the steps—it was a two-apartment house—she saw the name of Kane on the door leading to the second floor. Ringing the bell, she was opened to by Jennie, who was surprised to see so fashionably attired a young woman ascending her stairs.

"This is Mr. Kane's apartment, I believe," began Louise, condescendingly, as she neared the head of the stairs and looked in at the open door behind Jennie. She was a little surprised to meet a young woman, but not being sure under what conditions Lester maintained his quarters, could only vaguely surmise.

"Yes," replied Jennie.

"He's sick, I believe. I'm his sister. May I come in?"

Jennie, had she had time to collect her thoughts, would have tried to make some excuse, but Louise, with the audacity of her birth and station, swept past before Jennie could say a word. Once inside, Louise looked about her inquiringly. She found herself in the sitting-room, which gave into the bedroom where Lester was lying. Vesta happened to be playing in one corner of the room and stood up to eye the new-comer. The bedroom door, which stood open, showed Lester quite plainly lying in bed, a window to the left of him, his eyes closed. At the sight of him she exclaimed, "Oh, there you are, old fellow! What's ailing you?" and hurried in.

Lester, who at the sound of her voice opened his eyes, realized in an instant how things were. He pulled himself up on one elbow but did not know what to say.

"Why, hello, Louise," he finally forced out. "Where did you come from?"

"St. Paul. I came back sooner than I thought," she said lamely, a sense of something wrong irritating her. "I had a hard time finding you, too. Who's your—" she was about to say "pretty housekeeper," but turned about to find Jennie dazedly gathering up certain articles in the adjoining room and looking dreadfully distraught.

Lester cleared his throat hopelessly.

His sister swept the place with an observing eye. It took in an open wardrobe with certain garments of Lester's side by side with those of Jennie thus accidentally exposed to her gaze. There was a dress of Jennie's lying across a chair in a familiar way which caused Miss Kane to draw herself up warily. She looked at her brother, who had a rather curious expression in his eyes—slightly nonplussed, but cool and defiant.

"You shouldn't have come out here," he said finally before she could give vent to the rising question in her mind.

"Why shouldn't I?" she exclaimed, angered at the brazen confession—the moral badness aptly confessed. "You're my brother, aren't you? Why should you have any place that I couldn't come? Well, I like that—and from you to me."

"Listen, Louise," he said, drawing himself up further on one elbow. "You know as much about life as I do. There is no need of our getting into an argument. I didn't know you were coming, or I would have made other arrangements."

"Other arrangements, indeed," she sneered. "I should think as much. The idea!"

She was greatly irritated to think she had fallen into this trap; it was really disgraceful of Lester.

"I wouldn't be so haughty about it," he declared, his choler rising. "I'm not apologizing to you for my conduct. I'm saying I would have made other arrangements, which is a very different thing from begging your pardon. If you don't want to be civil, you needn't."

"Why, Lester Kane, how you talk!" she exclaimed, her cheeks flaming. "I thought better of you, honestly I did. I should think you would be ashamed of yourself living here in open—" she paused without using the word—"and our friends scattered all over the city. It's terrible and you know it. I thought you had more sense of decency and consideration."

"Decency, nothing," he flared. "I tell you I'm not apologizing to you. If you don't like this, you know what you can do."

"Oh!!" she exclaimed. "And from my own brother. And for the sake of that creature! Whose child is that?" she demanded, savagely and yet curiously.

"Never mind, it's not mine. If it were it wouldn't make any difference. I wish you wouldn't busy yourself about my affairs."

Jennie, who had been moving about the dining-room beyond the sitting-room, heard the cutting references to herself. She winced with pain.

"Don't flatter yourself. I won't any more," retorted Louise. "I should think, though, that you of all men would be above anything like this—and that with a woman so obviously beneath you. Why I thought she was—" she was again going to add "your housekeeper," but she was interrupted by Lester, who was angry to the point of brutality.

"Never mind what you thought she was," he growled. "She's better than some who do the so-called superior thinking. I know what you think. It's neither here nor there, I tell you. I'm doing this, and I don't care what you think. I have to take the blame. Don't extend your remarks to what you think."

"Well, I won't, believe me. I couldn't—" she went on. "It's quite plain that your family means nothing to you. But if you had any sense of decency, Lester Kane, you would never let your sister be trapped into coming into a place like this—I know that. I'm disgusted, that's all, and so will the others be, when they hear of it."

She turned on her heel and walked scornfully out, a withering look being reserved for Jennie, who had unfortunately stepped near the door of the dining-room. Vesta had disappeared. Jennie came in a little while later and closed the door. She knew of nothing to say. Lester, his thick hair roached back from his vigorous face, leaned back moodily on his pillow. What a devilish trick of fortune, he thought. Now she would go home and tell it to the family. His father would know, and his mother. Robert, Imogene, Amy—all would hear. He would have no explanation to make—she had seen. He stared at the wall meditatively.

Meanwhile Jennie, moving about her duties, also thought. So this was what her real position was in their eyes. Now she could see what the world thought. This family was as aloof from her as if it lived on another planet. To his sisters and brothers, his father and mother, she was a vile woman far beneath him socially, far beneath him mentally and morally, a creature of the streets. And she had so hoped somehow to rehabilitate herself in the eyes of the world. It cut her as nothing that had ever happened before in her life had. It tore a great, gaping wound in her sensibilities. She was really low and vile in her—Louise's—eyes, in the world's eyes, basically so in Lester's eyes. How could it be otherwise? She went about numb and still, but the ache of defeat and disgrace and basic shame was under it all. Oh, if she could only see some way to make herself right with the world, to live right. To be decent. How could that really be brought about, if ever? It ought to be, she knew that, but how?

CHAPTER XXXI

The storm of feeling which Lester anticipated Louise's report would arouse was not long in making itself felt even in Chicago. Outraged in her family pride, Louise lost no time in returning to Cincinnati, where she told the story of her discovery, embellished with many details. According to her, she was met at the door by a "silly-looking, white-faced woman" who did not even offer to invite her in when she announced her name, but stood there "looking just as guilty as a person possibly could." Lester also had acted shamefully, having brazened the matter out to her face, and, when she had demanded to know whose the child was, had refused to tell her. "It isn't mine," was all he would say.

"Oh dear, oh dear!" exclaimed Mrs. Kane, who was the first to hear this story. "My son, my Lester! And I have always entertained such high hopes for him."

"And such a creature!" exclaimed Louise emphatically, as though the words needed to be reiterated to give them any shadow of reality.

Mrs. Kane gripped her two hands together and opened her mouth in amazement and distress. Louise continued with other important details, such as the manner in which Lester had said he had not asked her to come, and the way in which he had let her come away without offering another word in explanation.

"And I went there solely because I thought I could help him. I thought when they said he was indisposed that he might be seriously ill. How should I have known?"

"Poor Lester!" exclaimed her mother. "To think he would come to anything like that!"

Louise sighed; after all Lester was her favorite brother, the one whom she had really more respect for than any one else in the world.

"I felt sorry afterward that I didn't stay," she said remorsefully, "but I was so angry at the time I hardly knew what I was doing. That creature ought to be shown exactly what she is."

"You did perfectly right, my dear," returned Mrs. Kane sadly, the volume of her feeling of reproach for Lester having been mingled with a quantity of motherly sympathy for the suffering his illness might have caused him. "Of course you couldn't be expected to stay under such circumstances. He can't be so very ill, or he would have notified us surely! Robert will have to go up and look after him in case he is really in need of some of us. We ought not to leave him alone sick if he needs us."

Mrs. Kane turned this difficult problem over in her mind and, having no previous experiences whereby to measure it, telephoned for old Archibald, who came out from the factory and sat through the discussion with a solemn countenance. So Lester was living openly with a woman whom they had never heard of. He would probably be as defiant and indifferent as his nature was strong. There was no looking at this from the standpoint of parental authority. Lester was a centralized authority in himself, and if any overtures for a change of conduct on his part were to be made, they would have to be very diplomatically executed.

Archibald Kane returned to the manufactory sore and disgusted, but determined that something ought to be done. He held a consultation with Robert, who confessed that he had heard disturbing rumors from time to time but had not wanted to say anything. He professed sorrow over the folly of Lester and was shrewd enough to guess that very little could be done about it unless Lester were himself the doer. This woman with whom he was now disporting himself must be some designing creature with whom he was temporarily infatuated, for certainly Lester would never go so far as to marry someone who was far beneath him. It was an evil relationship and a wild prank for a man of his brains and social standing to indulge in. By what round of secret machinations could a thing like this have been possibly brought about? In this case, he could not say.

Old Archibald decided after all that someone ought to go up and see Lester—Robert, of course. There was, in his judgement, the need of discussing this moral digression in a common-sense sort of way, and, if there were any possible way of doing it, of bringing Lester back to the application of his own good logic to the facts.

"He ought to see that this thing, if continued, is going to do him irreparable damage," said Mr. Kane. "He cannot hope to carry it off successfully. Nobody can. He ought to marry her, or he ought to quit. I want you to tell him that for me."

"All well and good," said Robert, "but who's going to make him? I'm sure I don't want the job."

"I hope to," said old Archibald, "eventually—but you'd better go up now and try, anyhow. It can't do any harm. He might come to his senses."

"I don't believe it," replied Robert. "He's a strong man. You see how much good talk does down here. Still, I'll go if it will relieve your feelings any. Mother wants it."

"Yes, yes," said his father distractedly, "better go."

Accordingly Robert went. He devoted the whole waking hours of his trip to a solid contemplation of the task he had before him, of the surliness with which Lester would accept any intrusion on his part, of the tact and good nature he would have to display, and lastly of the appeal he would have to make. Lester might not be amenable to argument, but an appeal, the citing of his innate regard for his father and mother—surely he would not remain wholly obdurate in the face of their feelings about the matter.

Without allowing himself to formulate any pictures of success in this venture, he rode pleasantly into the city, confident in having all the powers of morality and justice on his side, and feeling content in the thought that, if he failed to have any weight with his brother, he still had done his duty.

When he arrived in Chicago, the third morning after Louise's interview, he called up the ware-rooms, but Lester was not there. He then telephoned to the house and tactfully made an appointment. Lester was still indisposed, but he preferred to come down to the office, and did. He met Robert at his private office in his cheerful, nonchalant way, and together they talked business for a time. Then gradually his brother veered the topic to the real business which had brought him, and Lester looked him calmly in the eye.

"Well, I suppose you know what brought me up here," said Robert.

"I think I could make a guess at it," Lester replied.

"They were all very much worried over the fact that you were sick—mother particularly. You're not in any danger of having a relapse, are you?"

"I think not," said Lester.

"Louise said there was some sort of a peculiar *ménage* she ran into up here. You're not married—are you?"

"No," said Lester.

"The young woman Louise saw is just—" he waved his hand expressively.

Lester nodded.

"I don't want to be inquisitive, Lester. I didn't come up for that. I'm simply here because the family felt that I ought to come. Mother was so very much distressed that I couldn't do less than see you for her sake—although now that I'm here, I really don't see what's to be done about it. I thought I'd ask your opinion, though."

He paused and Lester, touched by the impartiality of the tone as well as by the respect in which his personality was held, felt moved to express himself, if for no more than affability's sake. Some explanation was certainly due.

"I don't know that anything I can say will help matters much," he replied thoughtfully. "There's really nothing to be said. I have the woman, and the family has its objections. The chief difficulty about the thing seems to be the bad luck in being found out."

He stopped, and Robert turned the substance of this worldly reasoning over in his mind. Lester was very calm about it. He seemed, as usual, to be most convincingly sane.

"You're not contemplating marrying her, are you?" he queried after a time.

"I hadn't come to that," said Lester coolly.

They looked at each other quietly for a moment, and then Robert turned his glance to the distant scene of the city.

"It's useless to ask whether you are seriously in love with her, I suppose," ventured Robert.

"I don't know whether I'd be able to discuss that divine afflatus with you or not," returned Lester with a touch of grim humor. "I have never experienced its prescribed sensations myself. All I know is that in the present case the lady is very pleasing to me."

They paused again, and before Lester could think of anything else to say, Robert began with:—

"It's all a question of your own well-being and the family's, Lester, as far as I can see. Morality doesn't seem to figure in it in any way—at least you and I can't discuss that together. Your feelings on that score naturally relate to you personally. But—the matter of your own personal welfare seems to me to be substantial enough ground to base a plea on. The family's feelings and pride are also fairly important, not that I think that anything any one of us could do would personally detract from the honor of any of the others, but there's a feeling about these things, and father's the kind of man who sets more store by the honor of his family than most men. You know that as well as I do, of course."

"I know how father feels about it," returned Lester. "The whole business is as clear to me as it is to any of you, though I don't see just what's to be done about it, offhand. These matters aren't always of a day's growth, and they can't be settled in a day. The girl's here. To a certain extent I'm responsible that she is here. While I'm not willing to go into details, there's always more in these affairs than appears on the court calendar. Unfortunately I'm the only one privileged to judge just at present."

"Of course I don't know what your relations with her have been," returned Robert, "and I'm not curious to know, but it does look like a bit of injustice all around, don't you think—unless you intend to marry her?"

"I might be willing to agree to that, too," said Lester, "if anything were to be gained by it. The point is, the woman is here, and the family is in possession of the fact. Now if there is anything to be done, I have to do it. There isn't anybody else can act for me in this matter."

Lester lapsed into a silence, and Robert rose and paced the floor a bit, coming back after a time to say, "You say you haven't any idea of marrying her—or rather you haven't come to it. I wouldn't, Lester. It seems to me you would be making the mistake of your life, from every point of view. I don't want to orate, but a man of your position has so much to lose. You can't afford to do it. Aside from family considerations, you have too much at stake. You'd be simply throwing your life away—"

He paused with his right hand out before him, as was customary when he was deeply in earnest, and Lester felt the candor and simplicity of this appeal. Robert was not criticizing him now. He was making an appeal to him, and this was somewhat different.

The appeal passed without comment from him, however, and then Robert began on a new tack, this time picturing old Archibald's fondness for Lester and the hope he had always entertained that he would marry some well-to-do Cincinnati girl—Catholic, if agreeable to him, but worthy of his station at least. And Mrs. Kane felt the same way; surely Lester must realize that.

"I know just how all of them feel about it," Lester interrupted at last, "but I don't see that anything's to be done right now."

"You mean that you don't think it would be policy for you to give her up just at present."

"I mean that she's been exceptionally good to me, and that I'm morally under obligation to do the best I can by her. What that may be, I can't tell."

"To live with her?" inquired Robert coolly.

"Certainly not to turn her out bag and baggage, if she has been accustomed to live with me," replied Lester.

Robert sat down again, as if he considered his recent appeal futile.

"Can't family reasons persuade you to make some amicable arrangements with her, and let her go?" he inquired.

"Not without due consideration of the matter, no."

"You don't think you could hold out some hope that the thing will be ended quickly—something that would give me a reasonable excuse for softening down the pain of it to the family?"

"I would be perfectly willing to do anything which would take away the edge of this thing for the family, but the truth's the truth, and I can't see any room for equivocation between you and me. As I've said before, these relationships are involved with things which make it impossible to discuss them—unfair to me, unfair to the woman. No one can see how they are to be handled, except the people that are in them, and even they can't always see. I'd be a damned dog to stand up here and give you my word to do anything except the best I can."

Lester stopped, and now Robert rose and paced the floor again, only to come back after a time and say, "You don't think there's anything to be done just at present."

"Not at present."

"Very well, then. I expect I might as well be going. I don't know that there's anything else we can talk about very much."

"Won't you stay and take lunch with me? I think I might manage to get down to the hotel if you'll stay."

"No, thank you," said Robert. "I believe I can make that one o'clock train for Cincinnati. I'll try, anyhow."

They stood before each other now, Lester pale and rather flaccid, Robert clean, waxlike, well-knit and shrewd, and one could see the difference time had already made. Robert was the clean, decisive man, Lester the man of doubts. Robert was the spirit of business energy and integrity embodied, Lester the spirit of commercial self-sufficiency, looking at life with an uncertain eye. Together they made a striking picture, which was none the less powerful for the thoughts that were now running through their minds.

"Well," said the older brother, after a time, "I don't suppose there is anything more I can say. I had hoped to make you feel just as we do about this thing, but of course you are your own best judge of this. If you don't see it now, nothing I could say would make you. It strikes me as a very bad move on your part, though."

Lester listened. He said nothing, but his face expressed an unchanged purpose.

Robert turned for his hat, and they walked to the office door together.

"I'll put the best face I can on it," said Robert, and walked out.

CHAPTER XXXII

In this world of ours the activities of animal life seem to be limited to a plane or circle, as if that were an inherent necessity to the creatures of a planet which is perforce compelled to swing about the sun. A fish, for instance, may not pass out of the circle of the seas without courting annihilation; a bird may not enter the domain of the fishes without paying for it dearly. From the parasites of the flowers to the monsters of the jungle and the deep, we see clearly the circumscribed nature of their gyrations—the emphatic manner in which life has limited them to a sphere—and we are content to note the ludicrous and invariably fatal results which attend any effort on their part to depart from their environments.

In the case of the activities of man, however, the operation of this theory of limitations has not yet been so clearly observed. The laws governing the social life of man are not yet so clearly understood as to permit of a clear generalization. Still the little opinions, pleas, arguments, and quarrels—if not actually like the forces which seize upon and cast men out of the world itself—are so similar in their results that they may well be considered a variation of the same thing. When men or women err—that is, pass out from the sphere in which they are accustomed to move— it is not as if the bird had intruded itself into the water or the wild animal into the haunts of man. Death is not the immediate result. People may do no more than elevate their eye-brows in astonishment, laugh sarcastically, or, in the case of friends going wrong, lift up their hands in protest, and yet so conditional is the well-defined sphere of social activity that he who departs from it is doomed. After having been accustomed to this environment, the individual is practically unfitted for any other state. He is like a bird accustomed to a certain density of atmosphere; he cannot live well at either higher or lower level. He is a victim of the theory of limitations, and any departure from his accustomed sphere can only prove his undoing.

When Lester parted from his brother in this spirit of dissatisfaction, he realized very clearly the reckless manner in which he had flown in the face of his family's feelings, the violence he had done those moral tenets of which his brother, for the time being, had been the personal representative. Even if Robert should choose for the family's sake not to report him as obstinately persisting in a course which they felt to be outrageous, nevertheless Robert was now in possession of the knowledge of his brother's shortcoming, and this in itself was a great difficulty. Would he be able to go home now after such a revelation as this? Could he think of facing his father and mother and the others after this drastic representation of his attitude? He thought about that. Truly his father would be deeply grieved, as his brother had said; his mother would be outraged in those fine sensibilities to which her condition as a proud and affectionate mother were heir. Robert, Amy, and Louise—how well he knew from the interviews he had had with the first and last of these how the family was in the future to look upon him.

And the worst of it was that honor did not dictate a plan of modifying the effect of Louise's discovery. Robert had come, and he had not been able to say anything which would soften the blow to those who had hoped that there might be some qualifying circumstances. Jennie was still here. Worst of all, he felt that for all the evil effects her staying was likely to entail, she had a right to be. Usefulness and adoration for him seemed to justify her. The very fact that she had nursed him so tenderly through his present illness seemed to preclude the possibility of thinking about her with anything save a kindly regard for her welfare.

He sat down in his easy chair by the window after his brother had gone and gazed ruminatively out over the flourishing city. Yonder was spread out before him life, with its concomitant phases of energy, hope, prosperity and pleasure, and here he was suddenly struck by a wind of misfortune and completely jolted to one side for the time being—his prospects and purposes enveloped in a haze. Could he continue as cheerily in the paths he had hitherto been wont to pursue? Would not his relations with Jennie be necessarily affected by the tide of opposition which had suddenly overtaken him? Was not his own home now a thing of the past, so far as his old easy-going relationship was concerned? All the atmosphere of unstained affection would be gone out of it now. That hearty look of approval which used to dwell in his father's eye—would it be there any longer? Robert, his relations with the manufactory, everything that was a part of his old life, had been affected by this sudden intrusion of Louise.

"It's damned unfortunate," was all that he thought to himself, and therewith turned from what he considered senseless brooding to the consideration of what, if anything, was to be done.

"I'm thinking I'll take a run up to Mt. Clemens tomorrow, or Thursday anyhow, if I feel strong enough," he said to Jennie after he had returned. "I'm not feeling as well as I might. A few days will do me good." He wanted to get off by himself and think. Jennie packed his bag for him at the given time, and he departed, but he was in a sullen, meditative mood.

During the week that followed, however, he had ample time to think it all over, and the result of these cogitations was that there was no need of making a decisive move at present. A few weeks more, one way or the other, would not make any practical difference. Neither Robert nor any other member of the family was at all likely to seek another conference with him. His business relations would necessarily go on as usual, since they were coupled with the welfare of the manufactory. No attempt to coerce him would ever be dreamed of by the family. Only this ghost of a shattered relationship with his family remained to haunt him— the lost esteem and confidence of his father and mother, the secret contempt and probably private satisfaction of his brother. "Bad business," he meditated—"bad business." But he did not change.

For some time, a period of a year, there was this unsatisfactory state of affairs without notable surface change, but with a slow, under-surface readjustment which was destined to show itself later. Lester did not go home for six months; then, an important business conference demanding it, he appeared and carried it all off as though nothing important had happened. His mother kissed him affectionately, if a little sadly; his father gave him his customary greeting, a hearty handshake; Robert, Louise, Amy, Imogene all concertedly, though without any verbal understanding, agreed to ignore the one important topic—to act as if nothing had ever happened. A feeling of estrangement was there, though, notably present in reality, and Lester felt it and soon left. His trips to Cincinnati thereafter were as few and far between as he could possibly make them.

CHAPTER XXXIII

In the meantime Jennie had been going through a moral siege of her own. For the first time in her life, aside from her family's attitude, which had afflicted her greatly, she had a taste of what the outer world thought. She was bad—she knew that. She had yielded on two occasions to circumstances which, as she sometimes thought, might have been fought out on different lines. If she had had more courage! If she did not always have this haunting sense of fear! Sometimes she thought she was cursed with a sense of fear, inherited from her father and mother. Things seemed to surround her and make her do differently from what she wanted to. Now was an occasion, she felt, when she ought to rise up and do something. She could get along. Lester would never marry her. Why should he? She loved him, but she could leave him, and it would be better for him. Her father would possibly live with her if she were back in Cleveland. He would honor her for at last taking a decent stand if she told him all. Yet leaving Lester was a terrible thought to her—he had been so good, and, as for her father, she was not sure whether he would receive her or not.

For some time after the tragic visit of Louise, she began thinking of saving a little money, laying it aside, for hitherto she had done nothing of that kind, but she was not morally able to do it. Lester had given her what he thought she needed. Since furnishing the house in Cleveland, she had sent home regularly fifteen dollars a week to maintain the family,—as much as they had lived on before, without any help from the outside. She spent twenty dollars to maintain the table, for Lester required the best of everything—fruits, meats, desserts, liqueurs and what not. The rent was fifty-five dollars, and clothes and extras a varying sum. He gave her nonchalantly fifty dollars a week, but somehow it had all gone. She thought how she might economize, but this seemed wrong. Better go without taking anything, if she were going, was the thought that came to her. It was the only decent thing to do.

She thought over this week after week following the advent of Louise, trying to nerve herself to the place where she could say something or act. Lester was consistently generous and kind, but she felt at times that he himself might wish it. He was thoughtful, abstracted. Since the scene with Louise in this apartment, it seemed to her that he had been a little different. If she could only say to him that she was not satisfied with the way she was living, and then leave. But he himself had plainly indicated, after his discovery of Vesta, that her feelings on that score could not matter so very much to him, seeing that he thought the presence of the child would definitely interfere with his ever marrying her. It was her presence he wanted on another basis. And he was so forceful—she could not argue with him very well. She decided if she went it would be best to write a letter and tell him why. Then maybe when he knew how she felt, he would forgive her and think nothing more about it.

The condition of the Gerhardt family was not improving. Since she had left, Martha had married. After several years of teaching in the public schools of Cleveland she had met a young architect, who had taken a great fancy to her, and they had been united after a short engagement. Martha had always been a little ashamed of her family, after she became old enough to discover its structural weaknesses, and now, when this new life dawned, was anxious to make the connection as slight as possible. She barely notified the members of the family of the approaching marriage—Jennie not at all, and at the time of the actual ceremony only wanted Bass and George because they were doing fairly well. Gerhardt, Veronica and William were not included and noticed the slight. Gerhardt was not for comment any more. He had had too many rebuffs. Veronica was resentful. She hoped that life would give her an opportunity to pay her sister off. William, of course, did not mind particularly. He was interested in the possibilities of becoming an electrical engineer, a career which one of his school teachers had pointed out to him as a field of great usefulness.

Jennie heard of Martha's marriage after it was all over, a note from Veronica giving her the main details. She was glad from one point of view, but realized that her brothers and sisters were drifting away from her. The connections, in all cases, were almost wholly and irretrievably broken.

A little while after Martha's marriage, Veronica and William left, going to reside with George, a thing which was brought about by the attitude of Gerhardt himself. Ever since his wife's death and the departure of the other children, he had fallen into a state of profound gloom from which he was not easily aroused. Life, it seemed, was drawing to a close for him, although he was only sixty-five years of age. The earthly ambitions he had once cherished were gone. He saw Sebastian, Martha and George out in the world practically ignoring him, contributing not at all to a home which should never have taken a dollar from Jennie. Veronica and William were restless. They objected to taking a smaller house, as he insisted should be done. They objected to leaving school and going to work, when it would have been better that they should be at work instead of living on money which he had long since concluded was not being come by honestly. He himself really should not be here, for after all he was not satisfied as to the true relations of Jennie and Lester. At first he had thought they were married, but the way Lester had neglected her for long periods, the way she ran at his beck and call, her fear of telling him about Vesta—somehow it all pointed to the same thing. She had not been married at home. Gerhardt had never had sight of her wedding certificate. Since she was away she might have been married, but he did not believe it.

And then here was the matter of the proper care and raising of Vesta, which still haunted him. What was the actual outcome of that? Jennie had written him that Lester knew now, that the child was with her, but was she? He had never been to Chicago to see. Jennie might be deceiving him as usual. And if Vesta was in the Kane home, was she legally adopted? Were they doing anything for her religiously? Was she being raised right? He pondered over these things long and wearily. It seemed an endless round of difficulty—of wrong action.

The trouble with Gerhardt was that he was intensely morose

and crotchety, and it was becoming impossible for young people to live with him. Veronica and William felt it. They resented the way he took charge of the expenditures after Martha left, quarreled with them because they spent too much on clothes and amusements, insisted that a smaller house should be taken, and hid a part of the money Jennie sent, for what purpose they could hardly guess. As a matter of fact, Gerhardt was saving as much as possible in order to have it eventually returned to her. He thought it was sinful to go on in this way, and this was his one method, outside of earning what he could himself, to redeem himself. If his other children had acted right by him, he felt that he would not now be left in his old age the recipient of charity from one who, whatever her other good qualities were, was certainly not leading a righteous life. So they quarreled.

It all ended one winter month when George, having received a raise of salary, and having long since tired of Gerhardt's quarreling and of his desire—his final insistence, in fact—to take smaller quarters, agreed to receive his complaining brother and sister on condition that they get something to do. Both agreed. Gerhardt was looking about Sundays for a little place when this occurred. He was nonplussed by it for a moment, but invited them to take the furniture and go their way. They were put in a sympathetic mood for the moment by this generosity of his and tentatively invited him to come and live with them, but this he would not do. He had decided to resort to his old trick of asking the foreman of the mill he watched for the privilege of sleeping in some out-of-the-way garret. He was always liked and trusted. And this would save him a little money.

So in a fit of pique he did this, and there was seen the spectacle of an old man watching through a dreary season of nights, in a lonely, trafficless neighborhood, while the great city pursued its gayety elsewhere. He had a wee, small corner in the topmost loft of a warehouse, away from the tear and grind of the factory proper, where he slept by day. He would sometimes get up in the afternoon and walk a little, strolling toward the business heart, or out along the banks of the Cuyahoga, or the lake, or where the big factories were speculating. As a rule his hands were behind his back, his brow bent in meditation. He would even talk to himself a little—an occasional "By chops!" or "So is it!" being indicative of his dreary mood. At dusk he would return, taking his stand at the lonely gate which was his post of duty. His meals he secured at a nearby working-man's boarding house—such of them as he thought he needed.

The nature of the old German's reflections at this time were of a peculiarly subtle and sombre character. What was this thing—life? What did it all come to, after struggle and worry and grieving? Where does it all go to? People die. You hear nothing more from them. His wife, now, she was gone. Where had her spirit taken its flight?

The trouble with his reasoning was that it was mixed in with some very dogmatic religious convictions which had not been upset by the direct testimony of life, but which had been shaken, confused, made anomalous—and still he believed they were so. He believed there was a hell. That people who sinned would go there. How about Mrs. Gerhardt? How about Jennie? He believed that both had sinned woefully. He believed that the just would be rewarded in heaven. But where were the just? He, actually, come to think, had not seen so many. Mrs. Gerhardt had not had a bad heart. Jennie was the soul of generosity. Take his son Sebastian, now—he was a good boy, but he was cold and rather indifferent to his father. Take Martha—she was ambitious but obviously selfish. She did not care for him. Somehow the children, outside of Jennie, seemed self-centered. They had made no effort to contribute reasonably—in fact, not at all, once they were able to do a little something. Bass walked off when he got married and did nothing more for anybody. Martha insisted that she needed all she made to live on. George had contributed for a little while, but had finally refused to contribute anything. Veronica and William had been content to live here on Jennie's money as long as he would allow it, and yet they knew it was not right. His very presence here, was it not a commentary on the selfishness of his children? And he was getting so old. He shook his head. Mystery of mysteries. Life was truly strange and dark and uncertain. Still he did not want to go and live with any of his children, he thought. Actually they were not worthy of him—none but Jennie, and she was not good. So he grieved.

This condition was not made known to Jennie for a considerable period of time. She had been sending her letters to Martha at first but, on her leaving, had sent them to Gerhardt. He had had Veronica write each week thanking Jennie and giving her the news, but now that Veronica was gone Gerhardt himself wrote saying that there was no need of sending any more money. Veronica and William were going to live with George. He had a good place in a factory and would live there a little while. He returned her a moderate sum he had saved—one hundred and fifteen dollars, with the word that he would not need it. Jennie did not understand, but as the others did not write her, she was not sure but what it might be all right—her father was so determined. By degrees, however, a sense of what it really must mean overtook her—a sense of something wrong, and she worried, hesitating between leaving Lester and going to see about her father, whether she left Lester or not. Would her father come with her? Not here certainly. If she were married, yes, possibly. If she were alone— probably. Yet if she did not get some work which paid well they would have a difficult time. It was the same old problem. What could she do? Nevertheless she decided to act. If she could get five or six dollars a week, they could live. This hundred and fifteen dollars Gerhardt had saved would tide them over the worst difficulties perhaps.

CHAPTER XXXIV

The trouble with Jennie's plan was that it did not definitely include a sane interpretation of Lester's attitude. He did care for her in a feral, Hyperborean way, but he was hedged about by the ideas of the conventional world in which he had been reared. To say that he cared enough for her to take her for better or worse—to legalize her anomalous position and face the world bravely with the fact that he had picked a wife who was suitable to him, whether she met with the ideas of those who were socially entitled to sit in judgement or not—was perhaps going a little too far, but he cared for her, and he was not in any mood at this particular time to contemplate the total loss of her.

He was getting along to that time of life when his ideas of womanhood were fixed and not subject to change. Thus far, on his own plane and within the circle of his associations, he had met no one who suited him as well as Jennie. She was gentle, intelligent, gracious, a handmaiden to his every need; and he had taught her the little tricks and necessaries of polite society until she was as comfortable a companion as he cared to know. When they went to the theatre he enjoyed her judgement of what constituted natural human motive—pathetic, humorous, or otherwise. If they were out for a drive he liked her comments on life and nature. In the home he enjoyed her capable management of all that concerned him and her, and her control of and relationship to Vesta were delightful. He had actually come to like the little waif, joked with and teased her and declared solemnly on several occasions that, when the time came, she ought to be sent to a suitable girls' school. Meanwhile the public school was, in his judgement, good enough for any child.

This condition holding, even in spite of the slaps it had had from an unkind fortune, had left him about where he was in the beginning—rather upset and annoyed by the trouble it had caused him but not satisfied to give it up.

Nevertheless, Jennie was going ahead in her brooding way, formulating a method of telling him which would be representative of her feelings and not unkind in its interpretation of his. She tried writing out her views, and started a half-dozen letters before she finally worded one which seemed to say partially what she felt in regard to herself, without being critical of anything he had failed to do. It was rather a long letter for her and ran as follows:

Lester Dear:

When you get this I won't be here, and I want you not to think harshly of me until you have read it all, for I am taking Vesta and leaving, and I think it is really better that I should. Lester, I ought to do it. You know when you met me we were very poor, and my condition was such that I didn't think any good man would ever want me, and when you came along and told me you loved me I was hardly able to think just what I ought to do. You made me love you, Lester, in spite of myself.

You know I told you that I oughtn't to do anything wrong any more and that I wasn't good, but somehow when you were near me I couldn't think just right, and I didn't see just how I was to get away from you. Papa was sick at home that time, and there was hardly anything in the house to eat. We were all doing so poorly. My brother George didn't have good shoes, and Mama was so worried. I have often thought, Lester, if Mama had not been compelled to worry so much then, she might be alive today. I thought if you liked me and I really liked you—I love you, Lester—it maybe wouldn't make so much difference about me.

You know you told me right away you would like to help my family, and I felt that maybe that would be the right thing to do. We were so terribly poor.

Lester dear, I am ashamed to leave you this way, it seems so mean, but if you knew how I have been feeling these days you would forgive me. Oh, I love you, Lester, I do, I do, but as I have thought of it for months past—ever since your sister came—I felt that I was doing wrong, and that I oughtn't to go on doing it, for I know how terribly wrong it is. It was wrong for me to ever have anything to do with Senator Brander, but I was such a girl then—I hardly thought what I was doing. It was wrong of me not to tell you about Vesta when I first met you, though I thought I was doing right when I did it. It was terribly wrong of me to keep her here all that time concealed, Lester, but I was afraid of you then—afraid of what you would say and do. When your sister Louise came, it all came over me somehow clearly, and I have never been able to think right about it since. It can't be right, Lester, but I don't blame you. I blame myself.

I don't ask you to marry me, Lester. I know how you feel about me and how you feel about your family, and I don't think it would be right. They would never want you to do it, and it isn't right that I should ask you, but at the same time I know I oughtn't to go on living this way. Vesta is getting along where she understands everything. She thinks you are her really truly uncle. I have thought of it all so much. I have thought a number of times that I would try to talk to you about it, but you frighten me when you get serious, and I don't seem to be able to say what I want to. So I thought if I could just write you this and then go, you would understand. You do, Lester, don't you? You won't be angry with me? I know it's for the best for you and for me. I ought to do it. Please forgive me, Lester, please—and don't think of me any more. I will get along. But I love you—oh, yes I do—and I will never be grateful enough for all you have done for me. I wish you all the luck that can come to you. Please forgive me, Lester. I love you, yes I do. I love you.

Jennie.

P. S. I expect to go to Cleveland with Papa. He needs me. He is all alone. But don't come for me, Lester. It's best that you shouldn't.

She put this in an envelope and sealed it and, having put it in her bosom for the time being, awaited the hour when she could conveniently leave.

It was several days before she could bring herself to the actual execution of her plan, but one afternoon, Lester phoning that he would not be home for a day or two, she put her necessary garments and those of Vesta in several trunks and sent for an expressman to get them. She thought once of telegraphing her father that she was coming, but, seeing he had no home, she thought it would be just as well to go and find him. George and Veronica had not taken all the furniture. The major portion of it was in storage, Gerhardt had written. She might take that and furnish a little home or flat. She was ready for the end, waiting for the expressman, who had not arrived, when the door opened and in walked Lester.

That worthy, for some unforeseen reason, had changed his mind. He was not at all psychic or intuitional, so he thought, but on this occasion his feelings had served him a peculiar turn. He had thought of going for a day's duck-shooting with some friends in the Kankakee marshes south of Chicago but had finally changed his mind, after he had telephoned Jennie that he would not be home, and had then decided to go out to the house early. What prompted this he could not have said.

As he neared the house he felt a little peculiar about coming home so early, but at the sight of the two trunks standing in the middle of the room he stood dumb-founded. Where was Jennie going, dressed and ready to depart? And Vesta in a similar condition? He stared in amazement, his brown eyes keen in inquiry.

"Where are you going?" he asked.

"Why—why—" she began, falling back, "I was going away—"

"Where to?"

"I thought I would go to Cleveland," she replied.

"What for?"

"Why—why—I meant to tell you, Lester, that I didn't think I ought to stay here any longer this way. I didn't think it was right. I thought I'd tell you, but I couldn't. I wrote you a letter."

"A letter!" he exclaimed. "What the deuce are you talking about? Where is the letter?"

"There," she said mechanically, pointing to a small centre table where she had laid it conspicuously on the top of a book.

"And you were really going to leave me with just a letter?" he said, picking it up, his voice hardening a little as he spoke. "I swear to heaven you are beyond me. What's the point?" He tore open the envelope and looked at the beginning. "Better send Vesta from the room," he suggested.

She did so mechanically. She came back and stood there pale and wide-eyed, looking at the wall, the trunks and him, but principally at him, and never moving. Lester read the letter thoughtfully. He shifted his position once or twice, then dropped the paper on the floor.

"Well, I'll tell you, Jennie," he said finally, looking at her curiously and wondering himself just what he should do about it. Here again was his chance to end this relationship if he wished. He couldn't say that he did wish it, seeing how peacefully things were running. They had gone so far together it seemed ridiculous to quit now. Still he did not want to marry her. "You have this thing wrong," he went on slowly. "I don't know what comes over you at times, but you don't view the situation right. I've told you before that I can't marry you—not now, anyhow. There are too many big things involved in this which you don't know anything about. I love you, you know that. What would I be doing running around with you for the past four years if I didn't? But my family has to be taken into consideration, and the business. You can't see the difficulties raised on these scores, but I can. Now I don't want you to leave me. I care too much about you. I can't prevent you, of course. You can go if you want to. But I don't think you ought to want to. Sit down a minute."

Jennie, who had been counting entirely on getting away without being seen, was now nonplussed and thrown out of her courage. She knew she ought to go, in a way, and yet she knew that she did not want to either. It was harder for her than for him. And to have him begin a quiet argument—a plea, as it were. It hurt her. He, Lester, pleading with her, and she loved him so!

She went over to him, and he took her hand.

"Now listen," he said. "There's really nothing to be gained by your leaving me at present. Where did you expect to go?" he asked again.

"To Cleveland," she replied.

"Well, how did you expect to get along?"

"I thought I'd take Papa, if he'd come with me—he's alone now—and get something to do, maybe."

"Well, what can you do, Jennie, different from what you ever have done? You wouldn't expect to be a lady's maid again, would you? Or clerk in a store?"

"I thought I might get some place as a housekeeper now," she suggested. She had been cogitating her possibilities, and this was the best thought which had been produced.

"No, no," he grumbled, shaking his head. "There's nothing in that. There's nothing in this whole move of yours except a notion. Why, you won't be any better off morally than you are right now. You can't undo the past. It doesn't make any difference anyhow. I can't marry you now. I might in the future, but I can't tell anything about that, and I don't want to promise anything. You're not going to leave me now, though, with my consent, and if you were going I wouldn't have you dropping back into any such thing as you're contemplating. I'll make some provision for you. You don't really want to leave me, do you, Jennie?"

During this solemn pronouncement of his feelings and beliefs, Jennie as usual had been growing in emotion. It was so hard for her to reason about the whys and wherefores of life. She tried to think things out, and by degrees she was getting a better conception of how the world was arranged, but it was slow work. In the face of his personality, his logic, his desire for her, her love of him, her own conclusions and decisions went to pieces. Just the pressure of his hand was enough to upset her. Now she began to cry.

"Don't cry, Jennie," he said. "This thing may work out better than you think. Let it rest for awhile. Take off your things. You're not going to leave me any more, are you?"

"No-oo!" she sobbed.

He took her on his lap. "Let things rest as they are," he went on. "It's a subtle world. Things can't be adjusted in a minute. They may work out. I'm putting up with some things myself that I ordinarily wouldn't stand for."

He finally saw her restored to comparative calmness, smiling sadly through her tears.

"Now you put those things away," he said genially, pointing to the trunks, "and I want you to promise me one thing."

"What's that?" asked Jennie.

"No more concealment of anything, do you hear? No more thinking things out for yourself and acting without my knowing anything about it. If you have anything on your mind now, I want you to come out with it. I'm not going to eat you! The thing you want to do is to learn to look the facts of life in the face. Talk to me about whatever is troubling you. I'll help you solve it, or, if I can't, at least there won't be any concealment between us. People can't live that way, Jennie. You know they can't. Don't you know that? It always breeds trouble."

"I know, Lester," she said earnestly, looking him straight in the eyes. "I promise I'll never conceal anything any more—truly I won't. I've been afraid, but I won't be now. You can trust me."

"That sounds like what you ought to be," he replied. "I know you will." And he let her go.

It was in consequence of this agreement that, a few days later, the condition of her father came up for discussion. She had been worrying about him for several days after her promise, but now it occurred to her that this was something to talk over with Lester. Accordingly she explained one night at dinner what had happened in Cleveland. "I know he is very unhappy there all alone," she said. "I hate to think of him like that. I was going to get him if I went back to Cleveland. Now I don't know what to do about it."

"Why don't you send him some money?" he inquired succinctly.

"He won't take any more money from me, Lester," she explained. "He thinks I'm not good—not acting right. He doesn't believe I'm married."

"He has pretty good reason, hasn't he?" he said calmly.

"I hate to think of him sleeping in a factory. He's so old and lonely."

"What's the matter with the rest of the family in Cleveland? Won't they do anything for him? Where's your brother Bass?"

"I think maybe they don't want him, he's so cross," she said simply.

"Excellent!" he replied. "They're fine children! I hardly know what to suggest in that case. The old gentleman oughtn't to be so fussy."

"I know," she said, "but he's so old now. He's had so much trouble."

Lester ruminated for a while, picking at his roast lamb. "I'll tell you what I've been thinking, Jennie," he said finally. "There's no use living this way any longer, if we're going to stick it out. I've been thinking we might take a house out in Hyde Park. It's something of a run from the office, but I'm not much for this apartment life. You and Vesta here would be better off for a yard. If I did that, you might bring your father on to live with us. He couldn't do any harm pottering around, if he'd come. He might help keep things straight."

"Oh, that would just suit Papa, if he'd come," she replied. "He loves to fix things, and he'd cut the grass and look after the furnace. But he won't come unless he's sure I'm married."

"I don't know how that could be arranged unless you could show the old gentleman a marriage certificate. He seems to want something that can't be produced very well. A steady job he'd have running the furnace of a country house," he added meditatively.

Jennie did not notice the grimness of his jest. She was too busy thinking of what a tangle her life was, how this last moral effort had come to nothing. Gerhardt would not come now, even if they had a lovely home—and it would have been so nice for him to have a home to come to. He ought to be with Vesta again. She would make him happy.

She ruminated thus until Lester, following the drift of her thought, said: "I don't see how it can be arranged. Marriage certificate blanks aren't easily procurable. It's bad business—a criminal offense to forge one, I believe. I wouldn't want to be mixed up in anything of that kind."

"Oh, I don't want you to do anything like that, Lester. I'm just sorry Papa is so stubborn. When he gets a notion you can't change him."

He thought over it for her, because she was so interested, and finally said, "Better wait until we get settled after moving. Then you can go to Cleveland and talk to him personally. You might be able to persuade him." He liked her attitude toward her father. It was so decent that he rather wished he could help her carry out her scheme. While not very interesting, Gerhardt was not objectionable to him, and if he wanted to do the odd jobs around a big place, why not? The subject was dropped for the time being, although it came up later in the same form.

CHAPTER XXXV

The proposition in regard to a residence in Hyde Park was not long in materializing. After several weeks had gone and things had quieted down again, Lester invited Jennie to go with him to South Hyde Park to look for a house, and on the first trip they found something which suited him admirably—and in consequence her—an old-time home of eleven large rooms set in a lawn fully two hundred feet square and shaded by trees which had been planted when the city was young. It was ornate, homelike, peaceful. Lester's reasons for looking for a place at this time were based on feeling. For one thing, he had grown a little weary of the Schiller Street apartment, largely because it had been the scene of a number of unpleasant things—the discovery of Vesta, the visit of Louise, the decision of Jennie to desert him. He thought that, in a large house with a lawn and flowers, she would be better contented, and he could find a satisfactory house in some inconspicuous neighborhood which would not trouble him on the score of publicity. All things told, he had done pretty well with the Schiller Street apartment in so far as public opinion was concerned—why not with a house on the far South Side? He hunted about and finally found this particular place, which, because it reminded him somewhat of his old home in Cincinnati, he liked very much. Jennie was fascinated by the sense of space and country, although depressed by the fact that she was not entering her new home under the right auspices. She had vaguely hoped that, in planning to go away, she was bringing about a condition under which Lester would have come after her and married her. Now all that was over. She had promised to stay, and she would have to make the best of it. The home was beautiful, but what was beauty without a right atmosphere? She suggested that they would never know what to do with so much room, but he waved that aside. "We will very likely have people in now and then," he said. "We can furnish it up anyhow and see how it looks." He had the agent make out a five-year lease, with an option for renewal, and set at once the forces to work to put the establishment in order.

It was painted, decorated, the lawn put in order, and everything done to give it a trim, satisfactory appearance. All the old furniture from the apartment was sent out, and such new as was deemed necessary was added. There was a large, comfortable library and sitting-room, a big dining-room with handsome furniture, a book-lined, ornament-bestrewn reception hall, a parlor with a baby grand piano, a large kitchen, a serving-room and, in fact, all the ground-floor essentials of a comfortable home. On the second floor were bedrooms, baths, a central reception hall and the maid's room. When it was finally completed, it had a comfortable, harmonious look throughout. A maid was hired and a man to look after the lawn and furnace and to run such errands as were necessary.

During this transfer Jennie was the soul of industry, albeit, as has been said, a little gloomy. She loved to look after her own things personally, and she was here, there and everywhere, working with her Swedish assistant, Mrs. Olsen, who had become general helper since the days when she cared for Vesta. "I wouldn't spend so much time on this job if I were you," Lester cautioned her sagely, but she only smiled.

"I like to do it, Lester," she replied. "I like things to do."

"You're the doctor," was all he would say.

In a very little while everything was in order, and Jennie, with Lester's permission, wrote to her father asking him to come to her. She did not say that she was married but rather left it to be inferred, seeing that the taking of a large house was testimony direct in favor of a sound matrimonial arrangement. She dilated on the beauty of the neighborhood, the size of the yard and so on. "It is so very nice," she added. "You would like it, Papa. Vesta is here and goes to school every day. Won't you come and stay here? It's so much better than living in a factory. And I would like to have you so."

Gerhardt read this letter with a solemn eye when it came. Was it really true? Would they be taking a larger house if they were not permanently united? After all, time was testimony in these cases, and they had been together some time now. Could he have been mistaken? Well, it was high time, whatever the truth was— but should he go? He had lived alone this long time now—should he go to Chicago and stay with her? It did have an appeal, but somehow he decided against it. That would be too quick an acknowledgement of general forgiveness. Still, of all his children, who had come to him or offered him release in this way? Jennie only. And her offer breathed sincere affection, that he knew.

When he wrote that he would not come, she was sincerely grieved. "Why will Papa act that way?" she thought. "Now I've made him such a nice offer and he won't come. And he would be so happy here." She talked it over with Lester and decided after a time that she would go and see him. Lester thought she could talk him into coming. Finally, with his consent, she made a trip to

Cleveland and hunted up the factory, which was a great rambling furniture company in one of the poorest sections of the city. She inquired at the office for her father. The clerk finally found his name as a watchman, looking all the time at her askance and wondering who she could be. Surely not a relative?—so well dressed! But he directed her to the distant warehouse, telling her any one would call Gerhardt, and when she came there a lumber-carrier climbed to her father's eyrie and informed him that a lady was waiting to see him. He crawled out of his humble cot and came down after a time, curious as to who it could be. When she saw him in his dusty, baggy clothes, his hair gray, his eyebrows shaggy, coming out of the dark door, her keen sense of the pathetic moved her again. "Poor Papa!" she thought. He came toward her, his inquisitorial eye softened a little by the sense of affection that had brought her. "What are you come for?" he asked cautiously.

"I want you to come home with me, Papa," she pleaded yearningly. "I don't want you to stay here any more. I can't think of you here."

"So," he said, nonplussed, "that brings you?"

"Yes," she replied. "Won't you? Don't stay here."

"I have a good bed," he explained by way of apology for his state.

"I know," she replied, "but we have such a good home now, and Vesta is there. Won't you come? Lester wants you to."

"Tell me one thing," he demanded. "Are you married?"

"Yes," she replied, lying hopelessly. "I've been married a long time." She could scarcely look him in the face, but she did her best, and somehow Gerhardt believed her. "You can ask Lester, when you come," she added.

"Well," he said, "it is time."

She made no answer, but the appeal of it all was working.

"Won't you come, Papa?" she pleaded.

He threw out his hands after his characteristic manner. The whole decency of it touched him to the quick. "Yes, I come," he said and turned, but she saw by his shoulders what was happening. He was crying.

"Now, Papa?" she pleaded.

For answer he walked back into the dark warehouse to get his things.

CHAPTER XXXVI

The progress of the general situation in regard to Lester, Jennie, and the home, after Gerhardt's arrival, was considerable. Gerhardt, having been duly installed, a rather emaciated old figure, bestirred himself at once about the labors which he felt instinctively concerned him. The furnace and the yard he took charge of, outraged at the thought that good money should be paid to any outsider when he himself had nothing to do. The trees, he declared to Jennie, were in a dreadful condition. If Lester would get him a pruning knife and a saw, he would fix these things in the spring. In Germany they knew how to do these things right, but these shiftless Americans knew nothing. Then he wanted tools and nails, and in time all the closets and shelves were put in order. He found himself a Lutheran church almost two miles away and declared that it was better than the one in Cleveland. The pastor, of course, was a heaven-sent son of divinity. And nothing would do but that Vesta must go to church with him regularly, and he was scandalized to see that Jennie did not go. It was partially Lester's fault, he saw that, for Lester was a wretched son of earth who had no religion in him and would lie abed Sundays. But as for Jennie—no good could result eventually from neglecting the church.

As for Jennie and Lester, they settled into the new order of living, enjoying the surrounding atmosphere very much. For him it meant establishment on a more pretentious basis and, as such, was more comfortable than was the old method, though in a way it was fraught with greater dangers and difficulties. For her it meant an opportunity to justify her claim to wifehood—to strengthen the bonds of affection which bound them, to appear more conspicuously, if not legally, in the role she so much craved. She did not anticipate all the difficulties, however, for the atmosphere here was different. He had introduced her so long as "Miss Gerhardt" and kept her so much in the background that now, owing to the conspicuous placement of the home, when he was compelled to acknowledge her before their neighbors, at least, as his wife, he felt a little strange and nonplussed. It had been so easy for Jennie, on the North Side, to shun neighbors and say nothing. Here, because things were so much more dignified and respectable, their immediate neighbors felt it their duty to call, and she had to play the part of an experienced hostess. She and Lester had talked this situation over. Neighbors were sure to come in and try to make friends. Lester and Jennie knew this would be the case. It might as well be understood here, he said, that they were husband and wife—it was necessary. Callers were to be received kindly, tea served if they wished, any story she saw fit told about her own early life, if it was told at all, only it must be the same story. Vesta was to be introduced as her daughter by her first marriage—her husband, a Mr. Stover (her mother's maiden name), having died immediately after the child's birth. Lester, of course, was the stepfather. Then they were to admit they had lived on the North Side. Hyde Park was so far from the fashionable heart of Chicago that Lester did not expect to run into many of his friends. He explained to her all the usages of entertainment, so that when the first visitor called Jennie was prepared to receive her, sure she was acting within the limits of what Lester desired and what was best for herself and all concerned.

They had not been in the house a week before this personage arrived in the shape of Mrs. Jacob Stendhal, a woman of considerable importance in this section, who, seeing that the house was ultra-respectable in its atmosphere and refined and tasteful, decided to call. She lived five doors from Jennie—the houses of the neighborhood were all set in spacious lawns—and drove up in her carriage on her return from her shopping one afternoon.

"Is Mrs. Kane in?" she asked of Jeannette, the new maid, whom Jennie had secured.

The girl, seeing the carriage, opened the door wide for entrance. "I think so, ma'am. Won't you let me have your card?"

The same was given and taken to Jennie, who looked at it curiously.

When she came into the entrance hall, which was in its way a reception room, Mrs. Stendhal, a tall, dark, inquiring-looking woman, greeted her most cordially.

"I thought I would take the liberty of intruding on you," she said most winningly. "I am one of your neighbors. I live on the other side of the street, some few doors up. Perhaps you have seen the house—the one with the white stone gate-posts."

"Oh, yes, indeed," replied Jennie, "I know it well. Mr. Kane and I were admiring it the first day we came out here."

"I know of your husband, of course, by reputation. My husband is connected with the Wilkes Frog and Switch Company."

Jennie bowed her head. She knew that the latter concern must be something important and profitable from the way in which Mrs. Stendhal spoke of it.

"We have lived here quite a number of years and admire this section of the city very much. I know how you must feel, coming as a total stranger to a new section of the city. I hope you will find time to come in and see me some afternoon. I shall be most pleased. My regular reception day is Thursday."

"Indeed I shall," answered Jennie, a little nervously, for she was on her mettle. This was a part of the social ordeal she knew she would have to become accustomed to. "I appreciate your goodness in calling. Mr. Kane is very busy as a rule, but when he is here I am sure he would be most pleased to meet both you and your husband."

"You must both come over some evening," replied Mrs. Stendhal. "We lead a very quiet life. My husband is not much for social gatherings. But we enjoy our neighborhood friends."

Jennie smiled her assurances of good-will. She accompanied Mrs. Stendhal to the door and shook hands with her. "I'm so glad to find you so charming," observed Mrs. Stendhal frankly.

"Oh, thank you," said Jennie flushing a little. "I'm sure I don't deserve so much praise."

"Well, now I will expect you some afternoon. Goodbye," and she waved her a gracious farewell.

"That wasn't so bad," thought Jennie as she watched Mrs. Stendhal drive away. "She is very nice, I think. I'll tell Lester about her." And she thought of the others who would come now, and what they would be like, and how she would get along with them. It wasn't so very hard after all, was it?

Among the other callers were a Mr. and Mrs. Carmichael Burke, who called a little later, a Mrs. Hanson Field, a Mrs. Timothy Ballinger and several others, all of whom left cards or stayed to chat a few minutes. Jennie found herself being taken quite seriously as a woman of importance—being the wife of so able a man, and she did her best to live up to it. Indeed, for the wife of so forceful and distinguished a person as Lester—as she now appeared to be, she did exceptionally well. She was most hospitable and gracious. She had a kindly smile and manner wholly natural, and she succeeded in making a most favorable impression. She was nervous at first, but her nervousness was not of the kind which showed itself in any visible tremor or any undue uselessness of motion. It made her chill and a little pale, but somehow, to her guests, she seemed all the more dignified and worthwhile for it. She explained to all in the pleasantest possible way that she had been living on the North Side until recently, that *her husband,* Mr. Kane, had long wanted to have a home in Hyde Park, that her father and daughter were living here, and that Lester was the child's stepfather. She said she hoped to repay all these nice attentions and to be a good neighbor.

Lester only heard about these calls in the evening, for he did not care to meet these people. If any of them came after eight, he made it a point to appear to be absent or working; but since most of the calling was done by the wives during the day, he was not greatly disturbed. Jennie came to enjoy it in a mild way. She liked people, and she was hoping that something definite could be worked out here which would make Lester see her as a good wife and an ideal companion. If she did this well enough, who knows—he might really someday want to marry her.

The trouble with this situation in so far as Jennie was concerned was that it had no real stability in point of character or possibility. As has been said, she was not of the social type—not even of this middle-world social type, which concerned itself here, in this neighborhood, with the affairs of well-to-do, aspiring, middle-class people. Every family resident here had some growing social and commercial connections. They were all trying to get along and get up, from positions of moderate trust and profit on the part of the men and budding social connections on the part of the women, to real financial success on the part of the former and real social recognition on the part of the latter. They would not long remain here, and most of them would not have remained any great length of time anyhow. Things were in a state of flux. Chicago was growing. The women, as a rule, were smart and interesting, but Jennie was better than that. Her queendom was really not of this particular social world, nor of the so-called higher one in which Lester naturally moved. She belonged to the world of dreamers who grow slowly and who come to a realization of things as they are only after a long time. Even when she did see, if she ever did, she would not have cared for these people. She was interested in nature and the drift of life. Because she loved Lester and was anxious to make a showing which would cause him to see that she was suited to his world, she worked hard at what might be called social affairs. She tried to make friends, to be nice and winning, and she did succeed in a way. These women liked her, but they were not big enough to like anything outside the conventional lines of living—or if they were, fear held them back.

Lester, for his part, and because of his conventional training, was prone to draw conclusions which, while sympathetic, were not wholly favorable to Jennie's social aspirations. He liked her immensely—might truly be said to have loved her, but his family and his social world still had a powerful grip on him. He had refused to marry Jennie solely to avoid that social comment which her presence as his wife would arouse; and now, having watched her here for some time, he figured that hers was not the temperament for introduction into formal social life, even if she had wanted to enter it, which he thought she did not. She did not care for it, he thought; could not make believe. She had none of the gayety and sparkle of the privileged figures of The Four Hundred, young and old. She had no sense of tradition, no family, no intimate knowledge of those various worlds—art, literature, society gossip—which make up the small change of social life. She would not have shone at a dinner. Many people might have found her tiresome, particularly those who are restless and eager for information concerning the little things which make up social brilliancy. But there was a mental and emotional pull to her nevertheless which bigger minds could understand. She thought only of big things in a vague way, formulating any idea or action slowly. But she thought in ways which usually transcended the common, more superficial method, much as the flow of a river might transcend in importance the hurry of an automobile.

But she liked social life of another kind, he saw—that quiet interchange of neighborly ideas and feelings which go to make up the substance and backbone of true social life. When it came to those pleasant things which concern taking an interest in one's neighbor's home, one's neighbor's children, one's neighbor's health and prosperity or sickness and failure, she was a personality to be reckoned with. Not that she did much in the way of talking and running—hers was a silent spirit—but she drew to herself those elements which, to a greater or less extent, felt right to her.

By degrees, those who lived in the immediate neighborhood, and there were not any who were social figures in any large sense, but all of whom had money and much comfort, came to see and feel that this was rather an exceptional home atmosphere which had been established here, and over which she presided. They saw Lester leaving in the morning, carried by a rather lively-stepping team of bays toward the city, and they saw Vesta emerge sometimes a little earlier, sometimes a little later, sometimes with her stepfather, who carried her to the school where her budding educational career had begun. His was a figure suited to impress any respectable home neighborhood, for he was strong, well set-up, handsome, conservatively dressed and with an air of distance and superiority which made any one note him as a personage. Vesta was sweet and gay, a lightsome, butterfly-type of child, always dressed in some extremely appropriate or childish novelty which set her off to perfection. She was seen to appear in quaint little dresses, big bows of ribbon, a flowered bag for her books, and to go hopping and skipping down the walk to the gate and down the side-walk, her mother looking smilingly after her. Jennie herself was seen to enter the family carriage with her husband and her young daughter, sometimes of an evening, sometimes of a Sunday afternoon, for a drive, or to stroll about the yard at times when the flowers were in season. There was a gay sleigh, which appeared with the first heavy snow, in which Jennie and Vesta were driven by Lester, the bells of the harness jingling merrily as they disappeared. It was quickly rumored, of course, that this was one of the sons of the celebrated Kane family, and that there was an endless supply of cash back of this rather charming social appearance.

CHAPTER XXXVII

The first impressions of a neighborhood are seldom enduring, as we all know well enough, and the first impressions of this particular neighborhood were subject to some modification, for they had been altogether a little too favorable. Jennie was charming to look at, gracious, but there were rumors which came from here and there. A Mrs. Sommerville, calling on Mrs. Craig, one

of Jennie's immediate neighbors, reported that she knew who
Lester was—"Oh, yes indeed. You know, my dear," she went on,
"his reputation is just a little—" she raised her eye-brows and her
hand at the same time.

"You don't say!" commented her friend curiously. "He looks
like such a staid, conservative person."

"Oh, no doubt in a way he is," went on Mrs. Sommerville.
"His family is of the very best. There was some young woman he
went with, my husband tells me—I don't know whether this is
the one or not—, but she was introduced as a Miss Gorwood, or
some such name as that, when they were living together as
husband and wife on the North Side."

"Tst! Tst! Tst!" clicked Mrs. Craig with her tongue at this
rather astonishing news. "You don't tell me. Come to think of it,
it must be the same woman. Her father's name is Gerhardt."

"Gerhardt!" exclaimed Mrs. Sommerville recollectively—
"that's the name. It seems that there was some scandal in connection with her before—at least there was a child. Whether he
married her afterward or not, I don't know. Anyhow I understand
his family will not have anything to do with her. At least she
hasn't been accepted in his circle here."

"How very interesting!" exclaimed Mrs. Craig. "And to
think he should have married her afterward, if he really did. He
appears to be the soul of devotion. I'm sure you can't tell with
whom you're coming in contact these days, can you?"

"It's so true. Life does get so badly mixed at times. I've no
doubt, as you say, that she appears to be a charming woman."

"Delightful!" exclaimed Mrs. Craig. "Quite naïve. I was
really taken with her."

"Well, it may be," went on her guest, "that this isn't the
same woman after all. I may be mistaken."

"Oh, I hardly think so. Gerhardt! She told me they had been
living on the North Side."

"Then I'm sure it's the same person. How curious that you
should speak of her!"

"It is, indeed," went on Mrs. Craig, who was speculating as
to what her attitude toward Jennie should be in the future.

Other rumors came from other sources. There were people
who had seen Jennie and Lester out driving on the North Side,

who had been introduced to her as "Miss Gerhardt," who knew what the Kane family thought. Everybody agreed that Lester was a remarkable person, that he might since have married her, that she might have been very unfortunate or was tremendously lucky, but she had a past and that had to be taken into consideration. Were they really married now—who knew? Of course her present wealth (or rather her husband's, if he was her husband), the charming manner in which they lived, the dignity of Lester, the beauty of Vesta—all these things helped soften the situation for her, for of course it was not possible by conversation to pull her down from her present position, if she had really attained it by marriage. She was apparently too circumspect, too much the good wife and mother, too really nice to be angry at.

An opening bolt of the coming storm fell upon Jennie one day when Vesta, returning from school, suddenly asked her, "Mama! Who was my papa?"

"His name was Stover, dear," replied her mother, struck at once by the thought that there might have been some criticism— that someone must have been saying something. "Why do you ask?"

"Where was I born?" continued Vesta, ignoring the last inquiry and interested only to clear up her own identity.

"In Columbus, Ohio, pet. Why?"

"Anita Ballinger said I didn't have any papa, if I wanted to know, and that you weren't ever married when you had me. She said I wasn't a really, truly girl at all—just a nobody. She made me so mad I slapped her."

Jennie stared solemnly before her. Anita Ballinger was the eight-year-old daughter of Mrs. Timothy Ballinger, who had come to call on her the first few weeks they had been settled in Hyde Park and had since shown many neighborly traits. She was a charming woman apparently, gracious, dignified, sympathetic. Jennie had thought her particularly considerate and helpful in her offers of assistance, and now her little daughter had said this to Vesta. Where did the child hear it?

"You mustn't pay any attention to her, dearie," soothed her mother as helpfully as she could. "She doesn't know. Your papa was Mr. Stover, and you were born in Columbus. You mustn't fight other little girls. Of course they say mean things when they fight—sometimes things they don't really mean. Just let her alone, and don't go near her any more. Then she won't say anything to you."

It was a lame explanation, but it satisfied Vesta for the time being. "I'll slap her if she tries to slap me," she persisted.

"You mustn't go near her, pet, do you hear? Then she can't try to slap you," returned her mother. "You mustn't quarrel. That isn't the way to be nice. Just go about your studies, and don't mind her. She can't quarrel with you if you don't let her."

Vesta went her way, but Jennie thought of this a long time, day after day. She could not say anything to Lester, and of course could speak to no one else, for there was no one else to talk to. She had to brood over this, knowing that the neighbors were talking—that her history was becoming common gossip. How had they found out?

It is one thing to nurse a single thrust, another to have the wound opened from time to time by additional stabs. Vesta brought home no additional comment immediately, but one day Jennie, having gone to call on Mrs. Hanson Field, who was her immediate neighbor, and who liked her very much in spite of what she had heard, was accidentally compelled to meet a Mrs. Williston Baker, who was there taking tea. Mrs. Baker was one of those more distant residents who knew of the Kanes, of Jennie's history on the North Side, and of the attitude of the Kane family. She was a thin, vigorous, intellectual woman, somewhat on the order of Mrs. Bracebridge, and very careful of her social connections. She had always considered Mrs. Field a woman of the same rigid circumspectness of attitude, and when she found Jennie calling there and being received, she was outwardly calm but inwardly greatly irritated.

"This is Mrs. Kane, Mrs. Baker," said Mrs. Field, introducing her guests with a smiling countenance and with every thought that the introduction would prove pleasing. Jennie was so young-looking, so flower-like in her unsophistication, even at twenty-nine. Mrs. Baker looked at Jennie ominously.

"Mrs. Lester Kane?" she inquired.

"Yes," replied Mrs. Field.

"Indeed," she went on freezingly. "I've heard a great deal about you."

She turned to Mrs. Field, ignoring Jennie completely, and

adding to some observation she had been making as to the social activities of some mutual friend. "She is so notably conservative," she added as a little reminder to Mrs. Field herself that she might be more cautious in her selection of those who were permitted to call on her. Jennie stood helplessly by, unable to formulate a thought which would be suitable to so trying a situation. Mrs. Baker immediately announced her departure, though she had come to stay longer. "I can't remain another minute. I promised Mrs. Neil that I would stop in to see her yet today. I'm sure I've bored you enough already as it is."

She walked to the door, not troubling to look at Jennie until she was nearly out of the room. Then she looked in her direction and gave her a frigid nod.

"We meet such curious people now and again," she observed finally to her hostess.

Mrs. Field did not feel able to defend Jennie in any way, for she herself was in no notable social position and was endeavoring, like every other middle-class woman of means, to get along. She did not care to offend Mrs. Williston Baker, who was socially so much more important than Jennie. She came back to where Jennie was sitting, smiling apologetically, but she was a little bit flustered. Jennie was out of countenance, of course. She could not talk gayly and genially now as she had hoped. The only thing either could do was to make lame, time-consuming remarks. Presently Jennie excused herself and went home. She had been cut deeply by this, and she felt that Mrs. Field now realized that she had made a mistake in ever taking up with her. There would be no additional exchange of visits there,—that she knew. And through it all there was no one to help her in the least, to stay her in her reflections that her life was a failure. It couldn't be made right, or, if it could, it wouldn't be. Lester was not inclined to marry her and put her right. She had the foolish notion that if he would marry her, somehow things would be different, but she had no notion as yet of the long, uphill fight he would have to make to establish her if he tried.

Jennie's misfortune at this time was that she did not understand quite the peculiar stratification of life which occurs everywhere, and which fixes the lives of people almost beyond their volition, unless they happen to be peculiarly strong and aggressive, and which succeeds in doing it very frequently even then.

She knew that Lester's family was against her, but she did not know that society demands so many things which even wealth and birth cannot give—the kind of society Lester liked. He was (outside of his passion for Jennie) very much for alertness of mind, swiftness of repartée, a certain amount of *hauteur*. It is true that he objected vigorously to this sort of thing when it was not backed by brains and fine feeling, but when it was, it appealed to him immensely. Few there were who really suited him, but there were a few, and they were joyously placed in his sphere. Letty Pace was one, the girl whom Lester had been most interested in before he had taken up with Jennie, but who had since married a Malcolm Gerald, wealthy and able, and was now in Europe. Mrs. Bracebridge was another, and Mrs. Knowles of Cincinnati—with whom he could have delightful moments of chatter and some good, hard, sophisticated talks. They did not have what Jennie had, but they had something else—almost as good at times. He was wont to try to figure out for himself just what it was about Jennie that appealed to him, and finally he concluded that it was her attitude toward life in general—simple, kindly, sympathetic, with an undertone of natural force that was like an organ-tone heard afar off. There was something there—as sure as he was alive. He knew that he did not take to or trouble with silly people. Jennie had something—a big, emotional pull of some kind which held him.

There was another side to this family life coming into play which was very delightful. If we will eliminate the attitude of these various people who originally, because of the obvious wealth and refinement of the new couple, had hastened to make friendly overtures, and who subsequently, when the news of their previous relationship arrived, showed by remarks, insinuations, absence, and direct insult, in Jennie's case, that they were not inclined to have anything to do with a home or personality, the morality of which was under suspicion (an attitude of which Lester was not yet aware, for Jennie did not tell him), the atmosphere was delightful enough. It has been indicated of Jennie, in dealing with the North Side apartment, that she was a fine housekeeper, companion, friend and helpmate. Here she was quite as much if not more so, only she showed to better advantage. After the first few weeks of effort, and because of the insistence of Lester, she had given over any attempts to do much of anything herself save superintend. Gerhardt was there, as has been indicated, to look after the details usually taken care of by a hired man, and he did so much more faithfully and effectively. In spite of his age, and he was very well along in years now—crotchety, fussy, inquiring—he was about the house and grounds, mornings and evenings, picking up sticks and pieces of paper that might have blown in, exchanging neighborly greetings with the stableman, the post-man, the milkman, the newspaper peddler and whoever else happened to have any regular or passing business with the estab-lishment. From having sunk to the place where he had considered all life more or less a failure—his own in particular—and having wanted nothing so much as to die, he had risen to the place where he now felt that there were a few more years ahead of him, and that he would be able to do considerable work in the world. He was rather partial to Lester as a man now, because that gentleman treated him considerately and with uniform courtesy, and he was inclined to feel that everything Jennie said in regard to her marriage was surely so this time because this house seemed so magnificent to him. These people coming in seemed to be sure that everything was all right. How could it be otherwise? So he busied himself about his multitudinous duties, never satisfied unless he had his hands in all that concerned the home.

One of his duties as he saw it—an idiosyncrasy of temper-ament to both Lester and Jennie—was to go about the house af-ter Lester or Jennie or the servants, turning out the gas-jets or electric-light bulbs which might accidentally have been left burn-ing, and complaining of extravagance. Lester's expensive clothes, which he carelessly threw aside after a few months' use, were a source of woe to the thrifty old German. He grieved over splendid shoes, discarded because of a few wrinkles in the leather or a slightly run-down heel or sole. Gerhardt was for having them re-paired, but Lester would have nothing to do with that. He an-swered the old man's querulous inquiry as to what was wrong "with them shoes" by saying they weren't comfortable any more.

"Such extravagance!" Gerhardt complained to Jennie. "Such waste! No good can come of anything like that. It will mean want one of these days."

"He can't help it, Papa," Jennie excused. "That's the way he was raised."

"Ha! A fine way to be raised. These Americans, they know

nothing of economy. They ought to live in Germany awhile. Then they would know what a dollar can do."

Lester heard something of this through Jennie, but he only smiled. Gerhardt was amusing to him.

One of the griefs of Gerhardt's life at this time was Lester's extravagant use of matches. He had the habit of striking a match, holding it while he talked, instead of lighting his cigar, and then throwing it away. Sometimes he would begin to light a cigar two or three minutes before he would actually do so, throwing away match after match. There was a place out in one corner of the veranda where he liked to sit of a spring or summer evening, smoking and throwing away half-burned matches. Jennie would sit with him, and a vast number of matches would be lit and tossed into the grass outside. At different times in cutting the grass here, Gerhardt found to his horror not a handful but literally boxes of half-burned match-sticks lying unconsumed and decaying under the fallen blades. He was discouraged, to say the least. He gathered up this damning evidence in a newspaper, a great stock of them, and carried them back into the sitting room where Jennie was sewing.

"See here what I find!" he demanded. "Just look at that! Just look at it! That man, he has no more sense of economy than a— than a—" the right term failed him. "He sits and smokes, and this is the way he uses matches. Five cents a box they cost—five cents. How can a man hope to do well and carry on like that, I like to know. Look at them."

Jennie looked. She shook her head. "Lester is extravagant," she said.

Gerhardt carried them to the basement. At least they should be burned in the furnace. He would have used them as lighters for his own pipe, sticking them in the fire to catch a blaze, only old newspapers were better, and he had stacks of these—another evidence of his lord and master's wretched, spendthrift disposition. It was a sad world to work in. Almost everything was against him. Still he fought as valiantly as he could against waste and shameless extravagance, but he could never succeed as well as he wished.

The crowning details of his economy related to his attitude toward Lester's discarded clothes. Gerhardt would have had all of Lester's old suits cut down for his own use if he could have worn them, but, being so saving himself, there was no hope. His clothes never wore out. He would wear the same suit of black— cut down from one of Lester's expensive investments of years before, every Sunday for a cycle. Lester's shoes, by a little stretch of the imagination, could be made to seem to fit, and these he wore. His old ties also—the black ones—they were fine. If he could have cut down Lester's shirts he would have done so; he did make over the underwear, with the friendly aid of the cook's needle. Lester's socks, of course, were just right. There was never any expense for Gerhardt's clothing.

The remaining stock of Lester's discarded clothing—shoes, shirts, collars, suits, ties and what not—he would store away for weeks and months, and then, in a sad and gloomy frame of mind, call in a tailor or an old-shoe man or a rag man and dispose of the lot at the best price he could. He learned by this process that all second-hand clothes men were sharks, that there was no use in putting the least faith in the protests of any rag dealer or old-shoe man. They all lied. They all claimed to be very poor. Some of them actually cried over hard times when they were buying, when as a matter of fact they were actually rolling in wealth. Gerhardt had investigated these stories, he had followed them up, he had seen what they were doing with the things he sold them.

"Scoundrels!" he declared. "They offer me ten cents for a pair of shoes, and then I see them hanging out in front of their places marked two dollars. Such robbery! My God! They could afford to give me a dollar."

Jennie smiled. It was only to her that he complained as a rule. He kept his money, though, and she suspected he had a small hoard hid away somewhere. As a matter of fact, he gave the most of it to his beloved church, where he was considered a model of propriety, honesty, faith,—in fact, of all the virtues which are supposed to be the concomitants of perfect religious old age.

In addition to Gerhardt there was Mrs. Frissell, the cook, whom Gerhardt considered a useless extravagance, marveling always that Jennie was not allowed to do her own cooking. There was also Jeannette Stevens, a most pleasing and attractive-looking maid, who admired Jennie and Lester extravagantly, un-derstood table service perfectly, was fond of looking after the details of the house, and thought Vesta and Gerhardt were ideal in their way, being members of the family. With these three efficient assistants, there was not so much for Jennie to do, and yet there was everything in the way of superintendence. She went from room to room during the day, seeing how things were. She had an eye for the order and fitness of things. There was the silverware to look after—to see that it was not tarnished; the linen to keep in stock in ample quantities; Lester's laundry as well as that of the others to send out. From Mrs. Bracebridge and from Lester's advice, she had learned how to stand about, calling on Jeannette to fix this and that. She would have done most things herself, had Lester not repeatedly cautioned her not to. "There's just one way to do this thing," he insisted. "Get someone else to do it, and see that they do it. You will learn more, do better, see what's going on clearer. Keep your own mind and hands easy. Then you can think." She did her best to follow this.

There were many things in which she came to understand him better than he did himself. She understood his moods—what a gray day meant; whether the approach of rain or snow would make him gruff and crusty; whether he was apt to want much or little for breakfast—she could tell it by the sound of his voice when he first got up. She could almost tell by the clock when he would want certain things, what he was doing, how he was feeling. Her intuitions concerning him were so keen that she could judge, by a movement of his head or a twist of his shoulder, whether he was wanting or thinking of something of which he was not willing to speak. Her glance would rove about and to her there would come, by telepathy perhaps, what it was. The next thing, if it were available, it was before him. Sometimes he would smile, sometimes say nothing at all, but he recognized this ability as being the complete proof of temperamental compatibility. At breakfast, at dinner, in the bath when he was shaving—everywhere she knew exactly what he was looking for and brought it. "That's it," he would say nonchalantly, hardly realizing that she had anticipated his need. So dependent on her was he that it irked him a little when she was not at his elbow.

During this time, and in spite of the ill winds that were beginning to blow socially, Jennie led the dream years of her existence. Lester, in spite of the doubts which assailed him at times as to the wisdom of his career, was fond of taking her in his strong arms and kissing her, telling her genially, in a general way, how things were going with him.

"Everything all right?" she would ask when he would come in of an evening.

"Right-oh!" he would answer, or "Sure!" and pinch her chin or cheek.

She would follow him in while Jeannette, always on the lookout, would take his coat and hat. In the winter-time they would sit in the library before the big grate-fire. In the spring, summer or fall he preferred to walk out on the porch, one corner of which commanded a sweeping view of the lawn and the distant street, and light his before-dinner cigar. He would then usually tell something that had happened or was going to happen—his father was going to revise the percentage system of rewarding old employés; or it was hard to get assistants with intelligence enough to carry out the schemes which he had devised; or he was thinking of taking a rest with her, leaving for Mt. Clemens or White Sulphur or Saratoga for a week or ten days. The way the lawn was kept, the condition of the horses, the state of his neighbor's property, or the sickness or death of any one always interested him. Jennie would sit on the side of his chair and stroke his head. Sometimes she would rub her cheek over his hair and pat his hand. "Your hair is not getting the least bit thin, Lester; aren't you glad?" she would say. Or, "Oh, see how your brow is wrinkled now. You mustn't do that. You didn't change your tie, mister, this morning. Why didn't you? I laid one out for you."

"Oh, I forgot," he would answer, or he would cause the wrinkles to disappear, or say that he would soon be getting bald if he wasn't now. She would pat his neck, hang on his arm as he walked, for she knew that he wanted her to.

In the drawing room or library, before Vesta and Gerhardt, she was not less loving, though a little more circumspect. She loved odd puzzles like Pigs in Clover, The Spider's Hole, Baby Billiards, and so on, and would have a new one every time she could find one. Lester liked these things himself. He would work by the hour, if necessary, to make a difficult puzzle come right. Jennie was clever at this herself. Sometimes she would show him how, and then she would be immensely pleased with herself. At other times she would stand behind him watching, her chin on his head, her arms about his neck. He seemed not to mind—was happy in the wealth of affection she bestowed. Her sense, her gentleness, her tact made an atmosphere which was immensely pleasing, and above all her youth and beauty appealed to him. It made him feel young—put age far off, convinced him that he was still in that light atmosphere which is of childhood. If there was one thing Lester objected to in himself, it was the thought of drying up into an aimless old age. He hated it, did not think it was necessary, did not propose to if he could help it. "I want to keep young or die young," was one of his pet remarks, and Jennie came to understand. She was so glad that she was so much younger now for his sake. She could always make him feel young if she tried, and she was so anxious to try.

One of the brightest notes in this whole home arrangement was the growth and development of Vesta, of whom Lester had steadily become more fond. Since leaving Schiller Street and now seeing her under these pleasant home conditions, he liked her better than ever. She learned rapidly, he discovered, and would sit at the big table in the library in the evening conning her books, while Jennie would sew and Gerhardt would read his interminable list of German-Lutheran papers which he was now allowed to have. It grieved the latter no little to think that Vesta should not be allowed to go to a German-Lutheran parochial school, but Lester would listen to nothing of the sort. "We'll not have any thick-headed German training in this," he said to Jennie when she suggested that Gerhardt had complained. "The public schools are good enough for any child. You tell him to let her alone."

There were really some delightful hours among the four. Lester liked to take the little seven-year-old school-girl between his knees and tease her. He liked to invert the so-called facts of life, to propound its paradoxes, and to see how the budding child's mind took them. "What's water?" he would ask and, being informed that it was "what we drink," would stare and say, "That's so, but what is it? Don't they teach you any better than that?"

"Well, it *is* what we drink, isn't it?" persisted Vesta.

"The fact that we drink it doesn't explain what it is," he replied. "You ask your teacher what water is." And he would leave her with this irritating problem troubling her young soul.

Food, china, her dress, anything was apt to be brought back to its chemical constituents, and he would leave her to struggle with these dark suggestions of something else back of the superficial appearance of things until she was actually in awe of him. She had a way of showing him how nice she looked before she started to school in the morning, a habit that arose because of his constant criticism of her appearance. He wanted her to look smart, insisted on a big bow of blue ribbon for her hair, that her shoes be changed from low-quarter to high boots with the changing character of the seasons, and that her clothing be carried out on a color scheme suited to her complexion and disposition.

"That child's light and gay by disposition. Don't put anything sombre on her," he once remarked.

Jennie had come to realize that he must be consulted in this, and would say, "Run to your papa and show him how you look."

Vesta would come and turn briskly around before him. "See?" she always said.

"Yes. You're all right. Go on." And on she would go.

He was so proud of her that on Sundays and some weekdays, when he and Jennie drove, he would always have Vesta in between them. He insisted that Jennie send her to dancing school, and Gerhardt was beside himself with rage and grief. "Such irreligion!" he complained to Jennie. "Such devil's fol-de-rol. Now she goes to dance. What for? To make a no-good out of her—a creature to be ashamed of."

"Oh, no, Papa," replied Jennie. "It isn't as bad as that. This is an awful nice school. Lester says she has to go."

"Lester, Lester, that man! A fine lot he knows about what is good for a child. A card-player, a whiskey-drinker!"

"Now hush, Papa; I won't have you talk like that," Jennie would reply warmly. "He's a good man and you know it."

"Yes, yes. A good man. In some things maybe. Not in this. No."

He went away groaning, but when Lester was near he said nothing.

It was the truth that beer, whiskey, cordials and liqueurs were amply stored in the basement and that Lester drank them. So did Gerhardt under persuasion. They were on the table. It was only when he was in a rage that whiskey was as bad as he now protested.

Old Gerhardt was so anxious that Vesta should get along well in school that he was inclined to be too insistent about her work. "You should pay more attention to your books!" he would exclaim when she would get up and wander to the window, or run to the piano, or leave what she was doing to come and tease him. He could not overawe her by his demands, however, for she had long since seen through his crotchety gruffness as meaning nothing in her case.

"Oh, you," she would say, pulling at his arm or rubbing his grizzled cheek. There was no more fight in Gerhardt when she did this. He lost control of himself—something welled up and choked his throat. He craved attention and affection, and getting it this way from Vesta, his little pet, made him careless of what she did. "Yes, I know how you do!" he would exclaim.

Vesta would tweak his ear.

"Stop now!" he would say. "That is enough."

It was noticeable, however, that she did not have to stop, nor did she have to study unless she herself willed it. Gerhardt had lost all desire to boss this child if she willed otherwise.

CHAPTER XXXVIII

During the time in which Lester had been putting his "matrimonial" relationship upon a more pretentious basis, the Kane family had been contemplating his stolid ignoring of the conventions with mingled pain and dissatisfaction. That it could not help but become a general scandal, in the course of time, was obvious to them. Rumors were already about at home. People seemed to understand in a wise way, though nothing ever was said directly. Kane senior could scarcely think what possessed his son to fly in the face of conventions in this manner and then deliberately persevere in his course. If the woman had been someone of distinction—some sorceress of the stage, or the world of art or letters, perhaps it would have been explicable if not commendable, but this creature of very ordinary capabilities, as Louise had described her, this putty-faced nobody—he could not possibly understand it.

And Lester was such an able man, by and large. He had good judgement of life and women. His companionship heretofore with women had been rather enviable. Look at the women in Cincinnati who knew him and liked him. Take Letty Pace, for instance. Why in the name of common sense had he not married her? She was good-looking, sympathetic, talented. There had been lots of girls of distinction and wealth who had set their caps for him in times past, and now he had come to this. The old man grieved bitterly, and then by degrees he began to harden. It seemed a shame that Lester should treat him so—treat his mother so, and his sisters. It wasn't natural or justifiable or decent. Archibald Kane brooded over it until he felt that some change ought to be enforced, but what it should be he could not say. Lester was his own boss. For so long he had been his favorite son.

Certain changes helped along an approaching dénouement. Louise married not many months after her very disturbing visit to Chicago, and then the home property was fairly empty except for visiting grandchildren. Lester did not attend the wedding, though he was invited. For another thing, Mrs. Kane died, making a readjustment of the family will necessary. Lester came home on this occasion, grieved to think he had lately seen so little of his mother—that he had caused her so much pain, but he had no explanation to make. His father thought at the time of talking to him but put it off because of his obvious gloom. Lester went back to Chicago, and there were more months of silence.

After Mrs. Kane's death the father went to live with Robert, for his three grandchildren afforded him some amusement in his old age. The business, except for the final adjustment, which would come after his death, was in Robert's hands. The latter was consistently agreeable to his sisters and their husbands and to his father, in view of the eventual control he hoped to obtain. He was not a sycophant in any sense of the word but a shrewd, cold, business man, shrewder quite than his brother gave him credit for. He was already richer by far than any two of the other children put together, but he chose to keep his counsel and to pretend modesty of fortune. He realized the danger of envy and preferred a Spartan form of existence, putting all the emphasis on inconspicuous but very ready and very hard cash. While Lester was drifting with his emotional relationship, Robert was working all the time.

It so came about that Robert's scheme for eliminating his brother from participation in the control of the business was really not very essential, for his father, after brooding long enough over the details of the Chicago situation, came to the definite conclusion that any large share of his property ought not to go to Lester. Obviously Lester was not as strong as he had thought him to be.

Long and close association with Robert, intimate observation of that individual's highly practical if chilly methods had led him to conclude that commercially there was no choice between them. Lester might be the bigger intellectually or sympathetically. Artistically and socially there was no comparison—but Robert got commercial results in a silent, effective way. If Lester was not going to pull himself together at this stage of the game, when would he? Better leave his property to those who would take care of it. Archibald Kane thought seriously of having his lawyer privately revise his will in such a way that, unless Lester should reform, he would be cut off with only a nominal income. But his father decided to give him one more chance—to make a plea, in fact, that he abandon his false way of living and put himself on a sound basis before the world. It wasn't too late. He really had a great future. Would he deliberately choose to throw it away? Old Archibald wrote Lester that he would like to have a talk with him at his convenience, and within the lapse of thirty-six hours Lester was in Cincinnati.

The result of this conversation was not any more satisfactory than the one which Lester had held with Robert after Louise's visit, although in a way it was somewhat more definite. His father, on a pretext of not feeling well, received him in his great, comfortable room in Robert's residence. After a few perfunctory inquiries as to the weather in Chicago and the general business prospects, old Archibald approached the proposition he had in mind direct.

"I thought I'd have one more talk with you, Lester, on a subject that's rather difficult for me to talk about," he said. "You know what I'm referring to?"

"Yes, I know," replied Lester, calmly.

"I used to think, when I was much younger, that my sons' matrimonial ventures would never concern me, but I changed my views on that score when I got a little farther along. I began to see, through my business connections, how much the right sort of a marriage helps a man, and then I got rather anxious that my boys should marry well. I used to worry about you, Lester, and I'm worrying yet. This recent connection you've made has caused me no end of trouble. It worried your mother up to the very last. It was her one great sorrow. Don't you think you have gone far enough with it? The scandal has reached down here. What it is in

Chicago I don't know, but it can't be a secret. That can't help the house in business there. It certainly can't help you. The whole thing has gone on so long that you have injured your prospects all around, and yet you continue. Why do you?"

"I suppose because I love her," Lester replied.

"You can't be serious in that," replied Archibald. "If you had loved her, you'd have married her in the first place. Surely you wouldn't take a woman and live with her, as you have with this woman for years, disgracing her and yourself, and still claim that you love her. You may have a passion for her, but it isn't love. If it were you'd have married her long ago."

"How do you know I haven't?" inquired his son solemnly. He wanted to see how his father would take to that idea.

"You're not serious!" The old gentleman propped himself up on his arms and looked at him.

"No, I'm not," replied Lester, "but I might be. I might marry her."

"Impossible!" exclaimed his father vigorously. "I can't be-lieve it. I can't believe a man of your intelligence would do a thing like that, Lester. Where is your judgement? Why, you've lived in open adultery with her for years, and now you talk of marrying her. Why, in heaven's name, if you were going to do anything like that, didn't you do it in the first place? Disgrace your parents, break your mother's heart, injure the business, become a public scandal, and then marry the cause of it. I don't believe it."

Old Archibald got up.

"Don't get excited, Father," said Lester quickly. "We won't get anywhere that way. I say I might marry her. I realize that all you say is true, or nearly so. It seems true anyhow. But I might marry her at that. She's not a bad woman, and I wish you wouldn't talk about her as you do. You've never seen her. You know nothing about her."

"I know enough," insisted old Archibald determinedly. "I know that no good woman would do as she has done. Why, man, she's after your money. What else could she want? It's as plain as the nose on your face."

"Father," said Lester calmly, his voice lowering ominously, "why do you talk like that? You never saw the woman. You wouldn't know her from Adam's off ox. Louise comes down here and gives an excited report, and you people swallow it whole. She isn't as bad as you think she is, and I wouldn't use the language you're using about her if I were you. You're my father and I respect you. I want always to do that. I've tried my best in most things to live up to your ideas. You're doing a good woman an injustice, and you won't, for some reason, be fair. You're usually exceptionally so. I can't understand it, but I don't want to quarrel with you. I respect you too much."

"Fair! Fair!" put in old Archibald quite before Lester was through. "Talk about being fair. Is it fair to me, to your family, to your dead mother to take a woman of the streets and live with her? Is it——"

"Stop now, Father!" exclaimed Lester, putting up his hand. "I warn you. I won't listen to talk like that. You're talking about the woman that I'm living with—that I may marry. I love you, but I won't have you saying things that aren't so. She isn't a woman of the streets. You know as well as you know anything that I wouldn't take up with a woman of that kind. She's a good woman. I tell you that, no matter what she's done, or what you think she's done. We'll have to discuss this in a calmer mood, or I won't stay here. I'm sorry. I'm awfully sorry. But I won't stand here and listen to any such language as that."

Old Archibald quieted himself. In spite of his opposition, he respected his son's point of view. He sat back in his chair and stared at the floor. How was he to handle this thing?

"Are you living in the same place?" he finally began.

"No, we've moved out to Hyde Park. I've taken a house out there."

"I hear there's a child. Is that yours?"

"No."

"Have you any children of your own?"

"No."

"Well that's a God's blessing," he declared.

Lester merely scratched his chin.

"And you insist you will marry her?"

"I didn't say that," replied his son. "I said I might."

"Might! Might!" exclaimed his father, his anger bubbling again. "What a tragedy! You with your prospects. Your outlook. How do you suppose I can seriously contemplate entrusting any share of my fortune to a man who has so little regard for what the world regards as right and proper? Why Lester, this carriage business, your family, your personal reputation appear to be as nothing at all to you. I can't possibly understand what has come over your judgement. I can't understand what has happened to your pride. It seems like some wild, impossible fancy. How can you do this way?"

"It's pretty hard to explain, Father. I can't do it very well. I simply know that I'm in this affair and that I'm bound to see it through. It may come out all right. I may not marry her. I may. I'm not prepared now, I know, to say what I'll do. I'll have to think a good deal more about it. I can't leave her all at once. There's no use talking about that. This thing didn't start in any silly, pointless way. It's been growing a long while. All I can say to you now is that I am thinking about this thing, trying to think it out. You'll have to wait. I'll do the best I can."

Old Archibald merely shook his head disparagingly.

"You've made a bad mess of this, Lester," he said finally. "Surely you have. But I suppose you are determined to go your way. Nothing that I have said appears to move you."

"Not now, Father. I'm sorry."

"Well I warn you, then, that unless you make some other arrangement—show some consideration for the dignity of your family and the honor of your position, that it will make a difference in my will. I can't go on countenancing this thing and not be a party to it morally and every other way. I won't do it. You can leave her, or you can marry her. You certainly ought to do one or the other. If you leave her, everything will be all right. We'll forget the past. I'll not mention it again. There will be no difference in my attitude one way or the other. You can make any provision for her you like. I have no objection to that. I'll gladly pay whatever you agree to. You will share with the rest of the children, just as I had planned. If you marry her, it will make a difference. I won't say what, but it will. I can't go on contemplating your throwing yourself away and not add my protest. I'll make it hard for you to do this—as hard as I can. If you take up with her finally after all this scandal, it will cost you something. Now you do as you please. But don't blame me. I love you. I'm your father. I'm doing what I think is my bounden duty. Now you think that over and let me know."

Lester sighed. He saw how hopeless this argument was. He felt that his father probably meant what he said now, but would he really, later? Would he cut him off? What could he do to counteract this? What could he say? How could he leave Jennie and justify himself to himself? Ought he really to do it? Would he be sorry? Would his father really cut him off? Surely not! The old gentleman loved him even now—he could see it. His father was troubled and distressed, and he did not know what to do. This attempt at coercion irritated Lester. The idea—he, Lester Kane, being made to do things—to throw Jennie down. He stared at the floor.

Old Archibald saw that he had let fly a telling bullet.

"Well," said Lester finally, "there's no use of our discussing it any further now—that's certain, isn't it? I can't say what I'll do. I'll have to take time and think. I can't decide this offhand."

The two looked at each other. Lester was sorry for the world's attitude, for his father's depressed feeling about it all. Kane senior was sorry for his son, but he was determined to see things through. He wasn't sure whether he had convinced and converted his son or not, but he was hopeful. Maybe Lester would come around yet.

"Goodbye, Father," said Lester, holding out his hand. "I think I'll try and make that two-ten. There wasn't anything else you wanted to see me about?"

"No."

The old man sat there after Lester had gone, thinking. What a twisted career. What an end to great possibilities. What a foolhardy persistence in evil and error. He shook his head. Robert was wiser. He was the one to control a business. He was cool and conservative. If Lester were only like that. He thought and thought. It was a long time before he stirred. And still his errant son appealed to him, somehow.

CHAPTER XXXIX

This information as to Lester's new arrangements in Chicago, communicated by degrees to the family, did not really make the opposition any more marked than it had been, though it fanned the flames anew. Although his sisters and brother were compelled to believe the information, they did not consider the arrangements natural or of any real enduring character. How could he—Lester—accept a home life under any conditions with a woman who knew nothing—an uneducated creature who was all wrong before she met him? And he the prospective heir of a half-million in his own right! Dear heaven! Could such a condition endure in a sane world? Imogene, Amy, Louise, Robert were to say the least disgusted. The subject was taboo. If Lester wanted to live with her, all right, but she should never darken their doors, believe that. He was now the black sheep of the family.

Meantime Lester had returned to Chicago. He realized that he had offended his father seriously, how seriously he could not say. In all his personal relations with his father he had never seen him so worked up. But even now Lester did not see that there was anything to do. He began to feel that he had probably made a mistake originally in letting an illicit passion get the better of his judgement, but since then he had not seriously erred. Of course policy dictated a very different course, but could he really, honestly, adjust his life to policy? It meant leaving Jennie—did he want to do that? This interview gave him a difficult problem to think upon, but he could not make up his mind. It seemed such a brutal thing to do. So he stood still. In the meanwhile the natural progress of his supposed married life in Chicago was not without its developments, which in their way were quite in accord with what had happened between his family and himself. Although in Jennie, Vesta and Gerhardt he had found three elements which, in their different ways, were gratifying—Jennie as his sweetheart and handmaiden; Vesta as a gay plaything and a charming work of art; Gerhardt as a character whose idiosyncracies he could not help smiling over—yet, nevertheless, there were outside considerations which were not so pleasant.

In Lester's private world, for instance, there were happening some things which indicated, quite as clearly to him as did these significant experiences with his family, that the contravener of social conventions, in certain spheres anyhow, and according to his or her ambition socially, commercially, politically or otherwise, pays rather dearly for his or her errors—unless he or she considers that what society is pleased to look upon as error is not error after all, and that the thing obtained is well worth in satisfaction what society is determined to take away in payment for it. In his own world, as has been said, there were many who knew of the earlier relationship with Jennie on the North Side and elsewhere and who were inclined to overlook it, so long as it appeared to be merely a temporary social transgression—an ebullition of lingering youthful enthusiasm. Now that he had established himself so conspicuously on the South Side and was letting it appear to some as if he were married, the nature of the new arrangement was coming up for careful inspection, and those who really liked him were asking themselves what they thought and what they intended to do. Those among his many distinguished friends—particularly those in the financial and social worlds—who liked him and were inclined to consider him a truly able man of sound judgement and perspective (in spite of the fact that he was only the son of a rich man and not a self-made one) were now inclined to look askance, to doubt their senses and his judgement—to consider that he must have a weak streak in him somewhere after all. What should Lester Kane be doing marrying, or at least living as man and wife with, a woman who was not of his own social station anyhow? How did he come to find her, and where? Was she really a servant girl as some people said? It appeared that her connection with Mrs. Bracebridge as a maid had been traced. Someone who had called there during her period of servitude had recognized her since, or claimed to. Was she dull or intelligent or what? What did he see in her?

These little things, so trivial to talk about apparently, are nevertheless so big and so significant in the affairs of the world. That indefinable thing, personal integrity, makes so much for business success, for social success, for intellectual success. People turn so quickly from weakness or the shadow of it. "Let us get away from failure and its earliest evidences" seems to be the subconscious and conscious thought or feeling of every element in nature. The process of "getting away" may take time; it may not appear to be in operation at first; its earliest manifestations may appear to be interminably slow, but depend on it, they are there, in full working order like the laws of gravitation and direction.

One day Lester happened to run across Berry Dodge, the millionaire head of Dodge, Holbrook & Kingsbury, a firm that stood in the dry-goods world where the Kane Company stood in the carriage world,—only Dodge had inherited his father's position as president. This was six months after Lester had begun residing in Hyde Park. Dodge showed some signs of something— Lester could not say whether it was diffidence or distance or what—some change of attitude which he had not noticed before. Dodge was one of his most valued social acquaintances, if not an intimate friend. Lester knew him about as he knew Henry Brace-bridge of Cleveland and George Knowles of Cincinnati. He visited at Dodge's home on the North Shore Drive, one of the most palatial residences in the city. Alice Dodge, his wife, was a clever woman, and there were two bright, sophisticated children. It was something to be included in the Dodge visiting list, though of course to Lester it was not as important as it might have seemed to some others less securely fixed.

"Why, Lester, I'm glad to see you again," said Dodge. They had met in Michigan Avenue near the Kane building. Dodge extended a formal hand, and seemed just a little cool. "I hear you've gone and married since I saw you."

"Something like that," replied Lester easily, with the air of one who prefers to be understood in a worldly way.

"Why so secret about it if you have?" asked Dodge, attempting to be gay, but with a little wry twist to the corners of his mouth. He was trying to be nice and to go through a difficult situation gracefully. "We fellows usually make a fuss about that sort of thing. You ought to let your friends know."

"Well," said Lester, feeling the edge of the social blade that was being driven into him, "I thought I'd do it in a new way. I'm not much for excitement in that direction anyhow."

"It is a matter of taste, isn't it?" replied Dodge a little absently. "You're living in the city, of course?"

"In Hyde Park."

"That's pleasant territory. How are things otherwise?" and he deftly changed the subject before waving Lester a perfunctory farewell.

Lester missed at once the inquiries which a man like Dodge would have made if he had really believed that he was married. Under ordinary circumstances his friend would have wanted to know a great deal about the new Mrs. Kane. He would already have known something of her in all likelihood—who her parents were, who her friends were, where she came from, or if he hadn't he would have wanted to know. There would have been all those little familiar touches so common to people on the same social plane, and he would have asked him to bring his wife over to see them, would have definitely promised to call. Nothing of the sort happened. The Dodges were aware of the nature of his shortcomings.

It was the same with the Burnham Moores, the Henry Aldriches, and a score of other people whom he knew equally well. They had all heard, apparently, that he had married and settled down. They were interested to know where he was living, what he was doing, whether it was really so. He had a hard time explaining. They were perfectly willing to joke him about being very secret, but they were not willing to discuss the supposed Mrs. Kane or the new relationship with him. They knew what the situation was. Everyone appeared to know. He was beginning to see that this last move of his was going to tell against him notably.

One of the worst stabs he had—it was the cruelest, because in a way it was the most unintentional—he received from an old acquaintance, Will Whitney, at the Union Club one evening. Lester was there, dining with Stoneman Hammond, a commercial friend of his, and Whitney met him in the main reading room as he was crossing from the cloak room to the cigar stand. The latter was a typical society figure—tall, lean, smooth-faced, immaculately garbed, a little cynical, and tonight a little the worse for liquor. "Hi! Lester!" he called. "What's this about a *ménage* of yours out in Hyde Park? Say, you're going some. How are you going to explain all this to your wife when you get married?"

"I don't have to explain it," replied Lester irritably. He didn't want anyone to hear. "I'm not up for cross-examination."

"When did that happen! Well, I swear! Ha! ha! You're a dark horse, sure enough," went on Whitney foolishly. "Don't you ever let on what you're up to? Eh? What?"

"Oh, it isn't so dark," said Lester. He noticed now that Whitney was just the least bit flushed. "Why should you be so excited about my affairs? You're not living in a stone house, are you?"

"Say, ha! ha! that's pretty good now, isn't it? You didn't marry that little beauty you used to travel around with on the North Side, did you? Eh! now! Ha, ha! Well, I swear! You married! You didn't now, did you?"

"Cut it now, Whitney," said Lester roughly. "You're under way. You're talking wild. Remember you're talking about my private affairs now. Brace up, will you?"

"Pardon, Lester," said the other aimlessly, but sobering. "I beg your pardon. Remember, I'm just a little warm. Eight whiskey sours straight in the other room there. Pardon. I'll talk to you some time when I'm all right. See, Lester? Eh! Ha! ha! I'm a little loose, that's right. Well, so long! Ha! Ha!"

Lester could hardly get over that cacophonous "Ha! ha!" It cut him, even though it came from a drunken society man. "That little beauty you used to travel with on the North Side. You didn't marry her, did you?" He quoted these things to himself. George, this was getting a little rough. He had never endured anything like this before—he, Lester Kane. It set him thinking. It made him weary of his dinner. It made him weary of his evenings. Certainly this recent move of his was going to make him pay. And his own family was so angry with him in the bargain.

CHAPTER XL

To contravene the social conventions of your time, to fly in the face of what people consider to be right and proper and to present a determined and self-willed attitude toward the world in matters of desire is quite an interesting and striking thing to contemplate as a policy, and quite a difficult one to work out to a logical and successful conclusion. The conventions, in their way, appear to be as inexorable in their workings as the laws of gravitation and expansion. There is a drift to society as a whole which pushes on in a certain direction, careless of the individual, concerned only with the general result. The drift for ages has apparently been toward the development of the home idea and the perfection of the family group, and, while this may have been a passing phase at the time that Lester and Jennie lived, much as its concomitant correlatives, the harem and the plurality arrangement of the Mormons, it was nevertheless dominant and destructive to anything in opposition. It showed itself in many little and unexpected ways, the moment the family might have been said to have become well-settled in its new environment, and it continued persistently during the remainder of the time they lived.

Neighbors talked, despite the fact that Lester was so well-known, so well-placed, so well able, apparently, to defend himself. It was soon pretty well-known, throughout the city (and the country, for that matter), that he had married unwisely or outside the conventional system for the Kane family, or rather its product was widely known. Lester, one of its principal heirs, had married a servant girl! He, an heir to millions! Could it be possible!

The American public likes gossip concerning the rich, or did at this time. It was inordinately interested in all that concerned the getting of money and the spending of it, for that was almost the sole and vital interest of the nation. A certain family had a million or two millions or ten millions of dollars. How were they going to spend it? Who were the daughters going to marry? How much cash were the children going to receive? With whom were they in love now? This was the business of the newspapers to chronicle, particularly in their Sunday issues, and this was the gossip of some of the smaller-fry society papers and magazines.

After Lester had been living as he now was, defiantly if moodily at times, for several years in Hyde Park, there began to appear references in this minor society leaflet and that to the fact that he had married unwisely, or rather in defiance of the wishes of his family, that he had married a girl of obscure origin, and that he was living out a rather distinguished romance in a rather retired and quiet way when he might have married famously and been one of the glittering social figures of the city. The fact that he might not be married seemed to be courteously ignored by these items, the romance of a real marriage between a man of wealth and a poor working-girl seeming to have a greater appeal for the paragraphers. It seemed rather astonishing to the poor and, in many cases, underpaid workers of the smaller press that any such thing should be. It was a choice morsel such as newspaper correspondents loved to telegraph from one city to another as reflecting the romance of the time and of life. A small society paper called the *South Side Budget* first referred to him anonymously as "the son of a famous and wealthy carriage manufacturer of Cincinnati" and outlined briefly what it knew of the story. "Of Mrs.————" it went on sagely, "not so much is known except that she once worked in a well-known Cleveland society family as a maid and was, before that, it is said, a working-girl in Columbus, Ohio. After such a picturesque love affair in high society, who shall say that romance is dead?"

Lester saw this item. He did not take the paper, but some kind soul took good care to see that a copy was marked and mailed to him. It irritated him greatly, for he suspected at once that it was a scheme to blackmail him. He did not know exactly what to do about it. He preferred, of course, that such comments should cease, but he also thought that if he made any efforts to have them stopped he might make matters worse. He was concerned as to what his family would think and his Chicago society friends, but he did nothing for the time being, hoping there would be nothing more. As time went on, however, this single item gave rise to others which he did not see, and about the time he was ready to act it attracted the attention of a newspaperman here and there in local journalistic circles. Inquiry was made by this person and that as to who was meant. Concealed references to him appeared in other small papers. Finally one Sunday editor, more enterprising than the others, conceived the notion of having this romance written up. It seemed so startling from every point of view. A full-page Sunday story with a scare-head such as "Sacrifices Millions for His Servant-Girl Love" could be seen by him, with pictures of Lester, Jennie, the house at Hyde Park, the Kane manufactory at Cincinnati, the warehouse on Michigan Avenue, and so on. He thought it was so fine that he consulted with the managing editor who, ignoring the prestige of the family, thought it advisable. The Kane Company was not an advertiser in any daily or Sunday paper. The newspaper owed them nothing. If Lester had been forewarned he might have put a stop to the whole business by consulting with the advertising department, putting an ad in the paper, or appealing to the publisher. He did not know, however, and so was without power to prevent the publication.

One thing the Sunday editor did which was commendable, though really more disastrous to Jennie and Lester, was to have the facts carefully looked up. Local newspapermen in Cincinnati, Cleveland, and Columbus were instructed to report by wire whether anything of Jennie's history was known in their cities. The Bracebridge family in Cleveland was asked whether Jennie had ever worked there. A garbled history of the Gerhardt family was obtained from Columbus. Jennie's residence on the North Side as Mrs. Kane, for several years prior to her supposed marriage, was discovered and the whole story rather nicely pieced together. It was not the idea of the newspaper editor to be cruel or critical, but rather complimentary. All the bitter things, such as the probable illegitimacy of Vesta, the probable immorality of

Lester and Jennie in residing together as man and wife when they were not—(the newspapermen could not actually establish the truth or falsity of their marriage or non-marriage)—the probable true grounds of the well-known objections of his family to the match, were to be ignored. The Sunday editor's idea was to have framed up a more or less Romeo and Juliet story in which Lester should appear as an ardent, self-sacrificing lover, and Jennie as a poor and lovely working-girl being lifted to great financial and social heights by the devotion of her millionaire lover. It was so fine that an exceptional newspaper artist was engaged to make scenes depicting the various steps of the romance, and the whole thing was handled in the most approved yellow-journal style.

Lester never knew how a photograph of him was obtained, though it was supplied simply enough by his Cincinnati photographer for a consideration. Jennie never knew that she was "snapped" by a staff photographer, coming out of her gate one morning to go downtown. She had on a neat walking suit and looked charming, so that did not make so much difference, for the photo did her looks justice, but she would have shrunk back in terror if she had known. The house was photographed, the Kane warerooms, and so on. Finally, apparently out of a clear sky, the story appeared—highly complimentary, running over with sugary phrases, but still, and in spite of itself, with the dark, sad facts looming up in the background. Jennie did not see it at first. Lester, who came across the page accidentally, tore it out. He was stunned and chagrined, irritated beyond words to express. "To think the damned newspaper would do that to a private citizen who was quietly minding his own business!" he thought. He went out of the house, the better to conceal his deep inward mortification. He avoided the more populous parts of the town, particularly the downtown section, and rode far out on Cottage Grove Avenue to the open prairie. He wondered, as the trolley car rumbled along, what his friends were thinking—Dodge and Burnham Moore and Henry Aldrich and all the long company of the well-to-do. This was a smash indeed. Why had he not attended to the previous item? A lawyer, working about among the newspapers, could have put a stop to this. Now it was too late. The damage had been done. Wrath was useless. The best he could do was to put a brave face on it and say nothing, or wave it off with an indifferent motion of the hand, letting it appear that he was married. One thing was sure—he could prevent further comment he knew. He returned to the house calmer, his self-poise restored, but he was eager to get to the office the next day in order to get in touch with his lawyer, Mr. Watson. He did not want to say anything to Jennie, for he did not feel that he could really talk to her about it.

The next day, early, he went to the office, feeling as though he had an exceedingly trying duty to perform. It was hard to ride or walk about and feel that you were in a way the cynosure of critical or wondering eyes. His employés would know it. The ones that had not seen the story would be told by the others. His family at Cincinnati would know it. Some Chicago papers were read there, and some one would see that his father's and brother's attention, to say nothing of his sisters', was called to it. He was satisfied that everyone in Chicago knew. It made him sick at heart.

Mr. Watson came at his request, on receipt of a telephone message. He was a large, bland man, slightly bald, blue-eyed, rather florid, smooth-shaven, who looked not unlike some of the published portraits of Robert G. Ingersoll, the famous lawyer-agnostic. He looked at Lester, smiling, for he intuitively anticipated that this hurried call might have something to do with the published story.

"You saw that story in the— about me yesterday, I suppose," said Lester.

"I did," replied Watson, who knew but of course had never indicated in any way what he knew.

"It's useless to say, Watson, that I'd have given considerable not to have had that appear."

"I understand perfectly," replied his counsel.

"The next best thing is to lock the stable door, now that the horse has been stolen. I don't want anything else to appear if it can be prevented."

"It can be," comforted Watson. "You can leave that to me."

"I know it. That's why I sent for you. I wish I had done so before. There was a small item published six months ago in the *South Side Budget* which gave me warning, but I did not take it. I wish sincerely now that I had."

"Let's not cry over spilled milk," replied his attorney. "I read the story—there was not anything libelous. Outside the fact that it establishes your marriage in the minds of the public, and certain references to the previous poverty of Mrs. Kane, I thought it was most complimentary. You can take one thing as a fact, though I know that it will not mean anything to you, one way or the other: it will make a sort of popular hero out of you with the working classes—the so-called proletariat."

Lester frowned a dark frown. He did not want to maintain this marriage idea.

"To the devil with them," he replied. "I'll welcome less attention from the proletariat and from the newspapers in the future. I want you to be sure to do everything in your power to stop it. There mustn't be anything else, if it can be helped."

"There won't be," said Mr. Watson determinedly.

Lester got up. "It's amazing—this damned country of ours!" he exclaimed. "A man with a little money hasn't any more privacy than a public monument."

"A man with a little money," said Mr. Watson, "is just like a cat with a bell around its neck. Every rat knows exactly where it is and what it is doing."

The shock that this story was to give Jennie did not materialize until a few days later when one of her neighbor friends, less tactful than the others and meaning no harm, called her attention to the fact of its appearance by announcing that she had seen it. Jennie did not quite understand at first. "A story about me!" she exclaimed.

"You and Mr. Kane, yes," replied her guest. "Your love romance."

Jennie colored swiftly. "Why, I hadn't seen it," she said. "Are you sure it was about us?"

"Why, of course," laughed Mrs. Stendhal. "How could I be mistaken? I have the paper over at the house. I'll send Marie over with it when I get back. You look very sweet in your picture."

Jennie winced.

"I wish you would," she said weakly.

She was wondering where they had secured her picture, what the article said, whether Lester had seen it, what he thought if he had, why he had said nothing if he had. He couldn't have seen it—otherwise he would have spoken. He was usually so direct about everything, good, bad or indifferent. Since he hadn't spoken, he probably had not seen it and would expect her to tell him—or would he? She was puzzled painfully by this unexpected development and was turning the matter over ruefully in her mind when her neighbor's daughter brought the page in question. It frightened her—the concise, direct, imposing headline standing out across the entire page—"This Millionaire Fell in Love With This Lady's Maid," which ran between a picture of Lester on the left and one of Jennie on the right. She was looking out of her photo, innocent of any intention to stare at anybody, but with a wondering, inquiring gaze which made her very pleasing to see. Lester was staring straight ahead in his determined, insistent way. There was an additional caption which explained how Lester, scion of the famous carriage-manufacturing family of Cincinnati, had sacrificed great social opportunity and distinction to marry his heart's desire. Below were scattered a number of other sketches— Lester addressing Jennie in the mansion of Mrs. Bracebridge, Lester standing beside her before an imposing and conventional-looking parson, Lester driving with her in a handsome victoria, the locale being, of course, one of the city parks, Jennie standing beside the window of an imposing mansion (the fact that it was a mansion being indicated by most sumptuous-looking hangings) and gazing out on a very modest working-man's cottage which was pictured in the distance. There was no attempt made to draw an exact likeness of her, but somehow the sketches looked not unlike her. She was nonplussed, hectored, staggered by what she saw, for she did not know how Lester would take it. She did not know how she ought to feel, really. How must he feel if he really had seen this, she kept saying to herself. She did not mind so much what it meant to her—as a matter of fact it was rather flattering, that she could see—but Lester, Lester, how must he feel? And his family! She had come, in her private conscience, to think rather badly of his family of late, for she had never seen them, had never had one word of welcome—only, on the contrary, Louise's bitter castigation—and she could not feel any personal friendship for them, but she felt sorry for Lester. He would mind. He loved his family. He always seemed to think they were the last word in matters social, intellectual and so on. Now they would have another club with which to strike him and her. Was she going to become a shining mark for the newspapers? She tried to keep calm about it—to exert emotional control, but again the tears would rise, only this time they were tears of opposition to defeat. She did not want to be hounded this way. She wanted to be let alone. Why couldn't she be—just a few years anyhow? She was trying to do right now. Why couldn't the world help her, instead of seeking to push her down?

CHAPTER XLI

The fact that Lester had seen this page was made perfectly clear to Jennie that evening, for he brought it home himself, having concluded, after mature deliberation, that he ought to. He had told her once that there was to be no concealment between them, and this thing, coming brutally as it did to disturb their peace, was nevertheless a case in point. He had decided to tell her not to think anything of it—that it did not make so much difference, though to him it made all the difference in the world. The effect of this chill history could never be undone. The wise— and they included all his social world, and many who were not of it—could see just how he had been living. The article which accompanied the pictures told how he had followed Jennie from Cleveland to Chicago, how she had been coy and distant, and that he had to court her a long time to win her consent. This was to explain their living together on the North Side. Lester realized that this was an asinine attempt to sugar over the true story, and it made him angry. Still, he preferred to have it that way rather than in some more brutal vein. He took the paper out of his pocket when he arrived at the house, spreading it on the library table. Jennie, who was close by, watched him, for she knew what was coming.

"Here's something will interest you, Jennie," he began dryly, when he had it properly unfolded.

"I've already seen it, Lester," she said wearily. "Mrs. Stendhal showed it to me this afternoon. I was wondering whether you had."

"Rather high-flown description of my attitude, isn't it? I didn't know I was such an ardent Romeo."

"I'm awfully sorry, Lester," said Jennie, reading behind the dry face of humor the serious import of this thing to him. She had long since learned that Lester did not express his real feeling—his big ills (ills so big that they could not readily be corrected by human effort) in words. He was inclined to jest and make light of the inevitable, the inexorable. This light persiflage merely meant, "This matter cannot be helped, so we will make the best of it."

"Oh, don't feel badly about it," he went on. "It isn't anything which can be adjusted now. They probably meant well enough. We just happen to be in the limelight."

"I understand," said Jennie, coming over to him. "I'm sorry, though, anyhow."

He folded up the paper as Gerhardt came in, and then Vesta arrived from somewhere, dancing and holding up a picture of a house she had drawn for her mother to see. She was taking drawing lessons at this time, and this was her chief interest. "Yes," said Jennie, "it's pretty." The maid came presently to announce dinner, and the incident of the newspaper story was over. But it was a sore subject with both of them.

For a long time this latest thrust of fate remained uppermost in Jennie's mind, for it was so indicative of the direction in which her life was flowing. It was perfectly plain to her after this that she had proved a great detriment to Lester in many ways. It would have been better for him, she thought, if he had let her go when she wanted to. It was weak on her part, she thought now, to have yielded, and yet she wanted so much to be with him. Dear heaven! Was there no remedy anywhere in life? And would he leave her now soon? Her own life was a failure. It would be just as well—better for him—if she went away now. Only he wanted her—she remembered that. He would not let her go. And she wanted so much to stay. Her love and respect for him swelled at the thought. He was really a good man in the best sense of the word—a big man, but he was making a failure of his life, and it was her fault. He ought never to have taken her at all.

Lester, on his part, was cogitating constantly. The evidence he had received up to now, that he was in a bad position socially, was convincing. His father had pointed it out to him rather plainly at the last interview, but this newspaper notoriety had capped it all. He might as well abandon his pretension to intimacy with his old world. It would have none of him, or at least the more conservative part of it would not. There were a few bachelors, a few gay married men, some sophisticated women, single and married, whom he knew who saw through it all and liked him, but they did not make society. Society was made by the most conservative, who were almost invariably the most powerful. Their very conservatism was their power. So he was practically out of it.

What he should do under these circumstances was really not a question with him at this time. If he had asked himself practically, he would have said that wisdom dictated that he leave Jennie at once, making suitable provision for her, but not going near her any more. He could be restored to favor if he were really clear of all this. But he did not want to do this. The thought was painful and objectionable. He did not want to show her that he was so mean as to force her to come with him, and then leave her at the first breath of ill fortune. What a rough thing it all was. Jennie was growing in mental acumen. She was beginning to see things quite as clearly as he did. She was not a cheap, ambitious, climbing creature. She wanted to be fair by him; she had his real interests at heart. She was a big woman in her way. It would be a shame to throw her down, and besides she was good-looking. He was forty-six and she was thirty-one; and she looked twenty-four or -five. It is an exceptional thing to find beauty, youth, compatibility, intelligence,—your own point of view softened and charmingly emotionalized in another. He had made his bed, as his father had said. Had he better lie on it?

It was only a little while after this disagreeable newspaper incident had taken place that Lester had word that his father was quite ill and failing, and that it might be necessary for him to go to Cincinnati at the first word. Pressure of work was holding him pretty close when word came that his father was dead. Lester was of course greatly shocked and grieved, and returned to Cincinnati in a retrospective and sorrowful mood. His father had been a great character to him—a fine and interesting old gentleman entirely aside from his relationship to him as his son. He remembered him now dandling him upon his knee as a child, telling him stories of his early life in Ireland, and of his subsequent commercial struggles when he was a little older, impressing the maxims of his business career and his commercial wisdom on him as he grew to manhood. Old Archibald had been radically honest. It was to him that Lester owed his instincts for plain speech and direct statement of fact. "Never lie," was Archibald's constant, reiterated statement. "Never try to make a thing look different from what it is to you. It's the breath of life—truth—it's the basis of real worth, while commercial success—it will make a notable character of any one who will stick to it." Lester believed this. He admired his father intensely for his rigid insistence on truth, and now that he was really gone he felt sorry. He wished he might have been spared to be reconciled to him. He half-fancied that old Archibald would have liked Jennie if he had known her. He did not imagine that he would ever have had the opportunity to straighten things out, although he still felt that Archibald would have liked her.

When he reached Cincinnati it was snowing, a windy, blustery snow. The flakes were coming down thick and fast. The traffic of the city had a muffled sound. When he stepped down from the train he was met by Amy, who was glad to see him in spite of all the row that had been. Of all the girls she was the most tolerant. Lester put his arms about her and kissed her, and then they walked to the carriage, the budding lights of the evening somehow fitting in gloomily with his mood.

"It seems like old times to see you, Amy," he said, "your coming to meet me this way. How's the family?—I suppose they're all here. Well, poor Father, his time had to come. Still, he had lived to see everything that he wanted to see. I guess he was pretty well satisfied with the outcome of his life."

"Yes," replied Amy, "and since Mother died he was very lonely."

They rode up to the house in kindly good feeling, chatting of old times and places. All the members of the immediate family, and the various relatives, were gathered in the old family mansion where the body had been removed, for sentimental reasons, to lie in state, when Lester came. He exchanged the customary condolences, realizing all the while that his father had lived long enough. He had had a successful life and had fallen like a ripe apple from the tree. He looked at him where he lay in the great parlor, in his black coffin, and wondered what the old gentleman knew now, if anything. He smiled at the clean-cut, determined, conscientious face.

"The old gentleman was all right in his way, all the way through," he said to Robert, who was present. "We won't find a better figure of a man soon."

"We will not," said his brother solemnly.

They strolled about, anxious to have the solemnities over with, for of course the family cared little about the details of death. Old Archibald wanted no show. They had long anticipated that he would die soon. Now it had come, and the thing to do was to wind it up as satisfactorily as possible. Lester was really anxious to get away and get back to Chicago.

After the funeral it was decided to read the will. Louise's husband was anxious to return to Buffalo; Lester was compelled to be in Chicago. A conference of the various members of the family was called for the second day after the funeral, to be held at the offices of Messrs. Knight, Keatley & O'Brien, counsellors of the late manufacturer.

Their offices were in a plain red-brick building in the heart of the city, and next door to an old graveyard. Lester, with Amy and Louise, journeyed there together on this chilly morning. There was lots of snow on the ground, crisp and sparkling. As they rode, Lester went over in his mind details of his early life here. He had had a vigorous young manhood in Cincinnati—lots of friends, lots of girls. The old house they were leaving, and from which his mother and father had now departed, had been the scene of many simple but joyous revelries. Once he had fancied he would some-time marry Letty Pace, who used to come here but who had since married Malcolm Gerald. She was very wealthy now, worth several millions, and she had been so nice to him. The old times seemed somewhat like a dream now,—like a tale that has been told. Could it be that he was getting along so far that things were beginning to be over? Yes—that was no doubt it. He was past forty-six, and life's finest excitements were behind him.

As he rode he had no suspicion that his father had acted in any way prejudicial to his interests. It had not been so long since they had had their last conversation, and he had been taking his time to think about things, and his father had given him time. No untoward event could have happened since their last conversation. He also felt that he had stood well with the old gentleman, except for his alliance with Jennie, and now that he was dead he felt that he would be properly provided for. He had not done so much. His business judgement had been valuable to the company. Why should there be any discrimination against him? He really did not think it possible.

When they reached the offices of the law firm, Mr. O'Brien, a short, fussy, albeit comfortable-looking little person, greeted all the members of the family and the various heirs and assigns with a hearty handshake. He had been personal counsel to Kane senior for twenty years, knew his whims and idiosyncrasies, and considered himself very much in the light of a father confessor. He liked all the children, Lester especially. He knew exactly how everything had been arranged but did not care to show, by look or word, how the very extensive property of the manufacturer had been disposed of.

"Now I believe we are all here," he said finally, extracting a pair of large horn reading-glasses from his coat pocket and looking sagely about. "Very well. We might as well proceed to business. I will just read the will without any preliminary remarks."

He turned to his desk and picked up a paper lying near the edge, unfolded it, cleared his throat and began.

It was a peculiar document in some respects, for it began with all the minor bequests first—small sums to old employés, servants, friends and so on. It then took up a few institutional bequests and finally came to the immediate family, beginning with the girls. Imogene, as a faithful and loving daughter, was left a sixth of the stock of the carriage company and a fifth of the remaining properties of the deceased, which aggregated (the properties—not her share) roughly eight hundred thousand dollars. Amy and Louise were provided for in exactly the same proportion. The grandchildren were given certain little bonuses for good conduct, when they should come of age. Then the document took up the cases of Robert and Lester in a very peculiar literary form.

"Owing to certain complications which have arisen in the affairs of my son Lester," it began, "I deem it my duty to make certain conditions which shall govern the distribution of the remainder of my property, to wit: One-fourth of the stock of the Kane Manufacturing Company and one-fifth of the remainder of my various properties, real, personal, moneys, stocks and bonds, to go to my beloved son Robert, in recognition of the faithful performance of his duties, and one-fourth of the stock of the Kane Manufacturing Company and the remaining fifth of my various properties, real, personal, moneys, stocks and bonds, to be held in trust by him for the benefit of his brother Lester, until such time as such conditions as shall hereinafter be specified shall have been complied with. And it is my wish and desire that my children shall concur in his direction of the Kane Manufacturing Company, and of such other interests as are entrusted to him, until such time as he shall voluntarily relinquish such control or shall indicate another arrangement which shall be better."

Lester swore under his breath. His cheeks changed color, but he did not move. He was not inclined to make a show. It appeared that he was not even to be mentioned separately.

The conditions "hereinafter set forth" dealt very fully with his case, however, though they were not read aloud to the family at the time, Mr. O'Brien stating that this was in accordance with their father's wish. Lester learned immediately afterward that he was to have ten thousand a year for three years, during which time he had the choice of doing either one of two things: first, to leave Jennie, if he had not already married her, and bring his life into moral conformity with the wishes of his father, in which case his share of the estate was to be immediately turned over to him; or, second, to marry Jennie, if he had not already done so, in which case the ten thousand a year, specifically set aside to him for three years, was to be continued for life—but for his life only. Jennie was not to have anything of it after his death. The ten thousand in question represented the annual dividends on two hundred shares of L.S. and M.S. stock, which were also to be held in trust until his decision had been reached and their final disposition effected. He was not to have the handling of them ever. If he refused to marry Jennie, or to leave her, he was to have nothing at all after the three years were up. At his death, the stock on which his interest was drawn was to be divided pro rata among the surviving members of the family. If any heir or assign contested the will, his or her share was thereby forfeited entirely.

It was astonishing to Lester to see how thoroughly his father had taken his case into consideration. He half-suspected, on reading these conditions, that his brother Robert had had something to do with the framing of them, but of course he could not be sure. Robert had not given any direct evidence of enmity.

"Who drew this will?" he demanded of O'Brien, a little while later.

"Well, we all had a hand in it," replied O'Brien, a little shamefacedly. "It was a very difficult document to draw up. You know, Mr. Kane, there was no budging him. He was adamant. He has come very near defeating his own wishes in some of these clauses. Of course, you know, we had nothing to do with its spirit. That was between you and him. I hated very much to have to do it."

"Oh, I understand all that," said Lester. "Don't let that worry you."

Mr. O'Brien was very grateful.

During the reading of the will Lester had sat as stolid as an ox.

He got up after a time, as did the others, assuming an air of nonchalance. Robert, Amy, Louise and Imogene all felt shocked, but not exactly, not unqualifiedly regretful. Certainly Lester had acted very badly. He had given his father great provocation.

"I think the old gentleman has been a little rough in this," said Robert, who had been sitting next him. "I certainly did not expect him to go as far as that. Certainly as far as I am concerned, some other arrangement would have been satisfactory."

Lester smiled grimly. "It doesn't matter," he said.

Imogene, Amy and Louise were anxious to be consolatory, but they did not know what to say. Lester had brought it all on himself. Amy ventured with an "I don't think Papa acted quite right, Lester," but he waved her away almost gruffly.

"I can stand it," he said.

He figured out, as he stood there, what this would bring him in case he refused to comply with his father's wishes. Two hundred shares of L.S. and M.S., in open market, were worth a little over one thousand each. They yielded from five to six per cent, sometimes more, sometimes less. At this rate he would have ten thousand a year, not more, and that was all his long services, his notable expectations were to bring him.

The family gathering broke up, each going his way, and Lester returned to his sister's home. He wanted to get out of the city quickly, gave business as an excuse to avoid lunching with any one, and caught the earliest train back to Chicago. As he rode he meditated.

So this was how much his father really cared for him. Could it be so? He, Lester Kane, ten thousand a year, for only three years, and then longer only on condition that he marry Jennie. The other provision did not interest him just now. What must he do—marry her? He was sick in the soul, for this apparently was the end of all his fine prospects unless he left Jennie, and he did not want to do that. The family would know that he had been made to.

"Ten thousand a year," he thought, "and that for three years! Why, hell! Any good clerk can earn that. To think he should have done that to me."

CHAPTER XLII

This attempt at coercion was quite the one thing which could definitely and firmly set Lester in opposition to his family, for the time being anyhow. He had realized clearly enough of late that he had made a very big mistake in not having married Jennie in the first place, openly and above board, and thus avoided scandal, or, alternately, in not having accepted her proposition at the time she wanted to leave him and let her go back to Cleveland. It might have been better all around. Certainly, since he had not been willing to do that, it was time now that he did something—either married her or left her. There were no two ways about it: he had made considerable of a mess of this. He would have to get out of it somehow, or stand his ground openly as her husband. He could not afford to lose his fortune entirely. He did not have enough money of his own. Jennie was unhappy, he could see that. Why shouldn't she be? He was unhappy. This hard determination of his father to coerce him made it all the worse. Did he want to lose the equivalent of $800,000? Did he want to drop permanently out of society? Did he want to accept the shabby ten thousand a year, even if he were willing to marry her? Could he accept the slow drift of commonplace life which was sure to descend on him—was obviously descending upon him now? He knew he was losing precious time debating, but what could he do about it? Did he want to leave Jennie now?

It was a tremendously difficult problem which was put up to him in this form, and he brooded over it steadily for days and weeks and months thereafter. The fact that such a complete finish could come to his personal financial fortunes had never really seriously occurred to him before, and now that it had actually happened he could scarcely believe it. To think that his father, a man who appeared to have been close to him sympathetically during so many years past, should have done this to him! "Why make conditions?" he thought. Why cut him off in a half-hearted arguing way? This war on Jennie was so damned silly, and yet in a way he knew it wasn't. He was at fault. He had made the silly situation. Why had he done it? Well, love, for one thing. His family for another. He thought he could compel public acceptance of a clandestine situation, and now he was seeing that he could not. Other people could fight as well as himself. Other people could dictate and make conditions. It was rough, surely, but it had to be met. On gray days when he looked out of his office window at the smoky lake front, at the tumbling waters of the lake, he actually grieved. Hell, what a tangle life was, what a mystery! How should he do to play his part decently? How act? Poor Jennie, what a mark for a pursuing nemesis she was.

As for himself, in regard to her personally, he knew he could not change. Although possibly not great or wonderful, she was a charming woman. He told himself he had gone over this matter before with himself. Why should he keep constantly turning it over in his mind? He loved her, of course. Why did he not want to marry her? Was it this possible fortune of $800,000 or more that was keeping him balanced in such a way as not to permit of action? Was it the dread of the utter loss of his social relationship—which he was sacrificing by degrees anyhow? He had to admit in all calmness that it was. These things meant something to him. By taking Jennie, he was burning his bridges behind him—crossing the Rubicon. And he might be sorry. He was used to another type of life after all.

On the other hand he saw that, think as he might, he was comfortable with her. It might be that she was not suited to his family's social station; he was quite willing to admit that. From the dashing, dressy, conversational point of view she was not. What difference did that make? She was a big woman in her way: she was sympathetic, intelligent, kindly. That was a lot more than could be said for some of the women who were so ready to look down upon her. As for him—well, they could all go to the devil. But what was he going to do about his future?

When Lester returned to his home after the funeral, Jennie saw at once that something was amiss with him. He pretended to be quite the same, barring of course a natural grief for his father's death, but she sensed beside that, which was sad enough for her since it grieved him, a something else. What was it, she wondered. She tried to draw near to him sympathetically, but in this he could not be healed that way. When hurt in his pride he was savage and sullen—he could have struck any man who irritated him. As for her, he merely looked at her, pretending off feelings owing to weather conditions as the cause of his gruffness. He was not willing to tell her anything as yet. She watched interestedly, wishing to do something, but he would not give her his confidence. He only grieved, and she grieved with him.

Days passed, and then the financial and executive situation which had been created by his father's death came up for careful consideration. The factory management had to be reorganized. Robert would have to be made president, as his father wished. Lester's own relationship to the manufactory would have to come up for adjudication. Unless he changed his mind about Jennie, he was not a stockholder. As a matter of fact, he was not anything. To continue to be secretary and treasurer, it was necessary that he should own at least one share of the company's stock. Would Robert give him any? Would Amy, Louise, or Imogene? Would they sell him any? His father had said that Robert was to be left in charge of the business. Would any of the other members of the family care to do anything which would in any way infringe on Robert's prerogatives under the will, or his control? They were all rather unfriendly to Lester at present. If Robert did not give or sell him any stock and he went asking the others, what would be the answer? He saw that he was facing a ticklish situation. It interested him, but he also felt that things were against him. The answer was—get rid of Jennie. If he did that, he would not need to be begging for stock. If he didn't, he was flying in the face of his father's last will and testament. What could he expect? He turned this matter over in his mind, slowly and deliberately. He could quite see how things were coming out. The die was cast. It was Jennie out and away from him or nothing! What would he do?

Despite Robert's assertion that, so far as he was concerned, another arrangement would have been satisfactory, he was really not at all dissatisfied with the outcome—quite the contrary. As he looked at it now, he saw that his dreams were slowly nearing completion. Lester, as he thought, would not be willing to give up Jennie for some time to come. He was too stubborn. Anyhow,

Robert had long had his plans perfected for not only a thorough reorganization of the company proper, but for an extension of his carriage-building and -selling capacity to a combination of carriage companies, and this new arrangement of making him trustee for his brother, to say nothing of the advice of his father to the other heirs and his own strong popularity with them, gave him just what he wanted. If he could get two or three of the larger organizations in the East and West to join with him now, selling costs could be reduced, surplus manufacture avoided, supplies bought in such quantities and at such terms as would effect a great saving, and the prices of carriages and wagons boosted to such a place that the various stockholders would be making twice as much on their money as they were now. He decided to pick up as much stock of the possibly constituent companies beforehand for himself as was available, and secretly, through a New York representative, he had been about this work for some time. Now, he said to himself, he could have himself elected president of the company, and, since Lester was no longer a factor, could select Amy's husband as vice-president and possibly someone else other than Lester as secretary and treasurer. Under the conditions of the will, the stock and other properties set aside temporarily for Lester, in the hope that he would come to his senses, were to be managed and voted by Robert. The will specifically stated this. His father had meant, obviously, that he, Robert, should help him coerce his brother. He did not want to appear mean, but this was such an easy way. It gave him a righteous duty to perform. Lester must come to his senses, or he must let Robert run the business to suit himself. Anyhow, with his sisters' stock being voted by him, and his father's admonition to them that they should leave him in control, he could command the situation whether Lester chose to reform or not. Amy's husband as vice-president would be a stool-pigeon.

Lester, in Chicago, attending to his branch duties, foresaw the drift of things at once. He realized now that he was permanently out of the company, a branch manager, at his brother's sufferance, and it irritated him greatly. Nothing was said at once by Robert to indicate that such a change had taken place—things went on very much as before—but Robert's suggestions were obviously law now. Before, Lester had conferred with him as a rule. Almost invariably Lester's ideas were sound. At the same time he was always amenable to suggestion, but this transfer of power made a secret difference. There was no Kane senior now to arbitrate. Lester was now really his brother's employé at so much a year. It sickened his soul.

There came a time, after a few weeks, when he felt as if he could not stand this any more. He had always been a free and independent agent. First the approach of the annual stockholder's meeting, which hitherto had been a one-man affair and a formality, his father doing all the voting, was now a combination of voters, his brother presiding, his sisters very likely represented by their husbands, and he not there at all. Without stock he could not hold his official position as secretary and treasurer of the company, and without that title—he had hoped to be vice-president at least—he could not be as significant in the carriage manufacturing world as he had been. It was going to be a great come-down, but as Robert had not said anything about offering to give or sell him any stock which would entitle him to sit as a director or hold any official position in the company, he decided to write and resign. That would bring matters to a crisis. It would show his brother that he felt no desire to be under obligations to him in any way or to retain anything which was not his—and gladly so—by right of ability and the desire of those with whom he was associated. If he wanted to move back into the company by deserting Jennie, he would come in a very different capacity from that of branch manager. He dictated a simple, straightforward business letter, saying:

DEAR ROBERT,—

I know the time is drawing near when the company must be reorganized under your direction. Not having any stock, I am not entitled to sit as a director, or to hold the joint position of secretary and treasurer. I want you to accept this letter as formal notice of my resignation from both positions, and I want to have your directors consider what disposition should be made of this position and my services. I am not anxious to retain the branch-managership as a branch-managership merely, and at the same time I do not want to do anything which will embarrass you in your plans for the future. You see by this that I am not ready to accept the proposition laid down in Father's will—at least not at present. I would like a definite understanding of how you feel in this matter. Will you write and let me know.

YOURS,—

LESTER.

Robert, sitting in his office at Cincinnati, considered this letter gravely. It was like his brother to come down to the "brass tacks" of the situation and to refuse to be coerced—at least at once. If Lester were only as cautious as he was straightforward and direct, what a man he would be! But there was no guile in the man—no subtlety. He wouldn't really do—ever—a snaky thing—and yet Robert knew, in his own soul, that to succeed greatly one must. "You have to be ruthless at times—you have to be subtle," Robert would say to himself. "Why not face the facts to yourself when you are playing for big stakes?" He would, for one, and he did.

Robert felt that although Lester was a tremendously decent fellow and his brother, he wasn't pliable enough to suit his needs. He was too out-spoken, too inclined to take issue. In any great affair which Robert might desire to turn in the future—and he was very anxious to turn one immediately, the stock of the company would be an issue—a juggling stick. Lester holding a share, and by virtue of this the secretary-treasurership, or his fourth, would be a partner to all the plans which he, Robert, was formulating—although of course Lester could not prevent them. It would be necessary, if he let him come now as secretary and treasurer, to explain to him just what he was doing, and he did not want to do that. Lester was a man who saw far and who would criticize honestly. Lester would be a barrier in his path. Did he want this? Decidedly he did not. He much preferred that Lester should hold fast by Jennie, for the time being anyhow, and he rather had the feeling that Lester would.

He thought a long time, and then he dictated a politic letter. He hadn't made up his mind yet just what he wanted to do. He did not know what his sisters' husbands would like. A consultation would have to be held. For his part, he would be very glad to have Lester remain secretary and treasurer, if it could be arranged. Perhaps it would be better to let the matter rest for the time being.

Lester cursed. What did Robert mean by beating around the bush? He knew well enough how it could be arranged. One share of stock would be enough for Lester to qualify. Robert was afraid of him—that was the basic fact. Robert did not want him in the company. Well, he would not retain any branch-managership, depend on that. He would resign at once. Lester wrote a letter then and there stating that he had considered all sides and had decided to look after some interests of his own for the time being. If Robert could arrange it, he would like to have someone come on to Chicago and take over the branch agency. Thirty days would be time enough. He dispatched this promptly, and in a few days there came a regretful reply, saying that Robert was awfully sorry, but that if Lester was determined he did not want to interfere with any plans he might have in view. Imogene's husband, Jefferson Midgely, had long thought he would like to reside in Chicago. He could undertake the work for the time being.

Lester smiled. It was interesting to see how his brother was making the best of a very subtle situation. Robert knew that he, Lester, could sue and tie things up, but he also knew that he would hesitate very much to do so. The newspapers would get hold of the whole story. This matter of his relationship to Jennie was in the air anyhow. He could solve it all better by leaving her. So it all came back to that.

CHAPTER XLIII

For a man of Lester's years—he was now forty-six—to be tossed out in the world without a definite connection, even though he did have a present income (including this new ten thousand) of fifteen thousand a year, was a disturbing and discouraging thing. He realized now that, unless he made some very fortunate and profitable arrangement in the near future, he could easily get to the place where it would be hard for him to make much of a showing of any kind. He could marry Jennie. That would give him definitely ten thousand for the rest of his life, but of course that would end his opportunity of getting his legitimate share of the Kane estate, and he hated to think of that. He could convert the seventy-five thousand dollars worth of moderate interest-bearing stocks which he owned, and which now yielded him about five thousand a year, and try a practical investment of some kind—say a rival carriage company—but did he want to do that? There were other carriage companies to be sure, but did he want to jump in, at this stage of the game, and begin a running fight on his father's old organization, an organization in which he might (and very likely) desire subsequently to share? Would any of the older and more substantial companies deem it advisable to tie up with him? Could he obtain a sufficient interest with the money at his command to compel an acceptance of his theories, or at least to give him a substantial voice in the business? If not, would he be able to organize a new company and drive through to success under the conditions which he knew to prevail in the trade? Robert, with his ruthless policy of buying, manufacturing and selling on the closest margin, as at present, was going to make it hard,—had as a matter of fact already done so—for everyone in the trade. There was the keenest rivalry for business as it was, with the Kane Company very much in the lead. Lester could probably convert his private holdings into cash and raise $75,000, but did he want to do this? Or did he want to begin in a picayune, obscure way? It took money to get a foothold in the carriage business, as things were now.

He thought of these things long and deeply, but the more he thought the less sure he was of what he could do. All the successful companies were big companies. Practically it might be said that three of them controlled the bulk of the American trade. Two others were minor but healthy companies doing a rougher grade of work. There were dozens of little local wagon-builders, but they had no grip and no distinction, and he could see plainly that they would have considerably less in the future. He pondered this fact solemnly. But it was quite impossible for him to decide at once.

The trouble with Lester was that, while blessed with a fine imagination and considerable insight, he lacked that ruthless, narrow-minded insistence on his individual superiority which is the necessary element in almost every great business success. To be a forceful figure in the business world means, as a rule, to be an individual of one idea largely, and that idea the God-given one that life has destined you for a tremendous future in the particular field you have chosen. It means that one thing—a cake of soap, a new can-opener, a safety razor, or speed-accelerator—must seize on your imagination with tremendous force, burn as a raging flame, and make itself the be-all and end-all of your existence. As a rule, a man needs poverty to help him to this enthusiasm, and youth. The thing he has discovered, and with which he is going to busy himself, must be the door to a thousand opportunities and a thousand joys. Happiness must lie beyond, or the fire will not burn as brightly as it might,—the urge will not be great enough to make a great success.

Lester did not have this enthusiasm. Life had already shown him by far the greater part of its so-called joys. He saw through the illusions that are so often and so noisily labelled pleasure; and the prestige which one could gain did not always appeal to him as important. Money was essential: for real distinction outside of the arts, a great deal of it was needed; and even in the arts the man with money was so much more distinguished. And he had already had money. He had some yet—enough to keep him comfortably. Did he want to risk it? He looked about him thoughtfully. Perhaps he did. Certainly he could not comfortably contemplate the thought of sitting by and watching other people work for the rest of his days.

This mood lasted a little while, and then he decided that he would bestir himself and look into things. He was, as he said to himself, in no hurry to make a mistake. He would first give the trade, the people who were identified with the manufacture and sale of carriages, time to realize that he was out of the Kane Company, for the time being anyhow, and open to other connections. So he announced that he was leaving the Kane Company and going to Europe, ostensibly for a rest. He had never been abroad. He decided after mature reflection that this would be a good time. Jennie would enjoy it. Vesta could be left at home with Gerhardt and a maid, and he and Jennie could travel around a bit, seeing what Europe had to show. He was interested to see Venice and Baden-Baden, and the great watering places that had been recommended to him. Cairo and Luxor and the Parthenon contained a slight fillip for his imagination. He was curious to see how they looked. Not that he cared very much—he fancied that the world was much the same everywhere, but it would be a slight diversion. Then he could come back and seriously gather up the threads of his intentions.

It came along toward spring, not long after his father had died. With a pleasant deliberation he studied out a tour. He made Jennie his confidante. He had wound up the work of the warerooms as quickly as possible a few weeks before, and now, having gathered together their travelling comforts, they took a steamer from New York for Liverpool. He had equipped himself with all the necessary information and conveniences for his trip, and together they browsed about London and Edinburgh, going direct from the former city to the Nile, because of the approaching heat. From there they came back through Greece and Italy into Austria and Switzerland, and then later through France and Paris to Germany and Berlin. He was interested greatly, and diverted, but all the time there was running through his mind the thought that in a way he was wasting his time. Great business enterprises were not built by travellers, and he was not looking for health. He had loafed himself in times past, but all the while he had been definitely connected up with his father's enterprise by letter and telegraph. Now it was different. He felt a little restless.

Jennie, on the other hand, was transported by what she saw and learned, although she was not unmindful of the fact that things were not entirely right with Lester. He had told her, of course, the main details of what had transpired without indicating their actual significance. He was out of the Kane Company, was thinking of buying into a company in order to manufacture for himself. He would probably be a great success, as he always had been, but he was not settled in his mind now. She came back a much wiser woman in so far as her knowledge of the organization of the world was concerned, a much better companion for him, but she was the same Jennie, brooding, mystified, nonplussed. Life was a strange, muddled picture to her, beautiful but inexplicable.

It is curious the effect of travel on a thinking mind. At Luxor and Karnak—places Jennie had never dreamed existed—she learned of an older civilization, powerful, complex, complete. Millions of people had lived and died here, believing in other gods, other forms of government, other details of existence. Lester explained sagely what he knew—short incisive comments mostly—but Jennie gained a clear idea of how vast the world is. Now from this point of view—of decayed Greece, fallen Rome, forgotten Egypt, and from the notable differences of the newer civilization, she gained an idea of how pointless are our minor difficulties after all—our minor beliefs. Her father's Lutheranism now—it did not seem so significant any more; and the social arrangement of Columbus, Ohio—rather pointless, perhaps. Her mother had worried so of what people thought—her neighbors— but here were dead worlds of people, some bad, some good, as Lester explained, differences in standards of morals being due sometimes to climate, sometimes to religious beliefs and the rise of peculiar personalities like Mahomet. He liked to show her how foolish were little conventions in the light of the sum of things, and vaguely she began to see. Supposing she had been bad—locally it was important, perhaps, but in the sum of civilizations, in the sum of big forces, what did it all amount to? They would be dead after a little while, she and Lester and all these people. Did anything matter except goodness—goodness of heart? What else was there that was real?

CHAPTER XLIV

It was while travelling abroad that Lester came across, first at the Savoy in London and later at Shepheard's in Cairo, the former favorite of his father and the one girl, before Jennie, whom it might have been said he truly admired—Letty Pace. He had not seen her for a long time. She had been Mrs. Malcolm Gerald for nearly four years, and a charming widow for nearly two years more. Malcolm Gerald had been a very wealthy man, having amassed a fortune (which, it was rumored, ran into millions) in banking and stock-brokering in Cincinnati, and he had left Mrs. Malcolm Gerald a very rich widow. She was the mother of one child, a little girl, who was safely in charge of a nurse and maid at all times, and she was invariably the picturesque centre of a group of admirers recruited from every capital of the civilized world. She herself was a talented woman, tall, graceful, artistic, a writer of verse, an omnivorous reader, a student of art, and a sincere and ardent admirer of Lester Kane.

In her day she had truly loved him, for she had been a wise observer of men and affairs from the beginning, and Lester had always appealed to her as a real man. He was so sane, she thought, so calm. His attitude was always so natural and frank, despite the fact that it was always tinged with a bit of what might have been called roughness by many. He was always intolerant of sham, and she liked him for it. He was always inclined to wave aside the petty little frivolities of common society conversation, and to talk of simple and homely things. Many and many a time, in years past, they had deserted a dance to sit out on a balcony somewhere, and talk while Lester smoked. He had argued philosophy with her, discussed books, described political and social conditions in other cities, discussed the fortunes and failures of their friends in a sympathetic and charitable mood, and she had hoped and hoped and hoped that he would propose to her. More than once she had looked at his big, solid head with its short growth of hardy brown hair and wished that she could stroke it with her hand.

She had imagined herself in his arms time and again, being held close and joyously caressed, and she had said to herself that if that day ever came she would be the happiest woman alive, for she knew that Lester would love her if he did it. She did not care so very much for his fortune or his family—her own parents were not poor,—but she did admire him. "Lester Kane is a man," she told her mother over and over, and it was a hard blow to her when he finally did desert her and took up with Jennie, for she had been waiting, hoping—until it was almost too late, she thought.

Then Malcolm Gerald, always an ardent admirer, proposed for something like the sixty-fifth time, and she took him. She did not love him, but she was getting along, and she had to marry someone. The callow youth of her local society world did not interest her. If she could not have Lester, she at least wanted a sedate, sane man, and Gerald was that. He was forty-four when he married her, and he lived only four years more—just long enough to realize that he had married a charming, tolerant, broad-minded woman. Then he died of pneumonia, and Mrs. Gerald was a rich widow—sympathetic, attractive, delightful in her knowledge of the world, and with nothing to do except live and spend her money.

She was not inclined to do either indifferently. She had long since had her ideal of a man established by Lester. These little whipper-snappers of counts, earls, lords, barons, whom she met in one social world and another (for her friendship and connections had broadened notably with the years), did not interest her a particle. She was terribly weary of the superficial veneer of the titled fortune-hunter whom she met abroad. A good judge of character, a student of men and manners, a natural reasoner along sociologic and psychologic lines, she saw through them and through the civilization which they represented. "I could have been happy in a cottage with a man I once knew out in Cincinnati," she once told one of her titled women friends, who had been an American before her marriage. "He was the biggest, cleanest, sanest fellow. If he had proposed to me I would have married him if I had had to work for a living myself."

"Was he so poor?" asked her friend.

"Indeed he wasn't. He was comfortably rich, but that did not make any difference to me. It was the man I wanted."

"It would have made a difference in the long run," said the other.

"You misjudge me," replied Mrs. Gerald. "I waited for him a number of years, and I know."

Lester had always had pleasant impressions and kindly memories of Letty Pace—or Mrs. Gerald, as she was now. He had been fond of her in a way, very fond. Why hadn't he married her? He had asked himself that question time and again. She would have made him an ideal wife, his father would have been pleased, everyone would have been delighted. Instead he had drifted and drifted, and then he had met Jennie; and somehow, after that, he did not want Letty Pace any more. Now after six years of separation he met her again. He knew she had been married. She knew that he was having some sort of an affair—she had heard that he had subsequently married the woman and was living on the South Side. She did not know of the loss of his fortune. She ran across him first in the Savoy one spring evening. The windows were open; the flowers were blooming; that sense of new life, which runs everywhere through the world when spring comes back, was in the air. She was a little beside herself for the moment. Something choked in her throat, but she calmed herself and extended a graceful arm and hand.

"Why, Lester Kane," she exclaimed, "how *do* you do! I am so glad. And this is Mrs. Kane? Charmed, I'm sure. It seems truly like a breath of spring to see you again. I hope you'll excuse me, Mrs. Kane, but I'm delighted to see your husband. I'm ashamed to say how long it seems, Lester, since I saw you last! I feel quite old when I think of it. Why, Lester, think, it's been all of six or seven years! And I've been married and had a child, and poor Mr. Gerald has died, and oh, dear, I don't know what all hasn't happened to me."

"You don't look it," commented Lester, smiling. He was pleased to see her again, for they had been good friends. She liked him still—that was evident, and he truly liked her.

Jennie smiled. She was glad to see this old friend of Lester's.

She was always glad to see that he had such friends. This woman, trailing a magnificent yellow lace train over pale, mother-of-pearl satin, her round, smooth arms bare to the shoulder, her corsage cut quite low, and a dark red rose blowing at her waist, seemed to her the ideal of what a woman should be. She liked looking at lovely women quite as much as Lester did, liked to call his attention to them, to tease him in the mildest way about their charms. "Wouldn't you like to run and talk to her, Lester, instead of to me?" She had often asked him this question in the past when some chic, daring or dashing figure of a woman would come into view. Lester would examine her choice critically, for he had come to know that her judgement of feminine charms was excellent. "Oh, I'm pretty well off where I am," he would sometimes retort, looking into her eyes; or, "I have seen as good." "I'm not as young as I used to was, or I'd get in tow of that," he'd jest.

"Run on," was her comment, "I'll wait for you."

"What would you do if I really should?"

"Why, Lester, I wouldn't do anything. You'd come back to me, maybe."

"Wouldn't you care?"

"You know I'd care. But if you felt that you wanted to, I wouldn't want to prevent you. I wouldn't want to be all in all to one man, unless he wanted me to be."

"Where do you get those ideas, Jennie?" he asked her once, curious to test the breadth of her philosophy.

"Oh, I don't know, why?"

"They're so broad, so good-natured, so charitable. They're not common, that's sure."

"Why, I don't think we ought to be so selfish, Lester. I don't know why. Some women think differently, I know, but a man and a woman ought to want to live together or they ought not to, don't you think? It doesn't make so much difference if a man goes off for a little while—just so long as he doesn't stay—if he wants to come back at all."

Lester smiled. He had learned to respect her intuitive knowledge. How she came by it he could not say—deep-seated observation and perspective, perhaps. No other member of her family seemed to have it, or at least he had not had the privilege of finding it out. He respected her for the sweetness of her point of view—he had to.

Tonight, when she saw this woman so eager to talk to Lester, she realized at once that they must have a great deal in common to recall and so did a characteristic thing. "Won't you excuse me for a little while?" she asked, smiling. "I left some things uncared for in our rooms. I'll be back."

She bowed herself away, a little envious—a little sad, remaining in her room as long as she reasonably could, and Lester and Letty fell to talking over old times in earnest. He recounted as much of his experiences, and what had happened to him recently, as he deemed wise, and Letty brought the history of her life up to date. "Now that you're safely married, Lester," she said daringly, "I'll confess to you that you were the one man I always wanted to have propose to me—and you never did."

"Maybe I never dared," he said, gazing into her superb black eyes and thinking that perhaps she might know that he was not married. He thought that she had grown more beautiful—physically, intellectually, and in every other way. She seemed to him now to be an ideal society figure—perfection itself—gracious, natural, witty, the type of woman who mixes and mingles well, meeting each newcomer upon the plane best suited to him or her.

"Yes, you thought! I know what you thought. Your real thought just left the table."

"Tut, tut, my dear. Not so fast. You don't know what I thought."

"Anyhow, I allow you some credit. She's charming."

"Jennie has her good points," he replied simply.

"And are you happy?"

"Oh, fairly so. Yes, I suppose I'm happy—as happy as any one can be who sees life as it is. You know I'm not troubled with many illusions."

"Not any, I think, kind sir, if I know you."

"Very likely not any, Letty, but sometimes I wish I had a few. I think I would be happier."

"And I, too, Lester. Really. I look on my life as a kind of failure, you know, in spite of the fact that I'm almost as rich as Croesus—not quite. I think he had some more dollars than I have."

"How you talk, girl, with your beauty and insight and money—good heavens!"

"And what can I do with it? Travel, talk, shoo away silly fortune-hunters. Oh, dear, sometimes I get so tired!"

She looked at Lester. In spite of Jennie, the old feeling came back. Why should she have been cheated of him by fortune? They were as comfortable together as old married people or young lovers. Jennie had had no better claim. Why had he picked her? She looked at him, and her eyes fairly spoke. He smiled a little sadly.

"Here comes my wife," he said. "We'll have to brace up and talk of other things. You'll find her charming, really."

"Yes, I know," she replied, and turned on Jennie a radiant smile.

Jennie felt something. She thought vaguely that this might be one of Lester's old flames. This was the kind of woman he should have had—not her. This woman was suited to his station in life, and he would have been as happy—perhaps happier. There would have been nothing of his family's opposition if he had married her, nothing of the newspaper notoriety, nothing of the social opposition which was already leaving him a rather lonely figure. She loved him truly but she loved him well enough to wish that he might not be made to suffer on account of her.

Mrs. Gerald was charming to her during the meal. She invited them the next day to join her on a drive through Rotten Row. There was a dinner later at Claridge's, and then she was compelled to keep some engagement which was taking her to Paris. She bade them both an affectionate farewell, but she was envious in a sad way of Jennie's good fortune. Lester had lost none of his charm for her. If anything he seemed nicer, more considerate, more wholesome. She wished sincerely that he were free. And Lester—subconsciously perhaps—was thinking the same thing.

On his part, and no doubt because of the fact that she was thinking of it, he had been led over in detail mentally all of the things which might have happened if he had married her. They were so congenial now—philosophically, artistically, practically. There was a natural flow of conversation between them all the time, like two old comrades among men. She knew everybody in his social sphere, which was equally hers, but Jennie did not. They could talk on certain subtle characteristics of life in a way which was not possible between him and Jennie, for the latter did not have the vocabulary. Jennie's ideas did not flow as fast as those of Mrs. Gerald. She had actually the deeper, more comprehensive, sympathetic, and emotional note in her nature, but she could not work it out in light conversation. Actually she was living the thing she was, and that was perhaps the thing which drew Lester to her. Just now, and often in situations of this kind, she seemed at a disadvantage, and was so. It seemed to Lester, for the time being, as if Mrs. Gerald would perhaps have been a better choice after all—certainly as good, and he would not now have this distressing thought as to his future.

They did not see Mrs. Gerald again until they reached Cairo. In the gardens about the hotel they suddenly encountered her, or rather Lester did, for he was alone at the time, strolling and smoking.

"Well, this is good luck!" he exclaimed. "Where do you come from?"

"Madrid, if you please. I didn't know I was coming until last Thursday. The Ellicotts are here. I came over with them. You know I wondered where you might be. Then I remembered you said you were going to Egypt. Where is your wife?"

"In her bath, I fancy, at this moment. This warm weather makes Jennie take to water. I was thinking of taking a plunge myself."

"Oh, dear," she said after a time, as they strolled about. She was in light blue silk, with a blue and white parasol held daintily over her shoulder. "I wonder sometimes what I am to do with myself. I can't loaf always this way. I think I'll go back to the States to live."

"Why don't you?"

"What good would it do me? I don't want to get married. I haven't any one to marry now,—that I want." She glanced at Lester significantly and then looked away.

"Oh, you'll find someone eventually," he said, somewhat awkwardly. "You can't actually escape for long—not with your looks and money."

"Oh, Lester, hush!"

"All right! Have it otherwise, if you want. I'm telling you."

"Do you still dance?" she inquired lightly, thinking of a ball which was being given at the hotel that evening. He had danced so well a few years before.

"Do I look it?"

"Now, Lester, you don't mean to say that you have gone and

abandoned that last charming art. I still love to dance. Doesn't Mrs. Kane?"

"No, she doesn't care to. At least she hasn't taken it up. Come to think of it, I suppose that is my fault. I haven't thought of dancing in some time."

It occurred to him that he hadn't been going out to functions of any kind much in some time. The opposition his entanglement had generated had put a stop to that.

"You come dance with me tonight. Your wife won't object. It's a splendid floor. I saw it this morning."

"I'll have to think about that," replied Lester. "I'm not much in practise. Dancing will probably go hard with me at my time of life."

"Oh, hush, Lester," replied Mrs. Gerald. "You make me feel old. Don't talk so sedately. Mercy alive, you'd think you were an old man."

"I am in experience, my dear."

"Pshaw, that simply makes us more attractive," replied his old flame.

CHAPTER XLV

That night after dinner, the music was already sounding in the ball-room of the great hotel, adjacent to the palm gardens, when Mrs. Gerald found Lester smoking on one of the verandas with Jennie by his side. The latter was in white satin and white silk slippers, her hair lying a heavy, enticing mass about her forehead and ears. Lester was brooding over the history of Egypt—its successive tides or waves of rather weak-bodied people; the thin, narrow strip of soil along either side of the Nile that had given these successive waves of population sustenance; the wonder of heat and tropic life; and this hotel with its modern conveniences and fashionable crowd set down among ancient, soul-weary, almost despairing conditions. He and Jennie had looked this morning on the Pyramids. They had taken a trolley to the Sphinx! They had watched swarms of ragged, half-clad, curiously costumed men and boys moving through narrow, smelly, albeit brightly colored lanes and alleys.

"It all seems such a mess to me," said Jennie at one place. "They are so dirty and oily. I like it, but somehow they seem tangled up like a lot of worms."

Lester chuckled. "You're almost right. But climate does it. Heat. The tropics. Life is always mushy and sensual under these conditions. They can't help it."

"Oh, I know that. I don't blame them. They're just queer."

Tonight he was brooding over this, the moon shining down into the grounds with an exuberant, sensuous lustre.

"Well, at last I've found you!" Mrs. Gerald exclaimed. "I couldn't get down to dinner after all. Our party was so late getting back. I've made your husband agree to dance with me, Mrs. Kane," she went on smilingly. She, like Lester and Jennie, was under the sensuous influence of the warmth, the spring, the moonlight. There were rich odours abroad, floating subtly from groves and gardens, the desert, the crowded, fetid alleys of the city. From somewhere camel-bells were sounding and strange cries—"*Ayah!*" and "*oosh! oosh!*" as though a drove of strange animals were being rounded up and driven somewhere. The strains from the ball-room mingled with it all like an undertone of something in a symphonic composition.

"You're welcome to him," replied Jennie pleasantly. "He ought to dance. I sometimes wish I did. I like to watch people dance."

"You want to take lessons right away then," replied Lester genially. "I'll do my best to keep you company. I'm not as light on my feet as I once was, but I guess I can get around."

"Oh, I don't want to dance that badly," smiled Jennie. "But you two go on. I'm going upstairs in a little while anyway."

"Why don't you come sit in the ball-room? I can't do more than a few rounds. Then we can watch the others," said Lester rising.

"No. I think I'll stay here. It's so pleasant. You go. Take him, Mrs. Gerald."

She smiled at her temporary guest, and Lester strolled off with her. They made a striking pair—Mrs. Gerald in dark, wine-colored silk, covered with glistening black beads, her shapely arms and neck bare, and a flashing diamond of great size set just above her forehead in her dark hair. Her lips were red and her cheeks bright. She had an engaging smile, showing an even row of white teeth, between wide, full, friendly lips. Lester was in his comfortable tuxedo, looking very vigorous.

"That is the woman he should have had," said Jennie to herself as he disappeared. She had thought so much over this marriage problem of late. She had grown so much mentally in the last few years. All the slaps she had been given by fate had tended to rouse her deep, phlegmatic spirituality and make her think. She had thought over every step of her life, time and time and again. Sometimes it seemed to her now as if she had been living in a dream. At other times she felt as though she were in that dream yet. Life sounded in her ears much as this night did. She heard its cries. She knew its large-mass features. But back of it were subtleties and curiosities that sank one within the other like the weird turnings of fancy in slumber. Why had she been so attractive to men? Why had Lester been so eager to follow her? Could she have prevented him? She thought of her days in 13th Street in Columbus, when she carried coal; and here she was tonight in Egypt, at this great hotel, the chatelaine of a suite of rooms, surrounded by every luxury, Lester still devoted to her. He had endured so many things for her! Why? Was she so wonderful? Brander had said so. Lester had told her so. Still she felt humble, out of place, holding handfuls of jewels that did not belong to her. Again she had that notion that she had had the first time she went to New York with Lester—namely that it could not endure. Her life was fated. Something would happen. She would go back to simple things, to a side street, a poor cottage, to old clothes. It could not be that this could endure.

And then she thought of her home in Chicago, the attitude of his social friends, and she knew it must be so. She would never be accepted, even if he married her. And she could understand why. She could look into the charming, smiling, genial face of this woman who was now with Lester and see that she considered her very nice, perhaps, but not of Lester's class. She was saying to herself right now, no doubt, as she danced with Lester, that he needed someone like her. He needed someone who had been raised in the atmosphere of the things to which he had been accustomed. He couldn't very well expect to find in her, Jennie, the familiarity with, the appreciation of, the niceties to which he had always been accustomed. She understood what they were. Her mind had wakened rapidly to details of furniture, clothing, arrangement, decoration, manners, forms, customs, but—she was not to the manner born. She hadn't the ease, she hadn't the poise, she hadn't the assurance. She couldn't get it. She might assume it right now if she wanted to be sharp, incisive, hard, cold, but she couldn't be, and it wouldn't be true and natural if she did. She didn't care enough. She really didn't care enough about society. She preferred large, simple things—the fields, the trees, the large aspects of nature in sun and rain. Natural beauty was calling to her. It was finer, much more appealing than people, although somehow they figured in it like a Greek chorus and were beautiful too. But Lester needed someone with the quick refinements, the subtleties of language and phraseology, the ability to make quick retorts and witty replies—to mix, mingle, bow, be polite, do a hundred and say a hundred sweet, gracious things in an hour. She could not, and Lester knew she could not.

As she sat here, she thought of these things and then, curiously, she wished she might die. Vesta was here—that stayed her, and Gerhardt, but if they were not it would be so much easier for him, for everybody, if she could just die. She had seen a great deal. Heavens, when she thought of it she had lived a wonderful life. Why should she not die?

While she was thinking—turning these curious thoughts over in her mind,—Lester was dancing with Mrs. Gerald, or sitting out between the waltzes talking over the subtleties of life, the mysteries of personalities, the characters of old friends. Mrs. Gerald was recalling places they had visited together, scenes they had enjoyed together, the eccentricities of his father, the good times they used to have at his house. While they danced to a strain of lovely music, he marveled at her youth and beauty. Certainly intellect made for distinction here. She was more robust than formerly, but still as slender and shapely as Diana. She had strength, too, in this smooth body of hers, and her black eyes were liquid and lustreful.

"I swear, Letty," he said impulsively, "you're really more beautiful than ever. You're exquisite. You've grown younger instead of older."

"You think so?" she smiled, looking up into his face.

"You know I do, or I wouldn't say so. I'm not much on philandering."

"Oh, Lester, dear, you bear, can't you allow a woman just a

little coyness? Don't you know we all love to sip our praise and not be compelled to swallow it all in one great mouthful?"

"What's the point?" he asked. "What did I say?"

"Oh, nothing. You're such a bear. You're such a big, determined, straight-talking boy. But never mind. I like you. That's enough, isn't it?"

"It surely is," he said.

They strolled into the garden as the music ceased, and he squeezed her arm softly. He couldn't help it. She felt so warm toward him that she made him feel as if he owned her. She wanted him to feel that way. To run to her if ever circumstance or fate permitted. She said to herself, as they sat looking at the lanterns in the garden, that if ever he were free and would come to her, she would take him. She would almost take him anyhow—only he probably wouldn't. He was so hard-reasoning, so straight-laced, so considerate. He wouldn't, like so many other men she knew, do a mean thing. He couldn't. But if he could and would—Jennie might look out for herself, and yet she felt sorry for her at that. She was lovely, but Lester needed another kind—herself—the Letty Pace that was.

After several hours of this Lester went to look for Jennie, but she had gone. He sat still another period with Mrs. Gerald and then finally excused himself. He and Jennie were going farther up the Nile in the morning—toward Karnak and Thebes and the water-washed temples at Philæ.

"When are you going home?" asked Mrs. Gerald ruefully.

"In September."

"Have you engaged your passage?"

"Yes, we sail from Hamburg on the ninth. The *Fulda.*"

"I may be going back in the fall," laughed Letty. "Don't be surprised if I crowd in on the same boat with you. I'm very unsettled in my mind."

"Come along, for goodness sake," replied Lester. "I hope you do. . . . I'll see you tomorrow before we leave." He paused, and she looked at him wistfully.

"Cheer up," he said, taking her hand. "You never can tell what life will do. We sometimes find ourselves right when we thought we were all wrong."

He was thinking that she was sorry to lose him, and he was sorry that she was not in a position to have what she wanted. As for himself, he was saying that here was one solution that he would probably never accept; but it was a solution. Why had he not seen this years before?

"And yet she wasn't as beautiful then as she is now, nor as wise, nor as wealthy." Maybe! Maybe! But he couldn't be unfaithful to Jennie nor wish her any bad luck. She had had enough without his willing and had stood it bravely.

The trip home did bring another week with Mrs. Gerald, for after consideration she had decided to go to America for awhile anyhow. Chicago and Cincinnati were her destinations, and she hoped to see more of Lester. Her presence was considerable of a surprise to Jennie, who had not expected her, and it started her thinking again. Lester had cooled off a little since he had come out of Egypt and strolled about Europe, but the opportunity this lovely creature presented could not but remain uppermost in his mind.

On the way home Jennie had more leisure in which to observe this woman, and in her quiet, observing, introspective way she could see what the point was. If she were not here, Mrs. Gerald would take Lester. She could not help liking her at that, for of all the society people she had met this one was the nicest to her. Letty went out of her way to do Jennie little services, to bring her delicacies, to make pleasant suggestions of things to do and so on. She made no attempt to monopolize Lester, but Jennie gave her ample opportunity to talk, for she wanted them to have a good time if they wished to. If Lester liked her, why shouldn't he talk to her? Basically she realized that she would have a hard time forcing him to neglect her or to turn entirely away from her. He was so considerate and fair that only a thing like death—her death— would straighten matters out for him. And she felt also that basically he liked her best—some of the emotional things about her anyhow. He had said so, and it was probably true. When they reached Chicago Mrs. Gerald went her way, and Jennie and Lester took up the customary thread of their living.

CHAPTER XLVI

On his return from Europe, Lester set to work in earnest to find a business opening. He was not sounded out, as he had hoped, by any of the big companies for the single reason, principally, that he was considered a strong man who was looking for control in anything he touched. The nature of his altered fortunes had not been made public. All the little companies that he investigated were having a hand-to-mouth existence, manufacturing a product which was not satisfactory to him, or coupled with individuals who were arbitrary or unsuited to his moods. He did find one company in a small town in northern Indiana, near Chicago, which looked as though it might have a future. It was controlled by a practical builder of wagons and carriages such as his father had been in his day—a man of about forty, who, however, was not a business man in the best sense of the word. He was making some small money on a past investment of about fifteen thousand dollars and a plant worth, say, twenty-five thousand. Lester foresaw that something could be made here if proper methods were pursued and business acumen exercised. It would be slow work. There would never be a great fortune in it—not in his life-time. He was thinking of investing here when the first rumors of the carriage trust reached him.

It appeared that in the short time after Robert had made himself president of the Kane Company, he had moved swiftly. Armed with the voting power of the entire stock of the company, and therefore with the privilege of hypothecating its securities, he laid before several of his intimate friends in the financial world his scheme of uniting the principal carriage companies and controlling the trade. It would not be a difficult matter, he argued, to persuade the two principal rivals of the Kane Company to cease their rivalry, to take three shares of stock in the new holding company for each share of stock they might hold in a constituent company, and to join in that work of economy—which meant six per cent on three shares where that sum had only been paid on one before. It could be done. He showed them how. He showed them where. Shrewd investors surveying his record and observing his present progress were inclined to agree. They promised him any necessary financial assistance within reason. So armed, he was prepared to visit the various carriage manufacturers, and while Lester was travelling in Europe he was busy perfecting a tentative organization.

The principal rival was the Lyman-Winthrop Company of New York, an old, established concern ante-dating the Kane Company but suffering in recent years from the growth of ultra-conservatism in its methods. Old Henry Lyman, the founder, was dead. Henry and Wilson Winthrop, the two sons of the original Samuel Winthrop, were in charge, but of these Henry was really the only important figure. Wilson was more or less of a society figure, interested in art and belles lettres and inclined to live on his income. Henry was handling the concern after the stable methods of his father. He was concerned to stick to the line of exclusive vehicles which his father had manufactured before him and leave to other companies the ruder vehicles that were so widely made. Wagons, trucks, wheelbarrows such as some companies went in for were not for him. Robert showed him in very short order, however, where thousands of dollars could be added to his income without affecting his private business in the least.

Briefly Robert's scheme was to transform the various carriage- and wagon-manufacturing companies into the United Carriage & Wagon Manufacturers Association, all the stock of the constituent companies to be transferred into the general treasury and new six per cent gold interest-bearing bonds issued in their place, at the rate of three for one. The private interests of the different manufactories were not to be interfered with in any way, except as the owners were willing to comply with.

The Kane Company, as the largest and parent company, was to be the centre of activities, but only in the sense that it would act as a clearing house for all the others. The trade orders of all the companies were to be filed there each week and immediately reported in bulletin form to all the others. There was to be a redivision of the work where possible, plants which were exceptional at making wagons and poor at making carriages being given all the wagons they could manufacture and being persuaded to turn over to the carriage companies all the orders for carriages which they received. Where possible, duplication of effort was to be eliminated, and salesmen, buyers, laborers to be cut down to the minimum necessary to do the actual work. Useless plants would be eliminated or run on part-time only. "If necessary, and if it will save money, we will shut up the Kane Company," said Robert, "and let the other plants do the work."

Mr. Henry Winthrop liked this. He liked Robert. He liked his letters of approval from financiers, and he liked, most of all, his business judgement, standing and acumen. If the others would come in, he would come in certainly—why not? He was in business to make money. They shook hands warmly, and Robert went his way.

His next call was at the Myers-Brooks Manufacturing Company of Buffalo, and with these people he was equally successful. It was not as large a concern as the Lyman-Winthrop Company, not as old, and was doing a much cheaper type of business, but it was thoroughly successful. Robert ingratiated himself as quickly as possible into the favor of Mr. Jacob Myers. He talked about the hard, cold facts of the situation. He showed where a parent company, acting as a clearing house, with the owners of the old companies as directors in the new, and with the facilities which a central financial organization would give them, could open up markets hitherto untouched for wagons and carriages. Wagons and carriages could be manufactured in America and sold in Russia, Australia, India and South America cheaper than they could be manufactured locally in these countries and sold. There could be supplies of lumber brought in from foreign countries, a move which would cut the cost of manufacture by nearly seven per cent. A great central organization could afford to, and would, look after the tariffs here and abroad so that they would be right. He was on fire with his ideas, and his hearers caught fire also. In six weeks he was able to call a meeting of all the carriage and wagon manufacturers whom it was deemed advisable to include at this time at the Evarts House in Indianapolis, and to persuade them to organize according to his plan. A charter for the new corporation was taken out in the State of New Jersey. Mr. Robert Kane, of Cincinnati, was elected president; Mr. Henry Winthrop of New York, vice-president; Mr. Jacob Myers, of Buffalo, treasurer; and Mr. Henry S. Woods, of St. Louis, secretary. In the due course of time, the stock-transfer scheme, as originally planned, was carried out. Robert found himself president of the United Carriage & Wagon Manufacturers Association, with a capital stock of ten million dollars, and with assets aggregating nearly three-fourths of that sum at a forced sale. He was a happy man.

While all this was going forward, Lester was completely in the dark. His trip to Europe prevented him from seeing three or four minor notices in the newspapers of some of the efforts that were being made to unite the various carriage and wagon manufactories. He returned to Chicago to learn that Jefferson Midgely, Imogene's husband, was still in full charge of the branch and living in Evanston, but because of his quarrel with his family he was in no position to get the news direct. Accident brought it fast enough, however, and that rather irritatingly.

The individual who conveyed this information was none other than Mr. Henry Bracebridge, of Cleveland, into whom Lester ran at the Union Club one evening after he had been back in the city a month.

"I hear you're out of the old company," Bracebridge remarked, smiling blandly. Some details of the reorganization had reached him months before.

"Yes," said Lester, "I'm out."

"What are you up to now?"

"Oh, I have a deal of my own under consideration. I'm thinking of handling an independent concern."

"Sure you won't run counter to your brother? He has a pretty good thing in that combination of his."

"Combination! I hadn't heard of it," said Lester. "I've just got back from Europe."

"Well, you want to wake up, Lester," replied Bracebridge. "He's got the biggest thing in your line. I thought you knew all about it. The Lyman-Winthrop Company; the Myers-Brooks Company; the Woods Company—in fact, five or six of the big companies are all in. I saw where he was elected president. I guess he can claim to be worth a couple of million now if it works out."

Lester stared. His glance hardened a little.

"Well, that's fine for Robert. I'm glad of it."

Bracebridge could see that he had given him a vital stab.

"Well, so long, old man!" he exclaimed. "When you're in Cleveland look us up. You know how fond my wife is of you."

"I know," replied Lester. "Bye-bye."

He strolled away to the smoking room, but the news took all the zest out of his private venture for him. Where would he be with a shabby little wagon company and his brother president of a carriage trust? Good heavens, he could put him out of business in a year! He would be running at Robert's sufferance. Didn't he know that? Why, he himself had dreamed of such a combination as this. Now his brother had done it.

It is one thing to have youth, courage, and a fighting spirit to meet the blows with which fortune often afflicts the talented. It is quite another to see middle age coming on, your principal fortune possibly gone, and avenue after avenue of opportunity being sealed to you on various sides. Jennie's obvious social insufficiency; the quality of newspaper reputation which had now become attached to her; his father's opposition and death; the loss of his fortune; the loss of his connection with the company; his brother's attitude; this trust—all combined in a way to dishearten and discourage him. He had tried to keep a brave face—and he had succeeded thus far, he thought, admirably, but this last kick appeared for the time being a little too much. He went home the same evening that he heard the news, sorely disheartened. Jennie saw it. She realized it, as a matter of fact, all during the evening that he was away. She felt blue and despondent herself. When he came home she saw that something had happened to him. Her first impulse was to say, "What is the matter, Lester?" but her next and sounder one was to ignore it until he was ready to speak, if ever. She tried not to let him see that she saw, coming as near as she might affectionately without disturbing him.

"Vesta is so delighted with herself today," she volunteered by way of diversion. "She got such nice marks in school."

"That's good," he replied solemnly.

"And she's dancing beautifully these days. She showed me some of her new dances tonight. You haven't any idea how sweet she looks."

"I'm glad of it," he grumbled. "I always wanted her to be perfect in that. It's time she was going into some good girls' school, I think."

"And Papa gets in such a rage. I have to laugh. She teases him about it—the little imp. She offered to teach him to dance tonight. If he didn't love her so, he'd box her ears."

"I can see that," said Lester, smiling. "Him dancing. That's pretty good."

"She's not the least bit disturbed by his storming either."

"Good for her," said Lester. He was very fond of Vesta, who was now quite a girl.

So Jennie tripped on until his mood was modified a little, and then some inkling of what had happened came out. It was when they were retiring for the night. "Robert's formulated a pretty big thing in a financial way since we've been away," he volunteered.

"What is it?" asked Jennie, all ears.

"Oh, he's gotten up a carriage trust." Lester was taking out the pin from his tie now, and was loosening that and his collar.

"It's something which will take in every manufactory of any importance in the country. Bracebridge was telling me that Robert was made president, and that they have nearly eight million in capital invested in it."

"You don't say," replied Jennie. "Well, then you won't want to do much with your new company, will you?" She understood quite well now that his scheme had been blocked and that he must bestir himself to find something else. She wondered at times whether something hadn't happened to his fortune—the family was so distant. His getting out of the company was strange to her.

"No, there's nothing in that possibility, just now," he said. "Later on I fancy it may be all right. I'll wait and see how this thing comes out. You never can tell what a trust like that will do."

Jennie was intensely sorry. She had never heard Lester complain before. It was a new note. She wished sincerely that she might do something to comfort him or make him feel better, but she knew that her efforts were useless. "Oh, well," she said, "there are so many interesting things in this world. If I were you I wouldn't be in a hurry to do anything, Lester. You have so much time."

She didn't trust herself to say anything more, and he felt that it was useless to worry. Why should he? He had an ample income, after all, absolutely secure for two years yet. He could have more if he wanted it. Only his brother was moving so dazzlingly onward. It seemed such a shame—such a weak showing—for him to stand still. He drifted along indifferently for a time, going downtown to his club, following up this clue and that as to interesting propositions which were presented to him. He was thinking, though, all the time, that he would have a hard time to get himself connected right—as effectively as he had been in the past—and that was a bad thought. It wasn't the way he should have thought, but recent events had made him curiously uncertain about himself.

CHAPTER XLVII

Lester had been doing some pretty hard thinking, but so far he had been unable to formulate any feasible plan for his reentrance into active life. The successful organization of Robert's carriage-trade trust had knocked in the head any further thought on his part of taking an interest in the small Indiana wagon manufactory. Rapidly nearing forty-seven years of age, he looked about him now and saw that the best and most interesting avenue to distinction was closed for him. He could not reasonably be expected to sink his sense of pride and place at this point and enter into a petty campaign for trade success with a man who was obviously immensely his superior financially. Robert was now the one successful man in his field. Lester had looked up the details of the combination and found that Bracebridge had barely indicated to him how wonderfully complete it was. There were millions in the combine. It would have every little manufacturer by the throat. Should he begin now in a small way and "pike along" in the shadow of his giant brother? Or should he return and claim his share of this immense fortune which was so justly his? Why, last year he had been counted the equal of his brother. Many of the uninformed still thought him so. And here he was with a beggarly income of fifteen thousand and a possible small wagon company to look to for further profit. He couldn't see it. It was too ignominious. He would be running around the country trying to fight a new trust, and that with his own brother as his possible tolerant rival; his own rightful share arrayed against him. It couldn't be done. Better sit still for the time being. Something else might show up. If not—well, he had his independent income and the right to come back into the Kane Company if he wished. Did he wish? The question was always with him.

It was while he was in this mood, drifting, that he received a visit from Samuel E. Ross, a real-estate dealer in Chicago whose great wooden signs, blazoning real-estate advantages, Lester had seen standing out on the windy stretches of prairie about the city. Lester had seen Ross once or twice at the Union Club, where he had been pointed out as a daring and successful real-estate speculator, and he had seen his rather conspicuous offices at La Salle and Washington Streets, windows replete with gold lettering stating his name over and over. Ross was a magnetic-looking person of about fifty years of age, tall, black-bearded after the Van Dyke pattern, black-eyed, with an arched, wide-nostrilled nose, and hair that curled naturally, almost electrically. Lester was impressed with his lithe, cat-like figure, and his long, thin, impressive white hands.

Mr. Ross had a real-estate proposition to lay before Mr. Kane. Of course Mr. Kane knew who he was. He himself knew all about Mr. Kane, he admitted freely. He had known of the Kane Company for years. As a matter of fact, he had once sold his father a piece of property in Cincinnati, not directly but indirectly. Upon reflection Lester recalled the transaction well. It had been profitable.

Mr. Ross's proposition was none other than one he had worked out to great advantage in a number of other instances. He frankly stated that his real-estate success had been built on other people's capital, or partially so. The first deal he ever made, he went to Mr. Martin Ryerson and pointed out a ten-acre plot in what was then the outskirts of the city (now no farther north than Indiana Street) which could be had for very little money. He showed Mr. Ryerson how this could be easily improved and sold off in small lots for a dozen times the purchasing price. He had no money, but Mr. Ryerson liked his looks and financed the operation. Mr. Ross cleared $25,000. Mr. Ryerson's profits were in the neighborhood of $50,000.

Lester listened with a pleasant sense of curiosity, but not much thought of financial investment.

The present proposition was one similar to that. He had recently, in conjunction with Mr. Norman Yale, of the wholesale grocery firm of Yale, Simpson and Rice, developed "Yalewood." Mr. Kane knew of that?

Yes, Mr. Kane knew of that.

Only within six weeks, the last lots in the Ridgewood section of "Yalewood" had been closed out by him at a total profit of forty-two per cent. Mr. George E. Marcasson of the Drovers and Traders Liability Company had been his silent partner in that. Lester knew Mr. Marcasson by reputation well. Ross went over a list of other deals in real estate which he had got through, all well-known properties. He was famous in the city as a real-estate speculator. Any bank would vouch for him. His success he attributed to this method of safeguarding himself, which brought to him in each deal a balanced outside judgement, critical, indifferent at first, apt to see all the flaws which he might not, and then, when convinced, sharing the risks and taking the usually certain subsequent profits. There were failures, he admitted. One or two had been made by him. There were mostly successes to his credit, however, nearly twenty-five in all—one for every year he had been in business. He came to Lester because he knew of his connection with the Kane Company. He knew he was now out of there. Lester might like a thing like this to interest him. Then he laid before Lester his specific proposition.

It was nothing more than that he and Lester should enter into a one-deal partnership, covering the purchase and development of a forty-acre tract of land lying between 55th, 71st, Halsted Street and Ashland Avenue on the Southwest Side. There were indications of a genuine real-estate boom there— healthy, natural and permanent. The city, as he understood it, was about to pave 55th Street. There was a plan to extend the Halsted Street car line far below its present terminus. The Chicago, Rock Island & Pacific, which ran near there, would be glad to put a passenger station on the property. He knew the officers and some of the directors of the road well. The initial cost of the land would be forty thousand dollars, which they would share equally. Grading, paving, lighting, tree planting, surveying would cost roughly an additional twenty-five thousand. There would be expenses for advertising—say, ten per cent of the total investment for two years, or three years at the outside—a total of $19,500, or $20,000. All told they would stand to invest jointly the sum of $95,000, or possibly $100,000, of which Lester's share would be $50,000. Then Mr. Ross began to figure on the profits.

The character of the land here, its saleability and likelihood of rise, could be judged by the land adjacent, the sales that had been made north of 55th Street and east of Halsted. Take now, for instance, the Mortimer plot at Halsted and 55th Streets, on the southeast corner. Here was a piece of land that in 1882 was held at forty-five dollars an acre. In 1886 it had risen to five hundred dollars an acre, as attested by its sale to a Mr. John L. Slosson at that time. In 1889, three years later, it had been sold to Mr. Mortimer for one thousand per acre, precisely what this tract was being offered to him for, and was now being parceled out into lots of 50 × 100 feet at $500 per lot. Was there any profit in that?

Lester admitted there was.

Ross went on in detail, showing just how real-estate profits were made. It was useless for any outsider to rush into the game and imagine that he could do in a few weeks or years what trained real-estate speculators like himself had been working on for a quarter of a century. There was something in prestige, something in taste, something in psychic apprehension. In his case, as he said, he had been uniformly successful. He liked to go in this way with able, successful men. If Lester would spare him the time, he would go all over this matter with him inch by inch, detail by detail, so that it would be so plain that he could not fail to see exactly how it was done. He, Ross, would be the presiding genius. He would do the work. He had a trained staff, he had giant contractors, he had friends in the tax office, the water office, the various city departments which made city improvements. If Lester would come in with him, he would make him some money—how much he would not say exactly. Fifty thousand dollars at the least—one hundred and fifty to two hundred thousand in all likelihood. Would Lester let him show him the details of this proposition?

After a few days of quiet personal speculation, Lester decided that he would.

CHAPTER XLVIII

Since Lester had been cut off by his father's will and had left the Kane Company, he had not made one single move which, in his judgement, had shown the least initiative or cleverness. If up to this time he had made any such, he would have felt better about life in general, his own personal ability, his judgement of men and affairs. As it was, he hadn't. If he went back into the family interests, as his natural commercial judgement counseled him to, if he left Jennie and took his share in the Kane Company, or married Mrs. Gerald, as he sometimes fancied that he might, or did both, he would still have no connection with any company which he would value as his own. He did not believe that he would want to hold any position with the Kane Company any more, particularly after he had been so ignominiously crowded out, and Robert had made it into a so much larger concern. He valued the interest which the enlarged company now presented but objected vigorously, mentally and physically, to being what he termed "a trailer." He wanted ever so much to get in on something which would be his own, to do some one thing which he could point to as having proved both interesting and profitable. He had not done this yet. He was merely drifting. And here was something which looked most promising.

True, a fifty-thousand-dollar investment was a rather large order for him to undertake in his present anomalous position. He did not know where he would be in another year or two. His most satisfying thought was that he might have parted from Jennie by that time, or married her and quit worrying about it, and also told his own family to go to the devil, for he could not forgive them for their connection with this affair; but he would feel so much better about it all if, at the same time, he could say to himself that he had made a successful commercial venture of some kind. The family would think so much more of him. Mrs. Gerald would respect him more. Jennie would, even though he were forcing her to leave him. He turned these points over in his mind and finally decided he might risk the sum demanded, seeing that it would not have to be paid in all at once and that it would not eat up all his extra capital. Fifty thousand dollars was two-thirds of all the stocks and bonds and ready money he had, outside of his present income, but the promise of reward was exceptional. He finally decided that he would risk it.

The peculiarity of this particular proposition was that it had in it the basic elements of success. Mr. Ross had the experience and the judgement and was quite capable of making a success of almost anything he undertook. He was in a field which was entirely familiar to him. He could convince almost any able man, if he could get his ear sufficiently long to lay his facts before him.

Lester was not convinced at first, although generally speaking he was interested in real-estate propositions. He liked land. He considered it a sound investment, providing you did not get too much of it. He had never invested in any, or scarcely any, solely because he had not been in a realm where real-estate propositions were talked of. His father had owned considerable land in Cincinnati. If he had gotten his just deserts, he would have been the possessor of a considerable portion of it. As it was he was landless and, in a way, jobless.

He rather liked Mr. Ross and his way of doing business. It was easy to verify his statements, and Lester did verify them in several particulars. There were his signs out on the prairie stretches, and here were his ads in the daily papers. It seemed not a bad way at all, in his idleness, to start and make some money.

The trouble with Lester was that he had reached the time

where he was not as keen for details as he had formerly been. All his work in recent years—in fact, from the very beginning—had been with large propositions, the purchasing of great quantities of supplies, the placing of large orders, the discussion of things which were wholesale and which had very little to do with the minor details which make up the special interests of the smaller traders of the world. In the factory his brother Robert had figured the pennies and nickels of labor-cost, had seen to it that all the little leaks were shut off. Lester had been left to deal with larger things, and he had consistently done so. When it came to this particular proposition, his interest was in the wholesale phases of it—not the petty details of selling. He could not help seeing that Chicago was a growing city, and that land values must rise. What was now far-out prairie property would soon—in the course of a few years—be well built-up suburban residence territory. Scarcely any land that could be purchased now would fall in value. It might drag in sales or increase, but it couldn't fall. Ross convinced him of this. He knew it of his own judgement to be true.

The several things in which Lester did not speculate sufficiently were the life or health of Mr. Ross; the chance that some obnoxious neighborhood growth would affect the territory he had selected as residence territory; the fact that difficult money situations might reduce real-estate values,—in fact, might bring about a flurry of real-estate liquidation which would send prices clattering and cause the failure of strong promoters—even such promoters, for instance, as Mr. Samuel E. Ross.

For several months Lester studied the situation as presented by his new guide and mentor and then, having satisfied himself that he was reasonably safe, decided to sell some of the holdings which were netting him a beggarly six per cent and invest in this new proposition. The first cash outlay was $20,000 for the land, which was taken over under an operative agreement between himself and Ross; this was to run indefinitely—as long as there was any of this land left to sell. The next thing was to raise $12,500 for improvements, which Lester did, and then to furnish some $2,500 more for taxes and unconsidered expenses, items which had come up in carrying out the improvement work which had been planned. It seemed that hard and soft earth made a difference in grading-costs, that trees would not always flourish as expected, that certain members of the city water and gas departments had to be "seen" and "fixed" before certain other improvements could be effected. Mr. Ross attended to all this, but the cost of the proceedings was something which had to be discussed, and Lester heard it all.

After the land was put in shape—about a year after the original conversation, it was necessary to wait until spring for the proper advertising and booming of the new section, and this advertising began to call at once for the third principal outlay. Lester disposed of an additional fifteen thousand dollars worth of securities in order to follow this venture to its logical and profitable conclusion.

Up to this time he was rather pleased with the drift of events. Ross had certainly been thorough and businesslike in his handling of the various details. The land was put in excellent shape. It was given a rather attractive title: "Inwood," although, as Lester noted, there was precious little wood anywhere around there. Ross assured him that the title was good business from a practical point of view, for Chicago, being as yet so largely treeless, and people looking for some section even partially equipped with trees, would be attracted by the name. Seeing the notable efforts in tree-planting that had been made to provide for shade in the future, they would take the will for the deed. Lester smiled.

The first chill wind that blew upon the infant project came when, after they had expended $6,000 for preliminary advertising, it was rumored in the papers that the International Packing Company, one of the big constituent members of the meat-packing group at Halsted and 39th Streets, having become dissatisfied with the treatment accorded it, not only in the space for handling cattle but in building facilities, would desert the old group and lay out a new packing area for itself. The papers explained that the company intended to go farther south, probably below 55th Street and west of Ashland Avenue. This was the territory that was located due west of Lester's property, and the mere suspicion that the packing company might invade the territory was sufficient to blight the prospects of any budding real-estate deal.

Ross was beside himself with rage. He was angry to think that the newspapers would quote a rumor of this kind, which so seriously affected his property, without first actually verifying and being sure that such was the case. He could not actually prove for himself whether the rumor was true. There had been, it was true,

a notable transfer of land, some two hundred acres in all, registered on the books of the county as having been sold to John C.
Bowne not long before, but who John C. Bowne was and whether
he was connected with the International Packing Company could
not be immediately verified. There was no one at the International Packing Company who could or would talk, and it was not
possible to learn anything from the city editors of the newspapers
beyond the fact that the rumor had come to them. Ross was at a
loss how to offset the damage done, for additional discussion by
him or any one else merely meant that the public would be more
thoroughly aroused to the fact that such a rumor had even been
current—which was all that was needed to definitely settle the
fate of the property. He decided, after quick deliberation, that the
best thing to do would be to boom the property heavily, by means
of newspaper advertising, and see if it could not be disposed of
quickly before any additional damage was likely to be done to it.
He laid the matter before Lester, who agreed that this would be
advisable, and the additional sum of $3,000 was spent in ten days
to make it appear that Inwood was an ideal residence section,
equipped with every modern convenience for the home-lover,
and destined to be one of the most exclusive and beautiful residence sections of the city. It was "no go." The prospective pur-
chasers did not come.

Lester, who was pretty shrewd in the matter of safe-guarding
his private interests, suggested that some more indirect method
might be advisable. Would it not be possible, while continuing
the general advertising—in order to give the place current prestige—to get some ulterior method of persuading people that this
was an ideal section—to fight rumor with rumor—and hire workers who, for a percentage, would "tip off" friends or associates in a
number of the big industrial enterprises in the city that this was an
ideal home section. He had seen this done in connection with his
father's employés at Cincinnati, and he thought it might be made
to work here. There was some little result from this—a few lots
were sold—but the rumor that the International Packing Company might move out into that territory was persistent and deadly;
and from any point of view, save that of a foreign-population
neighborhood, the enterprise was a failure.

To say that Lester was greatly disheartened by this blow is to
put it mildly. It was his first private venture since he had left the

Kane Company and, as the project had developed during the past year-and-a-half, he had taken a lively interest in it. To accommodate his mood and his business possibilities, he had taken an office downtown in the Rookery Building, where he was convenient to the offices of the Ross Company and where he could see some of the contractors whom he agreed to manage for Ross. He had talked about the proposition in a tentative way with Jennie, had indicated that he thought it would be a success.

Several times he had driven over the land with her, indicating in an off-hand manner what the possibilities were. She was immensely hopeful for him and for it, and now it was destined to come to nothing.

The worst part of it was that, having caught and chained this very interesting elephant of prospective prosperity, it was not easy to dispose of it. It might be sold out at a profit if given time enough, Ross argued. The International Packing Company might not move as indicated. Practically $50,000, two-thirds of all Lester's earthly possessions outside his stipulated annual income, was tied up here; and there were taxes to pay, repairs to maintain, actual depreciation in value to face. He suggested to Ross that the area might be sold at its cost value, or a loan raised on it, and the whole thing abandoned; but that experienced real-estate dealer was not so sanguine. He had had one or two failures of this kind before. He was superstitious about anything which did not go smoothly from the beginning. If it didn't go, it was a hoo doo—a black shadow—and he wanted no more to do with it. Other real-estate men, as he knew to his cost, were of the same opinion.

It finally turned out that the property was sold under the sheriff's hammer some three years later—but only after Mr. Samuel E. Ross had failed, endeavoring to handle a much larger venture. Lester, from having put in $50,000 all told, was glad to extract $18,000 and consider himself lucky.

CHAPTER XLIX

While this real-estate deal was first being mediated and engineered, Mrs. Gerald decided to move to Chicago. She had been in Cincinnati during the few months Lester had been looking about and had learned a great deal, from this person and that, as to the real facts of his life. The question as to whether he was really married to Jennie or not was an open one. The fact that he had lost his fortune, or would lose it unless he rearranged his affairs so as to eliminate her, was talked about in certain circles. The garbled details of her early life, the fact that a Chicago paper had written him up as a young millionaire who was sacrificing his fortune for love of her, the fact that Robert had practically eliminated him from any voice in the Kane Company, all came to her ears. She hated to think that Lester was making such a sacrifice of himself. She heard that he had let nearly a year slip by now without doing anything. In two more years his chance would be gone. Did Jennie know this? Would she let him make a sacrifice of himself? Would he go stubbornly ahead? She thought of her own love for him, persistent through so many years, and she could understand in a way how it might be with him. And yet he had said to her in London that he was without many illusions. Was Jennie one? Did he really love her, or was he just sorry for her? Letty wanted to find out for sure.

The house that Mrs. Gerald leased in Chicago was a most imposing one on Drexel Boulevard. The fact that she was coming for a season or two was announced in the various society columns. Jennie saw it, as did Lester, but he had word direct. "I'm going to take a house in your town this winter, and I hope to see a lot of you," she wrote him. "I'm awfully bored with life here in Cincinnati. After Europe it's so—well, you know. I saw Mrs. Knowles on Saturday. She asked after you. You ought to know that you have a loving friend in her. Her daughter is going to marry Jimmy Severance in the spring."

Lester thought of Letty's coming with mingled feelings of pleasure and uncertainty. She would be entertaining largely, of course. What had she heard since she had come back? Would she foolishly begin by attempting to invite him and Jennie? Surely not. She must know the truth by this time. Her letter indicated as much. She spoke of seeing a lot of him. That meant that Jennie would have to be eliminated, which was natural. Ought he to go? It was plain that there was coming a long conversation between himself and her some time. He would have to tell her all. Things couldn't be straightened out any other way. Then she could do as she pleased.

He did call finally, some time after she was settled, and there was a long heart-to-heart talk between them which cleared up a number of things. He did not think, when he saw her again, that he was going to explain anything, but seated in her comfortable boudoir one afternoon, about a year after seeing her in Europe, facing a vision of loveliness in pale yellow, he decided that he might as well have it out with her. She would understand. Anyhow, he was beginning to doubt the outcome of the real-estate deal and was consequently feeling a little blue, and, as a concomitant, a little confidential. He could not yet talk to Jennie about his troubles.

"You know, Lester," said Letty, by way of helping him to his confession—the maid had brought tea for her and some brandy and soda for him, and departed—"that I have been hearing a lot of things about you since I've been back in this country. Aren't you going to tell me all about yourself? You know I have your real interests at heart."

"What have you been hearing, Letty?" he asked quietly.

"Oh, I heard about your father's will for one thing, and the fact that you're out of the company, and some gossip about Mrs. Kane which doesn't interest me very much. You know what I mean. Aren't you going to straighten things out so that you can have what rightfully belongs to you? It seems to me such a great sacrifice, Lester, unless of course you are very much in love. Are you?" she asked archly.

Lester was truly in the house of the temptress, for Mrs. Gerald had made up her mind that if he were not married (and it looked to her as if he were not) and were going to leave Jennie, that he might as well come to her. She loved him. With her fortune of several million, to say nothing of his interest in the Kane Company, he would be a most imposing financial figure. Some of the companies in which Robert was interested as a stockholder and director were practically controlled by her interests. If Lester were in charge, he could force his brother off the boards, if he wished. She disliked the manner in which Robert had treated him, if local reports were true. Why shouldn't he marry her? He liked her, and she was an ideal companion for him—far more suitable than Jennie.

Lester paused and deliberated before replying. "I really don't know how to answer that last question, Letty," he said. "Sometimes I think that I love her; sometimes I wonder whether I do or not. I'm going to be perfectly frank with you. I was never in such a curious position in my life before. You like me so much, and I—well, I won't say what I think of you," he smiled. "But anyhow, I can talk to you frankly. I'm not married."

"I thought as much," she said, as he paused.

"And I'm not married because I have never been able to make up my mind just what to do about it. When I first met Jennie, I thought she was the most entrancing girl I had ever laid eyes on."

"That speaks volumes for my charms at that time," interrupted his *vis-à-vis*.

"Don't interrupt if you want to hear this," he smiled.

"Tell me one thing," she questioned, "and then I won't. Was that in Cleveland?"

"Yes," he said.

"So I heard," she replied.

"There was something about her so—"

"Love at first sight," interpolated Letty again, foolishly. Her heart was hurting her. "I know."

"Are you going to let me tell this?"

"Pardon me, Lester. I can't help a twinge or two."

"Well, anyhow, I lost my head. I thought she was the most perfect thing under the sun, even if she was a little out of my world. This is a democratic country. I thought at first, and that is where I made my mistake, that I could just take her and then—well, you know. I didn't think it would prove as serious as it did. I never cared for any other woman but you before and—I'll be frank—I didn't know whether I wanted to marry you. I thought I didn't want to marry any woman. I felt that I ought not to tie myself up in any way. I knew something about married life from general observation. I said to myself that I could just take her, and then, after awhile, when things were quieted down some, we could separate. She would be well provided for. I wouldn't care very much. She wouldn't care. You understand."

"Yes, I understand," replied his confessor.

"Well, you see, Letty, it hasn't worked out that way—I'm sorry to state and I'm not sorry to state. She's a woman of a curious temperament. She possesses a world of feeling and emotion. She's not educated in the sense in which we understand that word, but she has natural refinement and tact. She's a good housekeeper. She's an ideal mother. She's the most affectionate creature under the sun. Her devotion to her mother and father are classics in their way. Her devotion to her daughter—she's hers, not mine—is perfect. She hasn't any of the graces of the smart society woman. She isn't quick at repartée. She can't join in any rapid-fire conversation. She thinks rather slowly, I imagine. Some of her big thoughts never come to the surface at all, but you can feel that she is thinking and that she is feeling."

"You pay her a lovely tribute, Lester," said Letty.

"I ought to," he replied. "She's a good woman. But Letty, after I've said all that, I sometimes think that it's only sympathy that's holding me."

"Don't be too sure," she replied.

"I've gone through with a great deal. The thing for me to have done was to have married her in the first place. There have been so many entanglements since—so much rowing and discussion, that I've rather lost my bearings. As I told you a little while since, I hardly know what to think. This will of father's complicates matters. I stand to lose eight hundred thousand if I marry her—really, a great deal more, now that the company has been organized into a trust. I might better say two millions. If I don't marry her, I lose everything outright in about two more years. I could pretend that I have separated from her, of course, but I don't care to lie. I can't work it out that way without hurting her feelings, and she's been the soul of devotion. Right down in my heart, at this minute, I don't know whether I want to give her up. Honestly, I don't know what the devil to do."

Lester looked at her in a far-off, speculative way.

"Was there ever such a problem?" questioned Letty, staring at the floor. She rose, after a few moments of silence, and put her hands on his round, solid head. Her yellow, silken house-gown, faintly scented, touched his shoulders. "Poor Lester," she said. "You certainly have tied yourself up in a knot. It's a Gordian knot, my dear, though, and it will have to be cut. You are the one to cut it. Why don't you discuss this whole thing with her, just as you have with me, and see how she feels about it?"

"It seems such an unkind thing to do," he replied.

"You must take some action, Lester dear," she insisted. "You can't just drift. You are doing yourself such a great injustice.

Frankly I can't advise you to marry her, and I'm not speaking for myself in that, though I'll take you gladly, even if you did forsake me in the first place. I'll be perfectly honest, whether you ever come to me or not—I love you."

"I know it," said Lester calmly, getting up. He took her arms in his hands and studied her face curiously. Then he turned away. Letty paused to get her breath. This action of his flustered her greatly.

"But you're too big a man, Lester, to settle down on ten thousand a year," she continued. "You're too much of a social figure to drift. You ought to get back into the social and financial world where you belong. All that's happened won't injure you, if you reclaim your interest in the company. You can dictate your own terms. And if you tell her the truth, she won't object, I'm sure. If she cares for you as you think she does, she will be glad to make this sacrifice. I'm positive of it. You can provide for her handsomely then. Why shouldn't she?"

"It isn't the money that Jennie wants," said Lester gloomily.

"Well, even if it isn't, she can live without you, and she can live better for having an ample income."

"She will never want if I can help it," he said solemnly.

"You must leave her," she urged, finally. "You must. Every day is precious with you, Lester! Why don't you make up your mind to act at once—today, for that matter? Why not?"

"Not so fast," he said solemnly. "This is a ticklish business. To tell you the truth, I hate to do it. It seems so brutal—so unfair. I'm not one to run around and discuss my affairs with other people. I've refused to talk about this to any one heretofore— my father, my mother, any one. But somehow you have always seemed closer to me than any one else, and, since I met you this time, I have felt as though I ought to explain—I have really wanted to. I care for you. I don't know whether you understand how that can be under the circumstances. But I do. You're nearer to me intellectually and emotionally than I thought you were. Don't frown. You want the truth, don't you? Well, there you have it. Now you explain me to myself, if you can!"

"I don't want to explain you, Lester," she said softly, laying her hand on his arm. "I merely want to love you. I understand quite well how it has all come about. I'm sorry for myself. I'm sorry for you. I'm sorry for—Mrs. Kane," she hesitated. "She's a charming woman. I like her. I really do. But she isn't the woman for you, Lester, she really isn't. You need another type. It seems so unfair for us two to stand up here and discuss her in this way, but it isn't. We all have to stand on our merits. And I'm satisfied, if the facts in this case were put before her as you have put them before me, she would see just how it all is and agree. She can't want to harm you. Why, Lester, if I were in her position, knowing what I do now, or if you were married to me on our plane and any such complication came up, I would let you go. I would, truly. I think you know that I would. Any good woman would. It would hurt me, but I would. It will hurt her, but she will. Now, you mark my words, she will. I think I understand her as well as you do— better—for I am a woman." "Oh," she said, pausing, "I wish I were in a position to talk to her. I could make her understand."

He looked at her solemnly, wondering at her eagerness. She was beautiful, magnetic, immensely worth while.

"Not so fast," he repeated. "I want to think about this. I have some time yet."

She paused, a little crestfallen, but determined. "You want to act, and soon," she replied.

She tried to deceive herself into the belief that she was disinterested in giving this advice, but she wasn't at all. She wanted Lester, and she hoped that, after Jennie was away and he came to see her, somehow he would wake joyously to her charms—and then she would have him.

CHAPTER L

Lester had thought of this predicament of his earnestly enough, and he would have been satisfied to have acted shortly after this, if it had not been that one of those delaying and disrupting influences which sometimes complicate our affairs for us began to manifest itself in his Hyde Park domicile. Gerhardt's health began rapidly to fail.

For some little time during the summer while they were away, Gerhardt had been ailing. His appetite had been poor, and he had been complaining of pains in his back, a symptom, though he did not know it, of a disarrangement in the functioning of the pancreas, that factory of several secretions which does so much for the stomach. His digestive apparatus was not receiving in their proper proportions the three known chemical agents which it manufactures so liberally—why, no one might say. Perhaps the nerve governing the functioning of that organ was impinged on in some way, due to a general wasting of his frame. Anyhow, his health grew poor, and he took to his bed.

During the several years in which Lester and Jennie had been living in Hyde Park, he had been a most interesting factor in the home. He had, as has been shown, taken care of a long list of small duties, and now it was necessary to get someone else in his place. At first he protested that there was no need and that he would soon be up, but as days dragged by and he grew worse, if anything, rather than better, Jennie thought it advisable to hire a man to look after the furnace and run errands, and this was done. Gerhardt was beside himself with grief and protest. He did not want to get sick, and he did not want to die. He lay in his room, devotedly attended by Jeannette and Jennie and visited by Vesta, by Mrs. Frissell, the cook, by Henry Weeds, the stableman, and occasionally by Lester, who merely came to inquire how he was. There was a window not far from his bed which commanded a charming view of the lawn and of one of the surrounding streets, and through this he would gaze, wondering how the world was getting on without him. He suspected by turns that Weeds was not looking after the horses and harnesses as well as he should, that the newspaper carrier was getting negligent in his delivery of the papers, that the furnace man was apt to let the boiler blow up, or was wasting coal, or was not giving them enough heat. A score of little petty worries, which were nevertheless real enough to him. He knew how a house should be kept, he said. He was always rigid in his performance of his self-established duties, and he was so afraid that things would not go right. Jennie made for him a most imposing and sumptuous dressing-gown of basted wool, covered with dark blue silk, and bought him a pair of soft, thick, wool slippers to match, but he did not get to wear them much. He liked to lie in bed instead, read his Lutheran papers, read his Bible, and query Jennie as to how things were getting along.

"I want you should go down in the basement and see what that feller is doing. He's not giving us any heat," he would complain. "I bet I know what he does. He sits down there and reads, and then he forgets what the fire is doing until it is almost out. The beer is right there where he can take it. You should lock it up. You don't know what kind of a man he is. He may be a no-good."

Jennie would protest that the house was fairly comfortable, that the man was a nice, quiet, respectable-looking American— that if he did drink a little beer it would not matter. Gerhardt would immediately become incensed.

"That is always the way," he declared vigorously. "You have no sense of economy. You are always so ready to let things go if I am not there. He is a nice man! How do you know he is a nice man? Does he keep the fire up? No! Does he keep the walks clean? If you don't watch him he will be just like the others, no good. You should go around and see how things are for yourself."

"All right, Papa," she would reply in a genial effort to soothe him, "I will. Please don't worry. I'll lock up the beer. Don't you want a cup of coffee now and some toast?"

"No," Gerhardt would sigh immediately, "my stomach it don't do right. I don't know how I am going to come out of this."

Dr. Makin, the leading physician of the vicinity, and a man of considerable experience and ability, called at Jennie's request and suggested a few simple things—hot milk, a wine tonic, rest,—but he told Jennie that she must not expect too much. "You know he is quite well along in years now. He is quite feeble. If he were twenty years younger, we might do a great deal for him. As it is, he is quite well off where he is. He may live for some time. He may get up and be around again, and then he may not. We must all expect these things. I have never any care as to what may happen to me. I am too old myself."

Jennie felt sorry to think that her father might die, but she was pleased to think that if he must it was going to be under such comfortable circumstances. Here at least he could have every care.

It was when he first took sick that she did her best to get into communication with her brothers and sisters. She wrote Bass almost immediately that his father was not feeling well and had a letter from him saying that he was very busy and couldn't come unless his father was in serious danger. He went on to say that George was in Rochester, working for a wholesale wall-paper house, he thought—the Sheff-Jefferson Company. She might write him there. Martha and her husband had gone to Boston. Her address was a little suburb named Belmont, just outside the city. William was in Omaha, working for a local electric company. Veronica was married to a man named Albert Sheridan, who was connected with a wholesale drug company in Cleveland. "She never comes to see me," complained Bass, "but I'll let her know." Jennie wrote each one personally. From Veronica and Martha she heard finally that they were sorry, and to let them know. From George that he could not think of coming unless his father was very ill, but that he would like to know from time to time how he was getting along. William, as he told Jennie some time afterward, did not get her letter. So she understood how things were with them.

The progress of the old German's malady toward final dissolution preyed greatly on Jennie's mind, for in spite of the fact that they had been so far apart in times past, they had come very close together sympathetically since. He had come to realize very clearly that his outcast daughter was goodness itself, as far as he was concerned at least. She never quarreled with him, never crossed him in any way. She was always anxious that he should be well-dressed and well-fed, and she looked after him much as she did Vesta. Now that he was sick, she was in and out of his room a dozen times in an evening or an afternoon, seeing whether he was "all right," whether he wanted anything, whether he liked his breakfast or his lunch or his dinner. She entered into a sort of conspiracy with Mrs. Frissell to see whether his appetite could not be tempted by delicacies, but in a way they did him as much harm as good. His digestive organs were not functioning properly, and he would sometimes regret having attempted the things they offered. As he grew weaker she would sit by him and read, do her sewing in his room, send out to see whether the things he was worrying about were really as bad as he thought. He finally took her hand one day, when she was straightening his pillow, and kissed it. He was feeling very weak and despondent. She looked up quickly, astonished, a lump in her throat. There were tears in his eyes.

"You're a good girl, Jennie," he said brokenly. "You've been good to me. I've been hard and cross, but I'm an old man. You forgive me, don't you?"

"Oh, Papa, please don't," she pleaded, tears welling from her eyes. "You know I have nothing to forgive. I'm the one who has been all wrong."

"No, no," he said, and she sank down on her knees beside him and cried. He put his thin, yellow hand on her hair. "There, there," he said brokenly, "I understand a lot of things I didn't. We get wiser as we get older."

She went outside after a bit, ostensibly to wash her face and hands, and cried. Was he really forgiving her at last! And she had lied to him so! She tried to be more attentive, but that was not possible. He seemed happier and more contented afterward for having told her this, and they spent a number of happy hours together, just talking. Once he said to her, "You know, I feel just like I did when I was a boy. If it wasn't for my bones, I could get out and dance on the grass."

Jennie fairly smiled and sobbed in one breath. "You'll get stronger, Papa," she said. "You're going to get well. Then I'll take you out driving." She was so glad she had been able to make him comfortable these last few years.

One of the notable things of this period was Lester's consideration for her feeling and devotion.

"Well, how is he tonight?" he would ask the moment he entered the house, and he would always drop in for a few minutes before dinner to see how the old man was getting along. "He looks pretty well," he would tell Jennie. "He's apt to live some time yet. I wouldn't worry."

Vesta also spent time with her grandfather, for she had come to love him dearly. She would bring her books, if it didn't disturb him too much, and recite some of her lessons, or stand his door open and play for him on the piano. Lester had bought her a handsome music-box also, which she would sometimes carry to his room and play for him. At times he wearied of everything and everybody save Jennie and wanted to be alone with her. At these times she would sit beside him, quite still, and sew. She could see quite plainly that the end was only a little way off.

Gerhardt, true to his nature, took into consideration all the details of this approaching end. He wanted to be buried in the little Lutheran cemetery, which was several miles farther out on the South Side, and he wanted the beloved minister of his church to officiate.

"I want everything plain," he said. "Just my black suit and

those Sunday shoes of mine, and that black string tie. I don't want anything else. I will be all right."

Jennie begged him not to talk of it, but he would. One day at four o'clock he had a sudden sinking spell, and at five he was dead. Jennie held his hands, watching him breathe when she realized that he was nearing his end, and once or twice he opened his eyes to smile at her. "I don't mind going," he said in this final hour. "I've done what I could."

"Don't talk of dying, Papa," she pleaded.

"It's the end," he said. "You've been good to me. You're a good woman."

She heard no other words from his lips.

The finish which time thus put to this troubled life affected Jennie deeply. Strong in her kindly, emotional relationships, Gerhardt had appealed to her not only as her father but as a friend and counsellor. She saw him now in his true perspective, a hard-working, honest, sincere old German who had done his best to raise a troublesome family and lead an honest life. Truly she had been his one great burden, and she had never really dealt truthfully with him to the end. She wondered now if, where he was, he could see that she had lied. And would he forgive her? He had called her a good woman.

Telegrams were sent to all the children. Bass wired that he was coming and arrived the next day. The others wired that they could not come but asked for details, which Jennie wrote. The Lutheran minister was called in to say prayers and fix the time of the burial service. A fat, smug undertaker was commissioned to arrange all the details. Some few neighborhood friends called,— those who had remained most faithful—and on the second morning following his death the services were held. Lester accompanied Jennie and Vesta and Bass to the little red-brick Lutheran church and sat stolidly through the rather dry services. He listened wearily to the long discourse on the beauties and rewards of a future life and stirred irritably when reference was made to a hell. Bass was rather bored but considerate. He looked upon his father now much as he would on any other man. Jennie only wept sympathetically. She saw her father in perspective, the long years of trouble he had had, the days in which he had had to saw wood for a living, the days in which he had lived in a factory loft, the little shabby house they had been compelled to live in in 13th Street, the terrible days of suffering they had spent in Lorrie Street in Cleveland, his grief over her, his grief over Mrs. Gerhardt, his love and care of Vesta, and finally these last days.

"Oh, he was a good man," she thought. "He meant so well." They sang a hymn, "A Mighty Fortress Is Our God," and then she sobbed.

Lester pulled at her arm. He was moved to the danger line himself by her grief. "You'll have to do better than this," he whispered. "My God, I can't stand it. I'll have to get up and get out." Jennie quieted a little, but the fact that the last visible ties were being broken between her and her father were almost too much.

At the grave in the Cemetery of the Redeemer, where Lester had immediately arranged to purchase a lot, they saw the plain coffin lowered and the earth shoveled in. Lester looked curiously at the bare trees, the brown dead grass, and the brown soil of the prairie turned up at this simple graveside. There was no distinction to this burial plot. It was commonplace and shabby, a working-man's resting place, but as long as Gerhardt wanted it, it was all right. Lester studied Bass's keen, lean face, wondering what sort of a career he was cutting out for himself. Bass looked to him like someone who would run a cigar store. He watched Vesta wiping her red eyes, and Jennie, then he said to himself again, "Well, there is something to her." The woman's emotion was so deep, so real. "There's no explaining a good woman," he said to himself.

On the way home, through the wind-swept, dusty streets, he talked of life in general, Bass and Vesta being present. "Jennie takes things too seriously," he said. "She's inclined to be morbid. Life isn't as bad as she makes out with her feelings. We all have our troubles, and we all have to stand them—some more, some less. We can't assume that any one is so much better or worse off than any one else. We all have our share of troubles."

"I can't help it," said Jennie. "I feel so sorry for some people."

"Jennie always was a little gloomy," put in Bass. He was thinking what a fine figure of a man Lester was, how beautifully they lived, how Jennie had come up in the world. He was thinking that there must be a lot more to her than he had originally thought. Life surely did turn out queer. At one time he had thought Jennie was a hopeless failure and no good.

"You ought to try to steel yourself to take things as they come without going to pieces this way," said Lester finally.

Bass thought so too.

Jennie stared thoughtfully out of the carriage window. There was the old house now, large and silent, without Gerhardt. Just think, she would never see him any more, ever. They finally turned into the drive and entered the library. Jeannette, nervous and sympathetic, served tea. Jennie went to look after various details. She wondered curiously where she would be when she died.

CHAPTER LI

The fact that Gerhardt was dead did not really make so much difference to Lester sympathetically. He had admired the old German for several sterling qualities, but beyond that he had thought nothing of him, one way or the other. He took Jennie to a watering place for ten days after it was all over, and it was soon after this that he decided to tell her just how things stood with him anyhow, and to see what she would say. His cause in this respect was helped by the fact that Jennie knew of the disastrous trend of the real-estate deal, which was still pending. She was also aware of his continued interest in Mrs. Gerald, for, while he had not said much of her, there had been notes come to the house which he had casually mentioned or explained. He did not hesitate to let Jennie know that he was friendly with her. Mrs. Gerald had, at first, formally requested him to bring Jennie to see her, but she had never called herself, and Jennie understood quite clearly that it was not to be. Now that her father was dead, she was beginning to wonder what was going to become of her, for she was afraid Lester might not marry her. He showed no signs of intending to remedy anything.

It was by one of those curious coincidences of thought that, just at the time that he was ready to act, Robert had reached the conclusion that something ought to be done. He did not for one moment imagine that he could influence Lester in any way directly—he did not care to try—but he did think that some influence might be brought to bear on Jennie which would straighten the matter out before it was too late. Only two months of time remained. She was probably amenable to reason. If Lester had not married her by now, she must realize full well that he did not intend to. If someone—not any one coming from him apparently—were to approach her and explain how things were; if she were offered an independent income, might she not be willing to leave Lester and end this public trouble? He ought not to lose his fortune. After all, Lester was his brother. At the same time he did not care to see Lester's share, which was to be divided pro rata in case he did not take it, fall into the hands of the husbands of Amy and Imogene and Louise. They did not deserve it. Robert had things very much in his own hands now anyhow and could afford to be generous. He thought of asking Imogene to talk to Jennie in a friendly, sensible way, seeing that she was there in the same city, but he finally decided that Mr. O'Brien, of Knight, Keatley and O'Brien, would be better, for O'Brien was suave, good-natured, and well-meaning, even if he was a lawyer. He might explain to Jennie very delicately just how the family felt, how much Lester stood to lose, how obvious it was that he could not care for her as he should or he would have married her by now. If Lester had married Jennie, O'Brien would find this out. If not, a given sum—say, fifty or one-hundred thousand or one-hundred-and-fifty thousand dollars even—might be set aside for her use, and this might persuade her. Of course, its payment by degrees or in certain lump sums would depend on her conduct after the agreement had been reached. Robert had the idea that she was clinging to Lester because of his prestige, possibly—if so, nothing would avail—but if she really cared for him, this approaching trouble over his financial affairs might move her. Anyhow, she ought to be sounded out, and O'Brien, as the representative of his father, ought to do it. He turned this over in his mind and finally sent for O'Brien, giving him full instructions as to just how the thing was to be carried out.

Mr. O'Brien—round-faced, smiling, conciliatory—came as Robert suggested. He thought, he said, that something might be done. He had been thinking that it would be wise to communicate with Lester—to counsel with him, if possible. Lester might be brought to reason. Anyhow, if Jennie was reasonable or unreasonable, he might talk to Lester. The latter might decide to change. He said he would call up Lester when he arrived in

Chicago and find out where he was going to be at a certain hour—then call on Jennie a little before that so as to find her alone.

"You can arrange all that to suit yourself," said Robert indifferently. "I'm quite sure that something ought to be done. As an executor of the estate, you're entitled to know what his eventual decision is to be. When you find out, let me know."

Mr. O'Brien journeyed to Chicago. He called up Lester on reaching there and found out to his satisfaction that he was out of town for the day. He went out to the house in Hyde Park and sent in his card to Jennie, stating to the maid that it was most important and that he hoped she would see him. She came downstairs in a few minutes, quite unconscious of the import of his message, and he greeted her most blandly.

"This is Mrs. Kane?" he asked, with an interlocutory jerk of his head.

"Yes," replied Jennie.

"I am, as you see by my card, Mr. O'Brien, of Knight, Keatley and O'Brien," he began. "We are the attorneys and executors of the late Mr. Kane, your, ah—Mr. Kane's father. You'll think it's rather curious, my coming to you, but under your husband's father's will there were certain conditions stipulated which affect you and Mr. Kane very materially. I want to ask you as a favor, in the first place, if I may talk to you in confidence about this. I am quite sure I may as well say right now that Mr. Kane would object to my coming to see you very much if he knew. The conditions of the will, though, which affect your interests are so important—quite as important in their way as his, that I think you ought to know about them if he hasn't already told you. I—pardon me—but the peculiar nature of them makes me conclude that—possibly—he hasn't." He paused, a very question-mark of a man—the features of his face an interrogation.

"I don't quite understand," said Jennie. "I don't know anything about the will. If there's anything that I ought to know, I suppose Mr. Kane will tell me. He hasn't told me anything as yet."

"Ah," breathed Mr. O'Brien, highly gratified. "Just as I thought. Now let me tell you just a little about this, and then you can judge for yourself whether you wish to hear the rest or say anything at all. Won't you sit down?" They had both been standing. Jennie seated herself, and Mr. O'Brien pulled a chair near to hers.

"Now to begin," he said. "I need not say to you, of course, that there was considerable opposition on the part of Mr. Kane's father to this—ah—union, between yourself and his son."

"I know," Jennie was going to say, but checked herself. She was puzzled, disturbed, a little apprehensive.

"Before Mr. Kane senior died," he went on, "he indicated to your, ah—to Mr. Lester Kane—that he felt this way. In his will he made certain conditions governing the distribution of his property which make it rather hard for his son—your, ah—husband, to come into his rightful share. Ordinarily he would have inherited one-fourth of the Kane Manufacturing Company, worth today in the neighborhood of a million dollars, perhaps more, and one-fourth of his other properties, which now aggregate something like five hundred thousand dollars, I believe. Mr. Kane senior was really very anxious that his son should inherit this property. As it is—owing to the conditions which your—ah—which Mr. Kane's father made, he cannot possibly obtain his share except by complying with a—with a—certain wish which his father had expressed."

He paused, his eyes moving back and forth sidewise in their sockets. He was considerably impressed, in spite of the natural prejudice of the situation, with Jennie's pleasing appearance. She appeared to him to be a very charming woman. He could see quite plainly, he thought, why Lester might cling to her in spite of all opposition. He continued to study her furtively as he sat there waiting for her to speak.

"And what was that wish?" she finally asked, her nerves becoming just a little tense under the strain of the silence.

"I am glad you were kind enough to ask me that," he went on. "The subject is a very difficult one for me to talk about. Very difficult. I come as an emissary of the estate,—I might say as one of the executors under the will of Mr. Kane's father. I know how keenly your—ah—ah, how keenly Mr. Kane feels about it. I know how keenly you will probably feel about it. But it is one of those very difficult things which cannot be helped very well—which must be got over somehow. And while I hesitate very much to say so, I must tell you that Mr. Kane senior stipulated in his will that unless, unless—" again his eyes were moving sidewise to and fro—"he saw fit to separate from, ah, you—" he paused to get breath—"he could not inherit this or any other sum—or, at least, only a very minor one—some ten thousand a year, and that only on condition that he marry you." Mr. O'Brien paused again. "I should add," he went on, "that under the will he was given three years in which to indicate his intentions. That time is now drawing to a close."

He paused, half-expecting some outburst of feeling from Jennie, but she only looked at him fixedly, her eyes clouded with surprise, distress, unhappiness. It was filtering into her mind by degrees just what he meant. Lester was sacrificing his fortune for her. He was in danger of losing the opportunity of claiming it. His recent commercial venture was an effort to rehabilitate himself, to put himself in an independent position. All the recent periods of preoccupation, of subtle unrest and dissatisfaction which she had noticed, were due to this. He was unhappy, he was brooding over this loss, and he had never told her. It explained so many things. So his father had really disinherited him!

Mr. O'Brien sat before her, troubled himself. He was very sorry, now that he saw the expression of her face, that he had to do this. It expressed so much genuine regret, so much honest, unselfish woe. Still the truth had to come out. She ought to know.

"I'm sorry," he said, when he saw that she was not going to make any immediate reply, "that I have been the bearer of such unfortunate news. It is a very painful situation that I find myself in at this moment, I assure you. I bear you no ill will personally—of course you understand that. The family really bears you no ill will now—I hope you believe that. I am an emissary of the estate, a representative of the late Mr. Kane, as it were. As I told your— ah, as I told Mr. Kane at the time the will was read, I considered it most unfair, but, of course, as a mere executive under it and counsel for his father, I could do nothing. I really think it best that you should know how things stand, in order that you may help your, ah, your husband"—he paused significantly—"if possible, to some solution. It seems a pity to me, as it does to the various other members of his family, that he should lose all this money."

Jennie had turned her head away and was staring at the floor. When he finished his last sentence, she turned her glance back to him in a troubled way. "He mustn't lose it," she said; "it isn't fair that he should."

"I am most delighted to hear you say that Mrs.—ah—Mrs.

Kane," he went on, using for the first time her improbable title as Lester's wife without hesitation. He had been troubled in his mind, all the while he had been talking to her, as to what form he should use in addressing her. He did not think she was Lester's wife. He did not want to give her, at first, the advantage of thinking that he thought so. Now seeing that she appeared to be so amenable to reason, he was feeling a little softer. And the fact that he had a specific offer to make to her was coming back into his mind. "I may as well be very frank with you and say that I feared you might take this information in quite another spirit. Of course, you might as well know, to begin with, that the Kane family is very clannish. It has always been, as far as I can remember. Mrs. Kane, your, ah, your husband's mother, was a very proud and rather distant woman, and his sisters and brothers are rather set in their notions as to what constitute proper family connections. Of course they are not your, ah, husband's mentors in this matter, but they help to make what might otherwise prove a very pleasant relationship between you and them and him difficult. They look upon his relationship to you as irregular, and—pardon me if I appear to be a little cruel—as not generally satisfactory. As you know, there has been so much talk in the last few years that Mr. Kane senior did not believe that the situation could ever be rightly adjusted, so far as the family was concerned. He felt that his son had not gone about it right in the first place. One of the conditions of his will was that if your husband—pardon me—if his son did not accept the proposition in regard to separating from you and taking up his rightful share of the estate, then to inherit anything at all—the mere ten thousand a year I mentioned before, for the rest of his life—he must—ah—he must—pardon me, I seem a little brutal, but not intentionally so—marry you."

Jennie winced. It was such a cruel thing to say this to her face. And she had wanted to leave Lester because of this, or the lack of it. She was making a mistake—she saw that again clearly. Lester was making one. This whole attempt to live together illegally had proved disastrous at every step. Lester would so much better have left her at the time he discovered Vesta, or she him, when she wrote him the letter after Louise came. Now she was numb with a new complication, and there was only one solution to the unfortunate business—she could see that plainly. She must leave him, or he her. There was no other sensible answer. He must not sacrifice his fortune. That would be ridiculous—impossible to even think of it. She must leave him, or he must leave her. There was no other way. Lester living on ten thousand dollars a year! It seemed silly.

Mr. O'Brien was watching her curiously. He was thinking that Lester had and had not made a mistake. Why had he not married her in the first place? She was charming.

"There is just one other point which I wish to make in this connection, Mrs. Kane," he said now softly and easily. "I know, now that I see you, that it will not make any difference to you, but I am commissioned and, in a way, constrained to make it, and I hope you will take it in the manner in which it is given. Lester's brother Robert may have seemed a little hard in the attitude he has taken in connection with several commercial matters which have been connected with this will, but he has not been intentionally so—I don't know whether you are up on your husband's commercial interests or not?"

"No," said Jennie simply.

"Well, anyhow, in order to simplify matters and to make it easier for you, in case you should decide to assist your husband to a solution of this very difficult situation—frankly, in case you might possibly decide to leave on your own account, and maintain a separate establishment of your own—I am delighted to say that,—ah—any sum, say, ah,—"

Jennie rose and walked dazedly to one of the windows, clasping her hands as she went. Mr. O'Brien rose also.

"Well, be that as it may. In case you should decide to leave him, under any circumstances, it has been suggested to me that any reasonable sum you might name, fifty, seventy-five, a hundred thousand dollars"—Mr. O'Brien was feeling very generous toward her—"would be gladly set aside for your benefit—put in trust, as it were, so that you would have it whenever you needed it. You would never want for anything."

"Please don't," said Jennie, hurt beyond the power to express herself any further, unable mentally and physically to listen to another word. "Please don't say any more. Please go away. Let me alone now, please. I can go away. I will. It will be arranged. But please don't talk to me any more, will you?"

"I understand how you feel, Mrs. Kane," went on Mr. O'Brien, coming to a keen realization of her sufferings. "I know exactly, believe me. I have said all I intended to say. It has been very hard for me to do this—very hard. I regret the necessity. You have my card. Please note the name. I will come any time you suggest, or you can write me. I will not detain you any longer. I am sorry. I hope you will see fit to say nothing to your husband of my visit—it will be advisable that you should keep your own counsel in the matter. I value his friendship very highly, and I am sincerely sorry."

Jennie only stared at the floor.

Mr. O'Brien went out into the hall to get his coat. Jennie touched the electric button to summon the maid, and Jeannette came. Jennie went back into the library to be alone. Mr. O'Brien went briskly down the front walk. When she was really alone she put her doubled hands to her chin and stared at the floor, the queer design of the silken Turkish rug resolving itself into some curious pictures. She saw herself in a small cottage somewhere, alone with Vesta; she saw Lester off in another world, driving, and beside him was Mrs. Gerald. She saw this house vacant, and then a long stretch of time, and then—

"Oh," she sighed, choking back a desire to cry. With her hands she brushed away a hot tear from each eye. Then she got up.

"It must be," she said to herself in thought. "It must be. It should have been so long ago." And then—"Oh, thank God that Papa is dead. He did not live to see this anyhow."

CHAPTER LII

The explanation which Lester had concluded must come, whether it led to separation or legalization of their hitherto banal condition, followed quickly upon the appearance of Mr. O'Brien; for Lester was ready to talk to Jennie and felt that any day now might see the important conversation come to pass. On the day Mr. O'Brien had called, Lester had been gone on a journey to Hegewisch, a small manufacturing town, where he had been invited to witness the trial of a new motor intended to operate elevators—with a view to possible investment. When he came out to the house the next afternoon, interested to tell

Jennie something about it, even in spite of the fact that he was thinking of leaving her, he was struck by the sense of depression pervading it, for Jennie, in spite of the serious and sensible conclusion she had reached, was not one who could conceal her feelings easily. She was brooding sadly over her proposed action, realizing that it was best to leave, but having a hard time to summon the courage which would let her talk to him about it. She could not go without telling him what she thought. He ought to want to leave her. She was absolutely convinced that this one course of action—separation—was necessary and advisable. She could not think of him daring to make a sacrifice of such proportions for her sake, even if he wanted to. It was impossible. It was astonishing to her that he had let things go along as dangerously and silently as he had.

When he came in, Jennie did her best to put on a smile of greeting such as she was accustomed to wear, but it was a pretty poor imitation.

"Everything all right?" she asked, using her customary phrase of inquiry.

"Quite," he answered. "How are things with you?"

"Oh, just the same." She walked with him to the library, and he poked at the open fire with a long-handled poker before turning around to survey the room generally. It was five o'clock of a January afternoon. Jennie had gone to one of the windows to lower the shade. As she came back, he looked at her critically. "You're not quite your usual self, are you?" he asked, sensing something.

"Why, yes, I feel all right," she replied, but there was a peculiar uneven motion to the movement of her lips—a rippling tremor which was unmistakable to him.

"I think I know better than that," he observed, coming toward her slowly. "What's the trouble? Anything happened?"

She turned away from him a moment to get her breath and collect her senses. Then she turned back again. "It's something," she managed to say tentatively. "I have to tell you something."

"I know you have to," he urged, half smiling, but with a feeling that there was much of grave import back of this. "What is it?"

She was silent for a moment, biting her lips. She did not see how to begin. Finally she broke the spell with: "There was a man here yesterday—a Mister O'Brien of Cincinnati. Do you know him?"

"Yes, I know him. What did he want?"

"He came to talk to me about you and your father's will."

She paused, for his face clouded immediately. "What the devil should he be coming talking to you about my father's will for?" he exclaimed. "What did he have to say?"

"Please don't get angry, Lester," said Jennie calmly, for she realized that she must remain absolute mistress of herself if anything were to be accomplished toward the resolution of the problem. "He wanted to tell me what a sacrifice you are making," she went on. "He wanted to show me that there was only a little time left before you would lose it all unless you did something. Don't you want to act pretty soon? Don't you want to leave me?"

"Damn him!" said Lester fiercely. "What the devil does he mean by putting his nose in my private affairs? Can't they let me alone?" He shook himself angrily. "Damn them!" he added. "This is some of Robert's work. Why should Knight, Keatley and O'Brien be stirring around in my affairs? This whole business is getting to be a nuisance! What right has he to come here and interview you anyhow?" He was in a boiling rage in a moment, but it did not show in his face so much except for a darkening skin and sulphurous eyes.

Jennie trembled before his anger. She did not know what to say.

"Well," he exclaimed grimly after a moment, "just what did he tell you?"

Jennie pushed a book, which was lying on the table near her, to and fro nervously, her fear that she would not be able to keep up appearances troubling her greatly. It was hard for her to know what to do or say. Lester was so terrible when he became angry. Still it ought not be so hard for him to go, now that he had Mrs. Gerald, if he only wished to do so—and he ought to. His fortune was so much more important to him than anything she could be.

"He said," she went on, "that if you married me you would only get ten thousand a year. That if you didn't, and still lived with me, you would get nothing at all. If you would leave me, or I would leave you, you would get all of a million and a half. Don't you think you had better leave me now?"

She had not intended to propound this leading question so

quickly, but it came out as a natural climax to her statement. She realized, the moment she had said it, that if he were really in love with her he would answer, quickly, "No." There would be emphasis in what he said. If he didn't care—if it was all right for her to go—he would hesitate, delay for a moment.

"I don't see that," he jerked irritably, unconscious of her thought. "I don't see that there's any need for either interference or hasty action. What I object to is their coming here and mixing in my private affairs."

Jennie was cut to the quick by his indifference, his wrath instead of affection. To her the main point at issue was her leaving him or his leaving her. To him, this recent interference was obviously the chief matter for discussion and consideration. Their coming here and stirring things up before he was ready to act was the terrible thing. She had hoped, in spite of what she had seen, that possibly, because of the long time they had lived together and the things which (in a way) they had endured together, he might have come to care for her deeply—that she had stirred some emotion in him which would never brook real separation, though some seeming separation might be necessary. He had not married her, of course, but then there had been so many things against them. Now, in this final hour, he might have shown that he cared deeply, even if he had deemed it necessary to let her go. She felt for the time being as if (for all that she had lived with him so long) she did not understand him; and yet, in spite of this feeling, she knew also that she did. He cared, in his way. He could not care for any one enthusiastically and demonstratively. He could care for her enough to seize her and take her to himself, as he had, but he could not care enough to keep her if something more important appeared. He was debating her fate now. She was in a quandary— hurt, bleeding, but for once in her life determined. Whether he wanted to or not, she must not let him make this sacrifice. She must leave him, if he would not leave her. It was not important enough that she should stay. There might be but one answer. But might he not show affection?

"Don't you think you had better act soon?" she continued, hoping that some word of feeling would come from him. "There is only a little time left, isn't there?"

"Don't worry about that," he replied stubbornly, his wrath at his brother and his family and O'Brien still holding him. "There's time enough. I don't know what I want to do yet. I like the effrontery of these people! But I won't talk any more about it; isn't dinner nearly ready?"

He was so injured in his pride that he scarcely took the trouble to be civil. He was forgetting all about her and what she was feeling. He hated his brother Robert for this. He would have enjoyed wringing the necks of Messrs. Knight, Keatley and O'Brien, singly and collectively.

The question could not be dropped for good and all, however, and it came up again at dinner, spectrally, after Jennie had done her best to collect her thoughts and quiet her nerves. They could not talk very freely because of Vesta and Jeannette, but she managed to get in a word or two.

"I could take a little cottage somewhere," she suggested softly at one point, hoping to find him in a modified mood. "I would not want to stay here. I would not know what to do with a big house like this alone."

"I wish you wouldn't discuss this business any longer, Jennie," he persisted. "I'm in no mood for it. I don't know that I'm going to do anything of the sort. I don't know what I'm going to do." He was so sour and obstinate, because of O'Brien, that she finally gave it up. Vesta was astonished to see her stepfather—usually so courteous—in so grim a mood.

Jennie felt, curiously now, as if she might hold him if she would, for he was doubting; but she knew also that she should not wish to. It was not fair to him. It was not fair to herself, or kind, or decent.

"Oh, yes, Lester, you must," she pleaded at a later time. "I won't talk about it any more, but you must. I won't let you do anything else."

There were hours when it came up afterward—every day, in fact—in their boudoir, in the library, in the dining-room at breakfast, but not always in words. Jennie was worried. She was looking the worry she felt. She felt so sure that he should be made to act. Since he was showing more kindly consideration for her, she was all the more certain that he should act. Just how to go about it she did not know, but she looked at him longingly, trying to help him make up his mind. She would be happy, she assured herself—she would be happy thinking that he was happy, once she was away from him. He was a good man, most delightful in everything save perhaps his gift of love. He really did not love her—could not, perhaps, after all that had happened, even though she loved him most earnestly. But his family had been most brutal in their opposition, and this had affected his attitude. She could understand that, too. She could see now how his big, strong brain might be working in a circle. He was too decent to be absolutely brutal about this thing and leave her; too really considerate to look sharply after his own interests as he should, or hers—but he ought to.

"You must decide, Lester," she kept saying to him from time to time. "You must let me go. What difference does it make? I will be all right. Maybe, when this thing is all over some time you might want to come back to me. If you do, I will be there."

"I'm not ready to consider this question yet," was his invariable reply. "I don't know that I want to leave you. This money is important, of course, but money isn't everything. I can live on ten thousand a year if necessary. I have lived on it when I was younger."

"Oh, but you're so much more placed in the world now, Lester," she argued. "You can't do it now. Look how much it costs to run this house alone. And a million and a half of dollars! Why I wouldn't let you think of losing that. I'll go myself first."

"Where would you think of going if you went?" he asked curiously.

"Oh, I'd find some place. Do you remember that little town of Sandwood, this side of Kenosha, that I once said I liked? I have often thought I'd like to live there."

"I don't like to think of this," he said frankly, finally. "It doesn't seem fair. The conditions have all been against this union of ours. I suppose I should have married you in the first place. I'm sorry now that I didn't. Anyhow, things have been very much against us since we started."

Jennie choked in her throat, but said nothing.

"Anyhow, this won't be the last of it, if I can help it," he concluded. He was thinking that the storm might blow over, once he had the money, and then—but he hated compromises and subterfuges.

It came by degrees to be understood that, toward the end of February, she would look around at Sandwood and see what she could find. She was to have ample means, he told her, everything that she wanted. He might come out and see her occasionally, after a time, though it was against the will. And he was determined in his heart that he would make some people pay for the trouble they had caused him. He thought of the Auditorium Hotel, which was then being newly completed, as his prospective residence, and he decided to send for Mr. O'Brien shortly and talk things over. He wanted, for his personal satisfaction, to tell O'Brien what he thought of him.

At the same time, in the background of his mind, moved the shadowy, tenuous figure of Mrs. Gerald—charming, philosophic, sophisticated. He did not want to give her the broad reality of full thought, but she was there. She was possessed of millions also, and of distinction. Together they could repay an indifferent, chill, convention-ridden world with some sharp, bitter cuts of the power-whip if they chose. It seemed cruel to be speculating this way, but though he loved Jennie, and felt sorry for her, Mrs. Malcolm Gerald was always vaguely in his mind as someone who could put things right for him socially, and, by the same token, she was the one he should have had. He thought and thought. "Perhaps I'd better," he half concluded. When February came he was quite ready to act.

CHAPTER LIII

The little town of Sandwood, "this side of Kenosha," as Jennie had expressed it, was only a little distance from Chicago, an hour and fifteen minutes by any of the local trains which stopped there. It had a population of some three hundred families, dwelling in small cottages which were scattered over a pleasant area of lake-shore property. The land line of the lake gave in at that point and formed a miniature bay on which rested the few boats of those who liked sailing. There were a number of trees—quite a grove of pines in fact, which were the result of some fortuitous scattering of seed, and among these the various cottages were built by those who were willing to come so far for quiet, natural beauty and the advantages of the lake. They were not rich people. The houses were not worth more than from three to five thousand dollars each, but they were in most cases harmoniously constructed, the coloring was not bad, and the surrounding trees, green for the entire year, gave them a pleasing, summery appearance. Jennie, at the time they had passed by there—it was an outing taken behind a pair of fast-travelling horses—had admired the look of a little white church steeple, set down among green trees, and the gentle rocking of the boats upon the summer water. "I should like to live in a place like this some time," she had said to Lester, and he had made the comment that it was a little too peaceful for him. "I can imagine getting to the place where I might like this, but not now. It's too withdrawn."

Jennie thought of that expression afterward. It came to her when she thought of the world as trying. If she had to be alone ever and could afford it, she would like to live in a place like Sandwood. There she would have a little garden, say; some chickens perhaps; a tall pole with a pretty bird-house on it; and flowers and trees and green grass everywhere about. If she could have a little cottage in a place like this which commanded a view of the lake, she could sit of a summer evening and sew. Vesta could play about or come home from school. She might have a few friends, or not any. She was beginning to think that she could do very well living alone, if it were not for Vesta's social needs. Books were a pleasant thing—she was finding that out—books like Irving's *Sketch Book,* Lamb's *Elia* and Hawthorne's *Twice-Told Tales.* Vesta was coming to be quite a musician in her way, having a keen sense of the delicate and refined in musical composition. She had a natural sense of harmony and a love for those songs and instrumental compositions which reflect the sentimental and passionate moods of the soul, and she could sing and play quite well. Her voice was of course quite untrained—she was only fourteen—but it was pleasant to listen to. She was beginning to exhibit the combined traits of her mother and father—Jennie's gentle, speculative turn of mind combined with Brander's vivacity of spirit and innate executive capacity. She could talk to her mother in a sensible way about things—nature, books, dress, love—and from her developing tendencies Jennie caught keen glimpses of the new worlds which Vesta was to explore. The nature of modern school life, its consideration of various divisions of knowledge, the fact that there are complex worlds of art, literature, music, science, all came to Jennie watching her daughter take up new themes. Vesta was evidently going to be a woman of considerable ability—not irritably aggressive, but self-constructive. She was going to be able to take care of herself. All this pleased Jennie and gave her great hopes for Vesta's future.

The cottage which was finally secured at Sandwood—it was one which had been vacated the year before by a man whose wife had died after he had become nicely settled in what he had hoped would be his final home—was only a story and a half in height, but it was raised upon red brick piers between which were set green lattices and about which ran a veranda of varying levels. The house was long and narrow, its full length—some five rooms in a row—facing the lake. There was a dining-room whose tall windows opened even with the floor. There was a general reception room, whose sides carried shelves for books, and a parlor, laid with a smooth hardwood floor, whose windows flooded it with air and sunshine at all times. The plot of ground in which this cottage stood was one hundred feet square and ornamented with a few trees. The former owner had laid out flower-beds and arranged green hardwood tubs for the reception of various hardy plants and vines at different angles of the veranda railing. The house itself was white with green shutters and green shingles.

It was Lester's idea, since this thing must be, for the present anyhow, that Jennie might keep the house in Hyde Park just as it was, but she did not want to do that. She could not think of living there alone. The place was too full of memories. At first she did not think she would take anything much with her, but she finally saw that it was advisable to do as Lester suggested—to fit out the new place with a selection of what was here, silverware, hangings, furnishings and so on, and put the rest in storage.

"You have no idea what you will want to do or when you will need it," he said. "Take everything. I certainly don't want any of it."

The lease of the cottage in question was negotiated for two years, together with an option for an additional five years, including the privilege of purchase. So long as he was letting her go, Lester wanted to be generous. He could not think of her as wanting for anything and did not propose that she should. His one troublesome thought was what explanation was to be made to Vesta. He liked her very much and wanted her life kept free of complications.

"Why not send her off to a boarding school until spring?" he suggested at one point, but owing to the lateness of the season this was abandoned as inadvisable. Later they agreed to say that a complication of his business affairs made it necessary for him to travel for awhile and for Jennie to move. Later Vesta could be told that Jennie had left him for any reason she chose to give. It was a trying situation, all the more bitter to Jennie because she realized that, in spite of the wisdom of it, indifference to her was involved. He really did not care *enough,* as much as he cared.

The sex relationship, which we study so passionately in the hope of finding heaven knows what key to the mystery of existence, holds no more difficult or trying situation than this—of mutual compatibility broken or disrupted by untoward conditions which, in themselves, have so little to do with the real force and beauty of the relationship itself. These days of final dissolution in which this household, so charmingly arranged, the scene of so many pleasant activities, was literally going to pieces, was a period of great trial to both Jennie and Lester. On her part it was one of intense suffering, for she was of that stable nature that rejoices to fix itself in a serviceable and harmonious relationship, and then stay so. For her, life was made up of those mystic chords of sympathy and memory which bind up the transient elements of nature into a harmonious and enduring scene. This home was one such chord, united and made beautiful by her affection and consideration, extended to each person and to every object. Now the time had come when it must cease to be.

If she had ever had anything before in her life which had been anything like this, it might have been easier to part with it all now, though, as she had proved, her affections were not based in any way upon material considerations. Her love of life and of personality were free from the taint of selfishness. She went about among these various rooms selecting this rug, that set of furniture, this and this ornament, wishing all the time with all her heart and soul that it need not be. Just to think, in a little while Lester would not come any more of an evening! She would not need to get up first of a morning and see that coffee was made for her lord, that the table in the dining-room looked just so. It had been a habit of hers to arrange a bouquet for the table out of the richest blooming flowers of the conservatory, and she had always felt, in doing it, that it was particularly for him. Now it would not be necessary any more,—not for him. When you are accustomed to wait for the sound of a certain carriage wheel of an evening, grating upon your carriage drive, when you are used to listen at eleven, twelve and one, waking naturally and joyfully to the echo of a certain step on the stair, when your hand resting upon your lord and master's shoulder in sleep is the link that makes for peace and surety in dreams, then separation, the ending of these things, is keen with pain. These were the thoughts that were running through Jennie's brain, hour after hour and day after day.

Lester on his part was suffering in another fashion. His was not the sorrow of lacerated affection—of discarded and despised love, but of that painful sense of unfairness which comes to one who knows that he is making a sacrifice of the virtues—kindness, loyalty, affection,—to policy. Policy was dictating a very splendid course of action from one point of view. Free of Jennie, providing for her admirably, he was free to go his way, taking to himself the mass of affairs which comes naturally with great wealth. He could not help thinking of the thousand and one little things which Jennie had been accustomed to do for him, the hundred and one comfortable and pleasant and delightful things she meant to him. The virtues which she possessed were quite dear in his mind. He had gone over them time and again mentally. Now he was compelled to go over them finally, to see that she was suffering without making a sign. Her manner and attitude toward him in these last days were quite the same as they had always been,—no more, no less. She was not indulging in private hysterics, as another woman might have done; she was not pretending a fortitude in suffering she did not feel, showing him one face while wishing him to see another behind it. She was calm, gentle, considerate—thoughtful of him—where he would go and what he would do, without irritating him by her inquiries. He was struck quite forcibly by her ability to take a large situation largely, and he admired her. There was something to this woman, let the world think what it might. It was a shame that her life had issued forth under such a troubled star. Still a great world was calling him. The sound of its voice was in his ears. It had on occasion shown him its bared teeth. Did he really dare hesitate?

The last hour came, when having made excuses to this and that neighbor, when having spread the information that they were going abroad, when Lester had engaged rooms at the Auditorium, and the mass of furniture which could not be used had gone to storage, it was necessary to say farewell to this Hyde Park domicile. Jennie had visited Sandwood in company with Lester several times. He had carefully examined the character of the place. He was satisfied that it was nice but lonely. Spring was at hand, the flowers would be something. She was going to keep a gardener and man of all work. Vesta would be with her.

"Very well," he said, "only I want you to be comfortable."

She went over the old house in Hyde Park broodingly one budding March day. And then they left. All his own affairs were well taken care of. He had notified Messrs. Knight, Keatley and O'Brien through his own attorney, Mr. Watson, that he would expect them to deliver his share of his father's securities on a given date. He had made up his mind that, as long as he was compelled by circumstances to do this thing, he would do a number of other things equally ruthless. He would probably marry Mrs. Gerald. He would sit as a director in the United Carriage Association— with his share of the stock it would be impossible to keep him out; he would—if he had Mrs. Gerald's money—appear as a controlling factor in United Traction of Cincinnati, in which his brother was heavily interested, and in the Western Crucible Steel Works, of which his brother was now the leading adviser. What a different figure he would be now from that which he had been during the past few years!

Jennie was depressed to the point of despair. She was tremendously lonely. This home had meant so much to her, this lawn. When she had first come here and neighbors had begun to drop in, she had imagined herself on the threshold of a great career—that some day, possibly, Lester would marry her. Now, blow after blow had been delivered, and the home and the dream were a ruin. Gerhardt was gone. Jeannette, Henry Weeds and Mrs. Frissell had been discharged, the furnishing for a good part was in storage, and for her, practically, Lester was no more. She realized clearly that he would not come back. If he could do this, considerately, now, he could do much more when he was out and away later. Immersed in his great affairs he would forget, of course. And why not? She did not fit in. Had not everything, everything, illustrated that to her? Love was not enough in this world—that was so plain. One needed education, wealth, training, the ability to fight and scheme. She did not want to do that. She could not.

The day came when the house was finally closed and the old life was at an end. Lester travelled with Jennie to Sandwood. He spent some little while in the house trying to get her used to the idea of change—it was not so bad. He indicated that he would come again soon, but he went away, and all his words were as nothing against the fact of the actual and spiritual separation. When Jennie saw him going down the pretty brick walk at four in the afternoon, his solid, conservative figure clad in a new tweed suit, his overcoat on his arm, that sense of self-reliance and prosperity written anew all over his frame, she thought that she would die. The blue waters of the lake were spread out before her. The fresh, green grass of the spring was showing itself beautifully. No cloud was in the sky, and Vesta, by her side, had kissed her stepfather an affectionate farewell. Jennie had kissed Lester good-bye and had wished him joy, prosperity, peace; then she made an excuse to go to her bedroom to be alone. Vesta came after a time to seek her, but now Jennie's eyes were quite dry. Everything had subsided to a dull ache. The new life was actually begun for her— a life without Lester, without Gerhardt, without any one save Vesta.

"What a curious life I have led," she said to herself as she went into the kitchen, for here she was determined to do some of her own work at least. She needed to. She did not want to think. If it were not for Vesta she would have sought some regular outside employment. Anything to keep from brooding, for in that direction lay madness.

CHAPTER LIV

The social worlds of Chicago, Cincinnati, Cleveland and other cities saw, during the year or two which followed the breaking of his relationship with Jennie, a curious rejuvenation in the social and business spirit of Lester Kane. He had become rather distant and indifferent to certain personages and affairs while he was living with her, but now he suddenly appeared again, armed with authority from a number of sources, looking into this and that matter with the air of one who has the privilege of power, and showing himself to be quite a personage from the point of view of finance and commerce. He was older of course. It must be admitted that he was in some respects a mentally altered Lester. Up to the time he had met Jennie, he was full of the assurance of the man who has never known defeat. To have been reared in luxury, as he had been; to have seen only the pleasant face of society, which is so persistent and deluding where money is concerned; to have been in the run of big affairs, not because you have created them but because you are a part of them and because they seem natural to you, like the air you breathe, all this could not help but create one of those mortal illusions of solidarity which is apt under such circumstances to befog the clearest brain. It is so hard for us to know what we have not seen. It is so diffi-cult for us to feel what we have not experienced—like this world of ours, which seems so solid and persistent solely because we have no knowledge of the power which creates it. Lester's world seemed solid and persistent and real enough to him. It was only when the storms set in, and the winds of adversity blew, and he found himself facing the armed forces of convention that he realized that he might be mistaken as to the value of his person-ality, and that his private desires and opinions were as nothing in the face of a public conviction that he was wrong. The race spirit, the social avatar, the *"Zeitgeist,"* as the Germans term it, man-ifested itself as something having a system in charge, and the organization of society began to show itself to him as something based on possibly a spiritual—or at least superhuman—counter-part. He could not fly in the face of it. He could not deliberately ignore its mandates. The people of his time believed that some particular form of social arrangement was necessary, and unless he complied with that he could, as he saw, readily become a social outcast. His own father and mother had turned on him—his brother and sisters; society; his friends. Dear heaven, what a *to-do* this action of his had created. Why, even the fates seemed ad-verse. His real-estate venture was one of the most unlucky things he had ever heard of. Why? Were the gods battling on the side of a, to him, unimportant social arrangement? Apparently. Any-how, he had been compelled to quit, and here he was—vigorous, determined, somewhat battered by the experience, but still force-ful and worth while.

And the saddest part of it was that he was considerably soured by what had occurred. He was feeling that he had been compelled to do the first ugly, brutal thing of his life. Jennie deserved better of him. It was a shame to forsake her after all the devotion she had manifested. Truly she had played a finer part than he had, and worst of all his deed could not be excused on the grounds of necessity. He could have lived on ten thousand a year; he could have done without the million and more which was now his. He could have done without the society, the pleasures of which had always been a lure. He could have, but he had not, and he had complicated it all with the thought of another woman.

Was she as good as Jennie? That was a question which also rose before him. Was she as kindly? Wasn't she deliberately scheming under his very eyes to win him away from the woman who was as good as his wife? Was that admirable? Was it the thing a truly big woman would do? Was she good enough for him after all? Ought he to marry her? Ought he to marry any one, seeing that he really owed a spiritual if not a legal allegiance to Jennie? Was it worth while for any woman to marry him? These things turned in his brain. They haunted him. He could not shut out the fact that he was doing a cruel and unlovely thing.

Material error in the first place was now being complicated with spiritual error. He was attempting to right the first by committing the second. Could it be done *to his own satisfaction?* Would it pay mentally and spiritually? Would it bring him peace of mind? He was thinking, thinking, all the while he was readjusting his life to the old (or perhaps, better yet, new) conditions, and he was not feeling any happier. As a matter of fact he was feeling worse— grim, revengeful. If he married Letty he thought at times it would be to use her fortune as a club to knock his enemies over the head, and he hated to think he was marrying her for that. He took up his abode at the Auditorium, visited Cincinnati in a distant and aggressive spirit, sat in council with this board of directors, wishing that he was more at peace with himself, more interested in life. But he did not change his policy in regard to Jennie.

One of the persons who was thoroughly overjoyed to hear that he had rehabilitated himself, or was at least about the work of so doing in the eyes of the world, was Mrs. Malcolm Gerald. She was interested to learn, shortly after Lester left Hyde Park, that he was living at the Auditorium. She waited tactfully some little time before sending him word of any kind, but finally after a month she ventured to send him a note to the Hyde Park address (as if she did not know where he was) asking "Where are you?" By that time Lester had become slightly accustomed to the change. He was saying to himself that he needed sympathetic companionship—the companionship of a woman, of course. Social invitations had begun to come to him, now that he was alone and that his financial connections were so obviously restored. He had taken to himself a Japanese valet and was appearing, at this country place and that, alone—the best sign that he was once more a single man. No reference was made by any one to the past.

On receiving Mrs. Gerald's note he decided that he ought to go and see her. He had treated her rather shabbily, all told. For months preceding his separation from Jennie he had not gone near her place. There was no haste in his action, however, and he waited until time brought a 'phoned invitation to dinner. This he accepted.

Mrs. Gerald was at her best entertaining a company of talent and ability. She knew who the leading writers, artists, financiers, musicians, and personages in society were and could make them come. Her table glittered with a perfection of appointments. Alboni, the pianist, was there on this occasion, and Adam Rascavage, the sculptor. There was a visiting scientist from England, Sir Nelson Keyes, and, curiously, Mr. and Mrs. Berry Dodge, whom Lester had not seen socially in several years. Mrs. Gerald placed Lester at her right hand at the dinner table, but before the meal was served they exchanged the joyful greetings of those who understand each other thoroughly and are happy in each other's company. "Aren't you ashamed of yourself, sir," she said to him when he made his appearance, "to treat me so indifferently? You are going to be punished for this, Mister-Master."

"What's the damage?" he smiled. "I've been extremely rushed. I suppose something like ninety stripes will serve me about right."

"Ninety stripes, indeed," she retorted. "You're letting yourself off easy. What is it they do to evil-doers in Siam?"

"Boil them in oil, I suppose," he replied.

"Well, anyhow, that's more like. I'm thinking of something terrible."

"Be sure and tell me when you decide," he laughed and passed on to be presented to the distinguished strangers by Mrs. De Lincum, who aided Mrs. Gerald in receiving.

From the latest polar attempt by Borchgrevink, to the Art

Nouveau of France, to the attempt by some younger musicians in Italy and Germany to break away from classical traditions in music, to the determination of Díaz in Mexico to nationalize its railroads he drifted conversationally, talking now with Sir Nelson Keyes, Signor Tito Alboni, Adam Rascavage, Mr. and Mrs. Berry Dodge, Professor Jackson, the political economist, and others. Lester was always at his ease intellectually. He loved to ask questions—succinct, searching, vital. He could get at the big, novel points in science or art or the professions generally by asking solemnly what latest advance had been made. His confrères found him a fascinating intelligence. Sir Nelson Keyes was animatedly describing for his benefit, three minutes after his introduction, a theory, prevalent in scientific circles in England, that the earth from being in a perfect molten sphere tended toward a cold, hexagonal old age, sinking in upon itself between mountainous ridges, and eventually leaving a sunken, bony remnant of itself to be destroyed, possibly by collision or entombment in the sun.

Lester listened with interest to this. He liked new theories of life. No old one nor any new one had any stability or reality for him, but he was interested.

His next word was with Berry Dodge, who, greeting him warmly, asked: "Where are you now? We haven't seen you in— oh, when? Mrs. Dodge is waiting to have a word with you." Lester noticed the change in Dodge's attitude.

"Some time, that's sure," he replied easily. "I'm living at the Auditorium."

"I was asking after you the other day. You know Jackson Du Bois? Of course you do. We were thinking of running up into Canada for some hunting. Why don't you join us?"

"I can't," replied Lester. "Too many things on hand just now. Later, surely."

Dodge was anxious to continue. He had seen where Lester had been elected a director of the C. H. & D., a position to which a portion of his inherited property entitled him. Obviously he was coming back into the world again. He discussed trade conditions generally, and Lester listened, remembering that he had been cold-shouldered by this same man. How curious the world was. He drifted on to talk with Mrs. David Huston and one or two others before dinner was announced.

It was the same tintinnabulation of words through this very

interesting function, as it is ever on such occasions. All the women carefully gowned, all the men formal, the whole thing a picture full of beauty and color. He studied them, when lack of attention to others permitted, wondering whether Sir Nelson Keyes was troubled with rheumatism, he looked so angular and bony; whether Adam Rascavage was as calm as his eyes looked or as fussy and excitable as his beard and mustachios indicated; whether Mrs. Dickson Thompson wasn't becoming fat and stupid. Obviously Berry Dodge's long, thin head was becoming bald. It served him right.

"Aren't you coming to pay me a dinner call some afternoon after this?" asked Mrs. Gerald confidentially, when the conversation was brisk at the other end of the table.

"Truly I am," he replied, "and shortly. Seriously, I've been wanting to look you up. You understand, though, how things are now?"

"I do. I've heard a great deal. That's why I want you to come. We need to talk together."

He left after a long evening, in which he had traded in much of the new thought of the day, for observations of his own. As he took Mrs. Gerald's hand in parting she pleaded, "Do come, Lester. It's a shame the way you treat me."

"I'm coming," he replied. "Wait. I've had a great deal to do."

"I know," she replied, and looked the sympathy she felt.

Ten days later he was back again. He felt as if he must talk with her, for in spite of himself he was drawn. His long home life with Jennie had made hotel life objectionable. He felt at times as though he must find a sympathetic, intelligent ear, and where better than at this mansion? Letty was all ears for his troubles. She would have pillowed his solid head upon her breast in a moment if it had been possible. When he came she saw to it that they were not further disturbed.

"Well," he said when the usual fencing preliminaries were over, "what will you have me say in explanation?"

"Have you burned your bridges behind you?" she asked.

"I'm not so sure," he replied solemnly. "And I can't say that I'm feeling any too joyous about the matter as a whole."

"I judged as much," she replied. "I know how it is. I knew how it would be with you. I can see you wading through this mentally, Lester. I have been seeing you, every step of the way, wishing you peace of mind. These things are always so difficult, but, don't you know, I am still sure it's for the best. It never was right the other way. It never could be. You couldn't afford to sink back into a mere shell-fish life. You are not organized temperamentally for that, any more than I am. You have to keep stirring in the world. You may regret what you are doing now, but you would have regretted the other thing quite as much and more. You couldn't work your life out that way—now, could you? You wouldn't have been content to do it."

"I don't know about that, Letty, really I don't. I've wanted to come and see you for a long time, but I didn't think that I ought to. The fight was inside—you know what I mean."

"Yes, indeed I do," she soothed.

"It's still inside. I haven't gotten over it. I don't know whether this financial business binds me sufficiently or not. I'll be frank and tell you that I can't say that I love her, but I'm sorry, and that's something."

"She's comfortably provided for, of course," Letty commented rather than inquired.

"Everything she wants. Jennie is of a peculiar disposition. She doesn't want much. She's retiring by nature and doesn't care for show. I've taken a little cottage for her at Sandwood, a little place north of here on the lake, and there's plenty of money in trust, but of course she knows she can live anywhere she pleases."

"I can understand exactly how she feels, Lester. I know how you feel. She is going to suffer very keenly for awhile—we all do when we have to give up the thing we love. But we can get over it, and we do. At least we can live. She will. It will go hard at first, but after awhile she will see how it is, and she won't feel any the worse toward you."

"Jennie will never reproach me, I know that," he replied. "I'm the one who will do the reproaching. I'll be abusing myself for some time. The trouble is, with my peculiar turn of mind, I can't tell for the life of me how much of this disturbing feeling of mine is habit—the condition that I'm accustomed to—and how much is sympathy. I sometimes think I'm the most pointless individual in the world. I think too much. I know too much."

"Poor Lester," she said tenderly. "Well, I understand for one. You're lonely living where you are, aren't you?"

"I am that," he replied.

"Why not come and spend a few days down at West Baden? I'm going there."

"When?" he inquired.

"Next Tuesday."

"Let me see," he replied. "I'm not sure that I can do that." He consulted his note book. "I could come Thursday, for a few days."

"Why not do that? You need company. We can walk and talk things out down there. Will you?"

"Yes, I will," he replied.

She came to him, trailing a lavender lounging robe. "You're such a solemn philosopher, sir," she observed comfortably, "working through all the ramifications of this thing. Why do you? You were always like that."

"I can't help it," he replied. "It's my nature to think."

"Well, one thing I know," and she tweaked his ear with her soft, scented hand, "you're not going to make another mistake through sympathy if I can help it. You're going to stay disentangled long enough to give yourself a chance to think out what you want to do. You must. And I wish, for one thing, you'd take over the management of my affairs. You could advise me so much better than my lawyer."

He arose and walked to the window, turning to look back at her solemnly. "I know what you want," he said doggedly.

"And why shouldn't I?" she demanded, coming toward him. She looked him pleadingly and defiantly in the face. "Why shouldn't I?"

"You don't know what you're doing," he grumbled, looking out of the window, but her magnetism was reaching to him just the same. He looked back.

She stood there, as beautiful as a woman of her age could be, artistic, wise, considerate, full of friendship and affection.

"Letty," he said. "You ought not to want to marry me. I'm not worth it. Really I'm not. I'm too cynical. Too indifferent. It won't be worth anything in the long run."

"It will be worth something to me," she insisted. "I know what you are. Anyhow, I don't care. I want you!"

He took her hands, then her arms. He finally drew her to him and put his arms about her waist. "Poor Letty," he said; "I'm not worth it. You'll be sorry."

"No, I'll not," she replied. "I know what I'm doing. I don't care what you think you are worth. I know what you need—I know what I need." She laid her cheek on his shoulder. "I want you."

"If you keep on, I venture to say you'll have me," he returned, and he kissed her.

"Oh," she exclaimed, and hugged him tight.

He stood there, commenting to himself on the scene even as he caressed her. "This is rank charlatanry," he thought. "It's bad business. It isn't what I ought to be doing."

Still he held her, and when she offered her lips coaxingly he kissed her again and again.

CHAPTER LV

It is difficult to say whether Lester might not have returned to Jennie after all but for certain influential factors. After a time, with his control of his portion of the estate firmly settled in his hands and the storm of original feeling forgotten, he was well aware that diplomacy—if he ignored his natural tendency to fulfill even implied obligations—could readily bring about an arrangement whereby he and Jennie could be together. But he was haunted by the sense of what might be called an important social opportunity in the form of Mrs. Gerald. He was compelled to set over against his natural tendency toward Jennie a consciousness of what he was ignoring in the personality and fortunes of her rival, who was one of the most significant and interesting figures on the social horizon. For think as he would, these two women were now persistently juxtaposed in his consciousness. The one polished, sympathetic, philosophic—schooled in all the niceties of polite society, and with the means to gratify and make ornate her every wish; the other natural, sympathetic, emotional, with no schooling in the ways of polite society, but with a feeling for the beauty of life and the lovely things in human relationships which made her beyond any question an exceptional woman. Mrs. Gerald saw it and admitted it. Her charge against his living with Jennie was not that she was not worth while but that conditions made it impolitic. On the other hand, union with her was an ideal climax for his social aspirations. This would bring everything out right. He would be as happy with her as he would be with Jennie—almost—and he would have the satisfaction of knowing that this western social and financial world held no more significant figure than himself. It was not wise to delay, either, this latter excellent solution of his material problems, and after thinking it over long and seriously he finally concluded that he would not delay. He had already done Jennie the irreparable wrong of leaving her. What difference did it make if he did this also? She was possessed of everything she could possibly want, outside of himself. She had herself deemed it advisable for him to leave. By such figments of the brain, in the face of unsettled and disturbing conditions, he was becoming used to the idea of a new alliance.

As a matter of fact, the thing which prevented an eventual resumption of relationship in some form with Jennie was the constant presence of Mrs. Gerald. Circumstances seemed to conspire to make her the logical solution of his mental quandary at this time. Alone he could do nothing save to make visits here and there, and he did not care to do that. He was too indifferent mentally to gather about him, as a bachelor, that atmosphere which he enjoyed and which a woman like Mrs. Gerald could so readily provide. United with her it was simple enough. Their home, then, wherever it was, would be full of clever people. He would need to do little save appear and enjoy it. She understood quite as well as any one how he liked to live. She enjoyed meeting the people he enjoyed meeting. There were so many things they could do together nicely. He visited West Baden at the same time she did, as she suggested. He gave himself over to her in Chicago for dinners, parties, drives. Her house was quite as much his own as hers—she made him feel so. She talked to him about her affairs, showing him exactly how they stood and why she wished him to intervene in this and that matter. She did not wish him to be too much alone. She did not want him to think or regret. By degrees she won him to an attitude where his arms about her spelled a form of delight to him. It was comfort, forgetfulness, rest from care. Along with others he stopped at her house occasionally, and it gradually became rumored about that he would marry her. Because of the fact that there had been so much discussion of his previous relationship, Letty decided that if ever this occurred it should be a quiet affair. She wanted a simple explanation in the papers of how it had come about, and then afterward, when things were normal again and gossip had subsided, she would enter on a dazzling social display for his sake.

"Why not let us get married in April and go abroad for the summer?" she asked once, after they had reached a silent understanding that marriage would eventually come about between them. "Let's go to Japan. Then we can come back in the fall and take a house on the drive."

Lester had been away from Jennie so long now that the first severe wave of self-reproach had passed. He was still doubtful, but he preferred to stifle his misgivings. "Very well," he replied, almost jokingly, "only don't let there be any fuss about it."

"Do you really mean that, sweet?" she exclaimed, looking over at him from her chair, where she had been reading. They had been spending the evening together.

"I've thought about it a long while," he replied. "I don't see why not."

She came over to him and sat on his knee, putting her arms over his shoulders.

"I can scarcely believe you said that," she said, looking at him curiously.

"Shall I take it back?" he asked.

"No, no. It's agreed for April now. And we'll go to Japan. You can't change your mind. There won't be any fuss. But my, what a trousseau I will prepare!"

He smiled a little constrainedly as she tousled his head; there was a missing note somewhere in this gamut of happiness; perhaps it was because he was getting old.

In the meantime Jennie was going her way, settling herself in the markedly different world in which henceforth she was to move. It seemed a terrible thing at first, this life without Lester, for, in spite of the individuality she possessed, her ways had become so involved with his—all her thoughts and actions—that there seemed to be no way of disentangling them. Constantly she was with him in thought and action, just as though they had never separated. Where was he now? What was he doing? What was he saying? How was he looking? In the mornings when she would wake, it was with the sense that he must be beside her. At night, as if she could not go to bed alone. He would come after awhile, surely, and then—no, of course he would not. He would never come any more. Dear heaven, think of that! Never any more. And she wanted him so.

There were so many mean little trying things to adjust also, from time to time, for a change of this kind is never made without explanation. The explanation she had to make to Vesta was, of all, the most difficult. This little girl, who was old enough now to see and think for herself, was not without her thoughts and misgivings. Jennie had been an ideal mother—there was an indissoluble bond of affection between them, just as there had been between Jennie and her own mother—but Vesta recalled that her mother had been accused of not being married to her father when she was born. She had seen the article about Jennie and Lester in the Sunday paper at the time it had appeared—it had been shown to her at school—though even then she had had sense enough to say nothing about it, feeling somehow that Jennie would not like it. Lester's disappearance was a complete surprise to her, but she had learned in the last two or three years that her mother was very sensitive, and that she could hurt her in unexpected ways by talking. Jennie said nothing, but Vesta could see it all in her eyes. She loved her so that she was beginning to want to shield her, and at fifteen and sixteen she could do it nicely. Jennie was finally compelled to say to Vesta that Lester's fortune had been dependent on his leaving her, solely because she was not of his station. He did not want to, but if he had not they would have been almost poor. Vesta listened soberly and half-suspected the truth. She felt terribly sorry for her mother, though she pretended not to and concealed always what she thought. Because of Jennie's obvious distress, Vesta was trebly gay and courageous. She refused outright the suggestion of going to a boarding school, though she had once thought she would like to, and stayed as close to her mother as she could. She found interesting books to read with her mother, insisted that they go to see plays together, played to her on the piano, and asked for her criticisms on her drawing and modeling. She found a few friends in the excellent Sandwood school, and brought them home of an evening to add lightness and gayety to the cottage life. Jennie, because of her growing appreciation of Vesta's capabilities, drew more and more toward her. Lester was gone, but at least she had Vesta. That prop would probably sustain her in the face of a waning existence.

There was also her history to account for, by degrees, to the residents of Sandwood. In many cases, where one is content to lead a secluded life it is not necessary to say much of one's past, but as a rule something must be said. People have the habit of inquiring—if they are no more than butchers and bakers. By degrees one must account for this and that fact, and it was so here. She could not say that her husband was dead. Lester might come back. She had to say that she had left him,—to give the impression that it would be she, if any one, who would permit him to return. This put her in an interesting and sympathetic light in the neighborhood. It was the most sensible thing to do. She then settled down to a quiet routine of existence, waiting what dénouement to her life she could not guess.

Sandwood life was not without its charms for a lover of nature, and this, with the love of Vesta, offered some slight solace. Aside from the beauty of the lake which, with its passing boats, was a never-ending source of joy to her, the town was on a high road from Chicago to Milwaukee and points north, and trains were not infrequent and at times noisy, giving a comforting evidence of the activity of the world. There was a good bicycle road running north from Chicago which drew hundreds from the city in the hey-day of that craze, their presence lending some life to the lake-front road where they passed. She had her own horse and carryall—one of the horses of the pair they had enjoyed in Hyde Park. Other household pets appeared in due course of time, including a collie that Vesta named Rats; she had brought him from Chicago as a puppy, and he had grown to be a sterling watch-dog, sensible and affectionate. There was also a cat, Jimmy Woods, so named after a boy Vesta knew, and to whom she insisted the cat bore a marked resemblance. There was a singing thrush, guarded carefully against any roving desire for bird-food on the part of Jimmy Woods, and a jar of gold-fish. So this household drifted along quietly and dreamily indeed, but with always the undercurrent of feeling which ran so still because it was so deep.

There was no word from Lester for the first few weeks following his departure; he was too busy following up the threads of his new commercial connections and too considerate to wish to keep Jennie in a state of mental turmoil reading communications which, under the present circumstances, could mean nothing. He preferred to let matters rest for the time being and then, a little later, write her sanely and calmly of how things were going. He did this after a month, saying that he had been pretty well pressed by commercial affairs, that he had been in and out of the city frequently (which was the truth), and that he would probably need to be out of city a notable portion of the time in the future. He inquired after Vesta and the condition of things generally at Sandwood. "I may get up there one of these days," he suggested, but he really did not mean to do so, and Jennie knew that he did not.

Another month passed, and then there was a second letter from him, not so long as the first one. Jennie had written him entertainingly and fully, telling him just how things were. She concealed entirely her own feelings in the matter, saying that she liked the life very much, and that she was glad to be at Sandwood. She expressed the hope that everything was coming out for the best for him now, and tried to show him that she was really glad that he had gone. It was so much better for him. "You mustn't think of me as being unhappy," she said in one place, "for I'm not. I am sure it ought to be just as it is, and I wouldn't be happy if it were any other way. Lay out your life so as to give yourself the greatest happiness, Lester," she added. "You deserve it. Whatever you do will be just right for me. I won't mind." She had Mrs. Gerald in mind, and he suspected as much, but he felt that her generosity must be tinged greatly with self-sacrifice and secret unhappiness. It was one thing which made him delay.

The written word and the hidden thought—how they conflict! After six months the correspondence was more or less perfunctory on his part, and at eight months it ceased temporarily.

One morning, as she was glancing over the daily paper, she saw among the society notes the following item:

The engagement of Mrs. Malcolm Gerald, of 4044 Drexel Boulevard, to Lester Kane, second son of the late Archibald Kane, of Cincinnati, was formally announced at a party given by the prospective bride on Tuesday 6th to a circle of her immediate friends. The wedding will take place in April.

The paper fell from her hands. For a few minutes she sat perfectly still, looking straight ahead of her. Could this be so? she asked herself. Had it really come at last? She had known that it must and yet—and yet she had always hoped that it would not. Why had she hoped? Had not she herself sent him away? Had she not suggested this very thing in a roundabout way? It had come now. Here it was, directly before her. What must she do? Stay here as a pensioner? The idea was objectionable to her. And yet he had set aside a goodly sum to be hers absolutely. In the hands of a trust company in La Salle Street were a group of railway certificates aggregating seventy-five thousand dollars which yielded forty-five hundred dollars annually, which came to her direct. He had foreseen that she might not want to be a pensioner. This had all been straightened out by Mr. Watson. Could she refuse to receive this money? There was Vesta to be considered.

She was hurt through and through by this dénouement, and yet as she sat there she realized that it was foolish to feel angry after all she had said and felt. Life was always doing this sort of thing to her. It would go on doing so. Her life was marked for some reason. She was sure of it. If she went out in the world and earned her own living, what difference would it make to him? What difference would it make to Mrs. Gerald? Here she was, off in this little place, leading an obscure life, and there was he out in the great world doing the things he had once hoped possibly to do with her. It was too bad. It was not to be. Why cry? Why?

Her eyes indeed were dry, but her very soul seemed to be torn in pieces within her. She rose carefully, hid the newspaper at the bottom of the trunk, and turned the key upon it.

CHAPTER LVI

The engagement of Lester to Mrs. Gerald came to its formal fruition rapidly enough. Because of her charm and eagerness, and her persistent and consummate diplomacy, he found himself gradually contenting himself with the idea that this union was as it should be, and that all was for the best. He was sorry for Jennie—very sorry. So was Mrs. Gerald, but there was a practical unguent to her grief in the thought that it was best for both of them. He would be happier—was now. Jennie would be eventually, realizing that she had done a wise and kindly thing. Letty saw much of Lester during these days. They were together discussing the future of their consolidated interests and making love at the same time. Because of her indifference to the late Malcolm Gerald, and because she was realizing the dreams of her youth in getting Lester at last—even though a little late—she was intensely happy. She could think of nothing finer than this daily life with him—the places they would go, the things they would see. Her first season in Chicago as Mrs. Lester Kane, the following winter, was going to be something worth remembering. And as for Japan—that was almost too good to be true.

Lester wrote to Jennie of his coming marriage to Mrs. Gerald. He said that he had no explanation to make. It wouldn't be worth anything if he did make it. He thought he ought to marry Mrs. Gerald. He thought he ought to let Jennie know. He hoped she was well. He wanted her always to feel, in spite of this, that he had her real interests at heart. He would do anything in his power to make life as pleasant and agreeable for her as possible. He hadn't thought when he left that he would do this, but things had come up which had caused him to alter his mind. He wanted to be perfectly frank. He hoped she would forgive him. And would she remember him affectionately to Vesta? She ought to be sent to a finishing school.

Jennie understood how it was. She knew that Lester had been drawn to Mrs. Gerald from the time he had encountered her at the Savoy in London. She had been angling for him. Now she had him. It was all right. She hoped he would be happy. She was glad to write and tell him so, saying in an off-hand way that she had seen the announcement in the papers. He could read between the lines what she was thinking. Her very fortitude was a charm to him. Even in this hour. In spite of all he had done and what he was now going to do, he realized that he still cared for Jennie in a way. She was noble and a charming woman. If everything else had been all right, he would not be going to marry Mrs. Gerald at all now. And yet he did marry her.

The ceremony was performed on April fifteenth, at the residence of Mrs. Gerald, a Roman Catholic priest officiating. Lester was a poor example of the faith he occasionally professed. His father had been a good Catholic. He was himself an agnostic, but because he had been reared in the Church, he felt that he might as well be married in it. Some fifty guests, intimate friends, had been invited. The ceremony went off with perfect smoothness. There were jubilant congratulations and showers of rice and confetti. While the guests were still eating and drinking, Lester and Letty managed to slip out a side entrance into a closed carriage, and were off. There was pursuit, pell-mell, fifteen minutes later on the part of the guests to the Chicago, Rock Island and Pacific depot; but by that time the happy couple were in their private car, and the arrival of the rice-throwers made no difference. More champagne was opened; then the starting of the train ended all excitement, and they were at last safely off together.

"Well, now you have me," he said cheerfully, pulling her down beside him into a seat. "What of it?"

"This of it!" she exclaimed, and hugged him close, kissing him fervently. In four days they were in San Francisco, and two days later on board a fast steamship en route for the land of the Mikado.

In the meanwhile Jennie was left to brood. From the original notice, she had seen that he was to be married in April, and she had kept watch for additional comment ever since. There was none until some five days before the event, when it was stated that the ceremony would be performed on Thursday, April fifteenth, at 2:00 P.M. at the residence of the prospective bride. Individuals whom Jennie had heard of, through Lester and the papers, were named as prospective best man and bride's maid. In spite of her feeling of resignation, Jennie followed it all hopelessly—like a child, hungry and forlorn, looking into a lighted window at Christmas time.

On the day of the wedding she followed the various steps of these two fortunate individuals mentally, as closely as if she were present and looking on. She could see in her mind's eye the handsome residence, the carriages, the guests, the feast, the merriment, the ceremony—all. Telepathically and psychologically she received impressions of the private car and of the joyous journey they were going to take. The papers had stated that they would spend their honeymoon in Japan. Their honeymoon! Her Lester! And Mrs. Gerald was so attractive. She could see her now—the new Mrs. Kane—the only *Mrs.* Kane that ever was, lying in his arms. He had held her so once. He had loved her. Yes, he had! There was a solid lump in her throat as she thought of this. Oh, dear! Oh, dear! She sighed to herself and clasped her hands forcefully, but it did no good. She was just as miserable as before.

When the day was done she was actually relieved, for anyhow, then, nothing could change it. Vesta was sympathetically aware of what was happening but kept silent. She too had seen the report in the newspaper. She pretended to be gay and talked of other things, but it was of no avail. When the first and second day after had passed, Jennie was much calmer mentally, for she was seeing again that she was face to face with the inevitable. But it was weeks before the sharp pain dulled to the old familiar ache. Then there were months before they would be back again, though of course that made no difference now. Only Japan seemed so far off, and somehow she had liked the thought that Lester was near her—somewhere in the city.

The spring passed and the summer. In the fall Vesta started to school again. She was in the high school now, studying French and Algebra and Civil Government, things which interested Jennie as curious lines of thought because they were interesting to Vesta. She had thought a number of times of doing something more than this household work in order to occupy her mind, for in spite of her love of nature she was lonely. Her flowers and her lawn and her view of the lake, which was beautiful, seemed to require something more than just her love of them to make her happy. It was Lester, of course, but she kept thinking she ought to try to make herself happy without him. She would never have him any more. If she could only work. She drifted, though, thinking it was best to stay with Vesta, and then, after two years of indifference, came the last fell blow—and the world seemed to tumble about her ears.

It was early in October—one of the first premonitory chilly days—that Vesta came home from school complaining of a headache. Jennie gave her hot milk—a favorite remedy of her mother's—and advised a cold towel for the back of her head. Vesta went to her room and lay down. Instead of getting better, the headache grew a little worse, and the following morning she had a slight fever. This lingered while the local physician, Dr. Emory, treated her tentatively, suspecting after four days of fever that it was typhoid. There were several cases in the village. This doctor told Jennie that Vesta was probably strong enough constitutionally to shake it off, but it might be that she would have a severe siege. His other patients were suffering severely. Mistrusting her own skill in so delicate a situation, Jennie sent to Chicago for a trained nurse, and then she began a period of watchfulness which was a combination of fear, longing, hope and courage.

Never in her life before, with the exception of the time that Vesta had been sick at Mrs. Olsen's, had Jennie been in quite this position. She was alone now, dependent on her own resources, no one outside of the nurse, the doctor, and her neighbors, who called and volunteered their services, to confer with sympathetically. In times past she had had Lester, Gerhardt, her mother, Jeannette—individuals who had been with her a great deal and who were sympathetically in accord with her. On this occasion there was no one. She could not write to the other members of her family. She hesitated about communicating with Lester. He was probably not in the city anyhow. She saw by the papers where he and his wife were going to spend a season in New York. When the doctor, after watching the case for a week, pronounced it severe, she thought she ought to write anyhow, for no one could tell what would happen. Lester had been so fond of Vesta. He would probably want to know.

The letter sent to Lester did not reach him, for at the time it arrived he was on his way to the West Indies. Jennie was compelled to watch Vesta's general decline alone, for, although sympathetic neighbors, realizing the pathos of the case, were attentive, they could not supply the spiritual consolation which comes from contact with those we truly love. There was a period when Vesta appeared to be rallying, and both the physician and the nurse were hopeful; but afterward she became weaker. It was said by Dr. Emory that her heart and kidneys had become affected.

There came a time when the fact had to be faced that death was imminent. The doctor's face was grave, the nurse noncommittal in her opinions. Jennie hovered about, praying the only prayer that is prayer—the fervent desire of her heart that Vesta should get well. The child had come so close to her during the last few years. There had sprung up between them a strong bond of intelligent sympathy. Vesta understood her mother. She was beginning to realize clearly what her life had been. There had been innumerable occasions when she had caressed Jennie fondly, hugging her about the neck, kissing her, telling her that she was the dearest mother that ever was. Jennie, through her, had grown to a broad understanding of responsibility. She knew now what it meant to be a good mother and to have children. If Lester had not objected to it, and she had been truly married, she would have been glad to have had others. As it was, she had learned from just Vesta alone.

Again, she had always felt that she owed Vesta so much—a long and happy life at least to make up to her for the ignominy of her birth and rearing. Jennie had been so happy during the past few years to see Vesta becoming beautiful, graceful, intelligent and kindly. It was so plain that she was going to turn out to be an exceptional woman, and now here she was dying. Dr. Emory finally sent to Chicago for a physician friend of his, who came to consider the case with him. He was an old man, grave, sympathetic, understanding. He shook his head. "The treatment has been correct," he said. "Her system does not appear to be strong enough to endure the strain. Some physiques are more susceptible to this malady than others." It was agreed that if within three days a change for the better were not witnessed, then the end was close at hand.

No one can conceive the strain to which Jennie's spirit was subjected by this intelligence, for it was deemed best that she should know. She hovered about white-faced—feeling intensely but scarcely thinking. She seemed to vibrate consciously with Vesta's altering states. If there was the least improvement, she felt it physically. If there was decline, her barometric temperament registered the fact. Finally the time was up, and she knew, though she refused to believe, that the end was at hand.

There was a Mrs. Davis, a fine motherly soul of fifty, stout and sympathetic, who lived four doors from Jennie, and who understood quite well how she was feeling. She had co-operated with the nurse and doctor from the start to make Jennie's mental state as nearly normal as possible.

"Now you just go to your room and lie down, Mrs. Kane," she would say to Jennie when she found her watching so pathetically, or wandering to and fro wondering what to do. "I'll take charge of everything. I'll do just what you would do. Lord bless you, don't you think I know? I've been the mother of seven and lost three. Don't you think I understand?" Jennie put her head on her big, warm shoulder one day and cried. Mrs. Davis cried with her. "I understand," she said. "There, there, you poor dear. Now you come with me." And she led her to her sleeping-room.

Jennie could not be away long. She came back after moments of attempted resting, unrefreshed. Finally one midnight, when the nurse had persuaded her that all would be well until morning anyhow, there came a hurried stirring in the sick-room. Jennie was lying down for a few minutes on her bed in the adjoining room. She heard it and arose. Mrs. Davis had come in. The nurse had gone to call her from downstairs. They were both conferring as to Vesta's condition—standing close beside her.

Jennie understood. She came up and looked at her daughter keenly. Vesta's pale, waxen face told the story. She was breathing faintly, her eyes closed. Instinctively Jennie clasped her hands to her breast and strained mentally against what she feared. "She's very weak," whispered the nurse. Mrs. Davis took Jennie's hand.

The moments passed, and after a time the clock in the hall struck one. Miss Murfree, the nurse, moved to the medicine-table several times, wetting a soft piece of cotton cloth with alcohol and bathing Vesta's lips. When one-thirty came there was a stir of the weak body—a profound sigh. Jennie bent forward eagerly, but Mrs. Davis drew her back. The nurse came and motioned them away. Respiration had ceased.

Mrs. Davis seized Jennie firmly. "There, there, you poor dear," she whispered when Jennie began to shake. "It can't be helped. Don't cry."

Jennie sank on her knees beside the bed and caressed Vesta's still warm hand. "Oh no, Vesta," she pleaded. "Not you."

"There, dear, come now," soothed the voice of Mrs. Davis. "Can't you leave it all in God's hands? Can't you believe that everything is for the best?"

Jennie felt as if the earth had fallen. All ties were broken. There was no light anywhere in the immense dark of her existence.

CHAPTER LVII

This additional blow, which fortune so inconsiderately administered, was quite sufficient to return Jennie to that state of hyper-melancholia from which she had been with difficulty extracted by the few years of comfort and affection which she had enjoyed with Lester in Hyde Park. It was really weeks before she could realize that Vesta was gone. The emaciated figure which she saw in the bed for a day or two after the end did not seem like Vesta. Where was the joy and lightness? the quickness of motion? the subtle radiance of health? All gone. Only this pale, lily-hued shell—and silence. She would come into the pink and white bedroom where the bright waters of the lake were visible in the distance, shining in the sun, and look at this sylph-like figure, terribly thinned by sickness, and wonder where she was. What had become of all that she was? Vesta's hand would rest under hers, stiff and cold. Jennie had no tears to shed; only a deep, insistent pain to feel. If only some counsellor of eternal wisdom could have whispered to her that obvious and convincing truth— there are no dead.

Miss Murfree, Dr. Emory, Mrs. Davis, a Mrs. Whipple, and several others who were new friends of hers were all most attentive and considerate in this trying time. At her request, Mrs. Davis sent a telegram to Lester saying that Vesta was dead, but, he being absent, there was no response. The house was looked after with scrupulous care by others, for Jennie was incapable of thought for it. She walked about looking at things which Vesta had owned or liked—things which Lester or she had given her— and sighing over the fact that Vesta would not need or use them any more. She gave instructions that Vesta was to be taken to Chicago and buried in the Cemetery of the Redeemer, for Lester had, at the time of Gerhardt's death, purchased a small plot of ground there. She also asked whether the minister of the little Lutheran church in Cottage Grove Avenue, where Gerhardt had attended, could be seen and arrangements made for him to say a few words at the grave. He had known Vesta. This was done by Mrs. Whipple's husband, who went in to Chicago daily—he was a small manufacturer of candies. There were the usual preliminary services at the house. The local Methodist minister read a portion of the First Epistle of Paul to the Thessalonians, and a body of Vesta's classmates sang "Nearer My God to Thee." There were flowers, a white coffin, a world of sympathetic expressions, and then Vesta was taken away. Mr. Adam Borger, the undertaker, an undersized, preternaturally solemn individual of sharp business instincts, saw to it that the body was properly transferred—put in a great wooden case in the depot at Sandwood, taken out of it at

Chicago, and finally delivered at the Lutheran cemetery where it was re-incased when the services were completed.

Jennie moved as one in a dream. She was dazed, almost to the point of insensibility. Five of her neighborhood friends, at the solicitation of Mrs. Davis, were kind enough to accompany her. At the grave-side, when the body was finally lowered, she looked at it. One might have thought that she looked indifferently, for she was numb from suffering. She returned to Sandwood after it was all over, saying that she would not stay long. She wanted to come back to Chicago where she could be near Vesta and Gerhardt. Her thoughts were running to something she might do—anything—to get away from loneliness and the opportunity of self-commiseration.

It was after the funeral that the details began to come back by degrees—the long years of companionship, the love and care, the days in Cleveland, Schiller Street, Hyde Park, here. Because of certain associated memories, she thought at moments that she might like to stay here, but at other times she realized that it was impossible. She fixed her mind on the need of doing something, even though she did not need to. Because of observing Miss Murfree, she thought she would like nursing, though she feared that she was too old to obtain the training which was required. She also thought of William, the only member of the family who was unconnected, as one who might come and live with her, but she did not know where he was. Bass, on his visit at the time of Gerhardt's death, had said he did not know. She finally concluded that she would try to get in a hospital or store. Her disposition was against idleness. She could not live alone here, and she could not have her neighbors sympathetically worrying over what was to become of her. Miserable as she was, she would be less miserable stopping in a hotel in Chicago and looking for something to do, or living in a cottage somewhere near the Cemetery of the Redeemer. It also occurred to her latterly that she might adopt a homeless child. There were a number of orphan asylums in the city.

Somewhat over three weeks after Vesta's death, Lester returned to Chicago with his wife and discovered the first letter, the telegram, and an additional note telling him that Vesta was dead. He was truly grieved, for his affection for the girl had been real. He was very sorry for Jennie, and he told his wife that he would have to go out and see her. He was wondering what she would do. She could not live alone. There ought to be something which he could suggest which would help her. He took the train to Sandwood, but Jennie had gone to the Tremont House in Chicago, where he had once stopped with her. He went there, but Jennie had gone to her daughter's grave; later he called again and found her in. When the boy presented his card, she suffered an upwelling of feeling—a wave that was more intense than that with which she had received him in the olden days, for now her need of him was greater.

Lester, in spite of the glamour of his new affection and the restoration of his powers, dignities and influence, had had time to think deeply of what he had done. His original feeling of doubt and dissatisfaction with himself had never wholly quieted. It did not ease him any to know that he had left Jennie comfortably fixed, for it was always so plain to him that money was not the point at issue with her. Affection was what she craved, and although he had never been able to give her that in the measure to which it had been returned to him, he had at least stilled her longings for happiness in part by being with her. That being over, there was nothing for her. She was like a rudderless boat on an endless sea, and he knew it. She needed him, and he was ashamed at times that his charity had not outweighed his sense of self-preservation and his desire for material advantage. Today, as the elevator carried him up to her room, he was really sorry, though he knew now that no act of his could make right what was so thoroughly wrong. He had been to blame from the very beginning—first for taking her, then for failing to stick by a bad bargain—but it could not be helped now. The best thing he could do was to be fair, to counsel with her, to give her the best of his sympathy and advice. Things might be eased for her a little in this way.

"Hello, Jennie," he said familiarly when she opened the door to him in her hotel room, his glance taking in the ravages which death and suffering had wrought. She was thinner, her face quite drawn and for the time being colorless, her eyes larger by contrast. She looked as though she had cried a great deal, though she hadn't. "I'm awfully sorry about Vesta," he said a little awkwardly. "I never dreamed anything like that could happen."

It was the first real voice of comfort that had meant anything to her since Vesta had died—since Lester had left her, in fact. It touched her so that he had come to sympathize; for the moment she could not speak. Tears welled over her eyelids and down upon her cheeks.

"Don't cry, Jennie," he said, putting his arm around her and holding her head to his shoulder. "I'm sorry. I've been sorry for a good many things that can't be helped now. I'm intensely sorry for this. Where did you bury her?"

"Beside Papa," she said, sobbing.

"Too bad," he murmured, and held her in silence. She finally gained control of herself sufficiently to step away from him and, wiping her eyes with her handkerchief, asked him to sit down.

"Certainly," he replied in a conciliatory tone. "I'm so sorry that it should have happened while I was away. I would have been with you if I had been here. I suppose you won't want to live out at Sandwood now?"

"I can't, Lester," she replied. "I couldn't stand it."

"Where are you thinking of going?"

"Oh, I don't know yet. I didn't want to be a bother to those people out there. I thought I'd get me a little house somewhere and adopt a baby maybe, or get something to do. I don't like to be alone."

"That isn't a bad idea," he said—"that of adopting a baby. It would be a lot of company for you. You know how to go about getting one?"

"You just ask at one of these asylums, don't you?"

"I think there's something more than that," he replied thoughtfully. "There are some formalities—I don't know what they are. They keep control of the child, though, in some way. You had better consult with Watson and get him to help you. Pick out your baby and then let him do the rest. I'll speak to him about it."

Lester saw that she needed companionship badly. "Where is your brother George?" he asked.

"He's in Rochester, but he couldn't come. Bass said he was married," she added.

"There isn't any other member of the family you could persuade to come and live with you?"

"I might get William, but I don't know where he is."

"Why not try that new section west of Jackson Park," he suggested, "if you want a house here in Chicago. I see some nice cottages out that way. You needn't buy. Just rent until you see how well you're satisfied."

Jennie thought this good advice because it came from Lester. It was good to have him take this much interest in her—if nothing more. She wasn't entirely separated from him after all. He cared a little. She asked him how his wife was, whether he had had a pleasant trip, whether he was going to stay in Chicago. All the while he was thinking that he had treated her badly. He went to the window and looked down into Dearborn Street, the world of traffic below holding his attention. The great mass of trucks and vehicles, the counter-streams of hurrying pedestrians, seemed like a puzzle. So shadows march in a dream. It was growing dusk, and lights were springing up here and there.

"I want to tell you something, Jennie," said Lester, finally rousing himself from his fit of abstraction. "It may seem peculiar to you, after all that has happened, but I still care for you, in my way. I've thought of you right along since I left. I thought it good business to leave you—the way things were. I thought I liked Letty well enough to marry her under the circumstances. From one point of view it still seems best, but I'm not so much happier. I was just as happy with you as I ever will be. It isn't me that's important in this transaction apparently—it's the general situation. The individual doesn't count much in the situation. I don't know whether you see what I'm driving at, but all of us are more or less pawns. We're moved about like chess men by circumstances over which we have no control."

"I understand, Lester," she answered. "I'm not complaining. I know it's for the best."

"After all, life is more or less of a farce," he went on a little bitterly. "It's a silly show. The best we can do is to hold our personalities intact. It doesn't even appear that integrity has much to do with it."

Jennie did not quite grasp what he was talking about, but she knew it meant that he was not entirely satisfied with himself and was sorry for her.

"Don't worry over me, Lester," she consoled. "I'm all right; I'll get along. It did seem terrible to me for awhile—getting used to being alone. I'll be all right now. I'll get along."

"I want you to feel that my attitude hasn't changed," he went on. "I'm interested in what concerns you. Mrs.—Letty understands that. She knows just how I feel. When you get settled I'll come in and see how you're fixed. I'll come around here again in a few days. You understand how I feel, don't you?"

"Yes, I do," she said.

He took her hand, turning it sympathetically in his. "Don't worry," he said. "I don't want you to do that. I'll do the best I can. You're still Jennie to me, if you don't mind. I'm pretty bad, but I'm not all bad."

"It's all right, Lester. I wanted you to do as you did. It's for the best. You probably are happy since—"

"Now, Jennie," he interrupted; then he pressed her hand, her arm, her shoulder. "Want to kiss me for old times' sake?" he smiled.

She put her hands over his shoulders, looked long into his eyes, then kissed him. When their lips met she trembled. Lester also felt unsteady. Jennie saw his agitation, and tried hard to speak.

"You'd better go now," she said firmly. "It's getting dark."

He went away, and yet he knew that he wanted above all things to remain; she was still the one woman in the world for him. And Jennie felt comforted, even though the separation still existed in all its finality. She did not endeavor to explain or adjust the moral and ethical entanglements of the situation. She was not, like so many, endeavoring to put the ocean into a tea-cup, or to tie up the shifting universe in a mess of strings called law. Lester still cared for her a little. He cared for Letty too. That was all right. She had hoped once that he might want her only. Since he did not, was his affection worth nothing? She could not see it. She could not feel it. And neither could he.

CHAPTER LVIII

The drift of events for a period of five years saw a marked divergence in the affairs of Lester and Jennie—a period in which they settled naturally into their respective spheres without that exchange of relationship, or at least very little of it, which their several meetings at the Tremont would have indicated. The social and financial life which he was leading was rather binding at first. It led him in paths to which her retiring soul had never aspired. At the same time, these years took her back to the extreme simplicities which she had once fancied, at Cairo, would be hers again. There was a simple cottage in a very respectable but not showy neighborhood near Jackson Park, on the South Side, where she lived in retirement with a little foster child as her sole companion—a chestnut-haired girl, taken from the Western Home for the Friendless, whom she had obtained with the assistance of Mr. Dwight L. Watson, Lester's attorney. In this very pleasant neighborhood she was known as Mrs. J. G. Stover, for she had deemed it best, on consideration, to abandon the name of Kane.

Mr. and Mrs. Lester Kane, when resident in Chicago, were the occupants of a handsome mansion on the Lake Shore Drive, where parties, balls, receptions, dinners were given in rapid and at times almost pyrotechnic succession. Mrs. Kane, in addition to being a lover of brilliant social life, was a splendid executive. She was possessed of wit, tact and imagination, and her friends were numerous. To be recognized by her socially was a boon craved and appreciated by many. Her judgement of personalities outside of society, worthy of reception and public approval, was almost unfailing.

Lester had become, in his way, a lover of a peaceful and well-entertained existence. He had cut from his list of acquaintances and associates a number of people who had been a little doubtful or over-familiar or indifferent or talkative during a certain period which, to him, was a memory merely. He was a director, and in several cases the chairman of a board of directors, in nine of the most important financial and commercial organizations of the West—The United Traction Company of Cincinnati, The Western Crucible Steel Works, The United Carriage Association, The Second National Bank of Chicago, The First National Bank of Cincinnati, and several others of equal importance. He was never a personal factor in the affairs of The United Carriage Association, preferring to be represented by counsel—the aforementioned Mr. Dwight L. Watson—but he took a keen interest in its affairs. He had not seen his brother, Robert, to speak to him in eleven years. He had not seen Imogene, who lived in Chicago, in three. Louise, Amy, their husbands, and some of their closest acquaintances were practically strangers. The firm of Knight, Keatley and O'Brien had nothing to do with his affairs whatsoever.

The truth was that Lester, in addition to becoming a little phlegmatic, was becoming decidedly critical in his outlook on life. He could not make out what it was all about. In distant ages a queer thing had come to pass. There had started on its way, in the form of evolution, a minute cellular organism which had apparently reproduced itself by division, had early learned to combine itself with others, to organize itself into bodies—strange forms of fish, animals and birds—and had finally learned to organize itself into man. Man, on his part, composed as he was of self-organizing cells, was pushing himself forward into comfort, and different aspects of existence, by means of union and organization with other men. Why? Heaven only knew. Here he was endowed with a peculiar brain and a certain amount of talent, and he had inherited a certain amount of wealth—which he now scarcely believed he deserved, only luck had favored him. But he could not see that any one else might be said to deserve this wealth any more than himself, seeing that his use of it was as conservative and constructive and practical as the next one's. He might have been born poor, in which case he would have been as well satisfied as the next one—not more so. Why should he complain, why worry, why speculate—was not the world going steadily forward of its own volition, whether he would or no? Truly it was. And was there any need for him to disturb himself about it? There was not. He fancied at times that it might as well never have been started at all. "The one divine, far-off event" of the poet did not appeal to him as having any basis in fact. Mrs. Lester Kane was of very much the same opinion.

Mrs. J. G. Stover, living on the South Side with her adopted child, Rose Perpetua, was of no fixed conclusion as to what life meant. She had not the incisive reasoning capacity of either Mr. or Mrs. Lester Kane. She had seen a great deal, suffered a great deal, and had read some in a desultory way. Her mind had never grasped the nature and character of specialized knowledge. History, physics, chemistry, botany, geology and sociology were not fixed departments in her brain as they were in Lester's and Letty's. Instead there was the feeling that the world moved in some strange, unstable way. It was not known clearly by any one, apparently, what it was all about. People were born and died. Some believed that the world had been made six thousand years before. Some that it was millions of years old. Some, like her father, thought there was a personal God, some that there was no God at all. For her part she felt there must be something—a guiding intelligence which produced all the beautiful things—the flowers, the stars, the trees, the grass. Nature was so beautiful. If at times certain events were cruel, yet there was this beauty persisting. And color, tones, feeling, laughter, the joy of character, the beauty of youth—how these softened in between the harsh faces of hunger, cold, indifference, greed. She could not understand what it was all about, but still, as in her youth, it was beautiful. One could live, somehow, under any circumstances.

Lester came five times after she had moved into this house—once the first week, when she was nearly getting settled, and once two weeks later, when she was settled. Three months later he had seen the new adoption, Rose Perpetua, and had remarked her as clever. He invariably came in a light buggy, drawn by a handsomely matched team of bays. Six months later he came again, saying he had been away for three months, and then she did not see him any more for a year. After that she did not see him at all, but his picture was in the papers once as an arbitrator—one of a group—of a street railway strike. She saw Mrs. Lester Kane's name in the papers frequently and once saw where they were going to move to New York. It hurt her a little to think that now she might be all alone in Chicago, but it had to be borne. She had taken to heart a phrase she had once heard quoted—it did not help her entirely but it did offer a slight solace, somehow: "There is neither good nor ill, but thinking makes it so." That appealed to her at times as being true—only she could not stop thinking.

It has been said that Jennie was naturally of an industrious turn. She was, and this never forsook her. She liked to be employed, though she thought constantly as she worked. She was of matronly proportions these days—not disagreeably large, but full-bodied, shapely, smooth-faced in spite of her cares. Her eyes were gray and sad-appealing. Her hair was still a rich brown but with traces of gray in it. People spoke of her as sweet-tempered—her neighbors—and as kindly and hospitable. They knew nothing of her history, except that she had formerly resided in Sandwood, and before that in Cleveland. She was very reticent as to her past.

Jennie had fancied that because of her natural interests—although she did not need to—she might get to be a trained nurse. She had not looked into the matter long before she abandoned that, however, for only young people were wanted. She also thought that some charitable organization might employ her or accept her services as an assistant in some capacity, but she did not understand the new theory of charity which was then coming into general acceptance and practise—namely, only to help others to help themselves. She believed in giving—and was not inclined to look too closely into the protestations of those who claimed to be poor; and consequently her timid inquiry at one relief agency after another met with indifference, if not unqualified rebuke. She finally decided to adopt a boy—four years old—for Rose Perpetua's sake, and succeeded in securing one named Harry, who was given her last name of Stover. Owing to the fact that it was always possible for her to advise with Mr. Watson and with Mr. Hyatt Skale of the Union Trust Company, with which her funds were deposited, she stood in no danger of being swindled or misled. She had no desire for investment or for the devious ways of trade. The care of flowers, the care of children, the looking after and maintaining the order of a home were more in her province.

One of the interesting things in connection with this separation, once it had been firmly established, related to Robert and Lester, for these two, since the reading of the will a number of years before, had never met. Robert had thought of his brother often. He had followed his success, since he had left Jennie, with interest. He had read of his marriage to Mrs. Gerald with pleasure, for he had always considered her an ideal companion for his brother. He knew by many signs and tokens that his brother, since the unfortunate turn of their father's attitude and his own peculiar movements to gain control of the Kane Company, did not like him. Still they had never been so far apart mentally—certainly not in commercial judgement. Robert was prosperous now. He could afford to be generous. He could afford to make up. And, after all, he had done his best to aid his brother to come to his senses,—and with the best intentions. There were mutual interests they could share financially if they were friends. He wondered from time to time if Lester would not be friendly with him.

Time passed and then once, when he was in Chicago, he

wondered where Lester was at that moment. But he went away, and another year was nearly gone before he was back again. Another time when he was in Chicago he had some friends with whom he was driving turn into the North Shore in order to see the splendid mansion which he heard the Kanes occupied. He knew its location from hearsay and description.

When he saw it, a touch of the old Kane home atmosphere came back to him. Lester, in revising the property after purchase, had had a conservatory built on one side—not unlike the one they had had at home in Cincinnati. Mrs. Kane was very fond of flowers. It was pretentious and yet dignified, he saw—smart for its type. Still other days passed and then, knowing that he was to be in Chicago on a certain date, he wrote Lester and asked him if he would not like to dine with him at the Union Club. He was only in town for a day, but he would like to see him again. There was some feeling, he knew, but there was a proposition he would like to talk to Lester about. Would he come, say, on Thursday?

On receipt of this letter, Lester frowned and fell into a brown study. He had never really been healed of the wound his father had given him; he had never been comfortable in his mind since Robert had deserted him so summarily. He could understand well enough why Robert should have wanted to do what he had done at that time—he realized that the stakes his brother had been playing for were big—but after all he had been Robert's brother, and he would not have done the same thing to Robert—at least he hoped not. Now Robert wanted to see him.

He thought once of not answering at all. Then he thought he would write and say no. But a curious desire to look at Robert again, to hear what he had to say and what his proposition would be, came over him; he decided to write yes. It could do no harm. He knew it could do no good. They might agree to let by-gones be by-gones, but the damage had been done. Could a broken bowl be mended and called whole? It might be *called* whole, but what of it? Was it not broken and mended?

On the Thursday in question, Robert called him up from the Auditorium to remind him of the engagement. Lester listened curiously to the sound of his brother's voice. "All right," he said, "I'll be with you." He once thought of speaking to Letty about it and then decided not to. She knew very little of Robert and his doings. At noon he went downtown, and there, within the exclusive precincts of the Union Club, these two brothers met and looked at each other again. Robert was thinner than when Lester had seen him last—a little grayer. His eyes were bright and steely, but there were crow's-feet on either side. His manner was quick, keen, dynamic.

Lester was very much of another type. He was not quick, or noticeably dynamic or urgent, but solid, brusque and indifferent. Men spoke of Lester these days as a little hard. Robert's keen blue eyes did not disturb him in the least—did not affect him in any way. He saw his brother just as he was, for he had the larger philosophic and interpretative insight; but Robert did not see him exactly. He could not fathom just what had happened to Lester in these years. Lester was stouter, not gray, for some reason, but sandy and ruddy, fairly optimistic in his mood or, if not that, complaisent—satisfied to take life as he found it. Lester looked at his brother with a keen, steady eye. The latter shifted a little, for he was restless. He could see that there was no loss of that mental force and courage which had always been his brother's predominant characteristics.

"I thought I'd like to see you again, Lester," he remarked, after they had clasped hands in the customary grip. "It's been a long time now—nearly twelve years, hasn't it?"

"About that," replied Lester. "How are things with you?"

"Oh, about the same. You've been fairly well, I see."

"Never sick," said Lester. "A little cold now and then. I don't often go to bed with anything. How's your wife?"

"Oh, Margaret's fine. And the children. We don't see much of Ralph and Berenice since they married, but the others are around, more or less. I suppose your wife is all right," he said hesitatingly. It was difficult ground for him.

Lester eyed him without a change of expression.

"Yes," he replied. "She enjoys pretty fair health. She's quite well at present."

They drifted mentally a few moments while Lester inquired after the business, and asked about Amy, Louise and Imogene. He admitted frankly that he neither saw nor heard from them nowadays. Robert told him what he could.

"The thing that I was thinking of in connection with you, Lester," said Robert, when they had got to the place where the real substance of the meeting had to come up, "is this matter of the Western Crucible Steel Works. You haven't been sitting there as a director in person, I notice, but your attorney Watson has been acting for you. Clever man, that. The management isn't right—we all know that. We need a practical steel man at the head of it, if the thing is ever going to pay properly. I have voted my stock with yours right along, because the propositions made by Watson have been right. He agrees with me that things ought to be changed. What I wanted to say to you was that I have a chance to buy seventy shares now held by Rossiter's widow. That, with yours and mine, would give us control of the company. I would like to have you take them if you wish, though it doesn't make a bit of difference so long as it's in the family. I would rather you would take them, if you don't mind. Then you can put any one you please in for president, and we'll make the thing come out right."

Lester smiled. It was a nice proposition. Watson had reported trouble. He had always reported Robert's interests as co-operating with his. Lester had long suspected that Robert would like to make up. This was the olive branch—the control of a property worth in the neighborhood of a million and a half.

"That's very nice of you," said Lester solemnly. "It's a rather liberal thing to do. What makes you want to do it now?"

"Well, to tell you the honest truth, Lester," replied Robert, "I never did feel right about that will business, after it was all over. I never did feel right about that secretary-treasurership and some other things that have happened. I don't want to rake up the past—you smile at that—but I feel that I ought to tell you how I feel. I've been pretty ambitious in the past. I was pretty ambitious just about the time father died to get this United Carriage scheme under way, and I was afraid you might not like it. I have thought since that I ought not to have done it, but I did, and I suppose you're not anxious to hear any more about that. This other thing, though—"

"—might be handed out as a sort of compensation," put in Lester, quietly.

"Not exactly that, Lester," said his brother, "though it may have something of that in it. I know these things don't matter very much to you now. I know that the time to do things was years ago—not now. Still I thought sincerely that you might be interested in this proposition. It might lead to other things. I thought it might patch things up between us, frankly. We're brothers, after all."

"Yes," said Lester, "we're brothers."

He was thinking, as he said this, of the irony of the situation—the sardonic quality of his own idea of this brotherhood. Here was Robert, worth perhaps six or seven millions (it was rumored that he was worth that much—no one really knew) coming to him, when he himself was worth between four and five millions, to make up for something which should have been made up when he was worth only ten thousand a year—and in danger of losing that. Robert had practically forced him into his present relationship, and while Jennie had been really the only one to suffer, he could not help feeling angry. Robert had not cut him out of his one-fourth of his father's estate, it is true, but he certainly had not helped him to get it. Perhaps his father had actually taken counsel with him—he could not tell. Anyhow, here they were, and now Robert was thinking that this offer of his might mend things. It hurt him—Lester—a little. It irritated him. Life was strange.

"I can't see it, Robert," he said finally and determinedly. "I can appreciate the motive that prompts you to make the offer. But I can't see the wisdom of my taking it. Your opportunity is your opportunity. I don't want it. We can make all the changes you suggest if you take the stock. I'm rich enough anyhow. It's a sop on your part to plaster an old wound. I wouldn't, if I were you, make any such offer, Robert. I wouldn't think anything about it. I'd stand by my guns. By-gones are by-gones. I'm perfectly willing to talk with you from time to time. That's all you want. This other thing is simply a check to buy friendship with. So far as I'm concerned you have that. I don't hold any grudge against you. I won't."

Robert looked at him fixedly. He half smiled. He admired Lester, in spite of all that he had done to him—in spite of all that Lester was saying to him now.

"I don't know but what you're right, Lester, after all," he said. "I didn't make this offer in any petty spirit, though. I wanted to patch up this matter of feeling between us. I won't say anything more about it. You're not coming down to Cincinnati soon, are you?"

"I don't expect to," replied Lester.

"If you do I'd like to have you come and stay with us. Bring your wife. We could talk over old times."

Lester smiled an enigmatic smile.

"I'll be glad to," he said, without emotion. But he recalled that in the days of Jennie it had been different. They would never have receded from their stand in regard to her. "Well," he thought, "perhaps I can't blame them. Let it go."

They talked on about other things. Finally Lester remembered an appointment. "I'll have to leave you soon," he said, looking at his watch.

"I ought to go, too," said Robert. They rose. "Well, anyhow," he added, as they walked toward the cloak room, "we won't be absolutely strangers in the future, will we?"

"Not absolutely, no. Certainly not," said Lester. "I'll see you from time to time," and they separated amicably. There was a sense of unsatisfied obligation and some remorse in Robert's mind as he left. He stood on the steps of the club for a moment, as his carriage was turning in, thinking. Lester was an able man. Why was it that there was so much feeling between them—had been even before Jennie had appeared? Then he remembered his old thoughts about "snaky deeds." That was what his brother lacked, and that only. He was not crafty; not darkly cruel—hence. "What a world!" he thought.

On his part Lester went away feeling a slight sense of opposition to, but also sympathy for, his brother. Robert was not so terribly bad—not different from other men. He had refused to work with him at a time when that work might have resulted in big things for both, but he had been playing for big stakes at that time. Why criticize? What would he have done if he had been in Robert's place? Robert was getting along. So was he. He could see how it all came about—why he had been made the victim, why his brother had been made the keeper of the great fortune. "It's the way the world runs," he thought. "What difference does it make? I have enough to live on. Why not let it go at that?"

CHAPTER LIX

The days of man under the old dispensation, or, rather, according to that supposedly biblical formula, which persists, are threescore years and ten. It is so ingrained in the race-consciousness by mouth-to-mouth utterance that it seems the profoundest of truths. As a matter of fact, man, even under his mortal illusion, is organically built to last five times the period of his maturity and would last as long as the spirit that is in him if he but knew that it is spirit which persists, that age is an illusion, that there is no death. Yet the race-thought, gained from what dream of materiality we know not, persists, and the death of man, under the mathematical formula so fearfully accepted, is daily registered.

Lester was one who believed in this formula. He was under the illusion that we must die as prescribed. Everybody did. Why not he? He was nearing sixty. He thought he had, say, twenty years more at the utmost to live—perhaps not so long. Well, he had lived comfortably. He felt that he could not complain. If death was coming, let it. He was ready at any time. No complaint or resistance would issue from him. Life, in most of its aspects, was a silly show anyhow.

He admitted that it was mostly illusion—easily proved to be so. That it might all be illusory he sometimes suspected. It was very much like a dream in its composition—truly—sometimes like a very bad dream. All he had to sustain him in his acceptance of its reality, from hour to hour and day to day, was apparent contact with this or that material proposition—people, meetings of boards of directors, individuals and organizations planning to do this and that, his wife's social functions. Letty loved him as a fine, grizzled example of a philosopher. She admired, as Jennie had, his solid, determined, phlegmatic attitude in the face of troubled circumstance. All the winds of fortune or misfortune could not apparently excite or disturb Lester. He refused to be frightened. He refused to budge from his beliefs and feelings, and usually had to be pushed away from them, still believing, if he were gotten away at all. He refused to do anything save, as he always said, "Look the facts in the face," and fight. He could be made to fight easily enough if imposed upon, but only in a stubborn, resisting way. His plan was to resist every effort to coerce him to the last ditch. If he had to let go in the end, he would—when compelled—but his views as to the value of not letting go were quite the same, even when he had let go under compulsion.

His views of living were still decidedly material—well-grounded in creature comforts, and he still wanted, as he always had, the best of everything. If the furnishings of his home became the least bit dingy, he was for having them torn out and sold and the house done over. If he travelled, it must be exclusive of annoyance as far as possible. Money must go ahead of him and smooth the way. He did not want argument, useless talk, or "silly palaver," as he called it. Everyone must discuss interesting topics with him or not talk at all. Letty understood him thoroughly. She would chuck him under the chin mornings, or shake his solid head between her hands, telling him he was a brute, but a nice kind of a brute. "Yes, yes," he would growl. "I know. I'm an animal, I suppose. You're a seraphic suggestion of attenuated thought."

"Now, you hush," she would reply, for he could cut like a knife without really meaning to be unkind. Then he would pet her a little, as he had Jennie, for after all, and in spite of her vigorous conception of life, and her understanding of how things should be (and were not), she was, he realized, more or less dependent on him. It was always so plain to her that he could get along without her. For reasons of kindliness he was trying to conceal this, to pretend the necessity of her presence, but it was so obvious that he really could dispense with her easily enough. Now Letty did depend upon Lester. It was something, in so shifty and uncertain a world, for her to be near so fixed and determined a quantity as this bear-man. It was like being near a warmly glowing lamp in the dark or a bright-burning fire in the cold. Lester was not afraid of anything. He felt that he knew how to live and to die.

It was natural that a temperament of this kind should have its solid, material manifestation at every point. Having his financial affairs well in hand, most of his holding being shares of tremendous companies, where boards of solemn directors merely approved the strenuous efforts of ambitious executives to "make good," he had leisure for living. He and Letty were fond of visiting various American and European watering places—American, principally, in the early pressure of his affairs—Hot Springs, Arkansas; Hot Springs, Virginia; Saratoga, San Bernardino, Palm Beach; and, in Europe, Baden-Baden, Carlsbad, Scheveningen, Monte Carlo, the Riviera. He was inclined to gamble some, for he found that there was considerable diversion in risking interesting sums on the spin of a wheel or the fortuitous roll of a ball; and he took more and more to drinking, not in the sense that a drunkard takes to it, but as a high liver, socially, with all his friends, on every occasion and for every greeting. He was inclined to drink the rich drinks when he did not take straight whiskey—champagne, sparkling Burgundy, the expensive and effervescent white wines. When he drank he could drink a great deal, and he ate in proportion. Nothing must be served but the best—soup, fish, entrée, roast, game, dessert—everything that made up a showy dinner—and he had long since determined that only a high-priced chef was worth while. They had found a *cordon bleu,* Louis Berdot, who had served in the house of one of the great dry-goods princes, and this man he engaged. He cost Lester a hundred dollars a week, but his reply to any question was that he only had one life to live.

The trouble with this situation and this attitude was that it adjusted nothing, improved nothing, left everything to drift on toward an indefinite end. If Lester had married Jennie and accepted the very meagre income for him of ten thousand a year, he would have maintained this very same attitude to the end. It would have led him to a stolid indifference to the social world of which, now, necessarily he was a part. He would have drifted on with a few mentally compatible cronies who would have accepted him for what he was—a good fellow—and Jennie, in the end, would not have been so much better off than she was now.

One of the changes which was interesting was that the Kanes transferred their residence to New York. Mrs. Kane had become very intimate with a group of clever women in the eastern Four Hundred, or Nine Hundred, and had been advised and urged to transfer the scene of her activities to New York. She finally did so, leasing a house in 78th Street, near Madison Avenue. She installed, as a novelty for her, a complete staff of liveried servants, after the English fashion, and had the rooms of her house done in correlative periods. Lester smiled at her vanity and love of show.

"You talk about your democracy," he grunted one day. "You have as much democracy as I have religion, and that's none at all."

"Why, how you talk!" she denied. "I am democratic. We all run in classes. You do. I'm merely accepting the logic of the situation."

"The logic of your grandmother! Do you call a butler and doorman in red velvet a part of the necessity of the occasion?"

"I certainly do," she replied. "Maybe not the necessity exactly but the spirit, surely. Why should you quarrel? You're the first one to insist on perfection—to quarrel if there is any flaw in the order of things."

"You never heard me quarrel."

"Oh, I don't mean that literally. But you demand perfection—the exact spirit of the occasion, and you know it."

"Maybe I do, but what has that to do with your democracy?"

"I am democratic. I insist on it. I'm as democratic in spirit as any woman. Only I see things as they are, and conform as much as possible for comfort's sake, and so do you. Don't you throw rocks at my glass house, Mister-Master. Yours is so transparent I can see every move you make inside."

"I'm democratic and you're not," he teased, but he approved thoroughly of everything she did. She was, he sometimes fancied, a better executive in her world than he was in his.

Drifting in this fashion, wining, dining, drinking the waters of this curative spring and that, travelling to this city and that meeting, finally altered his body from a vigorous, quick-moving, well-balanced organism into one where plethora of substance was clogging every necessitous function. His liver, kidneys, spleen, pancreas—every organ, in fact—had been overtaxed for some time, keeping up the digestion, construction, elimination of the nutrients and wastes of his body. In the past seven years he had become uncomfortably heavy. His kidneys were weak, and so were the arteries of his brain. By dieting, proper exercise, the right mental attitude he might have lived to be eighty or ninety. As a matter of fact, he was slowly allowing himself to drift into the place where any catspaw of disease would carry him off quickly. The eventual result, the second year after he had removed to New York, was just that.

It so happened that he and Letty had gone to the North Cape on a cruise with a group of society friends. Lester, because of business details which Watson had frequently called to his attention, decided to return to Chicago late in November and let his wife go on to Europe alone. She would meet him in New York just before the Christmas holidays. What he had to do would require about two weeks of his time, and after that he would be free. He wrote Watson to expect him and engaged rooms at the Auditorium. Having sold his Chicago residence, he had no local stopping place.

One late November day, after having attended to a number of details and cleared up his affairs very materially, Lester was seized with what the doctor who was called to attend him described as a cold in the intestines—a symptom usually indicative of some other weakness, either of the blood or of some organ. Why he came to contract it was not obvious. It caused him great pain at once, however, and the usual remedies in that case were applied. There were bandages of red flannel with a mustard dressing. Some specifics were administered. He seemed to find some relief, but curiously he was troubled with a sense of impending disaster. He had Watson, who was with him most of the time, cable his wife—there was nothing serious about it, but he was ill. He had, at the advice of his physician, accepted the services of a trained nurse. His Japanese valet, Kozo, stood guard at the door to prevent annoyance of any kind. It was plain that Letty could not reach Chicago in under three weeks. He had the feeling that he would not see her again.

Curiously, not only because he was in Chicago, but because he had never been separated from Jennie mentally, he was thinking about her constantly at this time. He had intended to go out and see her, just as soon as he was through with his business engagements and before he left the city. He had asked Watson how she was getting along and had been informed that everything was well with her. She was living quietly and looking in good health, Watson said. Lester wished he could see her.

This thought grew as the days passed and he grew no better. He was suffering from time to time with severe attacks of griping pains that seemed to tie his viscera into knots and left him weak. Several times the physician had administered cocaine with a needle in order to relieve him of useless pain.

After one of the severe attacks he called Watson to his side, asked him to send the nurse away, and then said, "Watson, I'd like to have you do me a favor. Ask Mrs. Stover if she won't come here to see me. You'd better go and get her. And I advise you to send the nurse and Kozo away for the afternoon, or while she's here. If she comes at any other time I'd like to have her admitted."

Watson understood. He liked this expression of sentiment.

He was sorry for Jennie. He was sorry for Lester. He wondered what the world would think if it could know of this bit of romance in connection with so prominent a man. Lester was decent. He had made Watson prosperous. The latter was only too glad to serve him in any way.

He called a carriage and rode out to Jennie's residence at once. He found her watering some plants, her face expressive of surprise at his unusual presence.

"I come on a rather troublesome errand, Mrs. Stover," he said, using her local name. "Your—that is, Mr. Kane, is quite sick at the Auditorium—his wife is in Europe, and he wanted to know if I wouldn't come out here and ask you to come and see him. He wanted me to bring you, if possible. Could you come with me now?"

"Why, yes," said Jennie, her face a study. The children were in school. An old Swedish housekeeper, Mrs. Swenson, was in the kitchen. Jennie could go as well as not. But there was coming back to her in detail a dream she had had several nights before. It appeared, according to that dream, that she was out on a dark, mystic body of water, how or in what vessel was not clear, but there was water—still and smooth and lovely everywhere—a vast body of silent water over which was hanging something like a fog, only it appeared to be more of a pall of smoke or haze. She heard the water ripple, or sigh or stir faintly, and then out of the surrounding darkness a boat appeared. It was a little boat, oarless, or not visibly propelled, and in it were her mother and Vesta and someone whom she could not make out. Her mother's face was pale and sad, very much as she had often seen it in life. She looked at Jennie solemnly, sympathetically, and then suddenly Jennie realized that the third occupant of the boat was Lester. He looked at her gloomily, an expression she had never seen on his face before, and then her mother remarked, "Well, we must go now." The boat began to move, and a great sense of loss came over her, and she cried, "Oh, don't leave me, Mama."

But her mother only looked at her out of deep, sad, still eyes, and the boat was gone.

She woke with a start, half fancying that Lester was beside her. She stretched out her hand to touch his arm and then drew herself up in the dark and rubbed her eyes, realizing that she was alone. There was a great sense of depression still holding her.

After awhile she lay back, but the gloom would not leave. For two days it haunted her and then, when it seemed as if it were nothing, Mr. Watson appeared with his ominous message.

She went to dress and in a little while reappeared, looking as troubled as were her thoughts. She was very pleasing in her appearance yet, a sweet, kindly woman, well-dressed and shapely. She had never been separated mentally from Lester, just as he had never grown entirely away from her. She was always with him in thought, just as in the years when they were together. Her fondest memories were of the days when he first courted her in Cleveland—the days when he had seized her, much as the cave man had seized his mate—by force. Now she longed to do what she could for him. For this call was as much a testimony as a shock. He loved her—he loved her after all.

The carriage rolled briskly through the long streets into the smoky downtown district. The day was gray and sombre. The carriage arrived at the Auditorium, and Jennie was escorted to Lester's room. Watson had been considerate. He had talked little, leaving her to her thoughts. In this great hotel she felt diffident after so long a period of almost complete retirement. As she entered the room she looked at Lester with large, gray, sympathetic eyes. He was lying propped up on two pillows, his solid head with its growth of once dark brown hair slightly grayed. He looked at her curiously out of his wise old eyes, a light of sympathy and affection shining in them—weary as they were. Jennie was greatly distressed. His pale face, slightly drawn from suffering, cut her like a knife. She took his hand, which was outside the coverlet, and pressed it. She leaned over and kissed his lips.

"I'm so sorry, Lester," she murmured. "I'm so sorry. You're not very sick though, are you?"

"Yes, I'm pretty bad," he said. "I don't feel right about this illness. I don't seem to be able to shake it off. How have you been?"

"Oh, just the same, dear," she replied. "I'm all right. You mustn't talk like that, though. You're going to be all right very soon now."

He smiled grimly. "I don't think so. Sit down. I want to talk to you. I'm not worrying about getting well. I want to talk to you again."

She drew up a chair close beside the bed, her face toward his, and took his hand. It seemed such a beautiful thing that he should send for her. Her eyes showed the mingled sympathy, affection and gratitude. At the same time fear was in her heart.

"I can't tell what may happen," he went on. "Letty is in Europe. I've wanted to see you again for some time. I was coming out this trip. We are living in New York, you know. You're a little stouter."

"Yes, I'm getting old, Lester," she smiled.

"Oh, that doesn't make any difference," he replied, looking at her fixedly. "Age doesn't count. We are all in that boat. It's how we feel about life."

He stopped and stared at the ceiling. A slight twinge of pain reminded him of the vigorous seizures he had been through. He couldn't stand many more paroxysms like the last one.

"I've always wanted to say to you, Jennie," he went on when the pain had ceased, "that I haven't been satisfied with the way we parted. It wasn't the right thing after all. I haven't been any happier. I'm sorry. I wish now, for my own peace of mind, that I hadn't done it."

"Don't say that, Lester," she demurred. "It's all right. It doesn't make any difference. You've been very good to me. I wouldn't have been satisfied to have you lose your fortune. It couldn't be that way. I've been a lot better satisfied as it is. It's been hard, but, dear, everything is hard at times." She paused.

"No," he said. "It wasn't right. The thing wasn't worked out right from the start, but that wasn't your fault. I'm sorry. I wanted to tell you that. I'm glad I'm here to do it."

"Don't talk that way, Lester,—please don't," she pleaded. "It's all right. You needn't be sorry. There's nothing to be sorry for. You have always been good to me. Why, when I think—" she pressed his hands. She was recalling the house he took for her family in Cleveland, the manner in which he had let Gerhardt come, the money he had supplied her since.

"Well, I've told you now, and I feel better. You're a good woman, and you're kind to come this way. I loved you. I love you now. I want to tell you that. It seems strange, but you're the only woman I ever did love truly. We should never have parted."

Jennie caught her breath. It was the one thing she had waited for all these years—this testimony. It was the one thing that could make everything right—this confession of spiritual if not material union. Now she could live happily. Now die so. "Oh, Lester," she exclaimed with a sob, and pressed his hand. He returned the pressure. There was a little silence. Then he spoke again.

"How are the two orphans?" he asked.

"Oh, they're fine," she answered, entering upon a detailed description of their diminutive personalities. He listened comfortably, for her voice was soothing to him. Her whole personality was grateful to him. When it came time for her to go he seemed desirous of keeping her.

"Going, Jennie?" he asked.

"I can stay just as well as not, Lester," she volunteered. "I'll take a room. I can send a note out to Mrs. Swenson. It will be all right."

"You needn't do that," he said, but she could see that he wanted her, that he did not want to be alone.

From that time on until the hour of his death she was not out of the hotel.

CHAPTER LX

The end came after four days during which Jennie, as a friend of his wife's apparently, watched over him as she had always watched over everything which commanded her love, sympathy or sense of duty. She was by his bed constantly, never leaving it longer than was required to do some necessary thing. The nurse in charge welcomed her at first as a relief and as company, but the physician was inclined to object. Lester was stubborn. "This is my death," he said to Watson, with a touch of grim humor. "If I'm dying I ought to be allowed to die in my own way."

Watson smiled at the man's unfaltering courage. He had never seen anything like it before.

There were cards of sympathy, calls, notices in the newspapers. Robert saw an item in the *Enquirer* and decided to go to Chicago. Imogene called with her husband, and they were admitted to Lester's room for a few minutes, after Jennie had gone to hers. Lester had little to say. The nurse cautioned them that he was not to be talked to much. When they were gone Lester said to

Jennie, "Imogene has changed a good deal." He made no other comment.

Mrs. Kane was on the Atlantic, three days out from New York, the afternoon Lester died. He had been meditating whether anything more could be done for Jennie, but he did not see what. It was useless to leave her wealth. She did not want it. He was wondering where Letty was, how near her actual arrival might be, when he was seized with a tremendous paroxysm of pain. Before relief could be administered in the shape of an anesthetic, he was dead. It developed afterward that it was not the intestinal trouble which killed him, but a lesion of a major blood vessel in the brain. Blood was in his mouth and nose, and there was a spot of blood on his upper lip when Jennie, who was serving him at the time, came running with a fresh hot bandage which she had sought to prepare.

Jennie, who had been wrought up by watching and worrying, was beside herself with grief. He had been a part of her thought and feeling so long that it seemed now as though a part of herself had died. She had loved him as she had fancied she could never love any one, and he had always shown that he cared some. These late years had been a great trial, but after all he was not to blame. She could not feel the emotion that expresses itself in tears—only a dull ache, a numbness which seemed to make her insensible to pain. He looked so strong—her Lester, lying there still in death. His expression was unchanged—defiant, determined, albeit peaceful. Word had come from Mrs. Kane that she would arrive on the Wednesday following, and this was Saturday. It was decided to hold the body. Jennie learned from Mr. Watson that it was to be transferred not to New York but to Cincinnati, where the Paces had a vault. Because of the arrival of various members of the family, Jennie withdrew to her home; she could do nothing more.

The final ceremonies presented a peculiar commentary on the anomalies of existence. For instance it was arranged by wire with Mrs. Kane, when she reached New York, that the body should be transferred to Imogene's residence and the funeral held from there. Robert, who arrived the night Lester died; Berry Dodge; Imogene's husband, Mr. Midgely; and three other citizens of prominence were selected as pall bearers. Louise and her husband came from Buffalo; Amy and her husband from Cincinnati.

The house was full to overflowing with citizens who either sincerely wished to call, or felt it expedient to do so. Because of the fact that Lester and his family were nominally Catholic, a Catholic priest was called in and the ritual of that church was carried out. It was curious to see Lester lying in the parlor of this alien residence, candles at his head and feet, burning sepulchrally, a silver cross upon his breast caressed by his waxen fingers. He would have smiled if he could have seen himself, but the Kane family was too conventional, too set in its convictions, to see anything strange in this. The Church made no objection, of course. The family was distinguished. What more could be desired?

On Wednesday Mrs. Kane arrived. She was greatly distraught, for her love, like Jennie's, was sincere. She left her room that night, when all was silent, and leaned over the coffin, studying by the light of the burning candles Lester's interesting features. Tears trickled down her cheeks, for she had been happy with him. She caressed his cold cheeks and hands. "Poor, dear Lester," she whispered. "Poor, brave soul!" No one told her that he had sent for Jennie. The Kane family did not know.

Meanwhile, in the house on South Park Avenue, sat a woman who was enduring alone the feelings which this final climax brought to her. Now, after all these years, the subtle hope that had persisted in spite of every circumstance—that somehow life might bring him back to her—was gone. He had come to her, it is true—he really had come in death, but he had gone again. Where? Where her mother, where Gerhardt, where Vesta had gone. She did not see how she was to see him again, for the papers informed her of his removal to Mrs. Midgely's residence, and of the fact that he was to be taken from Chicago to Cincinnati for burial. The last ceremonies in Chicago were to be held in one of the wealthy Roman Catholic churches of the North Side, St. Michael's, of which the Midgelys were members.

Jennie was overawed. She would have liked so much to have gone and seen him again, to have had him buried in Chicago, where she could go to the grave occasionally, but this was not to be. She was never a master of her fate. Others invariably controlled. She thought of him as being removed from her finally by this process, as though distance made a difference. She decided at last to veil herself heavily and go to the church, where she could at least see him brought in. The paper had explained that the services would be at two in the afternoon; that at four the body would be taken to the depot of the Cleveland, Cincinnati, Chicago & St. Louis Railway and transferred to the train; and that the various members of the family would accompany it to Cincinnati. She thought of this as another opportunity. She might go to the depot.

A little before the time for the funeral cortège to arrive at the church, there appeared at one of its subsidiary entrances a woman in black, heavily veiled, who took a seat in an inconspicuous corner of the church. She was a little nervous, seeing that the church was dark and empty, lest she had mistaken the time and place; but after ten minutes of painful suspense a bell in the church tower began to toll solemnly. Shortly thereafter an acolyte in black gown and white surplice appeared and lighted groups of candles on either side of the altar. A hushed stirring of feet in the choir-loft indicated that there was to be requiem of some form for the dead. Some loiterers attracted by the bell, some strangers taken by the show of any funeral, some acquaintances and citizens not directly invited appeared and took seats.

Jennie watched all this with wondering gaze. Although she had lived all these years, she had never been inside a Catholic church. The gloom, the beauty of the windows, the whiteness of the altar, the golden flames of the candles impressed her. She was suffused with a sense of sorrow, loss, beauty and mystery. Life in all its vagueness and uncertainty seemed typified by this scene.

As the bell tolled there came from the sacristy to the left of the altar a procession of altar boys, dressed as had been the one who had lighted the candles. The smallest, an angelic youth of eleven, came first, bearing aloft a magnificent silver cross. In the hands of each subsequent pair of servitors was held a tall, lighted candle. The priest, in black cloth and lace, an open book in his hand, attended by an acolyte on either side, followed. The procession passed out the entrance into the vestibule of the church and was not seen again until the choir began a mournful, responsive chant, the Latin supplication for mercy and peace.

Then, at this sound, the solemn procession made its reappearance. There came the silver cross, the candles, the dark-faced priest, reading dramatically to himself as he walked, and the body of Lester, in a great black coffin with silver handles, carried by the pall bearers, who kept an even pace. Jennie stiffened perceptibly, her nerves running as with an electric current. She did not know any of these men. She did not know Robert. She had never seen Mr. Midgely. Of the long company of notables who followed two by two, she recognized only three, whom Lester had pointed out to her in times past. Mrs. Kane she saw, of course, for she was directly behind the coffin, leaning on the arm of a stranger, and Mr. Watson, who came farther along, solemn, gracious. He gave a quick glance to either side, evidently expecting to see her somewhere, but not finding her, he turned his eyes gravely forward and looked no more. Jennie followed it all, her heart in her mouth, for she seemed so much a part of this solemn ritual, and yet infinitely removed from it all.

The procession reached the altar rail, and the coffin was put down. A white shroud bearing the insignia of suffering, a black cross, was put over it, and the great candles were set beside it. There were the chanted invocations and responses, the sprinkling of the coffin with holy water, the lighting and swinging of censer, the mumbled responses of the auditors to the Lord's Prayer and to its Catholic addition, the invocation to the Blessed Virgin. Jennie was overawed and amazed, but no show of form—colorful, impressive, imperial—could take away the sting of death—of infinite loss. To Jennie the candles, the incense, the holy song were beautiful. They touched the deep chord of melancholy in her and made it vibrate through the depths of her being. She was as a house filled with mournful melody and the sense of death. She cried and cried. She could see, curiously, that Mrs. Kane was sobbing convulsively also.

When it was all over, the carriages were entered and the body borne to the depot. All of the guests and strangers departed, and finally, when all was silent, she arose. Now she would go to the depot also, for she was hopeful of seeing his body put on the train. They would have to bring it out on the platform. They did Vesta's. She took a car, and a little while later entered the waiting room of the depot, apprehensive lest she should be detected, but really safer than she thought.

The Kane family were scarcely aware of her existence any more. Mrs. Kane and Watson were too grieved and employed to bother at this point. She hung about, first in the concourse, where a great iron fence separated the passengers from the tracks, and then in the waiting room, hoping to discover the order of proceedings. She finally observed the group of immediate relatives waiting—Mrs. Kane, Robert, Mr. Midgely, Louise, Amy, Imogene, and a score of local residents who had come here to see them off. She did her best to identify them to herself as Robert, Amy, Imogene; and she succeeded, though it was not knowledge in this case but instinct and belief.

No one had noticed it, in the stress of excitement, but it was Thanksgiving Eve. Throughout the great railroad station there was a hum of anticipation, that curious ebullition of fancy which springs from the thought of pleasures to come. People were going away over the holiday. There was a great crowd of those who had baskets and bundles and a somewhat lesser crowd of those carrying handsome suit-cases and travelling-bags. Carriages were at the station entries. Announcers were calling in stentorian voices the destination of each new train as the time of its departure drew near. Jennie heard with a desperate ache the description of a route which she and Lester had taken more than once, slowly and melodiously emphasized. "Detroit, Toledo, Cleveland, Buffalo, and New York." There were cries of trains for "Fort Wayne, Columbus, Pittsburgh, Philadelphia, and points east," and then finally for "Indianapolis, Columbus, Cincinnati, Louisville, and points south." The hour had struck.

Several times Jennie had gone to the concourse between the waiting room and the tracks to see if, through the iron grating which separated her from her beloved, she could get one last look at the coffin, or the great wooden box which held it, before it was put on the train. It had not been there before. Now, however, she saw it coming. There was a baggage porter pushing a truck forward into position near the place where it was calculated the baggage car would stop. On it was Lester, that last shadow of his substance, encased in the honors of wood and cloth and silver. There was no thought on the part of the porter of the agony of loss which was here represented. He could not see how wealth and position, in this hour, were represented to her mind as a great force, a wall, which divided her eternally from her beloved. Had it not always been so? Was not her life a patchwork of conditions made and affected by these things which she saw—wealth and force— which had found her unfit? She had evidently been born to yield, not seek. This panoply of power had been paraded before her since childhood. What could she do now but stare vaguely after as it marched triumphantly by? Lester had been of it. Him it respected. Of her it knew nothing. She looked through the grating, and once more there came the cry of "Indianapolis, Columbus, Cincinnati, Louisville, and points south." A long red train, brilliantly lighted, composed of baggage cars, day coaches, a dining car set with white linen and silver, and a half-dozen comfortable Pullmans rolled in and stopped. A great black engine, puffing and glowing, had it all safely in tow.

As the baggage car drew near the waiting truck, a train-hand in blue, looking out of the car, called to someone within.

"Hey, Jack! Give us a hand here. There's a stiff outside!"

Jennie could not hear.

All she could see was the great box that was so soon to disappear. All she could feel was that this train would start presently, and then it would all be over. The gates opened, the passengers poured in. There were Robert and Amy and Louise and Imogene and Midgely—all making for the Pullman cars in the rear. They had said their farewells to their friends. No need to repeat them. A trio of assistants "gave a hand" at getting the great wooden case into its proper position in the car. Jennie saw it disappear with an acute physical wrench at her heart.

There were many trunks to put in afterward, and then the door of the baggage car half closed, but not before the warning bell of the engine sounded. There was the insistent calling of "All aboard!" from this quarter and that; then slowly the great locomotive began to move. Its bell was ringing, its steam hissing, its smoke-stack throwing aloft a great black plume of smoke that fell back over the cars like a pall. The firemen, conscious of the heavy load behind, flung open a flaming furnace door to throw in coal. Its light glowed like a golden eye.

Jennie stood rigid, staring into the wonder of this picture, her face white, her eyes wide, her hands unconsciously clasped, but one thought in her mind—they were taking his body away. A leaden November sky was ahead, almost dark. She looked and looked, the swirling crowd about her, until the last glimmer of the red lamp on the receding sleeper disappeared in the maze of smoke and haze overhanging the tracks of the far-stretching yard.

"Yes," said the voice of a passing stranger, gay with the anticipation of coming pleasures. "We're going to have a great time down there. Remember Annie? Uncle Jim's coming and Aunt Ella."

Jennie did not hear that or anything else of the chatter and bustle around her. Before her was stretching a vista of lonely years down which she was steadily gazing. Now what? She was not so old yet. There were these two orphan children to raise. They would marry and leave after awhile, and then what? Days and days, an endless reiteration of days, and then—?

THE END.

HISTORICAL
COMMENTARY

THE COMPOSITION AND PUBLICATION OF
JENNIE GERHARDT

Theodore Dreiser began writing *Jennie Gerhardt* on 6 January 1901, two months after formal publication of *Sister Carrie*. The *Sister Carrie* debacle would eventually become one of the best-known episodes in American literary history, but when Dreiser began composing *Jennie Gerhardt* he did not yet know what the publication, and subsequent "suppression," of his first novel would some day come to stand for. Only with time and retelling would the story gather symbolic weight.

Dreiser had submitted *Sister Carrie* to Doubleday, Page and Company in the late spring of 1900. It had been read there by novelist Frank Norris, who worked as a reader and an adviser for the firm. Norris was enthusiastic and recommended publication; on the strength of his reaction Walter Hines Page, the junior partner, assured Dreiser that the book would be issued in the fall. But at this point Frank Doubleday, the senior partner, returned from a trip abroad and read *Sister Carrie* in typescript. Doubleday, perhaps because of his wife's influence, took the position that the book was "immoral" and attempted to have his house renege on its commitment to publish. Dreiser was stubborn, however, and forced Doubleday to issue the novel.

After some blue-pencilling to remove profanity, sexual frankness, and names of real persons and places, *Sister Carrie* was issued by Doubleday, Page and Company on 8 November 1900. Norris sent out approximately 127 review copies; notices were mixed, with some reviewers expressing alarm at the novel's grim subject matter and amoral tone but others praising its bluntness and realism. Doubleday, Page, however, did nothing further to promote *Sister Carrie*, and the novel died on the backlist. This episode, with some embellishment, would later be central to Dreiser's own various accounts of his literary career. Indeed, *l'affaire Doubleday* would become, through the 1920s, a rallying point for opponents of puritanism and comstockery in American letters.[1]

In January 1901, however, when Dreiser was just beginning *Jennie Gerhardt*, much of this was yet to happen. Dreiser was certainly aware that Doubleday was making no great effort to sell *Sister Carrie*, but his friends and supporters were still praising the book and were assuring him that it would make its own way commercially once the reading public discovered it. Thus when Dreiser began composing *Jennie Gerhardt* he was still in motion—confident of his ability to write important realistic fiction and keen to follow his strong first novel with an equally good (or a better) second effort. [2]

Sister Carrie had been based on the misadventures of Dreiser's sister Emma, who had become involved in Chicago in 1886 with a married man named L. A. Hopkins. Hopkins had stolen money from his employers and had fled with Emma to Canada. Traced there by the authorities, he had returned most of the money; then he and Emma had traveled to New York, where they lived together as man and wife. With this tawdry material as his beginning point, Dreiser had fashioned a moving story of displacement, seeking, and ultimate disillusionment in *Sister Carrie*.

When he began to cast about for material for his next novel, Dreiser turned to the story of another of his sisters—this time to the life of his oldest sister, Mary Frances (Maria Franziska) Dreiser, or "Mame" as she was known in the family. As a teenager Mame had become involved with a wealthy older man, whom Dreiser calls "Colonel Silsby" in his autobiographical volume *Dawn*. Colonel Silsby had given money and presents to Mame and had visited her at the Dreiser home in Terre Haute, Indiana. Eventually she became pregnant—probably by Colonel Silsby, although she could not be certain. She gave birth to a child, delivered in the Dreiser home by her own mother, but the baby was stillborn. Mrs. Dreiser buried the child's corpse in the back yard.

Several years later Mame fell in love with Austin Brennan, a high-living, good-natured traveling businessman. He was older than she and was from a well-to-do Irish family in Rochester, New York. Brennan's family did not approve of Mame, but he was very much attached to her, and he formed a relationship with her that would endure until he died many years later. They married (apparently) and lived together in Chicago during the mid-1890s. Eventually they moved to Rochester, and John Paul Dreiser, the patriarch of the family, came to live with them there during his last years, along with Carl Dreiser, the illegitimate son of Sylvia, another of Dreiser's sisters. John Paul had been enraged by Mame's loose behavior as a young woman, but he and she had resolved their differences. He lived with Mame and Brennan until his death on Christmas Day 1900, some twelve days before Dreiser began composing *Jennie Gerhardt.*

Working from this material, Dreiser made a strong beginning on his novel. He was living in New York on East End Avenue, along the East River. The apartment was reasonably comfortable, and he was being looked after by Sara White Dreiser, his attentive wife of two years. He had saved some money from free-lance magazine work and had decided to devote the winter of 1901 to writing this novel. By the first week of February he had finished ten chapters; by early spring he had completed forty chapters in holograph, thirty of which had been typed. This mode of composition was similar to the procedure he had followed while completing *Sister Carrie* the previous winter and spring. The holograph sheets that he was turning out, in fact, are identical physically to those he produced during the composition of *Sister Carrie.* Dreiser was using black pencil throughout and was writing on half-sheets of inexpensive wove paper. He had the first thirty chapters of this text typed by Anna Mallon's typing agency—the same agency he had used for the typing of *Sister Carrie.* [3]

At this point, with approximately half of his novel composed, Dreiser decided to seek a publisher. He went initially to George P. Brett at Macmillan. Though a native of Great Britain, Brett had become thoroughly Americanized and had committed himself to publishing native writers, especially regionalists and realists. He had been interested in *Sister Carrie* in 1900 and apparently had expressed a willingness to take over the book if Frank Doubleday would not publish it. Brett was therefore the logical man for Dreiser to approach first with his novel in progress.

Dreiser's initial goal was a two-book arrangement. He wanted to have *Sister Carrie* republished and to tie its reissue to the publication of *Jennie Gerhardt.* His idea at this point was to finish and publish *Jennie Gerhardt,* then to follow with a reissue of *Sister Carrie.* He wanted the publisher of *Jennie Gerhardt*—whoever that might turn out to be—to acquire the literary rights, printing plates, and back stock of *Sister Carrie* from Doubleday, Page and Company. Then the two books, *Jennie* and *Carrie,* could be brought together under one roof and marketed as a pair.

Brett had indeed admired *Sister Carrie,* but he seems to have been skeptical about undertaking Dreiser's proposed two-book plan. The story of the author's battle with Frank Doubleday—a publisher whose literary judgment and business instincts were admired in New York book circles—was making the rounds. This novel in progress by Dreiser, a narrative involving an illegitimate child and an extramarital relationship, promised to be at least as troublesome to publish as *Sister Carrie* had been. And too, Brett's confidence in Dreiser could not have been bolstered by this letter:

My Dear Mr. Brett:—

I desire to know if you would consider a portion of my new novel—the first fourteen chapters—with a view to advancing me $400⁰⁰, so that I might go forward with the work and complete it by midsummer. I have already written more than forty chapters, but an error in character analysis makes me wish to throw aside everything from my fifteenth chapter on and rewrite it with a view to making it more truthful and appealing. I shall save considerable of that which is already done, but the new parts will necessitate three and perhaps four months additional labor—an amount of time I shall not be able to give without raising 400⁰⁰ either through some such method as this or by means of special writing for the magazines—the latter requiring the abandonment of my work on the novel for the next two months and possibly more. I do not know whether you will consider this a foolish intrusion or not but I cannot resist the temptation to help myself this way, rather than abandon my story. I would supplement the chapters in question with a synopsis of the remainder of the story and in case of its eventual rejection, when completed, would be glad to make any arrangement which would look to the speedy return of your investment.[4]

Brett's response was to praise *Sister Carrie* but to decline to advance money to Dreiser on *Jennie Gerhardt*.[5] Dreiser was disappointed but continued to shop his novel in progress to publishers. He approached at least three other New York houses that spring—The Century Company, A. S. Barnes, and McClure Phillips—but no one would take him on. The past history of *Sister Carrie*, together with the subject matter of the book on which he was working, made Dreiser a bad risk for an established house.

Dreiser decided to spend the summer of 1901 in an attempt to escape. He would "rough it" with his friend Arthur Henry on Quirk Island just off the shore of Connecticut, near the town of Noank. Dreiser and Henry would be accompanied by their wives, and the arrangement would be similar to the one they had maintained during the summer of 1899, just before Dreiser had begun composing *Sister Carrie*. In the relaxed atmosphere on the island, Dreiser hoped to remedy the problems with his characters, recapture the thread of his narrative, and carry his novel to a conclusion. This planned summer idyll, however, turned sour almost from the beginning. Dreiser was testy and cantankerous, and the four adventurers found themselves incompatible. So unpleasant was Dreiser's behavior that Henry was moved to set it all down in a thinly disguised account published the following year as *An Island Cabin*. This account so angered Dreiser that he broke off his friendship with Henry and never afterward mended it, though the two men did stay in occasional contact.

Back in New York that fall, Dreiser approached other publishers. Ripley Hitchcock at D. Appleton and Company, an editor who eventually was to play a major role in the publication of *Jennie Gerhardt*, wrote to praise *Sister Carrie*. Hitchcock was interested in publishing a "less drastic" second novel—by which he meant a story by Dreiser less offensive to conservative literary tastes than *Sister Carrie* had been.[6] Certainly Hitchcock came with good credentials: he had handled Stephen Crane's work for Appleton and had seen *The Red Badge of Courage* and the revised *Maggie: A Girl of the Streets* into print during the mid-1890s. But Hitchcock's idea that the new novel should be "less drastic" seems to have made Dreiser wary, and nothing came of this initial overture.

Dreiser decided instead to sign with an up-and-coming publisher named J. F. Taylor, who had begun in the book trade a few years before by buying up remainder stock from other houses and hiring salesmen to peddle it door to door. Taylor had been successful enough with this approach to hire a full-time editor named Rutger B. Jewett (later Edith Wharton's editor at Appleton). Jewett's assignment was to develop a list of original fiction; Dreiser, he hoped, would be one of the featured authors on this list. Dreiser signed a contract with J. F. Taylor and Company in November 1901; under its terms the house was to reissue *Sister Carrie* and publish the novel in progress once it was completed. Taylor and Jewett seem to have believed strongly in Dreiser— strongly enough, at least, to agree to provide him with a stake on which to finish his novel. Dreiser was to receive one hundred dollars a month while working on the manuscript; publication was scheduled for the fall of 1902.[7]

Early in November 1901, Dreiser turned over what he had written of *Jennie Gerhardt* to Mary Fanton Roberts, a friend who had agreed to edit the chapters for him. He and his wife then left New York and headed south to Bedford, a small town in the Blue Ridge Mountains of Virginia. There Dreiser hoped to live cheaply and finish his manuscript. In Bedford he made some progress but found it difficult to concentrate. (He was by this point well into a period of neuresthenia, or "nerve sickness," which would eventually bring his work on *Jennie Gerhardt* to a halt and, at its nadir, drive him close to suicide.) He began to have problems now with J. F. Taylor: Jewett wrote from New York that Taylor thought it inadvisable to reissue *Sister Carrie* in its present form. Taylor was urging Dreiser to change the title and supply a rewritten ending in which Carrie would be punished somehow for her transgressions. Taylor had suggested that she suffer rejection from Ames or (in a later proposal) that she reject Ames out of shame for her tarnished past.[8] Even more disturbing was Taylor's insistence that the novel Dreiser was now writing have more "moral coloring" than *Sister Carrie* had exhibited.[9] The new heroine, he felt, should be made to pay for her malefactions. These various entreaties and instructions irritated Dreiser and distracted him from his task of composition.

Dreiser and Sara spent Christmas of 1901 with Sara's family in Missouri. After the holidays they headed south again, visiting several modest spring-water spas and settling finally for almost two months in the small town of Hinton, West Virginia. Dreiser made some headway there with the revision and cutting of his narrative and then moved on to Lynchburg, Virginia, in March 1902. He was there only briefly before traveling to Charlottesville, where he lived alone for two months and continued to labor at recasting what he had written. (Sara returned to her parents during this period.) Dreiser was able to send ten revised chapters to Jewett in April and to mail ten more chapters to a typist in New York City at about this time.[10]

In early June, Dreiser left Charlottesville and headed north on a walking trip, hoping that fresh air and exercise would help him forget his worries about the novel and his mounting debt to Taylor. Almost the only satisfactory development, from Taylor's point of view, had been the selection of a title. Dreiser had wanted *Jennie Gerhardt* but had compromised on *The Transgressor,* a title with appropriately moral overtones. (Dreiser probably also realized that this title could be read ironically.) In an effort to encourage Dreiser, Jewett had a dummy front cover and title page manufactured for *The Transgressor* and had the first two pages of the story typeset and printed.[11]

A second batch of ten typed chapters was now forwarded to Jewett, but he was not altogether pleased with them, finding them overelaborated and prolix. Dreiser, admitting that he was stymied, gave up all pretense of meeting the fall deadline. The June 1902 check for one hundred dollars was the last he would accept from Taylor; he now owed seven hundred dollars to the firm with no immediate prospect of repaying the money. He shelved his novel and began to look for ways of writing himself out of debt.[12] He seems to have thought for a time of switching to another publisher, and again he had some contact with Hitchcock, but nothing came of their discussions.

Part of the difficulty was that the characters in the earliest version of *Jennie Gerhardt* had not been especially attractive. In the first version of the story, Senator Brander seduced and impregnated Jennie and then left her, with hardly a second thought, to take an ambassadorial appointment abroad. Jennie gave birth to her child and went to work in a factory. Some while later, Lester Kane met her on the street and engaged her in conversation. He pried her story from her, learned of her family's plight, and persuaded her to accept money from him. Later still (and with some ambivalence) she accepted an invitation to dine with him at a hotel that catered to wealthy patrons who needed a place to stage assignations. The affair was not consummated at the hotel, but after more gifts from Lester and promises by him to provide for her family, Jennie relented and went with him to New York as his mistress. Lester eventually established her in an apartment in Chicago, where they were discovered (as in the published novel) by one of his sisters.

Lester was an unsympathetic figure in this earliest version of the novel; he was essentially a rake, with nothing of the philosophical bent and stubborn independence that make him likeable in the published novel. And Jennie was shallow and duplicitous, with a matter-of-fact attitude toward bartering her sexual assets that was far different from the dreamy mysticism that she exhibits in the book. It is no wonder, then, that publishers who read this ur-version of *Jennie Gerhardt* shied away from it. Dreiser did make rather much progress in revising and recasting the narrative while he was under contract to J. F. Taylor, managing to deepen Jennie's character and to make both Senator Brander and Lester considerably more sympathetic. Indeed, it might be said that he made a good start at turning the novel in the direction it would eventually follow. But he was unable to compose new material and push the novel ahead, distracted as he was by his "nerve troubles."

Dreiser therefore gave up his struggle with the manuscript, at least for the time being. His stipend from J. F. Taylor was at an end; he now needed to find other sources of income. Since 1897 he had been able to earn good money on short notice by producing free-lance articles and interviews for New York magazines. He returned to that market now but found it largely closed to him— because of adverse publicity from the *Sister Carrie* affair, he later came to think. In truth Dreiser's writing was not up to its usual level. He was already crippled by neuresthenia, which probably had been brought on by a combination of factors: his problems with *Sister Carrie,* his apprehensions about his new novel, his dissatisfaction with his marriage, and his father's death the year before.

Dreiser now began a long period of wandering that took him from Philadelphia to Brooklyn and eventually back to New York. He literally came down to his last few cents and even contemplated suicide before being rescued by his brother Paul, a successful songwriter and vaudeville performer. Paul paid for a six-week stay at the Olympia Sanitarium near Purchase, New York—a rehabilitation center for wealthy dissipators. Then, on a doctor's suggestion, Dreiser went to work for the New York Central Railroad as what he called an "amateur" laborer. Fresh air and the monotony of physical work, he thought, would help him regain his mental equilibrium. By Christmas 1903 Dreiser was over the worst of his troubles, and in early January 1904 he joined the staff of the *New York Daily News* as an assistant feature editor of the Sunday edition. Dreiser attempted to turn his experiences into a book, but the holograph manuscript, entitled "An Amateur Laborer," was never completed.[13] Instead Dreiser reentered the world of magazine journalism, working for a time at Street and Smith, then editing *Broadway Magazine,* and finally rising to the position of editor-in-chief of a group of Butterick magazines—a highly paid and demanding position. *Jennie Gerhardt,* during most of this period, was shelved.

In early 1905, Dreiser did make a brief attempt to resume his career as a novelist. Uppermost in his mind was a reissue of *Sister Carrie,* but he also wanted to complete *Jennie Gerhardt* and carry it through to publication. In February he again offered both books to Ripley Hitchcock, who was no longer with Appleton. Hitchcock had left that firm, which was in financial straits, and had signed on with A. S. Barnes and Company, a house noted for its success with textbooks. Hitchcock was still interested in Dreiser but was unable to muster much support at his firm. He sent a copy of the Doubleday edition of *Sister Carrie* to a reader for an opinion as to whether Barnes should reissue it. The reader, A. R. Cross, reported that he had been so offended by the book that he had "put it in the fire, not wishing anyone to see such a book in my house and believing it would do more harm than good in the village library." C. D. Barnes, president of A. S. Barnes and Company, wrote "Amen" in large black letters at the bottom of Cross's letter, which Hitchcock then forwarded to Dreiser. Clearly Dreiser was not to be published by Barnes, no matter what Hitchcock's opinion of his work might be.[14]

Dreiser seems to have realized by now that no major New York house would take him on. He therefore decided in 1906 to cast his lot with B. W. Dodge and Company, a fledgling firm. Ben Dodge was an amiable alcoholic who had been in and out of publishing for years. Now he was looking for books and financial backing. Dreiser had *Sister Carrie* ready for republication and *Jennie Gerhardt* under way, and he could invest money that he had been saving from his salary at Butterick. Dreiser and Dodge therefore entered into an agreement: Dreiser would buy into the company and become one of its directors; the firm in return would reissue *Sister Carrie.* The book duly appeared in May 1907, with a sales campaign orchestrated by Dreiser, and it received generally favorable reviews. It sold well enough for Dodge to order another impression; thereafter it went to Grosset and Dunlap for an inexpensive reprint. *Sister Carrie* was now back in the public eye, but Dreiser was no closer to finishing *Jennie Gerhardt* than he had been five years before.[15]

Dreiser did manage during this period to make a new friend from among the tribe of Barabbas—the British publisher Grant

Richards, who had been an early admirer of *Sister Carrie*. Richards was recovering from a publishing failure and had been casting about in England for financial backing to begin another house. In February 1908 Dreiser sent his twenty revised chapters of *Jennie Gerhardt* to Richards, who praised them and began to press Dreiser to let him have rights for British publication. Dreiser held back, though, sensing (correctly, as it turned out) that an American house taking on *Jennie* might want to retain these rights for its own British subsidiary.[16]

In the spring of 1908 Dreiser met H. L. Mencken, a man who was to play a major role in his literary career and with whom he would form a complex, symbiotic relationship. Mencken was another admirer of *Sister Carrie*, and he began to encourage Dreiser to return to the writing of fiction. Grant Richards was urging the same thing, but the pressures of domestic life and of work at Butterick left Dreiser with no time for sustained creative work. A letter from Sara Dreiser to Richards, who had been urging her to get Dreiser back to his writing desk, reveals how difficult it would have been for him to devote significant energy to literary composition:

I have done all I can—not to become an irritation—toward urging him to get at it. I believe there is only one way to do it. That is for him to take two weeks or a month off, go way away from any possible communications with the Magazines & let him read & re-read all that is written until he is full of it all again—then he could write a chapter or two perhaps a week, and in that way it would soon be finished. You see there is much written that you haven't seen—It just isn't in good order. But the difficulty is getting him away from the Magazines. In four or five years he has had but one vacation of as much as a week's length. And he works over time every day & reads mss. every night and Sundays & Holidays. I have proposed this solution to him & he agrees that it would only take a little while to finish it if he could only begin again. I have also threatened to finish it myself if he doesn't soon. The plot is so clear & so perfect it seems to me that anyone could.[17]

Ironically, it was marital difficulty that caused Dreiser finally to break free of his job at Butterick and resume his career as a novelist. In the fall of 1909 he became infatuated with Thelma Cudlipp, the young daughter of Annie Ericsson Cudlipp, who was in charge of the Butterick typing pool. Dreiser's attachment to

Thelma came to light the following spring and became inter-mixed with office politics. In September 1910 he was given an ultimatum: either cease his attentions to Thelma or give up his job. Weary of office disputes and fed up with enervating editorial work, Dreiser resigned as of 15 October 1910. Seeking to make a clean break with his recent past, he also separated from Sara and took a rented room in the Riverside Drive apartment of Elias Rosenthal, a respected New York attorney, and his family.

Dreiser seems briefly to have considered reentering the magazine or book-publishing worlds in some managerial or editorial capacity, but he was in good enough financial condition to make an attempt at finishing *Jennie Gerhardt*. He was thirty-nine years old and seems to have sensed that this might be his last chance to launch a career as a writer. He therefore brought out the completed chapters of *Jennie Gerhardt* and began to show them around. His experience at Butterick had taught him the wisdom of dealing with editors through an intermediary, so this time he used a literary agent, Flora Mai Holly, to place his book.

At this point—November of 1910—Ripley Hitchcock made another appearance. He had moved on from A. S. Barnes to Harper and Brothers, a more appropriate house for Dreiser's work. Hitchcock was now willing to talk about a two-book contract for *Jennie Gerhardt* and *Sister Carrie*, provided that publication rights for the latter novel could be secured from B. W. Dodge. He encouraged Dreiser but, significantly, did not yet offer a contract. Dreiser was pleased but, in the absence of a formal agreement, did not feel himself bound to Harpers.

In a burst of optimism Dreiser predicted that he would have *Jennie Gerhardt* completed by 1 December. He was unable to finish the book that quickly, but by working steadily he did manage to produce a completed version by early January 1911. Dreiser showed this version to several persons whose literary judgment he trusted. Among them was Elias Rosenthal's daughter, Lillian, who praised the novel but advised Dreiser to have Lester marry Letty Gerald rather than Jennie. "Poignancy is a necessity in this story," she wrote in her critique, "and it can only be maintained by persistent want on the part of Jennie. The loss of Lester would insure this."[18]

Another reader was Fremont Rider, who had worked with Dreiser at B. W. Dodge and Company, at the *Bohemian*, and in the Butterick offices. Rider's letter to Dreiser no longer survives (apparently Dreiser sent it to B. W. Dodge, who forgot to return it), but in it Rider must also have urged Dreiser not to allow Jennie and Lester to marry. Dreiser agreed:

My Dear Rider:

I'm so much obliged for your interesting criticism for it is sincere, sound & helpful. I had already made up my mind to revise the story when I wrote you. A very little work will do it. I am convinced that one of the reasons of lack of poignancy is the fact that Lester marries Jennie. In the revision I don't intend to let him do it. And I may use your version for the rest. You are a good critic. Isn't it curious. I have had six excited opinions but yours is the first to confirm my private convictions. Thanks.[19]

To understand Dreiser's response in this letter one must turn to the surviving manuscripts and typescripts of *Jennie Gerhardt*. In the fall of 1910, when he resumed work on the novel, Dreiser found that he was reasonably well satisfied with the revising and rewriting he had done in the winter of 1901 and the spring of 1902. In this recast version, Jennie gives herself sexually to Senator Brander and becomes pregnant; Brander dies, and Vesta is born. In subsequent chapters old Gerhardt becomes enraged and casts Jennie out; later she returns with Vesta and is half-heartedly reinstated into the family. She goes to work for Mrs. Bracebridge and meets Lester. He pursues her and, after agreeing to help her family, enters into a liaison with her. Eventually they set up housekeeping in an apartment in Chicago. There, by accident, they are discovered by Lester's sister Louise.

Throughout these early sections of the novel, Dreiser had salvaged pages from his old typescript and even, in several places, had reached back to the ur-manuscript from 1901–2 to incorporate pencil-written half-sheets into his draft. This old material, both handwritten and typed, was now intermixed with new writing that was inscribed in black ink on full-sized sheets of white typing paper. This new draft, when completed, was a blending together of material from several stages of the composition of the novel. It is a remarkable document, a testament to Dreiser's ability to salvage old material and merge it seamlessly with new writing. It is not a first draft; it is instead a fair copy. Close inspection of the leaves salvaged from the ur-manuscript and typescript of 1901–2 shows that Dreiser thoroughly worked over these old sheets yet again, revising for style and clarity by adding or erasing words and punctuation, and in general adjusting the details of the text to his satisfaction. Many of the black-ink leaves show evidence of being one or two stages removed from a first draft. What resulted was a fair-copy MS from which Dreiser's typist could work. (This fair-copy MS, a crucial document, is among Dreiser's papers at the University of Pennsylvania. It has served as copy-text for the edition of *Jennie Gerhardt* presented here.)

Perhaps the most remarkable thing about this MS is how different it finally became from the earliest version of the novel. The bare bones of the story are unchanged, but characterization has been altered in quite significant ways. Senator Brander, for example, is kindlier: although unaware of Jennie's pregnancy, he means to marry her, but fate intervenes and he dies. Jennie is more innocent, less calculating about her loss of virtue, and less practical-minded about viewing sex as a commodity to be exchanged for food and shelter. Lester too is altered: he is a good deal less of a cad and is more honestly smitten by Jennie's wholesome beauty and sexual appeal than he had been in the urversion. His pursuit of her is less crass, and he is more deeply touched by her family's plight. Dreiser must have been pleased with these revisions.

Thereafter Dreiser brought his novel to its conclusion—working now entirely in black-ink holograph. But the narrative did not read in the way with which we are familiar today. Still working from the story of Mame and Brennan, Dreiser had Lester secretly marry Jennie, then admit to having done so in a conference with his father. It is difficult to know exactly how the novel proceeded from that point to its original conclusion because Dreiser, in revising, discarded almost all of the material that he had written. What is clear is that Dreiser took the advice of Lillian Rosenthal and Fremont Rider: he excised the marriage of Jennie and Lester from the narrative and had Lester marry Letty Gerald eventually. He effected this revision in an odd but practical way. First he went through the MS of *Jennie Gerhardt* (the composite document from which his typist had worked) and located those spots that needed to be revised if he were to remove all reference to the marriage. He marked these lines with plussigns (+) in the margins. Then he did the necessary revising on the leaves of the MS. He wanted to see just how much revising would be necessary and whether he could bring off the operation convincingly. He also wanted to save as many of the sheets of his typescript as he could from an extended revision that might ultimately have to be aborted. Dreiser introduced some interlinear revising on the sheets of the MS through chapter XLVIII and employed a combination of recopying and revision of the text after that. Once this labor was completed, he transferred a few changes by hand to the finished typescript and then had the typist recopy the rest of the material.[20]

The ribbon copy of this typescript no longer survives. It went to the eventual publisher, Harper and Brothers, where it was cut and revised extensively. Parts of it were returned to Dreiser, but these are not known to be extant today. What does survive, fortunately, is the carbon copy of this typescript. Dreiser transcribed his own revisions onto this carbon, in black ink, and he spliced the new chapters into it as well. He showed this carbon to several of his friends for opinions. A stamp on the first page, giving the address of Curtis Brown and Massie, a London literary agency, suggests that this carbon might also have been shown to some British publishers. Its travels thereafter are uncertain, but eventually it made its way into the Barrett Collection at the Alderman Library, University of Virginia. It is an important document because it preserves the essential form in which *Jennie Gerhardt* was submitted to Harper and Brothers.[21]

By 24 February 1911 Dreiser had finished his work on both the ribbon and carbon of the typescript. He now had two copies of the fully finished novel resting on his desk. On Dreiser's instruction Miss Holly, his agent, submitted the book first to Macmillan—since there was no contract with Harpers. But Macmillan was still not interested, so Holly sent it to Hitchcock at Harpers. Apparently Hitchcock had some difficulty in persuading his house to take on the book, but eventually he was successful. His offer to Dreiser, however, was conditional. Harpers would publish *Jennie Gerhardt* but only if Dreiser would allow the house to revise the text thoroughly and to cut certain offensive material from it. Dreiser was displeased but certainly not surprised. For years he had endured criticism of his blunt writing style, and he had been told virtually from the beginning that *Jennie Gerhardt* dealt with improper subject matter, some of which was probably

unpublishable. As he had written to Mencken while still composing the novel, "I sometimes think my desire is for expression that
is entirely too frank for this time—hence I must pay the price of
being unpalatable."[22]

Dreiser decided to accept Hitchcock's terms. It is important
to remember that, at this point in his career, Dreiser had virtually
no leverage with a powerful publishing house like Harper and
Brothers. In April 1911, Theodore Dreiser was not the irascible,
independent artist who would later deal in such high-handed
fashion with publishers like Horace Liveright, Bennett Cerf,
Richard Simon, and Lincoln Schuster. That later incarnation of
Dreiser was a public figure with a long record of literary visibility
and accomplishment; after 1925 he was also the author of the
best-selling novel *An American Tragedy*. Theodore Dreiser in
April 1911, by contrast, was a thirty-nine-year-old unemployed
ex-editor and journalist who had published only one book to
date—a controversial, "immoral" novel that had appeared more
than a decade before. He was known to a certain underground of
supporters but was not widely recognized for literary achievement, and he had certainly not written a best-selling novel.
Dreiser was in no position to dictate anything to Hitchcock.
Publication by a large, respectable house such as Harper and
Brothers (as opposed to another small-fry firm like J. F. Taylor or
B. W. Dodge) would be of immense value to Dreiser and would
validate his work publicly and professionally.

Evidence of Dreiser's nervousness over Hitchcock's plans for
Jennie Gerhardt survives in the contract, dated 29 April 1911, that
was now drawn up between author and publisher. Appended to
that contract was the following clause:

It is hereby understood and agreed that HARPER & BROTHERS will con-
dense and revise the said work in accordance with the general understanding existing with the AUTHOR, and that if the final outcome of such
condensation and revision should result in a radical disagreement of
views between HARPER & BROTHERS and the AUTHOR then the said
AUTHOR shall have the right to take the book elsewhere without any
pecuniary responsibility on his part to HARPER & BROTHERS for the
editorial work which they have done upon the story.[23]

Dreiser must have hoped that it would not be necessary for him to
exercise this option; he certainly had no other publisher waiting

in the wings should he and Harpers fall out. Probably he simply wanted the clause in the contract to act as a curb on Hitchcock's blue pencil. If that is what he hoped, then he was to be disappointed.

While he waited for the revising and cutting to begin, Dreiser sent *Jennie Gerhardt* to Mencken for a reading. Mencken's reaction was swift and positive:

> When "Jennie Gerhardt" is printed it is probable that more than one reviewer will object to its length, its microscopic detail, its enormous painstaking—but rest assured that Heinrich Ludwig von Mencken will not be in that gang. I have just finished reading the ms.—every word of it, from first to last—and I put it down with a clear notion that it should remain as it stands. The story comes upon me with great force; it touches my own experience of life in a hundred places; it preaches (or perhaps I had better say exhibits) a philosophy of life that seems to me to be sound; altogether I get a powerful effect of reality, stark and unashamed. It is drab and gloomy, but so is the struggle for existence. It is without humor, but so are the jests of that great comedian who shoots at our heels and makes us do our grotesque dancing.
>
> I needn't say that it seems to me an advance above "Sister Carrie". Its obvious superiority lies in its better form. You strained (or perhaps even broke) the back of "Sister Carrie" when you let Hurstwood lead you away from Carrie. In "Jennie Gerhardt" there is no such running amuk. The two currents of interest, of spiritual unfolding, are very deftly managed. Even when they do not actually coalesce, they are parallel and close together. Jennie is never out of Kane's life, and after their first meeting, [he] is never out of [hers]. The reaction of will upon will, of character upon character, is splendidly worked out and indicated. In brief, the story hangs together; it is a complete whole; consciously or unconsciously, you have avoided the chief defect of "Sister Carrie".

Mencken followed with two more paragraphs of praise and then added this admonition:

> If anyone urges you to cut down the book bid that one be damned. And if anyone argues that it is over-gloomy call the police. Let it stand as it is. Its bald, forthright style; its scientific, unemotional piling up of detail; the incisive truthfulness of its dialogue; the stark straightforwardness of it all—these are merits that need no praise. It is at once an accurate picture of life and a searching criticism of life. And that is my definition of a good novel.[24]

Dreiser was elated. "Yours is the sanest & best analysis I have received yet," he replied.[25] But he must have reacted with a grimace to Mencken's remarks about those who would wish to cut the novel, given what he knew of Hitchcock's plans for editing the text. In fact he had already asked his wife, who had been ill, to make an attempt at reducing the length of *Jennie Gerhardt* and to remove from it those words and passages that she thought Hitchcock might find offensive. Sara had taken the opportunity: perhaps if she could help Dreiser with his novel there might be some chance to repair their marriage. She had taken the carbon typescript of *Jennie* with her on a trip to a Virginia spa earlier in April. While she had rested and recuperated, she had gone through the typescript, marking long sections for removal and making numerous smaller alterations, usually with a view toward getting rid of suggestive passages. Her editing on this typescript is quite similar to the work she did on the manuscript and typescript of *Sister Carrie* in the winter and spring of 1900. Sara returned the marked typescript of *Jennie Gerhardt* to Dreiser in late April. He was upset by the changes she had made, apparently feeling that her revisions and cuts had damaged the novel. Her work was so unsatisfactory to him that he now had no choice but to take his chances with Hitchcock.[26]

If one is to understand the manner in which Hitchcock edited *Jennie Gerhardt,* one must know something of his personal background and professional career before he came to Harper and Brothers. His upbringing was different in almost every possible way from Dreiser's. Hitchcock was a New Englander, a native of Fitchburg, Massachusetts, whose father was a prominent physician and author and whose mother was a Latin teacher at Mount Holyoke. Hitchcock was a Harvard man (A.B., 1877); in fact, he sometimes took Dreiser to lunch at the Harvard Club in Manhattan. Hitchcock had served his apprenticeship in newspaper work and, in the early 1880s, had held the position of art critic for the *New York Tribune.* By 1890 he had moved into book publishing as an editor and literary adviser at Appleton. He stayed there for twelve years and then became a vice-president at A. S. Barnes. Finally he moved to Harpers in 1906, remaining there until his death in 1918.

Hitchcock's strengths were his flexibility and adaptability; during his career he worked with writers of many types and persuasions. Among his better-known authors were Woodrow Wilson, John Jacob Astor, Hall Caine, Zane Grey, Joel Chandler Harris, Arthur Conan Doyle, Rudyard Kipling, Frank R. Stockton, Gilbert Parker, and Hezekiah Butterworth. His specialty was the creation and management of books in series, such as Appleton's "Story of the West," the volumes of which were sold by subscription to libraries and individual buyers. In personality and behavior Hitchcock was genteel, courtly, reserved, unusually patriotic, and deeply religious. He was a member of the conservative eastern literary establishment and was on friendly terms with William Dean Howells. He was a prominent member of both the Authors Club and the Century Club and was an early inductee into the National Institute of Arts and Letters. Near the end of his life he was one of the judges for the new Pulitzer Prize in biography. Hitchcock is remembered today as the editor who published books by both Stephen Crane and Theodore Dreiser, but these were not the books for which he expected to be remembered. He wanted to be known instead for his work on Woodrow Wilson's A *History of the American People* and was especially proud of having edited Richard Henry Stoddard's *Recollections*. (Stoddard was an advocate of "roses, dew, and freshness" in literature and an opponent of any author who "mercilessly exposes the secrets of the heart.")[27]

Hitchcock also wanted to be remembered for his commercial successes. The greatest of these came in 1898, while he was still with Appleton, when he published Edward Noyes Westcott's novel *David Harum*. Hitchcock had taken Westcott's manuscript, which was long and disorganized, and had transformed it into one of the great best-sellers of the 1890s.

Westcott was a banker from Syracuse, New York. Afflicted with chronic tuberculosis, he was forced to take to his bed for an extended period of rest. To pass the time he wrote *David Harum*, a novel set in upstate New York. Westcott tried several publishers, all of whom rejected his manuscript. In December 1897 he sent *David Harum* to Hitchcock at Appleton. Westcott, now only three months from death, gave Hitchcock permission to cut, reorganize, and rewrite the book. Hitchcock moved much material about, reduced and tightened the story, revised the entire text for style, and cut the manuscript to increase its narrative pace. He also transferred a clever horse-swapping episode from the middle of the book to the beginning to "hook" readers into continuing.

Appleton published *David Harum* in September 1898, six months after Westcott's death. It was an immediate hit, selling as many as a thousand copies a day during its initial trade run and becoming a staple title thereafter on the Appleton backlist. By February 1904 it had sold some 727,000 copies; by 1935 it had been reprinted one hundred times; by 1946 its total hardback sales were estimated at 1,190,000—and this did not count a newly issued paperback edition of 240,000 copies. During its first period of popularity *David Harum* also became a successful Broadway play for Charles Frohman; later it was adapted twice for the movies. Hitchcock had pulled off what only a few trade editors had ever done before him: he had transformed a sow's ear of a manuscript into a phenomenally successful and lucrative silk purse. His employers at Appleton were certainly grateful, since the high sales of *David Harum* helped keep the leaky firm afloat in 1898 and 1899 before it finally succumbed to bankruptcy and reorganization in 1900. In fact, Hitchcock's books had been valuable to the firm throughout the late 1890s. Another of his best-sellers, Crane's *The Red Badge of Courage,* had helped keep Appleton from foundering in 1895 and 1896, and Joel Chandler Harris's Uncle Remus books had sold almost as well.[28]

If one is to understand Hitchcock's editing of *Jennie Gerhardt,* one must be aware of the fact that he spent virtually all of his book-publishing career with financially ailing firms. He was at Appleton from 1890 to 1902 and endured a major bankruptcy there in 1900. And he was at Harpers from 1906 to 1918—a difficult time financially for that house. By the time Hitchcock arrived in 1906, Harpers had already succumbed once to bankruptcy and reorganization. It was now under the direction of Colonel George B. Harvey, a flamboyant promoter of books. Harvey had introduced more efficient and businesslike methods, but try as he might he was unable to erase the enormous load of debt under which Harpers was laboring. Hitchcock was associated with the firm during this period; in fact, he had been hired by Colonel Harvey as part of a general effort to rehabilitate the house. Hitchcock was the man who had brought *Uncle Remus, The Red Badge,* and *David Harum* to Appleton; obviously he had a nose for a best-seller. He had helped keep Appleton out of bankruptcy court for several years. Harvey seems to have hoped that he could do the same for Harpers and help ease the weight of their debts. If Hitchcock could find, or "create," another *David Harum* for Harpers, then much of the ink in their account books would turn from red to black.[29]

Thus Hitchcock was under a good deal of pressure at Harper and Brothers to publish saleable books. All trade editors worked under such pressure, even in the early years of this century, but at Harpers the pressure would have been particularly strong. The economics of book publishing are such that one true best-seller, or a series of three or four strong sellers, can make up for a long list of failures and can rescue a house financially in a very short time. Hitchcock almost surely did not expect *Jennie Gerhardt* to be another *David Harum*, but he must have hoped that it would sell well—perhaps in the neighborhood of 50,000 copies. This helps to explain why Hitchcock took on Dreiser and *Jennie Gerhardt* in the first place. Despite his various contacts with Dreiser over the years, Dreiser was not Hitchcock's kind of author, nor was *Jennie Gerhardt* Hitchcock's kind of book. Publication of the novel, he knew, would involve some risk. Dreiser had already acquired a reputation from *Sister Carrie*; it was likely that protectors of the public decency would examine this new book quite carefully, no matter who published it. Suppression and banning were still very real possibilities for unconventional or sexually frank books in America during the first twenty years of this century. The Boston Watch and Ward Society and the New York Society for the Suppression of Vice were active and powerful, and there was a network of reviewers and columnists who were poised to attack morally objectionable literature. One of the foremost of such reviewers, in fact, was Hitchcock's own author Hamilton Wright Mabie, who wrote for *The Outlook*, a popular Christian magazine for middle-class American homes. Mabie, as it turned out, was shortly to play a role in the publication of *Jennie Gerhardt*.

Hitchcock had no desire to challenge the conservative literary establishment; indeed, he was part of that establishment himself. And he certainly did not want to publish a book that might be banned in Boston or New York. Such an outcome would do nothing for his firm's reputation or for its balance sheet. By the same token, Hitchcock knew that a novel that dealt in an acceptable fashion with "off-color" material could sell quite vigorously. He had seen this happen many times in the literary marketplace—in his own career it had happened with Crane's *Maggie: A Girl of the Streets*. He apparently felt that, with the right editing job, Dreiser's manuscript might be turned into such a book. It could balance on the ever-so-fine line between what was considered improper and what was thought to be acceptable; with luck, it could ring up a good sale at the bookshops. A novel that dealt with suspect material but that struck at some point the obligatory note of piety could become a strong seller. Harpers needed such a book—several of them, really. Perhaps Dreiser, who came to the house with a reputation for having dealt with "immoral" material in *Sister Carrie*, could (with Hitchcock's help) produce "less drastic" but very saleable books of this kind for Harper and Brothers. Hitchcock was not reluctant to take his blue pencil to a manuscript to bring about this necessary moral balancing act in a work of fiction. Many Crane scholars believe, in fact, that he was responsible for significant cuts and expurgations in both *The Red Badge* and *Maggie*, changes that alter both books philosophically and morally and make them less ironic and bitter.

The cutting and rewriting of *Jennie Gerhardt* began at Harpers in late April.[30] The editors there worked with the ribbon typescript, which is not known to survive, so it is difficult to know just who performed the labor. Hitchcock's letters to Dreiser indicate that he delegated a good deal of the work, probably giving general instructions to his subeditors and leaving the details of copy revision to them. Although Dreiser's ribbon typescript is no longer extant, it is possible to uncover the changes that Hitchcock's assistants made by collating the typed text of the extant carbon typescript against the text of the first edition. In so doing, one uncovers all alteration (authorial and nonauthorial) that occurred between the typing of the novel in early 1911 and its eventual publication in October of that year (see Table 3).

The collation reveals that *Jennie Gerhardt* was substantially cut between typescript and print. In all, some 16,000 words came out. The text that was left was thoroughly revised and often completely rewritten. The individual changes in wording (disregarding spelling, punctuation, capitalization, and other minor features of the text) number in the thousands. The editing of *Jennie Gerhardt* was immensely more thoroughgoing and relentless than the cutting and revision performed on the text of *Sister Carrie* more than ten years before by Sara Dreiser and Arthur Henry. The pages of Dreiser's typescript must literally have been covered with alterations and cuts. What emerged was a considerably different work of art—changed in style, characterization, and theme. Speaking generally, one can say that *Jennie Gerhardt* was transformed from a blunt, carefully documented piece of social analysis to a love story merely set against a social background. Part of what the Harpers workers did was plainly intentional; much of the rest of it was probably adventitious—the result of their desire to smooth out Dreiser's prose and to quicken narrative pace.

Many of the alterations are local and specific. Profanity is removed: Lester's oath, "Well I'll be God-damned!"—uttered when he learns of Vesta's existence—is excised, as is his later observation, "Hell, what a tangle life was, what a mystery" (204, 299). Slang in dialogue is removed so that characters speak grammatically. When Jennie protests to Lester, "I can't do this way," the text is altered to read, "I can't go on this way" (132). And Lester's joshing comment, "How you talk, girl," much later in the story, becomes "What talk from you" (312). Almost all mention of alcohol is cut. After editing, the reader no longer knows that old Gerhardt sometimes drinks from Lester's store of "beer, whiskey, cordials and liqueurs" (271), nor is the reader reminded that Lester visits a saloon before he goes to confront Jennie about Vesta.

Virtually all mention of sex is muted or removed, a practice that alters character and motivation. In the unedited text, for example, one learns that old Gerhardt, in the "ruddiest period of his youth" had been "wild and irreligious" (51, 52). Lester's desire for Jennie, in the unaltered text, is "feral" and "Hyperborean" but is only "elemental" in the published book (243). In a passage describing the "molten forces" in Lester's makeup, Dreiser had written that his protagonist had a "leaning toward women, a weakness he also thought he had well in hand. He was a man of breadth, he fancied; of vigor. His powers as a man and a well-favored one were self-conscious with him." All this was reduced to one sentence: "Another weakness lay in his sensual nature; but here again he believed that he was the master" (128).[31]

Two long scenes can stand as examples of the effects of the

Harpers editing on the behavior of major characters. In chapter
XX of the typescript Lester is, as it were, negotiating with Jennie.
She has agreed to be his mistress, and in return he is to look after
her nearly destitute family. The typescript text originally read as
follows:

"What is it, Jennie?" he asked helpfully. "You're so delicious. Can't
you tell me?"

Her hand was on the table. He reached over and laid his strong
brown one on top of it.

"I couldn't have a baby," she said finally and looked down.

He looked at her and the charm of her frankness, her innate
decency under conditions which were anomalous and compulsory, the
simple unaffected recognition of the facts of life lifted her to a plane
which she had not occupied before for him.

"You're a great girl, Jennie," he said. "You're wonderful. But don't
worry about that. [You don't need to. I understand a number of things
that you don't yet.] It can be arranged. You don't need to have a child
unless you want to, and I don't want to."

[He stopped and she opened her eyes in wonder and a kind of
shame. She had never known that.]

He saw the question written in her face.

"It's so," he said. "You believe me, don't you? You think I know,
don't you?"

"Yes," she faltered. (158)

The words within brackets above were cut. Also removed was a
sentence a few lines later that read, "She half wondered what it
was he knew and how he could be so sure but he did not trouble to
explain." At this spot the first edition reads, "Not for worlds could
she have met his eyes" (p. 266). These cuts and revisions remove
references to Jennie's complete ignorance of birth control—an
ironic lack of knowledge on her part, since she is by now the
mother of a child. Her ignorance, however, is entirely congruent
with her repressed upbringing and her lack of education. The cut
was apparently made to mask an overly direct reference to contraception—still a very controversial practice in 1911.[32]

Much later in the novel, when Lester must decide whether
to leave Jennie, he pays a visit to Letty Gerald at her home. Letty,
in the unedited version of the novel, is more openly calculating in
her pursuit of Lester. Dreiser writes, "Lester was truly in the house

of the temptress for Mrs. Gerald had made up her mind that if he were not married, and it looked to her as if he were not, and were going to leave Jennie that he might as well come to her" (337). That sentence and several more that follow it were cut. Two chapters later, as Lester is coming to the conclusion that he must disengage himself from Jennie, he thinks of the financial advantages of marrying Letty. "She was possessed of millions also, and distinction. Together they could repay an indifferent, chill, convention-ridden world with some sharp, bitter cuts of the power-whip if they chose" (361). Certainly such behavior—Letty's scheming and Lester's itch to use her money to punish his enemies—is not attractive. Perhaps that is why these sections were removed from the novel, or perhaps they were simply cut as digressions not essential to the plot. Some two dozen pages further in the typescript Letty succeeds in seducing Lester. Just before he kisses her, she says to him, "I know what you need—I know what I need." But this line was cut, as was the information, a few lines below, that Lester "caressed her" (375). The seduction still takes place, but it is not as explicitly described.

Some of the most important cuts were made in passages critical of organized religion. We know from Dreiser's biographers and from his own writings about himself that he resented his father's inflexible religiosity. He was also resentful all his life of the influence that the Catholic Church had had on his childhood and early education. Much of this feeling is evident in the unedited text of *Jennie Gerhardt* in passages strongly critical of old Gerhardt's religious fervor and of the Lutheran Pastor Wundt's intrusions into the Gerhardt home. But almost without exception such passages were cut. Mention of Gerhardt's "perverse, unreasoning zealotry" was removed (62); longer passages critical of the church and of unsound parochial schooling were done away with as well.

Thus far these cuts and revisions might almost have been predicted. They are parts of what must have been an intentional effort by the Harpers editors to "socialize" or "domesticate" Dreiser's novel for public consumption. But there are many other cuts for which the motivation is less clear. These passages seem to have been removed simply to hurry the plot along and to rid the text of what the Harpers editors must have seen as extraneous detail. In the progress, however, much of the social data that

Dreiser had included in his novel were lost. A lengthy description of the interior of the Kane mansion was removed, for example, and as a consequence the reader no longer knows that the Kanes have fashionable Louis Quinze furniture in their dining room, an antique Nuremberg clock in their hall, and canvases by Corot, Troyon, and Daubigny (members of the Barbizon school) on their walls (138). Dreiser had also included a long section in which he had described the daily life of Jennie and Lester in their comfortable Hyde Park home in Chicago. The section reveals much about Jennie's strong hold on Lester and tells us what she had to offer him—as opposed to what Mrs. Gerald could provide in her more opulent world. But this section too was cut, so the contrast could no longer be noted.[33]

Other scenes were removed, and some were reduced in such a way that the reader would have difficulty seeing their purpose. Early in the novel, in chapter XVII, Lester attends a coming-out party for a Cincinnati debutante. He does not particularly want to go but allows himself to be talked into attending by his sister Louise, who is more social-minded than he and who is determined that he shall choose a wife soon. Lester goes to the ball and finds it as dull as he had supposed it would be. He engages in some vapid conversation, but his mind is on Jennie, whom he has met only a few days before in Cleveland. Finally he becomes so bored with the affair that he resorts to punning. Mrs. Windom, a society matron who is attempting to introduce him to an eligible debutante, exclaims, "'I do believe I have made a match!'" "'Give it to me,'" answers Lester. "'My pipe's gone out.'" Mrs. Windom misses that bit of humor, so Lester tries again. Instructed by her to wait "on this spot" while she goes off to fetch the young woman, Lester replies, "'I'm afraid she'll spot me'" (145). This entire scene was cut, perhaps because Lester's puns were so bad. But that, of course, was the point: we are seeing Lester at a gathering of his own kind and are learning how weary he is of its empty social pretensions. "'It was a bore,'" thinks Lester a little later. "'Such youth. It was silly'" (146).

Lester abandons this stratum of society for some years in order to live with Jennie, but eventually social and economic considerations tempt him to reenter the class into which he was born. By chapter LIV of the typescript, he has left Jennie and has appeared again in his former world, "armed with authority from a number of sources, looking into this and that matter with the air of one who has the privilege of power" (367). At one of Letty Gerald's dinner parties, Lester pauses to look beneath the shining surface of the society into which he is about to be reintroduced:

It was the same tintinnabulation of words through this very interesting function, as it is ever on such occasions. All the women carefully gowned, all the men formal, the whole thing a picture full of beauty and color. He studied them, when lack of attention to others permitted, wondering whether Sir Nelson Keyes was troubled with rheumatism, he looked so angular and bony; whether Adam Rascavage was as calm as his eyes looked or as fussy and excitable as his beard and mustachios indicated; whether Mrs. Dickson Thompson wasn't becoming fat and stupid. Obviously Berry Dodge's long, thin head was becoming bald. It served him right. (371–72)

Lester seems to have some residual bitterness; perhaps he is already beginning to regret his abandonment of the simplicity and warmth that Jennie provided for him. But the paragraph was excised, probably for no other reason than that it had no obvious function in the plot.

The most important cuts have to do with Lester's and Jennie's personalities and with why they are drawn so powerfully to each other, despite the fact that they are opposites in almost every way. These cuts are most telling on Jennie's character, for they could be said to put the novel out of balance and tip it in favor of Lester. *Jennie Gerhardt,* as Mencken would say in his letter to Dreiser, is in many ways a novel about "the reaction of will upon will, of character upon character"—of Jennie on Lester and Lester on Jennie. Lester is a pragmatic cynic, Jennie an instinctive romantic; he is a pessimistic determinist, she an unreasoning mystic. In the unedited text of the novel (the text that Mencken read), Dreiser took pains to balance these two approaches to life against each other. He described Lester's philosophical orientation in several long passages and did the same for Jennie, in equally long sections. Lester's passages were left alone during the editing process, but nearly all of Jennie's were reduced or removed. Certainly they were not objectionable; probably they simply seemed dispensable to the Harpers editors. As a consequence, Lester and his point of view come to dominate the novel. Jennie is still present, but, except for a few passages, she seems not to have a point of view. Dreiser evidently did not intend this to be the case when he composed *Jennie Gerhardt*. He wanted Jennie's way of approaching life to have equal time with Lester's, equal explanation to the reader.[34]

Anyone familiar with Dreiser's own personality will recognize that these points of view were both parts of his own nature and were constantly at war in his own consciousness. He was simultaneously a pessimistic determinist and a religious mystic. He never really brought these two sides of his nature into harmony; in fact, one might argue that his best writing resulted from the friction generated between them. It might therefore be said that Lester and Jennie are representations of the two sides of their creator's artistic consciousness. The two characters stand for opposite sides of a dialectic that is being argued, but not resolved, in this novel. The cutting of *Jennie Gerhardt* between typescript and print, however, put the book out of balance. After the Harpers editors were finished, Lester had come to dominate the philosophical argument of the novel. Jennie's point of view had been all but silenced.

Jennie never states her point of view outright: language is not her métier. Her approach to life is instead revealed by her behavior, and this must be described by the narrative voice. One telling scene in this regard—a scene reminiscent of certain parts of *Sister Carrie*—was removed entirely. In chapter XXVI, Lester and Jennie are walking along 23rd Street in New York City and are approached by a beggar. Jennie is "quick to see ragged clothes, worn shoes, care-lined faces." " 'Oh, look,' " she says to Lester, pulling his sleeve, " 'let's give him something.' " Lester, however, is unsympathetic to the plight of the vagrants. " 'They are not always poor,' " he instructs her. " 'Some of these people are professional beggars. They make their living that way.' " Jennie is incredulous. She is familiar with ragged clothes, worn shoes, and other evidences of poverty in a way that Lester, with his privileged upbringing, can never be. Only someone who has never felt real want can hold his attitude. Oblivious to the sufferings of the beggars, Lester launches into a homily on the workings of chance. " 'Fortune is a thing that adjusts itself automatically to a person's capabilities and desires,' " he lectures. " 'If you see anybody who wants anything very badly and is capable of enjoying it, he is apt to get it.' " Jennie knows that this is not true—her experience has taught her otherwise—but as at other points in the novel, she is without language to express what she knows. The narrator, however, makes the point clear through her behavior. Lester strolls ahead, "quite sure he had expressed the whole logic of the case." Jennie, although unconvinced, "was overawed by his mighty sentences" and "only studied the crowd again" (195). The scene is heavy with irony. Before the novel is over both Lester and Jennie learn, in their own lives, that people who want things very badly indeed are not necessarily apt to get them. Whoever was cutting the typescript of *Jennie Gerhardt* at Harpers must have missed this point. The scene on 23rd Street must have seemed an unimportant digression, and so it came out in its entirety.

Mencken had praised *Jennie Gerhardt* in his letter to Dreiser because it had avoided "the chief defect of 'Sister Carrie' "—the tendency of the reader to be diverted by Hurstwood's fall and to lose sight of Carrie's own melancholy tragedy. In the version of *Jennie Gerhardt* that Mencken read, Dreiser had solved this problem by carefully balancing his portrayal of Jennie against his depiction of Lester. "The two currents of interest, of spiritual unfolding, are very deftly managed," wrote Mencken. "Even when they do not actually coalesce, they are parallel and close together." Ironically, the cutting of *Jennie Gerhardt* at Harpers had reintroduced the old problem from *Sister Carrie*: the male character had come to dominate the novel, and the female character (after whom this novel, like *Sister Carrie*, was also titled) had receded into the background. [35]

Much of the attention of the Harpers editors went to Dreiser's prose. They introduced thousands of changes—reordering sentences, altering syntax and wording, introducing new phrasings and expressions. Dreiser's own prose was blunt and unadorned; the Harper editors conventionalized and domesticated it. Their task was laborious, and the sheets of the typescript must perforce have been covered with alterations. In fact, the typescript was so thoroughly marked up that Hitchcock was reluctant even to let Dreiser see it.

The following example will stand as an example for what happened throughout the novel. In chapter XIX, Jennie is being pursued by Lester but has not yet agreed to become his lover. She has been readmitted into the Gerhardt household because her

father is away working in Youngstown, Ohio. The news arrives
that he has been seriously injured; both hands have been burned
severely, and he must return to his wife and younger children in
Cleveland. In the meantime a letter comes from Lester, urging
Jennie to join him. Old Gerhardt can no longer work, and "the
current expenses of rent, food and coal, to say nothing of the need
of incidentals," have now begun to "press very heavily" on the
Gerhardts. In the last paragraph of the chapter, Dreiser states
Jennie's dilemma:

> She still had Lester's letter unanswered. The day was drawing near.
> Should she write? He would help them. Had he not tried to force money
> on her? She decided after a long cogitation that she really ought to and
> consequently wrote him the briefest note. She would meet him as
> requested. Please not to come to the house. This she mailed and then
> waited, with a sort of soul dread, the arrival of the day. (152–53)

At the Harper editorial offices this paragraph was turned into
something quite different:

> Lester's letter had been left unanswered. The day was drawing
> near. Should she write? He would help them. Had he not tried to force
> money on her? She finally decided that it was her duty to avail herself of
> this proffered assistance. She sat down and wrote him a brief note. She
> would meet him as he had requested, but he would please not come to
> the house. She mailed the letter, and then waited, with mingled feelings
> of trepidation and thrilling expectancy, the arrival of the fateful day.
> (p. 158)

This stylistic reworking is typical of hundreds of other revisions
and recastings throughout the novel. Language is conventionalized, to be sure; more important, the tone is altered, becoming
softer and less forceful. The reader of Dreiser's original final
paragraph finished the chapter with a feeling of discomfort and
unease. The reader of the revised paragraph, by contrast, is let off
fairly lightly. Jennie is now to await "the fateful day" with feelings
of "trepidation" rather than "soul dread," and a note of "thrilling
expectancy" is in her heart as well. The reader of the revised text
is allowed to escape Dreiser's implications more easily, here and in
many similar passages throughout the novel.

The Harpers editors, in fact, were apt to descend on key

scenes or passages in which an emotional reaction was called for from the reader. Dreiser's tendency at such moments in the novel was to write his story "flat" and to avoid using words that would call forth sentiment from the reader. He seems to have wanted the events of the novel to speak for themselves. The Harpers editors, by contrast, almost invariably introduce such phrasing into the text, prompting the reader as to what emotional reaction would be appropriate.[36]

Inevitably, much of Dreiser's characteristic prose remains in the novel. Without rewriting the novel word by word, the Harpers editors could not have purged Dreiser's style from it altogether. What results, then, is a peculiar mixture: Dreiser's blunt sentences and flat rhythms as a base and the conventionally smooth and sometimes sentimental prose characteristic of much popular fiction of the early 1900s as a heavy overlay.

The novel as a whole loses much of its panoramic quality and cultural resonance as well. The story of Jennie and Lester remains, and it still touches the emotions, but it is played out against a sparser social background than the one that Dreiser had originally provided. Dreiser had more to say about class, money, marriage, and religion, but he was not allowed to speak. The book he had submitted to Hitchcock in the spring of 1911 was, in its own distinctive way, a powerful novel of manners. What emerged after the editing was a touching love story isolated from much of its social context.

Hitchcock's assistants began revising and cutting *Jennie Gerhardt* in late April. Dreiser's letters to Hitchcock, written during the weeks that followed, are no longer extant. Hitchcock's side of the correspondence does survive in Dreiser's papers at the University of Pennsylvania, however, and one can reconstruct much of what happened from these communications. Dreiser was apparently nervous about what was being done to his novel, and he wrote what must have been an impolite letter to Hitchcock in early May. The editor replied as follows on 5 May:

I have your letter of May third. Why you should abuse me I do not quite know, but I take it that the harsh terms you use are really an expression of affection.

Of course, you understand that the work on the manuscript takes time. Thus far, between one-third and one-half of the manuscript has been revised. I think that it can be finished within about ten days if all goes well. It is certainly being done very carefully and I know very intelligently.

The revising process seems to have taken longer than ten days. So extensive were the revisions and cuts that Hitchcock decided to have the novel retyped. He probably did this in part so that the typesetter at the Harpers printing plant could follow copy without difficulty. The original typescript sheets must have been so heavily marked up that it would have been difficult for a compositor to set galleys accurately from them. But Hitchcock seems also to have had the retyping done so that Dreiser would not be alarmed at the frequency and extent of the revisions and cuts in his text. By late May, Dreiser had the early chapters of the freshly typed text in hand, but he still wanted to see the old marked-up typescript. This desire he communicated to Hitch-cock through his agent. Hitchcock responded on 1 June:

Miss Holly tells me that you wish to see the original MS. and I am sending you a portion of it. I felt that it would be better for you to read through the clean copy and get your impression of the result as a whole without being distracted by constant reference to the changes in the original.

We have worked with the greatest care over the MS., with constant reference to the preservation of the artistic purpose of the whole and to the concentration of effect. I think that nothing vital has been omitted.

The necessity is upon us now of beginning to put some of the material into type. Therefore, I shall hope to hear from you soon.

Letters written to Dreiser by Hitchcock over the next several weeks show that Dreiser was allowed to see the newly typed chapters in batches. Apparently he was not altogether happy and complained about the cuts. In a letter dated 24 July, Hitchcock writes to beg Dreiser to let the text be typeset and proofed now without further wrangling:

I am hoping very earnestly that the proofs will go through smoothly. You will find, I am sure, that your judgment and preferences have received full consideration. I do not think I need speak again of the time and care given to the book. I noted all your comments and I have put back pages and pages of MS. in accordance with your request.

This letter demonstrates that the original cutting job done at Harpers was even more extensive than the collation of the carbon typescript with the first edition indicates. It shows too that Dreiser succeeded in getting Hitchcock to restore at least some of the excised material. The fiduciary, bureaucratic tone of Hitchcock's letters ("your judgment and preferences have received full consideration") makes it clear, however, that Hitchcock had final authority over what was to be included in the text.

If Dreiser had been profoundly at odds with Hitchcock over the editing of his text, he could at this point have invoked the clause in his contract and could have taken his novel elsewhere. But he was unwilling to cut loose, and understandably so. He was dissatisfied about many of the cuts, but Hitchcock had compromised and had reinstated some of the material. Besides, Dreiser had no alternate publisher waiting for his book and no reason to suppose that another major house would be willing to take him on, especially if it became known that he had withdrawn his manuscript after an argument with Harpers. Dreiser had waited eleven years for a chance to finish and publish *Jennie Gerhardt* and to reissue *Sister Carrie* with a reputable firm. Both of these things were guaranteed in the Harper and Brothers contract. He therefore decided to stay with them.

Type was being set by early August, and Dreiser was correcting galleys by the tenth of that month. The printing plates had been cast by 15 September; bound copies were ready by early October. At this point a curious episode occurred. Frederick A. Duneka, a vice-president at Harpers who is best known to literary historians as the co-perpetrator (with Alfred Bigelow Paine) of the *Mysterious Stranger* hoax after S. L. Clemens's death, sent an advance review copy of *Jennie Gerhardt* to his friend Hamilton Wright Mabie.[37] Mabie was associate editor of the Christian magazine *The Outlook*; he contributed a monthly book column to that periodical and wrote widely on literature for other magazines as well—among them *Ladies' Home Journal* and *Atlantic Monthly*. Mabie was widely respected and honored: like Hitchcock he was a member of the American Academy of Arts and Letters, and he held honorary doctorates from several institutions of higher learning. Mabie was one among a group of genteel, avuncular, anglophile critics who still had considerable influence on American readers and publishers in 1911. In addition to Mabie this group included Paul Elmer More, George Edward Woodberry, Barrett Wendell, and Henry van Dyke, all of whom would later be targets for Mencken and other literary rebels of the 1920s. Mabie, in fact, became a favorite whipping boy for Mencken in later years: Mencken often ridiculed Mabie's "White List of Books"—volumes that could be allowed into Christian homes and could be put safely into the hands of children.

By sending *Jennie Gerhardt* to Mabie, Duneka was performing a litmus test. If Mabie did not seriously object to the book, then Hitchcock had done a commendable job of editing it. If Mabie did object strongly, however, then other defenders of public morality would likely make trouble as well. Duneka's letter to Mabie of 6 October invites his reaction:

I have a special reason for sending this Dreiser book, (it is called "JENNIE GERHARDT", by the way) because it provoked more discussion before we decided to publish it than any book since Thomas Hardy's "JUDE".

The theme is rather unpleasant and it is a fair question whether any really good end is subserved. Of course, it is easy to say that it is a patent glaring phase of life which some author must touch, but this, after all, begs the question. The book is brutal in its directness, is written with almost violent sincerity, and in spite of its heroine being outside the pale it is about as suggestive as a Patent Office Report or Kent's Commentary.

I am wondering what you will think of it, and so I am venturing to bother you with it.[38]

Mabie responded to Duneka five days later. To Duneka's great relief, Mabie wrote that he had no great objection to Dreiser's novel:

I read Dreiser's book through, and at the end I liked it very much better than I expected to when I started it. In my judgment, that theme ought not to be dealt with too frequently in fiction, and always with the greatest reserve; but I think his treatment is a reverential one, and his picture of "Jennie" is very winning. One has no sense of moral dirt, except with regard to the men. Jennie is a distinct creation of a rather new type. There is a good deal of ability in the book, if Dreiser can be kept from getting obsessed by the general sex theme which has made so many writers of fiction insane.

Duneka was pleased. He responded on 13 October:

You do not know how glad I am to find that you discovered in Dreiser's Novel the reverential treatment which we somehow felt was there. The main question was: Would the reader find it?

I hate and loathe beyond possibility of expression the sex novel, and when it comes to the expression of this dirt on the stage, the constant occurence of it has driven me from the theatre. I do not go twice a year.

This exchange between Duneka and Mabie is important for several reasons. It suggests a great deal about the attitude of the higher-ups at Harpers toward Dreiser and *Jennie Gerhardt*. Harpers might have withdrawn *Jennie Gerhardt* from publication if Mabie had objected to it strenuously. (They would, in fact, withdraw from publishing *The Titan* three years later under very similar circumstances.) Mabie, however, had rather liked *Jennie Gerhardt*. Duneka therefore knew that Hitchcock had edited the novel just as it should have been edited. He had made it into a book acceptable to someone with the literary tastes and standards of Hamilton Wright Mabie. Mabie's letter of approval to Duneka had been the hoped-for confirmation of Hitchcock's skill.[39]

Dreiser, for his part, had continued to fret about the editing of *Jennie Gerhardt*. As early as 22 September he had had a set of the proofs of the book mailed to Mencken and had asked in a letter whether "the telling had been improved or otherwise" by the cutting and revising. A month later, on 20 October, he had sent Mencken a presentation copy of the first printing and had repeated the request: "Will you do me the favor to read it again & see whether in your judgment you think it has been hurt or helped by the editing?"[40] Mencken had by this time read *Jennie Gerhardt* twice, but both times in typescript—that is to say, in its uncut state. (His early review of the novel in the *Smart Set* was based on a reading of the typescript text, not the book.) How closely he read the novel in its printed and bound form one cannot know, but his counsel to Dreiser was to make the best of things:

On first going through "Jennie", in the printed form, the cuts irritated me a good deal, particularly in the first half, but now I incline to the opinion that not much damage has been done. As the story stands, it is superb.[41]

To his friend Harry Leon Wilson, however, Mencken rendered a more lengthy and very different opinion:

[Dreiser] is hopeful that "Jennie Gerhardt" will stir up the plain people, despite the fact that the Harpers cut about 25,000 words out of the ms. I read the ms. and it floored me. What the book will do, God knows. Such ruthless slashing is alarming. The chief virtue of Dreiser is his skill at piling up detail. The story he tells, reduced to a mere story, is nothing.[42]

It should be noted that Dreiser was also capable of playing the game both ways. Critic James Huneker, who had read *Jennie Gerhardt* during the late spring of 1911, had been critical of its "opaque" style; to him Dreiser wrote: "If you ever see the printed volume you will see a most marked improvement for it has been carefully edited. Nearly all of the objections you raise—repetitions, moralizings etc. have already been overcome."[43] Perhaps Dreiser can be pardoned for this behavior. Huneker was an influential critic whose opinion, if expressed in print, might do much for the novel.

Of course, it might also be argued that Dreiser's letter to Huneker represented his real feelings. In fact, Dreiser's final assessment of the editing of *Jennie Gerhardt* was probably mixed. As the critical returns came in, Dreiser realized that he had scored a success. Most reviewers had expressed approval, although some, such as the poet Edwin Markham, had condemned Jennie for "smirching her womanhood" and "staining her virtue."[44] Sales, on the whole, were strong—but not as good as Hitchcock had probably hoped. Through December 1912, *Jennie Gerhardt* had sold a little under 14,000 copies in America and England and had earned Dreiser something over $2,500 in royalties.[45] A sale such as this would not do much one way or the other for the Harpers balance sheet, but to Dreiser it must have been gratifying. Could the Harpers editing have been responsible in part for this success?

Dreiser also must have recognized that the kind of work that Harpers had done to *Jennie Gerhardt* was probably necessary if the book were to avoid prosecution for violating standards of public morality. Profanity, references to sex and alcohol, and perhaps some of the harsher criticisms of organized religion might have resulted in a ban on the book in Boston or New York. Pressure might have been brought to bear on Harpers to withdraw the novel from circulation. At this point, such developments might well have dealt a death blow to Dreiser's literary career. He therefore probably had no serious objections to most of the local and specific excisions from his text. What seems to have troubled him was the larger cutting and recasting of his narrative.

From Ripley Hitchcock's point of view, *Jennie Gerhardt* must have seemed a qualified success. He had invested a great deal of editorial energy and time—his own and his staff's—in the production of the book. Reviews in general had been favorable, but sales had been rather disappointing. Certainly *Jennie Gerhardt* had not turned out to be another *David Harum* or even a *Red Badge*. Dreiser had proved to be a difficult author, argumentative and balky about the editorial process. And after publication he had been full of complaints to Duneka about the advertising and marketing of his novel. Still, Dreiser might have a truly saleable novel in him—or even two or three such novels. Hitchcock and Harpers were prepared to continue to work with him to extract these novels and publish them under the Harper imprint. Dreiser and Hitchcock therefore collaborated again, almost immediately, on *The Financier*. Sales this time, however, were even less satisfactory than those for *Jennie*—only about 8,000 copies. And Dreiser continued to be quite difficult to handle—querulous about royalties, insistent over advances, and prone to dangle overtures from other publishers, such as Grant Richards and The Century Company, in front of Hitchcock's and Duneka's noses. All of these factors (and several more) finally came together shortly before the scheduled publication of *The Titan* in 1914 and caused Harpers to break off relations with Dreiser for good.

In the fall of 1911, however, none of this was foreseen. *Jennie Gerhardt* was in print and was selling reasonably well; most reviews were good; Mencken was lining up his artillery for future battles; *Sister Carrie* was to be reissued shortly. Dreiser was free of his marriage and of the drain of magazine editing. He was ready to begin the long burst of creative work from 1911 to 1914 on which, in many ways, the rest of his literary career would be based.

NOTES

1. For a detailed history of the composition and publication of Dreiser's first novel, see the Historical Commentary in the Pennsylvania Edition of *Sister Carrie* (historical editors, John C. Berkey and Alice M. Winters; textual editor,

James L. W. West III; general editor, Neda M. Westlake [Philadelphia: University of Pennsylvania Press, 1981], pp. 503–41).

2. Dreiser had already made one attempt to begin a follow-up novel to *Sister Carrie*. This was "The 'Rake,'" an autobiographical novel about the adventures of a young newspaperman named Eugene. Dreiser began this manuscript during the summer of 1900 while visiting with his in-laws in Missouri and completed ten chapters or so before abandoning it. Only a few pages of this manuscript survive, incorporated into the manuscript of *Newspaper Days*. This version of "The 'Rake'" was a predecessor to *The "Genius"*; it bears no relation to a later false start on *An American Tragedy*, also entitled "The 'Rake.'" This second fragment has been edited by Kathryn M. Plank and published in a special Dreiser issue of *Papers on Language and Literature* (Spring 1991). See Richard Lingeman, *Theodore Dreiser: At the Gates of the City, 1871–1907* (New York: G. P. Putnam's Sons, 1986), pp. 285, 292, 306.

3. This ur-manuscript of *Jennie Gerhardt* and the thirty chapters typed by Anna Mallon's typing agency are both in the Theodore Dreiser Collection, Van Pelt-Dietrich Library Center, University of Pennsylvania—hereafter cited as Dreiser Collection. Dreiser sold this manuscript to the collector W. W. Lange in 1922; Lange in turn sold the manuscript to the Phoenix Book Shop in 1928. It was purchased there by R. Sturgis Ingersoll, who donated it to the University of Pennsylvania in December 1948.

4. Dreiser to Brett, 16 April 1901, Box 71, Macmillan Collection, Manuscripts Division, New York Public Library.

5. Brett to Dreiser, 19 April 1901, Dreiser Collection; see also Dreiser's response to Brett, 26 September 1901, Macmillan Collection.

6. Dreiser recalled Hitchcock's expression of interest in "Down Hill and Up," Part II, unpaginated, Dreiser Collection.

7. Taylor's agreement with Doubleday to take over the plates and remainder stock and his agreement to support Dreiser during the composition of *Jennie Gerhardt* are both in the Dreiser Collection.

8. Jewett to Dreiser, 22 November 1901 and 30 December 1901, Dreiser Collection.

9. Jewett to Dreiser, 13 November 1901, Dreiser Collection.

10. This second typescript, which is filled with misreadings and typographical errors, eventually included the first thirty chapters of *Jennie*. It is preserved in the Dreiser Collection as well; the typist was named M. E. Gordinnier. See Lingeman, *At the Gates*, pp. 334ff.

11. The dummy front cover and title page of *The Transgressor* are in the Dreiser Collection. The cover is bound in red cloth; the lettering is hand-painted in white. Typescript copy for the dummy text (a blue-ribbon typescript) is also preserved with the dummy; this copy appears to derive from the Mallon typescript.

12. More than twenty years later Taylor recalled Dreiser's having told him that he had destroyed his manuscript, but there are no significant lacunae among the holograph documents dating from the 1901–2 period. It is possible that Dreiser burned one of his typescript copies but more probable that Taylor's memory was faulty. See Taylor to Dreiser, 14 August 1924, Dreiser Collection.

13. The finished chapters of the manuscript, together with fragments of

several uncompleted chapters, were published as *An Amateur Laborer*, ed. Richard W. Dowell; textual editor, James L. W. West III; general editor, Neda M. Westlake (Philadelphia: University of Pennsylvania Press, 1983).

14. Cross to C. D. Barnes, 5 February 1905, Barnes folder, Dreiser Collection.

15. James L. W. West III, "Dreiser and the B. W. Dodge *Sister Carrie*," *Studies in Bibliography* 35 (1982):323–31.

16. For Richards's recollections of Dreiser, see his *Author Hunting: Memories of Years Spent Mainly in Publishing* (New York: Coward-McCann, 1934). Richards is "Barfleur" in Dreiser's *A Traveler at Forty* (New York: Century, 1913).

17. Sara White Dreiser to Richards, 24 February 1909, Grant Richards Collection, University of Illinois Library, Urbana. See Lucia A. Kinsaul, "The Letters of Grant Richards to Theodore Dreiser: 1905–1914" (M.A. thesis, Florida State University, 1990).

18. Lillian Rosenthal to Dreiser, 25 January 1911, Dreiser Collection.

19. Dreiser to Rider, 24 January 1911, in Robert H. Elias, ed., *Letters of Theodore Dreiser: A Selection*, 3 vols. (Philadelphia: University of Pennsylvania Press, 1959), 1:110. Dreiser inscribed a copy of *Jennie Gerhardt* to Rider on 19 October 1911 as follows: "My Dear Rider, Here is Jennie, revised to your order. Will you [give] her shelter beside Carrie?" This copy is in the rare books collection at the Syracuse University library. Other evidence that Rider suggested that Lester and Jennie not marry is in Rider's letter to Dreiser, 6 November 1911, Dreiser Collection.

20. This revising can be followed in the MS by attending to the notes Dreiser wrote to his typist in the upper right-hand corners of the first pages of the chapters beginning with XXXIV. These notes typically read "Old—but corrected" or "New." In the Barrett carbon typescript, the change is signaled at p. 419 in chapter XXXIV by a shift from a wove unwatermarked stock to a bonded stock watermarked "A I STANDARD BOND." Thereafter the sheets are a mixture of wove and bonded paper until chapter XLIX, after which the novel was retyped on the bonded stock.

21. The history of this document is obscure. It came to the Alderman Library in January 1960 as part of the Clifton Waller Barrett Collection, but there is no record of its provenance among Barrett's papers. Many of the other Dreiser documents in the Barrett Collection date from the period of Dreiser's marriage to Sara Dreiser; Barrett may have acquired these documents (including this typescript of *Jennie Gerhardt*) from a relative of Sara Dreiser after her death in 1942.

22. Dreiser to Mencken, 10 March 1911, in Thomas P. Riggio, ed., *Dreiser-Mencken Letters: The Correspondence of Theodore Dreiser & H. L. Mencken, 1907–1945*, 2 vols. (Philadelphia: University of Pennsylvania Press, 1986), 1:65.

23. Two copies of this contract survive in the Dreiser Collection. One is Dreiser's own; the other is the Harper file copy, marked "Cancelled" in February 1923 when Dreiser was attempting to unite all rights to his books for a collected edition.

24. Mencken to Dreiser, 23 April 1911, *Dreiser-Mencken Letters*, 1:68–69.

25. Dreiser to Mencken, 28 April 1911, *Dreiser-Mencken Letters*, 1:71.

26. Sara Dreiser recalled her work on the typescript of *Jennie Gerhardt* in a letter of 19 April 1926 to Dreiser; in retrospect she expressed regret at having had to make cuts in the text. The letter is in the Dreiser Collection.

27. See Dorothy Dudley, *Forgotten Frontiers: Dreiser and the Land of the Free* (New York: Smith and Haas, 1932), p. 133.

28. For a fuller account of Hitchcock's career, see James L. W. West III, *American Authors and the Literary Marketplace since 1900* (Philadelphia: University of Pennsylvania Press, 1988), pp. 51–55. For an example of Hitchcock's reluctance to publish any book critical of a specific religious denomination, see the account of his dealings with Zane Grey over *Riders of the Purple Sage* (1912) in Frank Gruber, *Zane Grey: A Biography* (New York and Cleveland: World, 1970), pp. 103–4 passim. Hitchcock's papers are at the Butler Library, Columbia University, New York.

29. For accounts of the failures of both Appleton and Harpers, see John Tebbel, *A History of Book Publishing in the United States*, 4 vols. (New York: Bowker, 1972–81), 2:186–217; see also Charles A. Madison, *Book Publishing in America* (New York: McGraw-Hill, 1966), pp. 167–84. For specific information on the economic difficulties at Harpers, see Eugene Exman, *The Brothers Harper* (New York: Harper and Row, 1965), and Exman, *The House of Harper* (New York: Harper and Row, 1967).

30. Donald Pizer has written that Dreiser spent "several weeks" during the summer of 1911 cutting some 25,000 words from the novel, but the contract with Harper and Brothers and the surviving letters from Hitchcock to Dreiser demonstrate that this cutting was done at the Harper offices in April, May, and early June. What Dreiser worked with later, during the summer of 1911, was the *retyped* text of the novel, after it had already been cut and revised by Hitchcock and his assistants. Their initial cuts appear to have totalled some 25,000 words; Dreiser succeeded in having approximately 9,000 words restored, after he was shown the retyped text (see n. 42). Thus Dreiser was occupied during June and July of 1911 with restoring text to *Jennie Gerhardt*, not with cutting it. See Pizer, *The Novels of Theodore Dreiser: A Critical Study* (Minneapolis: University of Minnesota Press, 1976), p. 105 and pp. 356–57, n. 32.

31. One should note, in addition, Jennie's more frankly sexual response (in the unedited text) to Lester on pp. 121–23; see the word "urging" at 123.28. See also the section in chapter XIV in which guests at the Bracebridge home attempt to "lure [Jennie] into some unlicensed relationship" (119–20).

32. David M. Kennedy, *Birth Control in America: The Career of Margaret Sanger* (New Haven: Yale University Press, 1970); also *Margaret Sanger, An Autobiography* (New York: Norton, 1938).

33. For the strength of Jennie's hold on Lester, see also the passages at 244.2–16 and 257.20–259.29 of this edition that were cut from the Harpers text.

34. See, for example, the passage at 318.2–15, which was cut, and the passage at 395.31–396.13, which was largely removed.

35. To a considerable extent, Hurstwood's dominance of *Sister Carrie* was also caused by a round of heavy cutting. Arthur Henry and Dreiser removed

some 36,000 words from the novel, probably in response to a negative reader's report from Harpers. Most of the excised text is restored in the Pennsylvania edition of *Sister Carrie*. For an example of how much more fully Carrie's character reveals itself to a critic using the Pennsylvania text, see Thomas P. Riggio, "Carrie's Blues," in *New Essays on Sister Carrie*, ed. Donald Pizer (New York: Cambridge University Press, 1991), pp. 23–41. See also Kevin J. Hayes, "Textual Anomalies in the 1900 Doubleday, Page *Sister Carrie*," *American Literary Realism, 1870–1910* 22 (Fall 1989):53–68.

36. Two good examples of such passages (from among many in the novel) are Senator Brander's seduction of Jennie in chapter VII and Jennie's banishment from the Gerhardt home by her father in chapter VIII—especially the last paragraph of that chapter.

37. For an account of Duneka's work on *The Mysterious Stranger*, see John S. Tuckey, *Mark Twain and Little Satan: The Writing of* The Mysterious Stranger (Westport, Conn.: Greenwood Press, 1963). See also William M. Gibson, ed., *Mark Twain's Mysterious Stranger Manuscripts* (Berkeley and Los Angeles: University of California Press, 1969).

38. Duneka is referring to James Kent's *Commentaries on American Law* (orig. edn. 1826), a dry, comprehensive casebook for attorneys. The Duneka-Mabie correspondence quoted here is in the Harper Collection at the Pierpont Morgan Library, New York.

39. Mabie even gave a cautiously favorable notice to *Jennie Gerhardt* the following year on the occasion of the reissue of *Sister Carrie* by Harpers. See "A Few Books of Today," *Outlook* 102 (23 November 1912):650.

40. *Dreiser-Mencken Letters*, 1:78.

41. Ibid., 1:81.

42. Mencken to Wilson, 25 October 1911, in Guy J. Forgue, ed., *Letters of H. L. Mencken* (New York: Alfred A. Knopf, 1961), pp. 18–19. Mencken's estimate of 25,000 words cut from the novel likely came from Dreiser. It probably represents the amount removed at Harpers before Dreiser persuaded Hitchcock to restore some of the material. The final cuts between typescript and print total approximately 16,000 words.

43. See Huneker to Dreiser, 4 June 1911, Dreiser Collection, and *Letters of Theodore Dreiser*, 1:117.

44. Edwin Markham, "Theodore Dreiser's Second Novel," *New York American*, 25 October 1911; repr. in Jack Salzman, ed., *Theodore Dreiser: The Critical Reception* (New York: David Lewis, 1972), pp. 58–59.

45. Harper and Brothers royalty report, 31 December 1912, Dreiser Collection.

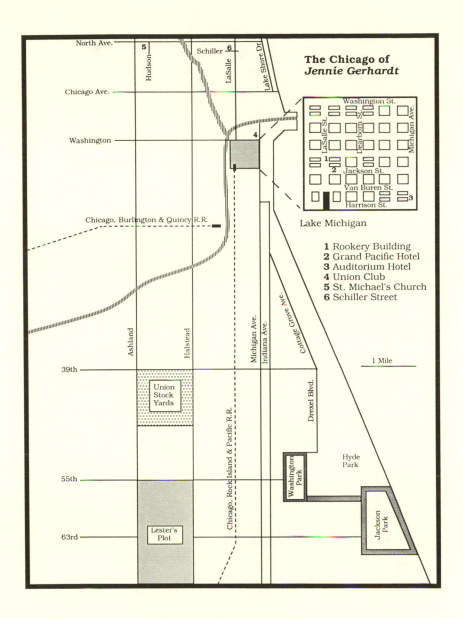

The Chicago of _Jennie Gerhardt_

North Ave.
Schiller
Chicago Ave.
Washington
Hudson
LaSalle
Lake Shore Dr.

Washington St.
LaSalle St.
Dearborn St.
Michigan Ave.
Jackson St.
Van Buren St.
Harrison St.

Lake Michigan

1 Rookery Building
2 Grand Pacific Hotel
3 Auditorium Hotel
4 Union Club
5 St. Michael's Church
6 Schiller Street

Chicago, Burlington & Quincy R.R.

Ashland
Halstead
Michigan Ave.
Indiana Ave.
Cottage Grove Ave.

1 Mile

39th

Union
Stock
Yards

Drexel Blvd.

Chicago, Rock Island & Pacific R.R.

Washington
Park

Hyde
Park

55th

Jackson
Park

Lester's
Plot

63rd

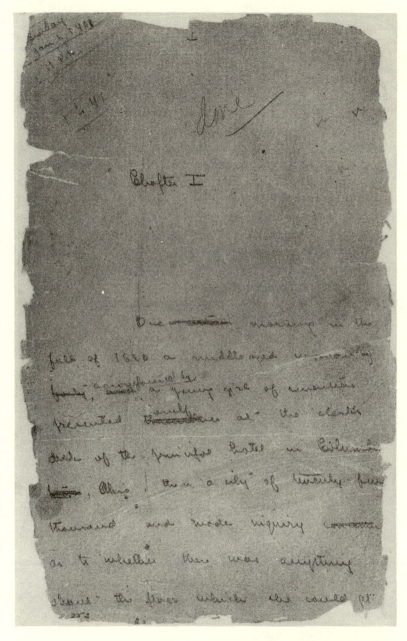

Figure 1. Leaf 1 of the ur-manuscript, 1901–2. (Theodore Dreiser Collection; Special Collections Dept.; Van Pelt-Dietrich Library Center; University of Pennsylvania)

The ✧ ✧ ✧
TRANSGRESSOR

By

THEODORE DREISER

NEW YORK
J. F. TAYLOR & COMPANY
1902

Figure 2. Dummy of *The Transgressor,* prepared by J. F. Taylor and Company. (Theodore Dreiser Collection; Special Collections Dept.; Van Pelt-Dietrich Library Center; University of Pennsylvania)

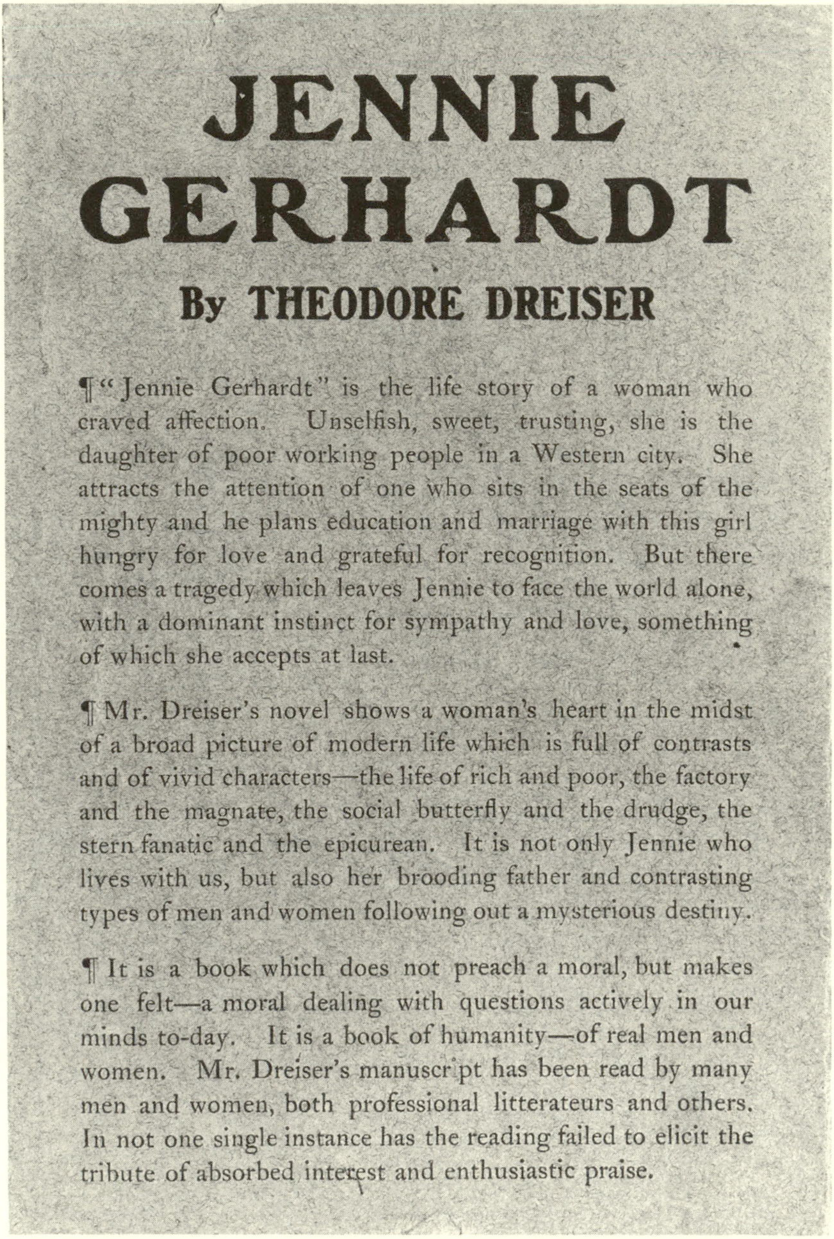

JENNIE GERHARDT

By THEODORE DREISER

¶ "Jennie Gerhardt" is the life story of a woman who craved affection. Unselfish, sweet, trusting, she is the daughter of poor working people in a Western city. She attracts the attention of one who sits in the seats of the mighty and he plans education and marriage with this girl hungry for love and grateful for recognition. But there comes a tragedy which leaves Jennie to face the world alone, with a dominant instinct for sympathy and love, something of which she accepts at last.

¶ Mr. Dreiser's novel shows a woman's heart in the midst of a broad picture of modern life which is full of contrasts and of vivid characters—the life of rich and poor, the factory and the magnate, the social butterfly and the drudge, the stern fanatic and the epicurean. It is not only Jennie who lives with us, but also her brooding father and contrasting types of men and women following out a mysterious destiny.

¶ It is a book which does not preach a moral, but makes one felt—a moral dealing with questions actively in our minds to-day. It is a book of humanity—of real men and women. Mr. Dreiser's manuscript has been read by many men and women, both professional litterateurs and others. In not one single instance has the reading failed to elicit the tribute of absorbed interest and enthusiastic praise.

Figure 3. Dust jacket of the Harper and Brothers 1911 edition. (Beinecke Rare Book and Manuscript Library, Yale University Library)

Figure 4. H. L. Mencken. Photo by Bachrach, 1913. (Courtesy Enoch Pratt Free Library, Baltimore)

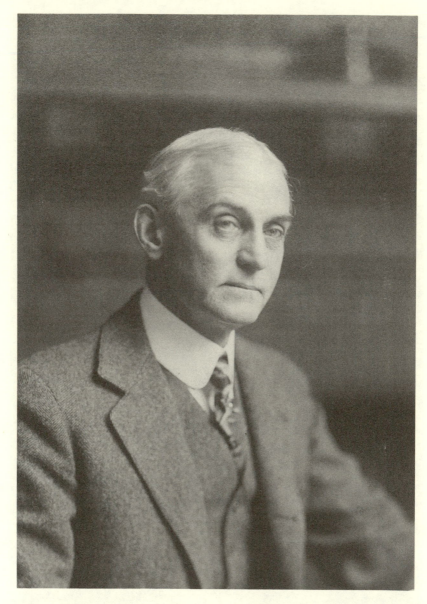

Figure 5. Ripley Hitchcock. (Ripley Hitchcock Papers, Rare Book and Manuscript Library, Columbia University)

Figure 6. Hamilton Wright Mabie. (From *The Outlook*, 10 January 1917)

which worried her, at times. She had not noted this in her daughter's moods before.

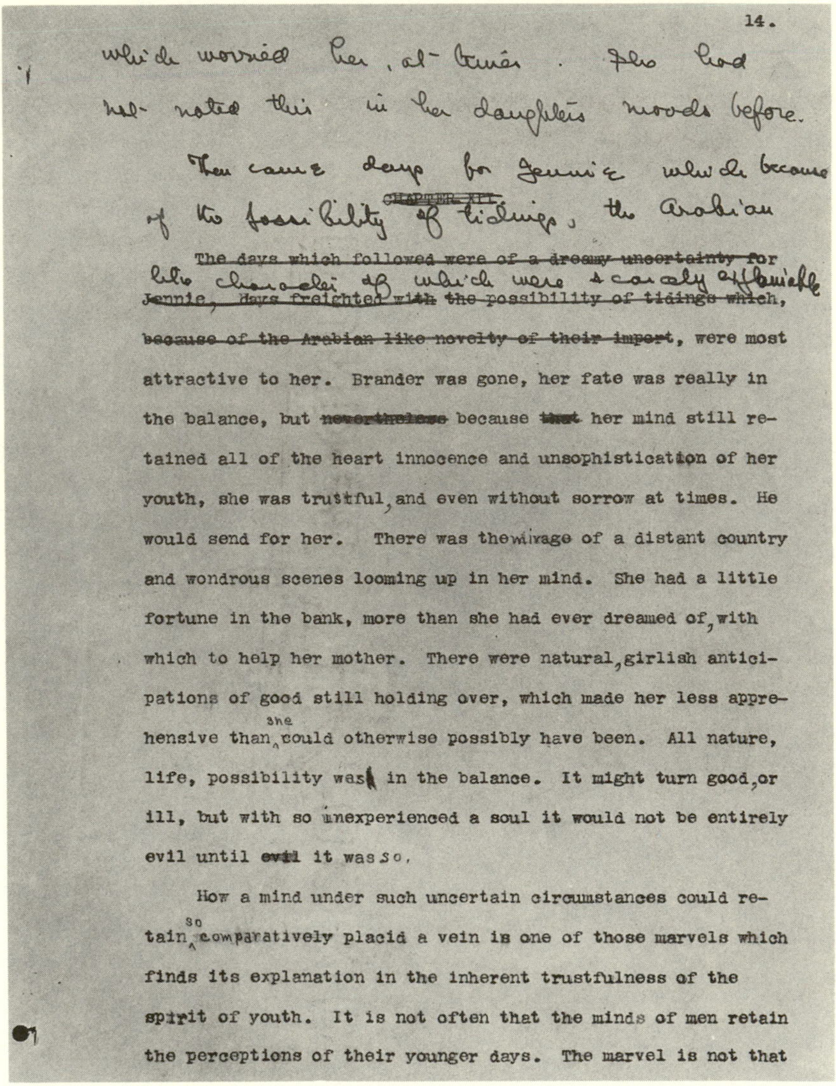

Then came days for Jennie which because of the possibility of tidings, the Arabian

CHAPTER XXI

The days which followed were of a dreamy uncertainty for *life character of which were scarcely appreciable* Jennie, days freighted with the possibility of tidings which, because of the Arabian-like novelty of their import, were most

attractive to her. Brander was gone, her fate was really in

the balance, but nevertheless because that her mind still re-

tained all of the heart innocence and unsophistication of her

youth, she was trustful, and even without sorrow at times. He

would send for her. There was the mirage of a distant country

and wondrous scenes looming up in her mind. She had a little

fortune in the bank, more than she had ever dreamed of, with

which to help her mother. There were natural, girlish antici-

pations of good still holding over, which made her less appre-

hensive than she could otherwise possibly have been. All nature,

life, possibility was in the balance. It might turn good, or

ill, but with so unexperienced a soul it would not be entirely

evil until evil it was so.

How a mind under such uncertain circumstances could re-
                        so
tain comparatively placid a vein is one of those marvels which

finds its explanation in the inherent trustfulness of the

spirit of youth. It is not often that the minds of men retain

the perceptions of their younger days. The marvel is not that

Figure 7. Leaf from the 1901–2 Mallon typescript, incorporated into chapter XX of the composite MS. All revisions (including the printed revisions toward the bottom of the page) are in Dreiser's hand. (Theodore Dreiser Collection; Special Collections Dept.; Van Pelt-Dietrich Library Center; University of Pennsylvania)

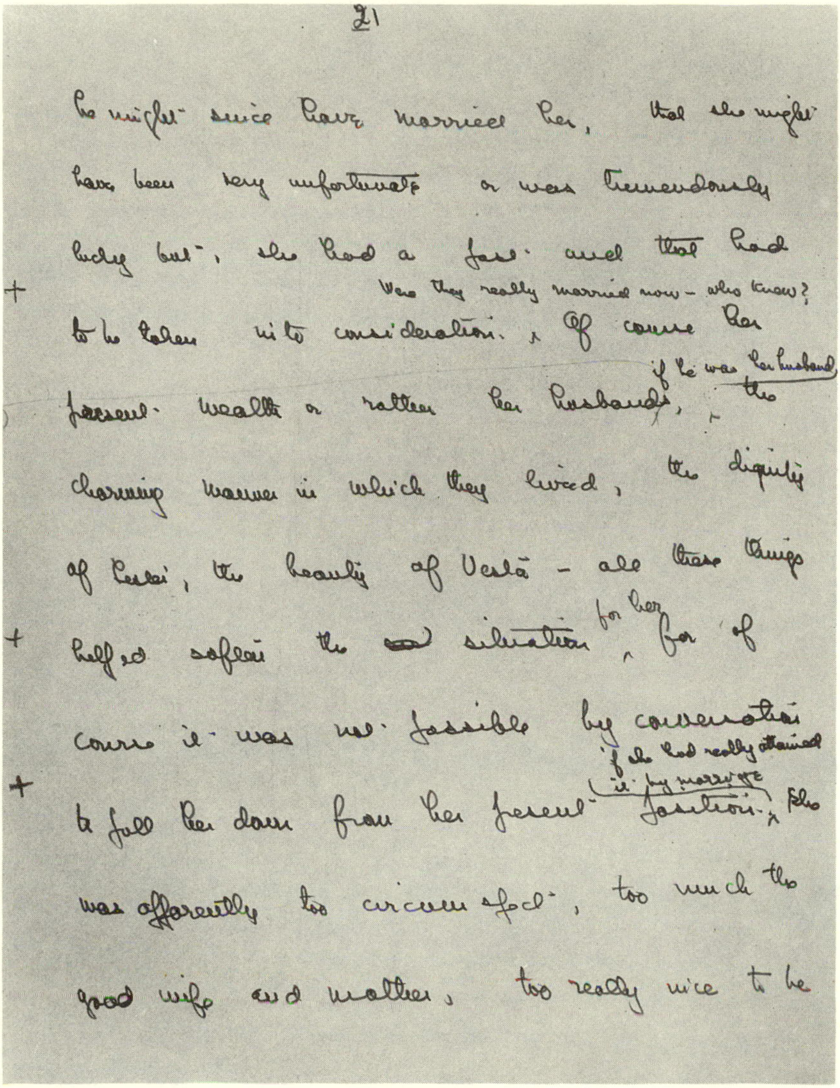
21

he might since have married her, that she might have been very unfortunate or was tremendously lucky but, she had a fate and that had to be taken into consideration. Was they really married now — who knew? Of course her present wealth or rather her husbands, if he was her husband, the charming manner in which they lived, the dignity of Lester, the beauty of Vesta — all these things helped soften the situation for her, for of course it was not possible by conversation if she had really attained it by marriage to pull her down from her present position. She was apparently too circumspect, too much the good wife and mother, too really nice to be

Figure 8. Black-ink holograph leaf from the composite MS, showing revisions to remove the marriage between Lester and Jennie. (Theodore Dreiser Collection; Special Collections Dept.; Van Pelt-Dietrich Library Center; University of Pennsylvania)

It can be arranged. You don't need to have a child unless
you want to, and I don't want to."

He stopped and she opened her eyes in wonder
and a kind of shame. She had never known that.

He saw the question written in her face.

"It's so," he said. "You believe me, don't you?
You think I know, don't you?"

"Yes," she faltered.

"Well, I do. But if you did I wouldn't let any
trouble come to you. I'll take you away. There won't be
any trouble about that. Only I don't want any children.
There wouldn't be any satisfaction in that proposition for
me at this time. I'd rather wait. But there won't be —
don't worry. You believe me, don't you?"

"Yes," she said. She half wondered what it was
he knew and how he could be so sure but he did not trouble
to explain.

"Look here, Jennie," he said after a time. "You
care for me, don't you? You don't think I'd sit here and
plead with you if I didn't care for you. I'm crazy about
you and that's the literal truth. You're like wine to
me. I want you to come with me. I want you to do it
quickly. I know how difficult this family business is
but you can arrange it. Come with me down to New York.
We'll work out something later. I'll meet your family.
We'll pretend a courtship, anything you like — only come

out

out

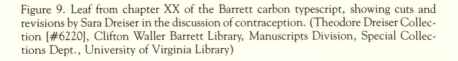

Figure 9. Leaf from chapter XX of the Barrett carbon typescript, showing cuts and revisions by Sara Dreiser in the discussion of contraception. (Theodore Dreiser Collection [#6220], Clifton Waller Barrett Library, Manuscripts Division, Special Collections Dept., University of Virginia Library)

HISTORICAL NOTES

Notes are supplied here for persons, places, terms, allusions, and other references in the text that might be unknown or obscure to the contemporary reader. If the name of a person or place in the text is not glossed, then the reference can be assumed to be fictitious, so far as the editor has been able to determine. As a general rule Dreiser used names of real hotels, restaurants, clubs, businesses, and other establishments unless his characters were directly associated with or employed by them or off-color behavior occurred at them. Thus Lester lives at the Auditorium Hotel in Chicago (a real establishment) after he leaves Jennie, but earlier in the narrative he and she rendezvous at an apparently fictitious hotel, the Dornton in Cleveland. Likewise, Dreiser mentions three real railroad lines in Chicago, but Lester becomes a director of the "C. H. & D." railroad (371), which is fictional. Dreiser followed this same policy in *Sister Carrie*; see the Pennsylvania edition, p. 557.

In each case below, the page-line reference is followed by the glossed word or words in bold type, then by the explanatory information. In addition to standard dictionaries, encyclopedias, guidebooks, and biographical reference works, the following sources have been consulted:

Abu-Lughod, Janet L. *Cairo: 1001 Years of the City Victorious.* Princeton: Princeton University Press, 1971.

Andreas, A. T. *History of Chicago, from the Earliest Period to the Present Time.* 3 vols. Chicago: A. T. Andreas Co., 1886.

Andrist, Ralph K. *The American Heritage History of the Confident Years.* New York: American Heritage Publishing Co., n.d.

Block, Jean F. *Hyde Park Houses: An Informal History, 1856–1910.* Chicago: University of Chicago Press, 1978.

Boller, Paul F. *American Thought in Transition: The Impact of Evolutionary Naturalism, 1865–1900.* Chicago: Rand McNally, 1969.

Bromiley, Geoffrey W., ed. *The International Standard Bible Encyclopedia.* Vol. 3. Grand Rapids, Mich.: William B. Eerdmans, 1986.

Casson, Herbert N. *The History of the Telephone.* Chicago: A. C. McClurg, 1910.

Champlin, John Denison, Jr., ed. *Cyclopedia of Painters and Paintings.* Vol. 4. New York: Empire State Book Co., 1885.

Danzer, Gerald A., and Lawrence W. McBride. *People, Space, and Time: The Chicago Neighborhood History Project.* Chicago: University Press of America, 1986.

Friedberg, Robert, and Jack Friedberg. *Paper Money of the United States.* 6th ed. New York: Coin and Currency Inst., 1968.

Fry, Herbert. *London.* Rev. ed. London: W. H. Allen, 1887.

Funk, Charles Earle. *A Hog on Ice and Other Curious Expressions.* New York: Harper & Brothers, 1948.

Gil, Carlos B., ed. *The Age of Porfirio Diaz.* Albuquerque: University of New Mexico Press, 1977.

Hakutani, Yoshinobu, ed. *Selected Magazine Articles of Theodore Dreiser: Life and Art in the American 1890s.* 2 vols. Rutherford, N.J.: Fairleigh Dickinson University Press, 1985, 1987.

Hill, Thomas E. *Souvenir Guide to Chicago and the World's Fair.* Chicago: Laird and Lee, 1892.

Koenig, Rev. Msgr. Narry, ed. *A History of the Parishes of the Archdiocese of Chicago.* Chicago: New World Publishing Co., 1980.

Lueker, Erwin L., ed. *Lutheran Cyclopedia.* Rev. ed. St. Louis: Concordia, 1975.

McClintock, Inez, and Marshall McClintock. *Toys in America.* Washington, D.C.: Public Affairs Press, 1961.

McGurn, James. *On Your Bicycle: An Illustrated History of Cycling.* New York: Facts on File, 1987.

Madigan, Mary Jean. "Introduction." *Nineteenth Century Furniture: Innovation, Revival and Reform.* New York: Art & Antiques, 1982.

Moses, John M., and Joseph K. Kirkland. *History of Chicago, Illinois.* Vols. 1 and 2. Chicago: Munsell & Co., 1895.

Myers, Bernard S., ed. *Encyclopedia of Painting: Painters and Painting of the World from Prehistoric Times to the Present Day.* New York: Crown Publishers, 1955.

Narbeth, Colin. *Collecting Paper Money: A Beginner's Guide.* Chicago: Henry Regnery, 1973.

Smith, Alan, ed. *The International Dictionary of Clocks.* New York: Exeter Books, 1984.

Smith, Eugene W. *Passenger Ships of the World, Past and Present.* Boston: George H. Dean, 1963.

Townsend, George Alfred. *Washington Outside and Inside.* Hartford, Conn., and Chicago: James Betts & Co., 1874.

Van Tassel, David D., and John J. Grabowski, eds. *The Encyclopedia of Cleveland History.* Bloomington: Indiana University Press, 1987.

Viskochil, Larry A. *Chicago at the Turn of the Century in Photographs.* New York: Dover, 1984.

Weinreb, Ben, and Christopher Hibbert, eds. *The London Encyclopedia.* London: Macmillan, 1983.

Williamson, Jefferson. *The American Hotel: An Anecdotal History.* New York: Alfred A. Knopf, 1930.

Winckler, Suzanne. *The Smithsonian Guide to Historic America: The Great Lakes States.* New York: Stewart, Tabori and Chang, 1989.

Yoder, Paton. *Taverns and Travelers: Inns of the Early Midwest.* Bloomington: Indiana University Press, 1969.

1.1   **in the fall of 1880**   The chronology of *Jennie Gerhardt* is as follows: Gerhardt *père* comes to America in 1844. Lester is born in 1847, Jennie in 1862. The novel begins in the fall of 1880; Vesta is born in early March 1882, when Jennie is twenty (or nearly so). Vesta is baptized, at the age of ten months, the week after Christmas 1882. Lester and Jennie meet during the early summer of 1883, when he is thirty-six. Old Gerhardt burns his hands in August of that summer; Vesta at this time is almost eighteen months old. Mrs. Gerhardt dies in November 1886, and Lester discovers Vesta's existence in the spring of 1887. Kane senior dies during the winter of 1893, when Lester is forty-six. Lester and Jennie leave on their travels to Europe and the Near East in the spring of 1893 and return on 9 September 1893. Old Gerhardt dies in the winter of 1896, and the lawyer representing the Kane estate visits Jennie shortly thereafter. Lester leaves Jennie in the early spring of 1896; she moves to Sandwood with Vesta, who is fourteen. Lester and Letty marry in mid-April 1897. Vesta dies in October 1899, at the age of seventeen. Five years pass. Lester turns fifty-seven and Jennie forty-two. Lester has his meeting with Robert in 1904. Lester dies in Chicago in November 1906, when he is fifty-nine. His funeral and the removal of his remains to Cincinnati take place on Thanksgiving Eve 1906. This chronology is of some importance, because in the Harpers text (and all subsequent texts), cuts in the narrative make it appear that Vesta's death occurs in the same year as Lester's marriage to Letty. In fact, more than two years separate the events, making it more plausible that Vesta has become Jennie's friend and confidante by the time of her death.

5.11   **lye hominy**   Corn soaked in a lye solution to remove the hulls, then boiled before being eaten.

18.27   **the Angelus**   The Angelus is a Catholic devotional exercise that commemorates the mystery of the Incarnation; it is performed at sunrise, noon, and sunset. The word also refers to the angelus bell, which is rung at those hours.

20.19   **enough votes to re-elect him**   In the early 1880s United States senators were still chosen by their state legislatures rather than by popular election.

26.17   **"Kriss Kringle**   An Americanization of the German *Christkind-lein,* or *Christkind'l,* a word that actually designates the Christ child, not Saint Nicholas.

26.22   **Christmas coming on Tuesday**   Christmas Day in 1880 in fact fell on a Saturday, but for the rest of this sentence to make sense (for the Gerhardt children to have two consecutive days free from their classes) there must be no school on "the Monday before." It seems best not to adjust the sentence by emendation.

50.2   **the Dukedom of Saxony**   This dukedom included Holstein and the land west of the lower Elbe. It became part of the German Empire in 1871 after Gerhardt had emigrated to the United States.

50.4   **the army-conscription iniquity**   In the 1840s Prussia, under Frederick William IV, was employing an efficient and ruthless system of forced military conscription under which it called up large numbers of men, trained them rigorously for several months, then released them and called up new men. Thus Prussia maintained both a standing army and a strong force of trained reservists. The system was subject to much popular resentment and caused some young German men, such as Gerhardt, to emigrate elsewhere.

51.9   **the Mennonite or perhaps the Dunkard religion**   Although they are separate sects, both the Mennonites and the Dunkards (or "Brethren") share an emphasis on strict performance of religious rites designed to restore the simple life of the apostolic church.

70.13   **the arc light had not yet been invented**   The arc light had in fact been invented by Charles F. Brush in 1876 but was not yet in general use for street lighting by the early 1880s, especially in poorer neighborhoods like the Gerhardts'. Most streets, if lighted at all, were illuminated by gaslamps. See 131.27 of this edition.

73.21   **Englishman Jefferies**   The quotation that follows is from Richard Jefferies' essay "Beauty in the Country," included in his collection *The Open Air.* Dreiser's version is nearly accurate; he was probably quoting from pp. 132–33 of the Harpers 1886 edition, the text that would have been most readily available to him.

78.35   **the Arlington**   The Arlington Hotel, erected by W. W. Cor-
coran on Vermont Avenue, was a small, elegant, expensive establishment with a capacity of 325 guests. It featured uniformed waiters
and an elevator (Townsend, pp. 180, 575).

96.14   **there are more things . . . than are dreamed of**   *Hamlet*, act 1,
sc. 5, lines 608–9.

101.8   **undiscovered bourne**   Dreiser is using *bourne* to mean "realm" or
"domain" and is alluding to *Hamlet*, act 3, sc. 1, line 79.

104.17   **boudoir**   A small, elegantly furnished room in which upper-class
women entertained their intimate guests.

115.9   **the baptism**   The Lutheran Church was not united nationally
when Vesta's baptism takes place. As a result, there were several different Lutheran prayer books in use in the United States at that
time. Dreiser did choose a Lutheran prayer book as a starting point
for this scene, but he was almost surely not aware of the various Lutheran prayer books then in existence, nor probably was he concerned to use the "correct" one. What he appears to have done was
to adapt Vesta's service from a Lutheran prayer book widely used in
the United States around the middle of the century. Dr. Donald L.
Huber, librarian and professor of church history at Trinity Lutheran
Seminary in Columbus, Ohio, has written to the editor as follows
(7 March 1991):

> Dreiser probably had a copy of the baptismal rite of the General
> Synod of the Evangelical Lutheran Church in front of him when
> he wrote the baptism scene in *Jennie Gerhardt*. He appears to have
> adapted the wording of his rite rather freely from *A Liturgy for the
> Use of the Evangelical Lutheran Church, Published by Order of the
> General Synod* (Baltimore: Evangelical Lutheran Church, 1847).
> The Fourth Formula in particular finds a number of echoes in
> Dreiser's imaginative reconstruction. Other services in use in the
> United States at the time bear little resemblance to his service.
>
> Dreiser's service is—from a theological perspective—quite un-
> Lutheran. The references to "education," "dedication," and so on,
> while common among American Catholics and Protestants down to
> this day, are different from the traditional Lutheran emphasis on
> baptismal grace. The Fourth Formula of the General Synod reflects
> this "Protestant" rather than Lutheran understanding because the
> General Synod was in fact self-consciously opposed to the Lutheran
> baptismal theology at that time.
>
> General Synod congregations were common in the East in the
> 1880s. They were also found in certain parts of Ohio. Assuming that
> Dreiser was unaware of the different kinds of Lutherans, it would
> have been natural for him to assume that there would be General
> Synod Lutherans in Cleveland in the early 1880s.

138.38   **Nuremberg clock**   During the sixteenth and seventeenth centuries Nuremberg was a center for German clockmaking. Nuremberg clocks were known for their accuracy and handsomeness; to

have a Nuremberg clock (an antique, by the 1880s) in one's hall would have been a symbol of status (Alan Smith, pp. 238–39).

138.39 **landscapes by Corot and Troyon and Daubigny** Camille Jean Baptiste Corot (1796–1875), Charles François Daubigny (1817–78), and Constant Troyon (1810–65) were French painters of the Barbizon school. Their aim was to paint nature as observed—a departure from the principles of classical theory.

139.6 **furnished after the period of Louis Quinze** At the Crystal Palace Exposition of 1851, Louis Quinze furniture—based on eighteenth-century French rococo designs—was prominently featured. Soon it became quite fashionable in America. Furniture in this style featured flowing curves, naturalistic carving, S and C scrolls, and cambriole legs (Madigan, p. 7).

144.20 **a writ of attachment** An order that enforces obedience to a judgment of the court, often by seizing persons or property. Lester is suggesting that he would rather have the courts force him to propose to the young woman than to sue voluntarily for her hand.

144.30 **aigrette** An ornamental tuft of upright plumes.

145.34 *embonpoint* A well-fed appearance; plumpness.

146.29 **the ladies' parlor** Single women often met with men in the ladies' parlor of a hotel. Originally designed to protect women from coarse behavior by men in the lobbies of taverns, the ladies' parlor had evolved into something very different by the 1880s. In big American hotels of the period, these rooms were well-furnished, softly lighted, and cozy; often they contained pianos (Yoder, p. 124; Williamson, p. 127).

153.28 **the large and ornamental public square** In the late 1870s and 1880s the public square in downtown Cleveland was developed by adding a waterfall, an artificial pond, a rustic pavilion, and several memorials (Van Tassel and Grabowski, pp. 809–10).

162.22 **green and yellow bills** The yellow-colored bills would have been U.S. gold certificates, which were a brilliant yellow-orange on the reverse side.

165.27 **"You'd make an excellent Mary Magdalene** Mary Magdalene is mentioned briefly in Luke 8:2 as a woman who follows Jesus and the disciples. She also plays an important role in the events surrounding the crucifixion and resurrection (Mark 15:40, 47; 16:1). Dreiser is making a common error by confusing her with another woman, the "sinner" in Luke 7, who washed Christ's feet with her hair and brought spices for his body after the crucifixion (Bromiley, p. 268).

178.18 *soi-disant* So to speak, so to say.

187.2 **a thought which has been . . . under the sun** Ecclesiastes 1:9: "The thing that hath been, it is that which shall be; and that which is done is that which shall be done; and there is no new thing under the sun."

187.15 **the Grand Pacific** One of the four largest hotels built after the Chicago fire of 1871, the Grand Pacific had five hundred guest rooms and covered an entire city block. It was constructed of olive-tinted Ohio sandstone, and its towers were made of iron. It remained in operation until 1919 (Moses and Kirkland, 1:565; Danzer and McBride, p. 405).

195.36 **the Southern Hotel in St. Louis**   When the Southern Hotel was completed in 1865, it was one of the largest hotels in St. Louis, occupying the block bounded by Broadway, Walnut, 4th, and Elm Streets. A fire destroyed this first building in 1877; the hotel was rebuilt in 1881 and continued to operate until 1912. Lester and Jennie would have stayed in the rebuilt hotel (Williamson, p. 102).

196.37 **the Union Club**   An exclusive and prestigious men's social club located at 12 Dearborn Place in Chicago (Moses and Kirkland, 2:583).

196.38 **An early patron of the telephone**   The telephone was invented by Alexander Graham Bell in 1875; after a decade of refinement, it was ready for popular use but would have been a convenience employed mostly by the well-to-do. Many business communications during the 1890s were still delivered by messengers.

204.38 **membranous croup**   An infection of the membranes of the throat and larynx that can lead to pneumonia.

222.4 **a wonder story**   A fairy tale or children's story. See Michael Vincent O'Shea, *Old World Wonder Stories* (Boston: D. C. Heath, 1902).

232.18 **divine afflatus**   Inspiration from on high. The words are usually employed ironically; see, for example, H. L. Mencken's "The Divine Afflatus" in *Prejudices: Second Series* (New York: Alfred A. Knopf, 1920).

237.16 **Mt. Clemens**   A popular Michigan mineral-water spa overlooking the Clinton River, eighteen miles northeast of Detroit.

241.36 **the Cuyahoga, or the lake**   Cleveland is located at the point where the Cuyahoga River empties into Lake Erie.

243.22 **Hyperborean**   In Greek mythology the Hyperboreans were a legendary race of Apollo-worshipers who lived in a land of perpetual abundance and sunshine beyond the reach of the north wind.

246.14 **the Kankakee marshes south of Chicago**   The Kankakee River, which for part of its length is low-lying and marshy, is approximately fifty miles south of Chicago.

249.37 **Hyde Park**   An upper middle-class suburb of Chicago located between State Street and Lake Michigan. In the late nineteenth century, many handsome mansions were built in Hyde Park by the executives of Chicago's most important firms (Block, pp. vii–ix).

258.19 **The Four Hundred**   In 1892 society leader Samuel Ward McAllister coined the designation "The Four Hundred" for members of elite New York society. Supposedly the phrase referred to the number of guests who would fit comfortably into Mrs. William Astor's ballroom (Andrist, p. 178).

269.15 **Mt. Clemens or White Sulphur or Saratoga**   White Sulphur

Springs, in southeastern West Virginia, and Saratoga, in east central New York State, were fashionable health spas for the wealthy. For Mt. Clemens, see the note at 237.16.

269.31   **odd puzzles like Pigs in Clover, The Spider's Hole, Baby Billiards** These were popular American parlor games of the late nineteenth century. "Pigs in Clover" became a craze in 1899 and sold at a rate of more than 8,000 games a day. It was played with marbles on a circular wooden board; the object was to herd the "pigs" past a series of obstacles into the "clover" at the center of the board (McClintock and McClintock, pp. 117, 193–96).

275.38   **You wouldn't know her from Adam's off ox**   You would not recognize her; you would not have the slightest knowledge of her. The off ox in a yoke of oxen is on the right and hence less readily visible to the driver, who walks to the left of the team (Funk, p. 96).

285.16   **a scare-head**   A newspaper headline in a large, bold, attention-catching type face.

287.20   **Robert G. Ingersoll, the famous lawyer-agnostic**   Ingersoll (1833–99) was an eloquent Illinois lawyer who lectured widely on agnosticism and Darwinism during the late nineteenth century.

306.27   **Baden-Baden**   A spa town in West Baden-Würtemberg, in the southwest region of Germany.

306.28   **Luxor and the Parthenon**   Luxor, on the upper Nile, is a town just south of the ruins of Thebes (see note for 319.24). The Parthenon is the temple of Athena on the Acropolis at Athens; it was completed ca. 438 B.C.

308.10   **the Savoy**   The Savoy Hotel was erected for D'Oyly Carte beside the new Savoy Theatre, where many of the famous Gilbert and Sullivan operettas were staged. The hotel was the most fashionable such establishment in London during the 1880s and early 1890s; it had wallpapers by Morris, tiles by De Morgan, numerous modern bathrooms for guests, and electric lights throughout.

308.11   **Shepheard's in Cairo**   Shepheard's Hotel, a favorite stopping place for Western visitors, was originally built in the 1850s on the site of the palace of Muhammad Bay al-Alfi. Lester and Jennie would have stayed in the second incarnation of the hotel, which was erected during the 1860s and was eventually burned in the Cairo riots of 1952 (Abu-Lughod, p. 100).

311.3   **corsage**   In current usage a corsage is a small bouquet worn on a woman's dress, but an alternate meaning of the word still current around the turn of the century was the body or "bodice" of a dress.

313.21   **a drive through Rotten Row. . . . dinner later at Claridge's**   Rotten Row is a long bridle path running across the bottom of Hyde Park. Traditionally it was the route taken by the king's carriage between Kensington Palace and Westminster—hence *route du roi*, corrupted to "Rotten Row." Claridge's, on Grosvenor Square, was long a leading West End hotel; its restaurant, at which Jennie and Lester dine, faced on Brook Street.

317.18   **chatelaine**   The lady or mistress of the rooms.

319.24   **toward Karnak and Thebes and the water-washed temples at Philæ**
Located on the upper Nile, Thebes was the capital of the ancient
Egyptian empire and site of the Great Temple of Amon. Philæ is an
island farther up the Nile, just above the Aswan Dam of today; it
was the site of the Temple of Isis and marked the ancient boundary
with Nubia.

319.29   *Fulda*   The *Fulda,* launched in 1882 in Glasgow, was a 4,816-ton
single-screw passenger ship in the North German Lloyd Line. In the
composite MS and in the Barrett typescript, Dreiser had had Lester
and Jennie return to America on the *Barbarossa,* a larger and more
luxurious vessel also in the Lloyd Line; but the *Barbarossa* was not
launched until 1896, three years after Lester and Jennie make their
return voyage (September 1893). The change to the *Fulda* was
introduced between Dreiser's typescript and the first edition and is
accepted here, despite the fact that the normal route of the *Fulda* ran
between New York and various Mediterranean cities. Lester and
Jennie depart from Hamburg (Eugene W. Smith, pp. 26–27, 100–
101).

321.22   **hypothecating its securities**   Using the securities of the firm as
collateral for loans or stock purchases.

321.27   **the new holding company**   Many late nineteenth-century entre-
preneurs used holding companies to combine the stock of several
related corporations in a trust that would limit competition. The
parent company might be a nonoperating or "pure" holding company, or, like Robert's company, it might be engaged in the business
itself, in which case it was called a "mixed" holding company.

327.36   **black-bearded after the Van Dyke pattern**   In the late nineteenth century many professional men wore mustaches and short,
pointed beards that were modeled after the whiskers of the Flemish
painter Sir Anthony Van Dyke.

333.25   **the International Packing Company, one of the big constituent
members of the meat-packing group at Halsted and 39th Streets**
In 1864, nine railroads together incorporated the vast 320-acre
Union Stock Yards on Halsted Street. The land was marshy, but
drainage quickly rendered it usable, and operations were begun in
December 1865. By 1895 the stockyards had expanded to cover
more than 420 acres (Moses and Kirkland, 1:394). The I.P.C. seems
to have been Dreiser's invention. See his article, "Great Problems of
Organization III: The Chicago Packing Industry," *Cosmopolitan* 25
(October 1898); repr. Hakutani, 2:119–29.

333.31   **below 55th Street and west of Ashland Avenue**   The packing
plant would be moving from due north of Lester's development to
due west. It would become a very close neighbor, and the problem of
odor would be acute.

335.4   **the Rookery Building**   After the 1871 fire, a temporary city hall
was built at the southeast corner of Adams and La Salle Streets. The

building was called "The Rookery" and remained in use until a new city hall was completed in 1873. Lester's office, however, would have been in the second Rookery Building, a handsome eleven-story edifice designed by Burnam & Root and erected in 1886 at 209 South La Salle Street. The lobby of this building was remodeled by Frank Lloyd Wright in 1905 (see Viskochil, plates 65–66).

342.3   **three known chemical agents**   The pancreas secretes several digestive enzymes, including insulin and glucagon; it regulates the amount of sugar in the blood.

347.13   **Cemetery of the Redeemer**   This cemetery appears to be Dreiser's creation; the German Lutheran burial ground in Chicago was in the southeast corner of Graceland Cemetery, not far from the U.S. Marine Hospital.

355.32   **Hegewisch**   Then a small town near Lake Calumet, incorporated into Chicago.

360.26   **Sandwood . . . Kenosha**   Kenosha, Wisconsin, is fifty miles north of Chicago. Sandwood, where Jennie lives, is apparently fictitious.

361.4   **Auditorium Hotel**   One of Chicago's most luxurious hotels, the Auditorium stood at Congress Street and Michigan Avenue and adjoined a theater and opera house of the same name. The rotunda of the hotel was finished in marble, and the dining room (on the tenth floor) overlooked Lake Michigan. Using dials on the walls of their rooms, guests could order iced water, newspapers, stationery, and other articles simply by moving the pointer to the desired item (Hill, p. 149).

370.41   **latest polar attempt by Borchgrevink**   Carsten Egeberg Borchgrevink (1864–1934) was a Norwegian explorer who made pioneering trips to the Antarctic in 1895 and 1898–1900.

370.41   **Art Nouveau**   An ornamental style found in many European cities, and especially in Brussels, between 1890 and 1910. Art Nouveau sought to break free of the rational, imitative historicism of the nineteenth century by emphasizing undulating, asymmetrical lines, often based on vegetative models. Its practitioners in America included glassmaker Louis Comfort Tiffany and architect Louis Henry Sullivan, whose best-known buildings were erected in Chicago.

371.1   **younger musicians in Italy and Germany**   During the first half of the nineteenth century, the romantic movement in music, which included such composers as Verdi (1813–1901) and Wagner (1813–83), was seen as a revolt against classicism; romantic music emphasized emotionalism, subjectivity, and nationalism. Probably the conversation at Mrs. Gerald's party would have concerned music by later Romantic composers—perhaps Brahms (1833–97) and Puccini (1858–1924).

371.3   **Díaz in Mexico**   Porfirio Díaz (1830–1915) was a soldier and later president of Mexico (1877–80; 1884–1911). He established a strong, centralized state; this in turn enabled him to oversee a massive increase in the number of railways. Between 1903 and 1909 several Mexican railways were combined into the Ferrocarriles Nacionales de México, a private company in which the government owned the majority of the stock (Gil, p. 89).

371.13 **a theory, prevalent . . . in England**   Dreiser has made reference here to the theories advanced by nineteenth-century geologists that a sufficiently constant source of heat within the earth could account for the formation of its land masses and topographical features by a process of gradual cooling over many millions of years. The key figures in the debate were James Hutton, Charles Lyell, and Charles Darwin on one side and Sir William Thomson (Lord Kelvin) on the other. Around the turn of the century, scientific discoveries began to throw weight on the side of the followers of Darwin. At issue was the earth's age: the Darwinians believed that the earth had been in existence for some four billion years, those in Lord Kelvin's camp that it was not nearly so old. Darwinians believed that very gradual change accounted for the earth's features; their opponents favored more catastrophic interpretations of geological evidence. Those of a skeptical turn of mind—Dreiser and Lester, for example—would have been attracted more strongly by Darwinian thinking. Christians seeking to accommodate the new findings of science with their religious beliefs would have favored Lord Kelvin's theories. See John Theodore Merz, A *History of European Thought in the Nineteenth Century*. 4 vols. (1904–12; repr. New York: Dover, 1965), 2:291–97, 363–67; also Lord Kelvin's *Popular Lectures and Addresses* (London: Macmillan, 1894), esp. the essay entitled "On Geological Time."

374.1 **West Baden**   Letty is inviting Lester to West Baden Springs in southern Indiana, a chic mineral-water spa of the period. The town would have been known to Dreiser in 1911 as the site of the West Baden Springs Hotel, an early twentieth-century engineering marvel of metal and glass. The hotel included a brick shell of six stories built around a domed atrium almost two hundred feet in diameter (Winckler, p. 120). Letty issues her invitation in 1896, six years before the hotel was erected, but Dreiser probably would not have been aware of this discrepancy, nor would most of his readers.

379.22 **the hey-dey of that craze**   The first great bicycle craze in America took place during the late 1860s; most riders practiced the sport in indoor rinks called by such fanciful names as *velocipedaria* or *amphicyclotheatrons*. Dreiser has referred here to a later popular-culture manifestation of the 1890s—outdoor leisure cycle-touring, practiced by such groups as the Century Riding Club of America and the League of American Wheelmen. Special bicycle roads, or "corridors," were constructed from large cities to picturesque outlying communities such as Sandwood (McGurn, pp. 41–45; 97–98).

383.14 **the Mikado**   An archaic title for the emperor of Japan. *The Mikado* is also the title of a famous comic opera by Gilbert and Sullivan, first produced in London in 1885.

388.33   **Thessalonians**   I Thessalonians 4:13–18 is a text sometimes read at funerals; it promises resurrection for dead believers: "For if we believe that Jesus died and rose again, even so them also which sleep in Jesus will God bring with him."

390.6   **Tremont House in Chicago**   A six-story hotel in the French Renaissance style, located at 31 West Lake in Chicago (Andreas, pp. 355–56).

394.9   **Western Home for the Friendless**   Dreiser probably had in mind the Chicago Home for the Friendless (established 1858) at 1926 Wabash Avenue. The purpose of this charitable institution was to protect destitute women and to arrange for the adoption of orphaned or abandoned children (Moses and Kirkland, 2:390–91).

395.28   **the poet**   A slight misquotation of Tennyson, *In Memoriam, A.H.H.* (1850): "One God, one law, one element, / And one far-off divine event, / To which the whole creation moves" (sect. 37).

396.28   **"There is neither good nor ill, but thinking makes it so."**   *Hamlet*, act 2, sc. 2, line 259.

404.36   **Carlsbad, Scheveningen**   Carlsbad was a hot-springs spa in Bohemia, a country now part of western Czechoslovakia; more recently the city has been known as Karlovy Vary. Scheveningen was a popular Dutch coastal resort on the North Sea.

405.9   *cordon bleu*   Le Cordon Bleu is a famous school of cooking in Paris. Its name derives from the blue ribbons (or baldrics) worn by members of the Order of the Holy Ghost, which is famous for its fine dinners. Lester and Letty's cook would have been trained at this school.

406.32   **North Cape**   A promontory of Mageroy, an island off northern Norway; it is frequently visited by tourist ships and is one of the very northernmost points of Europe.

411.31   *Enquirer*   The *Enquirer*, established in 1842, was Cincinnati's leading newspaper.

413.32   **St. Michael's**   This Catholic church stands at the northwest corner of North and Hudson Avenues; it is still one of the most handsome and imposing church buildings in Chicago. The church is named for Saint Michael the Archangel; there is perhaps some significance to the fact that, in apocryphal literature, this saint is represented as the protector of Christians at the hour of death, when he conducts their souls to God. In one of his two appearances in the New Testament (Jude 5:9) he disputes with the devil over possession of Moses' body—another appropriate allusion here.

TEXTUAL
COMMENTARY

EDITORIAL PRINCIPLES

This edition of *Jennie Gerhardt* has been prepared in accordance with the principles of copy-text editing enunciated by W. W. Greg, Fredson Bowers, and G. Thomas Tanselle. It presents a critical, eclectic text constructed from several documents; it does not reproduce the text of a single historical document. The edition aims to present, however imperfectly, an ideal text; it makes no claim to provide a "definitive" text. The history of *Jennie Gerhardt* is so complicated that definitiveness is not possible—as, indeed, it is not in any critically edited text. It is possible, however, to make a responsible attempt to reclaim a text that fulfills the author's final artistic intentions, and that has been the goal of this edition.

An author's text is often created during a lengthy compositional process and is the product of many different kinds, or sets, of intentions, some of which are contradictory and all of which continue to grow and change as the creative act progresses. It is often possible to identify these sets of intentions and to define them and differentiate among them. Some spring entirely from the author's creative imagination; some are influenced by commercial necessity (or by the author's perception of it); some are colored by the recommendations of other persons; some are suggested to the author or required of him by the publisher. All of these kinds of intention are present in the history of *Jennie Gerhardt*; it is possible to reconstruct or infer them either from the extant manuscripts and typescripts or from the correspondence that survives. It has been the policy in this edition to evaluate these various sets of intentions and to admit cuts and revisions into the copy-text selectively from the various textual witnesses that survive.[1]

Copy-Text

The copy-text for this edition of *Jennie Gerhardt* is the composite MS of 1910–11 in the Dreiser Collection at the University of Pennsylvania. This is a fair-copy document: in its early chapters it incorporates parts of the ur-manuscript and the typescripts of

1901–2; the bulk of its text, however, is inscribed in black-ink holograph. This is the text that Dreiser gave to his typist for copying; the resulting ribbon typescript, in turn, was the document that he submitted to Harper and Brothers in the spring of 1911.[2]

There are other possibilities for copy-text: the ur-manuscript (for the first several chapters), the Barrett carbon typescript at the University of Virginia, and the first edition. None of these is suitable for this kind of edition, however. The ur-manuscript is a different—and unfinished—version of the novel and has only a distant verbal relation to the composite MS of 1910–11; the Barrett carbon is simply a less-than-perfect copy of the composite MS; the first edition reflects the substantial revising and cutting that took place at Harpers and therefore represents a later, mixed, collaborative set of intentions. The aim in this edition is not to reflect those later mixed intentions; it is instead to recapture, as nearly as possible, Dreiser's own *active* intentions as they existed in the spring of 1911 when he submitted *Jennie Gerhardt,* through his agent, to Harper and Brothers. Such intentions are seen as extending horizontally throughout the compositional process and achieving a kind of systematic wholeness. An effort has been made to trace these intentions through subsequent incarnations of the text and to differentiate these intentions from among the various nonauthorial intentions that were operating simultaneously, and often at odds with one another, during the cutting and editing of the novel.

An author's *active* intentions can be put into words only in a general and imperfect way—but that, after all, is the essential condition of critical editing. For the purposes of this edition, Dreiser's *active* intentions of 1910–11 have been perceived as follows: From beginning to end, Dreiser thought of *Jennie Gerhardt* as an honest, moving portrait of a woman tragically compromised by circumstances of birth and fate. *Jennie Gerhardt* was to be his treatment of a woman of emotional greatness; the novel was also to embody a dialectical confrontation, never settled, between Jennie's quasi-religious mysticism and Lester's bleak, pessimistic determinism.

G. Thomas Tanselle, in his seminal article "The Editorial Problem of Final Authorial Intention," has adapted a taxonomy of intention from Michael Hancher's work and has applied it to textual editing.[3] The three kinds of intention that Hancher and

Tanselle distinguish are *programmatic, active,* and *final. Programmatic* intention is the author's intention to create something—a general plan to write and have published a sonnet, for example, or a novel. *Active* intention is the author's intention to be seen or understood as acting in a particular way. *Final* intention is the intention to make something happen—the hope that the poem or novel will change an audience's viewpoint or, alternately, the expectation that the literary work will bring recognition or remuneration. Of the three, *active* intention is the most important to the scholarly editor, for it "concerns the meanings embodied in the work" (Tanselle, p. 175).

These distinctions guide the scholarly editor in the process of emendation. Practically, in the case of *Jennie Gerhardt,* the editor must decide what variants from the published 1911 text to admit into the copy-text of 1910–11. Although the great majority of these variants undoubtedly resulted from the work of the Harpers editors, some of them must also have been Dreiser's work. Dreiser almost surely inscribed revisions and cuts himself on the ribbon typescript before submitting it to Harpers. Whether he transferred all of these revisions to the Barrett carbon cannot be determined. He also quite likely made corrections and revisions on the freshly typed text that Hitchcock sent to him for approval. And Dreiser surely made some alterations on the proofs of the novel. These embodiments of the text, however—the ribbon typescript, the Harpers typescript, and the Harpers proofs—are not known to be extant. The scholarly editor must therefore study the variants between the composite MS of 1910–11 and the Harpers first edition and exercise critical judgment to decide which of the many changes were likely introduced by Dreiser as continuations of his *active,* artistic intentions. These variants are admitted into the reading text of this edition.

One must realize, however, that some of the work of the Harpers editors can also be seen as carrying forward Dreiser's *active* intentions. Authors can delegate intention to editors or amanuenses, and these persons can act in the author's stead, correcting errors and repairing verbal confusions in ways that are satisfactory and beneficial to the author. Some of the work of the Harpers editors has been judged to fall into this category. Such changes have likewise been admitted into the reading text.[4]

Two extensive hand collations have been performed in the

creation of this edition. First, the composite MS (the copy-text) has been collated against the *typed* text of the Barrett carbon; this collation has uncovered the errors and misreadings introduced by the typist and has brought to light as well that typist's imposition of a new texture of accidentals on Dreiser's novel. A separate photo-reproduction of the Barrett carbon has been purged of typist corruption and of Sara Dreiser's alterations (which Dreiser rejected and which have only a tangential relationship to the published text) in order to create an accurate transcription of the copy-text. This document has been used as the typesetter's copy on which the various emendations from later forms of the text have been entered. The second collation is the major one for the edition. Here the *typed* text of the Barrett carbon has been collated against the 1911 first edition. Thousands of variants have been uncovered; they are a mixture of work by Dreiser, Hitchcock, and Hitchcock's assistants at Harpers, and they undoubtedly result from a mixture of *active, programmatic,* and *final* intentions on the part of both author and editors.

Those variants that, in the judgment of the editor of this edition, carry forward Dreiser's *active* intentions of 1910–11 have been emended back into the copy-text. Some of these variants were surely Dreiser's work; others were just as surely introduced by the Harpers employees for purposes of clarity and correctness. In a final round of emending, the editor of this edition has introduced some adjustments, nearly all of them minor, for clarity and accuracy.

Apparatus

Because of the importance of *Jennie Gerhardt* in the Dreiser canon, all substantive emendations have been recorded in the apparatus to this volume. The readings adopted from the Harpers text appear in Table 1 of the emendations lists; those introduced by the editor of this volume are given in Table 2. There is no other source of emendation. Limitations of space have prevented the presentation of all accidental variants and emendations in the published apparatus. Such a table would be unreasonably large and would be cluttered by an enormous amount of inconsequential data. Nor does the apparatus include such traditional tables as a historical collation or a record of alterations in the manuscripts. The texts of *Jennie Gerhardt* (and Dreiser's texts generally) survive in such multiplicity and variation that it would be impractical ever to publish an exhaustive apparatus for an edition such as this one. What is included in the present volume, however, represents a compromise: material that should genuinely be of use to readers of this edition. A full record of all accidental and substantive variation between the texts and a full record of accidental emendations in the copy-text has been deposited, however, in the Dreiser Collection at the University of Pennsylvania; it is available to specialists interested in the minutiae of variation and emendation for this edition.

Dreiser did not expect to exercise close control over the accidentals of his text—the spelling, punctuation, capitalization, and word division. It might therefore be argued that the punctuation supplied by typists, trade editors, and compositors in 1910–11 should be accepted en bloc because Dreiser gave it a kind of tacit approval. The Pennsylvania Dreiser Edition, however, entrusts the accidentals of its texts to scholarly editors who have studied the author's manuscripts and become familiar with his prose style. Dreiser punctuated his texts very lightly; in general he seems to have preferred a free or open system of pointing. This texture of punctuation has been preserved in this edition whenever possible. Dreiser's written prose, here and elsewhere, falls into certain syntactical patterns, and his pointing for some of these is predictably incorrect, even by the standards of his own day. For example, he set off modifying or appositional elements inconsistently (or sometimes not at all), he created floating participles, and he sometimes separated subjects and verbs with commas. Many of these errors or idiosyncrasies have been corrected or regularized for intelligibility, but others—if they cause no particular difficulty for the reader—have been preserved.

Dreiser was inconsistent in the matter of word division; for this edition his inconsistencies have been regularized to his most common usage. Dreiser's misspellings are predictable and have been corrected with reference to the *Oxford English Dictionary*; archaic or British forms of spelling or usage have been allowed to stand, however. The names of numbered streets in cities have been given in arabic numerals; the names of numbered avenues have been spelled out. A full record of the handling of accidentals in the reading text is on deposit in the Department of Special Collections of the Van Pelt-Dietrich Library Center at the University of Pennsylvania.

Certain inconsistencies have been allowed to remain in the text. Dreiser rendered large sums of money in two different ways—as words (fifty thousand dollars) and as numerals ($50,000). It is possible to discern a rough pattern in his usages: when he appears to want the sum of money to be embedded neutrally in the text, he gives the amount in words; when he wishes the sum or sums to stand out, he employs numerals. The numerals are used to particularly good effect in passages in which Lester reckons his net worth and contemplates what he will lose if he remains with Jennie. The choice has therefore been not to impose a particular style on the numbers in these cases.

One other inconsistency requires comment—the color of Jennie's eyes. At 8.26 they are blue, but much later in the text, at 396.36 and 409.21, they are described as gray. Dreiser was almost surely using these colors for their connotative value. Early in the novel Jennie's blue eyes suggest her openness and innocence; later her gray eyes betoken her innate sympathy and melancholy. One could emend all readings to "bluish-gray," but that would seem to go contrary to Dreiser's purposes. The inconsistencies are widely enough spaced in the text to present no particular problem for a reader; the decision has therefore been made not to emend.

Cruxes: Crux I

The first important decision that faces the editor of *Jennie Gerhardt* concerns the version of the novel that Dreiser completed in early January 1911, the version in which Lester and Jennie were married. Some editors might see Dreiser's decision to undo this marriage as having been influenced improperly by Lillian Rosenthal and Fremont Rider; these editors might argue for a reconstruction and restoration of the text in which the two major characters were wed. However convincing such an argument might be, the fact is that this earlier text of the novel no longer survives in its entirety. Dreiser must have discarded whatever materials were left from his revision; at least, no such fragments survive at the University of Pennsylvania or in any of the other major Dreiser collections in the United States. For the record, the editor of the Pennsylvania edition sees no persuasive evidence that Dreiser was improperly influenced in his decision to delete the marriage. That decision appears to have been more or less spontaneous on his part—a natural extension of the compositional process. If these fragments were ever discovered, of course, they would merit separate publication to complete the record, just as the extant chapters of the ur-version of *Jennie Gerhardt* might someday be published for the benefit of Dreiser scholars.

Crux II

A second textual crux in *Jennie Gerhardt* involves a deathbed scene and a set of double quotation marks. *Jennie Gerhardt* might be said to be structured around deathbed scenes: the death of Jennie's mother, then of old Gerhardt, then of Vesta, and finally of Lester. The most important of these scenes is the final one— Lester's death in a hotel room in Chicago. His wife, Letty, is away in Europe. Lester asks that Jennie, whom he has not seen in several years, come to him. She arrives, and they exchange small talk. A few lines later the emotional high point of the novel occurs—Lester's final and long-delayed declaration of love for Jennie. The passage is reproduced below exactly as it appears in the Harpers 1911 text:

"Well, I've told you now, and I feel better. You're a good woman, Jennie, and you're kind to come to me this way." I loved you. I love you now. I want to tell you that. It seems strange, but you're the only woman I ever did love truly. We should never have parted.

Jennie caught her breath. It was the one thing she had waited for all these years—this testimony. It was the one thing that could make everything right—this confession of spiritual if not material union. Now she could live happily. Now die so. "Oh, Lester," she exclaimed with a sob, and pressed his hand. He returned the pressure. There was a little silence. Then he spoke again. (pp. 422–23)

The reader will have noted that in the Harpers text of Lester's statement, a set of double quotation marks follows the word *way*. All that comes after—Lester's confession of love and regret—is outside the quotation marks so that, strictly speaking, he does not utter these words. One does not wish to make more of a single punctuation mark than is reasonable, but this error, if error it is, certainly comes at a crucial point in the narrative. Does Lester really tell Jennie that he loves her, or is his speech something that she imagines—something that she badly *wants* to hear but that in fact he does not say?

As it turns out, there is a reasonably simple explanation for the misplaced quotation marks. Lester's declaration and Jennie's reaction were added in a late stage of revision, and either Dreiser or the typist or compositor forgot to move the quotation marks to include the new words. In the composite MS and the Barrett carbon, Lester avoids the subject of love. He apologizes to Jennie for mishandling their relationship but says nothing more. The expansion of his speech and the addition of Jennie's reaction to it therefore must have been executed on the original ribbon typescript, on the fresh Harpers typescript, or on the proofs. Dreiser must have added the new lines in a margin or on a separate sheet of paper, together with directions for their placement in the text, but he must have forgotten to adjust the quotation marks to include the new words. The typist or compositor must have followed directions unthinkingly, and no one caught the error in a subsequent proofing. In fact, the reading was not corrected during Dreiser's lifetime.

There is a chance, of course, that the passage was added by one of the editors at Harpers who wanted Lester finally to overcome his inertia and declare his love for Jennie. This seems unlikely, however—even given the tendency of the Harpers editors to descend on key scenes in the narrative and revise them to increase their emotional intensity. The wording of Jennie's reaction—from "Jennie caught her breath" to "Then he spoke again"—is written in language characteristic of Dreiser. The dashes, the halting diction, the wording of "this confession of spiritual if not material union," the phrase "a little silence" all seem of a piece with Dreiser's style during this period of his career. It is likely that these words are Dreiser's and, by extension, that the confession by Lester that precedes them was written by him as well. These passages have therefore been emended into the text of this edition.[5]

For the record, the editor of the Pennsylvania edition believes that much of the thematic meaning of *Jennie Gerhardt* pivots on this scene and that the "flat" version, without Lester's declaration of love, is more consistent with the characterization and philosophical argument of the novel than is the scene in its revised form. The words uttered by Lester were almost surely added by Dreiser, however, and they should be emended into the copy-text. However, readers should ponder the transformation that would be wrought on *Jennie Gerhardt* if Lester's statement of love were *not* accepted as an emendation from the Harper text. By way of assistance in this exercise, the Pennsylvania edition includes as an appendix the text of the passage as it would appear without this emendation.[6]

Crux III

The composite MS, the Barrett carbon, and the Harpers first impression of *Jennie Gerhardt* all end with a coda entitled "In Passing." In this brief section Dreiser attempts, in heightened language, to summarize what has happened to Jennie and to present a series of questions about human life and man's relation to nature. In later Harpers reprintings, however, and in an undated A. L. Burt reprint, the coda is dropped, and the novel ends with the last words on page 431: "Days and days in endless reiteration, and then—?" All subsequent impressions of *Jennie Gerhardt* published during Dreiser's lifetime—including printings issued by Liveright, Doubleday, and Simon and Schuster—omit the coda.

Almost certainly Dreiser ordered the coda dropped from the text, but no document or testimony confirms his responsibility for the act. Still, it is most unlikely that an editor or other publishing-house employee would have made such a change unless acting under Dreiser's explicit directions. It is also unlikely that subsequent impressions by other publishers would have been issued without the coda unless such had been Dreiser's wish. One must conclude, therefore, that the decision to drop the coda was Dreiser's. That decision, whenever it occurred, is taken here to represent a continuation of Dreiser's *active*, artistic intentions and is followed in the text of this edition, which ends with the dash and question mark. The coda, however, is printed as an appendix.

Subsequent Textual History

During Dreiser's lifetime only one change was made in the plates of the Harper and Brothers edition. At 22.30 the erroneous reading "is" was altered to "it". There is an elaborate explanation of this small correction by one of Dreiser's first bibliographers, linking it (somewhat illogically) to a binding variant.[7] Book dealers have for many years used the "is [it" point as a means of differentiating the supposed first printing of the Harpers edition from subsequent printings, because the Harpers printings were not differentiated on their copyright pages.

As it turns out, the correction of "is" to "it" was probably a stop-press variant. A check of gutter measurements (a technique not employed by bibliographers until the 1960s) indicates that some copies of the Harpers edition were issued with the reading "is" and some with the reading "it" with no variation in gutter measurement. If "is" and "it" signaled different printings, the gutter measurements—the distance from the edge of one type page across the central gutter of a gathering to the opposite type page—would almost surely be significantly different.[8]

Only one other true edition of *Jennie Gerhardt*—that is to say, a complete resetting of the type—was published in Dreiser's lifetime. This was the Constable edition, published in London in 1928. Substantial portions of this text and corresponding portions of the Harpers text have been entered into computer files using the Kurzweil Scanner. Collation of the files has been performed using the programs in CASE—Computer-Assisted Scholarly Editing—developed by Peter L. Shillingsburg.[9] These collations have uncovered no evidence of authorial revision in the Constable text. The variations noted involve only the kinds of changes that typically occur when an American text is reset for the British book market. British punctuation of dialogue is introduced, as is a British system of word hyphenation. Words ending in *-or* and *-ize* in the American text are given *-our* and *-ise* endings. The word *offense* becomes *offence;* the word *center* becomes *centre*. The accidental texture of the Constable edition is much different from that of the Harpers edition, but for the purposes of this investigation the Constable edition is textually insignificant.

The Two Editions

The Harpers 1911 first edition of *Jennie Gerhardt* is an important textual artifact that merits study by Dreiser scholars. This was the text that brought Dreiser back into the public eye and launched the middle phase of his career. It is a collaborative, "negotiated" text, the product of conflicting aims and intentions on the part of Dreiser and his publishers. It is a socialized or domesticated text and can be read and studied as such, especially now that the Pennsylvania edition (with its ancillary material) is available for purposes of comparison. The 1911 text has its own validity and place in Dreiser's career; it is a good example of a text altered by conventional forces to fit the cultural climate of its time. It is the text that passed muster with Hamilton Wright Mabie, the text he approved for public consumption.

The Pennsylvania edition of *Jennie Gerhardt*, by contrast, presents the text that so deeply impressed H. L. Mencken. The text of the Pennsylvania edition is essentially the one that Dreiser brought to a point of stasis in the spring of 1911 and showed to Mencken for his opinion. This text, reconstructed from the documents that survive, now has its moment—its chance to be read, interpreted, and taught. This is not an edition of a familiar literary artifact. It is instead an edition of a new work of literature, heretofore unknown, and it should be approached freshly and interpreted anew.

NOTES

1. For an elaboration of this line of thinking, see James L. W. West III, "Editorial Theory and the Act of Submission," *Papers of the Bibliographical Society of America* 83 (June 1989):169–85.

2. The copy-text bears some markings and revisions in two extraneous hands—one the hand of Sara Dreiser and the other a loosely scrawled autograph that is clearly not hers and does not match the script of Mary Fanton Roberts. The changes in both hands were incorporated into the subsequent typescript; they appear to have resulted from his delegation of intention to his wife and to the unknown reader. Almost without exception these alterations are simple corrections of errors or minor clarifications of meaning; they have no significant effect on the meaning of the novel. Because they seem to have been made with Dreiser's active approval, the changes have been incorporated into the text of this edition.

3. Tanselle, "The Editorial Problem of Final Authorial Intention," *Studies in Bibliography* 29 (1976):167–211; Hancher, "Three Kinds of Intention," *Modern Language Notes* 87 (1972):827–51. See also Tanselle, "Classical, Biblical, and Medieval Textual Criticism and Modern Editing," *Studies in Bibliography* 36 (1983), esp. pp. 28, 49, and 67.

4. See "Editorial Theory and the Act of Submission," pp. 175–76.

5. Dreiser was probably influenced to make this change by a 13 March 1911 letter to him from C. B. De Camp, one of the persons he asked to read *Jennie Gerhardt* in its original typescript form. De Camp wrote in part: "You have [Lester] very naturally say but few words to Jennie on his death-bed, but I think you could make him just as naturally say a little more. . . . Now whether he loves Jennie very intensely or not, he has undoubtedly come to feel that there is a peculiar and spiritual relationship between them. I would have him confess it at the last—that theirs was a true marriage (or at least his truest marriage) and that there is a spiritual something in life that he was ignorant of." This letter is in the Dreiser Collection. See James L. W. West III, "C. B. De Camp and *Jennie Gerhardt*," *Dreiser Studies* 23 (Spring 1992).

6. For a more extensive discussion of the interpretive questions involved, see James L. W. West III, "Double Quotes and Double Meanings in *Jennie Gerhardt*, *Dreiser Studies* 18 (Spring 1987):1–11.

7. Vrest Orton, *Dreiserana: A Book about His Books* (New York: Chocorua Bibliographies, 1929), pp. 25–29.

8. Optical collation on a Lindstrand Comparator of a run of the printings of the 1911 edition reveals that, before the 1946 World impression, some twenty-six areas in the plates were reset to remedy problems with type batter or with crowded lines. No textual variants were introduced.

9. Shillingsburg, *Scholarly Editing in the Computer Age* (Athens: University of Georgia Press, 1986), part 3.

TEXTUAL APPARATUS

TEXTUAL TABLES

Table 1: Readings Adopted from the 1911 Edition

The table below records all substantive emendations adopted into the copy-text from the 1911 Harpers first edition. In each entry, the page-line citation refers to the pagination and lineation of the Pennsylvania edition. The first reading is the emended reading; it is followed by a left-pointing bracket that should be read as "emended from" and then by the original reading from the copy-text. Textual notes have been written for entries preceded by asterisked numbers; these notes follow Table 2.

4.1	said the clerk] he said
4.29	six-hundred] three-hundred
4.30	He had] He
4.33	on the mortgage] on this
5.1	longer—all these perplexities] longer,
5.10	the philanthropist] the credit-giver
5.38	that she] that the little one
6.2	Pastor Wundt] Father Wundt
6.10	scared from the railroad yards. Mrs. Gerhardt] scared off from doing that. She
6.25	were thus] were so
6.27	a population of fifty thousand] twenty-five thousand population
6.28	traffic, was a good field for the hotel business, and the opportunity had been improved; so at least the Columbus people proudly thought.] traffic, presented an opportunity for superiority in this line, which in this instance had been improved.
7.7	departing in accordance with the movement of the trains.] departing as the trains dictated.
7.11	terms] term
7.12	them to Columbus, invariably maintained parlor chambers at the hotel.] them here, invariably maintained parlor chambers.
7.16	but an otherwise homeless bachelor.] but a bachelor, and always in need of a comfortable room.
7.20	stir of this kaleidoscopic world.] merriment of this shifty world.
7.35	clumsy hands] faulty hands
8.3	bottom of the stairway.] bottom.
8.5	Through the big swinging doors there] About this time there
8.8	among the crowd] among the riff-raff

10.17   illness and trouble began] illness began
11.13   Sebastian] Sebastian had
11.15   Though only a] Though a
11.39   around the hotel entrance] around its entrance
12.16   those hotel fellows] those fellows
13.25   twenty-two. Jennie stood silently at her side.] twenty-two.
14.23   live?" [¶] To all of these questions] live?" all of which
14.36   During the colloquy Jennie's] All the time Jennie's
16.7   girl, softly.] girl.
16.20   which all the earth] which earth
17.20   formulating of conceptions] formulating conceptions
17.37   was sitting] was now sitting
19.6   he had studied law at Columbia University] he studied law at
          Columbia
19.11   that assiduity] that fulness
21.5   chamber that Saturday] chamber one Saturday
21.14   instead of on Monday] instead of Monday
22.34   the depressed local conditions in this branch of] the local condi-
          tion of this kind of
23.14   the door behind her.] the door.
23.33   which had made her feel uncomfortable] which made her far
          more comfortable
24.38   that, for] that, with
25.15   He had not realized, perhaps,] He did not know
25.18   nothing, procured] nothing, took
25.21   earn two, and sometimes three] earn three, and sometimes five
25.32   each of the children] each of them
27.22   an obstinate jerk] an opposing jerk
28.32   cars, the big plate-glass windows] cars, its windows
28.39   now appeared in the distance] now came vigorously forward
29.38   tramped along sympathetically] tramped sympathetically
30.15   groceryman] grocerman
30.18   mother and] moth- and
30.34   ordered the several articles] ordered everything
32.12   generosity of the unknown benefactor] generosity of some one
33.9   Nowadays when she came to the hotel upon her semi-weekly errand
          ] Whenever she came upon her errand
33.33   mop of black] mop of fine black
33.33   which hung about his forehead, and gave an almost leonine cast to
          his fine face.] which drooped about his forehead, and gave his
          face a touch of the lion.
34.4   she went on, even more bashfully; she realized now that he was still
          holding her hand.] she added.
34.31   his lips] his lip
35.1   her underlying respect for this great man, she said] her enduring
          respect, said
35.8   moved by a curious feeling] moved with a feeling

35.20	heavenly. Not that she fully understood his meaning, however.] heavenly. It was more as a word, though, than as anything else, that she understood his meaning.
35.32	time she came, and to] time, to
36.9	cheerily; then, seeing her hesitate, he added, "May] cheerily, and seeing her hesitate, "may
39.27	view. Since that one notable and halcyon visit upon which he] view. When in one chief and halcyon visit he
39.29	they had lived in] they came into
40.9	but the reflection] but it
40.19	his breast.] his bosom.
40.39	Jennie drew out the watch from his waistcoat pocket and] Jennie reached, and, taking it out,
41.23	discovered that a] discovered a
41.24	friendly, was secretly] friendly, secretly
41.35	about the clothes] about them
42.18	"Do I?"] "Have I?"
42.19	"Yes, but] "Yes, you have, but
42.29	washing must expect criticism if] washing is usually criticised, if
42.30	station is observed in] state is seen in
42.39	thought that it was] thought she was
43.9	admit at least part of the] admit the
43.12	attach any suspicion of evil] attach evil
44.34	passed about in] passed in
45.5	but perhaps it will be better to keep her away, at least for the present."] but it will be just as well to keep her away."
45.9	matter. [¶] Again that evening the senator sat in his easy chair and brooded over this new development. Jennie] matter. [¶] Jennie
45.22	recognition from the president which] recognition which
45.25	settled in his old quarters] settled here
45.28	door, he was greeted by Mrs. Gerhardt and her daughter with astonished and diffident] door astonished Mrs. Gerhardt and her daughter, who greeted him with diffident
46.6	the proposal. They parted with smiles and much handshaking. [¶] "That man] the matter. [¶] As he went out he did not fail to make another contribution, which, like all the others, was commented upon with delight. [¶] "That man
46.23	of laundering] of laundry
46.27	her well-shaped head] her shapely head
46.29	her as with] her with
49.3	not clearly understanding] not understanding
49.30	only joking] only jesting
50.5	Paris. From there he had set forth for America, the land of promise.] Paris. Having romance enough in him to venture merrily upon a lone and far journey, he set forth from there for America.
50.7	Arrived in this country] Arrived here
50.37	Lutheran proclivities] Lutheran doctrine

51.22   Pastor Wundt] Father Wundt

51.29   disobeyed his injunctions.] disobeyed.

51.30   was a sin.] was beyond the pale.

51.36   for all such.] for such.

53.7   him and his] him and all

53.14   was once young himself] was young once

54.31   Its opinions] Its opinion

55.22   shielding such weakness in one of their] shielding weakness and liberty in their

55.26   exclaimed Gerhardt] returned Gerhardt

56.35   daughter might] daughter-companion might

57.40   Gerhardt. "I shall] Gerhardt. "I haven't seen him. I shall

58.2   old. I shall tell him that.] old. I shall see him. If he wants to marry you he should see me. Besides he is too old. I shall tell him that.

58.5   of Gerhardt's] of the father

58.6   away, seemed] away, was something which seemed

58.7   attitude?] attitude as that?

58.8   him? Of course Brander did call again, while Gerhardt was away at work, and they trembled lest he should hear of it. A few days later the senator came and took Jennie for a long walk. Neither she nor her mother said anything to Gerhardt. But he was not to be put off the scent for long.] him? When he called again and Gerhardt was at work, they trembled lest he should hear of it, and they would be berated for not telling him. If they did tell of it, and had not ordered Brander to stay away, there would be trouble. In this condition, Jennie's walk with the ex-senator passed nervously, and the next day they said nothing at all. [¶] Gerhardt, however, who was fearful lest his commands should not be carried out, was not long in asking.

58.22   time carefully surveying the house, in order to discover whether any visitor was being entertained.] time surveying the house, and judging for himself whether there was anyone present.

58.25   nervous, he took] nervous, took

58.28   was on his way to the house at the time, observed her departure.] was coming up to see at the time, observed her going.

58.35   He sat down calmly] He remained calmly upon the ground

58.39   that any trouble of this character was pending, felt irritated and uncomfortable.] that anything of this character was pending, was troubled to know what the situation meant.

59.6   Brander.] Brander, who stood amazed.

59.7   furiously, unable] furiously, utterly unable

59.8   gravely. "Why should you] gravely. "Has she done anything that you

59.14   choose his words.] choose a word.

59.16   exclaimed Gerhardt, his excitement growing under] said Gerhardt, growing in excitement under

59.22   ruffled dignity.] unruffled dignity.

59.26   logic, and] logic in the matter and

59.27	of parental compulsion] of compulsion
59.31	full height, "that you will have] full dignity, "that I shall not go out of here, and that you will have
60.26	righteousness.] legal righteousness.
60.29	force and determination] grit and determination
60.33	you politicians] these politicians
60.39	from the angry father, "to have had such an] from her husband, "to have an
61.4	said, addressing Gerhardt] said, returning to the father
61.7	good-night." He bowed slightly] good-night," and he bowed rather slightly
61.27	bad] bad and infectious
62.14	the daylight hours] the hours
62.14	sleeping to] sleeping by day to
62.31	evening while] evening when
62.35	shippers complained] shippers repeatedly complained
62.36	cars from the Pennsylvania fields] cars shipped from Pennsylvania
62.39	railroad in this] railroad this
63.10	weakling. There] weakling of the kind usually encountered under such circumstances. There
63.12	his awkward predicament] his dreadful predicament
63.18	adversary. [¶] There] adversary. [¶] Instantly the detective began to revile him with abusive phrases which are so common among those who swear. [¶] "I'll put a bullet through you, you dirty little cur," he shouted. [¶] There
63.20	hurried Sebastian] took him
63.31	tonight. When] tonight. She frequently inquired of Jennie what she thought could have happened to him, and when
63.38	said Jennie, and then told the story of the evening's adventure in explanation.] said Jennie in explanation.
64.8	was under arrest.] was there.
64.34	finest part of] finest quality of
64.40	said the boy] said his boy
65.1	may go harder] may be harder
65.4	o'clock."] o'clock, I believe."
65.22	between the hours of two] between two
65.24	post of duty. But] post, but
65.28	anything. This] anything. That
67.29	yet very glad it was no worse.] yet glad it was no more.
67.33	right," said Bass soothingly.] right," he said to soothe him.
68.3	had. Jennie] had. The law always meant so much heavier fines to her. Jennie
68.9	a casual] a friendly
68.9	in at his office.] in when he got there.
68.11	money. Pastor Wundt might let] money. Father Wundt might have let
68.16	exhausted.] exhausted, but still mentally alert.

68.22   pawned a second time, and she had no other means of obtaining money.] pawned again.)

69.30   herself to dreams.] herself in dreams.

69.34   see Senator Brander.] see.

69.38   him for help?] him now?

70.38   nervous and pale] nervous within and pale

70.39   within her] in her

71.36   sighed, his sympathies touched and awakened.] sighed, and then swiftly in his own mind ran over once more the anomalies of life.

72.9   write a note to the judge asking him to revoke the fine, for the sake of the boy's character, and] write the judge to revoke the fine for the boy's character's sake (though as he said he would gladly pay it) and

72.12   friend, the sheriff,] friend

72.32   complicated by] complicated with

72.33   father. The] father who would oppose any union whatsoever. The

72.37   the keenest] the wildest

72.38   with intellect] with intelligence

73.4   with her beauty] with the beauty

73.8   endeavoring to appear] endeavoring to still a storm of affectional emotion and to appear

74.4   you have understood] you understood

74.6   world has ever touched] world touched

76.16   she answered evasively.] she evaded.

76.18   afraid. Your father went to your] afraid. He passed your

76.22   wistfully at her daughter.] wistfully.

76.27   he couldn't pay the fine."] he had nothing."

76.30   as though] as if

76.38   and intended] and proposed

76.40   he had promised] he promised

77.1   the following day] the same day

77.3   was already on his way to Washington, but] was called to Washington, suddenly, but

78.13   ex-senator] senator

78.18   but never suspected that there was anything serious in his indisposition. Then the doctor discovered that] but thought of nothing serious until a week after it transpired that

78.25   consciousness. Jennie] consciousness. For days the papers were most considerate of this item of news but, during it all, Jennie

78.26   of his illness and did] of its progress. She did

78.27   came home that evening.] came in the evening of the day of his death, bringing it with him.

78.31   the newspaper] the paper

79.1   amazement.] amazement, the tendency to weaken and grow pale overcoming her and causing her to quickly show what she felt.

79.21   and had seen Jennie] and saw Jennie

79.38   concluded that] concluded

79.39   and she went] and went
79.40   significance of the news began] significance began
80.6   out of the] out the
80.21   her family.] her mother.
80.25   frequently thereafter] frequently after that
81.5   to the washing] to a washing
81.7   suds.] suds of her labor.
81.23   father," Mrs. Gerhardt] father," she
81.40   unfulfilled. Gerhardt] unfulfilled. He
82.11   a door-lock] a doorknob at the time
82.16   summon] summon up
82.18   lifted the apron] lifted it
82.19   man with the] man of the
82.24   looked alert] looked strong
82.30   own train of thought] own thoughts
83.7   and stood | and so stood
83.23   too intense for him to] too massive to
83.26   having offered itself to his mind.] having taken his attention.
85.21   out," reiterated Gerhardt.] out," exclaimed his father, deigning
        even to answer him.
85.30   little girlish trinkets] little trinkets
86.7   Gerhardt, still speaking] Gerhardt, always exclaiming
86.30   interpolated weakly.] interpolated meekly.
87.4   could meet again.] could talk.
87.30   under foot.] under foot is the way society understands it.
88.5   world's selfish] world's petty
88.5   preserve oneself from the evil to come.] preserve yourself.
88.14   grow. Flashes of inspiration come to guide] grow. Great flashes of
        how to do are revealed to
88.15   or a condition] or form of condition
88.33   expressed her] expressed a
89.10   had walked together] had come along
89.27   as does a] as a
89.31   with Brander] with the late senator
89.36   He had been] He was
90.18   head here] head there
90.20   succeeded in finding work] succeeded
90.21   home. He was not going to try to meet the mortgage on the house—
        he could not hope to.] home.
91.12   Bass waited] He waited
91.27   would only] only would
91.32   something to do?"] something?"
92.13   after he left] after left
92.29   come into being by the one common road] come by the one
        method
92.33   upon the process by the extreme religionist, and the world, by its
        silence, gives assent to a judgement so marvelously warped. [¶

Surely there is something radically wrong in this attitude.] upon it by the religionist, and to this mouthing of ignorance the world has for centuries been held in awe. [¶] It is high time that the sane word were said in this connection, and that, with no malice to either the spirit of ignorance, the false modesty of passion, or the force of custom or religion.

93.11	depth of vileness] vileness
93.12	to predicate so inevitably] to indicate existed there
95.1	quietly singing] quietly humming
95.26	unexpected consequence] unexpected denouement
95.40	and waited.] and wondered.
96.10	through their multitudinous] through various
96.12	Lutheran upbringing] Lutheran tendency and upbringing
97.7	and it needed] and needed
97.16	and with that] and that
97.30	never] really never
97.33	and was well] and well
98.17	mind. Jennie] mind. This was that Jennie
101.7	one, now six months old,] one
102.1	view she said] view said
103.31	housework, although] housework, for
104.12	was a] was in a
104.31	She wished her to remain for the day and begin her duties at once, and Jennie agreed. Mrs. Bracebridge provided her a dainty cap and apron, and then spent] She invited her to remain for the day and begin her duties at once which Jennie agreed to. She secured a dainty cap and apron and then the lady spent
104.37	indicated. Mrs. Bracebridge] indicated. She
105.1	evening Jennie] evening she
106.24	out of the money which Senator Brander had sent to Jennie] out of a store, the original source of which it is needless to indicate
106.36	burden of responsibilities] burden of ability
107.22	need of anything, so long as the baby was properly taken care of] need of what even her mother insisted that she must have.
107.25	contributed. Later on he was allowed fifty cents] contributed. The fifty cents he was allowed
108.25	She protested that she needed] She needed
108.30	with the fullness] with a fullness
108.36	These were the every-day expressions of the enduring affection that existed between them.] These were common expressions.
108.38	between Jennie and her mother] between them
108.40	as being always] as always
109.3	craved!] craved, and once in awhile had indicated to Jennie, before it would be too late, only the secret treasury of her bosom may ever know.
109.17	dress, good form] dress, form
111.7	differently by his daughter. Yet he could not make up his mind how

to treat her for the future. She had committed a great sin; it was impossible to get away from that.] differently. Now, comforted by the fact, he hardly knew how to feel or what to say. "Such a family," he declared at last, vigorously. Then tossed up his hands and shook his head as if he gave them all up for a bad job.

111.11	home that night] home, however,
111.29	nod that Gerhardt knew of the child's existence.] nod that he had.
111.35	Jennie finally] She finally
112.21	When Jennie] When she
113.19	godfather to the child] godfather to it
114.9	her own choice] her own
114.19	brought forward this] brought this
114.19	offering upon the altar of natural affection,] offering,
114.21	"That is nice,"] "That is not so nice,"
114.21	"But how would] "How would
114.30	have every advantage, religious or otherwise, that it was possible to obtain.] have the advantage of all those religious forms and ceremonies which to her seemed essential.
115.2	difficulty, did not] difficulty as regards the child, did not
115.3	her so long] her as long
115.20	Gerhardt answered "Yes," and Mrs. Gerhardt added her affirmative.] Both Gerhardt and his wife felt the solemnity of the duty which this prescribed, and yet they were not slow to answer in the affirmative.
115.28	fared with his own children.] fared with others.
115.29	been thus sponsored.] been so sponsored.
115.30	pledge to care for their spiritual welfare. He was silent.] pledge.
115.32	repeated Gerhardt] repeated he
116.6	which followed:] which ran:
117.12	solemn admonition] solemn invocation
117.16	the tiny creature] the creature
117.17	which God in His sacrament had commanded.] which this sacrament commanded.
117.30	Slowly Gerhardt] Slowly he
117.33	church disappeared and a feeling of natural affection took its place.] church left him, and in its place a feeling of necessary kindliness was bred. It was still a little child, he thought.
117.36	thing, demanding his sympathy and his love. Gerhardt felt his heart go out to the little child, and yet he could not yield his position all in a moment.] thing. Steadily, the significance of its soul came on, a strong steady current which involved all that was important in his faith.
118.5	Gerhardt looked] He looked
118.7	the child] the little child
118.14	the meaning in his voice] the sound of his voice

118.15   enough. The presence of the child] enough. He might grumble and fuss in the future. The presence of such a creature

118.18   restraining him.] restraining him through it all.

118.35   sum of three dollars a week and then three-fifty.] sum of four dollars a week and then five.

119.11   have me?"] have her?"

119.21   morning to give him a message from his hostess.] morning to inquire for Mrs. Bracebridge whether he would shortly be ready for a start they were going to make somewhere.

119.27   She would] She should

120.9   is like a honey-pot] is as a honey pot

120.17   Lester Kane, the son of a wholesale carriage builder of great trade distinction in that city and elsewhere throughout the country, who was wont to visit this house frequently in a social way. He was a friend of Mrs. Bracebridge more than of her husband, for the former had been raised in Cincinnati and as a girl had visited at his father's house. She knew his mother, his brother and his sisters and to all intents and purposes socially had always been considered one of the family. [¶] "Lester's coming] Lester Kane, whom she had heard her mistress speak of as a man of considerable ability. "Lester's coming

120.26   Henry," Jennie] Henry," she

120.29   His father was so good to me."] His father is so influential, you know."

120.36   "I'll be decent] "I'll be nice

120.39   he replied dryly.] he said drily.

121.7   are," he began. "I'm] are. I'm

121.11   Lester," she said. "George] Lester. George

121.16   seemed, why] seemed, for why

121.19   man. [¶] Jennie] man. He was master, while present—not anyone else. [¶] Jennie

121.22   him now and then on the sly, and felt,] him a number of times when he was not looking at her and felt

122.4   coquetry about her, but] coquetry but

122.8   regret. Then, suddenly,] regret when suddenly

122.17   friendly. [¶] "Why] friendly. She knew his family well. It appeared she had been raised in Cincinnati and his father and mother were known to her from childhood. [¶] "Why

122.28   scarcely understood] scarcely realized

122.31   Now he] On this occasion he

123.6   "Thirteen fourteen,"] "1314,"

124.18   poor, the highly bred maidens of his own class, the daughters of the proletariat, but] poor, the scions of aristocracy, the daughters of commonplace conditions, but

125.13   is well-nigh irresistible; the spiritual nature is overwhelmed by the shock.] is particularly productive of just such results in the case of some of the really better minds.

126.11 questions that bothered him—such questions as the belief] questions such as the belief

126.13 universe, and whether a republican,] universe, whether government, republican,

126.14 aristocratic form of government was] aristocratic were

126.29 age and apparently] age and to look at

127.3 it," Lester returned.] it," he returned.

127.14 classical] classic

127.21 upon a business life] upon that life

127.37 flames which] flames of which

128.14 individual conduct.] individual error.

128.39 view feminine youth] view youth

131.5 leave the city.] leave.

131.7 do that—talk] do—talk

131.7 He must persuade her to come and live with him.] He must try to persuade her to come with him to be his sweetheart.

131.15 at the next] at this next

131.18 afterward] afterwards

131.21 and a little after seven he] and at seven fifteen he

131.23 result, and] result but

131.26 A few minutes after eight] At eight fifteen

131.27 but it gave sufficient light to] but sufficient to

131.36 cabman] cabmen

132.20 sympathy, with even a little pity.] sympathy, a little pity, his personal affection.

132.37 yielding, especially since] yielding, even if

133.6 play. Above all] play. Of all

133.9 over in his mind.] over.

*134.17 as a lady's maid.] for any four dollars a week.

134.18 to take you somewhere else.] to get you something else.

134.28 thought.] thought. There were four in his father's wealthy household.

135.6 between them spoke] between spoke

135.35 mind; certainly this was not the end of the affair. Kane knew that he was deeply fascinated.] mind that there was to be a great deal more between them. The former by the very process of talking to her, of hearing her voice, of noting her mental method of procedure was fascinated.

136.1 had had any] had any

136.36 was an imposing establishment which] was a charming institution which

136.39 brownstone. It was] brownstone, which was

136.40 trees in an almost park-like inclosure, and its very stones spoke of a splendid dignity and a refined luxury.] trees in a great yard and which breathed a world of dignity and comfort which the average mortal does not know.

137.5 he had realized] he realized

137.8   industry, he had built it up into a great business; he made good wagons, and he sold them at a good profit.] industry he went on from that building perfectly durable vehicles, making them as handsome and serviceable as he could, selecting the most desirable material and in every way putting in quality and quantity for the lowest reasonable price until he had become rich.

137.17   say—"Ah, there] say—"there

137.34   that Robert was,] that his brother was

138.17   seriousness and] seriousness at any time and

140.20   She pushed him away with her strong hands.] She pushed his chest with her hands.

140.22   dust more on with] dust it with

140.39   and Louise, in particular, made a point of it.] and they had entertained so freely.

141.5   and wondering when] and when

141.23   not," said Archibald] not," he said

142.19   make. Louise] make when they were through. Louise

146.28   and I shall expect] and expect

146.28   and I want] and want

146.31   I should] I shall

147.12   herself for the sake of Bass in Columbus, had] herself, had

147.24   of making this confession] of this exposure

148.3   on a Wednesday] on Wednesday

148.7   five dollars,] five dollars or less,

148.21   that Gerhardt] that he

148.27   "Did the letter] "Did he

148.37   results] result

148.38   "I know," said Mrs. Gerhardt,] "I know," she said,

149.5   Ma?" asked Jennie as she] Ma?" she inquired, the moment she

149.38   Did the letter] Did he

150.37   his bony] his interesting bony

151.4   said that he] said he

151.19   until Bass] until he

151.23   Bass's words] His words

151.27   recover the use of his hands.] recover a little of their use.

153.18   she could conceal] she conceal

153.19   perhaps—well, rich] perhaps—rich

153.22   she excused] she had excused

153.23   left the house for the hotel.] left.

154.30   he had asked] he asked

155.24   gets three dollars and a half."] gets five dollars."

156.8   extracted several ten-] extracted ten

156.9   bills—two hundred and fifty dollars in] bills—one hundred and fifty in

156.23   what would come next.] what more he would do.

156.37   home?" he asked. "That] home? That

156.37   daytimes."] daytimes," he suggested helpfully.

157.8	confidence such as this. He was by no means a hard man, and the thought touched him. But he would not relinquish his purpose.] confidence like that. He did not know how she would do it but he knew something of mothers and daughters.
157.14	New York; I'll] New York and I'll
157.15	you. As] you and, as
157.17	please. Wouldn't you like that?"] please. You'll be rid of all this worry about your family then. I'll see that you won't have to worry about them any more."
157.20	Mrs. Gerhardt] she
157.22	with good furniture and a yard filled with] with furniture and a yard with
157.27	She hesitated] She paused
157.36	Mrs. Bracebridge?" he suggested.] Mrs. Bracebridge—she might take you," he said, after a time.
158.1	maids on long trips.] maids.
158.28	plane in his esteem which] plane which
158.33	want you to."] want to."
159.15	asked, startled.] asked half startled.
159.31	appeared. Jennie] appeared. Admitting the lie, which seemed essential at this time, but which did not concern her mother, since Jennie
159.31	her mother the whole truth, and there] her the whole truth there
160.10	the purchased articles] the things purchased
162.3	"Why didn't] "Why don't
162.10	at each other] at one another
162.11	nature, endeavored] nature, endeavoring
162.18	two hundred] one hundred
162.35	mother had acquiesced] mother acquiesced
163.7	a nice trip] a fierce trip
163.17	parlor.] parlor. He had agreed to meet her there.
163.25	smoked, and finally] smoked, finally
163.30	part had been] part was
163.35	these simple] these few
164.1	Pullman state-room] Pullman section
164.33	soothingly. "Everything] soothingly, the thought that they were in sight of others troubling him greatly. Everything
165.33	out of the] out the
167.3	and the result surprised even himself] and surprised himself
167.8	state, Jennie] state she
167.36	stuff," he said. "I'll] stuff. I'll
167.37	arrangement." It was all very simple and easy; he was a master strategist.] arrangement." He was hoping that she would soon be able to make some arrangement for the family to move into a better house. He did not like the thought of the poverty stricken atmosphere behind her and a good home seemed to offer an eventual solution for their meeting if a separate one did not eventuate.

168.7 rejoicing. Of course she could not go back to her work, but Mrs. Gerhardt explained that Mrs. Bracebridge had given Jennie] rejoicing and the reason why she did not return to Mrs. Bracebridge was explained by her mother on the ground that the former had given her

169.34 chance," Lester] chance," he

169.39 perhaps sophisticatedly] sophisticatedly perhaps

170.5 easy-going ways were reprehensible, and bound to create trouble sooner or later.] easy acceptance of social and commercial difficulties was not the fore-runner of great financial distinction to say the least.

171.14 or perhaps both.] or both very likely.

171.31 father had argued from time to time.] father would retort.

172.35 turned the question] turned it

173.20 but Lester] but he

174.4 with Jennie] with her

174.23 Gerhardt went] He went

174.27 to hunt up another job as a watchman.] to be a watchman or something.

174.29 that Lester] that her Lester

174.31 Cleveland. The two women explained to Gerhardt that Jennie was going away to be married to Mr. Kane. Gerhardt flared up at this, and his suspicions were again aroused. But he could do nothing but grumble over the situation; it would lead to no good end, of that he was sure.] Cleveland. Mrs. Gerhardt suggested that if Gerhardt took unkindly to the proposition that she go away to marry him instead of having the supposed ceremony performed there, that she run away. It came about that way for at the mere suggestion that she did not expect to be married at home Gerhardt flared up. There should be nothing like that with his consent. He would have nothing to do with any such business. If she wished to lead a decent life and do things right—open and above board as they should be, well and good—Well and good! He would like that otherwise he would not stay—he would get out, if he had to starve on the streets. This worried Jennie and her mother greatly but Lester had fixed the day of her departure and there appeared to be no alternative.

175.3 Chicago; the old life had ended and the new one had begun.] Chicago and from then on to the end of her days that intimate, personal, immediate contact with her family was more or less broken.

175.16 had been in Chicago for a few days,] was in Chicago a little while

175.17 she wrote] she immediately wrote

175.19 Gerhardt, who had been] Gerhardt (who was

175.20 scene. He] scene) as was intended, and he

175.39 of fittings] of furniture

176.2 was supplied with every convenience, and there was even a bath room, a luxury the Gerhardts had never enjoyed before.] was furnished intelligently and the bath room, a thing the Gerhardts had never had before, supplied with its proper belongings.

176.4   was attractive, though plain,] was worthy though middle-class

176.5   that her] that at last her

178.24 Mt. Clemens, and Saratoga] Mt. Clemens, Saratoga

178.25 stretch, enjoy] stretch, and enjoy

178.27 Cleveland only for] Cleveland for

178.32 this condition of affairs] this rather tentative relationship

180.22 Gerhardt came running in from the yard,] Gerhardt who was out in the yard for some purpose came running in

182.22 to her] to its

182.24 to her] to it

182.30 and childhood] and young, new childhood

183.1   its helpless] its vile but

184.4   beautifully replete.] beautifully replenished.

184.5   hand, Gerhardt] hand, he

184.6   to drag] to hang

185.6   simple facts] simple love

186.8   once or twice] once

186.21 Robert had been;] Robert and

186.24 three and] three or

186.31 time, Robert] time his brother

186.32 beating Lester] beating him

186.32 did Lester] did he

186.40 and final value] and value

187.27 Robert. Should] Robert. Would

187.28 thought also came] thought came

187.33 how he could desert her] how that could be done

187.36 and well-established] and celebrated

188.2   father at first seemed to agree with Lester.] father was also, apparently at first in their favor.

188.3   argued out the question] argued

188.12 said Archibald Kane] said Kane, senior

188.16 said. He rose and strolled out of the office.] said and rose up and strolled out.

188.23 about his entanglement] about the continuation of this escapade

188.24 the long vacations] the time

188.24 taken from] taken off from

188.25 to Lester] to him

188.28 and mother] and brother

189.33 and country merchants could be more easily reached and dealt with] and merchants could so easily be reached and shown

189.37 undertake the construction of the new building and] undertake its construction and

189.39 reside in Chicago] reside there

190.5   live in Chicago] live there

190.18 living in Chicago] living here

191.22 comfortable. Jennie] comfortable. She

192.3 inform Jennie] inform her

192.4 health. Jennie proposed] health in case anything should happen during her absence. She proposed

192.5 thought that sometimes] thought sometimes

192.5 town, Vesta] town, she

192.6 apartment.] apartments.

192.11 to take Vesta away.] to get her.

192.25 on; now] on and now

192.26 struck he was] struck was

193.2 favorite haunt,] favorite place,

193.4 Bass, Martha] Bass, George, Martha

197.11 wardrobe at the apartment.] wardrobe here.

197.14 taking Jennie] taking her

198.13 the deception] the silly deception

198.14 as with Jennie's] as Jennie's

198.15 the disorganized home.] the shattered home.

198.36 with Vesta] with her

198.37 fairies] fairy

198.37 giants,] giant

199.6 might. She] might, and from having the child there, had toys there for her and little things she would be constantly making for her. She

199.6 risk Vesta's] risk her

199.37 two o'clock] two

200.7 had occasion] had another occasion

200.18 for an oversight] for a little oversight

200.18 effects of which she] effects she

200.20 lamb under] lamb—one of the wool betousled, neck-beribboned denizens of the hillsides of toyland under

200.25 children, had deliberately] children deliberately

200.26 behind the divan,] behind,

200.30 returned. [¶] That same evening, when he was lying on the divan,] returned. [¶] It also happened that one day when he was lying down

200.32 newspaper, he] newspaper that he

200.33 fully lighted] full lighted

200.34 under the divan.] under.

201.39 the amusement that he had expected.] the pleasure he thought it would.

201.40 Lester went] He went

202.5 about the incident of the toy lamb.] about it.

202.6 from Lester's memory] from his memory.

203.5 hearing, he went] hearing, went

203.6 who frowned] who fawned

203.13 and determined to inquire thoroughly into the matter. A moment later Jennie reappeared. Her face] and then giving way to one of his fits of choler decided instantly to speak to her about it now,—a decision which was made unnecessary by her pale and troubled appearance when she returned. She

205.35	quiet, and weak] quiet, weak
206.13	Where Jennie] Where she
207.9	fact. Art] fact. The thought of mere simplicity such as he had always deemed Jennie to be being capable of hoodwinking him thus was, not at the first blush of things at least, to be tolerated. Art
207.14	to Lester] to him
208.24	this business.] this.
208.26	about the] about among the
209.10	her. He] her, making her weak to the point of falling.
209.21	the coat] the latter
209.35	the familiar name of the dead but still famous statesman] the nationally famous name of his state
210.23	told your people] told them
211.13	condition so] condition that was
212.31	He went out,] He turned his face outward,
212.31	further] farther
212.35	a dissonance] a perfect harmony
213.4	matters considerably.] matters morally considerable.
213.5	of Jennie's] of her
213.8	if he had gone about it in earnest.] if he had thought to do it.
213.29	that the mixing] that mixing
214.4	see the child] see it
214.5	his own] own
214.16	as with ambition.] as ambition.
214.18	were distinctly wrapped up in their own affairs; Robert and he were temperamentally uncongenial. With Jennie he had really been happy, he had truly lived. She was necessary to him; the more he stayed away from her the more he wanted her. He finally decided to have a straight-out talk with her, to arrive at some sort of under-standing.] were distant or at least affectionally temperate. In the world of matrimonial possibilities he had not seen anyone whom he really wanted to marry. Out of all the pick of women only Jennie had appeared and she not entirely satisfactory but sympathetic. He could really live with her. She didn't irritate him. He thought of this day after day as he stayed away from her and then finally decided that he ought to go out and give her a theory of procedure.
214.24	She must] She ought to
214.24	quit] quit now
215.22	windows; then he turned to her] windows but came back to say
216.3	darkness] dark
216.5	leave the apartment and go to his club?] leave?
216.34	reunion] final reunion
217.7	that particular child.] such a child.
217.14	commercial-minded man.] commercial-minded soul who had to live with it.

217.16	Jennie] She
217.16	gave Vesta] gave her
217.17	night Lester telephoned that he] night he telephoned he
217.26	her own toilet] her toilet
217.35	Lester] He
217.37	that Vesta] that she
218.1	Jennie] She
218.7	Run into] Run in
218.37	for Vesta] for it
218.37	was Vesta's] was its
218.38	for Jennie] for her
218.39	morning Lester] morning he
219.18	in the minutest] in minutest
219.23	Not] It was not
219.23	this Lester] this he
219.24	newspaper, when] newspaper, that
219.27	house. Jennie was seated at the table, pouring out the coffee, when Vesta suddenly appeared,] house, when everything being settled and both at the table out she came—
219.30	room. Lester] room, at which Lester
219.39	mouth.] mouth. The independent self-sufficiency was a little bit too much for him.
221.7	and came] and come
221.30	me." Vesta smiled back at him, and now that the ice was broken she chattered on unrestrainedly.] me." The effect of these table conversations and the general attitude of Jennie toward her offspring was to soften him toward the whole situation. He could not help feeling that she was a charming mother and that the child was being well cared for.
222.39	that Lester] that he
222.40	him; he] him and
223.2	provided] providing
223.7	proper. Heretofore, he] proper. He
223.8	his business affairs] his affairs
223.9	From now] From then
223.15	his personal] his general
223.22	elimination. But Lester] elimination. He
223.23	of this,] of it
224.3	not attempt to detain] not stay
224.10	way. Well, what of it?] way. High! ho!
224.11	Robert, who, however, kept] Robert, however, who kept
224.16	after Lester] after he
224.18	fall, Lester] fall he
224.18	grippe. When] grippe and that one evening when he was at the apartment with Jennie. He concluded of course when
224.19	he thought that] that

224.36 the first real contretemps occurred. Lester's] the most unfortunate
of all the denouements thus far transpired. His

224.40 had originally planned.] had anticipated.

224.40 While Lester] While he

225.31 so fashionably attired] so distinguished

226.1 excuse, but] excuse had not

226.2 past before Jennie could say a word. Once inside, Louise looked
about her inquiringly. She found herself] past her hostess before
the latter could think to protest or act and being inside looked
around. She was

226.16 lamely] tamely

226.19 certain articles in the adjoining] certain things in the other

226.21 [¶ His] [¶ Naturally his

226.24 caused Miss Kane] caused her

226.27 but cool] but courageous

227.2 trap; it was really disgraceful of Lester.] trap.

227.17 demanded, savagely and yet curiously] demanded, curiously.

227.24 any more," retorted] anymore," exclaimed

227.25 you of] you above

227.27 was again going] was going

227.30 growled.] growled, jumping to her defense.

228.7 thought.] thought, "to bring about this unpremeditated visit."

228.30 she told the story of her discovery, embellished with many details.]
she reported all with a too painful accuracy.

229.7 as though] as if

230.4 Archibald Kane] He

230.25 said Mr. Kane.] said his father.

231.13 then telephoned to] then called up

232.14 at each other] at one another

233.9 by it.] by agreeing to anything.

233.23 now.] now or holding secret opinions that might be at variance,
or rather less than his spoken word.

233.27 for Lester] for him

233.28 that he] that Lester

233.29 least. And Mrs. Kane felt the same way; surely Lester must realize
that.] least. Mrs. Kane was also fixed in this hope. "Why they
actually tried to get up little innocent schemes by which they could
make you take an interest in some of the girls here at home," he
exclaimed in one place, and Lester's mind went out to his father and
mother in kindly sympathy as he sat here.

233.31 it," Lester] it," he

233.36 What that may be,] What,

234.29 and one] and as they stood one

235.3 listened. He said nothing, but his face expressed an unchanged
purpose.] listened, offering no further thought to his brother, but
looking as if he felt bound to stand upon his views as previously
expressed.

235.9	of animal] of every
235.10	necessity to] necessity in
235.15	parasites] parasite
235.19	from their environments.] from them.
235.21	operation] operations
235.22	limitations has] limitations have
235.24	clear generalization.] clear demonstration of the accuracy of this suggestion.
235.30	bird had intruded] bird intruded
236.2	doomed.] doomed—a family atmosphere colored by certain preconceived conventions or social notions of what is right and proper in an element truly.
237.24	present.] present since all the damage had been practically done.
237.25	any practical difference.] any difference.
238.35	for Lester] for her leige lord for he
239.5	without taking anything] without anything
239.12	abstracted.] abstract.
239.24	was not improving.] was tending to help solve this problem in a measure for her for by the lapse of time it offered a predicament which her presence alone could reasonably have solved.
239.28	Martha had always been] Martha was always
239.31	as slight] as dim
239.32	approaching marriage] approaching possibility
239.40	engineer, a career which] engineer which
240.8	after Martha's marriage] after this
240.26	call, her] call, the
240.28	Gerhardt had never had] He had never seen
241.9	on in this] on this
241.12	one who,] one whom
241.24	but this] but that
241.38	his brow bent] his sight lost
242.6	life? What did] life he asked himself now, over and over. What does
242.21	father.] father at this time.
242.26	nothing more for anybody.] nothing at all any more.
243.14	get some work which paid well] get something pretty good to do
243.23	been reared.] been raised that he was not able to free himself entirely as yet.
244.20	writing out her] writing her
246.6	Gerhardt had written] Gerhardt wrote
246.17	said. [¶] As] said. As a rule he did not care to leave his affairs before a reasonably late hour, but today he felt that he would like to go out, and so went. [¶] When
247.5	paper on the floor.] paper mechanically.
247.8	Here again was] Here was
247.8	relationship if] relationship again if

247.8	wished. He] wished. It was apparently coming up quite regularly of late. He
247.12	wrong," he went on slowly. "I] wrong. I
248.8	to promise anything.] to say anything about it.
248.29	her restored to comparative calmness, smiling] her calm and pleasant again smiling
249.40	on to live with us.] on here.
250.10	Jennie] She
250.36	go with him to] go to
251.20	entering her new home] entering it
251.28	then," he said.] then.
251.31	put the establishment] put it
252.15	wrote to her] wrote her
252.24	this letter with] this with
252.30	go to Chicago] go there
252.38	Lester and decided] Lester, decided
253.10	to who] to whom
254.16	go to church with] go with
255.8	story. Vesta] story. In the first place Vesta
255.11	after the child's] after her
255.13	that Lester] that he
256.3	latter concern must] latter must
256.5	Mrs. Stendhal spoke of] Mrs. Stendhal pronounced
256.7	coming as a total stranger to] coming a total stranger as you possibly do to
256.27	she watched Mrs. Stendhal drive away.] she entered and closed the door.
256.32	Among the other callers were] There was
257.8	home in Hyde Park,] home here,
257.10	was the child's stepfather.] was not the child's real but stepfather.
260.37	attitude toward Jennie should] attitude should
260.38	came from] came with this one from
261.14	An opening bolt of the coming storm fell upon Jennie] One of the opening bolts of a changing situation came to Jennie
261.34	daughter had said] daughter said
262.4	but it satisfied] but satisfied
262.16	to nurse] to brood over
262.24	family.] family through rumors rife elsewhere.
262.32	her guests with] her with
262.35	at Jennie] at her
262.40	ignoring Jennie] ignoring her
263.12	out of the room.] out.
263.17	position and was] position, was
263.20	more important] more significant
263.20	where Jennie] where she
263.24	remarks. Presently Jennie] remarks and then Jennie
263.26	now realized that] felt that

265.25   gas-jets or electric-light bulbs] gas or electric light jets or bulbs
265.27   Lester's expensive] Lester's excellent
265.28   aside after a few months' use, were] aside were
265.29   to the thrifty old German.] to him.
266.8   would begin] would tentatively begin
266.12   Jennie would] Jennie and his friends would
266.13   matches would be lit] matches were lit
266.33   wretched, spendthrift] wretched, wasteful
267.7   down Lester's] down his
267.7   so; he did make over the underwear] so, as he did his underwear
267.8   the friendly aid of the cook's needle] the aid of the machinations of the cook
267.11   The remaining stock of Lester's discarded clothing] In the matter of all the superfluity of clothing
267.12   would store away for] would hang on to great quantities of it for
267.14   the lot] the most of it
267.27   was only to her that he] was to her he
269.2   evening.] evening. The stableman would be driving the trap away from the side carriage entrance to the stable.
269.7   would sit in] would walk into
269.36   she would be] she was
269.39   sense, her gentleness,] sense, her youth,
270.1   all her youth] all youth
270.19   that Vesta] that she
270.24   child.] child. I went there.
270.38   constituents] constituency
271.1   a way] a habit
273.6   decent. Archibald Kane] decent. He
273.8   but what it should be] but how
273.25   consistently agreeable] consistently nice
273.31   and preferred] and the exciting character of his display. He preferred
274.5   got commercial results] got results
274.6   a silent,] a big, silent
274.9   it. Archibald Kane] it. He
274.11   he would be cut off with only a nominal income. But] he would be left with the income of a certain sum which would aggregate only ten thousand dollars annually and which would revert to the estate at his death. In case he should reform and by that he meant leave Jennie and settle down properly, he would fix it so that he would come in for his natural share. His salary and present perquisites would depend then anyhow (in case he should cling to Jennie) upon his effective conduct of the duties which were assigned him, duties which up to this time he had conducted satisfactorily enough. This would put a suitable and severe check upon him. But
274.15   away? Old Archibald wrote Lester that he] away? He wrote him he

274.18	was in Cincinnati.] was there.
275.27	Father," said Lester quickly.] Father," exclaimed Lester bristling.
278.16	but he was determined to see things through.] but in a way determined.
278.24	possibilities.] possibilities, possibly.
279.12	now Lester] now he
280.34	One day Lester happened to run across Berry Dodge,] For instance once, on meeting Berry Dodge,
281.11	again," said Dodge.] again," he said,
281.33	circumstances his friend would] circumstances he would
281.34	about the new Mrs. Kane] about Mrs. Kane
282.4	of other] of most able and interesting
282.19	was a] was such a
285.18	house at Hyde Park,] house he lived in,
285.27	prevent the publication.] prevent.
285.31	were instructed] were asked
286.4	objections] objection
286.12	in the most approved yellow-journal style.] in a rather masterly newspaper fashion.
286.32	as the trolley car rumbled along,] as he rode
288.30	laughed Mrs. Stendhal.] laughed her guest.
289.15	scattered a number of other pictures—] scattered all the pictures described and on one side a column of supposed love scenes,
289.37	club with which to strike him] club to strike him with
290.3	to do right now. Why couldn't the world help her, instead of seeking to push her down?] to be just right now—why couldn't she be?
291.3	of the inevitable,] of whatever was when he met
291.39	part of it would] part would
292.19	good-looking. He was forty-six and she] good-looking. When he was forty-six she
293.15	he was met by Amy,] he saw Amy
293.17	Lester] He
293.33	and had fallen] and fallen
294.35	gentleman, except for his alliance with Jennie, and] gentleman and
294.39	should there be any discrimination against him?] should his fortune be discriminated against.
294.40	it possible.] it would be.
295.4	been personal] been a personal
295.12	from his] from out his
296.12	that this was in accordance with their father's wish.] that it was their father's wish that they should not be.
296.23	two hundred] 200
296.28	after the three years were up.] after three years.
297.14	very badly.] very bad.
297.32	The family gathering] The party
297.33	home.] home, lonely.

297.39   condition] conditions

298.9   opposition to his family, for] opposition for

298.11   in not] in (1) not

298.13   or, alternately, in] or (2) in

299.39   When Lester returned to his home after the funeral,] He returned to his home and

300.10   not give her his confidence.] not tell her.

300.16   Lester's] His

300.19   treasurer, it was necessary that he should own at least one share of the company's stock.] treasurer as he was now he had to have stock.

300.26   to Lester] to him

300.41   Anyhow, Robert] Anyhow, he

301.2   but for an] but an

301.23   by Robert.] by him.

301.35   a branch manager] a manager

302.4   time, after] time, however, after

302.25   saying: Dear Robert,—I] saying "I

302.29   director, or] director, nor

302.31   and I want to] and to

303.9   subtle," Robert] subtle," he

303.12   Robert felt that] One of the facts was that

303.34   did Robert] did he

303.36   would be enough for Lester to qualify.] would arrange it.

303.39   once.] once. And if necessary go to law. The will might be broken.

304.6   if Lester] if he

304.15   So it all came] So he got

304.16   that.] that. [¶] It was a matter of astonishment and curiosity to Lester himself under these circumstances to see how he was parleying with himself. It was astonishing to him, the drift of events, now that he contemplated them in perspective. He sat about his office after this final word thinking how his attachment for Jennie had culminated in so many evils. Wasn't it curious?

304.19   income (including] income, outside of his formal salary of— (including

304.19   thousand) of fifteen] thousand) fifteen

304.22   future, he] future that he

304.26   legitimate share of the Kane estate] legitimate eight hundred thousand

305.29   necessary element in] necessary concomitant of

306.17   He would first give] He first gave

306.20   connections. So he announced] connections by first announcing

306.22   and going] and then going

306.38   gathered together their travelling comforts, they] gathered his traveling material

307.27   powerful, complex] powerful, interesting

307.38   mother had worried] mother worried

308.14   for a long time. She] for years, five or six in all, and since seeing her she

308.21   was invariably the] was the

308.21   group of admirers recruited from every capital of the civilized world.] group of middle-west loiterers abroad who were the quintessence of refinement of the several spheres and cities from which they had emanated.

308.24   art, and] art, picturesque in her beauty and

308.34   years past,] years passed

309.7   could stroke] could rub

310.14   himself that question time] himself time

310.15   pleased, everyone] pleased, all

310.18   years of separation] years of residence in Chicago and more

310.22   fortune. She ran across him] fortune. She did know of the wave of unpleasant notoriety that had followed his secret marriage but she still did believe that he was an ideal man and probably a delightful husband. When she met him

310.23   windows were open; the flowers were blooming] windows open, the flowers blooming

310.39   her again, for they had been good friends. She liked him still—that was evident, and] her for here he knew was embodied real friendship. She liked him, whatever else she might do, and

311.2   magnificent] magnificently

311.5   liked looking at lovely] liked lovely

311.25   curious to test] curious because of

311.27   so charitable] so rather charitable

311.30   but a man and a woman] but people

312.5   remaining in her room as] remaining as

312.10   Lester," she said daringly, "I'll] Lester, I'll

312.15   grown more beautiful—] grown and beautified,

312.16   and in every] and every

313.13   station in life, and] station and

313.22   was a dinner later at] was an additional dinner at

313.27   free. And Lester—subconsciously perhaps—was thinking the same thing.] free and open to her blandishments.

313.36   hers, but Jennie] hers) which Jennie

313.36   not. They] not, and they

314.9   Mrs. Gerald again until they reached Cairo. In the gardens] Mrs. Gerald any more until they reached Cairo—she had not contemplated going to Egypt when they were in England, but in the gardens

314.13   luck!" he exclaimed.] luck," exclaimed Lester.

314.17   be. Then I remembered you said you were going to Egypt.] be. You know you said you were coming down here.

314.25   I'll go] I'll come

314.31   he said, somewhat awkwardly. "You can't actually escape for long— not with] he comforted, thinking actually that he might take her if he were free. What a solution that would be of all his troubles if he were to decide on her! "You can't actually escape with

314.38   so well] so charmingly

315.7   his entanglement] his matrimonial venture

315.15   you were] you are

316.10   "Well, at last I've found you!" Mrs. Gerald exclaimed. "I couldn't] "Well, I've found you. I couldn't

316.12   Mrs. Kane," she went on smilingly.] Mrs. Kane," chattered Mrs. Gerald

316.18   drove of strange animals] drove of something

316.28   badly," smiled Jennie. "But] badly. But

317.11   sounded in] sounded about

318.31   still as slender and shapely as] still slender and shapely like

318.34   said impulsively,] said at one turn,

319.8   strolled into the garden] strolled through the windows

319.29   *Fulda*] *Barbarossa*

319.33   "I hope] "Delighted. I hope

320.7   it bravely.] it beautifully.

320.32   and Jennie] and she

320.34   Lester set to work in earnest to find a business opening.] Lester took up the thread of his previous investigations.

321.12   some small money] some money

324.32   private venture] private adventure

324.37   had done it.] had it.

325.1   sides. Jennie's] sides as he had recently by a chain of circumstances over which you have no control. Jennie's

325.6   and he had succeeded] and succeeded

325.9   news, sorely disheartened.] news a little crestfallen.

326.6   your new company] your company

326.12   I'll wait and see] I'll not try venturing that though until I see

326.33   Lester had been doing some pretty hard thinking, but so far he had been unable to formulate any feasible plan for his re-entrance into active life. The successful organization of Robert's carriage trade trust had knocked in the head any further thought on his part of taking an interest in the small Indiana wagon manufactory.] To be compelled to work—to make a strenuous effort in this world is one thing; to have that ample supply of means which is sufficient to deaden the sense of necessity according to one's light and yet not sufficient to warrant that ample security which makes men venturous and hospitable to new and daring enterprise in others is quite another. Lester Kane was now in this position.

327.11   wonderfully complete] wonderful

327.31   Lester had seen Ross] He had seen him

327.35   Ross] He

328.27   section of "Yalewood"] section of West Park

328.32   deals in real estate which] deals which

329.24   Then Mr. Ross] Then he

329.28	Streets] Street
329.35	50 × 100 feet at] 50 × 100 at
330.14	Would Lester] Would he
330.16	After a few days of quiet] After some quiet
332.9	to deal with] to brood over
333.20	efforts in tree-planting that] efforts that
333.22	future, they would] future would
333.23	upon the infant project] upon this very interesting adventure
333.30	itself. The papers explained that the company intended to go farther south,] itself. Farther south, the papers explained the company intended to go,
333.33	mere suspicion that the packing company might invade the territory was] mere rumors which, if generally noted, were
334.19	that Inwood] that this
334.39	this blow is] this is
335.17	indicated. Practically] indicated. Still Lester had practically
335.18	income, was tied] income tied
335.25	beginning. If it didn't] beginning. If it was going it was going with him and that from the very start. If it didn't
335.26	wanted no more] wanted little
336.11	himself. She] himself as not even to want to fight back. She
336.19	Letty wanted to find out for sure.] She wanted to find out very much, for sure.
336.20	The house that Mrs. Gerald] The house Letty
336.27	you. You ought to know] you. If you don't know
336.28	her. Her] her you'd better. Her
336.34	know the truth by this time.] know by now.
337.10	about his troubles.] about it.
337.12	Lester," said Letty, by way of helping him to his confession—the maid] Lester," she said by way of helping him and after the maid
337.23	seems to me such a great sacrifice,] seems such a great sacrifice to me,
337.39	before replying.] before answering her last question.
338.8	first met Jennie] first saw her
338.12	his *vis-à-vis.*] his vis-a-vis wisely.
338.28	before and—] before—and
339.20	lose eight hundred thousand] lose $800,000
339.39	she insisted.] she argued.
340.14	her the truth, she] her she
340.22	"You must leave her,"] "You must do that,"
340.30	to me than] to me intellectually than
340.36	explain me to myself, if] explain me if
341.13	a woman.] a woman, even if I have only seen her a few times.
342.17	room, devotedly attended] room, charmingly looked after
342.20	he was. There was] he was speculating on the wonder of life, the nature of his career, how old he was, whether he could not really live a few more years and things like that. There was

343.38 danger. He went on to say that George] danger. George,
344.4 man named Albert Sheridan,] man Albert Sheridan
344.22 Now that] Now when
345.4 hand] hands
345.23 how the old man was] how he was
345.24 tell Jennie.] tell her.
345.26 grandfather] grandpa
345.27 love him dearly.] love him.
346.33 rewards] reward
346.38 for a living,] for living,
347.21 looked to him like] looked like
347.22 store.] store to him.
347.24 there is] there was
348.2 way," said Lester finally.] way."
348.15 was soon after] was after
349.8 brother. At the same time he did not care to see Lester's share, which was to be divided pro rata in case he did not take it, fall into the hands of the husbands of Amy and Imogene and Louise. They did not deserve it. Robert had things] brother. He had things
349.17 explain to Jennie] explain to her
349.20 If Lester had married Jennie,] If he had married her
350.9 house in Hyde Park and] house and
350.21 were certain conditions] were things
350.22 affect] effect
350.35 "Ah," breathed] "Ah," snapped
351.6 "Before Mr. Kane senior] "Before he
351.7 to Mr. Lester Kane] to Mr. Kane
351.17 obtain his share] obtain this
351.19 had expressed."] had."
351.25 opposition. He continued to study her furtively as he sat there waiting for her to speak.] opposition. He wished that she would ask him what Lester's father's wish was and because he wished so hard that she would she did.
351.27 that wish?" she finally asked,] that?" she asked,
351.28 tense under the strain of the silence.] tense as he waited.
351.38 unless—" again his eyes were moving sidewise to and fro—] unless—" his eyes were moving to and fro, sidewise again—
352.2 you."] you within the same time."
352.4 intentions. That] intentions and that
352.12 periods] period
353.13 ah, your husband's] ah, husband's
353.19 as irregular, and—] as did his father, as outre and
353.20 cruel—as not] cruel, not
353.21 that Mr. Kane senior] that his father
353.22 ever be rightly] ever be nicely
353.25 me—if his] me, his
353.38 solution to the unfortunate business] solution to this

353.39   see that] see it
354.8   one other point] one point
354.32   you needed] you wanted
354.35   further, unable mentally and physically to listen to another word.]
           further, hurt beyond the ability to listen to anymore.
354.40   realization of her sufferings.] realization of how she was feeling
           and moving as if to go.
355.6   visit—it will be advisable that you should keep your own counsel in
           the matter.] visit if it can be arranged otherwise.
355.10   Mr. O'Brien] He
355.10   Jennie touched the electric button to summon the maid, and]
           She pulled a cord near where she was standing.
355.12   Jennie] She
355.30   pass. On the day] pass. He had gone the day
355.31   called, Lester had been gone on] called on
356.8   thought.] thought for it seemed pointless under the conditions.
356.15   Jennie] she
356.16   a pretty poor imitation.] a poor imitation of a very genial original.
356.25   shade. As she came back, he looked at her critically.] shade. She
           turned about and strolled back and he looked at her rather critically.
356.39   She was silent] She held her peace
357.9   realized that she must remain absolute mistress of herself if anything
           were to be accomplished toward the resolution of the problem.]
           realized that for once in her life if ever that she would have to be
           calm herself if she intended doing anything either fair or wise.
357.15   said Lester fiercely. "What] said Lester bringing himself fiercely
           into a defiant position. "What
358.3   "No." There] "No," or something like that. There
358.10   was cut to the quick by his indifference, his wrath instead of affec-
           tion.] was cut by his indifference, his wrath instead of affection to
           the quick.
358.21   there had been so many] there were all these
359.2   people! But I won't talk any more about it; isn't dinner nearly
           ready?"] people."
359.4   scarcely took the trouble] scarcely cared
359.9   dropped for good and all, however,] dropped without being dis-
           posed of however,
359.12   very freely] very well
359.13   managed to get in a word or two.] managed to say something.
359.15   in a modified mood] in a mollified mood
359.18   this business any longer,] this at this time anyhow,
359.35   showing more kindly consideration for her, she was] showing
           some growing signs of consideration for her (he was looking more
           kindly toward her each day), she was
360.14   his invariable] his persistent
361.22   Jennie had expressed] Jennie expressed
361.25   It had] It has

362.2   a pleasing, summery appearance.] a summery appearance and
          flavor which was pleasing to comment.
362.11   afterward] afterwards
363.2   herself. All this] herself. It
363.8   but it was raised] but raised
363.9   levels. The house] levels. It
363.16   was one hundred feet square and] was 150 × 150 and
363.17   The former owner had laid] The owner had already laid
363.25   her, but she finally saw] her but as discussion brought up various
          points she saw
363.26   suggested—to fit out the] suggested, fit the
363.32   two years, together with an option for an additional five years,
          including the privilege of purchase.] two years by Mr. Watson,
          acting for Lester, and an option on an additional five years, with
          privilege of purchase taken.
363.35   her as wanting] her wanting
364.3   business affairs made] business made
364.4   and for Jennie] and Jennie
364.28   though, as she had proved,] though, as has been indicated clearly
          enough,
364.30   free from] free of
364.39   that it] that that
365.25   as another woman might have done; she] as some women might
          have. She
365.31   take a large situation largely,] take a big situation bigly
365.32   this woman, let the world think what it might.] this woman,
          think what the world would.
365.33   shame that her] shame her
366.4   lonely. Spring] lonely. He suggested that she travel but she in-
          sisted that she could not alone—she did not want to. "I would rather
          come here," she said, where I can look at the lake." Spring
366.12   to deliver his] to pay over his
366.22   he had been during] he was at any time during
366.25   This home] This house
366.28   Now, blow] Now, after blow
366.29   delivered, and the home and] delivered, this house and
367.1   [¶] The day came when the house was finally closed and the old life
          was at an end. Lester travelled with Jennie] [¶] He went with her
          in a carriage to the depot. He traveled with her considerably
367.5   again soon,] again when occasion permitted soon,
367.6   fact of the actual and spiritual] fact of spiritual
367.10   thought that she] thought she
367.14   had kissed Lester goodbye and had wished] had—now mystically
          affectionate he could not understand. She wished
367.15   peace; then she made an excuse] peace, and then she made
          excuse
367.17   but now] but

367.17	dry. Everything had subsided] dry then. Everything had as usual subsided
367.24	would have sought some regular outside employment.] would get something to do.
367.25	direction lay] direction it seemed lay
367.27	Cleveland and other cities saw] Cleveland and several others, to say nothing of certain business atmospheres which were ramified in this fashion saw
367.30	Lester Kane. He had] Lester Kane. From having
367.31	affairs while] affairs during the period in which
367.32	her, but now he] her, he
368.2	was in some respects] was somewhat
368.4	been reared in luxury] been raised in luxury or at least solid, social comfort
368.18	convention that] convention and belief that
369.9	all with] all in-a-way with
369.31	directors, wishing] directors and that wishing
370.4	course. Social invitations] course. Invitations
370.33	she retorted.] she glistened.
370.39	on to be presented to] on to greet
370.39	strangers by Mrs. De Lincum, who aided Mrs. Gerald in receiving.] strangers who were being introduced to him by Mrs. DeLincos, who, for the occasion was Mrs. Gerald's associate.
371.25	change in Dodge's attitude.] change.
371.33	anxious to continue. He had seen where] anxious to talk again. He saw where
372.13	brisk at the other end of the table.] brisk otherwheres.
373.23	lake, and there's plenty of money in trust, but] lake, but
373.30	you."] you for it."
373.33	mind, I] mind—and you know how my mind works—I
374.22	my lawyer."] my counsel."
374.23	and walked] and strolled
375.2	worth. I] worth," she replied, "I
375.13	Lester might] Lester would
375.14	after all but for certain influential factors. After a time, with his control of his portion of the estate firmly settled in his hands and the storm of original feeling forgotten, he was well aware that diplomacy—if he ignored his natural tendency to fulfill even implied obligations—could readily bring about an engagement whereby he and Jennie could be together. But he was haunted] after all and after a time once his control of his portion of the estate was firmly settled in his hands and the storm of original feeling forgotten—(for he was well aware that diplomacy—if a tendency which usually dominated him to fulfill every implied obligation were ignored— could readily bring about an arrangement whereby he and Jennie could be together) if he had not been haunted

375.21   Mrs. Gerald. He was compelled] Mrs. Gerald, had not been compelled

376.1   ideal climax] ideal denouement

376.18   nothing save to make visits] nothing much save visit

376.26   enjoyed meeting.] enjoyed.

377.10   but he preferred to stifle his misgivings.] but this was in all likelihood the better way.

377.12   "only don't let there be any fuss] "only I would prefer that there would be no fuss

377.26   [¶] He smiled a little constrainedly as she tousled his head; there was a missing note somewhere in this gamut of happiness; perhaps it was because he was getting old.] [¶] He smiled jovially as she tousled his head, but he was still thinking that this was without its proper measure of joy. He was marrying and everything was coming out right,—but it wasn't

377.29   meantime] meanwhile

378.26   Vesta listened soberly and half suspected the truth.] Vesta thought of this and half suspected she knew not what.

378.33   together, played to her on the piano, and asked for her criticisms on her drawing and modeling.] together, talked to her of music and life in general.

378.39   her. Lester was gone, but at least she had Vesta.] her. Since Lester was gone, she at least had her.

379.2   Sandwood. In] Sandwood. It is in

379.3   life it is not] life not

379.5   if they are no] if no

379.9   be she] be her

379.24   Hyde Park. Other household pets appeared in due course of time, including a collie that Vesta named Rats; she had brought] Hyde Park, an animal which disported itself under the name Daisy. There was a gardener, an old Italian, who had done odd jobs about the village, but who once he found Jennie would have little to do with other work. His name was Gugielmo Conzone and when he realized through his sympathetic understanding of character that Jennie was kind and good natured he could not be driven away from her. The garden, the horse, the lawn, the furnace, were his particular perquisites. After a few days, when he found that there was a real job here he was about all the time. "Me lika dis," he frankly told Jennie. "Me maka you good work—you keepa me. Spada da gard. Watcha da fire. Keepa da horse. Cutta da grass." [¶] "All right," replied Jennie smiling, "we'll see." [¶] He ambled to his tasks, looking for all the world like a Sicilian cut throat, but being under the surface a kindly, home loving, child admiring old father who would not have harmed a fly. Jennie sensed something of this even while she feared that he might be half savage. "He looks terrible," she said to Vesta once, "but he has nice eyes. And I like his voice." [¶] "He'll probably steal Daisy and run away," was Vesta's comment, but he never did. [¶] In time there came to be a collie named "Rats" by Vesta—she brought

379.27	he had grown] he grew
379.28	affectionate. There was also a cat, Jimmy Woods,] affectionate, and a cat "Jimmy Woods,"
379.29	knew, and to] knew to
379.29	insisted the cat] insisted he
379.33	quietly and dreamily] quietly, dreamily,
379.37	too considerate] too wise
379.39	which, under the present circumstances, could] which, he knew, if he were really sincere in this action could
380.10	was a second] was another
380.14	be at Sandwood.] be here.
380.28	months it] months
380.30	saw among the society notes the following item: The] saw in the society notes of the morning where "the
380.33	a party] a house party
380.38	last? She had known that it must and yet—and yet] last? She knew it must and yet,—why, and yet
381.4	do? Stay here as a] do now? Stay here a
381.11	she refuse to receive this money? There was Vesta to be considered.] she turn it all back? Here was Vesta.
381.15	this sort of thing to] this to
381.23	Her eyes indeed were dry, but her very soul seemed to be torn in pieces within her. She rose carefully, hid the newspaper at the bottom of the trunk, and turned the key upon it.] But she did— not with tears of course but sad thoughts. And while so thinking she rose and hid the paper.
381.31	was Mrs. Gerald] was his fiancee
382.10	wrote to Jennie of his coming marriage to Mrs. Gerald. He said that he] wrote Jennie after a time that he was intending to do this. He said he
382.12	if he did make it. He] if he made it. He had fallen in love. He
382.12	marry Mrs. Gerald.] marry her.
382.22	that Lester had been] that he was
382.30	for Jennie in a way. She was noble and a charming woman. If everything else had been] for her *in a way.* She was charming. If everything else were
382.33	yet he did marry] yet he married
382.38	he had been reared] he was raised
382.39	in it. Some fifty guests, intimate friends, had been invited. The ceremony went off with perfect smoothness.] in it. There were some fifty guests necessarily invited. The rooms were full of flowers, presents, tables set with wines and refreshments and tactful ser- vants, and assistant hosts and hostesses everywhere. The ceremony went off without a hitch.

383.2   confetti. While] confetti. Outside the street was blocked with carriages. While

383.2   drinking, Lester] drinking, he

383.8   opened; then the] opened, but the

383.14   the land] the Empire

383.24   resignation, Jennie] resignation she

383.40   miserable as] miserable after as

384.3   She too had seen the report in the newspaper.] She had seen the item.

384.8   before the sharp pain dulled to the old familiar ache. Then] before she was only as unhappy as she had been before she first heard the news. Then

384.11   that Lester was near her—somewhere in] that anyhow he was near her here in

384.36   village. This doctor] village. The water which was drawn from wells appeared to be infected. He

385.18   know.] know. She was apprehensive and because of this may have done the case more harm than good.

385.27   had become] had been

385.31   Vesta should get well. The child had] Vesta get well. She had

386.4   Again, she] Another thing that made her feel wretched was that she

386.6   Jennie] She

386.7   see Vesta] see her

386.27   Jennie, and who] Jennie who

386.28   co-operated with] co-operated consistently with

386.30   as nearly normal as] as comfortable as

386.33   to do. "I'll] to do. If only Lester were with her now she thought. "I'll

387.14   one. Miss Murfree,] one. Mrs. Davis was conscious that the end was close and stayed by her protegée, fearing a breakdown. Miss Murfree

387.28   [¶] Jennie felt] [¶] She was talking to soothe her new friend, her own eyes wet. [¶] After a little she was able to lead her away but only for a little while. Jennie felt

387.34   she had enjoyed with Lester in Hyde Park.] she enjoyed with Lester from Cleveland to Hyde Park.

388.10   Jennie] She

388.22   that Vesta] that she

388.34   classmates sang] classmates with whom she had been popular sang

389.1   and finally delivered] and delivered

389.13   self commiseration. [¶] It was] self commiseration. [¶] One of the pathetic touches of the whole proceeding had been a large bunch of lilies which Gugielmo Canzona had brought to the back door of the house of the day after Vesta's death saying to Mrs. Davis who answered his knock: "Mees Kane here? She feela vera bad? Moocha tough! Moocha tough! I feela vera bad—righta here," he laid his hand on his heart. "Fina girl" Ev'ra bod like! Ev'ra bod say fine! Too bad! Too bad! You say Canzona very sorry. Please! I tanka you vera mooch. Gooda day." [¶] Gugielmo had dressed up in his best clothes which were a mass of peculiar creases to deliver these flowers and sentiments. He was really very sorry for he had admired Vesta very much. [¶] It was

389.31	Chicago and looking] Chicago looking
389.38	was truly grieved, for] was intensely sorry for her for
390.1	for the girl had been real.] for her was real.
390.7	He went there, but Jennie had gone to her daughter's grave; later he called again and] He returned there to find her out for she had gone out to her daughter's grave but later he called and
390.11	for now her] for her
390.13	influence, had] influence, greatly augmented had
390.25	and his desire] and desire
390.28	He had been] He was
390.39	he said a little awkwardly.] he added.
391.1	that had meant] that meant
391.2	since Lester] since he
391.3	sympathize; for the moment she] sympathize after all that she
391.4	over her eyelids] over eyelids
391.38	could persuade to come and live with you?"] could get?"
392.5	this good advice because it came from Lester.] this was advisible because he said so.
392.16	tell you something, Jennie," said Lester, finally rousing himself from his fit of abstraction.] tell you Jennie," he said finally after he had gazed out in silence, "that
392.22	it still seems] it seems
392.25	in the] in my
392.31	[¶] "After all, life is more or less of a farce," he went on a little bitterly.] [¶] "Life is more or less of a farce at best," he said.
392.36	and was sorry for her.] and sorry.
393.8	you to do that.] you to.
393.9	you don't mind.] you will be.
393.12	best. You] best. I won't mind. Really I won't mind now." You
393.13	then he pressed] then pressed
393.18	Jennie saw his agitation, and tried hard to speak.] She suspected this and tried hard to speak. She finally managed to.
393.20	she said firmly.] she admonished him.
393.21	He went away, and yet he knew that he wanted above all things to remain; she was still the one woman in the world for him. And Jennie felt comforted, even though the separation still existed in all its finality. She] He went out, but for the moment he wished that he were not. Hers was the loving magnetism for him. As for Jennie in spite of the peculiar nature of it all she felt relieved. She
393.29	only. Since] alone. Since
394.8	retirement with a] retirement—a

394.15	Chicago, were the occupants of a handsome mansion] Chicago, which was not often were the occupants of a distinguished mansion
394.18	pyrotechnic succession.] pyrotechnic order.
394.30	of a board] of a group
395.15	was endowed with a peculiar brain and a] was given a peculiar brain, having a
395.16	talent, and he had] talent, having
395.18	him. But he] him, but which he
395.19	deserve this wealth any] deserve any
395.21	and constructive] and organizing
395.38	Lester's and Letty's] Lester's and Mrs. Lester's
397.7	charity which] charity that
397.19	She had no desire for investment or for the devious ways] She had desire for investment or the ways
398.10	at home in Cincinnati.] at home.
398.17	come, say, on Thursday?] come?
398.20	him; he had] him by his harsh interpretation of his deserts; he had
398.25	Robert—at least he hoped not. Now Robert] Robert—certainly not. Now he
398.29	he had] he would have
398.30	him; he] him and he
398.35	the Thursday] the particular day
398.36	Auditorium to remind him of the engagement. Lester] Auditorium at his home saying he would be there. Lester
399.1	of the Union Club] of this club
399.14	sandy and ruddy,] sandy, ruddy,
399.15	found it. Lester] found it. Both were smartly dressed—in perhaps the same taste. Lester
399.22	nearly twelve] nearly ten
399.36	them nowadays. Robert] them, as a rule. Twice he had met Imogene in Chicago. Robert
400.20	million and a half.] million, five hundred thousand dollars.
400.39	sincerely that you might be interested in this proposition.] sincerely you might be interested to take this.
401.11	that. Robert] that. His brother
401.16	and now Robert] and Robert
401.18	him—Lester—a little] him a little
401.19	see it,] see that,
401.40	talk over old] talk things over for old
402.2	said, without emotion.] said.
402.5	"perhaps I can't] "perhaps he could not
402.9	go, too," said] go," said
402.12	not," said Lester. "I'll] not. I'll
402.17	been even before Jennie had appeared?] been before Jennie ever appeared."
402.18	his old] his own

402.22   opposition to, but also sympathy for,] opposition but also of sympathy for

402.33   or, rather, according to that supposedly biblical formula, which persists, are] or according to that biblical error which has been foisted on a believing world and so persists is

403.1   utterance that] utterance, by the example of this person and that dying under this race illusion at this time that

403.6   death. Yet the] death. The

403.7   persists, and] persists however and

403.28   apparently excite] apparently enthuse

403.37   had let go under] had under

404.13   to be unkind.] to be mean.

404.20   could dispense with her easily enough. Now Letty did depend upon Lester.] could.

404.23   was like] was something like

404.30   boards of solemn directors merely approved] boards of directors merely solemnly approved

405.7   fish, entrée, roast, game, dessert—everything that made up a] fish, two or three meals, everything that made a

405.8   since determined] since insisted

405.9   found a *cordon bleu,*] found an old man,

405.10   had served] had in his day served

405.11   he engaged.] he kept.

405.11   Lester a hundred] Lester fifty

405.30   complete staff of liveried servants,] complete service of uniformed attendants

405.4   materially, Lester] materially, he

405.14   wife—there was nothing serious about it, but] wife—nothing serious but

405.19   her again.] her any more. She was in Italy at the time.

405.22   time. He] time. As he had at other times, he

405.26   looking in good health, Watson] looking well, Watson

405.30   weak. Several times the] weak. Once the

405.33   attacks he] attacks and when he was feeling very weak he

405.37   and Kozo] and Hirobumi

408.29   then suddenly Jennie realized that the third occupant of the boat was Lester. He] then there was a change of scene and Lester was in the boat. She did not know where he had come from. He

408.32   and then her] and her

408.37   beside her. She] beside her as she so frequently did even yet when she awoke. She

408.38   his arm] his imaginary arm

409.3   appeared with his ominous message.] appeared.

409.5   as were her] as her

409.6   shapely. She had never been separated mentally from Lester, just as he had never grown entirely away from her. She was always with him in thought, just as in the years when they were together.] shapely. Because of her years of loneliness she like Lester had never really separated from him mentally. She was always with him in thought just as she was in the days when they were together.

409.10   were of the] were the

409.20   retirement. As she entered the room she looked at Lester with] retirement. She looked now at her lord and master as she entered just as she had in times past with

409.22   eyes. He was lying propped up on two pillows, his solid head with its growth of once dark brown hair slightly grayed. He looked at her curiously out of his wise old eyes, a light of sympathy and affection shining in them—weary as they were. Jennie was] eyes. She was

410.1   thing that he should send for her.] thing to her to be sent for by him.

410.20   she demurred.] she argued.

410.35   way. I loved you. I love you now. I want to tell you that. It seems strange, but you're the only woman I ever did love truly. We should never have parted." [¶] Jennie caught her breath. It was the one thing she had waited for all these years—this testimony. It was the one thing that could make everything right—this confession of spiritual if not material union. Now she could live happily. Now die so. "Oh, Lester," she exclaimed with a sob, and pressed his hand. He returned the pressure. There was a little silence. Then he spoke again.] way. [¶] She could see that sickness had taken away some of the natural phlegmatic sternness of his character.

411.6   she answered, entering upon a detailed description of their diminutive personalities.] she described, entering upon an account of their charms, abilities and idiosyncracies.

411.9   seemed desirous of keeping her.] seemed interested to keep her.

411.16   her, that he] her, he

411.25   physician was] physician in charge was

411.26   humor. "If] humor, after the physician had counseled with the latter to the end of having him influence Lester to be as quiet and much alone as much as possible. "If

411.30   There were] There had been

411.32   husband, and they] husband Mr. Midgely. They

412.7   arrival might be, when] arrival when

412.8   pain. Before] pain and before

412.9   anesthetic, he was] anesthetic, was

412.22   feel the] feel in this instance the

412.29   but to Cincinnati,] but Cincinnati

412.31   family, Jennie withdrew to her home; she could do nothing more.] family, she withdrew, leaving the final details of interment to those who were less close sympathetically than herself.

412.33   The final] These last final

412.35   body should be] body was to be

412.37	Berry Dodge; Imogene's husband, Mr. Midgely] Berry Dodge, Mr. Midgely
413.1	who either] who knew and who either
413.4	the ritual of that church was carried out.] the ceremonies of that church involved.
413.5	this alien] this to him alien
413.13	arrived. She] arrived and the details as arranged were approved by her. She
413.14	She left her room that night,] She came from her room in this house at night,
413.21	[¶ Meanwhile,] [¶ During all this to do,
413.30	Cincinnati for burial.] Cincinnati.
414.7	depot.] depot. In the pressure of other affairs Mr. Watson was unfortunately neglecting her. As a matter of fact he did not see how the situation was to be reconciled and wisely decided to do nothing.
414.33	followed. The] followed apparently reading solemnly. The
415.7	coffin, leaning on] coffin, on
415.10	her, he turned] her turned
415.12	much a part of this solemn ritual, and yet infinitely removed from it all.] much of it—yet so despised and ignored as it were.
415.14	procession reached] procession finally reached
415.16	candles were set] candles set
415.19	and to its] and its
416.1	to discover] to get track of
416.3	Amy, Imogene, and] Amy, and
416.10	of anticipation] of social anticipation
416.27	the coffin,] the casket
416.31	of his substance,] of substance,
416.33	loss which] loss that
417.5	train, brilliantly lighted,] train, lighted,
417.10	truck, a train-hand in blue, looking out of the car, called to someone within.] truck one of its assistants, a typical train-hand in blue looking out called to someone inside.
417.15	start presently,] start now
417.24	door of the baggage car half] door half
417.26	that; then slowly the great locomotive] that and then slowly this arbiter of her momentary destiny
417.28	great black] great lead black
417.29	of the heavy load behind, flung open] of a heavy load to be drawn opened up
417.32	[¶ Jennie stood rigid, staring into the wonder of this picture, her] [¶ Into the wonder of its composition Jennie stood looking, her
417.35	looked and looked,] looked,
417.38	yard.] yard and she sighed.
418.3	anything else of the chatter and bustle around her.] anything.
418.4	years down which she was steadily gazing.] years into which she was gazing.

Table 2: Editorial Emendations

Textual notes for the following emendations are signaled by an asterisk, refusals to emend by the word *stet*. The notes follow this table immediately.

4.35	but that meant for] but
13.16	were men] were
21.5	afternoon, he was aroused by a rap at his door.] afternoon, a rap at his door aroused him.
31.7	When Jennie] When she
32.6	mind," were] mind," was
33.5	and that assurance of] and the assurance, of
45.38	seemed to be] seemed
46.17	the ex-senator] he
50.20	full of.] full.
51.10	or perhaps the] or
51.32	until marriage] until the other
*53.35	setting off to work one evening] coming home from work
56.31	talking from] talking in
63.3	they had wanted] they wanted
63.20	hurried Sebastian] took him
64.6	At the] Arrived at the
66.33	who had arrested him leaned] who arrested him, leaned
68.15	home temporarily] home
*70.19	Columbus House] Capitol Hotel
71.10	her father] he
72.29	ensure] assure
73.21	The Englishman] The English
74.20	he had done, was] he did was
76.6	back that she] back she
79.24	came in to] came to
*81.4	horrible.] horrible. It was since the night she had consented to let Jennie go out in answer to his note, she fancied. No word of Bass's predicament had ever been whispered.
82.12	brought the hand] brought his hand
85.34	in the room where] in where
86.23	father had said about age] father said about age,
86.25	her the night of his jailing] her that night
90.10	details] detail
90.10	and of several] and several
90.38	that had so] that so
93.31	about him] about us
93.35	make] makes
94.21	men, such a heart] men, it

94.36	to await] to wait
95.29	times] times only
95.30	resulted only] resulted
97.10	live and be able to work for it, and she rejoiced] live to be able to work for it and rejoiced
97.18	With the money which Brander had left, there] Having the money which Brander had left there
98.14	When he had first come he] When he first came he
98.14	and had soon] and soon
99.3	but for the] but the
99.10	houses] house
99.27	this plan for] this for
99.36	worked, he having] worked, having
100.20	Jennie, Mrs. Gerhardt] Jennie, she
100.26	feeling that the] feeling the
101.4	all of her] all her
101.19	caught the child up] caught it up
101.25	she had said] she said
106.19	When she arrived at Cleveland, much of her feeling] Arrived at Cleveland much of this feeling
107.31	regular] regularly
107.39	twelve] eleven
108.17	circumstances had been] circumstances were
109.9	not among] not of
112.11	plain that it] plain it
113.2	since the child] since it
113.3	thought it over and wondered if the baby] thought over it and wondered if it
113.29	When the baby] When it
113.31	that his wife] that she
113.32	When the child] When it
113.37	parents. The child] parents. It
113.38	church—with Jennie] church, Jennie
113.40	that the baby] that it
114.2	decided that the child] decided it
114.2	taken on one] taken one
114.17	or with] or a
114.20	for an offering] for offering
118.21	for time seemed inclined to mend this gradually,] for this time seemed gradually inclined to mend,
119.7	soul such as hers,] soul,
119.8	but for her] but her
119.18	but as gently] but gently
119.28	will] would
125.4	appeared] appears
125.12	and are confused] and confused
125.30	is the] is of the

126.7   of such a choice] of the choice
126.22   of so much] of as much
126.28   freedoms] freedom
128.26   help noting] help reverting to
128.26   than the merely] than mere
128.31   him another] him, for another
128.31   was a] was, for a
128.40   of the eternal] of eternal
129.15   securing] secure
129.17   as creatures suited for] as more or less deserving creatures, it is
         true, but not unsuited for
129.38   wooing, the broad,] wooing, certain broad
130.1   lovers] lover
130.2   that their dalliance was sweet because it was new] that dalliance
         which is sweet because it is new
130.11   fair and honorable because] fair because
130.32   over that she] over she
131.19   and that this] and this
131.36   driving. He] driving, as he
136.12   toward the] toward
136.14   kind of] kind of a
138.34   certified by] certified to by
141.17   his father's hand] his hand
142.2   this home atmosphere] this homey home atmosphere
142.21   in at the] in the
143.20   met interesting] met more interesting
143.22   few men] few many
144.16   "This isn't] "I hope this isn't
144.21   gazed.] gazed in her direction.
144.29   pick them.] pick her.
144.36   return," she said. "I'll] return. I'll
145.13   be—" he] be—" something, he
145.22   but of ideas] but ideas
146.9   was a bore] was bore
146.9   silly. While] silly. And as
146.11   someone who] someone that
147.4   but also concerning her] but her
•147.16 said. [¶] The] said. [¶] As the presence and care of the little
         outcast Vesta was to have great weight not only in her present
         deliberations but their subsequent result, it may not be amiss to
         take a casual survey of her progress and present status. Ever since
         her recognition by Gerhardt at her baptism some ten months
         previous, she had been growing in health and intelligence until
         now, at eighteen months of age, she was a toddling girl of consider-
         able interest, her large, blue eyes and light hair giving promise of a
         comeliness which would closely approximate that of her mother,
         while her ability to pick up and apply such phrases and ideas as

were in commonest use about the house indicated a clear and intelligent mind. Mrs. Gerhardt had become very fond of her. Gerhardt had unbended so gradually that his interest was not even yet clearly discernable, but he had a distinct feeling toward her. As for Jennie, her affection was of that silent but ardent kind which only requires an opportunity of service to show its quality. [¶] How the gradual reorganization of the household atmosphere had been affected could hardly be traced, and yet it had its roots not only in the natural affinity of age for youth, and the gentle and affectionate attitude of Jennie, but many qualities of the child itself, whose temper was of a happy and playful sort, which goes such a long way toward making children tolerable to even the worst non-child-loving type. Gerhardt, for all his original, blustering wrath, was an easy victim. He had decided after the baptism that he would maintain only a tolerant and supervisory attitude in regard to her social and spiritual training, but, during the long days of sitting about the house, which had followed his injury and return home, he had experienced a change of feeling which was little short of a revolution. It began with the need of letting his eyes rest upon her at times when she would be at play, progressed through the seeming necessity of taking some small share of interest in her if for no other purpose than that of diverting his own weary mind, and finally evoluted to a personal movement or two which resulted in his complete undoing. [¶] "Such a child!" he used to declare to himself. "When they are little, then they are nice; once they are grown up, then they are not so nice any more." [¶] This readjustment of her father's attitude had been sufficient not only to arouse in Jennie an ardent desire to conduct herself so that no pain would ever come to him again but to cause her to feel that any additional folly on her part would not only be base ingratitude to him, but would tend to injure the opportunities of her little one—a thing which she would gladly have done almost anything to prevent. Her life was a failure, she fancied, but Vesta's was a thing apart, and even in going out to meet Lester, she had not in her own estimation done anything to injure her. Her object had been one of pure helpfulness. [¶] The

147.20	Must she tell] Must tell
147.23	want him to?] want to?
147.31	loosed] loosened
148.7	and enclosing] and the enclosure of
148.12	but the letter] but it
148.34	was that he] was he
149.33	thought all this while] thought this the while
150.1	from then on] from now on
150.6	The two fingers] The latter
152.11	affection, his gratitude for her tears] affection, gratitude for tears
152.28	eleven] nine
152.33	less per week,] less weekly

153.6	suffering was heightened] suffering heightened
153.7	really she was not] really not
153.14	the many] the whole
153.20	Lester] He
153.22	eleven] noon
154.35	he won't] he would not
155.6	suggesting dishes] suggesting things
155.14	Six] Five
155.22	Martha, William and] Martha and
156.2	be some situation] be something
158.7	done this] done it
158.10	through, under similarly] through with under similar
158.26	which were anomalous] which anomalous
159.1	you. I'd] you. I'll
159.31	it had appeared] it appeared
160.5	prize and anxious] prize, anxious
160.12	which would begin] which began
160.18	difficult thing] difficult
160.20	When Jennie] When she
160.29	past that she] past she
162.4	"It would] "It will
162.38	first," said Jennie, "and then I'll mention it afterward."] first and then I'll mention it afterward," she said.
163.30	fearful.] fearsome.
163.35	how smart] how well
163.39	arranged beforehand,] arranged for before hand
164.5	coming as] coming as they did as
164.15	one such town,] one,
164.17	they had lived] they used to live
164.22	handkerchief, he said] handkerchief, said
165.5	reassuringly. Jennie] reassuringly, and Jennie
•165.30	Jennie smiled] Jennie, who did not know what officiate meant, smiled
165.33	realization dwelling in her mind that her impulse to tell him had proved unavailing] realization that one impulse to tell him had proved unavailing, dwelling in her mind
166.4	stay, during] stay, in
166.19	training what] training of what
166.20	consisted of.] consisted.
166.25	and he bought] and bought
166.30	think, when she] think for the time she
166.36	gloves, which harmonized] gloves to harmonize
167.31	about the child] about her
167.33	things Lester] things he
169.2	for if one is in] for being in
169.3	limelight, one's every] lime light every
169.10	matters] matter

169.16	as he could.] as might well be.
169.23	would have it or no. Robert's] would or no. His
169.27	private lives] private life
169.37	or] nor
169.40	Actually Robert] Actually and calculatedly by his brother Robert
170.7	not much] not so much
171.1	contacts] contact
171.8	heaven's] heaven
171.25	that Lester] that he
171.26	had his father] had the latter
172.15	any woman] any of them
173.19	after Lester] after he
173.21	commonplace. These] commonplace. They
174.5	had been, why] had why
174.8	had taken on] had on
174.36	came, Jennie] came she
175.5	A curious thing should] It is a curious thing that should
175.5	here: although] here, that although
175.12	given her mother nearly all she had received from Lester] given nearly all she received
175.13	her, against] her mother against
175.17	this came] it came
175.22	money Jennie] money she
175.27	Really, Gerhardt] Really, he
175.32	advice, Jennie] advice, she
175.35	furniture was installed] furniture installed
176.34	was moved out.] was out.
176.35	through the new house, he] through he
176.36	descended upon him.] descended on him.
177.3	feet, at the] feet, the
177.5	walls, at the] walls, the
178.35	said she was married, and] said so and
179.22	on Lester] on the man
180.15	was on a] was one of those
180.16	morning,] mornings
180.23	bed,] bedside,
180.36	bad life] bad one
181.11	all of this] all this
181.23	an irritating] an aggravating
181.28	Jennie's—during] Jennie's—at
181.31	or of Jennie's] or Jennie's
181.36	for Jennie] for her
182.21	so she] so it
183.5	eventually acknowledge her to Lester and give her] eventually get married, lead a decent life and give Vesta
184.3	one of Vesta's] one of her
*185.11	and fifth] *stet*

185.30   services, which were legion, when he was with her, and to] ser-
          vices when he was with her, which were legion, to
186.5   charge equally with] charge with
186.8   Lester] He
186.16   was Robert] was he
186.17   he himself wanted] he wanted
187.5   of failure] of a failure
187.9   life was] life is
187.35   Cincinnati at about] Cincinnati about
188.22   the ultimate distribution] the distribution
188.27   put to] put up to
188.38   the three daughters] the daughters
188.40   Robert's] His
189.11   toward the general] toward general
189.26   time Robert] time his brother
190.11   Lester] He
190.30   Bass, Martha and George's being away ensured this.] Bass, Mar-
          tha and George, being away, assured this.
190.31   fifteen] fourteen
190.33   William] William, twelve,
190.36   narrated, Gerhardt] narrated the latter
191.16   that she] that it
191.17   crosses] cross
191.17   borne were] borne was
191.18   neglect, and this] neglect, this
191.24   of Vesta's] of her
191.27   leave Vesta] leave her
191.30   relocating Vesta] locating her
191.31   not] not so
191.34   transferring Vesta, Jennie] transferring her she
192.1   Vesta instead. Vesta.
192.13   he had been before.] he was before.
192.15   sending Vesta] sending her
192.21   was about to leave again,] was leaving again
193.15   animal nature,] animal natural,
193.26   world measures] world counts
194.30   He sensed what] He felt that
194.31   way she understood] way understood
194.34   presence, as] presence, like
195.5   specimen] specimens
195.5   he had scarcely] he scarcely
195.11   had now gone] had gone
195.39   and that her] and her
196.22   people—for her father, her] people, her father, his
196.32   of a home] of home
197.25   understood the] understood each
197.35   and he would] and would

198.16	she had had] she had
198.16	have word for] have for
198.39	finding that it] finding it
199.8	was that she] was she
199.12	adjust it] adjust herself to it
199.13	wife and a happy] wife, a happy
200.24	had climbed] had put it there, had climbed
200.35	see the cigar] see it
201.7	She was] "She is
201.26	speak. The bell] speak. It
202.16	third drawers. In the third drawer] third in the last of which
202.19	many odd things] many things
202.23	of whom,] of which
203.6	middle-aged woman] middle aged lady
204.2	as by the] as the
*205.1	death. Mrs. Kane] death herself and hastily dispatched a neighbor to say that Vesta was very ill and Mrs. Kane
205.5	discovery by] discovery of
205.6	[¶] Jennie left the flat and hastened] When she left the house she hastened
205.12	words, forgot all] words, all
205.14	she remembered] and remembered
205.17	present. But for her, perhaps but for] present; that but for her, perhaps
205.24	the street-cars] the cars
205.25	and a street-car's] and one's
205.30	misconduct and] misconduct toward it and
205.39	which Jennie,] which the other,
206.2	physician, practically all of whom] physician all of whom practically
206.15	cottage, Jennie] cottage she
206.16	path on] path by
206.20	Lester would be] Lester had been literally
206.29	action was] action on his part which for the moment it seemed to throw upon him, was
206.39	to Jennie's] to her
206.40	where Jennie] where she
207.16	it was] it is
207.23	and saw how] and how
209.7	stairs and,] stairs when
212.27	coat rack] closet
212.33	and were hearing] and hearing
212.36	clicked she moved] clicked moved
213.15	determined to do this, after] determined after
213.30	would have injured the] would injure the
213.30	how had] how did
213.35	could have wished] could wish

214.1	be something] be somewhat
214.1	He had been] He was
214.3	it also aroused] it aroused
214.28	her there at the apartment the] her the
214.30	put matters] put things
214.37	have gone if] have if
214.38	dinner that he did not come for, and] dinner for him and
214.40	that Jennie's] that her
215.4	take Vesta] take her
215.10	saw Lester] saw him
215.11	him. He] him, but as he had done the night he left her he
216.10	her own ungrateful] her ungrateful
216.17	All this] All the
216.21	wanted for long?] wanted long?
*216.28	was what he had implied.] was as he said
217.7	apartment—especially] apartment—particularly
217.15	watch Vesta closely, for Vesta] watch her closely for she
217.32	softly rolled collar] soft roll collar
218.19	impression] impressions
218.21	but the impression] but it
218.23	have married] have taken
218.26	and to keep Vesta there during Lester's visit.] and keeping Vesta there during his presence.
218.29	control her] control it
218.35	him, however, and had] him, had
218.36	thing as a baby on her mind,] thing on her mind as a baby
219.10	turned from his] turned his
219.11	turned from it] turned it
219.22	her first really] her really first
219.26	breakfast earlier and] breakfast and
220.7	That's] That
220.25	as far] so far
220.33	him, Vesta] him, she
220.39	was a real] was real
221.32	that interested him.] that interesting relationship to him.
222.22	to Jennie.] to her.
222.37	on Lester.] on him.
222.38	feasible.] feasible and hoped to return to it another time
223.20	people in responsible positions who were under obligation] people who in responsible positions were obligated
224.16	had begun] had been
224.22	he had counted] he counted
225.6	have been added.] have added.
225.13	had himself called] had called
225.13	for Lester in the past.] for Lester himself.
225.18	Street] Place
225.27	Street] Place

225.36   conditions Lester maintained] conditions he had had

227.12   know it.] know

229.12   which Lester] which he

229.20   all Lester] all he

230.16   about? In this] about in his

230.20   digression in] digression of his in

230.22   bringing Lester] bringing him

230.31   up now and] up and

230.35   was so very] was very

230.40   as by the] as the

232.26   as far] so far

232.34   of man] of a man

235.25   arguments, and quarrels] arguments, quarrels

235.27   so] still so

236.2   to this environment, the] to it the

236.4   atmosphere; he cannot] atmosphere and cannot

236.13   choose] chose

236.14   nevertheless Robert] nevertheless he

236.21   fine sensibilities] finest sensibilities

236.27   of Louise's discovery] of this discovery which Louise had made.

237.23   over, and the] over, the

237.23   cogitations was] cogitations being

237.31   haunt him—the] haunt the

237.37   change,] changes

238.6   happened. A feeling of estrangement was] happened. It was

238.8   trips to Cincinnati thereafter] trips thereafter

238.11   from her family's] from the family

238.30   do it.] do that.

239.27   they had been] they were

240.6   connections,] connection

240.6   cases, were] cases was

240.24   he had thought] he thought

240.34   was she?] was it?

240.35   Jennie] She

240.35   if Vesta] if it

240.36   was she] was it

240.37   for her] for it

240.37   Was she] Was it

240.39   difficulty—of wrong action] difficulty—of not right action

241.3   quarreled with them because] quarreled because

241.16   long since tired of] long heard of

241.17   and of his] and his

241.17   to take smaller] on taking smaller

241.22   a sympathetic mood] a melting mood

241.23   this generosity] this weakening generosity

242.40   Jennie] her

243.1   that Veronica] that she

243.8	By degrees] But by degrees
243.12	left Lester] left him
243.12	Would her father] Would he
246.16	and had then decided] and decided
247.3	principally at him] principally him
249.14	him like that] him that
251.6	reasons] reason
251.12	find a satisfactory house] find it
251.25	The home was] It was
251.37	room with handsome] room, handsome
251.39	kitchen, a serving-room] kitchen, serving room
252.7	and she was] and was
253.5	wondering who] wondering whom
253.7	call Gerhardt,] call him,
253.8	climbed to her father's] climbed to Gerhardt's
254.7	he himself had] he had
254.18	for Lester] for he
254.19	abed Sundays. But] abed—but
254.24	such, was more comfortable] such comfortable
254.29	not anticipate] not realize
255.12	North Side. Hyde Park] North Side. This particular neighborhood
257.1	and she succeeded] and succeeded
257.12	Lester only heard] Lester heard
257.15	wives during] wives of the men during
•257.21	The trouble] *stet*
257.23	was not of the] was the
257.28	and get up] and up
257.30	financial success on the part of the former and] financial on the part of the former, (or failure) and
257.31	recognition on] recognition or retirement on
257.31	latter. They] latter. In either case, if they were doing well or ill they
257.32	not have remained] not remain
258.8	his conventional] his ungained conventional
258.22	gossip—which make] gossip concerning which makes
258.24	particularly] particular
258.39	she drew] she felt and drew
258.40	felt right to] felt with
259.8	her stepfather,] her supposed father,
259.10	had begun] had been begun
259.17	and to go] and go
259.27	and that there] and there
261.13	angry at.] angry at, but she had a past and that had to be taken into consideration.
261.33	her offers] her proffers
262.11	course could speak to] course to

262.21	she had heard,] she knew
262.33	pleasing.] pleasing and interesting.
263.24	remarks.] remarks and then
263.26	Mrs. Field now] Mrs. Field
263.33	would marry her, somehow] would somehow
263.34	have to make to establish] have to establish
264.25	[¶] There] [¶] While these things were going on however, there
264.35	enough. It] enough. As
264.36	a fine] a delightful
265.19	seemed to be sure] seemed to prove
˙265.23	One of his duties] *stet*
266.11	veranda where] veranda which commanded a sweeping view of the town and the distant street where
267.31	in fact, of all] in fact all
267.35	cooking. There was also Jeannette] cooking and Jeannette
268.7	as that of the] as the
268.33	need. So dependent on her was he that it] need. Still it
268.38	career, was fond of taking] career of taking
269.11	that had happened] that happened
270.9	him feel young] him this way
270.13	and now seeing] and seeing
˙271.11	your papa] *stet*
271.16	when he and Jennie] when they
271.16	have Vesta] have her
271.35	protested. [¶] Old Gerhardt was so anxious] protested. [¶] An additional pleasing scene was of Lester and Jennie working out some puzzle, Vesta studying, Gerhardt reading. The latter was so anxious
272.33	rather enviable.] rather distinguished.
273.19	Lester] He
273.35	that Robert's] that his
276.24	thing?] thing he asked himself.
278.5	His father] He
278.6	distressed, and] distressed but
278.7	irritated Lester.] irritated him.
278.15	attitude, for his] attitude, his
278.18	Maybe Lester] Maybe he
278.34	believe the information,] believe it
278.34	consider the arrangements] consider it
280.9	worlds] world
280.38	had begun] had been
280.39	Hyde Park. Dodge] Hyde Park) the latter
280.39	something—Lester] something, he
281.3	Lester] He
281.5	at Dodge's] at his
281.5	North Shore Drive, one of the most palatial] North Shore Drive which was one of the most interesting and palatial
281.7	bright, sophisticated] bright, clever, sophisticated

281.9	might have seemed] might seem
281.11	They] for they
281.12	Dodge] He
281.29	waving Lester] waving him
281.34	would already have] would have
285.12	to who] to whom
285.13	small papers. Finally one] small fry papers. Finally some one
285.32	cities.] city.
286.13	of him] of himself
288.2	references] reference
288.4	that it will] that does
289.8	and one of Jennie] and Jennie
289.15	sketches] pictures
289.25	her.] her at that.
*292.20	thirty-one] twenty-nine
294.15	graveyard. Lester,] graveyard to which Lester
294.16	journeyed there together on] journeyed on
294.18	He had had] He had
294.26	that has been] that is
*295.22	a fifth] a fourth
295.24	roughly eight] roughly about eight
295.27	Then the document] Then it
295.34	fifth of] fourth of
295.38	remaining fifth] remaining fourth
298.1	soul, for] soul of him wondering, for
298.12	above board,] above aboard
298.13	or, alternately, in] or in
298.28	him now?] him?
299.3	him!] him appeared impossible.
299.13	front, at the] front, the
299.23	keeping him] keeping
300.41	come.] come, anyhow.
301.6	heirs and his] heirs as well as his
301.39	had conferred] had concurred
303.2	to the "brass] to "brass
303.15	which Robert] which he
303.20	course Lester] course he
303.27	that Lester] that he
303.39	Lester] he
304.5	days there came] days came
305.11	Lester] He
306.7	essential: for] essential: to
306.34	father had died. With] father died and with
307.25	mind. At] mind. Before
*308.10	the Savoy] the Carlton
308.31	roughness by many.] by many roughness.
309.23	years more—] years—

310.18	want Letty Pace] want her
310.19	she had been] she was
310.23	Savoy] Carlton
310.24	blooming; that sense of new life, which] blooming everywhere, that sense of new life in the air which
310.25	back, was in the air. She] back, she
310.36	Gerald has died] Gerald died
311.6	Lester did,] Lester,
311.9	him this question in] him in
311.12	that her judgement of feminine charms was excellent.] that she knew.
312.2	and so did] and did
•312.20	"Yes, you thought!] *stet*
313.13	her. This woman] her. She
313.13	station in life, and] station and
313.17	leaving him] leaving her
317.2	tuxedo, looking] tuxedo and looking
317.14	turnings] turning
317.23	she had had] she had
317.28	then she] then as she
319.19	herself—the] herself—namely, the
320.9	after consideration] after mature consideration
320.19	take Lester.] take her husband.
321.39	ante-dating the] ante-dating really the
321.40	suffering in] suffering within
322.9	so widely] so largely
322.11	order, however, where] order where
322.17	be transferred] be covered
322.21	comply with.] comply with apropos suggestions.
322.32	laborers to be] laborers being
322.34	and if it] and it
323.17	countries, a move which] countries which
324.6	Lester] he
324.6	been back in] been in
324.14	thinking of] thinking something of
324.35	at Robert's] at his
325.6	He had tried] He tried
325.12	saw that something] saw what it was—something
325.19	"That's good,"] "That's nice,"
325.40	Lester] He
325.41	was loosening] was unloosing
326.11	that possibility,] that,
327.7	enter into a] enter a
327.29	advantages, Lester] advantages he
327.37	black-eyed, with an] black eyed, an
328.2	He himself knew] He knew

328.17 looks and financed the operation.] looks. He financed the operation and

328.22 The present] His present

328.31 Ross] He

329.1 credit, however, nearly] credit, nearly

329.4 Lester] He

329.5 before Lester] before him

329.21 three years at] three, at

329.37 Ross] He

330.10 made city] made or marred city

330.14 this proposition?] this, anyhow?

330.18 Since Lester had] The reason for this particular decision at this time was due to the fact that in spite of the thought he was holding of leaving Jennie he was still in the mood of the man who feels that he must do something to justify himself to himself even if his return to the bosom of the Kane family, metaphorically speaking for of course he did not contemplate any actual social connection with them would solve his monetary problems for him. Since he had

330.20 or cleverness.] or any cleverness of judgement.

330.26 might, or] might if he left her or

331.19 finally decided] finally after mature deliberation decided

331.23 judgement and was quite] judgement which were quite

331.37 and Lester] and he

332.19 which Lester] which he

332.23 fact, might bring] fact, bring

332.27 months Lester] months he

332.33 was to run] was run

332.33 as long] so long

332.35 which Lester] which he

333.17 that the title was] that as a matter of policy it was

333.20 name. Seeing] name and seeing

333.24 when, after they had expended $6,000] when after expending $6,000

333.26 the meat-packing group] the packing house group

334.3 was and whether] was whether

335.17 all Lester's] all his

335.18 outside his] outside of his

335.31 venture. Lester] venture and Lester

336.30 of Letty's] of her

336.37 was plain] was so plain

337.9 deal and] deal previously described and

341.24 her, somehow] her that somehow

342.19 by Mrs. Frissell, the cook, by Henry Weeds,] Mrs. Frissell, the cook, Henry Weeds,

342.20 occasionally by Lester] occasionally Lester

342.22 and of one] and one

344.18 as far] so far

344.21	well-dressed and well-fed, and she looked] well dressed, well fed, and looked
347.15	looked curiously at] looked at
347.17	graveside. There] graveside curiously. There
347.19	as long as Gerhardt] so long as he
347.20	Lester] He
347.23	and Jennie, then] and then
347.39	he had thought] he thought
348.13	he had thought] he thought
348.25	she had never] she never
349.30	be sounded out,] be talked to
352.2	he marry] he marries
352.2	Mr. O'Brien] He
352.14	noticed, were] noticed, was
353.12	as far] so far
355.29	for Lester] for he
355.31	Mr. O'Brien had called, Lester had been gone on] Mr. O'Brien called, he had gone on
•355.32	town,] town in Wisconsin
355.35	house the next afternoon, interested to] house interested to
358.27	care for her enough to] care enough for her to
358.29	important appeared.] important appeared, or could be.
359.26	wish to.] wish.
359.40	everything save perhaps] everything perhaps save
361.7	tell O'Brien] tell him
361.13	and of distinction] and distinction
362.38	are complex] are involved
364.23	such chord, united] such, united
364.25	cease to be.] cease.
364.27	with it all] with this
364.28	her affections] Jennie's affections
365.16	comes] come
366.1	storage, it] storage that it
366.19	in United Traction] in the United Traction,
366.26	When she had first come] When she first came
366.29	the dream] that dream
367.12	spring was showing] spring showing
367.14	Jennie] She
367.17	Jennie's] her
368.9	breathe, all this could] breathe, could
368.19	realized that he] realized he
368.33	most unlucky] most fortuitously unlucky
369.28	knock his] knock other
369.39	him word] him any word
370.13	however, and he] however, for he
370.14	dinner. This] dinner and this
370.19	with a] with the

370.23	not seen] not met
370.24	before the meal] before this
370.41	Borchgrevink, to the] Borchgrevink, the
371.1	France, to the] France, the
371.3	music, to the] music, the
371.6	Professor] Prof.
371.14	tended toward] tended to
373.18	course," Letty] course," she
374.31	there, as beautiful] there, beautiful
375.25	on the social] on the then social
376.7	would not delay.] would not.
376.25	enjoyed meeting] enjoyed to meet
378.11	her own mother] her mother
378.29	distress, Vesta] distress she
378.32	her mother,] her,
379.17	her, the town] her it
379.31	against any roving] against roving
380.28	eight months] eight
381.34	Letty] She
381.35	of Lester] of him
382.13	let Jennie know.] let her (Jennie) know.
382.23	he had encountered] he met
382.37	father had been] father was
382.37	was himself an] was an
384.18	work in order to] work to
384.25	of indifference,] of more or less indifference
384.29	headache. Jennie gave] headache. When Jennie had given
384.31	and advised] and had advised
384.32	better, the headache grew] better it grew
385.1	then she began] then began
385.33	had sprung] had, as has been shown sprung
385.36	caressed Jennie] caressed her
386.2	have had others] have others
386.16	witnessed, then the] witnessed the
387.21	when Jennie] when she
388.30	daily—he was a] daily—a
389.7	thought that she looked indifferently,] thought indifferently,
389.26	death, had said] death said
390.6	Tremont House] Hotel Tremont
392.17	"It may] I may
392.33	personalities] personality
394.8	child as her sole companion—] child—
394.10	whom she] which she
394.11	Mr. Dwight L. Watson, Lester's attorney.] Mr. Dwight L. Watson, her sole companion.
394.25	way, a] way though, a

394.37	counsel—the aforementioned Mr. Dwight L. Watson—] counsel—Mr. Dwight L. Watson,
*394.40	eleven] seven
396.17	and had remarked] and remarked
396.20	she did not see] she had not seen
396.21	she did not see] she had not seen
396.25	that now] that after that
396.27	she had once] she once
396.36	hair was still] hair still
396.38	neighbors—and as kindly] neighbors—kindly
397.14	one named Harry,] one—Harry—
397.17	and with Mr. Hyatt Skale] and Mr. Hyatt Skale
397.28	He had read] He read
397.31	unfortunate turn] unfortunate termination
397.34	judgement. Robert] judgement. Lester
398.3	he had] he made
398.4	driving turn] driving purposely turn
398.17	happened to Lester] happened
398.22	why Robert] why he
398.22	to do what he had done] to do it
398.24	been Robert's] been his
398.28	at Robert] at him
398.37	his brother's voice] his voice
398.39	decided not to.] decided not.
399.7	dynamic or] dynamic nor
399.12	happened to Lester] happened
*399.22	twelve] ten
399.35	and asked about Amy,] and Amy,
400.18	with his.] with him.
401.7	worth that] worth so
401.7	coming to him, when] coming when
401.10	of losing that.] of that.
401.24	to plaster an old wound.] to stop a bad thought.
401.32	was saying] was doing
402.3	it had been] it was
402.23	Robert] He
402.26	he had been] he was
403.18	be illusory] be one
403.22	this or that material proposition—people] this material proposition and that—people
404.1	least bit dingy] least dingy
405.16	accepted the very meagre income for him of] accepted for him the very meagre income of
406.29	would carry] would have carried
407.16	His Japanese valet, Kozo,] His valet
407.18	Chicago in under] Chicago under
407.37	away] that was the valet's first name, away

408.16   housekeeper, Mrs. Swenson, was] housekeeper was
408.17   Jennie] She
408.20   what vessel was] what was
409.16   sombre. The carriage] sombre. It
409.31   this illness.] this business.
409.38   about getting well.] about that.
410.14   many more paroxysms] many paroxysms
410.16   pain had ceased,] pain ceased,
410.33   since.] since. [¶] "You mustn't think you have any reason to be
          sorry." She was choking with affection and sympathy.
410.35   way.] way."
410.37   parted."] parted.
411.5   he asked.] he added.
411.11   Jennie?" he asked.] Jennie?"
411.24   relief and as company,] relief and company,
412.34   existence. For instance it was arranged by wire with Mrs. Kane,
          when] existence. It was arranged for instance with Mrs. Kane by
          wire when
413.2   wished to call, or] wished or
413.2   to do so.] to call.
413.3   were nominally] were tentatively
413.5   see Lester] see him
413.25   come to her,] come,
413.26   had come in] had in
•413.32   North] South
413.39   made a] made any
414.32   lace, an open book in his hand, attended by an acolyte on either
          side, followed] lace, attended by an acolyte on either hand, an
          open book in his hand, followed.
416.6   and she succeeded,] and succeeded,
416.12   away over] away for over
416.28   It had not been] It was not

53.35   **setting off to work one evening**   Gerhardt works as a night watchman; he must therefore be departing for work late in the day if he is to bid good-night to Weaver at 54.35 and then question his wife the next morning at 55.13.

70.19   **Columbus House**   It has been established earlier that Senator Brander maintains permanent quarters at the Columbus House. Nowhere in the text has Dreiser suggested that Brander has moved to the Capital Hotel. The inconsistency probably results from a mixing of sheets from early and late versions in the copy-text or from a simple error by Dreiser. The emendation here has been made for consistency. The Columbus House is fictitious; the Capital Hotel, however, was a real establishment. An inconspicuous, somewhat shabby place, it stood on the north side of Broad Street opposite the State House in Columbus. It would not have been a likely hotel for Senator Brander to patronize. The leading hotel in Columbus at the time was the Neil House (see Theodore Dreiser, *Jennie Gerhardt*, ed. Lee Clark Mitchell [Oxford and New York: Oxford University Press, 1991], p. 368). Dreiser may have had in mind the Terre Haute House from his hometown when he described the Columbus House (see Theodore Dreiser, *Jennie Gerhardt*, ed. Donald Pizer [New York: Penguin Books, 1989], p. 433).

81.4   **horrible.**   Senator Brander has written no note to Jennie. Perhaps the reference survives from an earlier version of the text.

134.17   **as a lady's maid**   The change is adopted from the Harpers text because Jennie has not yet told Lester how much she earns.

147.16   **said. [¶] The**   Gerhardt is in Youngstown and so cannot yet grow fond of Vesta. Also, mention of his accident is made before it occurs. Hence the excision. These problems with logistics and chronology probably are carried over from an earlier version of this chapter.

165.30   **Jennie smiled**   Lester has not used the word *officiate* earlier. The phrase eliminated in this emendation occurs on a typescript sheet incorporated into the copy-text. The word *officiate* might tie in with an earlier, discarded page of this typescript, or it might be a mistranscription that Dreiser missed.

185.11   **and fifth**   It might be assumed that Vesta, at the age of five, is too old to be mispronouncing her words, as she does earlier in this chapter. In that case one might omit the words "and fifth" here. Earlier, however, at 183.17, Dreiser makes it clear that Vesta's conversations with her grandfather take place when she is a "toddling infant"—probably when she is between the ages of two and four. It therefore seems best not to emend this reading.

205.1   **death. Mrs. Kane**   Mrs. Olsen herself comes to fetch Jennie. Perhaps the neighbor had been delegated to stay with Vesta in the interim, or perhaps she is a remnant from an earlier version of the scene.

216.28 **was what he had implied.**   The original reading, "as he said," is not possible, since Lester has not said as much to Jennie. He has implied, however, that the final outcome might be "Vesta and herself alone"—a foreshadowing of what in fact does happen.

257.21 **The trouble**   From this point until the end of the chapter, no leaves survive in the composite MS. Copy-text for this passage therefore shifts to the Barrett typescript.

265.23 **One of his duties**   From this point until the reading "old age." at 267.32, there are no leaves extant in the composite MS. Copy-text therefore becomes the Barrett typescript.

271.11 **your papa**   Lester, of course, is not Vesta's father, but Dreiser seems at pains in this section to stress the fact that Lester, Jennie, and Vesta have formed a family unit. To all outside appearances, Lester is Vesta's stepfather; it would be natural for Jennie to call him her "papa." She also might want to encourage Lester to think of himself in this way.

292.20 **thirty-one**   Jennie is fifteen years younger than Lester; the newspaper article is published in the winter of 1893, just before Mr. Kane's death, when Lester is forty-six.

295.22 **a fifth**   Robert and Lester together inherit one-half of the stock of the carriage company (one-fourth each); the three sisters divide the remaining half equally among themselves (one-sixth each). The remaining properties in the estate are divided equally among the five children—hence the emendation here. The carriage company is apparently valued at approximately $2,560,000 and the entire estate at $3,360,000. Robert's and Lester's shares of the total estate are approximately $800,000; each sister's share is worth approximately $586,000.

308.10 **the Savoy**   Dreiser had originally put Jennie and Lester at the Carlton, a luxurious hotel in Haymarket, but their trip occurs in 1893, and the Carlton did not open for business until 1899. Hence the emendation.

312.20 **"Yes, you thought!**   Lester has not actually said what he thought, but this fact is not immediately apparent to the reader. It seems best not to emend here.

355.32 **town,**   Hegewisch is in Illinois. See the historical note at 355.32.

394.40 **eleven**   Lester and Robert have not met since the reading of their father's will in the winter of 1893 (see 397.25).

399.22 **twelve**   See note for 394.40 above.

413.32 **North**   The church Dreiser had in mind is on the North Side of Chicago. Other Catholic churches named for Saint Michael in Chicago of the period were small and ministered to immigrant congregations.

Table 3: First Printing] Barrett Carbon TS

The entries below record all substantive variants in chapters I, XXIII, and XLI of the Pennsylvania edition between the *typed* text of the Barrett carbon typescript and the text of the 1911 Harper and Brothers first printing. These chapters are typical for the novel as a whole. The variant lists give the user of this edition a general idea of the extent of variation between the text that Dreiser brought to a point of stasis in February 1911 and the text that was actually issued by Harpers in the fall of that year.

Undoubtedly, some of these changes were introduced by Dreiser as handwritten revisions on the ribbon copy of the typescript that he submitted to Harpers, or as changes marked on the fresh typescript that Harpers produced, or as alterations in proof. The revisions in chapter XLI having to do with Lester's marriage to Jennie, for example, were Dreiser's work and were even copied by him onto the Barrett carbon so that he might have his own record of them. The great majority of the changes, however, were almost surely the work of Ripley Hitchcock or of the sub-editors who worked under his direction. Some of these changes have been incorporated into the text of the Pennsylvania edition; see the entries in Table 1.

The table is keyed by page-line number to the first-edition text. The initial reading in each entry is the revised reading, as printed in the Harpers text. This reading is followed by a left-pointing bracket, which can be read as "revised from." Following the bracket is the original typed reading from the Barrett carbon.

CHAPTER I

1.14	She was a product of the fancy] The fancy
1.15	the untutored but poetic mind of her mother combined with the gravity] an untutored, but poetic mind, were all blended in the mother, but poverty was driving her. Excepting a kind of gravity
1.17	father. Poverty was driving them.] father, the daughter inherited her disposition from her mother.
2.1	to guess at the poverty that made it necessary. The clerk, manlike, was affected] to know. The clerk interrupted because he did not like to see the mother strain so nervously at explaining. Manlike, he was affected

2.4   hard indeed.] hard.
2.6   office, he called] office, called
2.12   "Yes, I believe so."] "Yes, I suppose so," returned the clerk.
2.15   said the clerk, pleasantly] he said pleasantly
2.19   succession of misfortunes] succession of events
2.23   lower walks of life] lower fields of endeavor
2.23   forced to] forced, for the present, to
2.24   dependent] depending
2.26   each recurring] each successive
2.27   He himself] He
2.28   Sebastian, or "Bass," as his associates transformed it, worked]
        Sebastian, worked
2.31   been trained to] been taught
2.35   complicated.] complicated. It was the ambition of both the father
        and mother to keep them in school, but the method of supplying
        clothes, books and monthly dues for this purpose, was practically
        beyond solution. The father, being an ardent Lutheran, insisted that
        the parochial schools were essential, and there, outside of the
        prayers and precepts of the Evangelical faith, they learned little.
        One child, Veronica, was already forced to remain at home for the
        want of shoes. George, old enough to understand and suffer from
        distinction made between himself and those better dressed, often
        ran away and played "hookey". Martha complained that she had
        nothing to wear, and Genevieve was glad that she was out of it all.
2.36   a six-hundred-dollar] a three-hundred-dollar
2.37   He had borrowed] He borrowed
3.1   when, having saved enough to buy the house, he desired to add]
        when he had saved enough to buy the house and lot, in order that he
        might add
3.3   and so make] and make
3.4   on the mortgage] on this
3.5   bad that he] bad he
3.7   Gerhardt was helpless, and the consciousness of his precarious situa-
        tion—the doctor's bill, the interest due upon the mortgage, to-
        gether with the sums] Helpless as he was, the doctor's bill, chil-
        dren's school, interest on the mortgage about to fall due, and sums
3.12   longer—all these perplexities weighed] longer, weighed
3.23   the philanthropist] the credit-giver
3.27   and this, with] and with
3.28   milk, made almost a feast] milk, sometimes seemed rich
3.30   was an infrequent treat] was a treat
3.34   hoping that the] hoping their
3.35   up. But as the winter approached Gerhardt began to feel desperate.
        ] up. The whole commercial element seemed more or less paralyzed
        in this district. Gerhardt was facing the approaching winter and felt
        desperate. [¶] "George," he would say, when the oldest of those
        attending school would come home at four o'clock, "we must have

some more coal," and seeing Martha, William and Veronica un-willingly gather up the baskets, would hide his face and wring his hands. When Sebastian, or "Bass", as his associates had transformed it, would arrive streaked and energetic from the shop at half-past six, he would assume a cheerful air of welcome. [¶] "How are things down there?" he would inquire. "Are they going to put on any more men?" [¶] Bass did not know, and had no faith in its possibility, but he went over the ground with his father and hoped for the best.

4.1	sturdy German's] sturdy Lutheran's
4.4	that she] that the little one
4.7	of purely human] of humane
4.9	Pastor Wundt] Father Wundt
4.18	scared from the railroad yards. Mrs. Gerhardt] scared off from doing that. She
4.21	hotel. Now, by a miracle, she had her chance.] hotel. Her son had often spoken of its beauty, and she was a resourceful woman. Genevieve helped her at home, why not here?
4.34	were thus] were so
4.37	having a population of fifty thousand] having twenty-five thousand population
5.1	traffic, was a good field for the hotel business, and the opportunity] traffic, presented an opportunity for superiority in this line, which in this instance
5.2	improved; so at least the Columbus people proudly thought.] improved.
5.6	stores.] stores, and, naturally, the crowd and hurry of life, which, to those who had never seen anything better, seemed wondrously gay and inspiriting. Large plate-glass windows looked out upon the main and side streets, through which could be seen many comfortable chairs scattered about for those who cared to occupy them.
5.17	usually] usually to be seen
5.17	departing, in accordance with the movement of the trains.] departing as the trains dictated.
5.21	terms] term
5.23	them to Columbus] them here
5.24	chambers at the hotel.] chambers.
5.26	permanent guest] permanent resident
5.26	a resident] a natural inhabitant
5.27	but an otherwise homeless bachelor.] but a bachelor, and always in need of a comfortable room.
5.32	and stir of this kaleidoscopic] and merriment of this shifty
5.33	daughter, suddenly flung] daughter, brought
5.33	of superior brightness, felt immeasurably overawed.] of brightness, saw only that which was far off and immensely superior.
5.37	sweep, had for them all the magnificence of a palace; they kept] sweep, overawed them so that they constantly kept
6.5	against the] against her

6.9   Genevieve, and started nervously at the sound of her own voice.]
        Genevieve nervously, more to be dulling the sound of her own
        conscience than anything else.

6.12   but clumsy] but faulty

6.17   Jennie, mortified] Jennie, actually reassured

6.18   vigorously, without again daring to lift her eyes.] vigorously with-
        out lifting her eyes.

6.20   With painstaking diligence they worked downward] In this man-
        ner they worked carefully downward

6.21   five o'clock; it] five o'clock, when it

6.23   bottom of the stairway.] bottom.

6.24   Through the big swinging doors there] About this time there

6.27   the crowd] the riff-raff

6.31   eyebrows.] eye-brows. He carried a polished walking-stick, evi-
        dently more for the pleasure of the thing than anything else.

6.35   acknowledged not only by] acknowledged by not only

7.4   bowed and smiled pleasantly. [¶] "You shouldn't have troubled your-
        self," he said.] bowed, smiled pleasantly, and addressing her said:
        [¶] "You shouldn't have troubled yourself."

7.7   landing an impulsive sidewise glance assured him, more clearly than
        before, of her uncommonly prepossessing appearance. He noted]
        landing, a sidewise glance told him, more keenly than even his first
        view, of her uncommon features. He saw

7.11   he saw were blue and the] he knew were blue, the

7.13   and the full cheeks—above all] and full cheeks, but most of all

7.14   that hopeful expectancy] that futurity of hope

7.15   middle-aged is] middle-aged and waning, is

7.17   way, but the impression of her charming personality went] way,
        carrying her impression

7.20   Senator.] senator from Ohio. [¶] A few moments after he had
        gone and Jennie had become engrossed with her labor as before, the
        fact that she also had observed him disclosed itself.

7.22   now?" observed Jennie a few moments later.] now?"

7.31   the glamor of the great world was having its effect upon her senses.
        ] the finery of the world was having its say.

7.33   brightness, the] brightness, and the

7.34   laughter surrounding her.] laughter which went about.

8.2   That feeling] All that feeling

8.16   and, after] and passing out into the side street, by the rear en-
        trance, after

8.16   away, they] away, the couple

8.20   by that half-defined emotion] by something of that

8.21   had engendered in her consciousness.] had driven swiftly home.

8.30   Jennie, half to herself.] Jennie, with a sigh.

8.32   mother with a long-drawn sigh.] mother after a time, when her
        own deep thoughts would no longer bear silence.

8.36   hopeless note] hopeless quality

9.5   house, they] house, both of the wayfarers
9.12   illness and trouble] illness
9.21   old shoddy] old red cotton
9.23   by in strained silence.] by strained and silent.
9.24   Mr. Bauman,] Mr. Bauman eventually,
9.26   He wrapped up] He laid out
9.26   and, handing Jennie the parcel, he added] and when about to
         hand it to them added
9.32   street, and] street again, and
10.2   the mother made her inquiry about the coal. "I got a little] the
         children had gathered in the kitchen to discuss developments with
         their mother. "I got some
10.9   the scanty] the scant
10.9   being prepared] being thus tardily prepared
10.10   the sick child's bedside] the cot-side
10.10   another long night's vigil quite as a matter of course.] another
         night's vigil that was almost without sleep.
10.12   While the supper was being eaten Sebastian offered a suggestion,
         and his] During the preparation of the meal, such as it was,
         Sebastian had made a suggestion. His
10.14   his proposition worth considering. Though only a] this valuable.
         Though a
10.17   very strongly] very much
10.20   age, he was a typical stripling of the town. Already he had formu-
         lated a philosophy of life. To succeed] age, he had already re-
         ceived those favors and glances from the young girls that tend to
         make the bright boy a dandy. With the earliest evidence of such
         interest, he had begun to see that appearances were worth some-
         thing, and from that to the illusion that they were more important
         than anything else, was but an easy step. At the car-works he got in
         with a half-dozen other young boys, who knew Columbus and its
         possibilities thoroughly, and with them he fraternized until he was a
         typical stripling of the town. He knew all about ball-games and
         athletics, had heard that the State capital contained the high and
         mighty of the land, loved the theatre, with its suggestion of travel
         and advertisement, and was not unaware that to succeed
10.22   something—one must associate] something—associate
10.23   seem to associate] seem to
10.26   this hotel] this hotel with its glow and shine
10.30   around the hotel] around its
10.34   nobodies, young] nobodies; those who gambled or sought other
         pleasures, and young
10.36   he admired] he both admired
10.37   main touchstone. If men] main persuasion. If they
11.2   and to act] and act
11.4   broadened.] broadened. [¶] It was he who had spoken to his
         mother more than once of Columbus House, and now that she was

working there, much to his mortification, he thought that it would be better if they only took laundry from it. Work they had to do, in some such difficult way, but if they could get some of these fine gentlemen's laundry to do, how much better it would be. Others did it.

11.5   those hotel fellows] those fellows
11.7   experiences.] experiences to him.
11.11 This plan struck Jennie] This plan struck her
11.23 hotel she spoke of it] hotel, Jennie spoke
11.36 That important individual] That individual
12.2   face. So he listened graciously when Mrs. Gerhardt ventured meekly] face. When they were working about him on their knees, he did not feel irritated at all. Finally they got through, and Mrs. Gerhardt ventured very meekly
12.4   been revolving] been anxiously revolving
12.9   again recognized that absolute want was written all over her anxious face.] again saw what was written all over her face, absolute want.
12.12 were charitable men] were of large, charitable mould
12.14 Senator Brander," he continued.] Senator Brander.
12.23 twenty-two. Jennie stood silently at her side.] twenty-two.
12.25 Senator. Attired in a handsome smoking-coat, he looked younger than at their first meeting.] senator. He was as faultlessly attired as before, only this time, because of a fancy smoking coat, he looked younger.
12.29 daughter,] daughter he had seen upon the stairs,
12.37 door. "Let me see," he repeated, opening and closing drawer after drawer of the massive black-walnut bureau.] door. While the two stood half-confused amid the evidences of comfort and finery, he repeated, "Let me see."
13.2   Jennie studied the room with interest.] Mrs. Gerhardt looked principally at his handsome head, but Jennie studied the room.
13.3   and pretty things] and things that seemed of great value
13.4   seen before.] seen.
13.6   and the fine] and fine
13.6   floor—what comfort, what luxury! [¶] "Sit down; take those two chairs there," said the Senator, graciously, disappearing into a closet.] floor, and all the scattered evidence of mannish comfort were to her distinctly ideal. [¶] While they were standing he moved over to a corner of the room, but turned about to say, "Sit down; take those two chairs there."
13.11 polite to decline, but now the Senator had completed his researches and he reiterated his invitation. Very uncomfortably they yielded and took chairs. [¶] "Is this your daughter?" he continued, with a smile at Jennie.] polite to disobey. [¶] He disappeared into a large closet, but came out again, and after advising them to sit down, said, with a glance at Mrs. Gerhardt and a smile at Jennie: [¶] "Is this your daughter?"

13.16   my oldest girl." [¶] "Is your husband alive?"] my oldest girl." [¶] "Oh, she is," he returned, turning his back now and opening a bureau drawer. While he was rummaging and extracting several articles of apparel, he asked: [¶] "Is your husband alive?"

13.19   live?" [¶] To all of these questions] live?" all of which

13.22   he went on.] he inquired very earnestly.

13.27   interesting] interested

13.32   During the colloquy Jennie's] All the time Jennie's

13.35   not keep his eyes off of her for more than a minute of the time.] not help repeating his attentions.

14.1   he continued, sympathetically] he said

14.3   but you are welcome to it.] but what there is, you are welcome to.

14.4   stuffing articles of apparel] stuffing things

14.5   side.] side, and all the while asking questions. In some indefinable way, these two figures appealed to him. He wanted to know just how their home condition stood and why this innocent looking mother, with the pathetic eyes, came to be scrubbing hotel stairways. [¶] In trying to question closely, without giving offense, he bordered upon the ridiculous: [¶] "Where is it you live?" he said, recalling that the mother had only vaguely indicated. [¶] "On Thirteenth street," she returned. [¶] "North or South?" [¶] "South." [¶] He paused again, and bringing over the bag said: [¶] "Well, here they are. How much do you charge for your work?" [¶] Mrs. Gerhardt started to explain, but he saw how aimless his question was. He really did not care about the price. Whatever such humble souls as these might charge, he would willingly pay. [¶] "Never mind," he said, sorry that he had mentioned the subject.

14.6   questioned Mrs. Gerhardt.] questioned the mother.

14.8   he said, reflectively;] he said, scratching his head reflectively,

14.18   people."] people." [¶] He brooded awhile, the ruck of his own trivial questions coming back, and then arose. Somehow their visit seemed for the time being to set clearly before him his own fortunate condition.

14.19   the room. [¶] Mrs. Gerhardt and Jennie] the chamber. [¶] As for Mrs. Gerhardt, she forgot the other washing in the glee of getting this one. She and Jennie

14.22   streets. They felt immeasurably encouraged by this fortunate venture.] streets.

14.28   girl, softly.] girl.

CHAPTER XXIII

180.1   A month later] It was only a little time after this, a month in all, before

180.2   His] Lester's

180.4   enough. Only Gerhardt seemed a little doubtful.] enough. She had come to be looked upon in the family as something rather out of the ordinary for somehow things seemed to happen to Jennie. She got in with astonishing people; she seemed to see more of the world; she was constantly doing something out of the ordinary. Gerhardt, the only one whom she was really anxious to placate was of course doubtful.

180.6   conscience, and really] conscience—too fine in fact—but

180.8   with Jennie] with her, even as terrible as he had

180.9   man? There was just one thing—the child.] man? He thought about this and finally concluded that it might be allright, but only after considerable talk between him and his wife. The latter had to explain the two drives which Jennie had on the two times when Lester had called. Her suggestion was that it was natural enough (and it was) that so fine a man should not want to stay in so poor a home and Gerhardt to a certain extent acquiesced in that thought. Certainly there was no harm in their driving Sundays. When the announcement was made, through Mrs. Gerhardt that he had asked her to marry him and was going to take her to Chicago for the time being, the children thought it was a great thing for her. Gerhardt frowned.

180.10   Vesta?" he asked his wife.] the child?" he asked.

180.11   "No," said Mrs. Gerhardt] "No," replied his wife

180.17   Gerhardt went] He went

180.18   him and he was only waiting to get well enough to hunt up another job as a watchman.] him. [¶] However there was nothing to do except wait. Time might not work things out so disasterously. As for him he was only waiting to be well enough to be a watchman or something.

180.21   mess of deception and dishonesty. [¶] A week or two later] mess of poverty and earn something. [¶] In another little while

180.23   Lester] her Lester

180.23   to join him in Chicago.] to come to Chicago.

180.24   well, and could not come to Cleveland. The two women explained to Gerhardt that Jennie was going away to be married to Mr. Kane. Gerhardt flared up at this, and his suspicions were again aroused. But he could do nothing but grumble over the situation; it would lead to no good end, of that he was sure.] well. He did not want to come to Cleveland. Mrs. Gerhardt suggested that if Gerhardt took unkindly to the proposition that she go away to marry him instead of having the supposed ceremony performed there, that she run away. It came about that way for at the mere suggestion that she did not expect to be married at home Gerhardt flared up. There should be nothing like that with his consent. He would have nothing to do with any such business. If she wished to lead a decent life and do things right—open and above board as they should be, well and good—Well and good! He would like that otherwise he would not stay—he would get out if he had to starve on the streets. This worried Jennie and her mother greatly but Lester had fixed the day of her departure and there appeared to be no alternative.

181.1 day came for Jennie's departure she had] time came she prepared

181.4 had been obliged to leave for the station.] had bid the others good-bye.

181.7 she went on hopefully.] she said.

181.8 move."] move." She talked as though she might not be going to stay in Chicago herself.

181.9 Chicago; the old life had ended and the new one had begun. [¶] The curious fact] Chicago and from then on to the end of her days that intimate, personal, immediate contact with her family was more or less broken. [¶] It is a curious thing that

181.12 Lester's generosity had relieved the stress upon the family finances] Lester's intimacy with her had relieved the stress of family finances since the night she gave her mother the money he had given her

181.16 not as yet] not yet

181.17 her. But, after Jennie had been in Chicago for a few days, she wrote to her mother saying] her. But Jennie had given nearly all she received and had advised her mother against the time when they could spend that the children should have good clothes, that a comfortable sitting room and dining room should be arranged, and that her mother was to have her almost faded dream, a parlor. After she was in Chicago a little while it came to pass for she immediately wrote

181.21 who had been] who was

181.21 He] as was intended, and he

181.24 them?] them? Mrs. Gerhardt spoke of the large sum of money she had sent, all she had been saving, and this also seemed a pretty strong proof of something affection certainly.

181.26 station in life, and was now able to help the family. Gerhardt almost concluded to forgive her everything once and for all.] station? The man was a strong man, no doubt of that. He was rather a nice fellow too. Really, he almost forgave her—not quite; but she was generous, that was sure.

181.29 it was that a new house was decided upon, and Jennie] it all, so far as the Gerhardt household was concerned was that a new house was really taken. At the end of a month, because of an enforced absence on the part of Lester and with his advice she

181.33 yard, which rented for thirty dollars, was secured and suitably furnished. There were comfortable fittings for the dining-room and sitting room, a handsome parlor set] yard which rented for thirty dollars was secured and suitable furniture installed, for Lester had cautioned her that she might want to be there a part of the time— that he might want to come occasionally. He advised her how to but intelligently. There was a complete and interesting set of furniture for the dining room, a nice quiet arrangement of furniture for the sitting room, a parlor set,

181.37 was supplied with every convenience, and there was even a bathroom, a luxury] was furnished intelligently and the bath room, a thing

182.2 never enjoyed before.] never had before, supplied with its proper belongings.

182.3 was attractive, though plain] was worthy though middle-class

182.4 that her] that at last her

182.7 this the] this now the

182.8 dreams?] dream?

182.9 waiting, and now] waiting for this. Now

182.11 ever even imagined—think of it!] ever seen.

182.14 beautiful!"] beautiful!" She rubbed her hands and looked at Jennie and once she squeezed her arm.

182.18 for his goodness to] for this service he had rendered

182.19 moved in Mrs. Gerhardt] being moved in her mother

182.23 spring, and] spring, as well as

182.24 family fell into] family, with the exception of Gerhardt, caught

182.25 such spaciousness!] such expansiveness.

182.26 carpets and Bass] carpets when he came home. Bass

182.29 that these] that this was the place she was to live from now on— these

182.31 dining-room were actually hers.] dining room. She finally settled herself in the kitchen, the best equipped of its kind she had ever had. "It's beautiful," she said.

182.32 of all.] of all. Somehow he desired to linger about the old place until all was out. When he was led through he was subtly affected by the comparative luxury which had descended on him.

182.35 table was the finishing touch.] table shocked him into a realization of one luxury hitherto not enjoyed.

183.6 to scratch] to catch

183.8 over." [¶] Yes, even Gerhardt was satisfied.] over." [¶] Experience in raising a family had taught him that.

CHAPTER XLI

289.6 coming so brutally] coming brutally as it did

289.8 make much] make so much

289.18 sugar-coat] sugar over

289.25 something that] something

289.25 he said dryly, pointing to the array of text and pictures.] he began drily, when he had it properly unfolded.

290.4 this affair] this thing

290.6 ills] ills (ills so big that they could not readily be corrected by human effort)

290.7 of the inevitable, the inexorable] light of whatever was when he met the inexorable

290.8 light comment] light perseflage

290.16   anyway." Dinner was announced a moment later and the incident was closed. [¶] But Lester could not dismiss the fact that matters were getting in a bad way.] anyhow." [¶] He folded up the paper as Gerhardt came in and then Vesta arrived from somewhere dancing and holding up a picture of a house she had drawn for her mother to see. She was taking drawing lessons at this time and this was her chief interest. "Yes," said Jennie, "it's pretty." The maid came presently to announce dinner and the incident of the newspaper story was over. [¶] For a long time this latest thrust of fate remained uppermost in Jennie's mind for it was so indicative of the direction in which her life was flowing. It was perfectly plain to her after this that she had proved a great detriment to Lester in many ways. It would have been better for him, she thought, if he had let her go when she wanted to. It was a little selfish on her part, she thought now to have demanded or accepted marriage of him. She was getting along well enough. Her own life was a failure. It would have been just as well— better—if she had gone away. Only he wanted her—she remembered that. He would not let her go. Her love and respect for him swelled at the thought. He was really a good man in the best sense of the word—a big man, but he was making a failure of his life and it was her fault. He ought never to have married her at all. [¶] Lester on his part was cogitating constantly. The evidence he had received up to now that he was in a bad position socially was convincing.

290.20   interview, and now this newspaper notoriety had capped the climax.] interview, but this newspaper notoriety had capped it all.

290.24   part of it] part

290.26   married,] married, whom he knew

290.28   him just the same] him

290.28   society. He was virtually an outcast, and nothing could save him but to reform his ways; in other words, he must give up Jennie once and for all.] society. Society was made by the most conservative who were almost invariably the most powerful. Their very conservatism was their power. So he was practically out of it. [¶] What he should do under these circumstances was really not a question with him at this time. If he had asked himself practically he would have said that wisdom dictated that he leave Jennie at once making suitable provision for her but not go near her any more. He could be restored to favor if he were really clear of all this.

290.35   creature. She was a big woman and a good one. It would be a shame to throw her down, and besides she was good looking. He was forty-six and she was twenty-nine; and she looked twenty-four or five.] creature. She wanted to be fair by him; she had his real interests at heart. She was a big woman in her way. It would be a shame to throw her down and besides she was good looking. When he was forty-six she was twenty-nine and she looked twenty-four or five.

291.4   another.] another. He had made his bed as his father had said. He had better lie on it.

291.7   after this disagreeable newspaper incident] after this disagreeable
           newspaper incident had taken place
291.9   failing; it] failing and it
291.10   at any moment] at the first word
291.11   when the news] when word
291.12   Lester, of course, was] Lester was of course
291.13   and he returned] and returned
292.4   he was met by] he saw
292.5   all their best differences.] all the row that had been.
292.6   Lester put] He put
292.13   his efforts."] his life."
292.19   mansion. Lester] mansion where the body had been removed, for
           sentimental reasons, to lie in state, when Lester came. He
292.20   condolences with the others] condolences
292.22   and had fallen] and fallen
292.23   Lester looked] He looked
292.24   and a feeling of the old-time affection swept over him.] and
           wondered what the old gentleman knew now, if anything.
292.27   was a big man] was all right in his way
292.30   solemnly.] solemnly. [¶] They strolled about anxious to have the
           solemnities over with for of course the family cared little about the
           details of death. Old Archibald wanted no show. They had long
           anticipated that he would die soon. Now it had come and the thing
           to do was to wind it up as satisfactorily as possible. Lester was really
           anxious to get away and get back to Chicago.
292.31   will at once.] will.
292.37   manufacturer.] manufacturer. [¶] Their offices were in a plain red
           brick building in the heart of the city and next door to an old
           graveyard to which Lester with Amy and Louise journeyed on this
           chilly morning. There was lots of snow on the ground crisp and
           sparkling. As they rode Lester went over in his mind details of his
           early life here. He had a vigorous young manhood in Cincinnati—
           lots of friends, lots of girls. The old house they were leaving and
           from which his mother and father had now departed had been the
           scene of many simple but joyous revelries. Once he had fancied he
           would sometime marry Letty Pace who used to come here but who
           had since married a Malcolm Gerald. She was very wealthy now,
           worth several millions, and she had been so nice to him. The old
           times seemed somewhat like a dream now;—like a tale that is told.
           Could it be that he was getting along so far that things were
           beginning to be over. Yes—there was no doubt it. He was nearly
           forty-six and life's finest excitements were behind him.
293.1   As Lester rode to the meeting he had the feeling that his father had
           not] As he rode he had no suspicion that his father had
293.3   so very long] so long
293.4   conversation; he] conversation and he

293.6	time. He always felt] time. No untoward event could have happened since their last conversation. He also knew
293.7	gentleman, except for his alliance with Jennie.] gentleman and now that he was dead he felt that he would be properly provided for. He had not done so much.
293.8	should there be any discrimination against him?] should his fortune be discriminated against.
293.10	think it possible.] think it would be.
293.15	counsel to Archibald Kane] counsel to Kane, Senior
293.16	years. He knew] years. Knew
293.18	especially.] especially. He knew exactly how everything had been arranged but did not care to show by look or word how the very extensive property of the manufacturer had been disposed of.
293.20	from his] from out his
293.24	lying upon it] lying near the edge, unfolded it
293.28	servants, and friends.] servants, friends and so on.
293.33	which roughly aggregated (the estate] which aggregated (the properties
294.2	and Lester.] and Lester in a very peculiar literary form.
294.16	as may hereinafter be set forth] as shall hereinafter be specified
294.29	that this was in accordance with their father's wish.] that it was their father's wish that they should not be.
294.33	things: First, he was] things: first
294.34	and so bring] and bring
294.36	father. In this event Lester's] father, in which case his
295.1	him. Secondly, he might elect to] him; or, second to
295.10	effected.] effected. He was not to have the handling of them ever.
295.10	If Lester] If he
295.11	after the three years were up.] after three years.
295.12	At Lester's] At his
295.24	little later.] little while later.
295.27	budging your father.] budging him.
296.8	that. So] that. Certainly as
296.14	himself. "I] himself. Amy ventured with an "I
296.15	Lester," ventured Amy, but Lester] Lester," but he
296.18	what his income would be] what this would bring him
296.24	more.] more, and that was all his long services, his notable expectations were to bring him.
296.25	The family gathering broke up] The party broke off
296.25	house.] house, lonely.
296.31	him!] him. Could it be so.
296.34	Jennie!] Jennie. The other provision did not interest him just now. What must he do—marry her? He was sick in the soul of him wondering, for this apparently was the end of all his fine prospects unless he left Jennie and he did not want to do that. The family would know that he had been made to.
296.35	years! Good Lord! Any smart] years! Why, hell! Any good

LESTER KANE'S DEATHBED SCENE: ALTERNATE VERSION

Below is the text of the deathbed scene in chapter LIX of *Jennie Gerhardt* as it would appear if one did not accept the crucial emendation from the Harpers 1911 edition. See the discussion on pp. 490–92 of the Textual Commentary.

He stopped and stared at the ceiling. A slight twinge of pain reminded him of the vigorous seizures he had been through. He couldn't stand many more paroxysms like the last one.

"I've always wanted to say to you, Jennie," he went on when the pain had ceased, "that I haven't been satisfied with the way we parted. It wasn't the right thing after all. I haven't been any happier. I'm sorry. I wish now, for my own peace of mind, that I hadn't done it."

"Don't say that, Lester," she demurred. "It's all right. It doesn't make any difference. You've been very good to me. I wouldn't have been satisfied to have you lose your fortune. It couldn't be that way. I've been a lot better satisfied as it is. It's been hard, but, dear, everything is hard at times." She paused.

"No," he said. "It wasn't right. The thing wasn't worked out right from the start, but that wasn't your fault. I'm sorry. I wanted to tell you that. I'm glad I'm here to do it."

"Don't talk that way, Lester,—please don't," she pleaded. "It's all right. You needn't be sorry. There's nothing to be sorry for. You have always been good to me. Why, when I think—" She pressed his hands. She was recalling the house he took for her family in Cleveland, the manner in which he had let Gerhardt come, the money he had supplied her since.

"Well, I've told you now and I feel better. You're a good woman, and you're kind to come this way."

She could see that sickness had taken away some of the natural phlegmatic sternness of his character.

"How are the two orphans?" he added.

CODA TO THE 1911 TEXT

Below is the text of the coda to *Jennie Gerhardt*. This coda is present in the copy-text, in the Barrett typescript, and in all observed impressions of the Harpers first printing of 1911. It was dropped from the text in a subsequent Harpers impression and did not reappear during Dreiser's lifetime. The judgment for the Pennsylvania edition has been that Dreiser was responsible for its omission. The text below has been edited by the same method applied to the rest of the edition: that is to say, copy-text has been the composite MS, emended against the first edition.

In Passing

It is useless to apostrophize a soul such as this which has reached the full measure of its being. Shall you say to the blown rose— well done! or to the battered, wind-riven, lightning-scarred pine, thou failure! In the chemic drift and flow of things, how little we know of that which is either failure or success. Is there either? To this daughter of the poor, born into the rush and hurry of a clamant world—a civilization, so-called, eager to possess itself of shows and chattels—what a sorry figure! Not to be possessed of the power to strike and destroy; not to be able, because of an absence of lust and hunger, to run as a troubled current; not to be able to seize upon your fellow being, tearing that which is momentarily desirable from his grasp, only to drop it and run wildly toward that which for another brief moment seems more worthy of pursuit. Not to be bitter, angry, brutal, feverish—what a loss!

And then how strange that there should be born into a soul a sense of its own fitness and place—that one should say to himself, in a spirit of deep understanding, "My kingdom is not of this world." Behold there are hierarchies and powers above and below the measure of our perception. It is given to us to see in part and to believe in part. But of that which is perfect who shall prophesy? Only this daughter of the poor felt something—the beauty of the trees, the wonder of the rains, the color of existence. Marveling at these, feeling the call of the artistry of spirit, how could it be that she should hurry—that she seek? Was it not all with her from the beginning?

Those days of her earliest youth, when she felt that life was perfect; those hours of stress, when it seemed that life could not be wholly bad; those moments of prosperity, when she realized in her own soul that she held them lightly and they would pass, leaving in their place the simplicities and the necessities only—were not these the hours of truest insight? Jennie loved and, loving, gave. Is there a superior wisdom? Are its signs and monuments in evidence? Of whom, then, have we life and all good things—and why?

THE END.

WORD DIVISION

Dreiser rarely hyphenated compound words at the ends of lines in the copy-text. Those few instances in which he did so have been resolved by reference to his usage at other points in the composite MS. Numerous possible hyphenated compounds are divided at the ends of lines in the present edition, however, and the critic or scholar must know how to render them in citations. The words below are all divided at the ends of lines in the Pennsylvania text. In quoting these words, the hyphenation should be preserved. All other compound words divided at the ends of lines in this text should be quoted as a single word.

3.31	scrub-woman
6.40	hand-rails
8.29	middle-aged
9.10	dining-room
9.19	half-repeated
11.24	car-works
18.31	cow-bell
26.10	candy-stores
26.11	self-respecting
28.31	drawing-room
51.4	all-importance
60.11	dining-room
74.4	hare-bells
76.1	ex-senator
84.5	self-commiseration
89.21	long-suffering
89.22	wind-up
93.34	non-understanding
94.16	evil-doing
109.15	self-sufficiency
111.6	All-seeing
118.35	three-fifty
121.2	clear-eyed
122.15	sitting-room
137.21	big-hearted
138.37	well-furnished
146.12	self-seeking
155.4	dining-room

156.8	twenty-dollar
169.21	straight-laced
175.14	sitting-room
176.30	dining-room
176.38	dining-room
178.16	self-reliance
187.13	self-consolation
198.37	wide-eyed
204.32	white-faced
205.3	soul-racking
217.31	blue-starred
235.34	well-defined
253.7	lumber-carrier
259.11	set-up
262.33	young-looking
262.34	twenty-nine
267.36	attractive-looking
283.33	well-known
285.15	full-page
287.20	lawyer-agnostic
289.17	conventional-looking
301.31	vice-president
302.12	vice-president
304.28	interest-bearing
306.36	ware-rooms
316.36	wine-colored
321.40	ultra-conservatism
326.34	re-entrance
328.28	forty-two
328.32	well-known
335.26	real-estate
339.6	rapid-fire
343.3	no-good
346.16	hard-working
349.22	one-hundred-and-fifty
390.24	self-preservation
394.25	well-entertained
396.34	full-bodied
400.17	co-operating
403.38	well-grounded
405.10	dry-goods

PEDIGREE OF EDITIONS

The following separate typesettings of *Jennie Gerhardt* have been published in the English language:

New York and London: Harper and Brothers, 1911.
London: Constable, 1928.
New York: Dell/Laurel, 1963.
New York: Library of America, 1987.

All three settings subsequent to the first edition of 1911 derive independently from that text. The Harpers 1911 text is currently in print, in a lightly corrected classroom paperback, from Viking Penguin. An uncorrected reprint of the Constable 1928 text is currently available in a similar format from Oxford University Press.

The University of Pennsylvania Dreiser Edition

This book was set in Linotron Goudy Old Style. Goudy Old Style was designed by F. W. Goudy in 1916 for American Type Founders. Goudy Old Style is based on the types used by the early Italian printers.

Printed on acid-free paper.